The Adventures of Elizabeth Stanton Series

Volume 10 Degradation

Vic Broquard

Published by:
Broquard eBooks
http://Broquard-eBooks.com
author@Broquard-eBooks.com
103 Timberlane
East Peoria, IL 61611

Artwork by Crooked Willow Studios

For Morgan and L. Ron Hubbard

Table of Contents

Chapter 1 Confusions

I know one thing for sure, it's June 1, 755. Well, I know another certain thing: we're living at 42 Hampton Way, Velona, otherwise known as the House of the Precocious Kids. It's been four years now since we all returned from our mission to Demokritos.

Yes, Dita and I still look like duckbills. Down in Demokritos, the Mano del Dio split our lips and inserted the clay lip plates that the Utu princesses wear. After a long discussion with Sandra, our able Healer, we decided surgery was out because most likely it would fail. In time, we have adapted to them fairly well. Because several vowel sounds cannot be made when we speak, we both now subtly use our telepathy on others when we speak, so that they understand what we are saying. We've become very adept at it and are now not so self-conscious about our lip plates. Dianna has helped us out greatly by making us some very light weight plates so that we do not need to have our front teeth removed as the Utu women do when their plates get too heavy to remain horizontal. Even though we only wear them when out in public, our lip loops continue slowly to stretch. Our upper plates are now three and a half inches in diameter, while our lower ones are four inches across.

Life has only grown more confusing for us. Okay, I guess I need to back up and outline the residents of our estate. My name — well for my older body — is Mrs. Bethany Brozena Malina and I am a Wid, that is, a Druwid who craves to know a lot about everything. I'm married to Dita Malina, who is really my lover from previous lifetimes, Renzo, and she is a Druwid Protector. Our dear friends are Mrs. Dianna Anka West Po, who is a healer and engineer. She is married to Mrs. Ania Anka West Po, who is a Druwid Judger and heavily into politics and group dynamics. Mrs. Ilenakova Kato da Cassa is also a Protector and is married to Mrs. Kali Kato da Cassa, who is a Judger.

Yes, we six married this way because at the time, we had lost our arms and by teaming up, we could deal with life far better. Of course, all six of us knew each other very well in previous lives. Dianna, for example, was the famous inventor Enyo; Ilenakova was the famous Sisterhood fighter, Lenkova Pazzio le'Goeur. We all now have had our arms either re-grown or touched by a miracle from the Guardian, the Son of God, Lord Jehosa.

If this is not confusing enough, when we six were still armless, we each adopted a young orphan — our little girls, as we call them. Others call them precocious witches, because of their incredible skills. My daughter, Alessa is a vivacious blonde, a Protector, and is thirteen. Dita's girl is Bianca, also a Protector and is fourteen with long black hair. Both our girls are emulating us with their hair, allowing it to grow as long as possible. Both

Dita and I have never cut our hair. My thick, very blonde hair reaches below my rump, while Dita's thick, straight, black hair is nearly as long. Our girls' hair reaches to the small of their backs. Yes, we four are perhaps a bit vain about our locks.

Dianna's daughter is Cosima, who is fifteen and now is an official Velona Detective Inspector. She has all the skills of us Druwids and then some. She discovered how to convince our growing bodies to re-grow their missing arms; she's exceedingly brilliant.

Elena is Ania's girl and is a fourteen year old Judger, like her mom. Fina is Ilenakova's daughter, now thirteen and a Protector, as you might guess. Kali's girl is Jemma, now fourteen and is a Judger, like her mother.

All six of our daughters are able to perform my special trauma therapy far better than I can. Ever since I taught them how to do it, they've run it on themselves, so much so, that they have regained a number of spiritual abilities including telepathy and the ability to move objects. This latter they used extensively when they still were armless. "Beats using your feet for everything," Cosima explained back then. Of course, now they are all going boy crazy, which is only adding to the confusion around the estate.

We are all watched over by four Forze Segrete members. This secret organization scattered throughout Tarra has as its purpose to monitor key individuals and protect them. These four have also become our parents; all are now thirty-one. Sandra and Arthur Bastiana are our Druwid Healer Specialist and Loremaster. His knowledge of plants and animals is staggering and her surgery skills are most remarkable indeed. Luisa and Enrico Angela are a Judger and Protector. All four of us knew all six of us and most of our precocious daughters in previous lives. Yes, we are a close-knit band indeed, spanning many lifetimes.

Now when we six were still armless, the Guardian believed that we would be assassinated by the Mano del Dio assassins of the Church of Jehosanity. Thus, he carefully prepared six new bodies for us so that we could still operate as a team. Sandra and Luisa each had triplets. Part of the deal was for some of us to end up with male bodies this time, namely Dita, Ilenakova, and Ania. The idea was simple, our six bodies are assassinated, and we get new ones of the right sex so that we can all have proper marriages. Well, that didn't quite work out.

Dianna and Cosima discovered that the Grey Creature's blasters could be recharged by sunlight. Besides blasting, these also provided a force shield to protect one from direct attacks. Using these, we only pretended to be assassinated, which was enough to convince the Mano del Dio. Now we six are trying to control and run two bodies at the same time!

All are now nine years old. My second body is Elizabeth Lilly, Kali's is Kallisto Ann, and Ania's is Alex. Our parents are Luisa and Enrico. Dita's second body is Renzo, Dianna's is Enyo, and Ilenakova's is Len. Sandra and Arturo are their parents. Thus, we six are running two bodies at the same time, terribly confusing at times.

Until the last few years, this was not much of a problem, since the babies did little. I found it convenient when I was down in Demokritos to use my little Elizabeth body to chat with everyone up here in Velona. However, now these new ones are nine years old and quite active! The Guardian promised that we would benefit greatly from trying to run and control two bodies at one time. Now, I am beginning to wonder about the wisdom of this. Dita calls what we are doing the spanning of our attention.

Consider how you may think of yourself: viewing the world from inside your head, from right behind your eyes. Now double that — two heads and two sets of eyes all relaying sights to you at the same time. I keep concentrating on one of them instead of the other, which causes no end of mishaps and confusions. Dianna has already "solved" her problem with this idea: when her Enyo body is older, she's going to have one sleeping while she runs the other body. "I can get twice as much done this way," she claims.

In these past few years, Dianna-Enyo has certainly been busy! She has developed an anti-gun vest, which stops the bullets from guns. Her older brother, Bale, is now working on getting them made in quantity, while her younger brother, Tom, is developing new and better guns to counter this new threat from Megalos, Demokritos, and the Mano del Dio, among others.

What I found fascinating is her latest development, a steam engine machine. Moving people and goods quickly from place to place has always been a problem. Horse drawn wagons have weight and speed limitations. She developed a machine that burns coal to boil water and thus make steam. The steam drives a piston affair, which then makes the wheels move. She made a whole miniature working model here at the estate. She calls it a train. Her new engine pulls a set of six cars on wheels, all of which run on parallel steel tracks. We now have a giant oval track completely around the perimeter of our estate. When she gave Bale and his advisors a ride and demonstration, he was so enthused about the idea that he took over the project.

Already, crews are building a rail line connecting the port city of Velona to all our major outlying cities. He has others working on building a large scale engine and sturdy cars to haul goods. It is scheduled to become operational this fall. If it proves successful, Bale then wants to run a rail line all across the eight Sea Prince sectors so that commerce between us becomes ten times faster than it is now. If this works out, Bale then wants to extend the line into the Greenway, so that their massive grain exports to us can be moved drastically faster. Already, Velona is one of the leading exporters in the world, second only to the vastly larger country of Demokritos.

Currently, Dianna is working with ship designers to see if her steam engine can be used to power an ocean going ship instead of the sail powered caravels, which are at the mercy of the winds. Because of its weight, they are now looking into the possibility of making an all steel ship. This I have to see! Everyone knows that steel sinks like a rock.

On the positive side of life, all of us have become very active patrons of the arts now. On Friday nights, we all go to the formal concerts and plays, particularly those put on by our close friends, the Matteo brothers, Dario and Luigi, and their wives, Ariadne and Alekto. Ariadne has already become a famous opera composer, while Alekto continues to compose new symphonies. Their music has become the topmost draw of any event in Velona! On Saturday nights, we all go to the various local dances, alternating between the waltzes, for us older folks, and the popular fast dances of the younger set. On Sundays, we still take time out for family outings, often horseback rides into the country with a picnic stop.

During the weekdays, Athena, now the wife of Andreas Myntas, an importer-exporter with his own fleet of five caravels, comes by to study with us. She is learning our skills as Druwids, as well as our therapy methods, the latter primarily from Cosima. She has not yet reached the specialization stage, but I suspect that she may become the first new Wid in half a century or more — either that or another Judger.

As expected, the massively wide hoop skirt dresses of Annelise have become the latest in high fashion in Velona proper. Constricting corsets are mandatory to wear these dresses, which usually flare out in a twelve foot in diameter circle around your feet. However, we often substitute the Alexa made high-heeled boots for those that are supposed to be worn with the Annelise outfits. The Annelise heels are at least six inches high or more, while the famous Alexa boots have a more manageable five-inch heel. Yes, our girls now insist on wearing these fancy outfits to all the affairs that they possibly can. However, we six have all put our feet down on wearing those wasp waist corsets all the time. They are allowed to only wear them when they are wearing the fancy dresses.

All this has led to boy troubles. Our teens are now all looking eagerly at boys. At the dances, they seem to attract them like flies to honey. Only Cosima has a steady boyfriend at this time, Gerardo West Po, Dianna's nephew, Tom's son, who is seventeen. Only last weekend, Alessa asked me, "Mom, why do all the boys our age strut around and act so silly? Aren't there any boys who are smart like us? How are we ever going to find a boyfriend? I mean, look, we six are smart, have Druwid skills that others dream about having, to say nothing of our spiritual skills, like moving objects without using our bodies. Are all boys just plain dumb?" Of course, all our other girls were listening in to hear my answer to Alessa.

"You just have to keep looking for the right person, Alessa. One day you will find one who will not only admire you for who you are but also respect you as well. Your heart will tell you when you've found the right boy for you. I will also say this: you need someone who can at least keep up with you. That's why Renzo and I are so much in love with each other; we can keep up with the other. We share a whole lot of things in common, though we each have other interests of our own. Dita is into fighting and I am not, for example. The key is not to get discouraged, but to keep on looking until you find Mister Right for you." So much for my philosophy lesson.

Within the last two years, some fashion ideas from Tashien found their way into mainstream Velona society. Makeup has now become almost a requirement when dressing up. Red is the most popular color for our lips, with a touch of rouge on our cheeks and a thing called eye shadow. Depending upon several factors of which I am not an expert yet, one wears various shades of eyelid color, green, blue, or black — all in various shades and styles. Sandra has become our expert in this arena. The other idea from Tashien is for women to have long fingernails, the longer the better, it seems — painted red, of course. They *have* to match your lips' color. All our girls now are sporting two-inch long claws. Well, okay, the rest of us are also letting ours grow as much as we can. Dianna isn't, she's always working on her inventions and cannot be bothered with such frivolities as she calls them.

Speaking of Tashien, I should briefly outline the geography of Tarra. Here in the northern hemisphere, the continent is shaped like an enormous dog bone. The center narrow area is the Desert of Desolation, where no living thing can be found. On either side of this enormous desert are two impassable mountain ranges. The western lobe is divided by the Med Sea. Along the northern coast of the Med are the Eight Sea Prince Sectors or countries. All across the northern part of the Sea Princes is the Appian Way, a tall mountain range. Velona sits at the mouth of the Med. Fortress d'Grange lies immediately north of Velona. Going eastward from Velona are the sectors of Barcella, Vito, Bonito, Pieta, Solamina, and Zargarb. To the east of Zargarb here at the eastern end of the Med is the desert region known as Juda Arad. Above the Appian Way lie the fertile farmlands of the Greenway and its twelve kingdoms. East of them is the Northern Steppes, where nomadic horsemen live. A range of mountains separates them from the cold lands of the Axemen of Volksholm.

The entire southern half is called the Southlands. Right below the Desert of Desolation is the giant island of Megalos. The eastern lobe of the dog bone continent is Tashien, a land of yellow skinned people, very densely populated. Further east across miles of ocean lies the island nation of Dorota. Here is where the Guardian now dwells and where he is working on freeing spiritual beings.

In the southern hemisphere lies a long oval continent. Demokritos occupies the western third. Vladimir lies in the middle, home of warlike horsemen. The highly civilized country of Annelise occupies the eastern third of that continent. Yet another continent lies far to the west and is largely unexplored. In this era, Tashien becomes an important factor.

This new portion of our lives begins then on Monday June 1, 755. Cosima and I are working with Athena on further developing her therapy skills. My Elizabeth body is out playing ball with the other kids, and I am having a hard time trying to focus on Athena while out running around and dodging the ball.

Sandra interrupted us and Chief Inspector Adolfo followed her into our study. "Excuse me, but the Chief Inspector wants to speak with Cosima."

"Hi, Chief," Cosima cheerily greeted him.

"Good afternoon ladies. Detective Inspector Cosima, I believe that I have another case for you."

"Say no more! I love challenges! Athena, we'll continue this when I get back. Do I need to change into pants or can I come in my dress?" she asked, tossing her curly brown hair out of her face. She was wearing a blue satin dress with several petticoats and her Alexia boots. Since she became of age and a Detective Inspector, she insisted on wearing only satin dresses and the higher heels. At least, I convinced her not to wear the high Annelise boots for every day. She hastily put on her gold neck chain with her Detective Inspector's badge hanging prominently on her chest. Her homemade detective kit, which looked more like a doctor's bag, seemed to float up and into her outreaching hand. Adolfo noticed this but said nothing. By now, he was very well used to seeing the unbelievable around 42 Hampton Way.

"I believe you are fine as you are," Adolfo replied, offering her his arm. "I must warn you, this is a particularly grim one." He assisted her into his waiting carriage and signaled his driver. While they were rolling through the densely packed streets of Velona, he explained further.

"Cosima, this morning dockhands found the body of a young teenaged girl lying in a back alley off 34th Street. It is in the slummier part of town. We've identified her as Agata Dalberto, the fifteen year old daughter of Alonso."

"Say, he's a relatively wealthy merchant — deals in paca wool, right?" Cosima asked, recognizing the name.

"Precisely. The family is taking it very hard and has put pressure on Bale to find the villain who did this to their daughter. According to her father, Agata was working at the Stitch Fine dressmaking shop and would never have gone into that section of Velona," Adolfo continued.

"What time was she last seen at the dressmakers? How far is that shop from her home? How did she normally travel to and from work?" Cosima asked, desiring to get a time frame established at once.

Adolfo opened his pad and skimmed. "Ah, they worked later than normal yesterday. She left work around six-thirty. Ten blocks. She usually walks. That area of town is normally rather safe. I've taken the liberty of telling Alonso that I was assigning this case to you. Ah, here we are. The crime scene has not been touched. I've left a patrolman on the scene since the body was found. No one has touched a thing. When you've finished examining her, let him know and he'll get the undertaker to remove the body.

He opened the carriage door, stepped down, and offered her his hand. The patrolman was surprised to see a well-dressed teenager with his boss, but now he recognized her badge. He'd heard of this precocious young girl, just never met her. He stuck close to them, listening in on their conversation.

Cosima knelt down and opened her case, removing her pad. Quickly, she jotted down the key information he'd previously told her. Then, she stood and went to examine the crime scene. "Well, she was definitely killed at this location."

"How do you tell that?" Adolfo asked, curious about how she could determine that after only a minute.

"Scuff marks on the cobblestones; scuff marks on her heels. I believe that she put up a struggle. Now let's see what the criminal has left for us to find." She began closely observing the scene. "There's a wealth of information here, Adolfo. Obviously, she was gagged; it's still in her mouth. Her panties are missing. Yes, she was raped, rather forcibly. See all the bruising? Now, cause of death? Strangulation. Observe the redness and bruising around her neck. She was lying on her back when he throttled her."

"How can you tell that? She was found on her stomach."

"The backs of her heels are terribly scuffed up and they match the shoe polish torn off while she moved her feet wildly as she tried to get him off of her. Her elbows show bad abrasions, adding to the notion that she fought him. Now let's see." She got out her magnifying glass and began a closer inspection.

"Now what do we have here?" Using her long fingernail, she scooped up some white ash powders, placed them into a jar, and sealed it.

"What was that?" Adolfo asked.

"I suspect opium ash, but I cannot be sure until I run some tests on it. If it is, then more than likely our murder smoked some before the crime."

"Why before and not after?" he asked, scratching his head.

"Lots of the ash has been ground into the cobblestones, probably during the ensuing rape and murder. He got high to enjoy his sex better. Now what have we here?" She pulled out a black hair, which was stuck between the girl's teeth and held it to the light between her two long red nails. She put the hair into another jar. "She bit him and a piece of his body hair got stuck between her teeth, probably done before he gagged her. Now let's undo the gag. Ah, here are her panties, stuck in her mouth. The murder improvised. However, this binding cloth is unusual. It does not come from her dress, which is cotton. I don't see any place where this has been torn off her undergarments. She does not have any other silk articles of clothing, and it is too big for a handkerchief. I suspect this silk cloth belongs to the murder." She put it into a small sack to study later.

"Now let me look more closely at these strange bruises along her upper arms and lower arms and wrists," Cosima said, very intent on her analysis. She focused her lens and moved along one arm and then the other.

"What do you make of it? She was probably tied up, right?" Adolfo concluded.

"Bingo!" Cosima exclaimed. She picked up a tiny bit of silk between her long nails and examined it under her lense. "Most unusual, but it fits the pattern," she concluded.

"What? What pattern? She was just bound, right?" Adolfo replied, scratching his head. Cosima was way ahead of his observations.

"Silk cord was used to bind her. He brought it with him and took it with him when he was finished. More importantly, the murder was likely one of those men from Tashien and an opium addict," she concluded.

Seeing the frowning face of Adolfo, she explained further. "Around here, our cord is definitely not made of silk. It's far too expensive and rare. Now you see these telltale marks left by the rope? He tied her up in a most peculiar way. If you or I were going to bind someone, we'd just tie the rope around their wrists. Not so here. See, the tie begins way up high on her upper arms. The rope went around her upper arms and then in spiraling loops all down her arms. With her arms behind her back, he then forced her hands up towards her head and then bound them. Then, many other loops were wrapped around her forearms and then around her waist. Her arms were then completely immobilized, but her upper arms would have been at her sides."

"Wow! Yes, yes, I see that now. How could I have missed that! That is the usual way the degenerate men of Tashien bind their whores or wives for play. We've often seen their women bound that way in their section of town. They say that is their custom. Brutal, if you ask me. So yes, we are looking for a man from Tashien, probably living in their section of Velona. Brilliant, Cosima."

"Well, we need more than this. Now let's see," she rolled the body over. "Ah, as I suspected. He held a knife to her back and forced her to walk here with him. See the knife cuts in the back of her dress near her waist? Now, let me measure her." She quickly retrieved her tape measure from her bag. "Ah ha. Now that gives us a better idea of his size. He was right around six-two."

"How can you possibly tell that?" Adolfo asked.

"Here, you stand behind me and pretend that you have a knife in your right hand. Let your arm hang down, you don't want to draw suspicion to yourself as you are walking these many blocks. See, your knife touches my dress here. If you measure that height from the ground, you can then get a good estimate of how tall the man was. Our bodies maintain a certain proportion to them as they grow. You've never seen a man with five-foot arms or even two-foot arms, you see. So based on the height of those knife cuts, he was right at six foot two. Further, that is rather tall for a man from

Tashien. There should not be too many men around that height in their sector of town."

"But let me take a closer look here, Adolfo, we need to find something that will positively place him here at this scene when we find him," she added. Cosima again used her magnifying glass to examine the girl's arms. After several minutes, she again exclaimed, "Ah ha. We have him now, Adolfo. Look here, please."

He squatted down beside her and looked through the lense, while she pointed out several spots with the tip of her long red nail. "The rope he used also took with it some of her own arm hair which is blonde. I will take several samples of hers. When we find the guilty man, we can examine his silk rope and find her hairs in it. Then, you will know for sure that you have the right culprit. Say, this looks like cat hairs on the front of her dress. I wonder if she has a cat. I'd better take some samples of this as well."

"Incredible, Cosima! I just don't know how you do all this, but once more, I can see why Bale appointed you to the Detective Inspector position!

"Thanks, but we haven't caught him yet. Now you can remove the body. It's legwork time. We need to see if anyone saw them walking the streets to this spot last evening. I need to visit with her parents, and then I'm going to walk her usual route home and see if I can determine the likely place where she was accosted by the murderer with his knife. That should then give us a likely route to go door to door seeing if anyone remembers seeing the pair of them walking here last evening."

"Excellent, let me know when you have the route pinned down. I'll put some policemen on the door to door canvas. It is imperative that we catch this murderer before he strikes again. Take my coach, Cosima. I'll hitch a ride with the undertaker," Adolfo suggested.

An hour later, Cosima discovered that the Dalberto's did not have any cats. She had the driver take her to the dressmaker's shop so that she could get the lay of the route that Agata would most likely follow. Then, she sighed and asked the driver to return to our estate. While she wanted to head into the seedier section of town and track down this opium addict and murderer, she knew my rules. One of we adults had to accompany her.

"Bethany, I'm going to need to go into some not so nice sections of town to find the murderer. Will you accompany me when I am ready to go?" Cosima asked.

"Sure. Just let me know when. I'll get Enrico to drive us, dear," I replied.

"Thanks. First, I need to run some tests on the evidence that I've gathered," she said, waltzing off to her room. Later she returned. "Yes, I was right. The murderer smoked some opium before he raped her and strangled her. So we are off to find us a murderer, Bethany. Don't forget to put your plates in," she reminded me. I'd forgotten to do just that and I slipped into my room and slid them into place. Then, we headed off back to the dressmaker's shop where Agata had worked.

On the way, Cosima related her findings. "I feel sure that we are going to have to go on foot through the crummy part of Little Tashien. You know, where they have all of their brothels and opium dens. We might have to search those dens too."

The population of the city of Velona is now well over one million. Approximately five thousand are yellow skinned immigrants from Tashien. Most came from their international port of Shansee, in the Tan Loc Province on their southern coast. Unable to speak our language well and because their own customs differ so much from ours, most have settled in the rather rundown portion of Velona, in an older section just north and west of the large docks. We call their section Little Tashien.

I had never been in this part of town, though Cosima had on several occasions in her official capacity as Detective Inspector. As our carriage rolled into their area, the buildings and houses looked old and fairly worn out. Only a few looked well kept, those were the brothels and the opium dens — most of which were located in a four block row. Here the streets were crowded with people; open markets had sprung up at every available location often blocking the sidewalk. Pedestrian traffic joined us in the street. Enrico halted the carriage.

"Ladies, we are not likely to get this carriage through there. It is too crowded," he called down.

"Okay, we need to go on foot anyway," Cosima replied, and we climbed out. "You guard the carriage, Enrico. We'll holler if we need you." He grinned, that she would need him he doubted very much! He was only thankful that she still followed my rules, bringing along an adult with her when she went into such disreputable sections of Velona.

Cosima double-checked her official badge, making sure it was quite visible, which it was. Our high heels clicking on the cobblestones, we two entered the mass of people moving along the street. We looked out of place — she in her blue satin dress and me in my red satin dress with my flowing blonde hair and large lip plates. Okay, I admit it, I alone would have looked very out of place, but I've grown comfortable with my appearance as weird as it is.

Here they wore traditional clothing from Tashien. Women dressed in simple, loose fitting dresses with simple flats. Drab, earthy colors predominated among both men and women. Usually, their hair was black, and the women wore theirs long as Dita and I did, only often braided. Many wore bamboo hats. However, as we drew closer to the brothel houses, we found many young women, who worked here selling their bodies for wages, out on the street attempting to drum up business.

These women were obvious, not by the finer silk, loose fitting, sheath style dresses, which would have also given them away, but by their tied arms. The customs followed by their employers was to bind these women's arms in a unique way. Cosima and I both stared at these women, who were wandering from person to person, looking for a taker. A soft silk rope was wrapped around their upper arms and then around their arms in several downward spirals. Their arms were forced behind their backs, wrists tied together but pointing upwards towards their necks. Many loops of the rope wrapped around their lower arms binding them securely as well. Finally, this was secured to the loops around their arms, such that their upper arms appeared to hang at their sides while their lower arms and hands were immobile, hands pointing upwards towards their necks.

One young woman came up to us and asked, "Want some pleasure? I give good pleasure, you will see?" She was rather pretty and attractive, and we could see her well-shaped breasts through her thin silk dress.

"Why do you do this? Selling your body?" I asked, just a bit annoyed with all this open solicitation of sex right here in the middle of a bustling street.

"Earn good money, pay very good. Hard find better job. Must feed three children. You want some pleasure? I give good pleasure to fine ladies. Very clean," she answered unashamed and unabashed. I could tell that she was both sincere and probably being very honest about her profession.

"No thank you, not just now," Cosima replied. "But I will give you a gold for some information. We are looking for a tall man, about six feet two inches high," she held up her arm to indicate the right height. "Have you seen any man that high around here, probably often visiting an opium den?" She put a gold coin in the woman's belt pouch for her, since she obviously could not do it herself.

"Three tall men. Visit Lin Ho's place just down there. Much thanks for coin!" she bowed repeatedly showing her appreciation for such a generous contribution. We walked on through the crowd, but were assailed five more times by other women seeking someone to pleasure before we arrived at Lin Ho's den. I read the sign for Cosima, who could not read their language. My Tashien was very rusty, like about a century out of practice. Still I could make out its name: Lin Ho's High.

We entered the relatively rundown building. The aroma of opium hung heavy in the air. A man sat behind a low wall here in the entrance room, which was only ten by ten if that. A closed door led into the back rooms where the customers would be taken. The man was perhaps fifty and in need of a bath, I thought. Cosima took charge.

"We are looking for a tall man, at least six feet two inches who regularly comes to smoke. This man probably owns a black cat and would not have been here from around six last night until probably nine. This is official police business, as you can see from my badge. Do you know of any such men?" she said formally.

"What's it to you? Are you and your strange looking lady friend here looking for a little relaxation?" he said, slightly annoyed with her direct questions.

"We can do this the easy way or I can fetch half of the policemen in Velona and raid your establishment here, looking for city code violations. Which will it be?" Cosima replied firmly.

"I've a business to run here, ladies. I don't need interruptions. There are few from Tashien that are as tall as you say. Cats, you say? Well, that might be Jin Ming," he replied.

"Thank you. Now has he come by today and perhaps made a purchase from you?" Cosima asked.

"Supposing that he has?" Lin Ho replied in a non-committal manner.

"Did he perhaps pay you with a green emerald on a gold necklace? The gem was about this big," she indicated with her fingers, flashing her long red nails.

"Perhaps he might have. Why?" We both sensed that he was now becoming slightly nervous.

"Official police business. I would like to examine that emerald and necklace now, please," Cosima stated flatly, wondering if she would need to threaten the man further.

He hesitated and then thought better of it. He retrieved his cash box, took out an emerald on a gold chain, and handed it to her. Two fighter types, strong men quietly appeared at the entrance door and at the door leading into the back rooms. We got a strong whiff of opium smoke, announcing the second man's arrival. Cosima ignored them, knowing that I had her back. She picked up the emerald and began examining it carefully. The green and gold contrasted sharply with the bright red of her nails.

"Ah, and did you not think to ask where this Jin Ming might have acquired a woman's necklace that has the name Agata engraved here on the back side of the mounting?" Cosima asked politely.

"No, money's money," he replied. "Why?"

"Well, this was stolen from a young teen named Agata Dalberto last night. I am afraid that I must take this as evidence in a crime. You may lay your legal claim to it at Central Police Headquarters, if you like. Now then, where can we find this Jin Ming?" she asked.

"But," he began to protest. He looked at her Detective Inspector badge prominently staring him in his face and decided otherwise. He gave us an address and directions as well.

"Thank you, sir. Again, if you wish to file a claim on this stolen property, file a notice at Central Police Headquarters. In the future, I would check on the authenticity of such items before you accept them as payment," Cosima suggested. We turned to leave. He made a hand signal and the burly man blocking the exit door stepped back outside, allowing us to leave.

We pushed on through the throng on the street, saying no to another four solicitations by tied women. At last, we ducked down a rundown alleyway. Ahead, Cosima spied the one room, small apartment. She knocked on its door. After a minute, we heard someone coming, footsteps echoed on a wooden floor just inside. The door opened and a tall man towered over Cosima whose height was five-five.

"Jin Ming?" she asked.

"Yah, what's it to you? My, you are a pretty thing. Come for some fun? Say your companion is intriguing. Double the fun," he said, leering at us both, trying to decide how to take us both.

"Good. As Detective Inspector of Velona, I am arresting you on suspicion of raping and murdering Agata Dalberto last evening. Will you come peacefully or do I need to use force?" Cosima replied in a rather bored manner. I realized that for her the puzzle was solved now. The rest was merely boring.

He whipped out a knife and moved towards Cosima. "Very well," she acknowledged his action. "Drop the knife!" she commanded. I saw her float over his body and take over total control of his body. The knife dropped to the ground. "Bethany, will you hold him here while I search inside for some additional evidence?" I moved over his body and lifted him slightly up off the ground, while he looked startled and shocked. He wiggled to get free of the unseen, hidden force that was holding him up. I just made sure that he couldn't kick me with his feet. Cosima slipped inside.

She returned with a silken rope and some cat hairs which she placed into two evidence bags. Cosima then searched his person but found no other weapons. After putting the knife into its sheath and placing that into her evidence bag, she took over from me. "Okay, Bethany, I have him now. We will return to Enrico and our carriage now." Indeed, I marveled at how easily she could possess his body and make it walk along with us. She had some amazing spiritual abilities, no doubt of that.

As we retraced our long path back to the waiting carriage, we again had to say no to several more propositions. Part way back a well-dressed man stepped out of one of the nicer looking brothels. He wore an immaculately made suit with polished boots. He nodded to us. "Excuse me. Would you ladies be interested in making some extra spending money? I could always use such good looking, attractive young women as yourselves. Ma'am," he said directly to me, "your lip ornamentations are very impressive. You would find that many men would be very much attracted to you. You could make a fortune in no time."

"Sorry, I am not interested in selling my body for money. I'm happily married. Good day," I replied politely. Honestly, the outright gall the man!

"Fine. If you change your mind one day, I will be here. The offer still stands," he replied and bowed. We continued on our way. I began to see a vast difference in customs between these people and ourselves, though the sheer magnitude of this would not become evident for some time yet.

An hour later, Cosima dropped Jin Ming off at the jail, promising to return in the morning with all the evidence needed to convict him of Agata's rape and murder. As soon as we returned, Cosima headed for her room to examine what she had taken from his place, the knife, rope, and cat hairs. Just before supper, Chief Inspector Adolfo returned, and I led him to her room.

"Cosima! This is incredible! I see that you already have the guilty man arrested and in our jail! Terrific work. How did you find him so quickly?" he asked, highly excited. I realized that with such a speedy capture, he would be able to inform the merchant that the crime was solved in less than a day! His police force would gain esteem from that for sure.

"Ah, good. You can save me a trip. Here, see for yourself," he handed him her magnifying glass. "On the right are cat hairs from his house, on the left are those I took from the victim. They are a match. Now here is the rope he used to tie her up in their peculiar manner. I have found six of her arm hairs still on the rope. They are in this labeled jar. Here is her emerald and necklace. You will note her engraved name on the mounting, which can be verified by her parents, who gave it to her as a birthday present last year. He traded it for opium. His body lay on top of hers; his rope tied her up; he had her emerald. I believe that will be enough to convict him or even better, use it to get a confession from him." Cosima tied up the loose ends, handing him all the evidence nicely labeled.

"Once again, Detective Inspector Cosima, allow me to thank you for a fantastic job solving this heinous crime. Very well done indeed!" She smiled, but I could tell that she was ready for another puzzle to solve. He gave her a hug and left with the evidence.

Reluctantly, Cosima removed her chain and badge of office, putting it beside her black evidence-collecting bag. She sighed, "Well, I wonder what's for supper? Kind of boring around here isn't it? Thanks for lending me a hand today, Bethany. Sure was a weird one." I gave her a hug as well and headed to my room to remove my lip disks, just as Dita, Alessa, and Bianca returned from a lengthy horse ride. "Hi Dita, you missed all the fun. I caught me a rapist and murderer this afternoon with Bethany's assistance," Cosima explained her day. Dita moaned; I knew that she would have loved to have been with us.

Chapter 2 Crime in Velona

The next evening, monarch Bale West Po, the political leader of Velona, dropped by after dinner. "Sorry for barging in unexpectedly, but I wanted to talk to you folks. I want this to be a frank and honest chat about some serious problems we are facing. I figured we could do it in an informal setting better than in my main conference room. Oh, by the way, excellent sleuthing, Cosima! Very well done. I heard today that the man broke down and confessed but laid the blame on his opium addiction." Cosima grinned, pleased to be acknowledged for her day's mystery solving.

"In that case, Bale, how about we fix up a large pot of tea?" I replied.

"Absolutely, this may well be a more than a one-cup meeting," he teased, knowing full well how much many of us loved our tea. A short while later, we all sat around our very large dining room table and sent the younger kids off to play quietly.

"As you know," Bale began formally, "Velona has been constantly growing every year. It seems we are something of a magnet for many in other countries as well. We've grown to well over a million citizens and there is no end in sight, as far as I can tell. We get immigrants from nearly all corners of the world coming here — hoping for a better life in my opinion. Our economy continues to grow by rapidly. We are a leader in new inventions, as witnessed by Dianna's new steam engine, which promises to revolutionize many areas, not just travel. Our artists are unrivaled anywhere on Tarra."

"However, there is a down side to our population explosion, a dark side, which I have been working to keep hidden from view, while attempting to fix it. I've come to realize that I am unable to do so. It's crime, gang. Oh, I suppose there will always be the street pickpockets hanging around, but really, that kind of petty theft is not what is troubling me. It's the sharp rise in more vicious, heinous crimes that has so baffled me."

"During the last five years, we've seen a sharp rise in rapes, beatings, and murders, along with major robberies and break ins. As you know, to combat this dramatic increase in crime, I've established the City Police Force and now have ten Detectives working the major cases with Cosima being our only Detective Inspector who handles the really baffling crimes. I keep adding more Detectives each year, but the number of these crimes just keeps on increasing in spite of all that I do to help capture the guilty parties."

"Until now, I have been unwilling to start to issue a large number of laws. I believe as you do that making a bunch of laws that are supposed to regulate personal conduct only antagonizes all of us who would naturally be doing the proper and right conduct. Those who would not follow such will just ignore the laws anyway. While none of us would ever consider raping another, the criminal elements would not be deterred in the slightest by our having a law on the books saying that thou shalt not rape another person. Those of us who would naturally not do such are only affronted, annoyed, and even invalidated and suppressed by having such a law on the books, as if we would ever think of doing such a thing. In short, official laws are not going to stop or halt or slow those who would naturally break them."

"Until now, I thought maybe the answer lay in fielding a sufficiently large police force so that the reprehensible are apprehended relatively quickly. Do you realize that as of now, we have more city policemen than we do actual soldiers protecting our country? Yes, it's true. Still the crime rate continues to escalate, as witnessed by the rape and murder the other day."

"I have to admit that I am at a complete loss on what to do next. I know that Lona has been doing her best as High Priestess in helping combat this issue. We both have the highest respect for you folks. So this afternoon, I decided to drop by tonight and ask you for advice and even such help as you can give." Bale finally relaxed; he'd laid it out for us.

Ania replied first, this was her province of expertise. "A person becomes criminal when he has lost respect for himself. Rightly or wrongly, he believes that he no longer can trust himself to do right actions and that he is no longer even worthy of his own respect. We've seen this happen in many ways to many people. For example, women, who were deceived by the Elders of Dorota and voluntarily had their arms amputated, upon discovering what they gave up and for nothing, literally lost all respect for themselves and committed suicide. We've seen men who cannot earn sufficiently to support their own families realize their failures and then take to criminal activities, in the mistaken hope that this will help. A person who does not respect themselves is a person you don't want to be around."

She continued, "So what do you do about the situation? Prevention and attack. First, identify the key areas in which people are struggling to make it and initiate programs to assist them in making it. For example, when we returned to Velona from Dorota and Megalos, we found that there were thousands of female victims in dire straits. We set to work on handling that situation, providing assistance in many forms: from providing free transportation to Dorota, to therapy sessions, to acceptance and honoring them by the Holy Rose Church and that of Jehosanity, and even to adopting some orphaned girls. To my knowledge, that avenue of lost respect of self has largely been handled."

"Prevention: find out what areas in which many are having great difficulties and set up programs to help them succeed — not handouts, but real help. If you like, Kali and I would be glad to lend you a hand on working this out."

Fired up, Ania continued, "Second is to attack the crime problem head on. Most believe that the only way to do this is to make the punishments so huge, so severe, and so overwhelming that a person will cease performing his criminal actions. Well, perhaps this may work if you carry it to an extreme. I mean, if it became public knowledge that anyone caught raping a woman or child would be summarily executed — if anyone caught robbing a business would be shot in the head — this would strike fear in some, but not all. They've lost their self-respect so it doesn't matter what you say you will do to them. Deep inside, they think that might just be the right thing to have happen to them — to be killed. So I agree with you, creating a new bunch of laws is not the answer."

"But how then do you attack the crime problem?" Bale asked, running his hands frustratingly through his hair. She'd just shot down the only real idea that he had had: more laws.

"Well, let's examine the underlying driving forces that have caused them to lose their self-respect. I'm just speculating now, but in the case of the rape and murder case that Cosima just solved, wasn't the man's opium addition the motive force behind his actions?"

"Well, yes, drug addiction has become a major problem within the last five years," Bale admitted. "While there have always been a few opium dens around, if one looked for them, within the last few years, their numbers have grown steadily."

"Right and the number of those heavily addicted have also grown substantially, I'll wager. Perhaps, Cosima can look into this for you. See just what percentage of the current crimes is tied to opium addiction," Ania replied.

Cosima raised her hand as if she were in school, "Excuse me, but I have already got those figures." Everyone turned to look at her. "Yes, well, I've been a bit bored, and I have been going over all of your police records for the last four years, working out the motives behind crimes. I was first looking to see if there were recognizable patterns. Let me get my notes," she added and dashed off to get them.

"One amazing young woman! Always two steps ahead of the rest of us," Dianna praised her teen. Armed with a pile of papers, Cosima raced back into the dining room.

"Ah, here, the percentage of drug crimes — that's my category for crimes in which drugs are heavily involved — either by stealing the drugs themselves or by stealing to support one's habit or as a byproduct of being on drugs — that percentage has been increasing rather dramatically. Four years ago, it was around ten percent; if this year continues on its current pace, that figure jumps to nearly sixty percent," Cosima explained.

"Wow! I had no idea," I exclaimed.

"That's incredibly alarming!" Dita added.

"I knew it was getting worse," Bale replied, "but I had no idea it was this bad."

"Yes, it's definitely getting out of hand. Now the next largest grouping

I found is related to a person having too little income to survive. You know, lack of a steady job, out of work, that sort of thing," Cosima continued. "Currently, that situation seems to be behind another twenty-five percent, more or less."

Ania resumed control, "So there would be the first two areas to directly attack. I know that you are planning to construct rail lines throughout Velona for the new steam engines to haul cargo quickly. Why not begin a project of offering those who desperately need employment jobs working on the construction of said rail lines? Besides, if you put enough of them to work on it, you will get the lines finished sooner."

"Now that is a good idea. I will get onto that first thing in the morning!" Bale said some hope returning.

"Now the opium situation," Ania continued, "is more problematical. While you could outlaw drug dens, we both know that they would just go underground and be even harder to control. Instead of doing that, why not go after those men who supply the opium to Velona? Confiscate their drugs and put them out of business?"

"Hey, we can help with that," Dita added. "Give us the names of the major owners of dens, and we can use bank records to figure out from where they are getting their drugs. You can then go after them."

"Brilliant. We don't want them going underground. Kill their supplies and the dens go out of business," Bale added, becoming even more cheerful. "I'll see that you have the list by noon tomorrow, Dita!"

Cosima wasn't finished, she interrupted, "At least another ten percent are strong armed extortionists, who insist on such things as protection money from store owners. Gangs have nothing better to do than to go around causing trouble and then demanding protection money. These seem to operate in the poorer sections of the city."

"Well, here, you could just arrest the gang leaders and take them out of circulation," Kali advised.

Cosima added, "The problem is that few shop owners voluntarily come forward. They are intimidated, bullied, or beaten into going along with the gangs and their suppression. It will be hard to identify them. Perhaps, we can do some undercover spying on likely areas and identify the guilty thugs."

"Excellent, excellent! I sure am glad that I decided to drop by tonight. I ought to have done this sooner," Bale exclaimed.

"Yes, well, let's work together now and do something about this mess. Kali and I will go undercover tomorrow. Cosima, you can point us into the right sections of town. No one will suspect us of being spies on the streets. No, Dita. You and Bethany will only draw tons of attention to yourselves," she added, seeing her pleading look. She knew that Dita would love to lend a hand, but considering our unique appearance, she was right. We would only attract the attention of others.

"Okay, then we will dive into the bank records," Dita volunteered.

"Big brother, Ania and I will help you work on the large construction project," Dianna added.

"Hey, what about us?" asked Alessa. "We all want to help too."

"You are right," I replied. "Alessa, you and Bianca can go with Kali and Ania. Ilenakova and Fina too. Elena and Jemma can lend either Dita and me a hand or Dianna, whoever needs some help. Enrico, you and the rest can be our coordinators, keeping track of us all as we go out and about, just in case trouble arises." This satisfied everyone. Bale thanked us profusely, and then the meeting became an informal chat, as Sandra brought in a large plate of cookies.

The next morning, Kali, Ilenakova, Ania, Alessa, and Bianca dressed in ratty clothing and had Enrico drive them to one of the poorer sections of the city. Here they fanned out and blended in with other women out visiting the markets. Their objective: spot and identify the thugs and gangs who were terrorizing the merchants and shops.

At noon, a messenger brought us a list from Bale. He'd listed twenty know opium dens and their owners. Dita and I headed for the Velona Banca del Dio and our basement records room. "Follow the money trail," Dita teased me. We began going over the banking records of the owners. "Rule out anything less than ten thousand," she added as soon as she opened the first of her ten owner's banking records.

"This is sort of fun," Dita suggested a while later. "I'm finding a pattern here, how about you?"

"Yes, there sure is. The question is: are all these dealers paying the same person? Keep digging, love," I replied, adding another financial transaction to my growing list. As the supper hour approached, she and I compared our halves of the opium den owners.

"Amazing, they are all paying large sums periodically to the same person," Dita observed. "Just who is this Bernardo Cosi anyway?"

"Well, he sure has a large amount of funds in his account," I replied.

"Maybe we should pay a visit to him and check him out," Dita suggested. "We can drop by on our way home."

"But what would we say to him? Why are you dealing to all the opium dens in Velona? Where do you get your opium from?" I asked. Dita grinned invisibly, but didn't reply as we packed up for the day. She, of course, was wearing her man's outfit, with tails and top hat, while I wore a red satin dress with a number of petticoats so that it billowed out a few feet. Dita loved my look and I respected hers. She felt vastly more comfortable wearing the pants, though she let her thick, long black hair flow down her back adding to her twin tails.

"Come on; we'd better put the darn metal lip plates back in before we go outside," she sighed. To avoid having our lips stretched even further, which would require ever-increasing size of the plates, we wore them only when out in public. We slipped the lightweight, golden colored plates back into our upper and lower lips. Inwardly, I thanked Dianna for her invention of these new plates. They were extremely lightweight, and she'd put a recessed curve on them so they fit nicely against our gums, adding to their stability and horizontal look. Only when our lips stretched enough so the plates sagged significantly did we have to have them enlarged. This we wanted to avoid as much as possible.

Dita held my hand so I could climb inside our carriage, and she hopped up to the tall driver's seat. Ten minutes later, she pulled up at a very nice home in the wealthier district of Velona. She helped me step down and arm in arm we walked slowly up to the main door, my Alexa boots clicking upon the stone pathway.

A servant opened the door and Dita asked, "Is Mr. Bernardo Cosi home?"

"No, sir, er ma'am," she replied, finally deciding that Dita was a woman.

"Well, then is Mrs. Cosi home? We would like to chat with her a bit."

"Whom should I say is calling?" she asked formally.

"Mrs. Bethany Brozena Malina and Mrs. Dita Malina. She's my wife," Dita added proud of me, especially since I was wearing red satin, her favorite color.

"This way," she replied allowing us inside. "If you will wait here, please, I will fetch Bella." We found ourselves in a fancy sitting room. Plush drapes outlined the windows and high quality furniture filled the room. We sat down on the love sofa facing the larger sofa. She removed her top hat.

"What's that smell?" Dita whispered to me.

"Opium," I whispered back.

Shortly, a middle aged woman entered, wearing one of the fancy Annelise dresses. She obviously wore a tight corset; her waist looked very small indeed. From her gliding and slow gait, we knew that she also wore those impossibly high heeled Annelise boots. She looked the height of fashion, but she was also armless! On the walls, we spied a number of holy crosses and knew at once that she was considered by her Church of Jehosanity to be a Holy Woman of the Eighth Degree. She had long brown hair, nicely curled, but her face was quite flushed, and she was breathing hard. Two servants quietly followed her into the room to assist her.

"I am Bella Cosi. I don't believe I have had the pleasure of meeting you. My, but you both are so attractive, such amazing lip ornaments," she said, staring at our duckbills.

"Thank you, Bella. You are a very beautiful woman yourself," Dita replied. "I'm Mrs. Dita Malina and this is my wife, Mrs. Bethany Malina." Dita moved over to her and gave her a hug. I followed suit. (Note that we both subtly used a bit of telepathy to make sure that others could understand our speech.)

"So pleased to meet you both! You are married, how unusual." As I hugged her, my lips touched her cheek, and I smelled opium on her breath. "My husband is at work still and isn't expected to return until six. We have quite some time to get acquainted. You are both so lovely, and I do love your hair, so utterly long, so lush, and so thick. My."

"Thank you. Might I ask what your husband does?" Dita asked. "We're from the Banca del Dio, and we're checking with our larger customers to see if there is anything that our bank can do for them."

"Oh, he is a merchant, runs Cosi's Paca. You know, that incredibly soft fur from those exotic animals. He sells apparel made from the paca wool. It's expensive but worth every penny. I will tell him that you dropped by. If there is something he needs, I will have him let you know. Do you mind if I ask you something personal? I mean, I've never known two women who are married before."

Dita grinned and nodded, Bella asked, "You must know how to really pleasure and please each other. Men just never do get it right, you know. I do so love to be pleasured. Like this, I can no longer do it myself. It is so frustrating. Don't think me rude or anything, but I would pay you both handsomely if you would take a few minutes now and pleasure me. I am so incredibly ready for it right now. It is so frustrating being unable to do anything for myself, please, I beg you."

I could tell that she was definitely under the influence of the opium, probably having just smoked some before we came. She was craving the touch sensation. So strong was her desire for it that we both felt it coming from her!

"I'm sorry, Bella. We have to get home fairly soon; we have two girls waiting for us to fix them their supper. Perhaps, we could take a rain check on your request. Would that be acceptable, Bella?" Dita said halfway sympathetically. Good old Dita knew just the right thing to say to get us out of an awkward situation!

"Oh, that would be splendid indeed. Oh yes, more than acceptable. I understand. I had two of my own to care for, but now they're all grown up and have flown the coop. Please, come back anytime. I am always here, except for Sunday church. You don't know how I crave such a simple thing as being pleasured." We both rose and gave her an affectionate hug, but she insisted on kissing our lips as they protruded from the large plates. I flushed, but endured it.

When we reached our carriage, I asked Dita to help me up to the driver's box. I wanted to chat. As we rolled along toward home, I said, "Well, she is likely addicted to opium, trying to suppress her despair over having become armless. I remember her name now, Dita; she was one of those duped by the Elders of Dorota into having them removed. She's lost her self-respect and has turned to opium to try to ease her pain." Dita agreed and we chatted as we rode home.

The next morning, we again hit the bank records. We poured over Bernardo Cosi's accounts, looking for funds that may well be linked to the opium trade and not his paca business. At lunchtime, we both stared at each other. Neither had expected what we had found!

"Half of the time, he sends large sums to Cardinal Reina Lano of the Church of Jehosanity here in Velona," I pointed out.

Dita added, "And the other half of the time, he sends sums to Cardinal Juan Malagon of the Church of Jehosanity, Bonito. That damnable church is at it again!"

"Perhaps not the church, Dita. We only have the two cardinals involved so far. Let's not jump to conclusions. How about some lunch?" We put our lip plates back in and headed out into the streets of Velona, heading for the many vendors who sold lunches. We dined at Luigi's because of their fancy outdoors tables. Here, you could dine surrounded by fresh air and many flowering plants in a cozy, romantic setting. Of course, while eating, we had to leave our lip plates in this time, making the process more difficult than usual. Still, we enjoyed ourselves. We had not been out like this in a very long time.

That afternoon, we began digging into the banking records of the two cardinals. Before too long, we discovered more intrigue. Cardinal Diego Estebano of the Barcella Church of Jehosanity also sent what appeared to be drug funds to Cardinal Juan Malagon of Bonito, but also sometimes to Cardinal Branco Beja of Vito's Church of Jehosanity. Further, we came across unexpected funds transfers. In both Vito and Bonito combined, there were now ten gun manufacturing companies. They were doing a huge amount of business!

Okay, at the mention of guns, we both were sidetracked! "Wow! Look at this, Bethany. The horsemen of the Northern Steppes have been buying a large number of these new guns, like a thousand," Dita exclaimed, looking at the figures.

"Incredible, Dita. Why would they want so many? Look what I've uncovered. Three of the kingdoms of the Greenway that either are bordering the Steppes or are closest to it have also purchased thousands of guns. Why? What is going on up there? We ought to find out pronto!"

"I agree, love. They could be planning to attack maybe Zargarb, do you suppose? That's about the closest country," she theorized. We speculated for a while, before diving back into the bank records. Still, the guns kept haunting us from the backs of our minds.

An hour later, we both said, "Ah ha!" simultaneously and broke into a laugh. We'd traced the drug funds from these two men back to the new Pope Christos of the Church of Jehosanity down in Megalos. "Glad that they got a new pope, but this one seems to be dealing opium," Dita said with a grin.

"Well, it does make the Church a whole lot of money. I wonder where Pope Christos is sending the drug funds? I don't recall ever hearing of poppy fields on Megalos. The opium must be coming from somewhere else," I replied. We both dug into the private records of Pope Christos. It didn't take us very long to discover that he sent very large sums periodically to one Yuen Ming in Shansee, Tan Lon Province, Tashien.

Since we still had an hour, we dug into Yuen's bank records. "Jeepers!" exclaimed Dita. "This man has millions in his bank account! Tens of millions! He's incredibly rich. This must all be his operation."

"Wow is right! I wonder if we can see where else he may be dealing his opium?" I asked. In short order, we found a connection to a man in Sud, Southlands. However, there was a very large number of transactions to accounts within Tashien — too many for us to search today.

Around the dinner table, we told everyone about our findings. Ania said didactically, "Well, it makes sense. Yuen sells to Pope Christos on Megalos, that's the closest place to Shansee. The Pope sends the drugs by caravel up to his two church-controlled countries and the cardinals in Bonito and Vito, where they then move the drugs to Barcella and Velona. I bet if you look further, then you will see them also going to the other Sea Prince Sectors as well. He must have quite an operation going to make tens of millions of gold."

"Now how do we break up this opium trafficking ring?" Ilenakova asked. "It would seem to me that if we intercepted the really big shipments that come in from Shansee to Megalos, then that would cripple the entire network. Beats just cutting off the supplies coming into Velona from Vito and Bonito."

"Right!" exclaimed Dita. "Go for the jugular!" We all chuckled.

Dianna interrupted, "You know, this gun thing has me more worried than the opium trade. Perhaps it ties into the rumors that I heard the other day, something about some army of Tashien invading the northeast seacoast of the Northern Steppes. Maybe there is a war going on up there that we haven't yet heard all about," she theorized.

"Damn! We'd better find out fast!" Ilenakova exclaimed; she hated wars.

"Yes, but gang," Cosima chose this point to speak up. "If you cut off the whole supply of opium, then we can expect the addicts here to become increasingly desperate for their fixes and thus a spike in crimes. Before you go cutting it off, we'd better let Bale know so that he can add more policemen to patrol the streets. Too bad there isn't any easy way to get a drug addict off drugs."

"Boy, our problems are mounting," Ania said. "We have a crime wave with which to deal, a possible invasion and war, and a major opium dealing ring to crack. This will take some doing!"

We had to stop our discussion to put our young children's bodies to bed. Controlling two bodies at the same time was terribly difficult, and we found that having them quiet helped a whole lot. Hence, we put them to bed early, around nine, just after dark.

When we all gathered around the dining room table a half hour later, Sandra had brewed us up another pot of tea, and we all sat down to explore ideas. Just then, Linda and the Guardian chose to make contact with us once more.

Chapter 3 The Guardian's Tale

The semi-ghostly forms of Linda and the Guardian appeared at the head of our large table and slowly solidified. Yes, we all found talking to solid bodies more comforting than talking to ghostly images. Linda realized this and insisted on their more solid forms.

The Guardian or Jes began, "Good evening. I have at last come to ask for your help, Bethany. Allow me to explain fully what is happening now. You all had a hand in dealing with the Grey Creatures and the mantis creatures, but let me clarify the situation. I am now very certain that Tarra used to be a penal colony for the unwanted spiritual beings of other worlds. By unwanted, I mean their artists, great thinkers, inventors, and even their criminals. Both the Grey Creatures and the mantis creatures periodically dumped their undesirable spiritual beings here on Tarra."

"Now spiritual beings are very hard to keep fixated here on this world. What's to keep Linda or me from taking off and returning to other worlds? In order to keep us all in prison, these races created a perfect prison — these fleshly bodies of yours. With our memories scrambled and by being forced into these human body's heads, we spiritual beings lost track of own identities and assumed the identities of the bodies. Thus, we remain imprisoned here."

"However, every prison must have its wardens to oversee the prison itself. Bethany and many of you have had a hand in eliminating the last of our wardens, the Grey Creatures and the mantis creatures. None of these have been seen on Tarra for over a century now."

"Good riddance!" Dita exclaimed with a passion.

"Indeed," the Guardian acknowledged her. "Now during your long voyage of exploration, done over a century ago, you came across another densely populated country hither-to-fore unknown, Tashien. As Bethany can attest, these people have very strange customs compared to all the other countries you've since discovered or have known. There, honoring one's ancestors used to be the sole driving force behind people's motivations for doing things in life. While on the surface, it sounds nice, in fact, this is a horrible aberration. People do horribly demeaning things on the sole justification that it honors their ancestors, which more often than not, it does not."

"Long ago, Bethany suggested to me that there might possibly be a third group of aliens here on Tarra — that an as yet unknown group of aliens were somehow controlling the people living in Tashien. Now that I have moved my large group of followers to Dorota, we lie not too far from the eastern coast of Tashien. Five years ago, I began sending some of my free beings over to that land to scout around. I wanted to find out if Bethany was correct or if there was some other action that had so utterly suppressed so many millions of spiritual beings. Make no mistake about it; the people living in Tashien are perhaps the most suppressed of any peoples on Tarra."

"Bethany, once more I must thank you for your astute deductions. Yes, there was in fact a third race of aliens using Tarra as their penal colony!" I gasped, as did many others.

"I knew it! I just knew that there had to be, Jes!" I exclaimed, so many things suddenly fell into place. My memories of my visit there over a century ago came back and the odd things fell into alignment.

"Yes, but this race was vastly different than the Grey Creatures or the mantis. They had strange bodies. Theirs were not alive as yours, not living bodies at all, but what I can best describe as a child's doll body. They stood some eight feet tall, but their forms looked like that of a rubber doll. I will place their images into all of your minds." I suddenly saw what could only be described, as Jes had said, a rubber doll, certainly not alive as our bodies were.

He continued, "These alien bodies did not need to eat, breathe, or even sleep, as human bodies must. In some ways, I admire them. Such bodies totally lack all the problems that our human fleshly bodies have. Anyway, they were discovered operating out of a remote cave in the Helios Grande mountains that separate Tashien from the impassable Desert of Desolation. My beings discovered that they used some form of electronic beams to control the people of Tashien. Great hemispherical dishes were located at periodic locations high in those mountains from north to south. They emitted an energy flow that caused the spiritual beings to become horribly suppressed in their emotions, down to the very low range that you have seen: useless, apathy, hopeless, victim, undeserving, and even numb."

"Now not all beings were that low, so very close to death. Some ranged a little higher, into the hostility and covertness range, and a few were at anger. Rare was the spiritual being who lived there who was significantly higher. All that was as of the year 749. While we were deciding what to do about the two doll wardens, two of my people continued to watch them and learn. They discovered that our two wardens were so utterly and completely bored with the whole operation that they finally 'died' — if such a rubber doll body can be said to have died. They dropped them and ceased to operate. We believe that they just more or less abandoned their posts here as wardens. Their electronic machines were shut off as well. We have taken the liberty of destroying them so that if others return, their imprisoning, suppressing machines will not operate."

We broke out into a spontaneous round of applause, which Jes appreciated. His smile told all. "Their suppressive control over the people of Tashien ended in the summer of 749. However, there has been an unforeseen problem. Well, I foresaw it, but many others did not. When that source of constant suppression over spiritual beings was eliminated, the emotional tones of the people then changed. Some have risen upwards from the depths of apathy to sympathy, covert hostility, and hostility."

"Until 749 as you all know, the Empress and her Emperor ruled over the tens of millions of inhabitants. While not perfect by any means, they maintained law and order, and a good measure of control over the lives of their people. All that changed abruptly when the Doll Creatures turned off their machines. As men rose somewhat in emotional tone, they became exceedingly hostile. We believe that some killed outright the current Emperor and Empress. Now the entire country of tens of millions is in utter anarchy and chaos. Overlords have appeared everywhere, fighting each other for control of the people and their goods and wealth and lives. Honestly, conditions are a deplorable mess there. The people have been degraded for so many centuries, that now that they are no longer forced into such degradation by the Doll Creatures, they are doing it to themselves."

"We have kept an eye on their chaos and violence for the last four years now. I hoped that in time, the people would continue to rise up in tone, cast off this current human-caused suppression, and rebound. However, it seems that the opposite has occurred. A few in power are doing to the masses just what the dolls were doing to them with their electronic beams. It is only growing worse each year."

"I believe that their turmoil is now beginning to spill over into other countries, something that we cannot have if we are to have a calm environment for us to operate freeing spiritual beings. So once again, my dearest Bethany, I must come to you to ask your help in solving this mess. Somehow, bring peace to that country. I believe some in the far north are now invading the Northern Steppes. I do not know what their goals may be."

"We're seeing it here, Jes. A man in Shansee is now distributing massive quantities of opium, funneling it into the Sea Princes," I replied. "We also know that there is a massive buildup of these new weapons called guns, heading into the Steppes and the nearby kingdoms of Greenway. We suspected that a war was happening, but it is good to hear confirmation from you. We have a huge crime wave hitting Velona now, brought on in part from these drugs from Tashien. So yes, those in Tashien are now destabilizing the world, and we must bring that to a halt. What do you want me to do?"

"Recently, I overheard the prayers of some devout followers who reside in Juda Arad. It seems that a young man has walked all the way there from Shansee, on foot no less. He has lost his fiancé somehow during this reign of anarchy. While I do not know how he knows, he knows about how over a century ago you helped Sho Lin Wu become Empress. He knows that at that time Velona and Tashien were allies. He has come to seek Velona's aid, and more specifically, yours Bethany, in finding his bride to be. While in the desert of the Arad, he ran into some of my traditional followers there and they have converted him to a belief in Lord Jehosa. They prayed together long and hard, which is why I overheard them. I took the liberty to answer their prayers. I told the young man to continue his journey to Velona and to seek the assistance of Mrs. Bethany Brozena Malina in his quest."

"You want me to help this young man find his bride to be?" I asked utterly incredulously. How could this possibly benefit anything? We were facing drastically larger problems than we had even suspected a few minutes ago and the Guardian was asking me to help a man hunt down a missing woman?

The Guardian smiled, ignoring my outburst of indignation. "Remember the old story: for the want of a nail, the shoe was lost, for want of a shoe, the horse was lost, for want of the horse the soldier was lost, and for want of the soldier the battle was lost? Well, while I cannot foresee everything, Bethany, somehow I believe that if we start in by helping this one person, then more and greater things will follow. Just what they will be I cannot say. I just have a strong feeling that this is the nail. I am bringing the nail to you, and I hope that you will find the shoe and fix the horse so that the soldier can go into battle that we may win the war."

"Okay, Jes, you know I will do it. When will he be arriving? What is his name?" I asked, mollified.

"He is arriving on a caravel from New Barq in two days. His name is Long Yan. He is twenty-three. I must caution you, Bethany. When you get to Shansee, you will see degradation as you have never seen it before. I suspect that you will find much changed there since your visit over a century ago. Persevere and I believe that we will win. Also, there is the matter of this war or invasion that must be handled. I know that you cannot be in two places at once."

"Hey! It is darn hard trying to run two bodies at the same time," Dita broke in.

"Yes, it is almost impossible," Dianna added.

The Guardian grinned, "And yet, you are managing, am I not correct?"

"Well, yes," Dita had to admit. "But it is not easy. We get so confused sometimes."

"Of course you do. Just persevere, Renzo-Dita, Enyo-Dianna," he replied.

"Okay, Jes, there are enough of us now that we can perhaps deal with all of these things at the same time. Dita and I will go with this Long Yan and help him find his fiancé. Some of the rest of us will deal with the opium problem, the war or invasion, and the crime wave here in Velona. It's a good thing that we have a strong, powerful group here," I suggested.

"That is all that I can ask of you." He looked around the table at all sixteen of us, pausing a moment to confront each of us in turn. I felt a surge of hope and power flowing from him to me as I met his gaze. The others did as well, I found out afterwards, though none of us knew really what it was all about, other than we felt truly content, hopeful, and strong. He then thanked each one of us personally and then he and Linda departed.

"Well, off we go again," Dita stated the obvious. "Damn, I forgot to ask him if he could fix our lips!" We all got a good laugh out of this one. She eventually calmed down and joined in our mirth.

"We are now being treated as equals and adults," Alessa pointed out. Bianca beamed.

"Well of course we are," Cosima replied, unable to fathom why she would not have been so treated. "I will work on the crime problems. I think I am the most qualified to do that, but I will need some help."

"Yes, I suppose that we ought to discuss who is going to tackle which problem," I took charge as Wid. "It seems that Dita and I are going into the lion's den in search of a missing woman. That doesn't sound too terribly dangerous. I think this war thing is going to be the toughest to handle."

"I'll tackle the war thing," Ilenakova volunteered. "Bianca, if you don't object, I'll take you with me."

"Woo hoo! No objections here," she exclaimed, extremely pleased that she would get to see some real action as a Protector. She'd feared that she would be left here in Velona.

Enrico volunteered, "I ought to go with those two. Three Protectors can be useful and, since wars are fought by men, they may well need a man's hand."

Kali spoke up, "I want to see if I can help deal with the opium trade. I hate that Church with a passion! The lives that they are secretly destroying are beyond words!"

"I'll lend her a hand," Ania added. "Fina, Jemma, any objections to lending us a hand?" Of course, they were as elated as Bianca.

"I'm on the home front and the coordinator," Dianna spoke up. "I will do all that I can to invent more useful things to help everyone out."

I continued, "Alessa, you are a Protector. I need you to protect Cosima. Elena, I want you to help me with the overall crime situation, lend a hand to Cosima and Alessa, and help watch after the six little children. We have tons of criminals to ferret out, especially so when their opium supply dries up. Sandra, Luisa, and Arturo will look after the six children and be ready to lend a hand with whoever needs it. Sandra will take over for us on the Banca del Dio records. We are going to be very spread out this time — like halfway around the world. You three be ready for whatever is needed."

"Let's appoint Luisa to be our central communications link," I suggested. "We all keep her apprised of our current situations and progress. That way, we all have one focus point, she can relay to everyone else." Luisa looked pleased. I knew that she and Sandra still held that their main objective was to protect our six growing child bodies. This they could continue to do and yet play a vital role.

"Hey, we have seven operational Grey Creature blasters," I pointed out. "They stop bullets. So, Enrico, I want you to take three with you. Ania, Kali, you take two and Cosima, you take the last two for your group. It is unlikely that Dita and I are going to be up against guns in Tashien, more like swords and fighting. Guns seem to be a western thing." Everyone agreed that this was a most reasonable request.

As Dita and I crawled into bed that night, she asked me, "Say, how are we going to find this lost woman of his anyway?"

"I have no idea, love, none at all, but Jes thinks that it is vitally important somehow. We will give it our best shot," I replied. "Now kiss me my love."

The next morning, we both had quite a shock. During the night, the Guardian had healed our lips. We stared at each other's lips. "He heard my prayers!" Dita exclaimed. I grinned. "Let me take a close look at yours, love," she said excitedly. "Wow, no scars at all. It's as if it never happened!"

We were the topic of talk at breakfast! She and I were both extremely relieved.

Chapter 4 Pian Wu Takes the Throne

It was early 749. Princess Pian Wu sat on her throne, reflecting on the news that she had been waiting all her life to hear. Her mother had died. "Finally!" she declared in relief. "Now it's my turn. She checked her six inch long nails to make sure she had not chipped their fiery red paint. Perfect. She checked the fall of her light blue silk dress, perfect. She held a mirror and gazed upon her makeup and hair. Her long black hair lay perfectly across her ample bosom. All was perfect. It had to be. She summoned her general. If he does what I ask, he is worthy of being my Emperor, she thought to herself. Pian was thirty-six, long overdue for donning the mantle of Empress of Tashien.

General Banzhou, a year older than she, tall and handsome, solid muscles, a virile man she thought, entered and bowed, before walking to her throne. "How may I assist my Princess this morning?" His voice had that subtle, sexy quality that had so enamored her when she had first met him some ten years ago.

"My dear General Banzhou," she said daintily, as befitting a princess, "our time has arrived. My brothers Nanping and Langzhou should have a fatal accident today."

"It is already arranged and needs only your permission to be executed," he smiled. He'd heard the news earlier and had set the long ago made plans into motion. Pian needed to remove from any possible consideration her two brothers and sister. Then, she would be the only choice for the High Council to consider for their next Emperor.

"Excellent, General Banzhou, excellent. Let it be done. Now, there is the even more critical situation of my younger sister, Shashi Wu, who is in Luoyang, in Linyi Province just north of us. Are our forces ready to take on the army that she has protecting her?"

"Yes, your majesty. Ours outnumber hers two to one. They await your orders and blessing," he replied, cunningly. He'd carefully worked out an assault scheme that was sure to clinch a swift victory. All depended upon it.

"Excellent. I want her banished to the ice lands of Dong Province. Yet, there, she may still be a threat. Before she is sent there, have her arms removed at the elbows so that she may forever be seen as a common whore, a concubine, a zen-kami, but no more," Pian said daintily. Without her hands and nails, she could never be considered for the position of Empress, because so much depended upon subtle flashing of one's nails and fingers.

"May I ask why not just her hands, my dear Pian?" he asked. They had planned to remove her hands when they had discussed what was to be done with her sister. Pian had obviously changed her mind.

"She deserves to be left some honor, my love. After all, she is the daughter of the late Empress, and she is my sister. If we cut off her hands, she will have no respect, no honor left at all. If we take but a bit more, to her elbows, then we are giving her back some honor, some respect. She can then be seen as a highly regarded sex toy, a zen-kami. I owe her some respect. I won't totally dishonor her, Banzhou, not completely."

"Yes, Pian, you are, as always, most wise and most kind. You honor your parents most well. It shall be done as you say. Expect her to be on her way to Xin within two days' time." He bowed respectfully.

"Excellent. There is one other outside possibility that we must consider, my love. I will not let chance enter the High Council decisions. I have a young cousin down in Nan Yang, Tan Lon Province. Her name is San Min Wu. She is only eighteen now, most likely far too young for the High Council's tastes. She has much to learn, you see. However, let us not take any undo chances. Since she has never had any aspirations for the High Throne of Tashien, not yet anyway, we will not take such drastic measures with her. Besides, she currently does not sit on a Province throne as my brothers do. So let's give her some honor as well. Arrange to have her abducted in secret and given to Yuen Ming. I am sure that he will know what to do with one with noble, royal blood."

General Banzhou grinned; he knew of Yuen. He was the biggest opium dealer in Tashien and owner of the finest pleasure palaces in Tan Lon Province. "My dear Pian is most wise and most generous as always. I am sure that she will find a place of great honor in his establishment. I will arrange it this morning, though it will take some days to get it carried out. We are in Zau, some five hundred or more miles from the mountainous Nan Yang. Still, it will be done long before the High Council could first get to her should they have such a desire." He bowed and she dismissed him with the proper flick of her long talons.

To her servant, she flicked the sign for high tea. It was time to celebrate the execution of her commands. In just a few days, she, Pian Wu, would be named Empress of all Tashien. Of that, she had no doubt now. She felt more relaxed than she had in weeks, especially since she had resolved what had been bothering her most about all this. No, her brothers would die honorably. It was her sister. Only last night had she finally realized that just cutting off her hands would leave Shashi totally dishonored. Her brilliant thought to remove them at the elbows and thus leaving her with some honor as a zen-kami had totally resolved her inner conflict that she had wrestled with for so long. Yes, Shashi deserved to be left with some honor; after all, she was her sister and daughter of the late Empress.

Thus, it came as no surprise a week later that the High Council representative came to her palace to ask Pian to become their next Empress. Two weeks later, Pian married and the general became Emperor Banzhou Wu, joining Empress Pian Wu on the Imperial Throne in Zau, Wontun Province in the summer of 749.

32

Barely one year later, in the summer of 750, chaos struck. The day before, all was completely normal throughout Tashien. The next day, tens of millions of people suddenly felt vastly different, as if some heavy yoke had been removed from them. Gone was the super-enforced tradition of honor your ancestors, though many, many people clung desperately to that notion — what else was there to hold on to? Some found themselves suddenly feeling totally useless, while others felt more of a hopelessness about themselves and their lives, particularly so among the very poor of Tashien. Some believed that they were mere victims of some horrible plot, while some rose to self-abasement. Some people were just plain numb, feeling nothing at all, while some screamed in terror from unknown threats. These people were just considered crazy and often executed. Despair struck the hearts of many, while anxiety and a general nervousness filled the minds of others, though they attempted to continue life as before.

A few rose to resentment, though some chose to carefully conceal such, particularly those who served those in power. No sympathy became the tone of many warriors, befitting what they did as a profession. Hate, anger, and open hostility arose in only a very few, particularly those in power or those who had always been actively seeking such. Many felt heavy pangs of grief, while others felt wholly undeserving. Emperor Banzhou and Empress Pian settled into this last zone. While neither spoke of it openly, wrestling with such feelings, they both felt that they were uniquely undeserving of life and their position, though they dare not admit why they had such feelings — not to each other, not to any others.

Thus, it was easy for the openly hostile, rebellious overlords to assault the palace and behead the both of them. The Imperial Throne passed into history on June 25, 750, and Tashien fell into utter chaos and anarchy. Overlords, long denied the power that they believed was owed them, now held power.

Solely by force of arms, brute force, wicked retribution, and wholly without conscience did these overlords maintain their control over their small sections of the country. By 754, Tashien was under the control of thirty different overlords. Most ruled with an iron hand if only to maintain their grip on their sections of the land. All vied with each other for more power. Many worked on building alliances in the vain hope of securing even greater power and control.

Chapter 5 Woes of Shashi Wu

It was early 749. Princess Shashi Wu sat on her throne in Luoyang, reflecting on the news that she had been given. Her mother had passed away down in Zau. Only twenty-two, while she had an angelic face and a young, perfect body, she had no aspirations to succeed her mother on the Imperial Throne. No, she had long ago assumed that her older sister, Pian, would follow her mother's footsteps and become the next Empress. She'd told this to Pian on many occasions. Still, she followed the advice of her boyfriend, Wu Zhou Cao, a highly educated, bright young man. Yes, her face was perfect; her long talons nicely done; her waist, perfectly small; her feet likewise tiny. She would be a perfect role model and choice for Empress had she desired the throne.

Wu Zhou had often sat with her, telling her such marvelous tales of the outer world. Breathtaking panoramas, artworks, incredible music quite unlike her own music, and marvelous inventions filled her mind from his stories. He'd actually taken a trip to Velona as a young, impressionable child, accompanying his father on a merchant trading vessel. Yet, Wu Zhou was not an intellectual; he was fighter-trained and commissioned in the Imperial Army, though still only a general's aide. One day, he knew that would change.

"We must protect you from Pian, Shashi," he said worriedly. "She is cunning and ruthless. You are a flower in spring, Shashi. It is not beyond hope that the High Council may step over Pian and ask you to become our next Empress."

"But I've told her repeatedly that I do not want it, Wu," she replied.

"Still, she may come after you, my love. We must prepare your defenses in case she sends her army after you," he pleaded.

"Well, if you think she will, then okay. Let's prepare for the worst. Honestly, I've done all that I can over the years to convince her that I am not and never will be a threat to her. I know how much she covets mother's throne. I am willing to back her all the way; she is my older sister, after all. The great honor should rightfully be hers. Still, I don't want anything bad to happen to you, my love. So let's get the defenses ready, but I don't think that they will be needed, really I don't. She's my sister, after all."

The next midday found his worst fears realized. Wu Zhou came rushing into her throne room, where Shashi sat in the company of her six personal servants. From the twisted expression on his face, Shashi knew something horrible had happened. "It's Pian's army, Shashi! They've surrounded your palace here. We are outnumbered heavily, though I have urged our brave soldiers to fight to the death to protect their Princess!" Now, sounds of battle filtered through the walls of her throne room. Wu

Zhou drew his sword. "I promise to protect you with my life."

He moved to her side, fearing the worst. For the first time in her life, Shashi felt fear; gone were all her pretenses of nobility, of honor, of being a Princess. "Why is she doing this to me? I am not a threat to her?" she cried out.

Before long, the throne room doors were flung open and a dozen fighters stepped into the room, gasping for breath. Their swords dripped blood onto the highly polished floor; their armor was covered in blood and many had cuts and tears, signs of fierce combat. They fanned out, but did not approach Wu Zhou and Shashi. Her servants screamed. However, she did not. Her heart was in her throat; she felt that she would gag if she tried to make the slightest sound! Her arms clung to her lover and final protector.

A uniformed general stepped solemnly and commandingly into the room. "By orders of Princess Pian Wu, I have come to carry out her judgment upon you, Shashi."

"Stand back! I am sworn to protect Princess Shashi with my life if needed," Wu Zhou cried out in desperation, knowing his resistance was both futile and far too little to stop them.

"Stay your sword, Wu Zhou Cao. After I carry out Princess Pian's orders, I will return your precious Princess Shashi to you along with her six servants. All seven will then desperately be in need of your assistance, if they are to survive. Pian does not wish to cause the death of her sister or her lover, Wu Zhou. When I return with them, you are to take them to Xin; she is banished forever to the ice of Dong Province. Still, as you will see, Princess Pian will leave her sister some honor. Her life will then be in your hands, Wu Zhou. I beg you to sheath your sword and prepare transportation for when I return with these seven in two days."

"Do as he asks, Wu! I need you now more than ever," Shashi pleaded with Wu, who finally did as his Princess asked. He could not go against her wishes.

"Wise is your protector and councilor," the general complimented Wu Zhou. "Men, pick up the seven and follow me. Wu Zhou, go now and prepare coaches for travel. You will need much. My men will not hinder you, on that you have my word."

Wu Zhou gave the formal bow of agreement and left. He could not face seeing these bloody men picking up his beloved Shashi. Two days, so little time, he thought, and so much to prepare. He must not and could not fail his Princess!

As promised, the general and his men returned to the throne room, where Wu Zhou waited impatiently for the return of his beloved Princess. The doors opened and the general walked in, followed by seven of his men carrying Shashi and her six servants. Wu Zhou gasped as he saw them. The six servants had their right lower arms bound in tight bandages. Pian had ordered the removal of their right hands! However, the sight of his beloved

Shashi was even more shocking. Both her arms were tightly bandaged at her elbows. These fiends had removed both of her lower arms at her elbows!

"You see, Empress Pian has given Shashi a high honor in her banishment. She is now a concubine of high honor, a zen-kami, befitting only the finest of Pleasure Houses. Take her now into permanent banishment in Xin." He bowed and left, as his men laid the unconscious woman on her throne. Her servants, barely conscious, sat beside her. Wu Zhou stared in utter shock for several minutes, until the whimpering of the servants brought him to reality once more.

Carefully, he carried Shashi out to the waiting carriage and put her inside. Then, he carried each of her servants as well. He sent for a doctor to accompany them. An hour later, he gave the driver the order to begin their long journey into exile. He sat beside her, holding her head in his lap, his fingers gently wiping her hair from her face. Tears trickled down his cheeks.

Some days later, when she finally regained consciousness after the doctor stopped giving her sleeping droughts, she too cried. "Wu, please kill me. Put me out of my misery. I am now completely helpless and of no worth to anyone," she wailed.

"You are of great worth to me, Shashi. I love you still. You must be brave. Honor your mother; she was a great Empress. Taking your life would bring great shame upon her and all our ancestors. At least think of them, if not me, your humble lover," he begged her, tears flowing from his eyes. He knew not what else to say to her. What could he say to give her hope for the future? She was indeed now so helpless. "I am here as always to love and protect you as I can."

She quieted down and began crying. Sometime later, Wu Zhou explained, "Shashi, I will not allow you to be known as an honored concubine or common whore. As soon as we get to Xin, we shall be married. Then, you will be my most honored wife. From there we will begin to rebuild. I have brought along all our things. Plus, I took the liberty of raiding the provincial treasury. I took all of their gold and gems. Shashi, we have a fortune with us, and we can buy nearly anything that we need. I took many hundreds of thousands worth. You will be rich."

"You still want me as helpless as I am now?" she whimpered, her eyes swollen and red.

"As always, you are the flower of spring to me," he replied honestly.

They settled in Xin just across the Upper Heng River in the cold northern province of Dong. During the next year, she and her servants finally healed and she began adapting to her new, harsh life, needing others to attend to her basic needs. She soon discovered that much had not really changed. Her servants had always attended to her needs anyway, only now she had a few more. The most embarrassing of these was being fed as a baby might.

Slowly, they began making plans for the future. Most importantly among these, both felt, was the acquisition of a mighty army. Never again did these two want to be at the mercy of an invading army. In this wild and icy country, an army was easily raised. Here, the desperate men eked out a living in the ore mines or felling great trees for lumber. Further north, the winters were long and filled with deep snow and ice. Even in Xin, the winters lasted far longer than both were used to enduring.

Then came the summer of 750 when chaos broke out across the entire country. Shashi rose to resentment bordering on outright hate — hate for what had been done to her — a life of helplessness in all things. Her hatred soon gave way to anger and at last a general hostility towards others who, in her mind, lived a life of luxury. Having arms was now to her a luxury. "I deserve far better than I've got!" she declared often. Wu Zhou himself rose to antagonism and a strong compulsion to lash out at others who had made his loving wife's life so miserable. He and she were now "owed" far better.

During the short summer of 750, they began to make plans to take their army and head south to seek revenge on her sister Pian. Those plans were abruptly dashed when they learned of the slaying of the Emperor and Empress. Soon word reached them of the constant fighting and treachery of the many overlords, who now had free reign over the lower, more valuable provinces.

"It'll take a bigger army than ours to defeat all the overlords," Wu Zhou complained bitterly.

"Dear, why don't we just go elsewhere? I remember all those stories you told me of the outer lands. We don't owe a damn thing to Tashien anymore. There is no reason to stay around this hell hole of a country anymore. Look what it has done to us and to me," she said bitterly, raising her short stumps.

"Hey, you are right as always, my spring flower. Why should we stay here, freezing most of the year? Damn them all! Let's move our entire army and all those who want to come with us to greener pastures, where it is at least warm!" Wu Zhou replied, suddenly inspired by Shashi.

Logistics became their first hurdle. He could not move their army southward to the southern large port of Shansee. Their far northern port of Ynan was iced in for all but three months in the summer. Besides, it was far too small to handle the vast number of boats that would be needed to transport a million and their gear. They could float down the Northern Heng to the port of Ning. Still, there remained the question of obtaining enough ocean going boats to sail to the outer lands.

Only one route remained open to them, the northern passage. The two spent hours looking at the map of Tashien and the outer lands, the dog bone continent. No way could they cross the Helios Grande range. Even if those tall mountains could somehow be crossed, no one could survive a trek across the Desert of Desolation, which lay beyond. Besides, once across it, another impassible mountain range loomed. The only possible route, until now totally unexplored, was to travel along the northern coastline. If they could somehow do this, they would arrive in the northeastern lands of the Northern Steppes. "It's supposed to be a land of nomadic horsemen, grasses as tall as your knees," he explained.

"And warmth!" Shashi added.

"Okay, there is a small town at the edge of the Helios Grande on our frozen northern coast, Chang. We should move there and send out exploration teams to scout the route. It may be possible to travel overland, maybe even by carriage, my love. Shall we?"

"Let's! It will be hard on us," Shashi explained, as if he already did not know the tremendous difficulties her one-handed servants had trying to dress up her and themselves against the bitter cold. In the bitter cold of Chang, life would be even more awful for them all.

Chang, they found most miserable. This wind-swept, port town clinging to the nearly barren rock of the far north was iced over except for the three summer months. During that time, many coastal vessels came to ferry out ore and great timbers, hauling them to the south, especially to the Tan Lon Province, where such great timbers were scarce. During their four years here, Shashi had a son, but he died of cold exposure one bitterly cold night. This only strengthened their resolve to move to the golden warmth of the Steppes.

By 754, his scouting parties returned with the anxiously awaited news. An army could easily make the two hundred-fifty mile journey along the northern coastline of the dog bone continent. The rest of that year, Wu Zhou worked diligently arranging their massive exodus. His army grew to just over five hundred thousand soldiers and their families. At first, he gave the peasants the opportunity voluntarily to join the exodus. While some welcomed the offer, he at last ordered another hundred thousand workers and their families to move with them. They would have need of carpenters, stone workers, and all manner of craftsmen, if they were to build a new city in this land of warmth and grass.

In 755, just as the ice finally melted along the coastline, the exodus to the new land began. A thousand soldiers and their families led the march, many of which were the scouts who knew what to expect. Wu Zhou and Shashi followed these men, bringing with them a long line of carriages, wagons, and makeshift sleds. The rest of his mighty army followed behind them. The tens of thousands of workers and their families walked in the very rear. Unknown to them as they started out, many more decided to join them as well, until the totals swelled to over a million.

Food was not their greatest concern. Only making eight miles a day, they were able to fish daily. Great loads of firewood fueled the numerous cooking fires at night. Water was their biggest concern. The desert on their left provided none whatsoever. However, the melting snows just inland provided for their needs, mostly. Nightly camping rituals consisted of collecting nearby snow and ice, starting a fire, boiling the water, and cooking their meals. By the time that the lowly peasants finally began their march at the very rear, the ice and snow had mostly all been used or had melted for the summer. Thousands of dead bodies lined the coast when the last of them reached their destination. This mattered not to Wu Zhou or Shashi. What was the life of just another peasant? Nothing, Tashien was full of them. These lowest of the low were used to feeling undeserving; they spent their lives in labor to honor their ancestors. Now, however, they too had risen in tone, free from the energy flows of the Doll Creatures. Many walked this trek in a state of numbness to all things, clinging to the faint hope that their promised warm land was not a myth. To rise any higher, they would hit despair and fear, which they could not handle. Better to just be numb about it all and walk on.

In late spring, the vanguard army finally reached the lush Northern Steppes, now fully abloom with spring flowers. Green grasses shot up everywhere. They stood and surveyed the low rolling hills with patches of forests dotting the horizon as far as they could see to the west and south. To their left, the foothills of the Kathas Mountains rose sharply. Good stone and timber was plentiful as well as mountain streams.

As planned, these thousand secured the area and began to build temporary quarters, awaiting the arrival of their leaders, Wu Zhou and Shashi. Thus, when the two arrived, a one-room log cabin awaited them. His arm around Shashi so that she could walk over this ground on her tiny feet, Wu Zhou led her out onto the Steppes.

"Oh Wu! This is so beautiful! So fresh, so warm! Thank you, thank you!" she exclaimed, really excited, and very much relieved to find the land was everything that he had promised her it would be.

Not long after they settled into the cabin, bands of horsemen began appearing in the distance. At first, these wild nomads kept their distance, surveying them, and appraising their strength. Daily, more and more of his soldiers arrived. At last, bands of these horsemen began sweeping in and attacking them. On foot, his soldiers were no match for the horsemen and their vicious charges and blades and arrows. That these men could ride without hands and still accurately shoot a short bow amazed Wu Zhou and his men. While their losses were heavy, what was the worth of a simple soldier? Not much, considering the vast numbers that he had with him. They felled many horsemen, though only about one for every six of his own losses. Wu Zhou considered these attacks mostly as harassment.

Now they had to begin to work out their next move. After much discussion, they chose to begin construction of New Xin here in the foothills. The higher elevation would give them added protection from the horsemen raiders, provide access to the northern ocean for fish, and access to the plentiful game that wandered the lush green lands. During the summer of

755, over a million "ants" began scrambling over the terrain; construction of a new permanent city had begun. Small wooden buildings began springing up like flowers on the Steppes. They had little choice but to prepare quickly for the coming winter.

"If worst comes to worse, Shashi, we can all migrate further south next year. Yet, we do not have such lush grasses in Dong Province, except in the far south. Perhaps the winters will be milder here. If not, I promise you that we will move to warmer weather. Far to the south lies the desert of the Arad, so it must be far warmer here than back in Xin." She hoped that it would be so.

Chapter 6 Preparations

"I say we take the high country route," Ilenakova decided. She, Enrico, and Bianca sat around out dining room table the next morning sketching out their planned route to the Steppes. "We can avoid any hassles with the more unsavory types in Vito and Bonito. Besides, it will be the fastest route there."

"How long will it take us?" Bianca asked, looking at the map.

"At least a month to the Arad. We only need to cross a tiny edge of that desert region. Of course, then it could well be another two weeks or more riding north until we find the horsemen or the battlefield," she stated calmly. In her previous lives, she had spent much time in the Zargarb area and was very familiar with the land there, albeit her knowledge was many years out of date.

Enrico suggested, "Our cover story can be that we are representatives from Velona coming to see if they need any assistance from our country. If there truly is a war going on there, they will be very pleased to have us come."

"Can we wait and meet this fellow that's coming for Bethany?" asked Bianca. "I'm rather curious about him." Ilenakova smiled; they all were most curious indeed to meet a man who walked on foot halfway across the world and all because of his love for a woman. Bianca wondered what kind of a man would have that strong a love. She just had to meet him.

Ania looked up from her maps. She, Kali, Jemma, and Fina were going over maps of the Megalos area, looking for likely ways to intercept the opium shipments. "We are delaying until he comes too. I think that we are all more than a little curious about him."

"Bale's giving us one of his gun caravels," Fina explained to Bianca. "With it, we can blow them out of the water."

"First, you have to know what ship it is that is transporting the opium and when it will be where. Only then can you intercept it," Kali pointed out. "This is not going to be easy. We are going to depend upon bank records to make an educated guess when a ship might be on its way. Of course, once we start sinking them, they will become cagier and cagier about their plans. I'm getting some papers signed by the Velona Banca del Dio which we can use if we need to examine banking records on Megalos. There is over a month's delay before those get up here to our bank. If we are going to have any chance, we must know when they pay for the opium. Even then, it will be a tricky operation. I'm sure that in time we will make a major dent in the overall supply."

Kali pointed out, "Further, we want to take them out before they get to Megalos. That way, the Church gets a double whammy. They paid for the opium which ends up at the bottom of the sea and they get to pay again." We chuckled, I hoped that this would work out so smoothly, but I had my doubts.

Dita and I then headed down to the docks to work out our passage to Tashien. Unfortunately, there were no scheduled caravels bound for there for many months. Reluctantly, we stopped by Bale's office on our way back. "Hi, what can I do for you two this — oh my god! Your lips!" He noticed them.

We grinned. "Yes, the Guardian has healed us thankfully!" Dita answered his unspoken question. "We've come by to ask a favor. We need to get to Tashien, Shansee, to be precise. Unfortunately, there's not any ship leaving for Tashien anytime soon. Could we possibly hitch a ride on the gun ship that you are sending down there with Kali and Ania?"

"Certainly, certainly. It is the Grande Pistola. I'll send word to the captain. Two more passengers?"

"Make that three for Shansee. We have to return one of theirs. Thank you, Bale. We owe you one," Dita replied.

"I think perhaps you have it backwards, lovely Dita of the twin tails. It is I who am deeply indebted to all of you," Bale replied humorously. She grinned and flipped her twin suit coat tails. We left and returned home, telling the others of our change in plans. Of course, they were delighted to have us along for the very long voyage.

We set about packing. "I am going to wear men's clothes," Dita pronounced, "enough of this silly pretending to be a woman for me. If they don't like it, then tough."

"Yes, but you ought to take at least one dress, just in case we need to not upset someone, dear." She grumbled but agreed to take my favorite yellow dress of hers. We decided to pack light and pickup other clothing there as needed. I then headed to the bank and saw to the transfer of sizeable funds to Shansee for us and to several other locations, including some on Megalos for the others. Once again, I chuckled at Dita. She brought one bag of clothing and one larger bag of weapons. Never can tell, she teased me.

The next morning we waited for the arrival of the caravel from New Barq. Dita and I decided that we alone would meet him, leaving the others to their last minute packing. It was a sunny, perfect Velona day, but then most days here in Velona were like this, especially in the spring and summer. Arturo had kindly driven our carriage here so that Enrico could continue his last minute packing. We three stood on the docks gazing out to sea, admiring the magnificent view. Gulls squawked overhead as workers scampered about loading and unloading a dozen caravels. Someone said that today was a lax day for shipping. I found that hard to believe.

At last, Dita spied the incoming caravel far off in the distance. Impatiently, we waited for another hour as it slowly made its way into the docks and moored. When the gangplank finally lowered, a young man, who was definitely from Tashien, walked down the plank.

I waved and shouted, "Over here. Over here. We're waiting for you." He waved back and walked towards us, his eyes sweeping all around him. He'd never seen a port as large as this or a city with so many towering buildings, especially the two enormous churches. He wore brown cotton trousers, very baggy, with a brown cotton shirt that seemed to have a thousand buttons running down its front. His black hair was long and done in a nice single braid down his back. His skin color was most definitely yellowish and his eyes gave him away as being from Tashien.

His command of our language was not that good, more like poor. "Hello. I be Long Yan. I be look for Velona helpers. You be they?"

"You bet we are. Welcome to Velona, Long Yan. Lord Jehosa's helpers have told us of your coming and a bit of what you desire. We have a ship ready to take us to Shansee tomorrow. First, let's go to our estate. Oh, yes, I am Mrs. Bethany Brozena Malina, and this is my wife, Mrs. Dita Malina."

"So pleased to meet such fine young women." He bowed low as if we were princesses or royalty. "Please to speak more slowly. She is you wife?" he asked slightly confused.

"Yes, she and I are married," I said more slowly, leading the way to our carriage.

"Such beauty times two," he replied politely.

I was wearing my red satin dress just for Dita and she kindly held my hand as I bunched up the billowing folds and petticoats and climbed aboard. She followed me and he climbed in afterwards. "Oh, I forgot to ask. Do you have any bags coming off the caravel?" I realized my blunder.

"No, just me. I walk long ways. Carry sword. Buy many boots," he replied. "Can I see city?"

"You bet you can. Arturo, can you take a sort of scenic route home," I called up. He chuckled and we were off. Dita began explaining the various sights as we drove by them. Long Yan was most impressed with the two enormous cathedrals.

A half hour later, we arrived back at our estate and the many introductions began. Poor Long Yan, there were so many foreign sounding names that he soon quickly lost track of who was who. Both Dita and I remembered the fancy Tea Ceremony from our journey to Tashien so long ago. We make a good attempt at recreating it for Long Yan, who was incredibly pleased that we did so. He'd been many months away from such civility, such reminders of his homeland. "You did good," he kept saying. "Most honored. Most pleased."

Next, we asked him to tell us his story, leaving out nothing. Instead of relaying it in his broken Velona dialect, I will paraphrase his tale for you.

"Five years ago, I was very happy. My childhood sweetheart and I were about to be married. We are madly in love with each other. Her name is San Min Wu. She is the most beautiful woman in the whole world, with such long black, shiny hair, such fair blue eyes, and a smile that electrifies me. We had not yet married because she is the niece of the Empress Nang Wu. We must wait until Empress Nang passes away and a new empress is chosen. There is no chance that San Min would be chosen, because Empress Nang has two daughters and two sons who are directly in line for the throne. Yet, we choose to honor Empress Nang by holding off getting married until the new Empress was chosen. Woe unto us for having done that. Perhaps if we had married, none of this would have ever happened."

"We live in Nan Yan, a large inland city on the Yan River. It is many hundreds of miles from Shansee, northwest of there. Then, in 749, Empress Nang went to join her ancestors. We, as did so many in our country, chose to spend a week in mourning for her. We'd hoped that when that period had passed, the High Council would have chosen a new Emperor, and Empress and we could marry at long last."

"Alas, that was not to be. On our seventh day of mourning, San Min suddenly vanished. Her two servants found her bed empty, but used. A window was smashed. Someone had come in the night and abducted her while she slept!"

"Frantic with fear and worry, I searched high and low for her. After months of searching, I found two river men — they drive boats up and down the Yan — who saw three men carrying a woman wrapped in bed sheets down the street late at night. According to these men, she was taken onboard a riverboat, heading downstream. I packed my few things and began to follow this — my only clue. There are many small villages and towns along the Yan and many small homesteads. I visited each and asked everyone if they had seen this boat and the woman of my heart."

"Perhaps I went too slowly. It took me many months to ask everyone I could find along the way. Finally, I found a man who recognized the men on the boat. He said that they worked for a local overlord named Ho Ba who lives in Giang. This is a city at the junction of the Yan River and the mighty Yonshu River, due north of Shansee."

"I spent much money in Giang, seeking information about what Ho Ba might have done with my precious San Min Wu. I even snuck into his compound in search of her and nearly got killed there. After months of trying, I finally found two of his men who told me of her, though it cost me the rest of my money to find out. Ho Ba had been ordered to send her on down to Shansee to the most powerful man, Wie Li Bosu, Yuen Ming!"

We interrupted him at this point. "Wait, Yuen Ming — the opium dealer and whorehouse owner?" I asked. If so, he was at the focal point of our opium trade, a man we had to stop.

"Yes, opium maker and dealer. I don't know this whorehouse word. He runs the most elegant and expensive Houses of Pleasure throughout all of Tan Lon. With a heavy heart, I traveled down the Yonshu to Shansee. If Yuen Ming has my San Min, then I don't know how I can find her or get her back. He is more powerful than the Empress; he has many men at his beck and call, evil men who kill without conscience. They are almost as bad as the Cao Bang, the band of thieves and assassins, who seem to be everywhere in Tashien."

"During this time, somehow our whole world has become chaos. The new Emperor and Empress were assassinated, some say by the Cao Bang. Who can say? Everywhere, everyone is out for themselves, so it seems to humble me. I get to Shansee and find that now the city is controlled by Yuen Ming, not by the Wu family as it has been for centuries. Still, I work a little to stay alive and search for my San Min. She must be here somewhere. I look for a year and find no sign of her; nobody has seen her."

"I paid an artist to make a sketch of her as I remember her to show to others. Still no one has seen her. I begin to despair. In my heart, I know that she yearns for me still. Then, I meet the prophet Yulin Wang in the street. We talk and I tell him of my plight. We sit and meditate. He opens my mind, and I can at last sense San Min! She is alive! She is waiting for me to rescue her! However, I do not know where she may be or how it is that I can do this thing, not against this most powerful Wie Li Bosu! Yulin offers me some guidance. 'Seek the Historian Jin Han's writings.' I did as he asked and read his tales of how those of Velona came to help Empress Sho Lin Wu so many years ago. I now see that in Velona lies my only hope."

"I began to walk there. I had no funds to buy passage so I walked. Most of the time, it was pleasant enough. However, in the land called Arad, the desert land, I nearly died of thirst. Some local men found me and saved me. They taught me of their God, this Jehosa. I told them my tale of woe, and they convinced me to pray with them to Jehosa for guidance. I did so. A miracle occurred. This Lord Jehosa does exist. He spoke to us telling me to continue my journey to Velona, and there to seek out Bethany Malina, and she would help me find my precious San Min. So impressed were these kind Arad men that they led me to this New Barq and bought me passage here to Velona. I owe them much."

"It is beyond me how it is that you may be able to help me defeat this Wie Li Bosu, but I am here to plead with you for your help," he ended humbly.

"You have our help," I answered him. "If San Min is still alive, we will find her and get her back to you. I promise you this. Now then, we also have a beef with this Yuen Ming fellow. He is sending his opium here to Velona, which is corrupting our city. We aim to put a stop to his drug trading."

"But he is Wie Li Bosu, a very powerful boss lord. Yet, I do not doubt the wisdom of our great historian Jin Han or this great God Jehosa. However, I do not have any way to pay for your assistance. I am sure that if you can get San Min back to me, she and I will work for you always until you say our debt is paid."

"Let's worry about that later. Right now, the primary goal is to find her and get her back safely," I replied.

Kali interrupted gently, "We have about five hours before the Grande Pistola is due to set sail. Perhaps Long Yan would like a quick tour of Velona."

"Yes, Long, you must have a tour before you go," Alessa spoke up. We can take you on a nice tour while our folks finish packing and all that." I could see that our little girls wanted to chat with him before he left. He graciously followed them out to the carriage and crowded inside, giggling and chatting away, far too fast for poor Long to grasp everything. Still, he seemed to be enjoying himself and their company.

After they left, Dita stated, "Okay, Kali, you put him out of business and we will take him out if we get the chance." Kali grinned, that's precisely what she had in mind, along with doing irreparable damage to the Pope and his Cardinals.

Later, we hugged and said our farewells to our girls, friends, and Forze Segrete. A bit later, we walked onto the Grande Pistola and met our captain, Dante Nestore. He was a lean man, but strong. He had a sixth sense about sailing caravels and was a terrific navigator. Enzo Orfeo was his bosun and second in charge, a burly man who took no back talk from the crew. In charge of the guns and thirty soldiers was Commander Mario Iliano, a veteran field commander of the Cannonae Batteries. He was widely known as one of the best shots around.

As we went below deck, we soon discovered that this caravel was fully loaded. In addition to the gun supplies, they had stored enough provisions to last some six months. However, despite the crowded conditions, we had enough private cabins for everyone. Besides us, the only woman on board was their cook Gina Nestore, the captain's wife. She was very happy to have so many women along for a change and invited us to spend as much time in her galley as we wanted. "Lot's o' tea for you all," she gaily informed us, which suited me fine. Now I could finally sip tea easily and not have to slurp it from a spoon!

After we all watched Velona slip into the horizon, we settled down for the long, two-month voyage. I decided that this was the perfect time for us all to learn or relearn his language. Tashien's language was vastly different and more complex than any other was. While Ania and Kali might not have any need to speak it, there was some chance that they might need or have to put in at Shansee for resupply. For two months, Long Yan spent long hours working with all of us.

One peculiar aspect that we learned from Long was that the length of a woman's fingernails was proportional to her social standing. That is, no one was allowed to have nails as long as six inches or more. Such was reserved for the princesses and Empress. Peasants who worked in the rice paddies, for example, had no length. In Tashien, the length was measured not from the base of the nail but rather how far it extended from the fleshy tip of the finger. Ours were already two inches long as was the current fashion in Velona. In the two months of our voyage, I expected that they might reach three inches. According to Long Yan, this would be a visual clue to everyone we met that we were very important women. As such, it might open more doors.

This gave me some ideas. I began to work out a method for finding his fiancé. Shansee was really the only port open to the western world, the outer lands. Hence, there should be no problem with our appearing on their streets. If we wore our Velona dresses, we would look to be tourists or visitors. As such, we may well get special treatment from the local establishments, especially if the length of our nails was a guide. True, merchants would tend to overcharge us, but I was not worried about funds.

I began to reason out a theory of what may have happened to San Min Wu, based upon my experiences with Sho Lin Wu so many years ago when I was last here. At that time, there was a power struggle for the throne. Her sister attempted to kill her so that she could be the only candidate for the throne of Tashien. Ruthless indeed was this struggle to become the next Empress. According to Long Yan, San Min was only a cousin to the woman attempting to obtain the throne for herself. He told us that she had defeated her sister's army and banished her to the frozen northern province. Further, he pointed out that he had heard that her two brothers had been killed shortly after the old Empress passed away. I guessed that this Pian Wu had ordered their assassinations, leaving her the only candidate for her mother's throne. It made sense, based upon my experiences there over a century ago.

San Min was only a cousin of this Pian Wu. Thus, she was probably only a distant threat to be appointed the next Empress. If Pian were thorough in her plots, she would be going after San Min as well. Still, she could not banish or exile her, because she had not the authority to do that outside her own siblings. Admittedly, I did not understand why Pian would have the authority to banish her own sister. Okay, if she couldn't banish her, how about killing her? No, she was only a cousin. The risks of being caught would be so severe as to ruin utterly any chance that she would be chosen to be the next Empress. Pian would have to risk that with her brothers, but not her sister. Certainly, she would not take that extra risk for only a cousin who probably had little chance of beating her out for the position. No, San Min would simply have to vanish and not be seen in her normal life in Nan Yan again.

In view of this, her midnight abduction began to make sense. She was removed from Nan Yan and taken hundreds of miles away to the large city of millions, Shansee. Okay, so far so good. Yet, if San Min were then just dumped into the slums of Shansee, surely within the past five years she would have been able to find a way to return to her home city, Nan Yan. No, she must somehow be being held a prisoner somewhere in Shansee.

I asked Long Yan if there were prisons in Tashien, a place where San

Min could have been locked up for all this time. His answer was, "What is a prison?" After explaining the concept, he said that there was none. If one dishonored his or her ancestors, then that was public humiliation enough. For more severe crimes, they were simply beheaded. No need for prisons in Tashien.

Okay, no prisons. Still, my theory was that San Min was being held against her will at some location in Shansee. She was given to this Wie Li Bosu Yuen Ming, the opium drug lord. Obviously, he also knew of her social standing as a princess, her breeding was that of the Wu family. She would be a valuable trading commodity at some point in the future. I was sure that he would not have killed her. The man was obviously into making money. I theorized that he kept her alive for solely monetary gain. This would make perfect sense.

Where she was being kept prisoner was the real question, I decided. I envisioned her locked in chains and bound to some heavy timber such that she could not get free. Indeed, she could be held almost anywhere. No, wait! I was forgetting the key aspect of this whole country, well what used to be the key aspect. Lord knows what we will find there now. Honor. San Min was nobility. If Yuen Ming held her in a filthy hovel all these years, he would be bringing total disgrace upon her. If that were her condition, she would be bringing disgrace upon her parents. Since he was the cause of that, he, too, would be bringing enormous disgrace down upon himself.

Though he was an opium lord and a whorehouse proprietor, would he still feel disgraced if he brought such a disgrace upon San Min? Ah, that was a good question, one I could not answer without first meeting this Yuen Ming personally. If he had no sense of honor at all, why, he could be keeping San Min in chains in some hovel. Yet, if he still held to the traditional view of honor, then he would have to keep her in far, far better living conditions, as befitting one of nobility.

So if she was being kept in some fancy place, we would stand a better chance of gaining entrance there if we too appeared to be of high social standing. Hence, I suggested that Dita and I allow our nails to grow instead of keeping them trimmed at our usual two-inch length. Fashion was now not our prime consideration.

Yet, I also realized that we probably could not just walk up to this Yuen Ming and chat, which would tell me lots about his nature. As the Wei Li Bosu, I would expect that he would be surrounded by large numbers of bodyguards at all times. He undoubtedly had many, many enemies who would love an opportunity to eliminate him and take over his business. We probably would not have any chance to get close to this drug lord. Still, the measure of a man can be ascertained by a careful examination of his possessions. In this case, according to Long Yan, Yuen Ming owned quite a lot of establishments in Shansee. By visiting these, we could see how he treated his possessions and thus gain insight into his personal nature.

When we arrived, I first wanted to wander the city and look at the many establishments owned by this Yuen Ming. Yet, as a tourist of visitor, this would make us more than obvious. We needed to look more like locals. Our skin was a light brown, while his was more yellowish. If we wore traditional Tashien clothes, we might pass as locals. At least we would not stick out as we would if we wore our Velona outfits. I explained my ideas to Dita and Long Yan.

"But what will this tell us?" Long asked somewhat confused by my suggestion.

"If his establishments are rundown, ill-cared for, then she may be anywhere. His level of honor would be low. On the other hand, if his properties were well kept, then he probably maintains a high level of honor in your society. This will give me clues as to where San Min may be being held," I replied. He still didn't see the connection totally, but accepted it.

While we were busy with our language lessons, Captain Dante Nestore had all hands working on the deck of the Grande Pistola. Naturally curious, we had to check out what he was doing. "Ah, fine day, ladies, careful on deck. As you can see, we are very busy," he teased us. Some thirty men were working with canvas and paint.

Seeing our curious expressions, he explained, "The Grande Pistola is a gun ship. Other ships get very nervous when we sail close to them. Whenever we sail into a harbor, everyone gets overly worried. I am concocting a disguise. They are painting the canvas to look like the sides of a ship. We will lower the canvas over the eight gun holes on each side. To a casual observer, we will look like any other caravel, that is, until we raise the canvas and open the gun ports. Clever, eh?" He grinned with satisfaction.

"Brilliant, Captain, positively brilliant," Kali exclaimed.

"Still, it will not stand up to close inspection. So when we get to Shansee, we will anchor in their harbor and use a dingy to get you ashore. No sense giving our presence away prematurely," Captain Dante added. "Further, when we are in attack mode, we will fly this skull and crossbones flag, indicating that we are pirates. That ought to further confuse the issue."

I relaxed a little. I was certain that my friends would be safe. Captain Dante knew what he was doing. He then asked, "Kali, I still don't see how we will know when an opium run is being made."

"Well, it all has to do with banking records," she explained. "You see, the Pope must deposit say ten grand into Yuen Ming's account at the Banca del Dio somewhere on Megalos. However, notice of that deposit has to be delivered to a Banca del Dio in Shansee, before Yuen knows that he now has the money. It is far too risky to send a courier with such large amounts, too great a risk of interception. Now the way that the Banca works is this. Each month, a Banca caravel picks up that month's set of records of transfers to Banca del Dio's in other countries and delivers them to the appropriate banks. No one tries to intercept a Banca del Dio caravel for two reasons.

First, they are well armed with some fifty fighters. Second, all that they are carrying is bank records, no real funds to steal."

"Now in the case here, on the first of each month, a Banca caravel leaves Megalos for Shansee, arriving around the end of the third week. Simultaneously, another Banca caravel leaves from Shansee heading for Megalos. When it gets to Megalos, it unloads the Banca records bound for Megalos and hands over the records bound for other countries, such as Velona or Demokritos. Other caravels then take those records on to these other places. There is a vast network of caravels plying the oceans taking banking records from country to country, until they at last reach the main Velona Banca del Dio, where the master set is stored. This gives us some big clues."

She continued, "So we know from the last three years' worth of records, that a large amount is transferred from the Pope to Yuen Ming before the first of each month. Yuen Ming receives notice of the transfer late in each month and then arranges for a ship to depart for Megalos with the opium. If he does not get notice of a transfer, he does not send a shipment. Thus, we only need to look for a shipment leaving Shansee late each third week or during the fourth week of each month."

Captain Dante grinned, "Well, that does explain a lot. Still, we must know which boat is carrying the opium."

Kali sighed, "Still working on that one."

Later, Kali chatted with us in private. "You know, it would be perfect if either Jemma or Fina could be in Shansee spying on the docks. When they see a ship being loaded with the opium, they could use their telepathy to let us know the details. Yet, I am leery of leaving our teens alone in such a chaotic country on their own."

Fina and Jemma both sat with a huff expression on their young faces. I couldn't resist a chuckle. "Why? You don't trust us, Bethany?" Fina finally retorted.

"Of course I trust you both. But you are both very young and this promises to be a very dangerous place, lawless in fact. We'd all worry about you constantly. Besides, if something went wrong, you'd have no way to leave the city," I replied.

They continued to sit like stone statues. I couldn't blame them, both wanted in on the action. "Well, Linda did say that there are some Forze Segrete members in all countries. When we get to Shansee, I will see if I can find some. If I can and if they are willing to watch over you two, then I will allow you to become spies in Shansee."

Both statues animated. Big grins replaced the stony stares. "Thanks, Bethany," Fina replied. "We can do this you know. We can look after ourselves."

As we neared our destination after some two months at sea, Dita complained to me, "With my nails this long, I am going to have a hard time holding my weapons! Are you sure having them this long is required?"

"Yes, for a while anyway, Dita. We are not here to fight. Lord knows that there is enough of that going on already. We need to go quietly about finding this woman. For that, we may need to gain access to establishments off limits except to those in higher society, whatever that means here in Shansee these days. After we get her rescued, you can cut them back as short as you like, but I do like how great your back scratches are," I teased her. Honestly, we both loved giving each other a loving scratch at bedtime. She grinned and was mollified for the moment, though I could see her frustrations while trying to grip a sword.

"Land ho!" came the welcome cry from the crow's nest. We all headed topside to watch our glide into the bustling port of Shansee, Tashien. As I said, this was still the only port open to ships from the outer lands. In the past, their rulers wanted to keep contact with we foreigners to a minimum and thus only opened this single, large port. Besides, none of their other port cities had sufficient water depth at their docks to support our deep keels.

As planned, Captain Dante hove to in their bay. He did not wish a close inspection of the Grande Pistola, a gun ship. Once the dingy was lowered and two crew members manned the oars, we climbed down the side rope netting and into the small safety craft. Dita, Long Yan, Fina, Jemma, and I took our seats. Yes, I decided to bring the teens along or there would be no living with them if they did not get a first-hand look at this strange city. If things were as bad as he claimed and if we could not find any Forze Secrete members, then Fina and Jemma would have to return to the Grande Pistola, wiser for their visit.

The docks were vastly different from that of Velona. Here, three caravels were either loading or unloading. In contrast, we saw dozens of their smaller, bamboo coastal craft docked, to say nothing of the hundreds of smaller fishing boats plying the wide harbor. As we climbed onto the docks from the dingy, we began to get a good look at the workers. In contrast to the sharp, business-like hustle and bustle of activity around the Velona docks, here, the men moved slowly, carrying over-burdened loads on their backs. One immediately got a sense of their emotions of hopelessness and uselessness. It was striking and annoying, I thought.

Their clothes were a drab brown, pants tied with ropes around their waists. Their drab cotton shirts were also dingy brown. Many wore a headband of brown to keep the sweat from their eyes. Hardly anyone noticed us as we walked along the planks to the solid ground. Here at the port, the land was entirely flat, though thickets of tall bamboo and a few trees could be seen in the distance. Rice paddies dotted the outer edges of the area and we could see the rise of many buildings ahead of us. Shansee was a city of nearly a million inhabitants, but most of the city was well back from the low-lying dock area.

As we walked past the large warehouses close by the docks, we spied numerous transportation vehicles, most were two wheeled, cart-like affairs, pulled by a person. Long Yan suggested that we first get a room at the main visitor's inn called the Santi. As we approached these vehicles, we became bombarded with, "Want ride? Take you anywhere." I had given Long Yan a money pouch so that he could act as our guide here. We piled into the first three riks as they were called, and Long said, "Take us to the Santi." Dita and I sat together in one. We watched as our man lifted up the two front bamboo poles and began pulling us along.

We moved along the outer fringes of the docks and got our first glimpse of the southern edge of the port city itself. The streets were as narrow as I remembered, packed with people, merchants, and shops. Signs hung over their heads, proclaiming everything from fresh fish to silken clothing. Shansee was certainly a busy place. However, we quickly veered to the right and headed eastward away from the bustling crowds.

A quarter of a mile later, we pulled up at the old Santi del Dio fortress and tower! I was shocked! We had originally built this over a century ago as a place of protection. When the Santi disbanded, the fortress was given back to Shansee. Now they conveniently turned it into an inn for their outside visitors! Well, we certainly would have secure quarters at least.

As we entered carrying our bags, a man came up offering to carry them, insisting on it. At the check-in desk, the manager asked, "Welcome to Shansee. How many rooms would you like? Would you like to see the layout and our prices first?" He pointed to a big map on the wall.

Curious, we all looked. The cheapest rooms were in the old ground level barracks where our fighters used to sleep. The rooms in the tower were increasingly expensive, with the ones at the very top costing the most. "Let's stay at the top!" exclaimed Fina, actually rather excited to be staying in an old Santi fortress tower. "I bet the view is *spectacular* from there." I got the subtle message.

"Yes, we will require a large suite on the top floor of the tower. It must have a good view of the docks and the city, please," I replied. I noticed that the manager was discretely observing our long nails and filed that away for the future.

"Ah yes, as it is, the entire top floor is currently available. I'm sure that you will find Suite 501 to be exactly as you desire. That will be ten gold per week; meals are included," he replied, watching carefully how I reacted to the steep price.

"Ah, perfect," I said, flashing my nails coyly. "Can we pay for three months in advance?" I wanted him to get the idea that money was no object, fitting with a person of high social standing. His face broke into a very broad grin and I knew that I had accomplished my goal. I handed him ten golds and a gem, which was the usual way to handle large sums. No one carried around pounds of gold. Rather, a bank transfer would handle the balance.

Once he received confirmation from his local Banca del Dio, he'd return my gem. He bowed and handed me several duplicate keys to our quarters.

He snapped his fingers and a bellhop came to show us around and to our suite. "Here is the dining room," he pointed out. Soon, it was up four flights of stairs to the top of the tower. I discovered that we had the entire western half of the tower. We had a good view of both the city and the docks. Perfect. I gave a gold to the bellhop, who had kindly lugged half of our bags up the stairs for us. As expected, he bowed and thanked me a dozen times, before leaving us.

"Wow! Silk sheets!" exclaimed Fina, who had already begun checking out the place.

"This must be where the top leaders lived," Jemma added. "What a grand view. We can easily keep an eye on the docks from here, especially with our spyglasses. Way great, Bethany. Thanks."

"Okay, let's unpack and then it's time to do some initial shopping. Dita and I must get some local clothing," I suggested. "Long Yan, you get some too. We need you to look like you are a noble gentleman as well."

He grinned, bowed, and thanked me for being so generous with my funds. We left the girls to explore the fortress and get themselves ready for spying, and we headed into the city by rik. The manager gave Long some directions to a fine clothier, and he relayed it to the two men who pulled our riks. Soon we were moving among the teeming streets, crowded with people.

Dita and I observed them carefully as we slowly were pulled along. The tone level was deploringly low. Hardly anyone was much above the fear level. However, we soon spied what we would call common street thugs, bullying others, outright robbing others, and once we spied a man stabbing an older man. Incredible as it seems, no one paid any attention to these thugs or the man bleeding to death on the side of the street. Just as I was about to do something for him, a woman stopped and began to assist him. Wow! Our eyes were beginning to open. This was not like our earlier images of Shansee at all!

At the clothier, we entered a fashion shop for the wealthy! Many fine dresses were on display as well as gentlemen's suits. Okay, don't give two women an unlimited budget in a fancy dress store! I admit that Dita and I went a little overboard. She picked out a white linen man's suite with all the trimmings and then one in silk, before she got to picking out a beautiful blue gown made of silk. It was thin and loose fitting, though its pencil thin bottom fell straight as an arrow to her feet. A walking slit allowed freedom of movement, though. The dressmaker insisted that this was the very latest in fashion for elegant ladies such as us. She duly noted our long nails, of course, and catered to the needs that she thus perceived we had.

I took a linen dress, a silk dress, a cotton dress, and then three more silk dresses, before we both got around to finding something for "everyday around the house" dresses. It took some explaining before she brought out a common peasant's drab brown cotton dress. "Ah perfect for lounging around," I exclaimed, putting our dressmaker more at ease. I figured with a little work, such as spilling some tea on it, we could get these drab dresses to blend in. Either way, once we were dressed in these outfits, we would definitely not appear as tourists or visitors, at least to the casual eye.

When we were finally done, Long Yan appeared in his new light brown silken suit, complete with top hat to match. He looked very pleased with his look and whispered, "I do wish San Min could see me now."

"Don't worry, soon she can," I whispered back. "Next stop is the Banca del Dio."

A half hour later, we entered a far wealthier section of the city. While the crowds were no less thick, they were better dressed. We noticed that if we were wearing our new dresses, we would blend in remarkably well. As we got out of the riks by the bank, several well-dressed men bowed to us. I nodded in return and caught them eyeing our nails, further confirming that we had made the right choice. Strange custom, I thought. It took only a couple of minutes to arrange the transfer of our balance to the Santi inn and to withdraw sufficient funds for daily expenses and the funds so far expended.

By the time we returned, it was suppertime. We five dined together, the girls trying out the local specialties: octopus and squid. Dita and I chose the many forms of chicken and the many kinds of vegetables. Tea was not an option, fortunately for me. If the teens were to stay here, I knew that they would be in good shape and I relaxed a bit about this aspect.

Our waitress was quite good, sensing our needs just as we did ourselves. As I poured the last drop from the teapot, which by the way was the finest china pot I had ever seen and which kept the tea hot far longer than those I had back home, she appeared with a fresh pot. Dita was as observant as ever, both she and I were impressed with her convenient and timely appearance with the fresh pot.

Just then, Dita observed our waitress making a small circle with three fingers of her other hand, as she sat the pot before me in a perfect position. Dita responded by duplicating the motion and adding the inscribed triangle. She rapidly duplicated Dita's sign and added the top triangle. "At dusk, it is a fine time to take a stroll around the outer walls. You can smell the ocean and hear the whippoorwills singing."

"Thanks, we shall do just that!" Dita exclaimed. I wondered why Dita said that. Once we were alone again, Dita whispered what she had just seen. Our waitress was indeed a member of our Forze Segrete! Well, it made some sense — her having a waitress job here at the main visitor's inn, where outsiders would most likely come upon their arrival. Fina and Jemma could scarcely contain their intense relief! In all likelihood, they could remain here spying on the ships, which would greatly aid Kali and Ania.

At dusk, we four began slowly walking around the outer walls of the old Santi fortress. Here and there, we paused to look around at the buildings. The smell of the ocean was in the air and the birds definitely were going to it from far beyond the stone walls. Our waitress, now off duty, suddenly and quietly appeared beside us. "Hello. I am Chan Dai, Forze Segrete. So pleased to meet you. We were not expecting anyone, but we always stay alert."

"Hi, Chan. I am Mrs. Bethany Brozena Malina and this is my wife, Dita Malina. We are the top Forze Segrete leaders from Velona. These two teens are the daughters of our close friends and associates. You may always speak freely around them, as if they were one of us. Jemma and Fina."

"Oh my! Top boss ladies! Oh, you should have sent word. So very pleased to meet you! Married?" she said quiet awed but then her curiosity aroused.

"Yes, happily so for many years. Dita likes to wear the pants," I teased. Chan grinned and we all shook hands. "Is there someplace where we can all safely talk?"

"This is the safest place. I am not allowed to go into the guests' rooms, unless I am bringing them food. Is the man you were with to be trusted?" she asked.

"We are here to help him find his lost fiancé. She was a cousin of the late Empress Pian Wu. San Min Wu. He is not Forze, so treat him as our friend but not one of us for now. Do you have others in your group?"

"We used to have six of us, but we've lost two already. Shansee has grown more and more violent with every passing week. Overlords are fighting each other everywhere; even routine travel is now a dangerous proposition. Here in Shansee, we have a vicious Wei Li Bosu in charge now. Yuen Ming. He owns many stores and controls many lives. There is now only my husband, Wen Dai, and Zhen and Fang Song. Wen is a publisher of books and is a respected man. Zhen and Fang are Xian masters and have a small martial arts school in town."

"Excellent. We would like to meet them soon. Actually, we have two different missions. There are more of us still on the caravel anchored in your harbor."

"Ah, yes, I saw it today. I thought that some might come ashore and I was alert as I always am for others of our force," she replied.

"Actually, that caravel is a gun ship. Our second mission is to put the opium dealer Yuen Ming out of business. His opium is causing terrible problems in Velona. These two teens here are going to act as spotters. When they see one of his opium shipments set sail, they will contact the gun ship which will then intercept it and blow it up," I explained the brief version of our goal.

"Oh that is very good! It will hurt Yuen badly! How can we help?" she asked growing very excited about the prospect of having an impact on their drug lord.

"I need someone to look after Jemma and Fina here. Dita and I will be gone quite a lot, searching wherever for his fiancé. They are quite powerful but they are only fourteen years old. It will really help to bring down this drug lord if they can stay here in the Santi. They can relay key information to the gun ship. Yet, I must be sure that they will be safe."

"I promise that we will protect them as we are pledged to do! If you ask the manager for someone to watch over them and suggest my name, he will then allow me to be able to visit the tower anytime. Of course, he will take half of the pay that I would get for doing it. Tomorrow, I will arrange a meeting with the others. I think that Fang would easily be able to accompany them around the city, if they need to go out. I will let you all know as I serve lunch. I should be going now. I don't want to draw undo attention to myself. I always take a walk around here before I leave for home each day. That way a brief chat does not seem unseemly. Until noon." She bowed and left, while we continued our walk for appearance's sake.

Once in our suite, Fina said to Jemma, "See, I told you it would work out for us!" Jemma poked Fina and then tickled her.

At six the next evening, our two riks pulled up outside Dia Publishers. We knocked and Chan opened the door to let us inside. She carefully glanced about to make sure that we were not being followed. The store was now closed for the day, and we followed her into the rear section of the building. Here they made their home. Three others sat around a modest table, already sipping tea. Chan motioned for us to sit as well and did the introductions. Her husband, Wen, was a dignified gentleman, who published printed material, especially books and the local Rag, as it was called. The Rag contained the latest news from around Tashien and Shansee. Thus, Wen was one of the few who were constantly informed of the latest happenings. However, these days, much of his business came from printing flyers for special events. He was thirty-one.

Sitting beside him was Zhen and Fang Song. Both had an athletic build and I suspected they were excellent fighters. He was thirty and she, twenty-nine. All four of them had black hair; all wore theirs long and braided down their backs. As I was soon to learn, few in Tashien ever cut their hair unless necessary.

"We are here on two different missions," I began the lengthy explanations. "First, Dita and I are going to try to find his missing fiancé, San Min Wu. Meantime, Fina and Jemma are going to spy on the docks and discover when Yuen Ming is sending another opium shipment to Megalos. They will report this to our gun ship, which is now anchored in your harbor. Of course, the gun ship will be leaving shortly. They will intercept that ship and blow it up, sending the opium to the bottom of the ocean." I explained in detail how we perceived the operation might go. All four were very impressed that both teens were masters of telepathy. Apparently, some of the martial arts masters in Tashien could also do telepathy, something I did not know before.

"Dita and I may well be gone for considerable periods of time. Thus, we need our teens to be watched over and kept safe from harm. We've officially hired Chan so that she can come up to their room as needed."

"Excellent. They should have a bodyguard when they leave the Santi. If you tell your manager that you have hired me, then appearances will be kept. I can come and go there as needed," Fang replied. "I sometimes do hire out as a bodyguard. This is well known and will not look suspicious."

"Terrific! I will do so as soon as we get back. Dita and I will rest easy knowing that you will be looking after them. As for us, don't be alarmed if we disappear for days or weeks. We will be trying to locate this missing woman. Who knows where the trail will lead us. She was abducted from Nan Yan, but we believe she might be here in Shansee. Who knows, though, just don't get alarmed if you don't hear from us for long periods. If we ever do need anything, Dita or I will use our telepathy to contact you." All four were very much impressed that we four had such powers.

"Can you tell us about this woman?" Zhen asked.

She was a cousin of the late Empress Pian Wu. San Min Wu disappeared from her bedroom in Nan Yan shortly after her aged aunt, the Empress, died and before Pian took the throne."

"Ah, undoubtedly Pian had a hand in her abduction," Zhen replied. "Often, there are large power plays when the Empress passes on. We heard that Pian had her army surround and capture her younger sister, Shashi Wu. She and her servants were banished to the northern ice lands of Dong Province. We also heard that Shashi may have been hurt; her protector had to carry her into the carriage, that much we know. Pian herself was killed four years ago when all this uprising began."

"That's what I concluded," I continued. "Long Yan says that he picked up the abductor's trail and followed them to Giang, where it seems that she was given to some of Yuen Ming's men. It seems likely that she may have been brought to Shansee for a time. Whether she has been moved since then, we do not know. It's been five years now. and Long Yan has not seen any signs of her. Yet, in a city of millions, that is to be expected."

"That is not good. Your path will be a most difficult one. Yuen Ming is devious and treacherous, a fierce opponent. He has eyes everywhere," Zhen warned. I took that to mean that he had many people in the streets who reported things they'd seen and heard up the lines to him. Made sense.

"What can you tell us about Yuen? Where does he live? What does he look like?" Dita asked.

"Few have actually seen him. When in public, he is always surrounded by many martial arts fighters. Some say that they are the best fighters in Tashien. I say that is not right. For one of us to stoop to being the bodyguard of a tyrant makes them less," Zhen vented his disgust for those fighters.

"It is said," Wen added quietly as was his demeanor, "Yuen considers himself of noble birth. Some have suggested that he could have become the Emperor. If this were so, he would be found only in the most elegant, highly respected company. That is to say, he would dine at only the finest restaurants, attend only the finest in entertainment theaters, and mix only with those of high social standing."

Fang added, "We see that you both are of such high standing — your nails give you away."

"If we wore the appropriate dresses, could we pass for such highly respected women and gain entrance to these restaurants and theaters?" I asked.

"Oh yes, your nails are of the right length to gain admittance anywhere. We saw Yuen from a distance one time. He is perhaps thirty-five or thereabouts. He is tall and thin, though he is very likely a master of the martial arts. When we saw him, he was very well dressed, as one might expect the Emperor to dress when in public," Fang added.

"Ah, but do not let looks fool you," the quiet voice of Wen spoke once more. "Yuen has no conscience. He will kill for the tiniest of infractions, the tiniest of insults. He has always been a major dealer in opium, which as only escalated enormously these last five years. Plus, he owns the majority of the Houses of Pleasure in Shansee."

"Say what exactly are these Houses of Pleasure?" I asked. When we were here before, we never heard of them, which is not unusual since we were with the Princess and Empress.

"They are places where our people go for all manner of entertainment. In fact, these Houses of Pleasure are perhaps the most popular and widely attended places in Shansee. They have music and dancing. A variety of spirits are served and many become quite drunk. Yes, there are even rooms where one can get a smoke of opium. Also, they have women who will perform all manner of sexual acts for you or with you. To be most honest with you, many go there for just that reason. Indeed, their women are both willing and pretty to look at. You can tell those women readily from their bound arms," Zhen explained, "which give them honor."

"We've seen some women in the Tashien immigrant section of Velona who had their arms bound. They were on the streets soliciting for sexual activities. We don't understand this at all," I replied, hoping to gain a better understanding of this strange cultural phenomenon.

"It is all about honor," Fang explained. "The rice paddy farmer has almost no honor at all. The Empress has the highest honor possible. All the rest of us lie in between these two extremes. Always, in our culture, we seek to gain honor for ourselves. The more honor we can obtain, the more that we can pass on to our offspring, our children, that they may have a better life. Women who use their bodies to pleasure others are considered to have a relatively high honor. What would keep any woman who was of low honor to simply go out into the streets and solicit to pleasure others and thus appear to have such a higher honor?"

Fang continued, "You see to avoid that, the woman must have her arms bound in a unique way. Only a silken rope, which does not bite or burn her skin, can be used. It is looped around her upper arms and spiraled down her arms. Her hands are placed behind her back and raised vertically to her neck where her wrists are bound. Then, the rope is wrapped securely around her forearms. Lastly, the ropes then tie back into the upper arm loops in such a manner that her upper arms are always at her sides, quite visible to all, and she is unable to move any of the rest of her arms. Thus bound appropriately, she can then ply her trade. Everyone knows that it would be impossible for a woman to so bind herself. Thus, a customer cannot be easily fooled by imposters, that is, a woman who is not of such a higher honor. They are well paid, as I understand it, and very well treated as a woman of such intermediate honor ought to be. We've heard that they really do know how to pleasure men and women, which make them so sought after of an evening."

Wen added, "It is said that if something is pleasurable to the senses, it can be found or had at these houses, but for a price. It is conceivable that if Yuen still has this San Min Wu woman, she may be held within one of his Houses of Pleasure." I was beginning to think along similar lines.

He went on, "These houses have been around for centuries now, but some of us now no longer believe in this whole honor approach to life. Our ancestors are quite dead, are they not? How is it that we can in the present dishonor those who are deceased? It defies logical thinking, though I must admit that many of us who now think and believe this way have only done so within the last few years. My father was a publisher and thus to honor him, I became a publisher too, though I would have rather been a writer or a painter."

"He's been dabbling in both recently," Chan spoke up for him and grinned. "Sometime you ought to see his paintings. They are really beautiful and speak to one's heart."

"Change has come at last to Tashien," Zhen philosophized, "but the cost of that change is becoming staggering beyond belief. If you go to these Houses of Pleasure, please use extreme caution. Also, as you walk the streets, beware of men dressed all in black. These are members of the Cao Bang, a countrywide band of thieves and assassins. If you spot one, go the other way fast. Do not cross them, for they will kill first and they never ask questions."

"Say," Dita asked her burning question, "is there any lawmen in Shansee? In Velona we have policeman who attempt to maintain law and order about the city. If we get into a fight, do we have to worry about being arrested or anything like that?" The Protector in her came through.

Wen replied softly, "When the princesses ruled, their army men would patrol the streets, maintaining order. Now, there is none. Our people have no one to turn to for aid. One must create one's own justice, if you can. We are most fortunate to have Zhen and Fang with us. Both are Xian masters and few will ever challenge them. Yet for those untrained in the art of self-defense, there is no option for them. They give up their money and hope that the thief will not harm them worse. Murder in the streets is commonplace and the undertaker now has a booming business. I am afraid that you have chosen the worst possible time in our long history to come for a visit. These days, you must make your own law or be silent."

Now I began to realize the immensity of the overall degradation of the millions of people here in Tashien. No wonder such vast numbers of people could not rise above the zone of fear. Those Doll Creatures had done their job well, using their electronics to force spiritual beings not only into the heads of the fleshly bodies, but to drive them so emotionally down into the depths, so close to death. Admittedly, their rigidly enforced honor system coupled with their electronics had created a society that seemed highly refined and well off, but such was only on the surface. Don't look at the lowly peasant in the rice paddies. Now that they had shut off their electronic controls, the few that rose into the hatred, anger, and hostility zones were taking the place of the Doll Creatures, further suppressing down the average person with such violence that they dare not rise above fear.

However, I took note of the promising fact that some, such as Wen, had begun to change their opinion of the old honor system and were taking a more rational look at existence. If there were enough like him, perhaps something could be done to change things. I hoped so. In any event, we were now about as prepared for our missions as we could be, under the circumstances. We gave our new friends warm hugs and returned to the Santi. I made sure that the manager knew that we had hired the martial arts fighter, Fang Song, to protect our teens. He grinned and said that was a very wise choice.

Chapter 7 The Search for San Min Wu

On August 25, 755, we began our search for San Min, leaving Jemma and Fina to begin their work with Kali and Ania. Dita and I dressed in our new Shansee outfits — she wore yellow while I wore red, each pleasing the other. Step One was to ride a rik around the city and become familiar with key locations, which would form our anchor points of reference. Additionally, we needed to pass by many of the establishments that Yuen Ming owned. I wanted to see first-hand how well they were kept, hoping to gain a bit more of an insight into this man.

Actually, travel by man-drawn rik was about the only way one could travel through these densely packed streets. Farmer's markets were nearly everywhere, to say nothing of numerous street merchants, those too poor to own a shop. In the wealthier sections, these street merchants were noticeably absent, but there were even more farmer's markets. Women congregated around these, picking up fresh produce and items for their household needs. At times, the scene looked commonplace and normal.

Soon, however, we began to see the dark side. Off to our left, a man was in the process of robbing a woman, who was terrified so badly, that she spilled her money pouch onto the ground. Dita became so enraged at the man that she moved out over the thief and twisted his neck, while the poor woman was trying to pick up her coins. She looked up and saw the man fall dead at her feet. So terrified, she ran off, leaving a few coins on the ground. Others who witnessed this, made a dive for the coins, while a few cautiously searched the dead man for anything of value. Their eyes darted all around in fear as they ripped off his shoes and clothes. They then ran off as fast as they could, leaving a nearly nude dead body on the ground.

"Welcome to a world of utter degradation," I commented sarcastically to Dita.

"Damn! Damn! Damn!" she exclaimed, unable to find any other response to what she had just seen.

Two blocks later, we witnessed a similar theft, though this time Dita remained calm. Little good it would do, she thought. Shortly afterwards, we passed by the first of the many establishments that was owned by Yuen Ming. This was a clothier and the shop looked immaculate from the outside. This we both noted as our man continued pulling us along the crowded street.

A bit further and we passed by a row of physician's offices. We were not yet very fluent at reading their language and asked our puller to read the many colorful signs. He did so and verified that this was called the Physician's Row. "Many doctors have their offices here. They treat those who can pay for their services. If I break my foot, I cannot pay, so I have to be careful," he explained. We noted that Yuen Ming also owned at least half of these offices. I wondered if he also controlled the doctors who worked there. I wouldn't be surprised if he did.

We continued on our quest. Not long after this, we entered the warehouse district, punctuated by large buildings in which goods were stored prior to shipment. Again, Yuen Ming owned a fair number of these as well. Once more, those that he owned were in remarkably good condition, contrasting sharply with many others. As noon was approaching, we asked our puller his name.

"Yi, great ladies," he replied.

"Well, Yi, we are getting hungry. Can you take us to a nice place where we may buy some lunch?" Dita asked.

"Oh yes, great ladies. Yi knows. Take you there now, not far." He pulled a little faster, we noted. About twenty minutes later, he pulled up beside a magnificent outdoor restaurant. "Here is fine place for great ladies to dine. Yi waits here for you."

"But you have to eat too," Dita protested.

"Yi brings his own lunch. See?" he pulled a dirty box out from beneath the rik. We smiled and went to see about our lunch. The place was called Xiu's — at least that was what we thought the sign read. We ordered a light lunch of seafood and salad, along with the customary black tea. The woman who took our order bowed and asked us to find a seat. She would bring it to us shortly.

At this open-air diner, there were over twenty tables; half were filled. We chose a spot where we had a view of the street and could watch the throngs going about their lives. The sun was hot and a cool ocean breeze kept us from overheating in the sunlight. After we at sat down, several other women who were near us, nodded our way. We smiled back, noticing that they wore dresses similar to ours, and flat shoes as well. Comfort was important it seemed. Dita also noticed that they had long nails as well.

Our waitress was kind and polite. She brought us our order and carefully placed each dish, plate, and sticks in their proper position, before placing the teapot and cups. I gave her a nice tip as well. Just as we were about to try to figure out how to eat with the two sticks, the two women next to us came over and bowed.

"Hello. I am Xia and this is my dear friend Xian. We couldn't help notice that you are new to Tashien. Would you like some assistance on the proper way to use the sticks?"

"Oh thank you! Yes, we would, please, come and join us," Dita replied, eager to get any advice about eating with the sticks. She couldn't remember how she had managed this when she was last in Tashien, as Renzo over a century ago. I noticed that their nails were as long as ours, only theirs were brightly painted, ours were plain.

We quickly got a good lesson in how to eat with the sticks, as they were called. We chatted away and I asked them where we could get such a good-looking nail polish. Of course, Xia was very eager to tell us about a fabulous salon that we just had to visit. We had her write down its name and address for us.

"So what do you think of Shansee so far?" Xia asked. "We see that you have adopted our fashions. They are perfect for this weather are they not?"

"Well, it certainly is a beautiful city, so much to see and do," I replied honestly. "Yet, we could not help noticing that there seems to be a lot of crimes being committed right out in the streets as we pass by."

"Oh yes, lots of lawlessness. Our advice is to never bring more than ten gold on your person when you are out. Thieves love to rob us. We've been robbed twice now. Mostly it is just a big bother, and we have to return home or to the Banca to get more coins. If you get accosted, just hand over your money pouches; they won't dare harm women of high standing."

"Why is that?" asked Dita becoming curious.

"Well, for one thing, our husbands are wealthy and have many fighters working for them. If the thieves harmed us, they know that our husbands would extract a most severe punishment on them. Besides, if we were harmed, Yuen Ming would soon hear about it. He's the perfect gentleman, you see. If he hears that one of we women of high honor was harmed, he always sends his fighters to obtain justice. Yan had that happen to her, you know. A month ago, the thief actually cut her arm because she was so slow in handing over her pouch. Her nails got in the way of such quick movement, as you well know. Anyway, when Yuen heard of this, he sent his doctors to make sure that Yan was fine, and the man who cut her was found beheaded in an alleyway the next day. Yuen is such a gentleman. Why, he even owns this diner here."

"Wow, we had no idea. Does Yuen socialize much? I mean is there someplace where we could go and perhaps meet this perfect gentleman?" I inquired, playing along.

"Well, sometimes he is at the Purple Palace," Xian broke in, "and sometimes he goes to the Royal House Palace. Those are the most elegant Houses of Pleasure in all Shansee. You two just must put in an appearance there. They have the most elegant dining in all Shansee, and the music is fabulous. You won't regret it."

"Oh yes, our husbands take us there every Friday night, though you would need to wear something more elegant than these everyday dresses that we are now wearing to even get into those two places," Xia added.

"Oh my. Say, could you also recommend a dressmaker where we could purchase fitting dresses? Dita and I would love to visit these palaces," I asked. We were getting an awful lot of key information rather easily, I thought. They added the name of their dressmaker to the paper with the nail salon. Xia also wrote down the two addresses of the palaces for us.

"Say, one day why not come and pay us a visit? Our houses are adjacent to each other. Come for afternoon tea perhaps?" Xian asked.

"Of course, we would love to visit. I'm just not sure when, though," Dita replied.

"Of course, you probably have a busy schedule as we do. Just send word to us by messenger when you are free. We can let you know if we would be free then too. I take it that you are both staying at the Santi?" Xian asked.

"Of course, we have a suite at the top of the tower. Marvelous view," Dita replied.

"Oh yes, very best location. Nearly all visitors to Shansee stay at the Santi. You have made a wise choice. That is their very best suite," Xian confirmed our choice and approved highly of it. We grinned. They then excused themselves; after bowing to us, they left. Shortly, we left ourselves. However, I also purchased several egg rolls and had them wrapped before we went back to our rik and Li.

"Here, Li, add this to your lunch box," I said, handing him the egg rolls. He thanked us repeatedly, calling us very great ladies over and over. Next, we continued our exploration of the city. First, we passed through a residential section where those with substantial funds lived. Gone were the street vendors and the throngs. The streets were not crowded and we saw children out playing ball in the streets.

A while later, we doubled back and re-entered the bustling commercial district. Once more, our eyes were filled with the unmistakable signs of deep degradation. Fear and hopelessness flooded our senses. It was as if you walked into a room and could sense the tone of the people inside. It was that strong. At last, I asked Li to take us to the nail salon. I wanted time to think about what we had seen. Again, Li waited patiently for us, but now had something to eat.

Inside the nail salon, the women treated us with great respect and honor. Our nails were pampered and then carefully painted a bright red. We asked what the most popular color most women of our stature chose and it was bright red. I intended for us to fit right in with this social strata. I needed to see just what all went on inside these two places and perhaps to see this Yuen Ming personally.

Once we were finished, it was getting late and we headed back to the Santi. I paid Li twice what he was asking, and said, "We need you again tomorrow, Li. If you will be so kind as to pick us up here say around nine in the morning and pull us again, we will be quite grateful." He was extremely pleased and honored, bowing repeatedly until we entered the gates of the old Santi fortress.

The girls loved the look of our nails and begged us to allow them to let theirs grow long and to visit the same salon. We agreed, how could we not? On the other hand, Long Yan wanted to know if we had made any progress. I told him that progress would likely be slow and methodical. "Be patient. We will find her in time," I explained, hoping that would satisfy him for the moment.

Dita and I then chatted that evening, planning our next move. She suggested, "You know, before we spend money on some fancy dresses just to be allowed into these elegant houses, we ought to verify that San Min really was brought here. We know that Long found riverboatmen who claim she was handed over to some boatmen in Yuen's employ. However, we do not know that she was brought to this city. For all we know, she could well be up-river at some other town. We could be chasing our tails here."

"I see your point, love. I suppose that we could visit the river docks and ask around about her. Yet, the event would have been close to five years ago. They might not remember. We also run the risk of raising suspicions, if we start asking a whole lot of boatmen about San Min," I replied.

"Valid point. If we do this, undoubtedly Yuen will hear about it. He might try to harm us or something. Yet, without knowing for sure that she was brought here, it seems silly to go looking. Also, what if she was brought here and then taken somewhere else? This whole thing seems an impossible task," she replied.

"Well, if Long Yan can walk halfway across the world in search of help, the least we can do is give it our very best efforts."

Dita straightened out her long hair and suggested, "You know, I have an idea that will put a little distance between us and the boatmen. After all, we do not have to talk directly with them. We've seen many kids in the streets, poor ones. What if we hired some of them to go around and make the inquiries for us? Then, if Yuen got curious, it would only be some street kids doing the asking."

"Well, that's better than us doing it directly, Dita. I wonder if he would hurt children? No, who could possibly harm a child? I think you have a good idea, love. Tomorrow, let's see what we can find in the way of helpers and continue our exploration of the city."

The next day, we had Li take us to the river docks. He protested that it was not a safe place for great ladies to visit, but we insisted. I recalled the fancy docks near the palace where Sho Lin Wu had taken us aboard her royal barge for the long trip up to the Imperial City of Zau. However, I had no idea that the river docks were so huge. They stretched over five miles along the Yonshu River. At the southern edge, the wide, slow moving river fanned out into a marshy river delta dotted with rice paddies. From the first bit of solid ground there, the docks ran northward through the city, which was entirely here on the western shore. Small shacks and farms dotted the other side, along with bamboo forests.

Unlike the ocean-going docks, the river docks were a rougher neighborhood. We had barely begun moving along them, when a young man with a knife stopped Li, threatening him with his waving knife. "Your money ladies," he called out, nervously shifting his weight from foot to foot.

Dita said calmly, "Young man, put down that knife and walk away alive. Continue in this folly and you die." She was quite mad and provoked by his threatening our kind puller, who struggled to make a subsistence living.

"Your money or your life," he cried out again.

"Okay, have it your way," Dita replied. She moved over his body and gave his neck a twist. The thief fell to the ground dead. "You may continue, Li. He seems to be having a problem with his neck." Li, who had been shaking in fear, instantly complied, and we began moving once more.

A couple of blocks later, he turned to ask, "What happened to the thief? I saw him twist his neck and fall."

"Yes, that's what happened, Li, he twisted his neck too far, probably worried someone would come after him. You were very brave there," Dita explained, well mostly. Li looked satisfied. Twice more during the five-mile ride we were accosted by a thief demanding our purses. Twice more, Dita broke their necks. Li just could not believe his incredibly good luck. All three had turned their necks so far — they must have been terrified was his only conclusion. After all, he certainly was.

We doubled back, down several blocks inland from the tall warehouses that lined the river docks. Now we were into the street crowds once more. We then encountered a new phenomenon. Suddenly a pack of young boys, none looked older than ten, accosted us, jogging alongside of us. "Please Great Ladies, a small coin for us? We are poor and starving. One small coin, Great Ladies?"

Dita asked Li to stop, which he did. Li warned us, "Beggar kids. Don't give them your money; they will just keep on asking you for more."

Dita stepped out and was surrounded by a dozen boys; all looked awfully gaunt and thin for their age. Most were in need of a bath and many square meals. "Which one of you is your leader?" she asked.

"I am," the tallest boy spoke up and took a step toward her.

"Boys, how would you like to earn a gold coin each?" Their eyes nearly bulged out of their heads. "We are looking for our missing cousin. She was abducted some five years ago from Nan Yan and brought down here by riverboat by some of Yuen Ming's men." She went on to explain what she wanted them to do, to ask around and see if they could confirm that a young captive woman was brought into the city from a riverboat some five years ago. Dita gave them a description of San Min, though to my ears it sounded pretty much like that would fit nearly every woman we met. Everyone had very long hair, and nearly all of it was black. Ah well, so much for the description.

"Now if you can find out if she was brought into the city, I will give you all another two gold coins. If you have some other friends who want to help you search, I will give them a gold coin too. Every day at noon, we will be dining at Xiu's. If you find out anything or get more boys, meet us there."

She made sure that they knew where the diner was located. Then, she handed each of the ten boys a gold coin. They promised her and thanked her repeatedly, until we were out of hearing range. As she looked back, she saw them all dashing off to the river docks. "Well, our plan is now in motion," Dita stated factually.

We continued our travels about the city. Day by day, our familiarity grew. Each noon we dined at Xiu's. One noon, the boy in charge appeared with another twenty boys and Dita promptly gave them the promised gold coin as well. She also noticed that the leader now looked a bit healthier. She hoped that he had spent his money on food.

As the days passed, we began to draw up a good map of the huge city. At the southernmost edge lay the ocean-going docks, surrounding a half-moon bay. Just west of the docks was the tiny spur of land unoccupied except for the Santi inn. Beyond the inn, the marshes and rice paddies began, covering the miles-wide river delta. Many blocks of warehouses surrounded these docks. Right down the center of the docks and running perfectly straight northward was the main road called Tiger Street. I am using the translations of their names, because they make more sense to our ears. This was the widest street in the city and left the city behind some ten miles further north, heading on up to Giang.

About three quarters of the way up was the second widest street, a cross street called Princess Path. The palace and formal gardens of the Princess Sho Lin Wu began to the right of Tiger Street and above the Princess Path. Here was the palace with which we were familiar from our visit over a century ago. The great Yonshu River formed the eastern edge of the city. From the palace southward to the warehouse district lay the huge merchant's district. It also extended to halfway across the width of the city, many blocks further west than Tiger Street. Xia's diner was located about ten blocks south of Princess Path and six blocks east from Tiger Street. Just west of Tiger Street and Xia's lay the huge Central Gardens, a six block wide and twelve block long formal gardens.

Stretching west of the merchant's district and south of Princess Path was the middle class residential section of the city. South of that and on down to the warehouse district were the slums, which occupied a good sixth of the entire city area. Above the Princess Path was the wealthier residential district. The only other main road out of Shansee was down at the ocean-going docks, where the River Road headed on west, following the coastline.

Also of note, about twenty blocks west of Tiger Street, on the south side of the Princess Path, lay the Purple Palace, and ten blocks further west was the Royal House Palace. Other fine restaurants, dance halls, theaters, and concert halls lay in between these.

Yes, we spent an afternoon wandering about the magnificent Central Gardens. The breathtaking beauty and artistry that went into these gardens was a wonder to behold. On our tenth day of scouting out the city, we finally headed down the Princess Path, heading westward from Tiger Street.

As we got to within three blocks of the Purple Palace, we began seeing bound women walking the crowded streets! As Li brought us closer, many of these women began walking up to our rik. Their arms were immobile, bound tightly with colorful silken ropes, perhaps a half inch thick. The palms of their hands were touching and vertical, nearly touching the backs of their necks, tied securely behind their backs in such a way that their forearms hung properly at their sides, giving the illusion that their arms ended at their elbows.

They wore the thinnest of silk dresses, which barely hid their breasts. All were very good looking, very attractive. They seemed well fed, and their long black hair was well brushed and groomed. Indeed, I could find no fault with their appearance. Each one was more than attractive, I thought.

"Pleasure ladies? I give good pleasure to great ladies? Would you like great pleasure today? I am really good at giving pleasure to beautiful women." We were bombarded with their pleas and suggestions.

At one point, Li had to stop; the traffic was blocking further forward travel for a brief moment. Three of these women were now begging, pleading, and asking to pleasure us. Dita finally relented, feeling a bit sorry for these women. "How can you pleasure me with your arms tied up like this?" she asked.

"We have our ways," one young woman replied coyly and with an infectious smile; the other two giggled, certain that we had no idea at all of their arts.

"Well, show me how you can kiss me while we are waiting and I'll give you a gold coin," Dita requested and stepped down to the street. Eagerly and without any hesitation, the young woman leaned over and gave Dita a most passionate kiss. The other two followed her immediately before Dita could change her mind. Dita's face was flushed, and I knew that she had gotten more than she had bargained for! Now I watched as Dita struggled to get the coins out of her purse; our long nails did have their disadvantages; this was one of them. At last, she managed to drop the promised coins into the money pouches they had tied to their waists.

"See, I told you. We have our ways. Come on in to the palace sometime, and we can really show you much pleasure!" Flushing even more, Dita climbed back into the rik, and Li began pulling us once more.

I teased her, "Some kisses, eh?"

"You wouldn't believe them. Oh, if I had my Renzo body," she teased me back. I poked her a good one and she laughed.

Soon we arrived outside the Purple Palace. Yes, the building was indeed royal purple! It was made of stone and rose five stories, one of the tallest buildings around. The palace was also quite large — at least three times the width of a normal home. It bordered on a Velona estate home of the wealthy. Many people were going into and out of its ornate, gold leafed doors. All were very well dressed. Also, we saw some of these bound women leading both men and women inside, obviously takers of their pleasure offers.

On down the street we finally saw the other one, the Royal House Palace. This one was twice the width of the other palace but was only two stories tall. Even more bound women were escorting men and women into the four entrance doors of this place. A sign read Friday Night Dances.

As we passed on by continuing down the Princess Path, Dita commented, "Well, thus far, these two places are the finest looking buildings outside of the old palace complex of Sho Lin. They are very well built and their exterior is very well maintained." I concurred. All the properties of Yuen Ming that we had so far seen were indeed well kept. I concluded that Yuen Ming took care of his possessions and valued them. This reflected upon his personality. We were dealing with a knowledgeable man and a careful man, not prone to making bad errors of judgment. He would be a formidable opponent, we surmised.

On September 8, we got our first real break. As we dined at Xia's at noon, twenty boys came by and Dita went out to the street to talk with them. "We found out for you," the leader boy said excitedly. "We found some men who said that they brought a woman down from Giang about that time. But Yong here, he did one better! He found another boy who saw some men carrying a young woman into the Purple Palace late at night. She was struggling and fighting them. He says it was about that time too. Can we have our coins now?"

"Brilliant! You have all done very well indeed! Yes, you may. Oh, darn these long nails anyway. Here why don't you just take the whole pouch? Divide it up evenly between yourselves. There's likely to be about four coins for each of you. Thanks fellows!" The boys began greedily dumping out the coins. Soon they were ecstatic! They were rich, four gold each! Dita returned to me and relayed the good news.

"Looks like we go visit Lin's Dresses next. Fancy gowns we need to gain entrance," I joked.

A half hour later, Li parked outside Lin's Dresses, an upscale shop indeed. Inside we saw several other women with equally long bright red nails making purchases as well. An hour later, we left, each carrying a large, carefully wrapped package. "Damn, it's back into corsets we go," Dita complained as we began the long ride back to the Santi inn.

"Well, that's true, but that's about all," I consoled her. First, we would have to tight lace the corset down to an eighteen-inch waist once more. At least this corset ended just below our bust line. From there, everything was quite different. We now had black silk stockings so thin that you could easily see through them. She warned us that they tore readily and we had gotten three pairs, just in case. She demonstrated how to don them with our long nails, quite necessary to avoid ripping them. Next, they fastened to six garters on the corset. We then slipped into sheer, silk panties that hardly hid anything — certainly not in Dita's case, for her hair was black. The dress was a sheer silk, lightly colored, with the familiar pencil tight skirt. It was designed to fit our body's shape — our bust was highly accentuated. Gold filaments were intertwined within the fabric at various intervals, reflecting light that was enticing to the eye. One thing was certain, the dresses highlighted our many curves! Our shoes were flats, matching our gown's colors. Again, gold threads were woven into the fabric of the sides of the shoes. I found the shoes quite comfortable and easily slid off our feet. The sheer silk hose felt very exotic to us and slippery. In fact, the outfit was ten times more comfortable and easy to wear than the Annelise outfits. Besides, there were no high heels, a fact Dita did appreciate.

Back at the Santi, we finally had some encouraging news to share with Long Yan. He was most pleased to hear that we had uncovered the fact that she has been taken into the Purple Palace. However, that she was in the hands of Yuen Ming distressed him greatly. Still, he, as well as we, knew that there was little that he could do about it. "Be patient, as you have been, Long. Allow us to do our job," I consoled him.

Our plan was simple. Tomorrow evening, we would don our new outfits and pay the Purple Palace a visit. We had absolutely no idea what to expect inside, we would just be playing it all by ear. Our objective was simple: try to see every woman in the place and see if we could spot San Min Wu. Then what? We had no idea yet. First, we had to find her, if she was still even there in that place. For all we knew, Yuen had moved her elsewhere long ago. It had been five years now.

Chapter 8 The Purple Palace

On September 9, we finally arrived outside the Purple Palace around six in the evening. It was just getting dark outside. Although we told Li not to wait for us, he insisted that he would. Already the place was swarming with elegantly dressed couples, single men, and women entering the gold trimmed doors. As always, there were bound women milling around, asking and begging for their services. Dita politely took my arm and said, "Would you care to join me?"

"But of course, Dita dear. Now I don't want your eyes to wander onto all of these pretty women inside. No mischievous thoughts, dear." She tossed her long hair back and laughed.

"Dear, this *is* a pleasure palace and I am a man at heart," she replied as we stepped through the doors, held open by a doorman.

Just inside, the enticing flagrance of apple blossoms seeped into our olfactory senses. The carpet was purple and soft. We found ourselves in a line waiting to pay for admission, along with a dozen others ahead of us. I noticed six strong men, well dressed, but obviously martial arts bouncers for this palace. Soft stringed instruments played somewhere in the background, the music sounded strange to our ears, unused to traditional Tashien sounds, particularly their musical scale of notes, which used many quarter-tones.

As we stepped up to the immaculately dressed man behind the counter, he spoke softly, "Welcome to the Purple Place, Great Ladies. Is this your first visit?"

"Well, yes, it is. We've been told that this *is* the place to visit and here we are," Dita replied, quite factually.

He smiled, "Excellent. May I suggest that you accept one of our kami as your hostess? She can show you around, wait on your needs, assist you with obtaining the very best in pleasure that you may seek. She is very knowledgeable on all the available pleasures to be found here as well as some very special pleasures and their fees. Your admittance fee of five gold totally covers her services for the evening as well as all pleasures to be found here on the main floor. Should you desire more expensive tastes, your kami can arrange such for you."

Dita handed the man her money pouch, "Thank you. That is most kind. Could I trouble you to take our entrance fee from my pouch? With these nails it is troublesome for me to do so, and I do so not want to scratch my nails; we just had them done." Oh, was Dita ever learning, I thought!

"Of course, so many women allow me to do so for them. No, it would not do to have a mar upon such a fine set of nails. Ah there we go. Here is your kami for the evening. Her name is Mei. I am sure that you will find her most knowledgeable and able to satisfy your every pleasure need."

A tall young woman with long black hair and a very pretty face stepped up to us. Her hair draped over her shoulders and down to her waist, much as our very long hair did. However, here and there a bit of purple silk rope revealed that her arms were tightly bound in the now familiar proper and elegant manner. Her voice was soft and sensual, "Good evening, Great Ladies. I am Mei and I am here to serve your every need. If you will follow me, I will show you around." She bowed low to us and we returned the bow as best we could, constrained at our waists by the tight corsets.

She wore the thinnest of loose-fitting silk dresses, so sheer that her breasts were clearly visible as was the fact that she wore no panties. She did have a garter belt holding up similar sheer silk hose to those that we wore. Her shoes matched ours. The back of her thick, long, black hair hung down to below her waist, mostly concealing the purple silk rope which bound her arms behind her, though we could see glimpses of the ropes and the inverted 'T' shaped bulge where her forearms were bound together with her hands, palms facing, pointing upwards towards her neck. As we followed her, Dita's eyes never left her undulating hips, which she swayed erotically as she walked slowly ahead of us. I was thankful for Dita. I remembered when I had my Ket Bethany body. In situations like this, I always had this embarrassing bulge in my pants! At least she didn't have to worry about that embarrassment or maybe she did miss it, I began to wonder.

"Here is our music room. I will lead you to some excellent seats where you may listen a while," Mei said softly so as not to detract from the music that was playing. We were in a room about fifty by thirty feet. Up front was a quartet of musicians sitting on the floor playing traditional Tashien instruments. One was a set of unusual drums, one was some kind of stringed drone instrument, and the other two were stringed instruments vaguely similar to lutes or guitars. Half of the audience portion of the room had soft, plush chairs arranged in numerous rows; about half were filled with couples and individuals. Some were sipping beverages, though more than a few also had a lovely kami sitting quietly on the floor beside them.

Mei led us to the right side of the audience where sheets of the thinnest gossamer silk hung down from the ceiling, providing the illusion of a barrier wall around very soft, plush velvet divans. Mei used her head to push aside a gossamer hanging and motioned for us to enter. "Sit and lie back. Let the music touch your inner senses," she whispered. We each sat down and laid back on the pair of divans, especially arranged for couples. We saw that there were several other divans near us that were already occupied. As we lay down, Mei moved in between our divans and sat on the floor near our heads. "Close your eyes and enjoy," she suggested. We needed no further encouragement.

I found the music incredibly relaxing, soothing, and for me quite spiritual in nature. I drifted into a reverie with the enchanting sounds.

Indeed, this was a pleasure for one's ears and inner self. A bit later, I heard a slight moan from Dita. I opened my eyes and saw that Mei was now standing over her allowing her long hair to slowly touch and move along Dita's legs and up to and over her breasts. Again, she moaned softly. I knew that Dita was really enjoying this eroticism. Soon, Mei put her lips together as if to say shh to me and indicated that I should again close my eyes. I did so and she used her hair touch on me. I tried to keep from moaning but simply could not. The combination of the enchanting music and the incredibly light touch totally did me in.

How long we sat and listened, I didn't know. At last, the musicians finished their program, and the guests slowly, as if still in a trance, rose. Mei whispered, "This way. We will go to the dance room and get you some refreshments." Others were just as quiet as we were in getting up and leaving. It was as if the whole audience was under some kind of spell or trance. We didn't want this mood to ever end.

The dance room was quite a contrast. On the stage, a young singer belted out a popular dance song while a chorus of women dancers wearing the scantiest of apparel that left nothing to the imagination performed highly choreographed dance movements, reflecting the ideas that the singer was belting out. Here the audience was seated at some fifty tables, usually two to a table, though a few had four and some had only one. Again, we saw many kami sitting on the floor beside the tables, patiently waiting on the needs of their customers.

Mei led us to a back table and bade us sit. Dita pulled out my chair for me and assisted me to sit, which I really didn't need, but was the elegant, polite thing for her to do, as any gentleman would do for his lady. "Mei will get you your refreshments. What would you like?" she asked.

"Gosh, we have no idea what is available," I replied. Mei then gently rattled off a lengthy list that included everything from various teas to wines to meads to even opium-laced drinks. "Well, alcohol beverages will dull our senses," I replied. "We love tea, but you have so many kinds. What tea would you recommend, Mei?"

"Ah, I know just the tea for your Great Ladies; you will delight in its taste. Mei will bring it, you enjoy the show." She bowed and left. All the tables had candles burning and I noticed that they gave off the apple blossom odor that we had detected as we entered earlier.

"God, Bethany, she is good! I am so embarrassed, dear! My panties are soaked. I hope that no one will notice that," Dita whispered, her face quite flushed.

"Enjoy dear. But we are supposed to be looking for San Min. Perhaps she is now one of these kami women. In here, we can see a whole lot of them. Get looking," I ordered. Slowly, we scanned the various kami who numbered over thirty. Some were waiting patiently beside their customers, while others were moving about the huge dance room. In a short while, Mei returned carrying a teacup in her mouth. She bent over and placed it in a perfect position for me. She bowed and left once more. A bit later, she returned with a second cup for Dita. On her last trip, she carried a fine china teapot with a handle much like a tea kettle held tightly between her teeth. She sat it down perfectly and gently before Dita, who did the honors of pouring our tea. Mei bowed and quietly sat down on the plush purple carpet beside us.

"Wow, this is a good tea," I commented.

"Yes, it is made by adding jasmine blossoms to the oolong leaves. There is a hint of ginseng in it as well," Mei whispered. We sipped and watched the dance show. I could not help noticing that some kami brought cigars to their male customers, carrying them between their lips. Others were kissing their clients; others were doing all other manner of enticing, prurient actions with their guests.

When the current song set ended, a number of stage hands began to change the stage quickly. Meanwhile, the audience began chatting, and the noise level rose sharply. Mei explained, "They are setting up for their next set. Now I can explain more things that are available for your pleasures. There is a play that is going on in the next room, you know, with actors and such. It is rather long and is repeated every hour. If you would like to see it, we can go there when it is to begin again; it will be after the dancer's next set. Your entrance fee covers these three shows, the music, the dances, and the play. You can watch and listen all night long, if you like. There is also a food room where we can go where you may dine if you become hungry. That is also part of your basic fee."

"On the second floor, are other pleasures for which you must pay an additional fee," Mei continued her explanation. "There, you may engage me or any kami of your choosing for any and all bodily pleasures. We are very, very good at giving you sensual pleasures. Mei is very good, you see. There you may also smoke some hashish to heighten your pleasures. Many do so and then allow us to pleasure them, before they return down here to drift off in the music."

"On the third floor, you may also purchase an opium high. This is our most expensive fee, but it covers also having three kami delivering to you the most exquisite of pleasures available. Many come here often just for this, you see."

"Incredible," Dita replied. "We have seen a lot of your kami. So if we wanted to go to the second floor for more pleasures, then you would accompany us there? Do all the kami that we see around us go to the second floor when needed? Or are there some kami who only work on the second floor."

"Oh I see. You mean are there other more beautiful, more skilled kami on the second floor. No, we here service both the main floor and the second floor. However, none of us service the third floor. Up there, the kami have far more training and skills with which to better meet the pleasures found there. If Mei continues to give excellent pleasures here, then one day Mei will be invited to learn how to be one of the very special kami who give the greatest of pleasures on the third floor. Mei hopes that day will come soon. It brings us a great honor to be chosen to work there."

'What's on the fourth and fifth floor?" Dita asked the obvious.

"Nothing. It's the owner's offices. Would you both like a cookie? Mei can bring you a special cookie that goes very well with this tea?"

We agreed and she left to fetch it. Meanwhile, our eyes surveyed the crowd, concentrating on all the kami. We did notice that there were a dozen bouncers standing quietly at the back of the room, well dressed, of course. Shortly, we saw why they were needed. One lone gentleman, who had too much to drink, became loud and upset over something. Quickly, two bouncers moved directly to his table. One touched him on his neck and the man went instantly limp, caught by the second bouncer. Between them, they escorted the temporarily paralyzed man out of the room, presumable also out of the palace.

Mei returned with a large cookie held between her teeth. She mumbled for Dita to take a bite, which she did. Mei then held it close to me, indicating that I was to take a bite. I did, back and forth we went until Mei took the very last bite herself. It tasted like a combination of wild rice and oats, but there was something greenish in it that I couldn't identify. Then, the show began once more.

When it finished, Dita and I were just a little spacey, more than a little turned on. "We just have to go listen to the music again," Dita insisted. I agreed, and Mei led us back to the music room. We lay back on the velvet divans once more just as the musicians began another set. Oh, how sensuous the music seemed this time, so utterly different than the last time. Again, Mei did her thing with her hair, and at last, Dita could stand it no longer! Neither could I.

"We have to have you take us to the second floor, Mei. You must pleasure us, please, please," Dita begged. I also insisted, as we floated up to the second floor. I was only dimly aware of Dita handing out more coins. We did see some of the kami that we'd seen before going in and out of some of the rooms here on the second floor. Again, the stairway and the floors were plush purple carpeting. Mei led us to a bedroom, which I can only saw was the most elegant bedrooms that I'd ever seen! The bed was large, soft, and covered in slippery purple satin sheets. We two lay down on it, and in the very dim light, Mei knelt beside Dita.

Before long, I heard Dita moaning in relief. I was also incredibly turned on, and I just could not figure out why this should be. Then, Mei came around to my side of the bed and knelt down beside me. A bit later, I moaned in relief. Mei knew her job well. We thanked her repeatedly, as she led us back down to the main floor. We just couldn't take any more of that music, and so we chose to watch the play and calm down.

Finally, around midnight, the Purple Palace closed its doors. Mei walked us to the main doors, and Dita gave her a good tip, placing several gold coins between her teeth as Mei bowed to us. Outside, the many riks were moving out carrying the many customers home. At last, Li came trotting up to us, "Li waits. Take Great Ladies home now." We were quite grateful that he had waited. Dita made sure that he was rewarded for his long wait, once we returned home.

In the quiet of our bedroom, we two sank onto our bed, emotionally drained, our minds racing. "God, she was good," Dita commented. "Why did we react like that? I know that I am attracted to women, but that's me, really. I usually have control over those feelings, Bethany. Is it normal for a woman to so lose it like I did there?"

Suddenly, I realized what had happened. I sat up like a rocket. "We were drugged, Dita! That cookie must have contained marijuana, hashish, or something like that. We didn't go nuts until sometime after we ate the cookie. It wasn't the tea; that was very good, and we didn't go nuts after just drinking it. It had to be the cookie which so set us off!"

"Boy do I feel better about what happened," Dita said greatly relieved. "Just now, I am so embarrassed about it."

"Hey, don't be. I was just as horny as you were and just as out of control. It was the drug, that's all. I'm feeling fine now, just a little hungry, that's all. Well, we didn't see San Min there yet. We are going to have to go back and repeat it again. Perhaps we missed her this first time. Then, if we don't spot here, we are going to have to get to the third floor somehow. Perhaps she is one of the specially trained kami up there."

"Yes, but I don't want to smoke opium!" Dita exclaimed.

"Neither do I, but we must see if San Min is up there somehow. We'll think of something. Then, there are the fourth and fifth floors to search."

Chapter 9 Moves and Countermoves

On the fourth floor of the Purple Palace, Yuen Ming held a conference with his top enforcers. "What in hell is going on with our opium shipment to Megalos?" Yuen was violently angry; he seldom got angry, and his men were twitching nervously, expecting the worst.

"Bosu, we do not know. The boat was supposed to arrive there some days ago. Shall we send a replacement?" one asked.

"Hell yes! Make sure it leaves for Megalos today! The Pope is not sending more funds until he gets what he paid for. Someone will pay for this."

"Bosu, we could send out a ship to try and find out what happened to it. Perhaps the crew got greedy. We can find them and eliminate them," another suggested.

"Yes, make that happen. I want their heads! Yet, it may be that the Pope has become greedy and has stolen the shipment. We must consider that possibility as well. Have them also investigate that as well. If he double crossed me, I will have his head!" Yuen exclaimed angrily. "Now see to it!" Several men rushed out of the room and down the stairs.

"Perhaps they ran into a hurricane," one top enforcer suggested. "Or perhaps some really bad weather forced them off course."

"There haven't been any hurricanes that I know about," Yuen growled, but saw the man's point. Perhaps the scout vessel would discover something.

"Bosu, there is another small matter that has appeared," Qiang Peng, his second in command brought up, hoping to cleverly turn his Bosu's attention to other matters. So far, they were lucky. He had not killed any of the top enforcers yet, anyway.

Yuen waved his fingers, a sign for Qiang to continue. "A number of slum rats have been asking around the river docks about a woman who was abducted five years ago and brought here by your men. They mentioned the name of San Min Wu. Of course, your river men will not reveal anything to them, but I thought it most curious."

Yuen's anger subsided, just as Qiang hoped it would. "You don't say? San Min, eh. It's been five years now, hasn't it? Slum rats? Hell, they weren't even born then." He exaggerated, but Qiang took his meaning. "Someone has put them up to asking. Find out who, Qiang."

He bowed and left, grateful that no one lost their head this morning. It had been a close call; a whole load of opium had gone astray — worth perhaps a million gold. Someone would pay, of that Qiang was certain. He was thankful it had not been one of the top enforcers.

Qiang returned mid-afternoon. "Bosu, I have news. You were right.

Someone has put the slum rats up to it. It seems that two Great Ladies from Velona have been asking around about San Min. They have paid the slum rats gold coins to interrogate your river men. They dine at Xia's at noon every day. The slum rats are to report anything they find out to them there."

"Most curious indeed. A mystery, Qiang. Why would two Great Ladies all the way from very distant Velona come here looking for San Min, of all people?"

"They are a strange pair, Bosu. They are lesbians — married even," Qiang added.

Yuen chuckled. "Well, in that case, I need to show them what they are missing!" He laughed evilly. "Pay one of the slum rats a gold. Have him tell them that he saw my men bringing a woman to the Purple Palace five years ago. That ought to entice them to pay us a visit." He laughed once more.

Qiang bowed and left to handle it. Later he returned. "Bosu, it has been done. The slum rat did as I asked. I watched them deliver the message. I believe that the two women bought it."

"Excellent, Qiang. Excellent. Now I need you to hang around the entrance of the Purple Palace. Let me know when you spot them entering. I want you to point out our new adversaries to me." Both men laughed evilly.

On the evening of September 9, Qiang, dressed as a bouncer, spotted the two women from Velona entering the Purple Palace. He covertly pointed them out to Yuen, who grinned. "Perfect. As cows led to the slaughter, these two are. Totally predictable." While they were in the queue to gain entrance, he came up to the manager and whispered into his ear, "The two foreigners are in line back there. They are new here. I want you to assign Mei to them tonight." The manager bowed and did as he was asked. Mei was one of their best kami.

Later, when Mei went to fetch the pot of tea, Yuen stepped up to her. "Good evening Mei. How are your two new guests enjoying themselves?"

"They are delighted, as to be expected, sir," she replied softly and meekly.

"Ah that is good. You are doing a fine job as always, Mei. I want you to do me a special favor for these women. In a bit, see if you can get them to accept a cookie. I will have one waiting. Then later, they will not be able to resist your magnificent charms any longer, Mei."

She blushed at the high compliment her boss had just given her. A short while later, she returned, and Yuen placed the special cookie between her teeth and gave her a kiss on her cheek, causing her to blush noticeably.

Staying in the background, he observed the two women. The black haired woman was absolutely stunning. Right then Yuen decided that he would teach her first; the blonde one would learn later on. Right on cue he saw them heading for the second floor. "I have you now!" he exclaimed to himself. He ignored them the rest of the evening, confident in his victory.

Fina and Jemma found that Fang was most knowledgeable. From their observation post at the top of the old Santi tower, they had an unobstructed view of the ocean-going docks. Fang knew the work crews of Yuen and was able to point them out to the teens, who continually used their spyglass to watch the activities on the docks. Fang pointed out the Ducky to the girls. "That is one of Yuen's ocean going boats. Perhaps this is what you are looking for," she suggested.

As they watched, men began carrying large, oilskin wrapped bales onto the small craft, dwarfed by the taller caravels currently in port. "I wish we could see inside those bales, just to be sure," Jemma cautioned.

"Too risky," Fang replied. "If it is opium, then one or more of Yuen's top enforcers will be standing guard, along with at least a dozen fighters. I'll go down and take a peak. You keep your eyes open up here."

A half hour later, the teens saw Fang standing idly against the side of a warehouse, observing the dock scene. They trained their spyglasses in the direction that she was looking and saw a number of what appeared to be common thugs, though one was better dressed in a white suit. "That one must be the enforcer," Jemma concluded.

"We'll know for sure if the Ducky heads off towards Megalos. From this height, we can see far out to sea and can tell if it's headed that way," Fina added.

Later, Fang returned and they exchanged ideas. Around four, the Ducky began tacking out of the harbor. Now the teens watched carefully from the tower. "Yes, it's going out to sea," Fina exclaimed, becoming more excited.

"Yes, but will it head towards Megalos?" Jemma cautioned.

"I'd say so; they took on considerable provisions," Fang added. "Far too much to just sail to some of Tan Lon's smaller coastal fishing ports."

They watched it until the Ducky became just a tiny dot on the very distant horizon. It was on a course for Megalos. Now, Jemma did the honors. She sat down and cleared her mind, focusing on Kali. In a moment, she reached Kali.

Hi mom. We got our first one. It's called the Ducky, Jemma sent. She and her mother exchanged data and chatted a while, before Fina pulled on Jemma's arm telling her it was time to eat supper.

"Okay, Captain Dante, we have our first boatload of opium to sink," Kali found him, relaying the word. Of course, Captain Dante was very impressed to discover that they really did have a magical telepathic contact. He had not really believed that this was so until now. Kali relayed the data, and the two headed to his cabin, where he had his navigational charts laid out on his table.

"We're here. The Ducky is about here," Captain Dante explained. "These Tashien junkets only go about half our speed. We can take them anywhere we like. I think right about here would be an ideal spot; it's about halfway between Shansee and Megalos." Kali agreed and he barked out his sailing orders.

Four days later, they heard the call from the crow's nest — the call that they had been anxiously expecting. "Ducky ahead!" Captain Dante took several spyglass measurements over the next hour, plotting the speed and course on his chart.

Kali watched as he drew his intercept plans. "We will sail alongside them and give them a broadside as we pass them. We circle around and come at them from their other side, if they are still afloat." Kali didn't figure that the Ducky had much chance, however, and she was right.

An hour later, Captain Dante called out, "Raise the canvas on the starboard side now." The bosun relayed his orders, and eight men rapidly began pulling up the ropes that held the canvas disguise covers over the gun hole ports. "Raise the starboard gun ports." Again, Dante's command was echoed twice more as it finally reached his men below deck. "Take starboard range checks now. Prepare to fire Standard Small Ship Volley on my mark." Kali listened to his commands as they were echoed several times to the gun crews below deck.

"Now we wait, Kali. This will be very easy," Captain Dante explained. Kali and Ania stood at his side, watching the approaching Ducky. Kali suddenly realized the actual situation on the Ducky. As they sailed near them with this impressive caravel gun ship flying the Jolly Roger flag of pirates, there was absolutely nothing the crew of the Ducky could do. The gun ship was twice as fast as the Ducky was; they could not out run or out maneuver the caravel. All they could do was to pray that the artillerymen miss-calculated their shots. They were sitting ducks!

"Standby to fire on my mark," Captain Dante called out. The bosun relayed it and others relayed it below decks. "Fire!" The command echoed followed by eight thunderous blasts from below their feet. Great billows of acrid gunpowder swept over those standing on the deck. Kali and Ania coughed and covered their noses. A moment later and the heavy iron balls arrived on target. One ripped through the mail mast, crushing it as if it was a mere matchstick. Two others smashed giant holes into the starboard sides of the Ducky. More importantly, others struck just below the water line, splintering the hull. At first, the Ducky lurched violently to port from the impact and then slowly came back upright. As the Grande Pistola sailed past the stricken ship, Kali saw the Ducky beginning to lean heavily to starboard.

"She's taking on water fast," Captain Dante called out. "Great shooting men!" His compliment was once again echoed throughout the ship and cheers arose from the men below deck. Now he ordered a change of course, turning around to head back to the sinking Ducky. Below decks, the gun crews were reloading, getting prepared for a second volley if such was needed. Ten minutes later, the Grande Pistola floated past the remains of the Ducky. A few boards now floated on the surface, along with a lot of whitish powder.

"Well, so much for that shipment of opium, Kali. Strike one!" Captain Dante cheered. "Stow the guns. Close the gun ports. Lower the canvas."

"Well done, Captain," Kali replied. "That cost them at least a hundred grand!" The three smiled. Now they were beginning to make an impact upon the opium imports to Velona. Actually, a million's worth was lost.

"Don't get too excited. These Tashien boats are very flimsy affairs. If that were a caravel, why we would still be battling it out," he explained.

Years before this, down in Constanza City, the new Pope Christos had just been elected by the conclave of cardinals. After the incredible fiasco in Demokritos where Cardinal Drakon Erebos had been arrested and found guilty of high treason and executed, Pope Leo had graciously passed away. Now the cardinals elected him, a young man in his late thirties to succeed him. Pope Chrisos was an excellent judge of people, which is why he had manipulated the cardinals into choosing him as their next leader. It was plainly obvious to Pope Christos that this new Emperor Kreon and Empress Frona were merely reacting to the misguided treachery of the late Cardinal Drakon. That Frona was a Holy Woman of the Eighth Degree, he found encouraging.

How to make amends with this new Emperor and to rebuild the stature of the Church of Jehosanity on Demokritos was his top priority upon taking his Holy Office. He appointed a new man to head the church there, one Cardinal Danski, a young ambitious man like himself. Next, he sent Cardinal Danski to Demokritos to meet personally with the new Emperor. His objective: mend ties with the rulers. How: offer a sizeable monetary donation. Pope Christos knew that any Emperor could always use a sizeable donation to his treasury, especially if it were given with no strings attached.

Pope Christos denuded the entire church's funds to set up such a bribe, well over three million. Thus armed, Cardinal Danski set sail for Demokritos to mend the church's fences with this new ruler. It worked out exactly as Pope Christos had planned. Instead of a horrible backlash against the Church, there was only some grumbling and griping, especially once Emperor Kreon acknowledged that the Church of Jehosanity had apologized for the treasonous conduct of the late Cardinal Drakon and had given a generous contribution to Demokritos to help with rebuilding efforts.

Now, Pope Christos faced an even bigger problem: money. Repairing the damage done had cost the Church all its operating funds. True, in time tithes would slowly refill their coffers, but in the meantime, he needed more funds, lots more funds.

That's when he was contacted by two Cardinals who were here for the conclave, which had ultimately chosen him to be their next Holy Pope. "Thank you for seeing us," Cardinal Branco Beja began, as he and Cardinal Juan Malagon sat down in the Holy Pope's private office. As you know, we have been totally unable to infiltrate many of the other Sea Prince Sectors, as we would like to have. Specifically, Velona and Barcella have long been a thorn in the Church's side. Your Holiness, Juan and I have come up with a plan to remedy this and fill our Church coffers at the same time."

Pope Christos looked up, quite startled. "Lord Jehosa had just answered my prayers!" he thought to himself. Looking as pious as possible, he said, "Please, continue. I am very interested to hear of this remedy."

"You might not be aware of this, but the Emperor and Empress of Tashien have been executed. Overlords now run the country. A representative of one of these has approached us with a proposition. With a little wrangling, I believe I have worked out an excellent agreement. This overlord Yuen Ming controls all the opium production in Tan Lon Province. He wishes to expand his markets significantly. Here's the idea. He sells his product directly to you, for say ten grand. You send the product along to us in Vito and Bonito, where we route it to the cardinals in Velona and Barcella, for example. They then sell it to the local opium dealers for twenty grand. We clear a hundred percent profit."

"Very intriguing proposition. Over time, many in Velona will become addicts; their crime rates will soar. Our Church can then step in and bring order and so establish our Church on the populace," Pope Christos replied, grasping their plan in its whole. Juan smiled; their choice of the new pope was indeed the right one. "What kind of volume are we talking about? What would be our needed initial outlay of funds? As you know, the Church is rather strapped for funds now, considering the mess Cardinal Drakon made for us down in Demokritos."

"The initial purchase ought to be for a million worth," Cardinal Branco replied. "I am aware of the mess. If you please, Your Holiness, Juan and I have another suggestion to make."

"I'm listening," Pope Christos replied. He knew that the Church just did not have such funds. He'd just sent it all to appease Emperor Kreon.

"We realize that the Church cannot afford this at this time. Besides, we would not want the Church to be ever seen as the ones promoting the sale of opium, now would we? No, no indeed. The purchase should come from our private, personal funds. Between Juan and me, we can raise most of that initial amount. If you could perhaps swing the balance of two hundred thousand, we would be in business. Always the funds are transferred between our personal accounts. When you finally get the profit funds, then you can donate them directly into the Church's account and seem to be a great benefactor of our Church," Cardinal Branco explained.

"Of course, the both of you would also like to be seen donating significant funds into your Churches as well," Pope Christos added.

"Well, that would indeed be more than acceptable to us. We both want to do our part in bringing down Velona and Barcella, in particular.

"Excellent, Cardinals. I agree. Let's implement it. I will have my funds available within a week. How do we expedite this trading arrangement with this Yuen Ming fellow?" Pope Christos replied, his prayers were answered in spades!

During the next few years, the volume of drugs steadily increased. By 752, he had a standing order of one million worth each month. Before the first of each month, he visited the Constanza City's Banca del Dio and transferred one million from his account into Yuen Ming's account. The caravels of the Banca then sailed on the first of each month to Tashien, where upon arrival his transaction was logged into Yuen's account. At this point Yuen sent the shipment via their flimsy ocean vessels to Constanza City. Here the Mano del Dio transferred the cargo onto a caravel bound for Vito or Bonito. None of the Mano del Dio men knew what this secret cargo actually contained. Theirs was not to ask questions of their Pope, but to follow his orders.

Pope Christos paced his office. The September shipment had not arrived on time. Indeed, it was now two weeks late. At last, he decided against sending another million to Yuen Ming. He wrote a letter instead, asking why their shipment had been delayed so long. He alluded to the fact that more money would not be forthcoming until he had received the previously paid for goods. He sent the letter with the Banca del Dio as part of their routine mail cargo.

"Well, even if this now dries up, it has been well worth it. I've pumped over fifty million into the Church's coffers thus far," he said to himself, satisfied. He could now begin to tackle other projects, which required heavy financing.

Hi, mom. Jemma here. They've sent another ship to replace what was lost. However, there is also a second ship, which is going out to investigate what happened to the Ducky. They are sailing together now. I'm not sure how you can tell which is which.

Leave that to us, dear. Thanks. Keep up the good work and stay behind the scenes. I suspect things will soon get violent there, Kali sent.

"Captain Dante, they've sent out a replacement shipment and a second ship is traveling with it, supposedly trying to find out what happened to the Ducky," Kali reported to the captain.

"Okay, to the navigation charts, we can sort them out," he said confidently. "However, once we sink this one, we are going to have to do something about getting our fresh water re-supplied. Food's holding out, not the water."

Three days later, they spotted the two ships heading their way. Unfortunately, so were a squall and a fog bank. "How do we know which is which?" asked Kali.

"That one there, see, she's riding low in the water. That means she has the cargo," Captain Dante replied. As before, he began issuing the prefiring orders. As they closed the distance, once more heading eastward as the unsuspecting boats from Tashien headed westward, the canvas covers were raised, and the eight gun ports opened. Kali saw the two crews reacting wildly, in a hopeless attempt to survive somehow.

Boom! Boom! The eight guns fired their well-aimed barrage just seconds apart. Again, thick acrid smoke drifted onto the main deck. Ania and Kali were prepared this time, holding handkerchiefs over their noses. The cargo ship lurched violently and split in half! Meanwhile, the other vessel made a sharp turn into the dense fog bank as the squall line hit the Grande Pistola. By the time that Captain Dante had the caravel turned around and headed back, the cargo ship had vanished as had the other ship.

"I'm afraid that we've lost them in yonder fog. We could heave to and wait it out, perhaps spotting them tomorrow. Or we could head off to find fresh water," Captain Dante explained. After a brief discussion, they chose to replenish their critically low water supply.

"Our best bet is to put in at a small Southlands port. We dare not dock in Megalos, not with this being a gun ship. We can get away with it at one of the small ports in the Southlands, but that will mean a two-week delay to get there and another two weeks to get back here," he explained.

"Well, if they send another boat in the meantime, I guess we will just have to work on picking off the secondary caravel transport out of Megalos," Kali replied. They agreed to the plan and the Grande Pistola headed westward, sailing far south of Megalos. Kali relayed the news to Jemma. It would be nearly October 20 before the Grande Pistola would be back off the coast of Tashien.

"Gosh, Fina, we are going to be really bored here. There's hardly anything to do, cooped up here in this tower," Jemma complained.

"I know, but we are under orders. We must be alert for more shipments and such," Fina replied, "but still, it is so boring."

"Better safe and bored than dead," Fang reminded the teens, who giggled.

Chapter 10 Journey to the Steppes

Ilenakova, now twenty-eight, had shortened her light brown hair to shoulder length in preparation for this long overland trip. They would be roughing it once more. Her blue eyes shown with excitement and anticipation of a long journey by horseback. She realized how much she had missed this aspect of life, cooped up in the big city. She double-checked her various weapons; all were sharpened and ready. Now she checked her horse and the packhorses for the second time. She wore leather pants and a cotton shirt, ready for the long trail ahead.

Enrico, now thirty-one, checked his many weapons as well. While the eldest and the one who ultimately had to answer for their safety on this trip, Enrico was rather worried. He'd never been beyond the borders of the Velona Sector and knew his guidance would be severely limited. He would just have to trust Ilenakova. Still he definitely felt that he needed to look after young Bianca. This was her first big trip anywhere.

Bianca was now of age, that is fourteen, and she acted as if she was now her own woman, her own boss, fiercely independent. With full recall of her former life as Janisseko Bottellio, famous as a Sisterhood Fighter Group Leader of Bonilla, she felt supremely confident that she could handle anything, especially now that she was a fully trained Protector, taking after her adopted mother, Dita. In fact, since Dita had never cut her hair, Bianca had allowed hers to grow long as well. Hers now reached to the small of her back, far short of Dita's, but nevertheless impressive, she thought. Today, she had tied a ribbon at the back of her head, forming a loose ponytail. She too checked her weapons and found them ready, but of course, she already had known that; she'd prepared them three days ago. Of the three, Bianca was the most excited about the trip. This would be her first real trip and a chance to show everyone that she was more than up to the challenges of the open road.

At last, their packhorse was re-checked enough times, and the three mounted, waving goodbye to everyone. Slowly the trio rode out of the gates of 42 Hampton Way and into the cobblestone streets of the wealthier section of Velona. Ilenakova rode point; Bianca followed her, while Enrico brought up the rear leading their packhorse. An hour later, the trio left the last outskirts of the huge city of over a million inhabitants far behind them. Still, they passed many farmsteads, though suburbia slowly continued to encroach on these farms. They passed many work crews who were building the rail line for Dianna's fancy steam powered engine and Ilenakova felt a pang of regret. If this new invention worked out, horses may become outdated.

Their horses were the smaller breed, which originated in the

Northern Steppes, where Dita had originally purchased them. She had gotten some of the finest available and their breeding had produced many excellent trail horses. Finally free of congestion and the majority of traffic, Ilenakova let her mare have a good run. The three galloped at top speed for several miles, loving every second of this freedom. Finally, they settled down into the long ride ahead of them.

Ilenakova's planned route was to head due north on the main spoke road, until they reached the hillier country, just south of Fortress d'Grange. Here, they would veer north and east and finally reach the Paese di Dio, God's Highway, a high, green plain separating the Eight Sea Princes and the impassable mountain range known as the Appian Way. By traveling the length of the Paese di Dio, they would bypass all the other Sea Prince sectors and potential troubles in Vito and Bonito, which were under the control of the Church of Jehosanity and where violence was commonplace. Yes, many now referred to these two sectors as the slums of the Sea Princes.

They chose not to stay at inns, but rather to camp out. Ilenakova wanted to make sure that they had everything needed, before they reached the Paese di Dio. Once they hit the high country, there would be no civilization for the length of the entire Sea Princes. If they had forgotten something, now was the time to find out. At the northern Velona town of Alda, they would pick up additional supplies for the long journey. When they reached Zargarb Sector at the other end, they would need to find a town to replenish them, before cutting north and east into the Northern Steppes.

The second day out of Velona, around noon, Ilenakova turned to Bianca. "I think someone has been following us all morning long."

"You think it spells trouble?" Bianca asked, eager for some additional excitement.

"Probably not, I keep seeing glimpses of a single rider behind us. Keep alert; it's probably just another traveler heading to Alda too," she suggested a plausible theory.

Purposely, Ilenakova dallied at their lunch break, figuring the rider would pass them by if they took an overly long noon break. He didn't, which raised her suspicions as well as Bianca's and Enrico's. "He could be a thief scouting us and then will bring his band down on us while we camp tonight," Bianca suggested as they climbed back on their horses to continue their north ride.

As they rode on, Bianca found herself frequently turning in her saddle to see if she could catch a glimpse of the rider behind them. Twice she thought she saw him on a dark brown horse. Eventually, they stopped for the night, near a stream in a grove of trees where they could set up a good defensible camp. They kept their eyes and ears pealed, but saw no sign of the mysterious rider. However, Ilenakova decided to post a guard. Each of them would take three-hour shifts, watching over the other two sleeping companions. None saw or heard anything out of the ordinary during the night.

The next day, Ilenakova again felt that someone was trailing them. This was beginning to get on her nerves. "I have an idea. See that large boulder ahead? I am going to peel off and get behind it, hidden from view. You two continue riding along the road. When our mysterious rider comes by here, I will come out behind him and you can turn around and come back. We will have him caught between us. Let's see what's going on."

"Hey, love the idea. I wish that I had thought of that!" Bianca exclaimed, all for the subterfuge. A minute later, Ilenakova pulled off to the left and circled around the large boulder, while Bianca and Enrico continued walking on down the road.

"Can't out fox me," Ilenakova thought to herself, drawing her broadsword, just in case. She waited. Soon, she heard the walking hoof beats of another horse coming up the road. "Got you now," she thought. She waited patiently. Wait. The rider paused. She heard someone dismount. Well, now is the time, she decided and cantered out from behind the large orange granite outcrop.

"Hello," a pleasant sounding young man said, as she appeared, her sword held high in her right hand, ready for action. The lad was sixteen, she guessed, with shoulder length light brown hair and fair blue eyes. He had a youthful look. He had dismounted and was examining the tracks that she'd left. "I wondered why you went around that boulder."

"Why are you following us?" Ilenakova demanded to know, just as Bianca and Enrico came galloping up to them.

"Hello," the lad said to Bianca and Enrico as they arrived, a dust cloud sailing into the lad and Ilenakova.

"Who are you and why are you following us?" Ilenakova repeated sounding as stern as possible.

"I am Louis. I'm merely riding north. This is still a free country, is it not?" She saw that the lad carried a bastard sword slung across his back and his horse had bulging saddlebags. His dark roan was nearly a foot taller than their short Northern Steppes mounts.

"I've seen you at some dances in Velona," Bianca said.

"Aye, I have seen you there as well. You kindly allowed me to dance once with you, if you remember that. It was some time ago, though, unfortunately. I am Louis."

"Bianca here. So you are not following us?" she asked.

"If by traveling this road northward means that I am following you, then yes I am," he replied. He had a strange way of answering, Bianca thought.

"Well, we are headed to Alta. You might as well ride along with us," Ilenakova said, mounting her horse. She didn't see anything suspicious about the young boy, but having him with them where she could keep an eye on him sounded better than always wondering if he was behind them.

"Thank you, that would be most enjoyable," Louis said with a grin, mounting his tall horse. He fell in beside Bianca.

"Fine day for a ride," he began to chat with her.

"Well, yes," she answered politely.

"Looks like you are all headed off on a long trip. Packhorse and all," he hinted.

Bianca saw that she could not easily discount their burdened packhorse, and replied, "Well, as a matter of fact we are starting on a long trip. Where do you live, Louis?"

"Around. Sometimes I am in Velona. I enjoy the dances and the music. Don't you?" he answered. Bianca thought that he was being a tad too mysterious, though.

"Oh yes indeed. We try to go to the local dances each week and see the concerts too. Where do you live when you are not in Velona?" she asked, attempting to uncover a bit more about this young man. He grinned, that was not the response she desired, though.

"Oh here and there. I have a ranch further north, very pretty, excellent location. Your horses come from the Northern Steppes, don't they?" he asked.

"Yes, they breed really fast horses that have a great endurance, which is why we got them. Mom bred these from the original mares and stallion that she bought several years ago," she explained. The two continued to chat as they rode along.

As dusk came, Ilenakova found a good spot to camp. Louis asked, "You are not staying at the inns. Interesting."

"We like roughing it," Bianca answered, unwilling to say more.

"Well, mind if I join you? There is not much light left, and I won't be able to get to Alta yet tonight," he asked. Bianca looked at Ilenakova, who nodded. Better to have him with them where she could keep an eye on him than having him out there somewhere.

Louis made his small camp next to theirs, independently made his campfire, and cooked his dinner. All the while, Bianca kept glancing his way, seeing what he was up to, but she saw nothing unusual, except that he was just as familiar with roughing it as she. Ilenakova established their guard shifts once more, unwilling to have them all asleep with Louis nearby. She took the first watch and saw Louis turn in over near his fire, which was now dying out.

At midnight, she roused Bianca. "Your turn. Keep an eye on Louis. He might try something," she whispered. Bianca wiped the sleep from her eyes and took a seat on a rock near their fire pit, whose embers still flickered red. She tossed a few sticks into the pit to have a bit more night. She glanced at Louis and saw that he was getting up and stretching. He waved to her and she found herself answering. Shortly, Louis, unarmed she noted, walked over to her and sat down on another rock beside her.

"Nice night, isn't it, Bianca."

"Yes, how come you are up?"

"Oh, just stretching. I saw you up and came over to say hi. You don't mind do you?"

"Well no. I am on guard duty, though."

"I can see. I feel really well protected." She couldn't tell whether he was teasing her or jesting or was sincere. "You know that you are a very beautiful woman?" She blushed.

"Well, I suppose so," she answered in a non-committal way.

"I suppose you get your good looks from your mother, Dita, isn't that her name?"

"Yes."

"Dita's about the most gorgeous woman I've ever seen anywhere," he complimented.

"Well, I suppose so," she again didn't want to say more.

"I notice that you don't date much. I haven't seen you out and around Velona at the various hangouts where we young folks are at," he said staring at the embers.

"Well, I've had lots to study and learn. We haven't had much time to just hangout." She didn't want to say more, but felt the need at least to give him a reason.

"I can understand that. Most of the kids hanging out are dull anyway. Stars are bright tonight. I always like the stars, you know. Gives me a sense of peace, and using them I always know where I am at — never get lost if you know your stars," he chatted.

She became curious. "How so? How is it that you can't get lost?"

"Oh, see that one there? It never seems to move and points to the north. If you can see it, then you know which way is north." He explained a bit more. "Well, I suppose I ought to get to sleep. See you in the morning, Bianca. Night."

"Night, Louis." She smiled. He was very well mannered, she thought, and cute.

The next day, they entered Alta around noon. This was the northernmost town in Velona. Just a few miles further north was the rocky border with Fortress d'Grange and a few miles up the canyon to the northeast lay the Paese di Dio, where they would head out to the east. They headed to the supply goods store and began to pick out the many dried provisions that they would need for the long overland journey.

Bianca caught sight of Louis also in the store, picking up supplies. "How curious," she thought. Eventually, the two met over the bags of dried fish. As each began picking up some bags, she asked, "How come you are in here? Going on a long trip?"

"Might ask you the same, but yes, I am planning a trip just now. I've decided to do it. Do you believe that you need to follow what your heart tells you to do, Bianca?" he asked.

What a strange question, she thought, not at all what she expected, especially coming from a man. "Well, of course, one should do the right thing." She hastily took several bags and joined the others. A bit later, all three had their arms full of items and headed to the counter to pay for them. Quietly, Louis came up behind them, his arms full as well.

"Well, we have made only one goof," Ilenakova commented, looking at their pile of stores, and realizing that they also needed to take along a large water barrel.

"A second packhorse!" Bianca exclaimed. "Duh, how stupid of us."

Enrico asked the shopkeeper, "Is there anywhere around here where we could purchase a packhorse and rack saddle?"

He looked up from his figuring and noticed Louis standing quietly in line. "Well, it's your lucky day. Yes, Louis here. He has a fine herd of horses. If anyone has one to spare, it's young Louis here."

Both miffed and embarrassed at the same time, Ilenakova turned and asked, "We have underestimated our needs. It seems we need to purchase a second packhorse."

"Sure, I have plenty. My place is just north and east of here, if that is not too far out of your way. I'd be glad to loan you a good one, rack saddle too," Louis replied, with a grin.

North and east? Thought Ilenakova. He must be very close to the Paese di Dio. She didn't think there was anyone living that close. "No, that is not out of our way. We can pay you for the horse and saddle," she said, still a bit surprised with the way things were moving.

"Sure, we can just pile your things and mine onto my horse and I'll walk. It's not too far to my spread," Louis replied.

After the shopkeeper figured Louis' tab, he asked, "Want me to debit this from your account with me?"

"Sure, thanks. See you later on." He carried his pile of dried food outside. After tying all the sacks onto his horse, he led the way north out of town.

"I didn't know that you lived way out here," Bianca chatted to their timely benefactor.

"That's because I didn't say. I like my privacy. It took some doing to get my spread. I love it out here. I am as close to the Paese di Dio as you can get. Do you know what that is?"

"Absolutely. It's one fantastic place, God's Highway. Love it there," Bianca replied.

"I've never seen you out there," Louis replied, and Bianca realized that she'd said a bit too much. "But then I am not always here on my spread. It's rather a wild place. I don't believe in fences and the like. Here's my marker. Look there; see them. There's a few of my horses."

Louis continued, "Biggest problem I have is keeping them from spending all their time grazing up on the Paese. Ilenakova, if you want, see if you can round up one of them. You pick which one you want. They are all good horses." She obeyed, cantering on up the slope.

"Say where is your ranch house?" Bianca asked.

"Oh, we're nearly there. It blends in and I can look out on the Paese from my window."

As they climbed up out of the last gully, the green grasses of the flat, sloping Paese di Dio came into view, along with the tall, gray peaks of the Appian Way. Off to their right, Bianca saw a small, one room cabin with a single door and one window facing the Paese.

"See how it blends in," Louis asked as he led them towards his cabin. "Perhaps one day I will build a stone home, but I am waiting because I want my wife to have a big say in how it is designed and looks," he replied.

"Oh, so you have a fiancé?" Bianca inquired, dismounting before his door.

"Not yet, but I am hopeful that soon I will. Hang on a second while I fetch some saddles." He went inside and came out with two packsaddles. Ilenakova rode up leading one of his horses. He quickly saddled it and put a leading bridle on it. Enrico and Ilenakova began to pack their new supplies onto the saddle.

"Where can we fill the water keg?" Bianca asked.

"There behind the cabin; a small spring bubbles the finest tasting water."

Louis began whistling and Ilenakova stopped to watch. Shortly, several other horses came trotting up to him. He petted each and gave them a nibble of carrots. One he chose and threw the other packsaddle on her. "You off on a trip as well?" she asked.

"Yes, I've decided that indeed I am!" he said determinedly.

"Where are you headed?" she asked, slightly annoyed with this lad.

"Not exactly sure yet, but I'll know soon," he replied. She didn't like his impertinence at all! Why didn't he just stay here and take care of his ranch?

Bianca carried the now heavy barrel, and Enrico hoisted it up and lashed it securely to the pack frame. "Thanks again for the use of the horse. We'll return it on our way back, though that may be a long time. Are you sure you don't want us to pay for it?" she asked, realizing that it would be many months before they returned.

"No thanks. Keep her as long as you have need of her. She's a fine horse, level headed," he replied. The three mounted, and Bianca now had to lead their second packhorse. As she turned to take a last look at Louis, she saw him packing his supplies onto his other horse. Strange fellow, but cute, she thought.

They climbed up out of the last gully and stepped onto the tall green grassland of the Paese di Dio. Here the land was about fifty miles wide, gently sloping up to the craggy, impassible mountains of the Appian Way. They were a mile high, and the air was thin, but crisp and clean. They paused a moment to take in its beauty.

"It's just as I remembered it!" Ilenakova exclaimed.

"Same here, just as I remembered it," Bianca added, taking in the breathtaking beauty of this high country. She heard hoof beats behind her and turned to see Louis leading his packhorse coming up behind them.

"Hello once again. Going my way again, I see," he definitely teased her.

"I thought you said you were going on a trip," she replied.

"I am. I'm heading east along the Paese for a while. How about you folks? Heading that way too? How about some company," he said.

Damn, we cannot get rid of this guy! Ilenakova was definitely becoming annoyed with him. "Look, we are on a special mission for the monarch of Velona. It is a very, very dangerous mission. We cannot have you following us around. You could get killed in the crossfire," she decided to be very frank and blunt. She had to get rid of this annoying lad.

"Isn't that interesting? Well, I know that Dianna West Po is Bale's younger sister and that you all live together. So I am not at all surprised that he has you on some dangerous special mission for him. I can take care of myself. Besides, there is no danger at all up here along the Paese di Dio. There are a couple of shepherds that I know about, but no one else. I ride up here quite a lot, as you can imagine, what with my ranch as close as you can get. I just could not put the ranch up in this land. I believe that it belongs only to God and not to man, though man may pass through here and be touched by God. Shall we ride on? It's beautiful, is it not?"

"Louis! We can't take you along with us," Ilenakova was becoming exasperated with him.

"You are not taking me along with you. I am just riding along the Paese di Dio a while and truly enjoy your company. Where's the harm in that?" Louis replied, completely unflustered by her insistence.

Enrico tried to intervene. "Look son, we are not kidding. This is a very dangerous mission. We can't have you with us."

"I am fighter trained and am a skilled camper and travel light. I won't be in your way. Besides, if you don't let me tag along for a while, I will just tag along after you. If Bianca is heading off into a dangerous situation, then I am determined to tag along. You will then have two men with you which may be better than one, should trouble come," Louis countered.

"But we are all highly skilled fighters," Ilenakova continued to press him. "Wait a second!" She suddenly worked it out. "You are in love with Bianca, aren't you?"

Bianca turned to face Louis and saw his face turn red as a beet. She grinned sensing that Ilenakova was dead on — that she knew it. Poor Louis mumbled, "Well, sort of — for a very long time now, I have been wanting the chance to meet her and talk with her and see, but if you are taking her into danger, then by god I am tagging along! You cannot stop me. Well, I suppose you can, but I will just track you anyway." He saw Ilenakova frowning and began thinking that he might have to pay his only trump card.

"Can't we just meet at a dance or something when I get back?" Bianca tried gently to convince him to take a different approach. What did he mean by a long time now? Who was he anyway? "Besides, you obviously know a good deal about me, and I don't know who you are, other than Louis."

He sighed, "I was hoping not to reveal my sir name just yet. I guess I really don't have any choice, but please, Bianca, don't let it influence you."

"Okay, I won't," she agreed. "So out with it."

"I'm Louis d'Grange, heir to dad's throne in Fortress d'Grange," he admitted.

"Wow! Cool, why didn't you want to tell us that?" Bianca asked, rather surprised.

"I can't tell you how many young girls have tried to hit on me hoping to take advantage of my becoming the ruler of d'Grange when dad dies. I want someone who will respect me for who I am, not whether or not I am a monarch. I figured if I remained anonymous and then if we, well, you know what I mean. I wanted you to like me because I'm me, not my heritage. Besides, you just said that this dangerous mission was on important Velona business. We are allies, and I am the official representative of your closest ally, so I ought to be in on this too." He played his final card.

"Look, Louis, we are going to be gone a long time, months. What will your dad say if you are mysteriously gone for so long? Besides, if anything happened to you, he would have our heads!" Ilenakova countered.

"I am on my own, especially for the last two years. I did send word to dad that I am with you and will be gone sometime. So if anything happens in d'Grange, dad will be able to contact me by contacting Bale West Po first. Dad wants me to get experience in the wide world so I'm better qualified to take over for him. This looks like a way to me. I have my own funds and supplies, so I won't be a bother. I really do want to get to know you better, Bianca."

Ilenakova looked rather flustered, so Enrico stepped in, "Well, it probably won't hurt to have the boy travel along with us across the Paese di Dio, Ilenakova. By then, he may tire of this and head back here."

"It ought to be up to Bianca. Do you really want this stranger riding along with you? If you'd rather he just wait and take you to a dance when we get back, just say so and I'll skedaddle him out of here," she replied.

"Well, we did dance once, so I suppose it won't hurt to have him ride along with us for a while. We can chat some," Bianca decided. Besides, she was curious about him. He barely knew her and yet was attracted to her. As royalty, he probably had all sort of other girls after him and yet he was interested in her. This intrigued her and so she wanted to find out more about him.

"Well, then, okay. We are heading for the Arad at this point, going across all the Paese di Dio. Do you really want to ride that far with us?" Ilenakova tried another approach to dissuade him from coming.

"Sure, that's fine with me. It bypasses the thief-plagued Bonito and Vito sectors. Good plan," he said, feeling far more hopeful now.

"Well, then let's get going. We've already wasted enough time as it is," she gave in and kicked her horse into motion at last. Bianca, leading the second packhorse, fell in behind her, while Louis, leading his packhorse, moved beside her. Enrico brought up the rear with their second packhorse.

"Thanks for agreeing to let me tag along," Louis said. "I didn't mean to embarrass you so or to put you on the spot, Bianca. I was just hoping we could ride along and chat. You know, get to know each other a bit."

"That's okay, Louis. This is my actual first real outing. So what's it like being an heir to a throne? What are you interested in? Say, how come you have a ranch in Velona and why is it right by the Paese anyway?"

"I love horses and the Paese di Dio. Even if I become their ruler, I plan to take vacation trips often to my ranch. As I said, I won't actually build any real permanent structures there until I marry. I want her to have a big say in what is built there." Louis chatted away, telling her about himself.

A bit later, he explained, "You see, I have found it difficult to have any really close friends. As soon as they find out who I am, they began using me for their own ends and purposes. That's when dad and I decided it might be best if I just leave our city for a while, get this ranch, and make my way around your sector. Still, making any real friends is hard. It seems the second that they find out dad's the ruler of d'Grange, everything changes with them — for the worst. That's why I really tried so hard not to tell you right away. I didn't want you to do that to me too."

"Well, you don't have to worry about that. I've no interest in you just because you are the heir apparent to d'Grange. I certainly won't marry anyone for that kind of a reason. So tell me, how come you are so attracted to me?" she asked coyly, wondering just why he was.

"Oh, lots of reasons. You are quite cute and attractive, just like your mom, but that's not really the main reason. I know a little about you, your moms, and other siblings, for want of a better way to say it. Around Velona, your place is known as the Estate of the Precocious Witches. When I heard those rumors, I had to see for myself. I found it fascinating to see balls levitating and flying around without anyone's hands on them. Little things like that intrigue me. I can see where that would make others think of you as witches. You don't go riding around on broom handles, do you?" he teased.

"No, of course not," she teased him back.

"Didn't think so. I just think that all of you in 42 Hampton Way are able, powerful people, the kind of people that I would really like to know well and become friends with, if possible. I don't know why, but I am really drawn to all of you. It's a strange feeling, you know. It just feels right somehow. And then there is another reason, Bianca, but maybe this is too personal for you to say anything about."

"What? Out with it," she teased him in a friendly way. Her curiosity was aroused.

"I knew you when you were a little girl. Now you are grown up and of age."

"And. . ." she nudged, wondering what he meant.

"Well, when I first met you ages ago, you, well, you had no arms. Later on, when I next met you at the dance, there you were with arms again. You have to admit that is more than a little unusual. I admit that I did some checking after that dance. I found people nearby your place that did see all of you, including your parents, without any arms at all — like the women from Dorota and those that were duped by their Elders there in Velona. Yet, now all twelve of you have perfectly normal arms. I find that inexplicable and yet a wonderful miracle. I certainly took notice of you. I admit that when I saw you as a little armless girl, I did like you then. I guess that's why I have paid so much attention to you later on, after we met again at the dance. Since no one in Velona is talking about some dozen 'Holy Miracles,' I began to think that you must be very special people."

"I've checked out Cosima, though I know that she is dating Gerardo West Po. That girl is a fabulous detective! Exceedingly sharp mind. I took even more notice of you after discovering that. I found myself falling for you, but I was too shy to actually approach you and ask you out. I feared that you would tell me to just get lost or something. If you are all as powerful as I believe you to be, I can understand it if you are not at all interested in someone like me. Then too, your folks are all women married to women, most unusual. Still, I've decided to give it a try. When I saw you all packing up for a long trip, I decided I'd give it a go and began following your trail. I am a good tracker, and it's hard for me to get lost. Anyway, if you only like other women, just say so or if you really are only interested in men who are powerful as yourselves, please just be up front with me."

"Oh, I like boys," Bianca hastily answered. "I'm not like my mom or our moms. Actually, we all think of ourselves as sisters, really. We're all adopted, you see. You are right. Our real parents were duped by the Elders from Dorota. We six lost our arms when we were very young, around three years old or so. Our folks, well, they couldn't handle it and committed suicide rather than face life. We were so lucky that they all adopted us."

She continued, "You are right. It was Cosima's doing. She figured out how to make our growing bodies re-generate new arms. That is one of the amazing things about our bodies, while they are growing up, they can repair an enormous amount of damage, though it takes a special trick that she discovered to get them to do it after the body is born. Cosima tried it on some who were fully grown, and her technique didn't work then. Have you ever heard of the old Druwids?" she asked, curious about how much he really did know.

"Sure, they are a historical legend. They are all dead now, but they used to be the most powerful people around here. So many did so many fabulous things for the Greenway and the Sea Princes. In fact, they had an awful lot to do with the founding of our own Fortress d'Grange. It's said that they could bring down bolts of lightning and cast flaming balls of fire. I don't know if it's true or not, but our history books certainly say so. Too bad that they are all dead now. Our world could use more of them," he replied.

"Well, they are not all dead yet. There are still a few of us around, though we are adapting to the new times we live in," Bianca replied.

"What do you mean by 'us?'" he asked, suddenly curious about her choice of words.

"Well, some of us are still here," she answered, worrying that she'd said too much.

"Well, my grandparents and great-grandparents were Druwids, but there are none in d'Grange that I know of anymore. They used to tell me all manner of stories about them, Ket Bethany in particular. Are you saying that you are one of them?" he decided to ask her directly.

"Well, it ought to be kept a secret," she admitted.

"My lips are sealed!"

"Okay, yes, I'm a Protector. Actually, all three of us are Protectors. So is my mom. I take after her, but Bethany is our Wid, our leader. In the old days, they used to form into Circles of Seven, but now, as you have said, most are dead. We are now just about the last still living."

"Wow. Well, now finally everything about all of you makes sense! I knew that you had to be one powerhouse of a girl! Yes! Wow. I am very, very honored to meet you, Protector Bianca!" he exclaimed. "So much makes perfect sense to me. Ah well," he sighed.

"Ah well what?" Bianca asked.

"Well, of course you really won't be interested in someone like me. I am not a Druwid. I don't possess the kind of powers you all are supposed to have. Still, I will honor my pledge; I will protect you with my life."

"Why not interested in you? Oh, you think that I would only be interested in other Druwid guys! I get it," she suddenly saw what he was alluding to. "Oh don't be silly! I'm interested in guys that are not jerks. Honestly, all six of us are having a terrible time meeting guys that don't act so darn silly around us. Oh, I get it. Girls all act silly around you when they find out that you are heir to your dad's throne," she finally knew what he had run into with girls his age.

"Yes, that's right. Say, we both are having the same problem, but for different reasons. We have at least that in common," he grinned. It was a hopeful start, he thought.

The ice broken between them, they continued chatting away as they rode across God's Highway. When they stopped for the night, Bianca noted that Louis was very proficient in setting up a campsite and dealing with living out of doors. So much so, that Ilenakova decided to have him share night watch duties, allowing them to all get a bit more rest. She was still unwilling not to have someone watching over them while they slept.

As the days passed, Louis heard about the therapy sessions that Bethany had taught to Bianca and her sisters. Bianca found that Louis was keenly interested in this therapy and asked many questions about it. "How come you are so curious about it, Louis?" she finally asked, as they rode along.

"Well, I don't exactly know. It's one of those things that intrigue me. Have you ever come across something that you think you should or ought to or know about, and yet you've never really knew existed before, but you still think it is somehow familiar? Well, that's the best explanation I can give you. It's the same thing with you. I mean when I first danced with you and saw that you now had arms, my mind was blown. It struck me that you must be a very powerful person. That's when I knew that somehow I had to get to know you better. You've been in my thoughts ever since and I can't shake them, though I have tried. Isn't that just plain weird? I mean, neither of us knows the other, and yet I am somehow drawn to you by something I cannot quite see."

"I know what you mean. The Paese here is so familiar to me, as if I know it and love it up here, but I've never been this far along the Paese. Mom has brought us up to see it, but that's about all. However, I know why it is so familiar to me," she confided. "I have a good recall on some of my previous lives, and one time I used to be one of those powerful Sisterhood Fighter Group Leaders and scout. I knew every inch of the back country of many sectors. As we ride along, I keep getting memories from those days. Because of the therapy sessions I've had, it all is understandable and makes sense to me."

"Wow. That is terrific that you can remember like that. Maybe someday I can get some of those therapy sessions too. I'll have to meet with Bethany or Dita when they get back and see if I might be able to get some," Louis sounded a hopeful note.

"Hey, you are remembering all this too?" Ilenakova had eased back to the pair and overheard their conversation. "It's all coming back to me too, Bianca. What a strange feeling suddenly to remember all these things that you one knew and the things you once did in a former lifetime. Pretty interesting, I think."

"And useful too, I'll bet," Louis added. She grinned. He had no idea, she thought to herself.

That evening while they were sitting around the small campsite, Bianca decided why not give Louis a therapy session. She didn't know exactly why she'd had this impulse, but what the heck, there was little else to do but stir the embers. Wood was scarce up here and they purposely used only a little for cooking suppers. Otherwise, they would have to detour to the right and head down from the Paese into the sectors and scrounge for firewood, something none wanted to waste time doing.

"Tell you what, Louis, why don't I give you a therapy session right now. You game to give it a try?" Bianca asked.

"Are you sure? Well, yes, absolutely! That would be really great," he replied suddenly becoming very enthusiastic about the prospect.

After she explained a little about the process, she said, "Well, the hardest part is getting started. Usually, we start with the recent accident, illness, or harm that someone just had. You know, like one time I fell down and busted up my knee. Alessa right away had me go back to a moment just before I fell down and hurt it. So, have you had any recent injuries or something like that?"

"Er, no, I've not gotten hurt or ill. I guess it might not work on me then," he said with a downcast sigh.

"Well, have you had any unusual or strange feelings or emotions?" she asked, wondering if indeed, she might not have any way really to get started. This was always the hardest part, she remembered Dita explaining to her.

"Well, actually yes I have this one that keeps haunting me, Bianca, but it is so hard to describe. Kind of a fear," he answered.

"Good. Close your eyes. All right. Now I want you to go to a time when you were having this haunting one, this kind of fear," she ordered. Inwardly, she relaxed, she'd found something and knew that the worst for her was over.

Soon, he was telling her about it. "Well, I am dancing with you that Friday night, and after we were done, Cosima cut in on us. I am feeling separated from you. Suddenly, I have this horrible fear that I am losing something I desperately need." He described a bit more about it. After several times over it, Bianca asked if there was an earlier time he had this fear.

"I am six years old. Dad, Count Lionel d'Grange, is telling me, 'Son, one day when you grow up, you will become the ruler of Fortress d'Grange. You will take my place here.' I suddenly realize what that means! I sense that I am missing someone who absolutely must be close to me! Without this person with me, I cannot rule. I am scared and very frightened! I nearly pee my pants. My stomach even hurts."

Bianca had him go over this several times, and Louis' fear only grew stronger and stronger. At last, she asked him if there was something even earlier that was similar. Suddenly, a massive ball of grief appeared, Louis began crying. "Maggie has died! I am so alone now! I cannot live without her! I cannot possibly rule without my Maggie with me!" He cried heavily for a couple of minutes. Bianca was quiet and allowed him to re-experience the loss. She had him go through it several more times, before he suddenly saw the whole thing.

"Oh my god. I was Leroy d'Grange! Back in the 635, I ruled d'Grange! Maggie Helmut — she was my wife, and she was one of your Loremasters! She was a Druwid. I depended on her for so much! She even taught me a whole bunch of things. I remember now. 'Observe what is really there, not what you think or believe is there.' She tells me that a whole lot! Well, no wonder I had this terrible fear of becoming a ruler again! I was so dependent on Maggie back then, and now I don't have her at my side. Well, that is silly isn't it? Hey, there was a whole bunch of Druwids around us back then. Yes, I remember; they were the d'Grange Circle! I was always learning cool, great new things from them. Wow, do I ever miss them. Oh! That's why I was so attracted to you and your sisters! Oh! I wasn't wrong; you are Druwids! No wonder I am so attracted to all of you. I have a strong bond with Druwids. Isn't that interesting? Well, now I don't feel this kind of reactive force driving me to connect with all of you. What a relief! Oh! I was seeing you as Maggie, Bianca! Duh! How stupid of me. Well, I'm sorry for my behavior. I would like to get to know you, Bianca and you too, Ilenakova, Enrico. Can we all maybe just start over? I'm Louis d'Grange and will one day be the ruler of Fortress d'Grange. As such, Velona and d'Grange have always been strong allies as well as with the Druwids. I want to continue our long standing friendship and trust."

Bianca quietly ended his session. "Apology accepted, Louis d'Grange. Indeed, let's start over as friends."

Even Ilenakova shook his hand with a smile. "Allies have to stick together, Louis. I'll tell you what our mission is all about. Then, if you think it is too dangerous, you are free to return to your ranch." She outlined the presumed war going on in the Northern Steppes. Some army from Tashien had invaded the horsemen's land. A huge supply of guns is being sent to arm these horsemen. "We are going to see firsthand what is happening and offer them the assistance of Velona."

"Wow. Okay, count me in. I will offer them the aid of Fortress d'Grange as well. We don't want another war on our hands! If it had not been for the cannonae, the Centurion legions of Demokritos would have swept through all the Sea Princes, much like the horsemen did way back when. As the heir, it is my duty to see firsthand what the situation actually is so that I can advise Lionel, my dad, what is happening there," Louis replied.

Ilenakova accepted this completely as did Enrico. "Welcome aboard, Louis," he added, shaking the lad's hand. Bianca grinned; she rather liked this young heir.

"Oh, no wonder I so love plants and animals and have gotten my own ranch with a hundred head of horses!" Louis suddenly realized. "Maggie taught me her love of such things, and I still have not forgotten it."

Bianca realized that the Druwids did have lasting influences upon the people of Tarra, long after they were gone. She felt a sense of pride.

Some days later, they discovered a massive trampled-grass path and stopped to investigate. "Look, they came up out of the canyons here," Ilenakova announced, pointing out the signs.

"That must be Vito down there, if my estimates of how far we've come are accurate," Enrico commented.

"Probably a good fifty riders have passed through here, more than three days ahead of us," Louis added to the observations.

"Now why would a band of some fifty riders come up here out of Vito?" Bianca wondered aloud. "They are heading the same way as we are."

"Where did you say the gun shipment was traveling?" Louis asked Ilenakova.

"They would be traveling the coast road through the Sea Princes and then head up the northeast spoke road to the Arad. Oh, I get what you are thinking, Louis. I think you may be on to something," she exclaimed growing concerned.

"You think these men are out to rob the gun shipment?" Bianca asked, catching on quickly.

"Well, that would be a fine prize for thieves to nab," Enrico suggested.

"If I were them, I wouldn't try to take the shipment while it is within the Sea Princes. There would be too many questions and too much of a counter-attack threat," Ilenakova considered aloud. "I'd wait and take them when they are in the Arad. It's still a no-man's land. Few counter-attacks are likely. Damn, we had better hurry up our pace. I hope that we aren't too late."

"If we are, they will likely be bringing them back this same way, sneaking back into Vito," Bianca proposed. "I certainly would. So if we run into them coming our way, we had best be prepared to counter-attack them to retrieve the gun shipment."

"Right. Mount up. Let's double our pace," Ilenakova ordered sternly. They rode hard that day, but saw nothing but the beaten grass path of the riders ahead of them.

As the days passed, Louis pointed out that they were gaining on the band ahead of them. As mid-July came, the Paese di Dio's width began to narrow; they were above Zargarb Sector now. The area was keenly familiar to Ilenakova. She'd been up here many times in her previous lives. "We're about two days from the border with the Arad, gang. We are running low on supplies. Louis, we were planning to head down into Zargarb to re-supply, but under the circumstances, I say we press on."

"Makes sense. I still have some food left. Let's pool it and make do. We are getting close to them. I think that they are at most a day ahead of us now. Press on!" Bianca liked his youthful enthusiasm. He'd said what she would have said: press on. They continued following the plain trail, riding as fast as they dared push their horses. As the Paese di Dio finally ended, they veered southeast. Here the canyons quickly gave way to far more arid land. They were nearing the border of the desert land of Juda Arad, where it met Zargarb.

Now the tracking became more difficult. Bianca began picking up some tips from Louis, whose observations were backed up by Ilenakova. Even Enrico was having a more difficult time with the tracking over the sometimes hard-packed ground. None had any difficulty when the path led over the sands. "They cannot be too far ahead of us now," Louis concluded, and Ilenakova backed him up. Bianca asked how they could tell, and Louis explained as they rode on.

Late in the afternoon, Ilenakova, riding point, spied a distant dust cloud. She urged them into a canter. An hour later, the sounds of gunfire could be heard in the distance. The group broke into an all-out gallop, closing the distance to the field of battle as rapidly as they could.

As they crested a small rise, they spied six wagons below on the dirt track heading northeast. Many bodies lay on the ground around them while over a dozen men were now resorting to close quarter sword combat, defending the wagons. A dozen bodies of the raiders lay in a more distant perimeter around the battlefield. Obviously, they were felled by the initial gunshot volleys. Still, some forty raiders were attempting to finish off the remaining men guarding the wagons and the gun shipment.

"Spells first. Let's even the odds!" Ilenakova cried as she charged down the slope. Bianca struggled to concentrate. She'd not practiced casting a ball of fire while charging on a galloping horse before. Evidently, neither had the others, she noted as their spells detonated around the time hers did, and she didn't feel so badly about being so slow with it.

Three balls of fire some thirty feet across engulfed the back outer perimeter of the raiders, who were attempting to move in to assist the close quarters combat. The clothing of fifteen men erupted into flames. They screamed and fled, vainly trying to dose themselves in the sand. Louis watched the flying dismount of Ilenakova and was amazed at her grace and skill. In the same motion, she drew her broadsword and headed into the thick of the battle.

Bianca chose to rein in and dismount. No way was she going to try what Ilenakova had done. Enrico and Louis were right behind her. The three drew their swords and rushed in after the fearless Ilenakova. Louis held his large bastard sword high and then swung at the first raider he encountered.

Taken by surprise, the remaining raiders pivoted to face this new, unexpected threat. Already, they had most of the remaining men who were guarding the guns wounded, yet their prize was suddenly in dire jeopardy by this strange appearance of the four. Ilenakova battled three raiders at the same time, Bianca, Enrico, and Louis found themselves facing two each. Bianca kept her focus and concentrated on parrying and looking for an opening. At last, she saw a weakness and exploited it; one raider's grabbed his stomach and crumpled to the ground. Another scrambled over him to get at her.

At her side, Louis was taking a heavy toll on the raiders, who were using either short swords or broadswords. With the longer reach of his sword, using two hands on it, he was connecting before his opponents could get close enough to hit him. Occasionally, he also took out one who was to his right, who was attacking Bianca, giving her a bit of a relief.

Enrico hacked away on her right, felling half as many as Louis. Just ahead of them, Ilenakova continued in her berserk manner to cut through the raiders as if they were butter. A wild battle lust shown from her eyes. She was immensely enjoying this battle; this was the life for her! Thirty minutes after her flying dismount, sweating profusely, she finally stopped swinging her blade, for no more men came charging at her. She paused and looked back. Louis, Bianca, and Enrico were holding their knees and gasping for breath. Blood was everywhere as were the pile of bodies.

"Damn, ended way too soon," she gasped to her friends. "You okay? Any injuries?"

"Okay here, few cuts, nothing major," Bianca replied.

"Alright, let's lend a hand to the gun shipment protectors," she ordered, wiping her blade on her pants and sheathing it. The four moved over the fallen raiders to assist the wounded. Enrico chose to stand guard, just in case some of the wounded raiders had thoughts of continuing the fighting. He was loathed to just go around making sure that they were dead by stabbing the bodies.

"Who are you?" asked one of the men, holding a bloodied arm.

"Friends from Velona and d'Grange, heading for the Steppes to see if the horsemen needed any help from our countries," Ilenakova replied.

"Ah, friends, yes we need allies. I am Viktor Martoski, Bear Clan leader from the Steppes. I was sent to fetch our order of guns. I am deeply in your debt for your timely assistance," he said, grimacing from the pain in his arm.

"Glad we were in time. We've been trailing these raiders all the way from Vito. Now, let me examine your arm and get you patched up. My friends and I know a bit about field doctoring," she asked. He allowed her to examine his sword wound.

"I'll deal with the raiders, Enrico. I am afraid I don't know how to deal with all these injuries," Louis said. Enrico joined the two women, while Louis began to drag the fallen, dead raiders' bodies into one large pile. He allowed several of their wounded to leave the battlefield on foot. Meantime, a dozen wagon drivers crawled out from under their wagons and began to assist their wounded Vito guards.

By dusk, the three had the wounded Vito men patched up as best they could under field conditions, which included nearly a total lack of any medical supplies. Ilenakova insisted that they head back into Zargarb immediately to seek better medical care. Louis had rounded up the scattered horses, and, as the sun set, he watched eighteen Vito guards riding back down the desert track. By morning, if they made it, they ought to be in Zargarb Sector and near some towns, where they could seek assistance.

Viktor's arm had been stitched up as best as could be done by Ilenakova. Additionally, six of his men survived the battle and were also patched up, but the Druwids insisted that they ride on the wagons the next day. "We'll stand guard tonight and ride north with you, Viktor, to help protect your valuable shipment of guns," Ilenakova explained, much to his relief. He knew just how much he was indebted to his unexpected allies.

Around the campfire, the four chatted while the others slept. "You are an impressive fighter," Louis complimented Ilenakova.

"Thanks. I admit I do enjoy a good fight for a good cause. I have to say that when I had lost my arms as a little girl, I almost took my own life because I knew that I would be unable to fight again. Now, I am glad that I did not. Thank you Cosima! Say, Louis, you handled yourself very well today. Big blade," Ilenakova replied with a teasing smile.

"Big blade for a big boy," he teased her back. "Your balls of fire were totally unexpected and incredibly impressive! I'm glad I came along. I was able to help. I made sure that Bianca wasn't hurt."

"Yes, thanks. I'm still growing stronger and this was my first real battle. Boy, you sure do get tired after a bit, don't you," Bianca admitted.

"Well, if the truth be known, Louis, the outcome might have been different had you not been with us," Enrico stated factually. "Glad you persisted. Thanks."

The next morning, Ilenakova chatted with Viktor Martoski. He explained, "My arm is sore and we really do need to get to a doctor soon. I've issued orders to veer to the northwest and make for Meslokov instead of Bodova as planned."

"Say, we are rather out of date on our knowledge of your country," Enrico explained. "Have your people settled down in some permanent towns?"

"Yes and no. Yes, under the leadership of our czars and now Czar Chekov Strokova and Czarina Mara, some of our people and clans have created seven permanent cities. We are becoming modernized and we even have a Banca del Dio in these seven cities! Meslokov is not far from here, just across the Dragon's Teeth in the hills across the Elbe River and the Appian Way. Then further up the Elbe is Kelnosky on the Greenway side of the Appian Way. Up at the Volgost Mountains that form our northern border and where the Elbe River comes through the mountain valley is Rodgost. Midway between the Elbe and the eastern Kathas Mountains is Zimyeva, where the Czar and Czarina dwell, our capital city. Further east from there is Kyposki. All three of those lie in the foothills of the Volgost

Mountains. Across the center of the Steppes is Rynov and further east of there and about half way up is Bodova. The invasion force from Tashien is located at the furthest northeastern point of the Steppes, where the Volgost Mountains end. There is a bit of seacoast there. We suspect that the invasion force came along the northern coast of the Desert of Desolation."

He went on, "However, as always, about half of our clans refused to abandon their traditional ways and still roam across the vast grasslands, moving their villages two to four times a year. Czar Chekov has formed up a defensive army just north of Bodova. They are waiting for the arrival of these new guns. He believes that they may make a big difference in the battles."

"Just how big is the invasion force?" Ilenakova asked, hoping to get a better feel on the actual situation here in the Steppes.

"We don't know exactly. They are like ants! Swarming in from the northeastern seacoast, thousands and thousands of them. Already, scouts are watching them building shelters in the foothills of the Kathas Mountains. All signs point to their desire to stay long term in our land. The Czar has promised to drive them back to Tashien, but so far, we have been unsuccessful," Viktor answered.

"Your warriors are strong and fierce," Ilenakova complimented him. "How is it that you have not been able to drive them back already? Your horsemen are powerful."

"Aye that we are indeed. Yes, our bands attacked them many times already. We have slain many of their foot soldiers. Some say that we kill ten of theirs for every one of ours who dies. Yet, even with such staggering losses, they just continue to pour into our grasslands. They are like a plague of ants, swarming over our land. The Czar is hoping that these new guns will drive them back to the sea."

"Czar Chekov has gotten some support from three of our neighboring Greenway kingdoms. After all, if the swarm passes to the west, they will bear the brunt of it. Their kings are wise and have sent many soldiers to help us fight them on the Steppes and not on their lands. I am sure that Czar Chekov will want to enlist all the aid that your countries can send as well."

"Well, we are here as ambassadors. We'd like to see firsthand this army of ants and then visit with Czar Chekov," Ilenakova replied.

Viktor grinned, "Well, you stay with me and you'll get to do both. After we resupply and care for the wounded in Meslokov, we will be taking these guns northeast to Bodova, where the army is forming. The Czar himself will lead the next major attack on the ants of Tashien."

Three slow days later, the six wagons pulled into their southernmost city of Meslokov. The wide Elbe River gently flowed past the western edge of the city, across which the sharply rising, craggy granite peaks of the Appian Way stood like silent specters watching over the city. The houses were built uniformly from wood, but had an unusual shape. Their sides were octagonal as were their windows. Beginning at the second story level, the octagonal walls sloped upwards, forming a huge roof — a chimney protruded from the very center. The nomads lived in rounded hide huts upon the Steppes. Those that moved into a city emulated those style homes in wood. Overall, the city had a most fascinating look about it.

The four visited the Banca del Dio and withdrew some spending money and then replenished their exceedingly low food supply. That night, Viktor advised them to stay at the Levka Inn and they got a good look at the inside layout of one of the larger octagonal buildings. The door led into the very center, where the innkeeper's bar and the chief's kitchen lay in an octagonal shape around the large stove and fireplace combination. The rest of the main floor was filled with tables and chairs for the patrons. Sleeping quarters were on the sloping side-walled second floor. The four found the accommodations warm and comfortable, especially because each bedroom had its own window with a view. Naturally, the four chose two rooms that overlooked the Appian Way and the Elbe River.

The next day around noon, Viktor sent for them. The gun caravan was ready to continue its overland journey. After packing their gear and refilling their water keg, the four met the six wagons at the edge of the city. Here, Viktor had added some fifty horsemen to ride protection across the Steppes.

For days, the caravan wandered across the open rolling grasslands, with patches of forest interspersed. The four found the rustic, idyllic setting refreshing, though they all noticed no signs of any permanent road. They were heading in a straight line for Bodova, according to Viktor. Twice, they spotted a small nomad village in the distance, but the caravan did not stop.

Often at night, some of the horsemen poked fun at Louis' giant horse, as they called her. Indeed, his mare stood nearly a foot and a half taller than their well-bred Steppes horses. Ilenakova was thankful that the three of them rode Steppes bred horses. Poor Louis took daily continual teasing from these warriors. "How's the weather up there? Do you often get nosebleeds way up there? How's the view?" Many other less pleasant taunts were thrown his way as well.

On August 15, the wagons rolled to the top of a hill and now below them stretched the large city of Bodova, some five miles around. Ilenakova observed that the overall outline of the city as also octagonal, emulating the many wooden buildings within the sprawling city. However, the wagons did not enter Bodova, but circled to the east, heading directly to the large encampment of the Czar's army.

"Wow!" Bianca exclaimed as she got her first view of the thousands of hide huts of the encampment. Czar Chekov had amassed fully ten thousand warriors for the coming offensive intended to drive the invaders out of their land. Tethered horses were everywhere, but there were well-worn tracks where constant foot traffic and horses had passed, forming dirt streets. She wondered how long the army had been encamped here.

As Viktor and his band rode into the sprawling encampment, many leather-clad fighters came out of their portable huts to shout, cheer, and yell good wishes to them. Many stared long and hard at the strangers and especially young Louis astride his tall mare. Somewhere in the middle of the incredible maze of huts, the wagons halted. Viktor explained that this was the Czar's hut and to let him do the talking first. Everyone dismounted as a man and woman came out of the hut.

Czar Chekov was tall and thin, but still he looked every inch a fighter. He wore the same leather armor as all the other men, except he had a large emerald hanging on his breast from a gold chain around his neck. His long curly blonde hair fell unruly to his shoulders and his face appeared as if he had not shaved for a couple weeks. His sharp blue eyes missed nothing. The Czarina Mara had similar light blond hair, tied back in a ponytail. She stood a half foot shorter than her husband did and wore similar leather with a similar emerald about her neck.

"Ah, Viktor, back at last with our guns," his voice was clear and sharp. "I see you ran into some trouble."

Viktor looked puzzled. "Yes, the guns have arrived, my Czar. How did you know that we were ambushed?"

"You are days late and have brought other Bear Clan fighters with you than those you left with. Tell us what happened. Are all the guns here?" Czar Chekov asked the most important question.

"All guns as delivered," Viktor reassured him. "Yes, all went well until we reached the Arad. There we were beset upon by a large band of robbers, presumably from Vito Sector. We were heavily outnumbered and down to our last few men when we received timely and unexpected assistance from these four official representatives from our allies, Velona and Fortress d'Grange. Apparently, they were on their way to see you and had been following these raiders. They were able to finish off the raiders. Had they not come, very likely we would have lost the shipment. I left those of my men who survived in Meslokov with the doctors."

The Czar looked at the four and then focused solely on Enrico. "On behalf of our country, it seems that I owe you many thanks. Please, I am Czar Chekov Strokova, grandson of the great Czar Illi Strokova. My wife, Czarina Mara. Our hut is your hut." He extended his hand to Enrico.

"Well met, Czar Chekov. I am Enrico Angela; this is Mrs. Ilenakova Kato da Cassa and Miss Bianca Malina. We are representatives from Velona, sent by our monarch Bale West Po. This is the heir and son of Lionel d'Grange, monarch of Fortress d'Grange. We have been sent by our countries to find out about this invasion from Tashien and if there is anything that your southern allies can do to help you." He shook Chekov's hand firmly.

"Welcome allies from the south lands. Yes, in these hard times, the more allies that one has, the better. Again, thank you for your timely intervention on our behalf. However, I believe that these new gun weapons may be all that we need to drive these yellow swine back to Tashien. Tonight, you shall join our hut for a celebration. Mustov will see that a hut is prepared for your stay. First, we shall learn how to use these new weapons. Then, we ride to battle. You are welcome to come and watch as we drive them back into the sea," Czar Chekov replied very confident that these new weapons were precisely what was needed to achieve complete victory.

Mustov, a warrior and a grim faced man, led the four to a hut six rows down from the Czar's. Here the four tethered their horses, which began to graze on the lush grasses near the hut. The four carried their gear inside. A fire pit was in the center; the smoke vent was in the top of the hide dome. Bent saplings formed the frame around which the hide was laid. The floor was simply a set of hides thrown onto the grass beneath them. They piled their gear and then headed outside to watch and observe the army and their use of the guns.

Before long, the one thousand guns were handed out and Viktor began explaining their operation to small groups at one time. Soon, the echoing sounds of gunfire brought thousands out to watch. Essentially, these were one shot affairs, the kind that were now in widespread usage. After firing, one had to fill a metal cylinder with more powder, pour its contents into the barrel, add a lead bullet wrapped in a circle of cotton, and then tamp it down solidly. A bit of powder was then put in a flash pan and the trigger lever cocked. When the trigger was pulled, a bit of flint struck the steel flash pan igniting the powder, which then ignited the powder in the barrel. The explosion then drove the bullet out.

A dozen dummy targets, more like scarecrows, were lined up in a row at the edge of the encampment. Each group of a dozen handpicked men took their first shots at the targets. When the bullets hit, the severe damage that they would do was plainly evident. Louis, who had never seen the guns before, commented to Bianca, "They are slow weapons. They have one shot before the enemy can close upon them. Not so effective in a war, perhaps."

"That may be, but at close range, one shot can kill a person from say twenty-five feet away. That makes them deadly weapons in a city," she observed. He agreed with her suggestion.

That night, they dined in the crowded hut of the Czar. He seemed supremely confident of victory and chatted with his four new guests. They learned that some nomads had first spotted the arrival of these invaders this spring at the extreme northeast corner of the Steppes. Hence, that they had come by following the shoreline from Tashien seemed entirely plausible. Yet, Ilenakova could not fathom what these invaders desired. Even the Czar seemed to know nothing that would give her a clue.

Back in their own hut, as they laid out their bedrolls, Ilenakova discussed the scant information that they had learned, "Look, what could possibly be their motives in invading the Steppes? There are only seven cities, a relatively new thing for these nomadic people. The invading army has not moved due west to attack the three cities along the Volgost range, as I certainly would have done to secure a position in this land. They have not swept out onto the vast Steppes where Bodova would become a prime target. They have not swept southwest to Zargarb either. Instead, they are hugging along the foothills of the Kathas range. Why? What's their military objective? I can find none. I must be missing some key data. Do these horsemen have a huge stash of gold or something in the foothills of Kathas?"

"Dunno," Enrico replied thoughtfully. "It does seem that their advance does not fit in with our estimations. Perhaps, Ilenakova, these invaders think differently than we do, that their objectives are not the ones that we, if we were leading the advance, would choose."

"I agree with Enrico," Louis put in, "if I was leading the invasion, I would do one of three things: go after the horses of these nomads, drive westward to capture the grain fields of the Greenway, drive southwest to conquer the relatively wealthy Zargarb Sector. It seems a mystery why they would so hug the foothills of Kathas."

"Well, I wonder what their methods of combat are going to be," Bianca said what she was more curious about. "Whatever that is, apparently they lose ten men to every one of the horsemen. That can't go well with an invading army's morale. Why, if that happened to our Velona troops, they might retreat or route."

"Damn, nothing about this makes any sense," Ilenakova cursed in disgust. "Here we are and we don't know a darn thing more than when we left."

"We will get to see more soon enough, once they launch their planned assault on them," Enrico advised.

For over a week, the sounds of gunfire echoed throughout the encampment. The thousand men practiced daily and, once routinely hitting the targets, began to fire while mounted. These horsemen were famous for fighting from their saddles. Indeed, as cavalry, they once were the most feared of all enemies in the Arad and Sea Princes sectors.

Late August, Czar Chekov issued the order to move out. Viktor came to show us how to pack up our hut and stow it on our packhorse. "You are supposed to stay with my group. When we go into combat, we go in groups of twenty-five riders. I lead my group. The Czar wishes me to lead my group as his protectors. Indeed, this is a high honor for me to serve as the personal guard of the Czar. This way, you will get an excellent view of the battle."

That sounded hopeful, for it was precisely what we needed: to see the enemy in action and observe their battlefield tactics.

The army of ten thousand rode due northeast. Mile after rolling hill mile, the grasslands of the Steppes passed by. It was a beautiful country, no doubt of that. Patches of forest occasionally dotted the hills and valleys.

Evenings, the air grew chilly; fall was nearing.

Finally, on September 11, scouts returned with word of the enemy forces. Battle would be joined on the morrow.

Chapter 11 The Purple Palace Mistake

On September 10, we decided to re-visit the Purple Palace. Somehow, we had to get to the third floor and check out all the kami who worked there. "Perhaps we can fake it," Dita suggested. "You know, they give us the pipes or the what-evers and we go into the room and pretend to do the opium. Then, we can sneak around and see what's there and maybe even what's on the two upper floors. Why does he need two more floors? Honestly, each floor is as large as an estate. He can't need that much space for his offices."

"Okay, but promise me, under no conditions do we actually smoke this opium drug. There's no telling what might happen to us if we lose total control in that place," I urged a strong measure of caution.

"Agreed. Whatever they gave us last time was just a sensual stimulus. I can override those effects if I have to, dear. We can do this. Of course, if we don't find San Min there, then what do we do?"

"Dita, I don't know, but if she's not there, I think we will have to use more persuasion on the Yuen Ming fellow, real persuasion of the type he will understand," I replied as we began dressing for our evening out.

"Damn these long nails anyway, there goes a rip," Dita complained, as she accidentally ripped a hole in our thin hose.

"That's why we got three pairs; now you are down to two and a half pairs, dear," I teased her.

"No make that just two pairs. I ripped the other one too. How about lending me a hand?" Dita pleaded.

Shortly after six, Li pulled us up before the Purple Place once more. Again, a substantial number of people were headed in as we climbed out and joined those entering. Once more, we got in the entrance queue, waiting our turn to pay and enter.

"Good evening, Great Ladies," a man stepped close to us. "I am Yuen Ming, the owner of this fine establishment." We whirled to face our opponent. He was thirty-five, immaculately well dressed in a white silk suit, with a black tie that was as black as his hair and eyes. He wore a small moustache. We noticed that his build spoke of a well-trained martial artist; he carried himself well, a powerhouse that could explode at any moment.

His voice was soft and soothing, "My Mei told me about your visit last night. I do hope that you found her an excellent kami."

"Oh yes, she is all that and more," Dita readily admitted, recalling how Mei had really gotten her excited last night.

"I don't believe that we have formally met," he hinted. Where were our manners, I wondered.

"I am Mrs. Bethany Brozena Malina, and this is my wife, Mrs. Dita Malina. We are on an extended vacation here from Velona. So far, we have found your country delightful. Your music is very different from that in our country."

"So pleased to meet such Great Ladies from Velona. Yes, Mei is one of my very best first-floor girls. The musicians are the finest in all Tashien and once played for the Princess and the Empress. However, with the collapse of the Imperial Throne, the musicians were unemployed, and I hired them."

"They certainly are top quality musicians," I replied.

"Say, how would you both like a grand tour of the Purple Palace?" he asked. "I will ask Mei to join us."

"That would be welcome indeed. Oops, we need to pay our entrance fee," Dita replied, discovering that we were now up to the manager.

Yuen waved his hand, "They will be my guests for this evening, Cho. No charge. Now let's find Mei, and I'll give you a personal tour. Ah, there she is now. Isn't she just a lovely young woman?"

"Thank you very much. And yes, Mei is very attractive," Dita replied honestly from her unique point of view.

Mei grinned and bowed to us. She was bound tightly as she had been last night. Yuen put his arm around her waist and led us on the tour. Dita put hers around me and we followed. We both noticed that six martial arts bodyguards followed us at a discrete distance. While he explained about this and that, Dita and I began looking over the many kami who were either waiting for customers or were now with them. He took us into the music room and we got to meet the four musicians personally. We told them how much we enjoyed their music and they were pleased, bowing to us both.

A bit later, we met some of the actors who performed in the plays. As we were escorted around, many other's eyes followed us. The wealthy of Shansee were definitely taking note of the two strangers from Velona, that's for sure. Mei walked tall and proudly with us. I guessed she felt extremely honored to be chosen by Yuen to accompany us. I decided to ask about well-being of the kami.

"Oh yes, the kami are very well paid for their services. Tell them, Mei," Yuen asked.

Mei softly replied, "Yuen Ming is very kind. I take home twenty-five gold a week. Here in Shansee, that is a very large amount."

"Customers never mistreat you?" I asked.

"Oh no! If anyone does anything ill, they are removed from the palace immediately! Right?"

"Oh quite right. You have noticed all of my bouncers. Have you not? They are highly trained to be able to remove an unruly customer with both speed and grace. Seldom is there any stir so created. Usually, it is one who has had too much to drink," Yuen replied. "Would you care to see the second floor?"

"Sure, we only got to see the one room last night. Mei was just wonderful," Dita replied, once again, quite honestly.

"We have forty rooms, all similarly furnished. Nothing but the finest materials is used, as you may have noticed." He went on to describe the various, but obvious, facts, and showed us several currently empty rooms, all of which were identical, save for the number on the door. "Madam Li here keeps track of which rooms are currently empty and tells the kami which to use when she brings someone up here."

After a bit more showing of the rooms, Yuen asked, "Now, would you like to see our third floor? Mei will be working up here later tonight. She has done so well, that I have promoted her to our special clients." Mei looked exceedingly proud and happy. We grinned and agreed.

"Up here, we have very expensive and special pleasures for our distinguished customers. Yes, they come here to smoke opium and relish in the incredible sensory stimulation that our kami provide. Each customer gets to pick their kami from our group of a dozen. Ah, here is their waiting room." He opened the door, and we saw a dozen more kami, who were bound just as Mei was bound. We saw little or no difference in their appearances. None looked like San Min, though.

"Now then, some prefer a sitting room in which to partake of their pleasures, while others prefer a bedroom setting. As a result, we have plenty of both types of rooms up here. This gentleman is in charge of accepting the fees and handing out the items required." He proceeded to show us even more rooms, which were as he had suggested, all equipped with the finest of objects.

"I am sure that with your financial means, you could easily afford extended visits to this floor," he finished off.

Good old Dita was not yet satisfied, "Oh yes, that is but a trifle for us. We are independently wealthy women. Say, do you have anything even more expensive, more exotically pleasurable than this floor? We can pay most any price."

"Well," he hesitated just the right amount, as if he were weighing his options. Somehow, I had the feeling this was all an act, though. I wish now that I had acted upon it. "As a matter of fact, I do. There is very, very expensive floor here — one, which only the wealthiest can possibly afford. One thousand is required even to gain access. There I have the most exquisite and rarest of all exotic pleasures for your senses. Would this be totally out of your expense range?" he asked politely, setting us up, I wagered.

"Oh certainly not! As I said, that's but a mere trifle for us," Dita replied, eager to catch a glimpse of this mysterious floor. Mei opened her eyes wide. This was the first that she had even heard of another floor, and the cost was staggering, a thousand just to enter it! "Please, this interests us. If we find it appealing, we may come here a thousand times and not dent our funds." He opened his eyes a bit wider, though he made no other reaction to the sum that she indicated.

"In that case, Great Ladies of Velona, I will personally escort you on a tour. Very, very few have ever visited this most exotic of pleasure rooms. I keep it very well guarded and protected. The safety of such customers is my highest priority. Mei, will you please bring our two Great Ladies some tea, while I arrange for their visit. You many come with us as well." Mei was extremely pleased and delighted. She dashed off for the tea at once.

"If you will wait here in this sitting room, Mei will return with some tea to pass the minutes. As you can imagine, I must attend to a few things on the lower floors to get the evening rolling for my many other guests. I will be back in less than a half hour and will then be able to devote my full attention to you and our very, very special pleasure room. I will see that you are protected. One of my guards will be assigned to watch over your room here to make very certain that nothing untold happens to such very Great Ladies of Velona! Very Great indeed!" He poured it on thick. He bowed deeply and then left us. Shortly, Mei returned, but the matron carried in the pot of tea and the three cups. Evidently, Mei would be joining us.

"Good evening. Rare indeed is it when Yuen plays host to such very Great Ladies," the matronly woman chatted as she poured our tea. "Mei, I am so proud of you. Such a deserving promotion you've had." She held the cup for Mei to sip.

"I know. I am so very pleased. It is such a high honor to be chosen. I've worked so very hard to always give the best of pleasures to our customers," Mei replied, obviously very delighted with her promotion.

Suddenly, my inner sense of danger startled me. I nearly dropped my cup. "My dear, what is the matter?" the matron said, obviously distressed that I felt something was very wrong. "Did some tea go down the wrong hole? If so, see if you can cough it up." She was obviously trying to guess why I was reacting so startled. Dita also looked very surprised and startled as well. Now even Mei looked very worried.

"What is the matter?" asked the matron again, her voice tone sounded quite concerned. I started to say something, but my voice sounded terribly distant and disconnected. The room faded into darkness. I heard a thump and realized my body had fallen out of my chair. Thump. Thump. Two more thumps. Had Dita fallen? Mei too? It had to be the tea! The matron had not been drinking; she'd been helping Mei. No fourth thump. No, footsteps. "I'm going for help. Something is very wrong," I heard the matron say fearfully. Then, blackness swept over me.

I came to a bit and opened my eyes. The world looked strange. I saw a face staring down at me. She looked like San Min — the sketch that Long Yan had shown us — only slightly older. My voice called out, "San Min Wu?" The woman looked startled and said yes, but then some cloth covered my face and all went very black once again. I heard a voice say "Sleep." Yes, sleep, that was a good idea. I am sleeping, I thought. I registered nothing more, not for a long time.

I awoke very groggy and moaned slightly. Where was I? What was happening to me? She was there, that face. San Min. Her lips moved, "Here, you are supposed to breathe this. It will help you." Something is in my mouth or nose. I can't help but breathe. Oh, it seems so good, so sweet, so relaxing, and so fabulous. Whatever this is, I like it. I feel pain in my feet and elbows. No, this sweetness is making it go away. "Sleep now." Yes, I need sleep. I am so tired.

Voices, I hear voices, voices speaking from a great distance away. "Eat this." Food. I am hungry. I am eating. I am eating. "Sleep now." Ah, that is so much better. Yes, I feel full and sleepy. I must sleep now. Other voices are calling me. Who are they?

Is it my feet that are aching so? My elbows are definitely throbbing. Am I awake? Am I dreaming? I feel so good. Yes, it is San Min again. I need to talk to her. Where is my body anyway? How do I speak like this? "Eat this." Yes, is that my mouth eating? How can I tell? Maybe I am dreaming that I am eating. I hear other voices, voices that I should know, but who? Voices inside my head. I am eating now. It tastes so good. More. Full. "Sleep now." Yes, sleep. I am sleeping. Yes, I am.

My feet do hurt, so do my elbows. Yes, that is pain. I just know it. What is happening? Where am I? What's going on? Dita! Where's Dita? I must sit up. Where's my body? "Eat now." Eat? Oh, is that food that is there? In my mouth? I am hungry. "Sleep now." Sleep, yes, I seem to need a whole lot of sleep. This must be some really crazy dream that I am having. I am so tired. Sleep. More familiar voices echo in my mind. I must be dreaming.

"Oh! I hurt so! My feet are throbbing and so are my elbows! What's going on?" I heard my voice call out. Yes, I am sitting up. The room is strange. I've never seen it before. So much purple. The Purple Palace. "Help!" My eyes finally focused on the here and now. It was daytime. Light shone through purple curtains. I was sitting on a narrow bed with my head and back propped up. I saw my aching elbows. I screamed! I was missing my arms below my elbows. Someone had cut off my lower arms! I saw my feet; they were encased in some kind of metal boots. Big screws held them tightly against my ankles.

"It's all right. I am here. We are here. I am San Min. You are one of us now. Mei is here too. We will be taking care of you, Bethany. Mei told me your name. Here, you need to take a hit from this pipe," San Min put the end of a pipe into my mouth. "Yes, breathe it in deeply. This will really help you now. We know what to do." San Min was insistent. Opium! I was inhaling opium! I didn't want to, but I couldn't help myself. San Min was holding the pipe between her elbows. God, she didn't have any lower arms either! What was going on here? I coughed and she removed the pipe.

My body felt delightful. The pain dissolved. San Min leaned over me and dragged her hair gently over my lips, down my cheeks, over my breasts.

Oh god, this feels so exquisite, so sensuous! "More," my mouth speaks so distantly. Her arms — their touch is electrifying! I am so hot! More, more. Oh my god! I had an explosion between my legs.

"There, now you can sleep with pleasant dreams, Bethany," the gentle voice of San Min spoke. I closed my eyes and drifted into a deep slumber, one filled with a total ecstasy of sensuousness. I hear other harsh voices coming from inside my head. Too harsh. I'm ignoring them; they are interrupting my pleasure.

Sunlight woke me. I sat bolt up! I stared at the bandages on my elbows and the metal cases on my feet. This time, I was alert and awake. I turned and saw Dita lying on a narrow bed close to mine. She was still sleeping peacefully. Her lower arms were gone too, and she had these metal things on her feet too. Mei, yes, there was Mei lying on a bed next to Dita. She'd lost her lower arms as well and had these metal things on her feet like us. Well, we were alive and had found San Min, I realized. San Min! I called out, "San Min? San Min Wu?"

She was sitting on a soft chair across the room. I saw her rise, "Ah, good morning, Bethany. I am here. I am coming." I watched as she came over to me moving extremely slowly, as if in slow motion. No, she was taking very small steps; that was it. At last, she stood beside my bed. "How are you feeling this morning? I think that they will be taking the bandages off you three today. Are you ready to eat something?"

"No. I have too many questions. Yes, I am hungry, starving in fact," I replied, still trying to gather my wits about me. Two other young women holding a pot with their forearms came shuffling over to us. San Min leaned down and struggled to get a good grip on a big wooden spoon. At last, her upper arms grasped it, and she moved her body around to scoop us some food from the pot, which the other woman had sat on my bedside. With a twist of her body, San Min move the spoonful towards my mouth. I leaned a bit and took the whole bite, very nearly pulling the spoon from her feeble grasp.

San Min adjusted her grip on the spoon and maneuvered to get another bite for me. I saw another young woman shuffling towards us carrying two more spoons. Now Dita was wakening, and someone was helping her up to eat as well.

"Bethany! Oh god! Not again!" Dita called out, finally coherent herself. "Are you otherwise okay?" she finally asked. "I think we've been had once again."

"Yes, we have. This is San Min Wu. We've found her," I replied and then moved to get the next bite that she held for me. When I could turn to look at Dita, the other woman was feeding her, while the other two were rousing Mei.

Mei gained consciousness as well. "What has happened to me? Oh no!" she cried out.

One of the women said softly, "It's okay, Mei. You have been promoted to the very top. We are the very exclusive pleasure givers — the ones that people pay a thousand gold to visit. You have been given the absolute highest of honors, a zen-kami. You will see. Now you must eat to gain back your strength. It's been weeks now."

"Weeks?" I nearly choked on my food. "How long has it been, San Min?" I was afraid to hear her reply.

"About eighteen days now. They kept you pretty well doped up. That way you do not have to experience much pain at all. They will be removing the bandages today. Your feet still have to heal more fully. You three are now like us four, very special pleasure givers, zen-kami," San Min answered, while struggling to get another bite up to my mouth.

Sometime later, we three were all full at last. We watched as the four carried the pots and spoons back to a distant table. All four moved so slowly, but I could not really see why this was so. I could see that they wore elegant shoes, much the same pattern as our flats had been, and cotton tops with gold thread interwoven in them. A bit later, they returned with three pipes.

"You must now smoke from these pipes," San Min explained. "It is opium, which will help you recover more fully. We four will give you all great pleasure that you may sleep most pleasantly."

I wanted to refuse it and tried to do so. However, one whiff of the fumes from the pipe and my body craved it! I found myself inhaling deeply, though occasionally coughing from it. Then, waves of utter sensuousness seeped into my entire body. San Min again lowered her hair onto my face. Oh, how delightfully that soft touch felt! Over my lips it slipped. I had to kiss it. My lips felt so full; waves of sensuousness filled my being. Oh, was San Min ever good at this! Her arms began gently touching me, electrifying in their touch! "More!" I exclaimed, and she smiled, continuing to slide her arm gently over my body, touching all the right spots, each of which acted like a bolt of lightning throughout my body. Wham! That incredible explosion swept over my entire body once more. I was beyond heaven now!

"You sleep peacefully now, Bethany. We can talk more later on." Oh, her voice was so gentle, so delightful, and so perfect. I heard Dita's heavy moaning and knew she too was in total ecstasy. Mei moaned even louder, and I smiled as I drifted off into a most relaxing, sensuous sleep.

Sunlight woke me again. San Min was beside me. "Morning sleepyhead," she teased me. "Look, they have removed your bandages. See, they have done a very good job. Your arms look just like mine, so smooth and pointy now." I gazed at what was left of my arms. Indeed, there would be very little scaring; the surgeon had done well. My upper arms tapered gradually down to about an inch across where my elbows used to be. I compared my stumps to San Min's and saw that they matched well. She seemed pleased.

"I am supposed to ask you if your feet still hurt," San Min said softly.

Her voice sounded so angelic. I wanted her to pleasure me again. "Yes, but in a little while. First, you must eat some and then a smoke. Then I will be very happy to pleasure you once more, Bethany. But I am supposed to ask if your feet still hurt."

"Well not any more. They feel like they are in a heavy cast or something," I replied.

"That is a good sign. Maybe they will take those metal casts off you soon now. Time to eat some more. I will feed you." I watched as the other three young women carefully carried the large loops attached to the pots over to our bedsides. Once more, San Min struggled to pick up the wooden spoon and then awkwardly maneuvered it into the pot to get a bite for me. Even more awkwardly, she struggled to get it over to me. Again, I leaned as much as I could to help her. As I ate, I watched the others helping Dita up and Mei too. Soon we three were all eating.

Once we had finished, I felt like talking some more. "San Min, Long Yan asked us to come to find you and rescue you. He loves you deeply."

"I love him too, but it is not to be. I am here and cannot get away. He cannot get to me. How is he?" she asked. I saw a deep emotional battle going on within her. I had just opened up the terrible loss that she had. A tear formed and trickled down her cheek. She wiped at it with her arm. I softly described how he looked and how he had walked all the way to Velona to get help.

Dita added, "We are here to rescue you, San Min." I realized that she was being a tad optimistic just now.

"No can be rescued now. We are helpless like this. We can only give pleasure to those Yuen Ming says," San Min replied, very near tears. I wished I hadn't opened up that old wound just now.

"Hey, I have got to have another smoke of that stuff!" Dita exclaimed. Suddenly, I was also absolutely craving it as well.

Mei squeaked, "Me too! What's going on?"

"We all need it now. The opium. We have to have it every day or we just go frantically crazy," San Min said sadly. "We're opium addicts now. All of us. The pipe will come soon."

Sure enough it did. San Min and the others allowed us three to smoke our fill first, before they had their fix. They were in better shape to hold out longer than we three were. Not long after that, San Min pleasured me, and I exploded once again into utter ecstasy, wild beyond all belief and imagination! I heard distant voices in my mind again, but blocked out those harsh sounding voices. I only wanted to hear the gentle voice of San Min; she was an angel! I slept.

"Wake up sleepyheads," the delightful voice of San Min woke me. Sunlight streamed in the window, beautiful sunlight, the perfect shade. The dust motes floating in the air were as sensuous as I felt. "See, you now have shoes again. No more metal cases. Your feet are tiny like ours," San Min replied. I looked down at my feet and saw the familiar style shoes that I had worn; only these looked somehow different. I moved my feet so I could get a better look at them. I gasped. They were indeed tiny! "See, I show you," San Min said and slowly walked to my feet. Using her stubs, she pulled one of my shoes off so I could see the bottom of the shoe and my foot.

My foot looked whole, only its arch seemed different. Then I realized that my arch was now extremely high — so high, in fact, that I could no longer put my heel flat on the floor at the same time as my toes! Far from it. I would be walking on my toes, which were flat on the floor as usual, but the back of my heel was very nearly in line with the backs of my toes. As I looked at the soles of the shoes, there was the usual rounded front for my toes. A huge high heel of wood ended with a heel that was about an inch around, but located almost against the backside of the toes. My foot was still the same overall length, but now I was walking on my toes with only a bit of heel behind the front soles. The overall impression that was given was that I had very small, very tiny feet.

San Min explained, "Almost a century ago, women in Tashien often bound their feet to have tiny feet. The tinier a woman's foot, the more honor she had. Our Empresses used to have the tiniest feet in the whole country. However, that was deemed barbaric and was extraordinarily painful or so everyone says. Now, they no longer bind feet. They just reform your foot's arch. Now that your feet have healed, you, too, have very dainty, tiny feet, just like us. It is a high honor. Everyone will give you much respect for such small feet."

"Now you must stand and practice walking. Here, we will help you." She put her stump around my back and I attempted to stand up.

"Whoa! This is weird! I'm standing on my toes. Oops, I've really got no heel or rest of the foot to help maintain my balance," I analyzed my struggling efforts just to stand in one spot without falling over. Normally, my foot was about nine inches in length, from toe tip to heel. Now it was not even four inches long! Even more dramatic was the fact that the top of my foot arch, which used to be behind the back ends of my toes, was now almost even with the tips of my toes. My arch was incredibly high. I finally realized what they had done. They had purposely broken my foot arch and forced it into this new position. The metal cases held the broken arch in the new position while the bones had re-grown into this new position. No wonder my foot would not go flat onto the floor anymore. If I were to walk at all, I would have to walk solely on the base of my toes, with only a tiny bit of heel support. Hence, keeping my balance was indeed challenging just standing!

Another woman came to my other side and put her arm around me too. "Now take very small steps, like we do," San Min ordered. I tried to do so and wobbled, nearly falling. I would have, if it weren't for the support from the two women, though without hands, if I had fallen, they could have done nothing really to stop me. This first time, I made about two feet of distance, before returning to the safety of the bed. Two others held on to Dita as she took her first steps. I won't repeat the expletives that she uttered! Then, it was Mei's turn. None of us took more than a walk two feet away from our bed.

Now I was starving again. A bit later, we were fed and then the craving for opium struck all three of us. I was nearly frantic with desire before the pipe smoke entered my craving lungs. I felt the flow of utter ecstasy flowing all throughout my body once more, the greatest sensations I have ever known! No, that came shortly thereafter, as San Min once more gave me fabulous pleasure. I then slept soundly as if I was floating in heaven.

It was days later that I finally realized that this had been going on for many days now. Waking up, practicing walking, eating, craving, inhaling the sweet ecstasy, and then the overwhelming passions flowing throughout my entire body. Each time we walked farther and farther from our beds, which I slowly thought most promising, when I was actually thinking, which was seldom, except for the brief times after waking. I also began to notice that the delay in giving me my opium fix was increasing and the amount was also being lowered very gradually. That must be accounting for my increasing periods of semi-clear thinking.

One morning, I was now practicing walking on my own. We had a shuffling type of gait, never taking more than a few inches at a time for fear of losing our balance. Indeed, San Min complimented us on just how well we were doing. I sat down at the distant table. "Say, I don't even know your names. I am Bethany Brozena Malina and this is my wife, Dita Malina. We are married and come from Velona. We came to rescue San Min."

The three other women giggled. "You know me. I am Mei Bi. This is Chan Bao, Dai Son, and Hon Feng." All were quite pretty to darn attractive to say the least, though Dita would be a better judge of this. All were in their mid-twenties. Three of them had earned a promotion, or so they thought, just before San Min came, some five years ago. Yuen had explained that in their current form, they represented the highest womanly beauty to be found anywhere in Tashien. We learned that they were very well treated, but only extremely rarely was anyone brought up here to be pleasured — perhaps once a month at the very most. For the most part, all four were exceedingly bored when they were not pleasuring themselves after a smoke.

"Say, does anyone know what day it is? How long have we been here?" I asked, suddenly realizing that we must have been gone for many days to be so well healed up.

"We don't know the day. It is someday. It is raining outside. Does that help?" asked Chan.

"Each day is like the next here. How can we tell?" replied Hon, quite honestly.

"Have you ever tried to escape?" I asked the provocative question.

The three had never considered it. San Min sighed. "Yes, I did. But we cannot walk much. There are so many fighters around who would pick us up and carry us back here if we tried. And well, well, we have to have our pipes now, just like you do. We cannot live without it. If we leave, how would we get it? I tried once — not to smoke for a whole day. I went almost mad before they helped me get the pipe re-lighted. We cannot escape even if we wanted to escape."

"She's right; it would take an army to bust in here, love. There are so many martial arts bouncers around, it would take a whole bunch to get way up here to us, dear," Dita admitted what I sensed. Coming from a Protector, I felt confident in her analysis. However, before I could do much more clear thinking, my body began its cravings once more. San Min insisted that we eat something first, but I fought her all the way, desperately craving the relief that could only come from that pipe! Ah, at last, relief and ecstasy flowed throughout my body! Pleasure hit and then my intense sexual arousal came, followed by an equally intense explosion of relief. I slept soundly.

Voices. I heard voices again. Asking me to wake up. Somehow, I managed to wake. Dita did too. Damn! There was Yuen Ming standing tall before our beds. He was slowly taking off his exquisite suit. "Ah, my latest pretty flowers. Now Yuen will teach you both what it is that you pathetic lesbians have been missing — a *real* man! Now you will learn what *real* pleasure means!" He laughed evilly and smugly. I wanted to smash his face, but realized I had no hands to slap him with any more.

"I have been waiting very patiently for this *exquisite* moment! Now you will soon see what you have been missing! First, I will teach Dita here what a real man can *do* to her body. Prepare yourself for the *real* thing!" He now had removed all his clothes and stood naked before our beds. Mei watched in shock. San Min and the other three sat huddled together quietly as far away from us as they could get in the room. Dita was sitting up on her bed staring at him as he leered at her nearly naked form. We now realized how we were dressed. We wore only the thinnest gossamer dresses, quite see-through. We had a garter belt around our waists and wore that super fine, black silken hose, which cost a fortune. We did not even have panties on, which greatly aided our use of the chamber pots, I realized in a flash. Gosh, we had been so out of it all. Now, with our enemy standing naked before us, all six of us were forced into the present time.

In a rush of realizations, I understood what he intended to do — rape us. But I also realized that he had picked on the wrong woman to rape! Dita was really Renzo; she'd never yet adapted to being a woman. She saw him as another man and would be utterly repulsed by him, especially if he were to force himself off on her. I knew what would happen before it did!

He leered evilly at her, lasciviously eyeing her intensely shapely form. He took one step towards her bed and she reacted as any man would. She lashed out, but in her own unique way. I saw her move out of her body and over his. He never knew what happened to him. His neck twisted around twice, accompanied by the sound of breaking vertebrae. His lifeless body slumped to the floor. "Damn you anyway! That will teach you to pick on me and my wife!" Dita barked vehemently. The other five women stared in utter disbelief.

"He's dead! How? I saw his head twist around and around," San Min finally found her voice; she was in shock as were the others.

"I did that to him. Twisted his damn neck like a chicken," Dita spat out and then spat on his body. "Never mess with Dita!" She spat a second time.

"Oh god! Now they will come and find him dead and kill us all!" wailed Chan. Hon, Dai, and Mei panicked and began crying, knowing that she was right. Soon, the other men would come and kill us all.

"Time that we get out of here," I said calmly. Gather up everything we might need. Lots of opium, please! Wrap everything in a bed sheet. Hurry up. Dita, we have to get someone to help us fast."

"I know. I will find us a way out. See if you can get Long Yan and maybe Zhen Song to help us. We need a wagon. We're not going to do much walking, I'm afraid," Dita replied. She moved out of her body and out of the room. I concentrated, for the first time in days, my mind felt clear, although I knew that as soon as the adrenalin wore off, I would be craving opium once more and would *have* to have a pipe!

Long! Yes, it's me Bethany. No time to explain. We have San Min with us. She's fine. You must get to Zhen Song's martial arts place as fast as you can. We must have a wagon to transport us in a very short while. Run if you can. More later.

I took a deep breath and found Zhen's mind. *Zhen. It's Bethany. No time to explain. You must get a wagon to the Purple Palace to pick us up. Long Yan is on his way to you. Our lives are dependent on your getting here with a wagon as soon as possible. I will tell you more in a bit. Hurry. We've killed Yuen Ming. Soon they will be on to us. Yes, Dita killed him. Hurry.*

Mom! Alessa here! Where have you been? We've been frantically trying to reach you. Are you in bad trouble? My little girl! Wow!

Yes, we are alive. Been kidnaped again, mutilated, and have been forced to become very addicted to opium. Right now, we are trying to escape. More later. Got to go. Thanks dear.

Dita had returned to her body. "Bethany, ah good. Yes, I found a back stairs that is not well guarded. We can get out that way and into the back alley. Have the wagon meet us in the alley. If they aren't there when we get down, tell them that we will continue walking down the alley to the west. Hurry."

I quickly re-contacted both men and told them where to meet us. By now, the five others had gathered up all the opium they could find; actually, it was quite a large stash indeed, at least ten grand worth of the dismal stuff. They had wrapped everything in a bed sheet as I had asked. All five were trembling in fear.

"Okay, Dita has found us a way out of here. A wagon is going to soon pick us up, but we may have to walk a ways before they get here. Dita, lead on, I'll get the sheet bag."

"But how? We cannot lift it," San Min raised her arms in a futile gesture.

"Like this." I moved over and picked it up — that is, I did it, not my body. They simply saw the sheet bag floating up in the air all by itself. All five gasped.

"Okay, coast is clear for the moment," Dita called out. San Min started to ask how she could know that, but stopped short as she saw the doorknob turn, apparently of its own accord. Dita stepped into the dark hallway. She nearly fell because she took too big a step. She swore softly to herself. We seven women, scantily dressed, began a terribly slow, shuffling walk out of our captive room. All our arms were wiggling wildly as we attempted to hurry as much as possible while not falling down. Our steps had to be carefully taken I soon realized and concentrated as best I could.

Going down stairs on your very tiptoes is challenging if you have arms to hold on to the railing. As we were, it was most treacherous. At last, I simply gave up, lifted us all up, and began lowering our bodies down the stairs. The women gasped once more, but realized this was a vast improvement. Dita moved on out in front of us. Good thing. As we rounded the first bend, a guard was standing there. He looked up, shocked to see us and began to react. Dita twisted his neck and shoved his body back out of the way.

It seemed like forever before we reached the back alley door. Dita eliminated three more guards on the way. At last, she opened the door for us, and I lifted everyone outside, sitting our bodies gently onto the cobblestone alleyway. Dita shut the door and then mangled the locking mechanism. "There, now it cannot easily be opened. No wagon. We walk now. Damn, this is hard!"

Quickly, San Min and the others knew how to handle this. They moved to our sides and put their arms around us. Chan and Mei were on either side of Dita, who put her arms around the two. San Min and Hon put theirs around me and I, they. Dia latched on to San Min. Ever so slowly we began our westward shuffle down the alleyway. Rain poured down and we soon were drenched in the cold rain. It must be late in the year, I concluded. I began shivering and felt my companions also shivering. I hoped that Zhen would come soon.

Ahead, a couple of Yuen's bouncers came half-drunk out of the back of a nearby pub. They saw us and looked shocked. Then they began to come toward us. One by one, Dita wrung their necks. "Looks like I am leaving a clear trail for Zhen to follow," she whispered.

"How did you do that?" Chan asked, nearly stumbling herself. Dita held her somehow.

"They must be great Olin Masters," San Min whispered.

"Wow! Real Olin Masters, yes that explains it. They have kijutsu powers!" Chan whispered back, very excited and very relieved to have an explanation for what was happening to her. "I — I a-am g-g-e-e-t-ting c-cold," she added. I was shivering like mad. The soaking cold rain continued to drench us, and the nearly see-through gauze of a dress offered no protection at all.

The uneven alley surface made each step a challenge in balance. My toes were aching, taking a beating I'd seldom given them. We had to press on; if the wagon was intercepted, we had to get away. Two dark figures moved out of the shadows, one saying in a leering, condescending, insinuating voice, "Well, look what we have here."

Dita said, "I'll warn you once. Leave us alone!" She nearly lost her balance while trying to watch them closely. One stepped up to block her way. His neck twisted around, and his body flew off to the side of the alley, out of our painstakingly slow path. The other man bolted and ran off on down the alley. I hoped that he was not going for reinforcements!

I heard the sound of a horse coming from behind us and halted our group. Shivering uncontrollably, I turned to look. It was a wagon. "Dita — a wagon. Maybe it's them!" We huddled together in the middle of the alley and waited, shivering so badly that we were of little support to each other. That craving was starting to affect me once more, and I suspected it was hitting the others too. Soon we would have to have a pipe or begin to lose all semblance of rationality.

As the wagon drew close, I recognized Long Yan and Zhen Song, who was driving. "San Min! San Min! It is Long Yan! We've found you at last!" He jumped off the still rolling wagon and ran up to her, grabbing her soaking, shivering body tightly in his arms, lifting her off her feet. She was too cold, too scared, too much fighting needing another pipe to respond much at all, her body shivering uncontrollably.

"Long, get them in the wagon fast! Cover them with the blanket. Hurry up man!" Zhen called out, jumping out of the wagon as well. He grabbed me and carried me into the back of the wagon. I stumbled to the front and sat down before my legs gave out completely. One by one, the others joined me. Last in was our bed sheet, a large package. Long Yan climbed in last, while I heard Zhen climb back into the soaking wet driver's box.

"L-Long. We n-need an o-opium pipe f-fast. I-in the s-sh-eet," I tried to explain before I completely lost all control. Although he was now just as soaked as us, he dried his hands on a blanket and rummaged through the stuff the others had stowed in the sheets. Soon he had found the pipes and loaded one. San Min held it in her lips and supported it with her short arms. Tears flowed down Long Yan's face as he saw the reality of her arms and struggled to get the slightly wet match to light. Smoke! Sweet, sensuous smoke! We all smelled it, as San Min greedily inhaled. We involuntarily inhaled the smoke that she exhaled. Yes, we were that desperate for our fix! Soon, she passed the pipe on to Chan and before too long we all had inhaled deeply the soothing ecstasy, which would wash away all our fears and troubles and cold. I was only vaguely aware of Long covering us all up with a bunch of blankets. The slow rocking of the wagon seemed like a mother's cradle to me as I drifted off into the most pleasant of sensuous dreams once more.

Chapter 12 Fears Grow

"A gun ship?" screamed Yuen Ming; his hand found the table in front of him and the force of his reaction shattered the table into halves. His nervous top enforcers blinked, but were relieved that it was not one of them who had received the blow.

"Yes, it flew the common pirate flag. A caravel. Somehow, the pirates have one of these new gun ships and are blowing us out of the water. Our scout ship narrowly escaped by sailing into a fog bank and squall," the aide reported more fully. He proceeded to relay all that the captain had told him.

Yuen paced the room, thinking. "Look, does this Pope fellow — does he have a gun ship in his fleet?" No one knew. He paced more, and then said, "Okay. Post a letter to this Pope fellow. Tell him what has happened to his last two shipments. Tell him that it is now his problem as well as ours. If he wants another shipment, he has to send a ship here to get it. No! Wait! He's not going to believe this at all. If I were him, I would suspect that I was cheating him out of a million. No, we must arrange for another shipment. Only this time, it will be the shell game. Get ten boats ready to sail. One will carry you, Bai; you will report directly to this Pope fellow and tell him this is the last shipment he's getting, unless he can guarantee safe passage from here to Megalos. Put the goods on one ship, put rocks on the other nine. At sea, have the captains mingle their boats constantly, mix them up good. The gun ship will be unable to tell which is the right one this time. If they go after one, the other nine can escape. Yes, this will confuse the gun ship sufficiently. Make it so, gentlemen, before I get angrier than I am!"

The enforcers dashed out of his office, very grateful for the new lease on life that he'd just granted them. His top aide and best martial artist, Tao Shi, remained. "Now then, what have we learned about our mysterious visitors from Velona?"

"They are staying in the penthouse suite at the Santi, as expected. It seems that they have two teenaged girls there with them. However, the teens do not leave the complex. Probably a wise move. They came with little baggage but they do seem to have appreciable funds. The manager said they had no hesitation about the price of the suite and paid for a three months stay."

"Excellent. Are the doctors ready for tonight's work?" Yuen grinned evilly.

"Yes, they will enter using the back alley doors as ordered. All is in readiness. Are you sure they will come back tonight?"

"I am almost certain of that. They got their taste of pleasure last night. I'm sure that they will be unable to stay away. After I take them and have them totally under my power, then I will thoroughly question them.

After all, who can resist not telling all when their cravings are in full bloom? It will be a while before that time comes, but I can be a patient man. To be on the safe side, I will also take Mei out of the picture. No loose ends that way."

Yuen Ming kicked at his broken table. "Any word on this gun ship attacking our many other coastal ships, delivering our product around Tashien?" he asked.

"None at all. All is normal, if this overlord thing can be considered normal," Tao replied. He decided to ask what had been bothering him all along. "Bosu, what could these two women of Velona possibly want with San Min Wu? You've had her for five years now, and no one in Tashien is the wiser. All presume that she is also dead, but that her body has not been found. I don't understand all this interest in her."

"Tao, all life is a game. All life is interconnected. Between San Min and these two, there is a connection. It is that we have not yet seen what it is. The playing of the game is what life is all about. Hence, we will play along, and now I will play my hand. Then, my faithful Tao, then we will finally know the connection. Perhaps when we know it, we will say it was nothing important at all, who can say. Still, we must enjoy the chase and the playing of the game. It helps that this Dita is one of the greatest beauties that I have ever seen. Tao, take your pleasure from the playing of the game, as I do."

Tao grinned and bowed. To him, this game seemed to be going down a strange path. Why not just take the women, torture the information out of them, and then just kill them? Why go to all this immense trouble and expense of turning them into the ultimate pleasure toys? Of course, they would then talk, talk themselves silly. Still, he thought that he could easily beat the information out of them. He bowed and left.

After Bethany and Dita left for their second evening out at the Purple Palace, Fina and Jemma finally got cabin fever. "How come they get to go out to these really fancy places, and we have to stay cooped up here all the time. There's nothing going on at the docks at night, we ought to be able to have some fun too," Jemma whined.

"Maybe we could sneak out and have some fun. As long as we got back before they did, they would never know," Fina suggested, coyly. They chatted about how they could do this, planning a nighttime escapade for tomorrow night.

A knock on their door startled both teens. "Who can this be at this hour?" Fina whispered. Jemma opened the door a crack and then let Fang Song inside. She looked a bit worried.

"Hi. Any word from Bethany or Dita?" Fang asked softly.

"No, we know; it is really late. They were back before now last night," Fina answered.

Fang twisted a strand of her long black hair, deep in thought. At last, she reached a decision. "Okay, kids. Pack all your things. I will leave a note for Bethany, if she returns here. It is no longer safe for you two to stay in this room or this inn."

"Why?" Jemma was all ears now. Gone was her boredom. Something exciting was happening!

"I spotted several of Yuen's men hanging around here, and one asked the manager quite a lot of questions about all of you. Now that he knows that you are here and that Bethany and Dita are here as well, my instincts tell me that it is not safe for you to stay here any longer. Come on; pack your bags. Leave theirs, just yours. We need to sneak out without being seen somehow. I haven't worked that part out yet," Fang answered her.

With renewed enthusiasm, the teens packed their single duffle bag. "Okay, what's the plan?" Jemma asked excitedly. This was now becoming a real adventure!

"Well, for tonight, you will stay at our home. Tomorrow we will work something out. However, the first thing is to sneak out of here. We do not want anyone seeing us leave," she replied.

"Well, leave that to me," Jemma volunteered, stepping out of their room ahead of Fang, who decided against protesting her action. She ushered Fina out and quietly closed their door. No one was in the hallway and Jemma was already descending the stairs, before Fang could catch up to her.

Partway down the long stairs and near the third floor, a man was coming up. Jemma gestured for them to press against the side wall. While Fang saw that this would do little good, the man would walk right past them, she did so, preparing to knock the man out as he passed her. Jemma whispered, "The stairs is empty." To Fang's surprise, the man walked right on past the three of them, completely oblivious to their presence. Once he entered a room, Jemma continued their descent.

When they reached the main floor, the night manager and two security men were on duty. They would have to walk right past them. Fang was about to suggest that they use the back entrance, which she had picked its lock to enter a few minutes ago, when Jemma began a soft chant. All three men began to doze! Jemma motioned them to follow her, and she walked right straight on out past the three men. Once outside, Fang whispered, "You must have great Olin Master kijutsu powers!"

"I don't know what that is, but I am a Judger, and I just convinced them that they ought to sleep a while. Simple, really. Now where do we go?" Jemma replied in a whisper, looking all around for unseen observers.

"There are two guards at the main gates. I knocked them out when I entered. Perhaps they are still out cold," Fang whispered back. The three walked silently to the main gate. Both men were rubbing their heads, wondering what had happened to themselves.

"I think we should sound the alarm," one said groggily.

Jemma acted swiftly, chanting once more. She whispered, "Oh, we just fell asleep and banged our heads, that's all. Nothing to worry about."

The other man then said, "Oh, we just fell asleep and banged our heads, that's all. Nothing to worry about." Fang held her hands to her mouth. This was an amazing feat of kijutsu! Both men yawned, as Jemma finished her whispered chant. They lay down and began to doze. Now Jemma walked straight on past them, as if they were not there.

At this point, they were out in the open. For a quarter of a mile, there was no cover at all, just the flat roadbed. Fang moved them along as swiftly as possible. At last ducking into an alleyway off the docks, Fang whispered, "Okay, we are now in the streets of Shansee. It is very dangerous to walk them so late at night. Bad men are out and about, thieves, ruffians, and drunks. We must be very careful. It is a mile and a half to our place."

"Okay, if we run into any men, let me handle them," Jemma requested, thoroughly enjoying her outing. Indeed, she put six more men to sleep on their hasty trip to Zhen Song's Xian Martial Arts Academy. In the back of their establishment, the Songs had a meager residence. The girls had to sleep doubled up in one smaller guest bed. Still, this was all very exciting for them.

The next morning, Jemma complained over breakfast, "Something's wrong. I cannot contact either Bethany or Dita. This is not like them."

Zhen said calmly, "She did say for us not to worry about them, that they may well need to disappear for some time and be out of contact with us. You two and your spying mission is our top priority. Still, I think it prudent to bring Long Yan here as well. There are enough of our students around the academy during the day to ensure his safety."

"Yes, he will be worried when he doesn't find us in our room this morning," Fina acknowledged him. "At least now I can finally don my various weapons, like a real Protector ought to be wearing."

Zhen smiled and asked, "You are a young fighter in your country?"

"Of course, I am a Protector. So is Dita."

"Come, get your things, let us see what all you can do, Fina," he grinned at Fang.

A short while later, Fina had her collection of swords and daggers fastened and was ready for action. She'd put on her leathers and was quite ready for some practice. Already, six of his students had arrived for their morning lessons.

"Tian, bring your sword and let's see how Fina can do against you," Zhen ordered. Tian bowed, retrieved his slightly curved blade, and walked into the center ring, where Fina had just positioned herself. He bowed to her, and she emulated his move. "Action," Zhen spoke crisply. Fang and Jemma stood near him. She was most curious to see how these teens handled themselves, especially since they were going to be out on the streets now, if they were going to continue to spy on the opium dealings.

The two traded strikes and parries as they tested out each other.

Then, they escalated into stronger moves. Zhen and Fang were impressed that Fina could at least hold her ground against Tian, who was one of their best young students. Suddenly, Tian did an unexpected thrust, locking his blade against hers, and then he did a full body twist and turn, which drove her short sword from her grasp, sending it flying away from her. Zhen figured this was the end of the round, but Fina back flipped out of harm's way and then crouched low, stalking Tian, who continued to close, his blade ready to strike, waiting for Zhen's stop command. It didn't come. Fina unexpectedly swung her leg up and around his blade, hitting the precise pressure point on his shoulder. Tian's arm dropped limply to his side, the sword clanking on to the floor.

Now they traded fist thrusts for a bit, though Fina here was way out of her league, and at last, Tian managed to flip her onto her back and rested his foot gently on her throat. "Stop," Zhen called out, and Tian backed away, held his had to pull her to her feet, then bowed to her.

"Now that was indeed a fine demonstration, Fina. I am most impressed with your skill. How did you manage to numb his arm? Just luck?" Zhen asked.

"No. I know thirteen precise points, and the amount of pressure to apply. I hope your arm stops tingling soon, Tian," she explained, a bit worried about his arm, which he was still massaging. "I can see that I still have a whole lot to learn. I can't do so much without a weapon, except hit the pressure points."

"Well, I am satisfied, Fina. I believe that you and Jemma will not be a liability while on the streets of Shansee, as long as Fang is with you. If you wish, you are both welcome to train with us here at the Xian Academy," Zhen explained.

"Hey, that would be terrific," Fina exclaimed, eager to learn new ways of combat. "After all, my job as Protector is to keep Jemma safe."

Say, what is this Protector and Judger thing?" Fang asked. "Come let us take tea and chat before we hit the streets." Fina was very eager to tell her all about us and our special skills. Later, with the teens dressed in drab brown peasant clothes, though armed well, Fang led them the mile and a half to the docks.

On the way, Jemma had an idea. "What if we got some flowers and pretended to have a tiny flower shop there close to the docks where we could easily see what's going on?"

"Clever, I like it," Fang replied, and they stopped and picked up several large handfuls along the way. They found an out of the way spot nearby the docks and set up their flower stand. To others, they looked like really down on their luck peasants attempting to sell slightly wilted flowers at a location where sales were highly unlikely. Still, it gave them a perfect cover, but the teens found it very boring.

Yet, their diligence was rewarded. Two days later, they spied workers bringing the usual bales of packed opium to the docks once more. They watched as the drugs were loaded onto another Tashien junket, but both were dismayed to see ten ships sail off together. Jemma quickly reported this to Kali.

During the evenings, Fina began to receive Xian lessons and Tian became her twin. Jemma did a little practicing of these new martial arts moves, but soon gave it up. She was not interested in fighting. Instead, she continued to try to make contact with Bethany and Dita, but with no luck. They were there, but just not responding to her telepathic contact for some unknown reason. Zhen continued to tell her not to worry, that Bethany's orders indicated that this might happen. Still, Jemma worried, especially as October came with still no word.

When Kali received word on this next shipment, they were half way to the Southlands to resupply. Fresh water was nearly gone. No way could they possibly intercept this shipment. It would easily get to Megalos weeks before they could get back there. Certainly, the Pope would quickly load the drugs onto one of his caravels and send it on its way to Vito or Bonito. There were so many caravels plying these waters off the Southlands that they would have no way to know which vessel carried the drugs.

Hi, Kali here. Bad timing, Jemma. We are out of fresh water and are heading to a small Southlands port to resupply. By the time that we can get back to Megalos, the caravel will have long since set sail. Looks like we will miss this shipment.

Mom, Jemma answered, *I have an idea. I'll get back to you soon.*

"Hey, Fina, mom's got a problem," Jemma began explaining what the Grande Pistola was doing. "They could intercept the caravel off of Megalos and around the Southlands, but they won't know which one to hit. I have an idea, but I am going to need your help."

She explained her idea and Fina readily agreed. "After all, I am supposed to be your Protector. So let me protect. Tell her about it and let's get going."

Jemma grinned and contacted her mom again. *Hi. We have it all worked out. I am going to follow the ships — sit on their crow's nest if I have to. When they load the opium onto a caravel there in Megalos, I will go sit in its crow's nest. When you are finally ready to intercept it, I can let you know which ship it is. Fina will watch over my body here at the Song's residence while I am off at sea. This will be perfect. You can't let them get another shipment through, we mustn't!* Kali agreed and the plan was set into motion.

Both Zhen and Fang were incredibly curious about the plan and kept a careful eye on the teens. This was a terrific use of kijutsu powers, of that they were certain. Jemma's body seemed to be just a vegetable, sitting and sleeping, and she even had to be fed by hand, while Jemma herself was now out over the ocean, sitting on the top of the main mast of the ship carrying the load of opium to Megalos. Naturally, Fina now had to take care of Jemma's body, as if she were a total invalid, unable to do anything for herself. Jemma wasn't around it, of course.

Still, Fina took some time off to continue her daily practice sessions with Tian. These times, Fang watched over Jemma while she had her lessons. Fina found herself forming a strong bond with this young lad a couple years older than she was. It seemed that he always had a surprise move for her during their sessions. It was almost as if he could anticipate or somehow know what her next move would be and thus counter it.

Still, she liked him quite a lot. He was handsome and strong. His eyes always met hers, and she felt very much at ease around him. For several days, she mused about whether she could possibly give him a kiss and whether he would like her. One day after a sweaty round of intense hand-to-hand work, both were standing with their hands on their knees, catching their breaths. She found herself dreaming about what it would be like kissing him. Then, she saw his face redden. Somehow, he knew what she was thinking! Hell, I might as well do it, she thought to herself, steeling up the nerve to kiss him. She leaned close and gave him the kiss that she had wanted to give him for days now. To her surprise, he responded in kind, their arms slid around each other, and he pressed her close to him; for a time they passionately embraced.

That day, the two realized that they were in love with each other. Tian now began to spend time sitting with Fina as she sat with Jemma's body and took care of it for her. The two chatted about their lives, dreams, and goals. Tian certainly got an education from her. Fina learned that Tian was an orphan whom Zhen had taken under his wing and that he'd showed great promise as a student. She also learned that at the core of their martial arts was the skill to know or anticipate what your opponent's next move or thought would be. Yes, Tian was indeed reading her mind in many ways. By the time that October came, the two were almost inseparable.

By October 5, the Grande Pistola was again on its way to Megalos. While some people at the small harbor town grew suspicious of their caravel, Kali and Ania promptly used their Judger skills on them, planting ideas that convinced them there was nothing out of the ordinary with this ship, in spite of the fact that one canvas cover got loose, revealing the gun ports. Captain Dante was very surprised at how well these two women totally manipulated the minds of others, removing all traces of suspicions in them.

Now even more miraculously, Kali and her unseen daughter were guiding them to the caravel out of Megalos that was carrying the load of opium. The next day, they spotted the caravel heading their way.

Okay, we have the ship sighted. You get out of there, Jemma, Kali sent.

Okay, but I want to watch it from a distance, before I go back. Kali chuckled. She knew Jemma was intensely curious and wouldn't obey her if she ordered her back to Shansee. Now, the combat was once more in the hands of Captain Dante. Only this time, the target would be much more difficult. While it was larger, it was faster and vastly sturdier than the flimsy bamboo craft of Tashien. Actually, to date, no one had yet attacked a caravel with a gun ship, though Kali didn't know this at the time.

Captain Dante weighted his options, carefully estimating the speed of the caravel target. They would be well matched on speed. If he took the usual approach of firing a broadside while sailing past them, by the time they reversed course, they might not be able to catch them. He could drop sail and let them sail past him. This would give his men perhaps two volleys before the caravel would be past them. Again, by the time they got back up to speed, the caravel would be out of their reach once more.

He also considered that their captain was well aware that there was a pirate gun ship in these waters and would be prepared to take defensive actions. He sighed; the outcome would likely be decided by whoever made the first mistake. He made his decision and ordered half of the sails lowered. The Grande Pistola began to slow down, as the opium-laden ship continued to close on them, running full sails. Kali and Ania watched from the deck as Captain Dante relayed the now familiar series of orders.

As the canvas covers raised and the port side gun ports opened, they could see the crew of the approaching caravel dashing about their deck, following their captain's frantic orders. Captain Dante issued one new order, however. "Load with a quarter sack of extra powder." Kali wondered what that was all about, perhaps to pack an extra wallop? At last, as the other ship came along side, she saw their crew hoisting every bit of extra sail that they could hang! Out run the gun ship was their obvious plan. No, now they were turning towards the gun ship! "Fire!" Dante's voice barked, relay-echoed twice more before the deafening booms thundered and the thick acrid smoke blew back into their faces.

"Reload! Hoist all sail! Hard to port!" Dante screamed. He saw now that the enemy ship intended to ram the Grande Pistola. Two balls missed completely because of the last second turn made by the sly enemy captain. However, the extra powder caused two of the heavy balls to hit higher than normal, ripping out a good deal of the ship's rigging lines; their mainsail now fluttered about, adding nothing to their speed. One ball tore away their bow spirit, one hit below their starboard waterline. Seawater gushed through the two-foot hole, and the sailors fought hard to make an emergency repair. Two other balls crushed through the cabin bulkheads, severely weakening the base of support of their main mast itself.

For a moment, it appeared as if the two ships were circling each other, going round and round, but soon they drew closer again. Just as Dante yelled, "Fire!" the other captain yelled, "Fire!" We saw seven men shooting their guns at our crew and us as the thunderous booms once more shook the very air around us. This close, the damage was severe, all eight penetrated her hull; she leaned heavily and her crew began abandoning ship.

Kali felt a sharp stinging in her chest; looking down, she realized that she had been shot! Thank goodness she had the Grey Creature's blaster in her pocket. She only had a nasty bruise. Two other crew members were not so lucky. Both Kali and Ania rushed to aid the bleeding men. Two others came to help them carry the wounded men below deck and laid them onto the dining room table, where they could be doctored. On deck, Captain Dante saw a lifeboat hit the water and their men heading for it. The caravel was definitely sinking now. He ordered a course change, heading due south, hoping to indicate to the survivors that they came from somewhere to the south. Once they had left the sinking ship far behind them, he went below to check on his two wounded crew members.

No one had any real idea of how best to treat a gunshot wound. Kali, Ania, and the ship's doctor were working together to assist the two men, who were now quite drunk on rum — their intense pain very dulled. Once the bullets were finally removed, Kali and Ania combined their limited healing skills with those of the doctor. "We'll watch them constantly," Kali explained, wiping the blood off her hands, as Captain Dante appeared beside the men. Bandaged, they were carried into their cabins, the two women followed, unwilling to take any chances with the men's lives. Oh for Sandra' healing skill right now, thought Kali.

By October 20, the Grande Pistola was once more back in the waters not far from Shansee, lying quietly far south of the city. Both crew members were well on the road to recovery.

Jemma eased back into her body, only to wake up and see Tian and Fina passionately kissing nearby. She cleared her throat and watched as the two looked a bit embarrassedly at her. "Oh you're back," Fina stated the obvious. Jemma then had to describe the big battle scene in full detail, twice actually — once for Tian and Fina, and again for the other three adults, when they heard that Jemma was back.

"Any word from Bethany?" Jemma remembered to ask at last.

"None at all. I still keep trying to contact her and Dita, but no luck yet," Fina replied.

"Damn. Shouldn't we start searching for them or do something?" Jemma begged.

"We really don't have any idea where they are," Zhen answered her. "While we know they went to the Purple Palace, there is no guarantee that they are still there. Even if we wanted to get in there, the place is too heavily fortified with Yuen's guards. It would take a small army to get inside if he doesn't want us in there. Bethany told me to be patient and wait for her message. We should do that." Jemma didn't like this, but what else could she do?

That night, she decided to again leave her body and go check out the Purple Palace for herself. Later she returned defeated. She didn't know where it was located in the city. The next day, they again took up their spying position, selling wilted flowers by the docks. However, she got Fang to give her good directions so she could find the Purple Palace that night.

After everyone was asleep, she moved out of her body and this time found the palace. She slipped in through the roof and tried to see what was what. "Rats, all is dark. I should have figured that," she thought. Dejectedly, she returned to her body, vowing to try this in the day time.

In the afternoon of October 20 while they all sat bored at their makeshift flower stall, Jemma quietly moved out of her body and headed over to the Purple Palace. Again, she entered through the roof and began looking around through the rooms. Shortly, she came upon the large room where the seven women were being held. She gasped as she saw the women lying in their beds. All were missing their lower arms! There were Bethany and Dita, and she thought one was San Min! She tried to contact Bethany once more but got no response. Then, she saw the opium pipes lying on the table and realized why she couldn't get through. Hastily, she returned to her body and began telling Fang and Fina what she had seen. Fang decided that they needed to return at once and talk to Zhen about this startling discovery.

Of course, Long Yan was elated that Jemma had seen his beloved San Min. That Bethany and Dita were with her was comforting to him, but that all seven had somehow lost their lower arms was shocking to all. "Now it makes sense, why I cannot reach Bethany," Jemma pointed out. "She's being kept high on opium all the time."

"Well, when she does contact us, we're going to need some way to ferry them to safety," Zhen mused. "I think I ought to get us a wagon and get prepared. Come on, Long, let's go see what we can get."

While they were out, Jemma began making plans for their rescue. "We can go in from the rooftop. I know just where they are. Maybe we can cut a hole in the roof right over their room and lower them a rope."

"Yes, but they don't have hands to climb with," Fina countered. "Besides, it's those two who can lift things without their bodies. Drugged up, they certainly cannot do that, let alone contact or respond to us, telepathically, that is."

"How would we get to the roof without being seen?" Fang countered, though still liking the idea. "I'll talk to Zhen about casing the place. If we could get to the roof, we might be able to cut through the roof, but that's a noisy proposition. Still, it has potential, Jemma."

An hour later, a soaked Zhen and Long entered their academy. "Monsoon has started. We got soaked, but we've now got a wagon in case it's needed."

"We'd better throw some towels and blankets in there, Zhen. With all this rain, they might get soaked too," Fang reasoned and set about the task. The downpour dashed all Jemma's hopes for casing the place today.

It was midnight when Bethany finally contacted Zhen. He sat up like a rocket! Bethany is somehow in my head — no, oh, telepathy. Kijutsu. He listened and grew more and more surprised and worried. "Okay, on my way now!" he called out, waking Fang.

He quickly woke everyone, but Long Yan came rushing with the news that Zhen already had received. Hastily, Zhen explained what little Bethany had told him. "Yes, Dita has somehow, miraculously killed Yuen Ming! That will set off a massive power struggle by tomorrow! The city streets will not be safe for days. Long and I will take the wagon and get them. Fang, you are to keep the teens safe. Get Tian to aid you. I don't know what to expect or when I will return. Things will go wild around Shansee for some days. Right now, we have to get them to a place of safety before Yuen's men find out that they've killed him and go after them with vengeance."

The two hitched up the horse and headed out into the rain. Before they covered a few blocks, both men were soaked from the fall's heavy rain. They had several miles of city streets to cover and their progress was slow due to the pouring rain. Zhen needed to think this through. With Yuen dead, the city would be in turmoil as the various fractions fought each other for the spoils. If they knew that Bethany and Dita were responsible for his death, certainly they would search high and low for them. No place in the city would be safe for them. Besides, now they were practically invalids and could likely do nothing even to care for their own needs. Couple that with their now being opium addicts and the situation looked grim indeed.

Finally, they reached the alley that ran behind Princess Path. He turned the horse and they rolled down the uneven surface, avoiding some obstacles along the way. Another mile or less and they would be behind the Purple Palace. Still, Zhen could think of no safe place to take them.

The rear of the palace appeared, along with dead bodies lying in the waters flowing down the alley. "They must have started walking on ahead," Long Yan sounded a hopeful note, straining to see ahead in the downpour. As they continued along the alley, more dead bodies appeared.

"Well, they are leaving us a trail a blind man could follow," Zhen made a stab at a bit of humor.

"I see them! Just ahead! There. Look, they are stopping, turning to look!" Long Yan exclaimed, his heart racing. In a moment, he would finally be reunited with his lost love! As they drew close, he could wait no longer. He jumped off the wagon as Zhen was halting it and ran to San Min, grabbing a hold of her tightly!

Zhan noticed that a bed sheet bag was floating along behind the group of seven and smiled, more kijutsu powers, undoubtedly. "Get them into the wagon and wrapped in blankets fast!" he called out.

Two minutes later, Zhen looked around. No one had seen them; he climbed back to the driver's box and urged the horse onwards. The poor beast now had to pull nine instead of two and barely managed to get the wagon moving, his hooves slipping on the slippery, wet stone of the alleyway.

He got a whiff of the opium smoke and knew that they would likely be out for some time. He thought to himself, "Just as good. They are wet and cold, to say nothing of the shock they have experienced. Think! Where can I take them? I have to get them out of the city." He turned out of the alley and shortly continued on west down Princess Path. He knew that it eventually led out of the city and into the rural countryside. Of course, from there, it went nowhere in particular, for it was not a main road. Those were the north road to Giang and the coastal road, which led to the many coastal fishing villages.

"They need the warm beds of an inn, a warm fire, and good hot meals, but that is out. Inns would be the first place anyone would search. Besides, they would be dead giveaways without their arms. Everyone would remember their passing. Inns are out. They can't do much walking either, so it is by wagon or possibly by boat. At least the city guards won't be out stopping traffic this late at night in this cold deluge. Caught a break there. Whatever am I going to do with them now?"

Zhen then remembered that San Min was from Nan Yan, and he started thinking along the lines of getting them to her old home city. Inspiration struck. In Nan Yan there was an Olin Masters Monastery, where adepts were training in their school of martial arts. They often provided sanctuary for the needy. That would be a perfect place for them to hide out for a while. Travel overland would be too risky, too challenging. They needed anonymity, which they could not get overland. Riverboat was the best, he thought. Now a plan began forming. He knew an old husband and wife team who were honorable and trustworthy. They owned and operated a small riverboat, plying the local river systems carrying grains mostly. He had just chatted with them the other day, and Kang and Bi Jie were still docked, unloading their rice cargo.

He'd just reached the outer western edge of Shansee; now he turned north on a muddy side road. Two miles later, he turned east once more and headed some eight more miles to the banks of the Yonshu River. Here, he parked the wagon in a heavy bamboo thicket, close to the river's edge. He outlined his plan to Long and quietly began walking back into Shansee, arriving home around five in the morning, cold, tired, and soaked to the bone.

The others awoke when he entered. While Jemma and Fina dried him off, Fang brewed hot tea, laced with honey. Then, she set to work making him a hot breakfast. Finally warmed, Zhen outlined what had happened. "I have them hiding in a bamboo thicket just north of the city. If they are quiet, they should not be discovered. They are going to need warm clothing, some funds, and some hot food soon." He told them of his plan and Fang volunteered to go at once to contact the Jies. "No, let me. I need you to see about getting them some warm clothes to wear. Keep them simple, because they no longer have their lower arms." She agreed, while Jemma and Fina pooled their stash of coins to give to Fang. What was left over, they would give to Bethany. The three women then headed off to get the clothes, planning to be at the store the minute it opened.

Fed and warmed, Zhen headed back out in the early morning light to find his boat friends. By the time that he arrived at their berth along the river docks, Bi was already cooking their breakfast on their small riverboat. "Come for breakfast, have you Zhen?" she kindly called out to him as he walked across the board connecting their boat to the docks.

"No, I have a very special mission, a secret mission that I beg you to undertake for me," he began. Kang overheard them and climbed up out of the cargo hold, where he had been sweeping up the remnants of the last load of rice.

The couple was in their late fifties and had rolled with the punches of life for the last forty years. Zhen explained what had happened and what he wanted them to do. "They'll have to remain in your cargo hold so no one can see them. We'll bring along some clothes and funds to help cover your expenses. I know that it is a long trip."

"No problem. We are always ready to help those in need," Bi replied, "won't we Kang?"

"Sure, Bi. We are ready to go today. We don't have a return cargo, so there's plenty of room."

"Thank you for helping to save their lives. Fang is out getting them some clothes now. I'll go back, bring them and what funds we have, and ride with you to where I left the wagon. After I help get them safely aboard, I'll take the wagon back into the city," Zhen explained. The two men shook hands and he left.

"Kang, you'd better lay in a good supply of rice, fish, tea, beans — oh, just get a bunch. We'll have eight more mouths to feed," Bi urged her husband. "Oh, and lay in more charcoal. We will probably need to run the cargo hold heater some too," she added. He grinned, already thinking of that.

Around ten, Zhen returned, carrying a large bundle on his back, much like a common laborer might. He'd packed the clothing tightly, but still they occupied a goodly volume. He climbed aboard and stowed the bundle in the hold. He and Kang undid the mooring lines, and Kang began leading the two oxen up the well-worn trail beside the river. Oxen were used to pull boats upriver, but they could move down river on their own. Inside, Zhen handed Bi a money pouch. "This is their funds. You should use as much of it as you need to cover your expenses, Bi."

"Thanks, Zhen. We'll take good care of these unfortunate women.

Now, sit a spell and take some tea."

"No, I best walk with Kang so we don't pass the spot where I left them. Another time, Bi." She grinned, showing her three missing teeth.

An hour later, Zhen and Kang tied the oxen to a stand of bamboo, and he slipped into the thicket. He found Long dumping out a chamber pot. "Hi, glad they had the presence of mind to bring along a couple of these. They are starving and chilled to the bone."

"We'll get them warmed up and fed in no time. Come on; we best carry them onto the boat. Are they awake?" Zhen asked. They were. He crawled into the back of the wagon and saw the women looking somber, their hair a mess, huddled in the blankets.

"Okay, I will be quick. I have a riverboat nearby. They have a warm cargo hold and we have some warm clothes for you. They will take you up river to Nan Yan and to the Olin Masters Monastery there. I think that the monastery will give you sanctuary for a time. That will be the safest place for you right now. Their names are Kang and Bi Jie; I trust them. Now, Long and I are going to carry you into the boat now."

One by one, the two men carried the blanket-wrapped and still wet women through the thicket and onto the boat, handing them down to Kang. Bi took each one from Kang and helped them maneuver to the rear, where she had the charcoal warmer going. "Lordy, Kang, these women are freezing!" she exclaimed.

Zhen carried Bethany down last. He shut the hold doors. Only the three lanterns illuminated the hold. Long bundled up their bed sheet of confiscated items and brought it aboard, finally joining San Min.

"Thanks, Zhen. We owe you our lives," I said. "We can hold out for a while. I think your plan is a good one. Can you all help us dry off and get into the warm clothes? Forget modesty. We are so cold! Then, we ought to eat something. Probably we all can last that long."

"You got it," Zhen explained. "Yuen has them all heavily addicted to opium now. They will need their pipes at some point. We best hurry while they are still lucid."

"Damn that evil man anyway," Bi commented, as she began taking off Dita's flimsy excuse of a dress.

"Don't fret. I wrung his neck. He's quite dead," Dita explained. Of course, Bi didn't believe this shivering woman with two stumps could have done that, but Zhen explained that indeed, Yuen Ming was now very dead.

"My, there will truly be hell to pay now! I am glad that we are out of the city. There will be a whole lot of street fighting going on now. Everyone will be fighting for a share of what he had," Kang added.

Ten minutes later, I finally began to truly warm up. While the peasant clothes were loose fitting and halfway easy to get on, they were thick and warm! I quickly discovered that it would be terrifically hard for us to stand up and move around easily, because the bottom was slightly curved and the boat rocked. If we had arms, no problem. The way we were, it was an almost "no can do." Bi, Kang, Zhen, and Long began to feed us, but San Min insisted that if they could get our special wooden spoons out of the sheet bag, we could feed each other more or less.

"Time enough for that once we are underway," Bi replied. "Just now, sweetie, you sit there and let us help you. You need food and warmth immediately." San Min smiled at the kindness of this old river woman and allowed herself to be fed this once.

Fed and warming up, the cravings began to make themselves known once more. Zhen saw this coming too. "Bethany, the best advice that I can give to you is to slowly reduce the amount of opium that you do. Fight off the cravings as long as you can each day and then when you absolutely must have it, smoke less of it each day. Opium addiction is a tough thing to break, but you seven must find the will power to do it. Just don't try to come off it cold turkey. The Jie's cannot handle you. Finally, if the monks give you a hard time, tell them that I am asking that they give you sanctuary for my sake." He gave me a hug and promised to take good care of our teens. I hated to see him leave. He was so strong and powerful! God, this was the opium effecting my judgment once more!

Kang left and shortly we all felt the boat moving once more. Long began to circulate the opium pipes between us, while Bi busied herself working on our tangled mass of hair. All seven of us had long hair. Bi was going to be very busy. God, I needed that smoke! Soon, the sweet, sensuous ecstasy flowed through out my body. My sense of touch seemed heightened beyond measure. I drifted off into sweet, relaxing dreams. Once more, I was lost to the world, as were the rest of my six companions.

Long had purposely given us a lower dose of opium this first time and we seven awoke around suppertime, lucid once more. Suddenly, Alessa made contact with me!

Mom! Thank god I finally got through to you! Jemma has told us what happened. Are you really addicted to opium? We finally figured that something like that has been going on with you, only Jemma confirmed it. Are you in pain? She said you lost your arms again and something about your feet. I am ready to start in therapy with you. Sandra is working out a way to deal with the addiction, if we can. Cosima is here and is going to contact Dita and work her, since Bianca is tied up elsewhere. She talked as fast as she could. I realized now that she had been trying to contact me for weeks! How scared she must have been!

Hi. I am physically okay. I have lucid periods, but they don't last too long. Yes, Yuen had our arms removed at the elbows, and he has somehow broken our feet arches and forced them into a strange super arch so that the backs of our heels are nearly at the back ends of our toes! It looks like we have tiny feet. I need to eat supper and probably will have to have a fix after that. Try again in the morning or better, let me contact you when I have another lucid period. I love you and miss you. Thank you for helping us.

Dita said, "Hey, Cosima is going to run therapy on me. I told her she'd better wait a bit yet until we are able to stay clear for a bit longer. You know that they have been frantically trying to get to us for nearly six weeks? It's October 21! Food!" she suddenly saw the steaming pot and her stomach insisted on being fed.

Mei was also lucid now and very worried, "What's going to happen to us now?" I detected a trace of fear in her voice.

"Well, stick with us, and we will lend you a whole lot of support and help," I tried to think of something to reassure her. "We've known many women who have been in worse shape than we all are now and they have learned new ways of doing life things and have been very successful women."

"But all I know how to do is give others pleasure," Mei protested, "and now, I am so helpless myself."

"Yes, but you pleasured us incredibly well when your arms were completely immobile, tied up in those ropes," Dita added.

Chan spoke up, "Mei, we were supposed to show you how to use your arms as well as everything else you already know. We just haven't had the chance yet. You really can do far more with your arms too."

"Say, how long did they keep your arms tied up like that? How come they even tie you up in the first place?" Dita asked between spoonful's.

"Usually for maybe five days running. We had to learn to sleep bound," Mei explained. "Then, they would untie me and I would bathe and help feed and dress and comb other kami's hair for a day. Then, I would be rebound again. We all took turns being unbound for a day or so."

"That's awful! Why do they do that anyway?" Dita asked again.

"Oh, you get used to it; it's not so bad, really. It is our custom. It has been done that way for centuries. This way, everyone knows at once that we are kami, the official pleasure givers. Customers do not get cheated, because they know that we are the true ones."

Chan added gloomily, "They also know that we cannot steal from the customers and that we had darn well better perform well or else. Say, we were supposed to be being paid a lot of gold. I wonder whether that is true or not?"

"Bet we never do see a gold," Hon said acridly. That gave me an idea. I was still lucid enough and made contact with Alessa.

Hi, can you check the Tashien bank records for the Purple Palace and see if any of the women have an account? Specifically, see if there is one for Chan Bao, Mei Bi, Dai Son, Hon Feng, and San Min Wu. They were supposed to be being paid lots of gold for their work. She agreed and promised to get back to me about that in the morning. While the master records in Velona would be three months or more out of date, if they did have an account, there should already be funds in there.

"Hon, I am having my daughter check the bank records. By tomorrow we will know if Yuen actually did set aside your pay."

"How can you do this?" Hon asked.

"Dita and I can use telepathy to talk to anyone we know anywhere in the world," I kept it simple. All of them stared even harder at us.

"Oh, kijutsu powers. I forgot," Chan finally said. This, the other accepted as well.

While the rains continued in Shansee, later that morning Jemma had an idea. She was particularly annoyed with what Yuen had done to us and to the other women. She took this as a personal affront. "Fang, Fina, I want to go to the Banca del Dio as soon as possible. We need to withdraw some more funds." She lied, but the request seemed plausible, since she and Fina had donated all their gold to Bethany earlier in the morning.

Around noon, the three entered the bank. "You two stand watch and don't let anyone come close to me or the teller that I am with." She winked at Fina, who noticed their secret signal. Fina knew that Jemma was up to something devious indeed. She and Fang stood guard behind Jemma as she walked up to the teller.

"Ah, good morning, Bosu Yuen Ming. How may we assist you this wet morning?" the teller replied. Fina grinned. Fang gasped and held her hand to her lips to cover her surprise.

"Well, I need to transfer some funds to Velona. I am buying a fleet of these new caravels. Can you tell me how much I dare transfer at this time? By the way, you look very attractive this morning. New dress?"

The teller smiled, "Why yes, I just got it yesterday. Let me consult your records. Ah yes, you have sixty million, three hundred forty thousand on hand. Of course, more is likely to be coming in shortly, if your businesses continue to make their usual deposits," she replied. Fang gasped once more.

"Oh this will be sufficient then. I wish to transfer the sixty million to the following account in Velona. Mrs. Bethany Brozena Malina. She is handling the purchase for me." A bit later, she had Jemma sign the document and thanked him. Jemma turned and walked out of the bank, with several others recognizing Yuen Ming, nodding and greeting him. Fina and Fang found others recognizing them as two of Yuen's close associates.

Once outside in the pouring rain and clear of the bank, Jemma cancelled her Judger spell. "Well, that ought to help them don't you think?"

"Sixty million gold? Jemma, what did you do?" Fang asked.

"Oh, a little trickery that we Judgers can do. I know this was not legal, but this way, Yuen is paying for what he has done to others. Bethany will want to give all of it to the women she's with and to others whom Yuen has severely harmed. She doesn't need the money, because she has her own millions. This way, Yuen is paying for what he's done."

"My god! I had no idea that you were this powerful! The teller will swear that she actually saw you, even though Yuen is dead," Fang replied flabbergasted.

"Yes, and also that he was accompanied by two of his close associates," Jemma added with a smirk. "Never mess with Bethany or Dita. That's what they always are saying. Now I say, it's *costly* to mess with a Jemma!"

Fina pounded her on her back, "Brilliant Jemma, brilliant!" Jemma had a self-satisfied, smug smile on her face, though the rain was coming down by the buckets full on her face.

During my next lucid spell the next morning, Alessa relayed that there was no bank records anywhere for any of those five names. However, she relayed what Jemma had done and I had a roaring laugh!

"Ladies, Hon was right. Yuen cheated all of you. He never did set up a bank account for any of you. While he said you were making a lot of money, in fact, you were given none at all." Their faces were uniformly stunned. "However, one of our teens in Shansee has rectified that omission on Yuen's part. Yesterday, she got the Banca del Dio in Shansee to transfer sixty million in gold to my account in Velona. When it gets there in a few months, I will have them set up accounts for all of you and transfer millions into your accounts. Yuen is paying you back in spades!" Their stunned looks changed to ones of total shock and total disbelief.

Dita stated flatly, "Never mess with Dita or Bethany! Never!" I roared with laughter. My mirth and her statement caused the whole group finally to burst out in laughter, the first laughter any of these women had done in a long, long time. Slowly, we were bringing them up to higher emotional tones, which they sorely needed. However, soon all seven of us were fighting off the intense cravings of the opium once more. With Long's help, we fought it much longer today, a whole hour even, but it was pure torture, knowing that just in front of us were the pipes and the opium, just waiting to release us from our tortures and despairs.

Chapter 13 The Battle on the Steppes

As Bianca, Enrico, Ilenakova, and Louis laid in their hut on September 11, 752, which by the way they now could put up properly in less than a half hour, Alessa made contact with Ilenakova, Enrico, and Bianca. *Bianca! Your mom has gone missing! No one can contact her. We think that she and Bethany are in some kind of bad trouble! We will continue to try to get through to her.* They exchanged what little information that Alessa knew.

Louis saw that all three were somehow "not here," and remained quiet and on guard. Then, they all seemed to "reappear" into the here and now, but Bianca began crying. "Bianca, what's the matter? What just happened?" His voice held a tremble of worry in it.

"Mom! She and Bethany have gone missing down in Shansee, Tashien," she cried.

"They were on a mission too, trying to locate some man's missing fiancé," Ilenakova explained. "It was supposed to be a simple go find out what happened to her type of mission and now no one can seem to contact them."

"Huh? I don't understand. How can you know all this? What just happened?" Louis asked even more startled.

"Oh, I'm sorry," Enrico realized that Louis didn't know that Alessa had contacted them. "Louis, Bianca here and her sisters all can do telepathy. Bethany and Dita are perhaps the best telepaths around. Alessa just contacted us and told us the news."

"Oh! Incredible! Now that *is* very useful! Wow!" Louis exclaimed, suddenly grasping the immense value of this aspect of the Precocious Witches of 42 Hampton Way.

"Okay. I am going to try to contact mom myself," Bianca declared and attempted to calm her nerves and grief. She sat still as a rock for many minutes, before she broke into tears once more. "I can't reach them. I can sense them, but not make contact."

"Well, dear, at least you know that they are alive still," Ilenakova consoled her.

Louis took her hand and swore solemnly, "Bianca, when we have finished this mission, I promise you that I will take you to this Shansee wherever that is and go in search of Dita with you. I give you my word."

The unexpected gesture of kindness hit her hard and she leaned over and rested her head on his shoulders, putting her arms around him tightly. His arms encircled her and he held her until she recovered a bit. "Thanks, Louis," she whispered.

At dawn, preparations crescendoed. The ten thousand soldiers ate a good breakfast; none knew when they would get a chance to eat again.

Purposely, Czar Chekov allowed the morning to pass by, because he wanted the sun at their backs and not in their eyes when they attacked. Morale was high, Ilenakova noted. She and Enrico paid close attention to the way that Chekov ran his army. Velona's information on these hardy fighters from the Northern Steppes was at least a century out of date.

Late morning, Viktor signaled the four to join him as the horde mounted up and rode off in various directions to take up their assigned battlefield positions. The four followed behind the Czar and Czarina, who rode to the top of the next hill. From here, they and the others would get a bird's eye view of the battlefield.

In the far distance in the foothills of the Kathas range laid the city under construction, New Xin. Wooden cabin buildings flowed up and down the hills no more than a half mile from the northern seacoast. Flooding out upon the grasslands, more of the army from Tashien marched to the beat of some drums heading to join tens of thousands of others already in position. The Tashien army stretched in a mass from the sea coast on down to at least five miles south of the city, a wall of soldiers wearing leather armor and carrying bows and curved swords for the most part, ill-equipped to fend off charging cavalrymen.

To the four, the large size of the Czar's army, which had seemed huge before, now seemed utterly dwarfed! His men had fanned out along the southern and central sections of this massive army. One could easily see the organizational groupings of some twenty-five men per squad. At last, Czar Chekov seemed pleased, raised his hand, and brought it sharply down. Suddenly, the ten thousand men began wildly yelling and rows upon rows broke into an all-out gallop, closing the distance to the front lines.

At dawn, Huan Chan, a foot soldier in General Wu Zhou Cao's mighty army, rose and dressed. He was given his morning bowl of rice with fish bits. He ate slowly, knowing that he was most unworthy of this feast that he was being given. His squad leader came around to tell the members of the coming battle and that this was their ceremonial meal. Still, he ate slowly, "Most unworthy of this bounteous gift from General Wu Zhou Cao — I eat so as not to dishonor my father, who fought for the Princess Shashi Wu and died eight years ago," he thought to himself. Later, he donned his armor, again feeling most unworthy of wearing it.

He fell in line with his squad members, most of who felt as he. "Today, we fight for General Wu Zhou Cao. Show him that you are worthy of his grace. Prove to your ancestors that you are indeed worthy soldiers. We are to show no mercy. Kill the raiding horsemen that our Princess may remain safe. Show her the highest honor. To victory, men!" All raised their hands in a victory shout and began to march onto the battlefield shortly after nine in the morning.

Sometime later, Huan Chan stood on the grass behind his fellows, one unworthy, undeserving ant in the colony standing behind other unworthy, undeserving ants. Hours passed, and he knew just how unworthy he was — he needed to relieve himself. No true soldier of the great general would need to relieve themselves while upon the battlefield. This only added to his feelings of worthlessness. Still, he stood unwavering, holding onto the idea that he must not dishonor his ancestors.

He heard what sounded like firecrackers for some time, along with the thunderous hoof beats of countless horses. Still he stood like a statue — all thoughts focused on honoring his ancestors. If Huan could do nothing else in his lifetime, he would at least accomplish this small task. Now an opening appeared in front of him. Men were lying on the ground, dead or bleeding to death. Bang! Huan felt a sharp pain in his chest. He forced his body to remain rigid, awaiting the order to charge into battle. Honor of his ancestors was all that he had left for which to live; he would not dishonor them. He felt his legs crumple, his eyes closed, his body slumped to the ground. Still the order to charge never came. Shocked, he seemed to be floating above his body now. It was lying dead on the grasslands, like thousands in front of him.

"I have honored my ancestors," he thought, as he realized it was over for him. Suddenly, he wondered, "If I am not my body down there, then what am I? Have I failed utterly in my unworthy task? Cannot I even properly die to honor my ancestors? Have I become so useless that I cannot even die properly? I have now disgraced my ancestors. Woe is me. I am doomed. I cannot even do this small task properly!" he thought.

"What am I to do now? Oh, I must go back to Tashien and try to do this once more and see if I can get it right this time," he concluded and floated off over the Kathas Mountains, heading toward Tashien.

As the four watched along with Viktor and the Czar and Czarina, the gun shooting units came charging toward the front lines. When they were some twenty-five feet from them, they fired their guns and galloped away, veering away from the enemy's front lines. After circling back to their starting position, they halted and spent several minutes reloading their guns. That done, they repeated their initial charge path.

The Tashien soldiers let lose volleys of arrows, so thick at times, that the Czar's riders were hit multiple times! Men were dying on both sides, the four observed. However, the enemy leaders did not seem to understand just what these new weapons were nor did they have a reasonable reaction to them. Their men stood their ground and were mowed down by the gunfire. Now the cavalrymen were forced to trample over the fallen Tashien soldiers just to get sufficiently close to fire upon others accurately!

"I don't understand them at all!" exclaimed Ilenakova. "They are just standing there shooting arrows and getting shot or chopped or trampled to death. What kind of a general allows such butchery of his own men?"

"Their morale still holds," Enrico commented. "Thousands have already died and the front ranks do not even seem to have noticed! By now, any other army would have routed, fleeing the battlefield for cover or shelter or anything."

"How can anyone just stand there and take that kind of punishment?" Bianca asked flabbergasted.

Czar Chekov answered her, "You now see what we are facing. They are always like this. We demolish their front lines, and yet no matter how many we slay, they continue as if the battle has not yet started! Ants, swarms of ants. Damn, even the massive carnage of the guns is making no real difference!"

"Dear, I don't see that these new guns are worth so much," Czarina Mara commented. "It is taking our shooters minutes to reload their guns and return to the battle. Our usual swordsmen and bowmen are not so constrained. See, they continuously battle them and take fewer casualties because they are in so close that they cannot use their bows against our men. These guns are not what they have been made out to be, I don't think."

"You are right. Perhaps with enemies other than these ant swarms, the guns will be of great benefit. Here, they are not doing as well as our cavalry. I shall call a halt to the use of the guns," Czar Chekov replied and issued an order. One rider headed off to deliver his order to the galloping riders.

By mid-afternoon, Czar Chekov reluctantly gave the signal to cease their attack and to withdraw to their encampment. Many riders assisted their fallen comrades as well as rounding up stray horses and the bodies of their fallen. The Czar did not want a single gun to fall into the hands of the ants.

While he sat on his horse, watching his men retreat, he said, "You see how hopeless this has become! I've lost perhaps a thousand men with double that many wounded who will live to fight again. Can you estimate their numbers lost? It must easily be ten times that number. Still, with such losses, they have not moved a foot from their initial positions! How can we possibly defeat such an army, my allies? I am most thankful that you have witnessed this for yourselves. We are all doomed utterly if these ants ever decide to move out from this location. What on Tarra could possibly stop them?"

"Truly, you are right, Czar Chekov!" Ilenakova answered. "Even if we armed every man in Velona, we could not stop them! Such battlefield losses without the slightest impact are beyond words! Indeed, we are all doomed if they choose to move out. Zargarb would not stand a chance of not being overrun."

"Speaking of that," Louis wondered, "has anyone tried to talk to them to find out what their intentions are? Do they plan to remain here at the coast? Are they intending to move out and attack the Sea Princes, the

Greenway, or your cities, Czar Chekov?"

"Well, we tried once, but got nowhere," he admitted. "None of us can understand a word that they say and they can't understand a word that we say to them. Communication with them is hopeless. Still, I would rest easier if I knew what they at least *say* that their intentions will be, though you cannot trust what your enemy would actually say."

"I speak a little of their language. Czar, if you will permit it, I will go down there and see if I can parley with them and find those answers for you and for Fortress d'Grange," Louis volunteered.

"Louis! You aren't going down there into the enemy alone!" Bianca replied, startled, surprised, and pleased at the same time. She liked the style and resourcefulness of Louis. "We three also speak a little of their language. We have a fair number of immigrants from southern Tashien in our countries. We'll go with you, Louis, that is, if it's okay with Czar Chekov."

"I cannot be responsible for your safety!" the Czar immediately distanced himself from their parley plans. "Look, if they hold you for ransom or whatever, as you have seen today, I cannot even punch one hole in their formation, let alone come to your rescue. However, I will not stop you from making the attempt. Certainly, our three countries desperately need to know what these ants' plans and intentions might be. Still, I think it a foolhardy thing to do because we just cannot possibly come to your aid."

"We understand that fully," Enrico replied. "We cannot possibly expect you to come to our aid. If we get into trouble, it is our problem, not yours. Still, if we can somehow find out what they are intent upon doing, then perhaps that will be of great value to us all."

"Thanks. Gang, I think it best that we leave our weapons here with Czar Chekov, when we ride out to parley. If they see weapons, they might react in a hostile manner. Even so, they might confiscate our weapons and not give them back. I don't want to be in a war without my sword," Enrico suggested.

While the four began to make a pile of their weapons, Czarina Mara prepared a white flag for them to carry. "Go with the Czarina's blessing, brave allies," she said, handing Louis the flag.

Czar Chekov spoke loudly so that Viktor and all his men could hear. "Never let it be said that our allies are not brave! These four are going down onto the battlefield unarmed to parley with the enemy, who outnumber us greatly. All hail our valiant allies from Velona and d'Grange!" He led a round of loud cheering, which caused Louis to break into a smile.

"We will be back later on. It might take us days to learn all that we can. Thanks," Louis replied. Slowly, he led the four down from the tall hill overlooking the carnage field below. As the four rode slowly, they saw some enemy soldiers digging mass graves. They swore that some of the bodies thrown into the pits were still alive! All four were shocked at this sight.

As they neared these burial details, several held bows upon them.

Louis called out, "We came to parley with your general. Please take us to him. We are unarmed." He hoped his accent wasn't so bad that they wouldn't understand him. At last, several motioned for the group to follow them. Slowly they passed through the receding ranks of thousands of soldiers, heading back into the city in the foothills. A large garrison force began to make camp upon the grasslands, evidently to stand guard against any further assault by the cavalrymen.

Ten times, they had to repeat their request, as they were led to higher and higher ranking soldiers. At last, they faced General Wu Zhou Cao himself. He was thirty and a tall, well-muscled young man. From his voice tones and his manner, the four could see that he was a highly educated, bright young man. "Well, you do not look like these barbaric horsemen, though three of you ride their tiny horses. Rather, you have the look of ones from Velona. I once visited there as a young child."

"Indeed, my three companions are from Velona, and I am from Fortress d'Grange. Yes, they had to borrow three of their horses. We've come to parley with you, general. I am Louis d'Grange." He introduced the other three.

Ilenakova and Bianca both noticed that the general seemed rather hostile toward them. Polite and refined, nevertheless, there was a cold, hostility in his voice. "I am General Wu Zhou Cao. I obey my wife, the Princess Shashi Wu. If you wish to parley, you must do so in her presence."

"That is acceptable to us, thank you," Louis replied politely.

"Ha! You may not find it so acceptable once you know. Still, I believe the Princess will have many questions for you as well. We are highly civilized. You shall be our guests for some days as we exchange information. It is well that finally we have some refined people from the Outer Lands with which to converse. I will have my men search you for concealed weapons. Then, you will be led to our palace guest room. There, I will send our Court Historian to discuss how it must be if your women are to participate and meet with the Princess. If your women agree to the terms, they will be allowed to join you, when the Princess and I summon you after dinner. If the terms are unacceptable, then only you two men will be allowed into the presence of our Princess." He signaled and quickly several soldiers thoroughly searched the four for weapons. Finding none, a squad of soldiers led the four into the city under construction.

As they rode into the huge city, signs of hasty construction lay in all directions. The four concluded that they were working as fast as possible to construct cabins before the winter snows came. They passed a huge number of wagons, laden with food and other supplies. Many of the returning soldiers had already begun continuing their construction work duties. Hardly anyone stopped even to look at the four strangers! Bianca just could not believe this; these minions cared not that four strangers were entering their city.

Near the center of the city in the foothills stood a larger wooden building, the Royal Palace — all four read the Tashien characters that proclaimed this. "Leave horses. Follow me," a guard said, speaking as if these four could perhaps only barely understand him. They entered a side door into a one-room guest room. Two beds lay on one side of the room. A table and four chairs occupied the center. A washbasin and towels along with chamber pots stood in one corner. There was an inside door which was securely latched from the other side.

The four entered and decided to wash up quickly. "We ought to look as presentable as possible," Enrico suggested. As they were wiping off, a man wearing a silk suit entered from the locked inner door. He had long black hair tied into a ponytail. His moustache was long and turned down at the sides of his mouth. A small goatee complimented his look. He bowed politely to the four.

"I am Wang Lon, the Court Historian for Princess Shashi Wu." His voice was polite and soft, with a hint of no sympathy for them in his tone. I understand that you wish to meet with General Wu Zhou and Princess Shashi. Do you know of her?"

Enrico spoke, "No, we do not."

"Then, allow me to explain fully. More than five years ago, Princess Shashi was indeed a royal princess. She ruled in Linyi Province. However, when the Empress, her mother, died, her sister Pian wanted to be the chosen new Empress. Never had Princess Shashi ever indicated to Pian that she wanted also to be chosen Empress. Indeed, Princess Shashi had often told her sister that she did not want the throne, but to marry General Wu Zhou. Still, the evil in Pian's heart could not risk the chance that the High Council would pass over her."

"In those days, Princess Shashi was a princess. She has small feet, a small waist, and at that time very long nails. We found her to be a kind, loving Princess indeed. Yet, evil was the way of Pian. She cast a terrible disgrace upon her own sister. Her army conquered that of Princess Shashi and then Pian had her banned to the Ice Province of Dong. However, to make sure that the High Council could not still choose Princess Shashi over her, Pian ordered the doctors to turn Princess Shashi into a zen-kami. There could be no greater disgrace brought upon our poor Princess, but to be turned into an untrained zen-kami! General Wu Zhou Cao has married her and he insists that we still call her Princess Shashi, even though she could not possible be so considered a Princess by any standard. She is now really a zen-kami."

"Excuse us, Wang Lon, what is a zen-kami? We are not familiar with that term," Enrico spoke for us four, who looked completely baffled. None of this made sense.

"Forgive me. In Tashien, those men and women who are trained to give sensual, physical pleasure to others are called kami. All cultures have their vulgar prostitutes who ply their trade. Yet, in our highly cultured society, we have elevated those who are specially trained to give sensual pleasures to others — both men and women — to a high social standing of which they are most deserving. It is an honor to be so pleasured by a kami. Yet, we find it vital for anyone to be able instantly to recognize an honored, healthy, highly trained, and clean kami from a filthy, disease-ridden common prostitute. Thus, many centuries ago, our people adopted such a means. The kami have their arms bound in a very special way with silk ropes, bound in such a way that their upper arms are at their sides, while they are immobile. You see, a kami does not ever need their arms to give the ultimate of pleasure to their customers. When you see a bound kami, you know that you are getting the real thing. No one could bind themselves in such a manner, you see."

"Extremely rarely, a kami so excels at their trade that they are awarded the zen-kami status. Oh, those are very rare indeed, complete with an honor nearly that of a Princess. To become a total zen-kami, these men and women have their lower arms removed completely and their upper arms properly shaped into an aesthetic form. It is said that one night of utter ecstasy with a zen-kami would cost one a thousand gold and that such would be well worth the expense. However, I cannot verify that from first-hand knowledge. I can say that our kami do know their trade exceedingly well. Perhaps one day, I will be wealthy enough to spend one night in total bliss with a zen-kami, who can say?"

"So you see, our Princess was disgraced and cast out of her birthright of being a Royal Princess and cast down into being a zen-kami. Most horribly, she has no training and knows nothing of that trade, not even that of a kami. Thus, she is forced to appear to everyone as if she is a zen-kami, not a Princess, and worse, she does not know how to be a zen-kami. It is a most unbearable position that our Princess Shashi is in for the rest of her life. So, to at least make her feel more comfortable in the presence of other women, it is her orders that these other women appear before her as bound kami. Thus, in our culture, Princess Shashi is elevating all women who appear in her presence to at least that of a kami, a most respected, most honored woman or man, though there are so few of them."

"If your men will wear our civilized clothes, they will be allowed free run of this Royal Palace and meet with our General and Princess. If your women will consent to also wearing our civilized clothing and to be bound as a kami, they may also have free run of the palace, meet with, and appear in the presence of our Princess. Should they not wish to do so, then your women will be confined to this room during your stay here in New Xin."

"It does not hurt nor cause any permanent harm. You have two men who can look after your needs, if you choose to dress as a kami. However, it is your choice. Do you need time to consider?" he asked politely.

"No, we wish to talk with the General and the Princess," Ilenakova replied. "If we must be tied up, so be it." Bianca agreed, though she was slightly ill at ease with this whole proposition.

"I promise to be your hands for you, Bianca," Louis whispered to her. She smiled. If need be, she could just use her spiritual ability to move objects as she had done as a young girl before her arms had been re-grown.

"Excellent choice. I will return with appropriate attire for all of you and send someone to properly bind you," he replied and bowed to all four. "Dinner will be served at your table here in about one hour. As I understand it, after that, you will be meeting with the General and our Princess."

A couple of minutes later, he returned with clothes and the four began changing. The men wore silk shirts with fine white linen pants and jackets. The women were given a thin, silk gown that tingled their skin. All wore traditional cloth slip-on shoes. Once the women were dressed, another young woman entered carrying thick, silken ropes. The four watched as she nimbly set to work on binding Ilenakova and Bianca properly. Indeed, there seemed to be a certain ceremony to the actual process. First, the rope was wrapped around their very upper arms and then in spirals around their upper arms down to their elbows. Then, with their lower arms behind their backs and palms touching while pointing up to their necks, their wrists were secured. Many wrappings of the ropes secured their lower arms together, and at last, the ropes encircled their waists and tied off. Both of their upper arms were left hanging at their sides, as if they were not even bound up. Yet, they could not move their arms the slightest amount.

The woman, who had not spoken yet, at last did so. "As long as you remain bound, you may come and go as desired. If you remove them, you are to be locked in this room. Please, do not remove the bindings. You both appear now as perfect kami." She bowed to the two women and left.

"Are you okay, Bianca?" Louis said worriedly. "Does it hurt at all?"

"I'm fine, no, but I cannot even wiggle them. I guess Louis, you are going to have to help me with everything now," she teased him. He flushed, wondering if perhaps he ought to have insisted the women not have come to the parley.

Just then, several women entered carrying trays of steaming food and tableware. Carefully, as if following some kind of ritual, they set the table for them and placed the various dishes in very precise locations, before silently bowing and leaving them.

"Guys, you are up," Ilenakova teased. "Honestly, we don't want to make the same mistake that Bethany and Dita did last year when they were down in Demokritos. Bianca, no showing off your talents. So guys, you get to feed us."

Louis helped Bianca get seated and began to do just that. "I'm sorry, Ilenakova. I didn't understand what you were just telling us about her mother."

"We are spiritual beings, just like you, Louis, only we have recovered many of our native skills, Bianca especially more so than me," Ilenakova answered. "When they were on their mission down in Demokritos, Bethany and Dita used far too many of their special skills in situations where others could see them happening. Oh, show him, Bianca, with your teacup." Bianca grinned. Louis watched as the cup rose up to her lips, and she took a nice sip, and the cup sat back down on the table.

"How did. . ." he didn't finish his question.

"Right, seeing *unexplainable* things happening — things beyond one's understanding, forces one to have to invent the 'how comes,' usually assigning totally wrong reasons. Honestly, Bianca doesn't need anyone's help with anything, while I do need some," Ilenakova continued her explanation. "Yet, if we start doing things that will blow someone's reality, shocking them, then they tend to have rather nasty reactions."

"Yes, they did some really evil things to mom and Bethany out of their own ignorance. The stupid Cardinal Drakon thought that they were Daughters of Lucifer, the devil," Bianca explained. "As such, he believed that he needed to take terrible actions against them. We don't know what these people believe here. We aren't going to take any chances with them. She's right. I really won't need any help with anything."

"Not even going to the bathroom?" asked Louis, trying very hard to grasp these revelations, though many jived with his own clandestine observations of the women of 42 Hampton Way over the years.

"No, silly. However, she's right. We don't want to take any chances, so we will appear that we are now two mostly helpless women, a kami, or whatever. I hope that you don't mind assisting me, Louis," Bianca added.

"Not at all, Bianca. Just let me know if I miss something," he replied sincerely.

"Sip of tea please," she replied with a grin. "This is rather kinky, Ilenakova," she teased.

Enrico added, "Well, we blew that one when we came charging in and fired off three balls of fire against the Vito raiders. However, we lucked out, because the survivors were so tied up fending off the thirty raiders that they really didn't get a look at what we did there. Let's play it right this time, gang. I don't want anything bad to happen to any of us."

About an hour later, a woman with her right hand missing came to get them. "My Princess will see you now. If you will follow me?"

"Thank you," Louis replied, putting his arm around Bianca's waist beneath her long hair, which he adjusted to fall properly for her. Enrico did the same with Ilenakova. He resisted asking the woman about her missing hand, however. Shortly, they entered a larger room, well lit by a dozen lanterns. At the far end sitting on a plush chair was a young woman of twenty-seven. Shashi wore a blue silk gown; her feet looked tiny, but that was just the illusion her terrifically high heels gave. Rather her shoes matched the ones that Bianca wore; only they had an enormous heeled wedge. Her very long black hair was draped across her chest, falling below her waist. Her face was quite attractive, but their attention was drawn to her arms, which ended at her elbows. The surgeon had removed some of the upper arm muscles so that her upper arms were more conical in shape, ending about an inch in diameter where her elbows had been. Sitting on a similar plush chair to her right was General Wu Zhou, looking much as he had. The woman who had brought them here went to sit beside five others, who like her, were missing their right hands. They all sat off to Princess Shashi's left. Soft mats lay on the floor in front of them. The four bowed to her, and she waved her short right arm, indicating that they were to sit. The men helped balance the women as they sat down.

"Welcome to my court. I am Princess Shashi Wu. My sister, Pian, did this to me, as my Historian has probably told you. She also cut off the right hands of my hand maidens. We were sent into exile in Dong Province. Now then, who are you and why are you fighting us?" she asked.

At once, Bianca spotted the fact that she was holding onto a terrific resentment and that it reflected off onto others. Her husband was simply full of hostility. She could see why this would be so for each of them. Enrico introduced his group, one by one, with each bowing slightly as they were introduced. However, Bianca sensed that Princess Shashi would feel far less threatened if one of the women did the talking. She sent this to her companions via telepathy, which rather surprised Louis.

"First, Princess Shashi, thank you for seeing us," Ilenakova tried her best to be social and polite. "We did not take part in the battle today against your army. Down in Velona and d'Grange, we heard that there was some bad trouble up here in the Northern Steppes, and our rulers asked us to come and see what was happening here."

"Ah, Velona. Wu Zhou has told me much about your country. Perhaps one day we can visit it," Princess Shashi showed a hint of curiosity buried deep within her resentment.

"The barbarians of the Northern Steppes have been our allies for many years," Ilenakova used the term that Wu Zhou had used earlier. "The grasslands from here to the far distant Elbe River is their homeland. We talked with them. They believe that you are invading their country and attempting to conquer them. Louis decided that we ought to come and visit with you to hear your side of the story before making any conclusions." There, she'd been about as polite about all this as she could possibly be. Bianca noted this as well.

Shashi replied, "You have to understand that we were all banished in utter disgrace to the icy realms of Dong Provence, where the snows are gone only the three summer months. Life there is exceedingly harsh, even more so for me. I am unable to do even the simple things of life. The bitter cold makes my arms ache terribly. In order to survive, we just had to find a warmer climate. Obviously, we cannot move to the south in Tashien. We are banished. This is our only alternative to find a warmer, more hospitable place to live. We brought everyone and everything with us. We will not go back. We would rather die where it is warm than to go back to living in that cold hell hole," Princes Shashi explained, her deep resentment coming through loud and clear to all.

"No one can blame you for that," Bianca replied sympathetically, hoping for a bit of advantage with her.

"Is that why your soldiers just stood there and died without retreating?" Ilenakova asked the general.

"Of don't be silly, woman," he said hostilely, "they are *mere* soldiers, simple peons. They are of *no* significance whatsoever. Their lives are worth nothing if they cannot give them to protect their Princess. They died with honor serving Princess Shashi." His hostility and his belief in the utter worthlessness of the lives of all those soldiers Ilenakova found appalling.

"But they are men," she replied, unable to grasp how he could be so brazen, so crass.

Princess Shashi echoed his values, "They are mere soldiers, whose function in life is to give their lives so I may be safe. Think nothing of them. We certainly do not. In Tashien, we have millions and millions of people. One can own as many soldiers as one has money to pay their meager rations and to equip them. Yes, their lives are a bit better than the peasant farmer in the rice paddies is. Still, they died with honor, which is everything for them. Is it not with you? To live a life with honor?"

Ilenakova's temper was rising; Bianca stepped in cleverly. "Honor, yes, I believe all men and women should live their lives with honor. We also believe that our self-respect ranks as high as honor. If one no longer respects himself or herself, they ultimately follow a path of self-destruction and of dishonor."

"Excuse me," Enrico interrupted their philosophy flow. "Correct me if I am misunderstanding you, Princess Shashi. You are trying to find a new, warmer climate, one that is far more hospitable for you and your people. Is this correct?"

"Yes, it is our main objective here," she replied, as if he were an imbecile.

"I know something of the Northern Steppes and their often brutal winters. These grasslands sometimes are covered in over a foot of snow. While it does melt in the spring, the winters here can be harsh and bitterly cold as well," Enrico explained. "However, there is a much warmer location than here where you are. If you follow these foothills southwards for some three hundred miles or so, you will arrive in Juda Arad, which is a hot, semi-arid desert land, unsuitable for most everything. Yet, just south of that desert land and here in these foothills, the winters are warm with no snow. The climate is much warmer there, significantly more so than way up here. Also, there the coastline is suitable for ships coming the short distance from

Shansee, so you could get food and supply shipments in from Tan Lon Province, if you like. As far as we know, those foothills are uninhabited at this time. Besides, you would also be only a relatively short ways from the Sea Prince Sector of Zargarb to the west or Shansee to the east. You would be closer to civilization than way up here."

Princess Shashi looked at Wu Zhou and then Enrico. "We did not know this. We had so hoped that the winters would be mild here. The land offers so much more promise than Dong Province. Is this true? Will there be that much cold and snow up here?"

"Yes, I am afraid that is the truth," Ilenakova backed him up. She described some of the winters here in the Steppes that she had personally seen in previous lifetimes, though she didn't tell them that aspect. Bianca watched very carefully their reactions to this news and realized that this was of major importance to the Princess and thus to Wu Zhou, whom she now grasped was doing everything that he could to make his wife's life more tolerable! She saw her opening and took it.

Bianca then said, "There is still time to get down there and situated somewhat before winter comes up here. General Wu Zhou, could you send some most trusted scouts along with Enrico here? He can lead your men to the location that we have in mind so that they can appraise its worth. He can also visit with the leader of the barbarians and explain to him your plight. Their leader is terrified that your intentions are to conquer his grassland country, which we now can see is not the case at all. You are just looking for a warmer homeland."

Enrico began to protest, as she knew he would. "Bianca! I am supposed to be protecting you and Ilenakova."

"Yes, but this is extremely important, Enrico. Unless they want to become trapped up here in a few more months in the cold and snow, they need to move south, below the Arad and soon. Usually, precipitation there is a light rain and the pastures of the foothills are quite fertile, even in the winter. They need to see that this is so and Czar Chekov must know that the Princess is not attempting to conquer their land," Bianca insisted.

General Wu Zhou, a keen judge of character, picked up on Enrico's distress and sensed that it was sincere, that he was here to look after the welfare of the women. Yet, this young teen was right, though, he would need proof before they moved. If she was right, they would barely have time to move everything before the snows came, assuming that they did. Further, the Princess had promised everyone to lead them all to a warmer climate. If this winter proved cold, she might lose honor in their eyes. He had to take this gamble.

Wu Zhou spoke quietly, "You have a most honorable plan, Bianca. Yes, we would need such proof and quickly. If these barbarians understand that we do not want their grasslands, perhaps they will stop harassing us. I will send five men with Enrico in the morning." Enrico had no choice in the matter now that he realized his would be a key role.

Princess Shashi added, "Enrico, as long as your women remain as kami, I will send some of my handmaidens to assist them with their needs. As long as they remain as kami, I will protect them from all harm as I do my own handmaidens. I can give you no better guarantee of their safety." Enrico bowed and accepted her pledge. They chatted about what this land was like for some time. At last, the Princess ended the session as the hour was getting late.

Back in their room, Enrico was still a bit angry. "Look, I am supposed to be protecting you both. Now you've gone and sent me off on this side mission. Yes, I can see how pivotal this actually is going to be, but still, I am pledged to your protection."

"You heard the Princess, we will be safe enough," Bianca said. Still, Enrico thought she was being very naive.

"I give you my word that I will protect both of them with my life," Louis swore to Enrico, who at last gave in. "Now then, even more of a problem, how are we to sleep? There are only two beds. I can sleep on the floor."

"Oh don't be silly, Louis. If we must play our part, then we will need all manner of assistance. You must sleep with me in one bed and Enrico with Ilenakova in the other," Bianca replied. "Besides, I don't know how we can possibly sleep tied up like this."

"Okay, I see your point. I will be here for you, Bianca," Louis hastily promised.

She giggled, "Well, here comes the nasty part. I need to use the chamber pot." His face reddened, but he assisted her fully, as did Enrico with Ilenakova. He then helped her lay down so that she didn't have to fall down into bed and crawled in beside her. "Let me rest my head on your shoulders; that may make this more comfortable to sleep." He lovingly snuggled her close to himself, as she slept on her side.

The next morning, a servant brought them their breakfast. After they ate and freshened up, one of the handmaidens came to fetch Enrico, who gave the two women a farewell hug and shook Louis' hand firmly. "Take good care of them," he whispered in his ear. Louis so promised. After he had gone, the one-handed maiden returned saying that the Princess wanted to chat with the two women. Louis, an arm around each of them, followed them into the same large meeting room.

"Louis, why don't you take a walk around our house and city for a while? I would like a private chat with Bianca and Ilenakova," the Princess said. "Besides, my handmaidens need to brush out their hair." He flushed; he had not thought of doing that for her. He agreed and left the room.

While two women set to work on Bianca's long hair and one brushed out Ilenakova's relatively short hair, Princess Shashi chatted. "Something you said last night has made me wonder all night long. You say that self-respect is so important among your people — as much so as honor. Yet, look at me. How can I have any self-respect when I am like this?" She waved her short arms. "I can do nothing for myself. Worse yet is that as a zen-kami, I know absolutely nothing about how to pleasure anyone. Would it be possible for me to somehow entice a zen-kami to come to me here and teach me how it is done, that I may at least learn the only profession left open to me now?"

"I do not know about the zen-kami, Princess, but I do know much about self-respect and how it may be regained, once it has been lost. You see, many years ago, a young monarch was butchered by an evil man, who cut her arms off even shorter than yours. I believe hers were barely six inches long, mere stubs of arms. Yet, she received the special therapy and training that we in Velona know how to do. She recovered her self-respect and went on to become one of the most famous monarchs and sole ruler of her Sea Prince Sector of Barcella."

"Another young woman was brutally attacked by another evil man, who cut off her arms completely! She too received our special therapy and training and became the ruler of Zargarb. She was loved by all her people and did a fantastic job running her country. So, yes, it is possible for one who has been so brutalize, so disgraced, so humiliated as yourself to regain your own self-respect, to learn how to do many things for yourself, and to become a competent, respected leader of your people," Bianca explained. Now at last, Ilenakova realized just where Bianca was headed with all this talk.

"Tell me more about these women of Zargarb and Barcella," Princess Shashi asked a wee bit of hope in her voice and in her eyes. Ilenakova, who knew much more about the two women, chatted about them for another half hour, doing her best to impress the Princess. Astute Bianca already knew that she had Princess Shashi all setup.

With her hair nicely brushed and draped in front of her, Bianca suggested, "I am very good at delivering the Velona therapy."

"Bianca, what must I do to get this wonderful therapy of yours? Do you want gold?" Princess Shashi asked, determined to get some of this herself, somehow, someway.

"No, something as precious as this cannot be bought with money. I will give it to you freely, but when we are finished, if you have found it to be valuable, then I may ask something of you that you can do in return," Bianca replied.

"Oh, thank you, Bianca. What must I do? How is it done? When can we start?" Princess Shashi was eager to experience it. Hope, however small, had kindled in her heart.

"It is a private thing and when we start, we must not be interrupted," Bianca explained. A bit later, the six handmaidens and Ilenakova moved to the side room, where they made their quarters nearby so that they could help their Princess Shashi. Ilenakova began chatting with them.

Alone in the throne room, Bianca said, "Okay, close your eyes. Good. Now I want you to return to the time when the men came to take you away to perform their surgery on you." She was off and running.

The first pass through took only a minute, the whole incident was buried under some kind of drug anesthetic. "I am scared; they lead me and my maidens out of my throne room. They are impatient with my slow gait, and they pick me up and carry me into the doctor's room. He puts a cloth over my face. I am crying and screaming not to do this. I fall asleep. I wake up and I see my beautiful hands and perfect nails are gone! I scream loudly. I hear the screams of my handmaidens too." She described additional aftereffects of the surgery.

A dozen more times through and the drug veil had lifted. Now she was experiencing the operation itself, the pain, the sensations, and feelings in her elbows, and the conversation of the doctors and assistants who were performing the operation on her. Unfortunately, lunchtime came, and Bianca was forced to suspend the session so that they could eat. Ilenakova and her handmaidens came back in to the room, along with Wu Zhou and several servants bringing their noon meal.

"What has happened to you, my Princess?" Wu Zhou asked, seeing her red eyes and the wet cheeks, being dabbed by one of her maidens. "Has Bianca hurt you somehow?" He was exceedingly hostile towards Bianca.

"No, she is helping me, Wu Zhou. I am now re-experiencing the operation. Somehow, I am able to see and feel what they did to me. It is helping me. I feel much better, Wu. It is their therapy," she attempted to explain. Mollified for the moment, he began eating his rice and fish, while a handmaiden fed Princess Shashi, and another two fed Ilenakova and Bianca, insisting that Louis feed himself and not Bianca.

After lunch, Louis asked Ilenakova to come with General Wu Zhou and himself. He wanted to show her much about these people, especially their soldiers and weapons. She agreed, for she was incredibly bored just sitting around, to say nothing of being continually bound as a prisoner. As they walked out of the main house, she commented, "I feel as if I'm being treated as a prisoner here, tied up like this." She was indeed grumbling and complaining.

"Oh, no. You are not a prisoner!" General Wu Zhou broke out of his chronic hostilities. "Rather just the opposite. You are giving my wife, our Princess, the highest honor possible by being like a kami! You must understand just how devastated she is over the loss of her arms and hands. She went from being a royal Princess whose honor is only just less than the Empress herself, the highest possible in Tashien, to that of a zen-kami, a substantially lower honor. Shashi is utterly crushed by this. So by your appearance as a fellow kami, you are giving her the highest honor that you possibly can. Honor is so important to us."

"For us, self-respect is just as important," Ilenakova zinged him. She was good at retaliation in the hostility range, being a fighter herself. "What is honor without self-respect? Tell me that."

He glared back at her. "Look, even if your self-respect is gone, you still have honor to lead and guide you. Look at the millions of worthless soldiers that we have here. They have no self-respect at all, yet they still have their honor to their ancestors to fulfill. Without that, they would be nothing more than criminals," the general countered.

"In Velona, we value people and the contributions that they can make to our society. But I see your point. You instill a drive for them to achieve honor for their ancestors in place of any thrust in life for themselves, their families, and their group. Have you taken a good look at what that has achieved with these peasants and soldiers? How alive are they? How much do they actually contribute to the betterment of your group? Sure, they stand and die, forming a human barrier to protect your Princess."

"Yet, look at those whom you call barbarians. They have a high sense of self-worth, self-respect, self-pride. I watched the battle. One of them was worth between ten and twenty of your honor-driven soldiers. Personally, I would rather command an army of the barbarians than I would command an army of your honor-driven soldiers. As a general, surely you have seen that," Ilenakova retorted and countered.

"Well, yes, that was obvious on the battlefield, but I have to play the hand that was dealt to the Princess Shashi and myself," he countered her, justifying his position.

"What if that hand could be drastically altered for the better?" Ilenakova asked. "Would you be willing to change?"

"Seeing is believing," he countered. The three continued their inspection of New Xin.

Meanwhile, Bianca resumed her therapy session with Princess Shashi. By suppertime, Bianca had the heavy pain off the entire incident, but still it would not erase; it would not relieve with a mountain of laughter. She still held on tightly to the massive loss of her honor and self-respect. They stopped for supper and afterwards, Princess Shashi was too tired to continue. Bianca had to wait until the morning to continue.

After their dinner, Bianca asked Louis to massage her arms; they were aching and burning now. So were Ilenakova's for that matter. He did his best for both women, before they too went to bed.

The next day after the morning rituals were finished, Bianca continued her therapy with the Princess. Bianca asked her, "Could there be something similar to this that happened to you earlier in time?"

Princess Shashi sat there and looked at the images in her mind. There was nothing at all similar in her childhood. "Oh I have these strange images here, but they are probably just my imagination." Bianca ignored that and had her go to the start of one of these that looked promising. She asked her to go through it and tell her what was happening as she re-experienced it.

Shashi began to speak and then became quiet for a time. Bianca sat on the floor mat and waited patiently, though she was intensely curious about just what Shashi was viewing. "Oh my god! I have lived before!" Shashi exclaimed, suddenly opening her eyes and confronting Bianca for the first time with her eyes. "I was the Empress! Oh my god! I was Sho Lin Wu! Some wonderful people from Velona came to Shansee and literally saved me from doom and utter disgrace! Bethany, that was her name. Oh my god! When she came to visit me afterwards, she too had somehow lost her arms completely. She had others with her that had no arms as well and they all did the most marvelous, miraculous things, even though they had no arms. Oh my god! I am my own granddaughter!" Princess Shashi broke into a howling laughter, which just would not stop, even though Bianca ended the session quietly.

When everyone joined them for lunch, Princess Shashi was still laughing so hard that it was nearly impossible for her handmaidens to feed her. The six became infected with her wild cheerfulness and laughter, smiling among themselves as well. Poor General Wu Zhou just stared utterly dumbfounded at his wife. He could not believe what he was seeing. "I've never seen her remotely this happy, so cheerful, so vibrant and full of life," he commented to Bianca. "Will this last?"

"I am not yet finished with her therapy, General, but you should see marked improvement in her outlook on life. She ought to be far more cheerful from now on, especially when I finally finish," she whispered to him.

Since Shashi was still laughing and enjoying her massive relief, Bianca and Ilenakova began therapy on two of her handmaidens, intent upon wiping out their trauma of having their right hands cut off. These women's fear, terror, and pain were somewhat less because they only lost the one hand. Aiding the duo was also the fact that these handmaidens had not suffered the grievous loss of self-respect and honor, as had the Princess. As a result, by that evening, the two handmaidens were now quite cheerful, they had faced their traumas and had erased them as well.

Again, in the quiet of their one room bedroom, Louis massaged the aching arms of Bianca and Ilenakova. Although he said nothing, he feared that their arms would suffer irreparable damage by being so continuously tied and held immobile. While the women were off doing therapy sessions the next day, Louis went in search of the woman who had bound them. Close to noon, he finally found her. Much to his relief, she explained that after six days of binding, she would release them for a day. If not, they would indeed begin to suffer the possibility of permanent damage. "I am keeping an accurate record. Have no fear, young man. Their well-being is my prime charge from my Princess." Louis felt relieved and relayed this news to them at lunchtime.

During the morning session, Ilenakova worked on another of her handmaidens, while Bianca resumed her therapy sessions with Princess Shashi. This distorted, aberrated feeling or sense of honor she wanted tackled head on; it was not right conduct in her worldview. Thus, she had Shashi begin contacting the most recent time that she felt this powerful urge to assign all importance to honor.

Slowly the session progressed. In the late afternoon, Shashi uncovered something quite strange. "I am floating out of my body. Yes, they are burying it. I can see them. I feel this strange energy flooding over me. Weird. I am drawn to it. What am I seeing? Like white dolls, only huge, really huge. What is it that they are saying to me? I am hearing ideas in my mind. Something like: 'You must always remember to honor your ancestors.' Yes, that was it. Over and over, they say that to me until I think that my mind is bursting from it! I can't take it anymore. Now I am being sucked down into the world again. There is a mother giving birth. I am grabbing that baby body now."

Bianca had her go over this one several more times and the content became clearer to the Princess. At last, she blew off its effect on her; she began laughing once more. "They were forcing me to dwell utterly on honoring my ancestors! Well, I like them and would do that anyway," she laughed.

"I feel different, Bianca, really different," Princess Shashi exclaimed. "What was that all about and who were those really strange people? I think it was up in the Helios Grande Mountains."

"Well, I don't know who they were, only the results of what they did to you and your people," Bianca explained. She felt the Princess needed to hear a bit of her conjectures and the two chatted for some time.

That evening, Shashi talked with Wu Zhou at length about all this. The following morning, General Wu Zhou asked Bianca, "Does your therapy only work on those who have suffered a recent injury or trauma, such as my wife and her handmaidens?"

"No, of course not. We usually prefer to give them the therapy first because the trauma often can so horribly impact their lives," Bianca answered him, guessing what was on his mind.

"Once you have finished with her handmaidens who have suffered horribly merely because they were her personal assistants, would it be possible for me to receive this therapy? It probably won't do me any good, but Shashi believes it might. I owe it to her to try. I have never seen her as happy as she has been these last few days. It is truly a miracle," he replied, more honestly and humbly than he had ever spoken to her before.

"Sure, give us a few days more," Bianca answered him, giving him some hope as well.

Once the handmaidens were finished, the binding woman came to them. "It is time that your arms are freed for a whole day. Of course, you must remain here in your room while unbound, but a bath barrel will be brought in, and you may indulge yourselves in a long hot, soaking bath. I believe that it will help with your arms."

A bit later, untied after six days of constant binding, Bianca and Ilenakova's arms were aching and stiff. Louis massaged their arms and helped them with a long, hot bath, three hours long, keeping the servants busy bringing in more hot water. "Serves them right for binding us so long," Ilenakova growled. Her arms were still half-numb and sore.

Later on, two servants came to assist them with washing their hair and then combing it out, a detail that Louis was relieved to have them do. He knew nothing about such matters.

Bianca commented, "Well, I can see the General's mind at work here. He did not want a session today because he does not want to be alone with me with his eyes closed and my arms free. I have not yet fully earned his implicit trust. I can't say that I blame him, though." Ilenakova chuckled, she agreed with Bianca. She certainly would not want to lower her guard to a person whom she had only known for six days.

As they ate their supper, Bianca commented, "Well, I still cannot contact mom. I am growing more and more worried about her and Bethany. Whatever could be going wrong with them?" It was a rhetorical question; none could answer her. "Well, Enrico is still doing fine. He's paralleling the eastern side of the Arad now. He hopes to be at the river in four more days."

The next morning after breakfast was finished, the woman returned to bind the two once more. Ilenakova grumbled, but Bianca put on a brave face. This had to be done, definite progress was being made — she was certain of that. If only she could work a miracle on General Wu Zhou, then things may begin to improve.

This time she sat on the mat in the throne room while Wu Zhou sat on the plush chair in front of her. She had him close his eyes and realized at once that she had been right. Only when she was bound before him did he feel that he could relax his guard completely. She began by having him locate the most recent time that he felt this strong, impulsive urge to honor his ancestors, figuring this was the right approach to take.

All morning long and into the afternoon, she listened to the constant barrage of demeaning, dehumanizing vocalizations coming from his incidents. Late in the afternoon, she finally had gone early enough that he too contacted an event with the doll people between his lives in Tashien. After six times through this one, the General began roaring with laughter. He'd severed the decisions that had kept this honor-aberration of his solidly in place. "I've been fighting those people for centuries now, only I kind of forgot about them and was just fighting everyone who countered me or my wife!" She ended the session quietly once more.

As the servants brought in dinner for the whole group, Bianca observed that the couple was indeed dramatically changed. Gone was their hostility and resentment against life and others. A genuine happiness now filled both of them and it radiated out from them both quite noticeably, in fact.

As they were dining, Wu Zhou said, "Bianca, Ilenakova, Shashi and I have been talking and we have decided to release you from the requirement to appear as a kami when in her presence. After dinner, we will send Sho Tou to you to unbind you."

"Thanks, we appreciate it," Ilenakova replied at once, greatly relieved.

"Thank you both," Bianca added. "However, I think that it may well be wise of us to remain bound as a kami. You see, while you and your handmaidens now understand the situation and know that we mean no disrespect to the Princess, you have a million of your people beyond this room who do not see it this way, not yet anyway. If we break with your long established tradition, this will certainly cause an undo stir among your people. Many will think and believe that we are being disrespectful. I believe that it is wise if we remain bound as a kami." Ilenakova growled, but saw that she was quite right. Their people would see it precisely as a big dishonor.

"Besides, tomorrow, she and I want to start showing Princess Shashi how to do things for herself. Bound as a kami and as helpless as she appears, it will be easier to teach her new ways," Bianca continued.

Princess Shashi bowed to the two. "Thank you both for doing this for me. You are wise and right, of course. Will it really be possible for me to do some things for myself?"

"Yes, as long as you are willing to learn, we have much that we can teach you," Bianca answered.

"There is another matter that we must handle," General Wu Zhou brought up. "Today, it snowed a few flakes. Shashi and I trust your judgment now totally. While our men ought to be getting to this new promised land about now, we do not feel that we should wait another dozen days for their return before taking action. Tomorrow, the Princess will make a speech to our people, and then we will begin our long overland move southward. We must be seen as giving our people the promised warmth of winters."

"Excellent, General Wu Zhou. That is indeed good news," Ilenakova replied enthusiastically. She preferred action to all of this sitting around on her butt. "By the time the real snows come here, we should be so far south so that the little snow that falls will not be a problem."

That evening back in their private bedroom, Louis again performed his nightly ritual, massaging their arms and shoulders once more. When he was done, Bianca felt very playful. She used her foot to tickle Louis, whom she discovered was quite ticklish. "Hey, stop that," he laughed.

She jumped up and said, "You can't catch me to tickle me back." She darted around the room with Louis chasing after her. Of course bound as she was, she knew that he would soon catch her, which he did, tickling her back. At last, she leaned forward and gave him a surprise, passionate kiss. Later, once he had them both tucked into bed, he crawled in beside her and got her head onto his shoulders, in her usual sleeping position.

She whispered, "I really do like you a whole lot, Louis." She kissed him once more, and he responded in kind.

The next morning after breakfast, the three stood silently behind the Princess and the General as they stood on the porch of their wooden house. Before them, the streets were packed densely solid with as many of their people who could possibly crowd in to hear their address.

Princess Shashi spoke loudly and clearly. "These are our dear friends and allies from Velona and Fortress d'Grange, Sea Princesses. They are leading us all to a better new homeland than here. Already, we have seen the first snowflakes of winter coming. None of us likes to live in the cold and snow. I promised you that I would lead all of us to a new homeland, one that was warm in the wintertime. This is just what our friends are helping me do. Already, we have sent out scouts with one of them to get a first view of this new, promised land. By now, they are on their way back with the news. However, we cannot delay another two weeks. Starting today, we are going to dismantle our homes and load the wood onto our wagons and move south. Some of us will go on ahead of the others to begin to prepare homes for the rest who will be bringing up the rear."

"In this new homeland, we shall all be a free people, free from the burdens that we had to bear back in Tashien. Together, you and I will form a new country and new cities. I'm told that the southern ocean lies at our doorstep there. We will be getting in fresh supplies directly from Shansee. We will not starve."

"Since we are now going to become a free people, I want all of you to begin thinking about what that will mean for you and your families. Honor me and our great General by asking yourselves if you could do any job, any work, that you wanted to do instead of what you have been doing, what would that be? Once we are situated with temporary roofs over our heads, we will begin to make those wild dreams of yours come true. A free person is able to choose his or her own destiny. We will make that somehow possible for every one of you. So honor me by giving this some thought. One day down south where it is always warm, we will be asking you what it is that you really do want to do in life, and we will try our best to help make that a reality. Now then, the General needs to begin giving you our plans for moving as soon as possible. None of us want to endure more cold and snow."

The crowd broke into spontaneous clapping, though most politely so. It would take more than mere words to shake so many out of their feelings of uselessness, apathy, hopelessness, and feelings of being nothing but a victim of life. Now the General began outlining the moving process. Some would remain and begin dismantling the many buildings. All the wood would be saved and later reused down south, greatly speeding the construction of so many needed homes. Others would begin to pack up supplies and possessions and begin to head on south, the vanguard of the migration.

Chapter 14 The Migration South

"Where do we begin?" asked Princess Shashi. They were back in the throne room once more. Her servants already had begun to start the lengthy packing. Now Shashi timidly waited to see if there was anything that she really could learn to do for herself.

"First, have someone remove our shoes and socks, please, yours too," Bianca explained. "We use our feet where others use their hands. We are going to begin with learning to feed ourselves. It is hard, mind you, but it can be done. It just takes a lot of practice and patience. At first, things will seem impossibly slow to you, but persist. Once you have mastered a skill, you will no longer be dependent upon another to do this action for you."

Slowly, the two worked with Shashi. The usual wooden sticks were definitely out, instead, they chose to use a cooking spoon for the moment. It was easier to grasp between their toes. They experimented raising the teacups, which had no handles, but even Bianca found it too difficult to manage effectively , having to hold it with both feet. A handmaiden found some other cups, which had a handle, and these proved workable.

Bianca interspersed this training with some additional education. "We have found that if four women such as yourself live together, they can accomplish much, where one alone cannot. Still, Shashi, there will be much that you can do for yourself."

"It is hard, but if I can at least feed myself, that will be something. I've been meaning to ask, what replaces the honor goal? Self-respect only?"

"We have found that there are seven aspects to life," Bianca began explaining her basic Druwid beliefs, which Shashi rapidly saw was truth and simplicity, if one only looked.

Speaking of looking, both Bianca and Ilenakova got very good looks at her feet. They could see that her arches had somehow been greatly increased, so much so that her feet would no longer go flat on the floor. When she stood on her toes, the back of her heel was almost directly above the back ends of her toes. Hence, her shoes gave the appearance of her feet being extremely tiny, a thing of great beauty for these people. They now saw why it made walking so difficult for her as she was basically walking supported only by her toes. Her heels, which ought to have been some six inches or more from the back ends of her toes, were now almost at the same spot, making her basic foot contact with the ground incredibly small. She was forced to take small, tiny steps if only to keep her balance.

When the General joined them for supper, Princess Shashi proudly fed herself for the first time since her mutilation so many years ago. Ilenakova and Bianca likewise fed themselves, if only to give her moral support. "See, I can sort of do this, Wu," Princess Shashi exclaimed, proud of her minor achievement. Although he thought this was a strange way to eat, his emotions got the better of him, and he had to wipe his eyes. She was so happy now and so full of life.

For the next few days, they continued to work with her, slowly getting her able to do some things for herself. Then came the moving day. Bianca and Ilenakova were unbound and allowed one last hot bath, before they and Louis packed their few possessions. He took a few hours off to ride back to the Czar's encampment, explain what was going on, and retrieve their many weapons.

Czar Chekov was extremely pleased to learn that these ants were about to leave the Northern Steppes entirely, moving south of the Arad! He swore that the alliance between them was the strongest possible. "Always, the riders of the Steppes will be ready to come to your aid. Send us word, and we will come." He shook the hand of Louis firmly.

"At least we haven't lost our swords," Ilenakova commented when Louis returned with her many weapons.

"Yes, but I will pack yours on the packhorses. I will be riding beside your wagon," Louis explained.

In the morning, after breakfast, the woman returned once again to bind the two as a kami. Louis helped them don their coats, and they said goodbye to their now familiar room. Already, workers had begun hammering off the outer wall boards. Louis lifted each into the wagon, where they sat with Princess Shashi and her six handmaidens. Her eyes were bright and hopeful; Bianca saw that she was eager to get moving to their new warm land. Already a light sprinkle of snow was falling. It wouldn't stick yet, but it was a harbinger for sure. Louis tied their two packhorses behind the wagon and mounted his tall mare.

Shortly, General Wu Zhou rode up and asked the Princess if she were ready. "Absolutely! Let's get to the warmth!" He grinned, this time they would succeed; she would finally be warm in the winters.

Their driver got the two horses moving and their wagon slowly joined the long caravan heading out of New Xin heading southward. From their seats, they got a good look at the long line of wagons and people. Many soldiers were walking and carrying heavy packs as well. The line extended out a mile before them and several more behind them as they left the city.

Ilenakova began making a careful estimate of their slow progress. She wanted to know how long she must endure just sitting here in a wagon and being tied up. Still, she saw the reverence that others gave to her; they did acknowledge her for honoring their Princess. "Damn, we are not likely to make more than twelve miles each day."

"Does that mean we are facing six weeks to get there?" Bianca asked, doing the math in her head.

"Yep, six weeks of this. Say, how are we going to have a day free of these ropes? Surely we cannot remain bound that long," she asked.

"Oh no. In six days, you will be free for a day as always. You may ride in the wagon behind us on those days," Princess Shashi answered her. "You know, I really would like to learn just how the zen-kami work their magic. I owe Wu Zhou so very much. He has taken care of me all this time without a single complaint. If I can learn to give him the pleasure that a zen-kami can, then that would give me a way to really honor and thank him."

Bored, Bianca decided to continue working on educating Shashi. She began with the most fundamental skill, observing the obvious. This fascinated the Princess as well as her handmaidens, who joined in with the lessons, to help pass the time.

An hour before dark, they halted and men began scurrying like ants, erecting the numerous canvas square tents, which would be their shelters each evening. Once they were setup, the women set to work preparing a hot dinner, using charcoal stoves. "At least we don't have to worry about cooking," Bianca teased Ilenakova as they sat watching the women preparing the meal for all of them. Louis was unpacking their gear in the tent next to that of the Princess. They would have a lot of space with only the three of them inside this huge square tent, he noted.

That evening after he had once more massaged their arms and shoulders and gotten them tucked in, he crawled under the blankets beside Bianca. "You know, I have an idea, Bianca. Once we get these people settled into their new land, why don't we see if we can hop a boat for Shansee and see if we can find your mother and Bethany?"

She leaned over a bit and gave him a loving kiss before whispering, "Thanks, Louis. That's a good idea. We would be well over half way there. If we cannot get a boat, we could ride along the coastline below the Desert of Desolation and so get to Tan Lon Province. Good thinking." She didn't tell him that she already had a similar thought. Resting her head on his shoulders, she again tried to contact Dita and failed as usual.

Day after day, they continued their slow southerly progress. Steadily the temperatures dropped during the night as winter was slowly approaching. At last, Enrico and the six scouts met them and the scouts eagerly gave their stellar report to their General and Princess. The new land was all that had been promised!

Bianca had contacted Enrico every evening, bringing him up to date with what was going on in New Xin. Thus, when he returned with the scouts on October 5, he already knew what to expect. "You look tired," Ilenakova suggested with a wry grin as he rode up to her wagon.

"Yes, we rode hard and fast — long days in the saddle. I had hoped for a long, hot bath when I returned," he teased her.

"Oh no. Then you can't share our tent tonight," she teased him back. He feigned a mock protest.

"Well, then," he said dismounting and tying his horse to the back of the slow moving wagon and climbing in to sit beside Ilenakova and Bianca,

"I guess I will just have to eat this chocolate bar by myself."

"No fair!" Ilenakova protested, squirming her body around somehow to snatch a bite. He purposely held it out of her reach. Bianca dutifully leaned over and took a bite herself.

"You can sleep in my tent," Bianca suggested, quietly slurping on the melting chocolate. Enrico relented and held it for Ilenakova to take a bite herself.

"Did you miss me?" he asked. Both women leaned their heads on his shoulders in response.

"Well, tell us about the trip," Ilenakova insisted, now that the chocolate bar had vanished. "We've been sitting around tied up." Nearby, Princess Shashi giggled at her description, as he began telling them about their long trip.

When he finished, Princess Shashi lamented, "Gosh, I wish I could ride a horse for a while. Being cooped up here in this wagon is butt breaking."

"Your wish is my command, Your Highness," Enrico replied.

"Hey, don't forget us," Ilenakova teased him. He retrieved their two short Steppes mares and saddled them while walking, a challenging feat at that. Then, he gently lifted Ilenakova out of the moving wagon and sat her on one mare, helping her get the reins in between her teeth. Next, he lifted Bianca out and onto her mare.

"Okay, Princess, your turn." He lifted the startled Shashi out of the wagon and set her astride his horse. After tying the reins together, he inserted the loop between her arms. "I think you can manage without having to bite down. Let's see how it goes, shall we? If you have too much trouble, you can bite down on them as Ilenakova and Bianca are doing. See, you can ride as well as the rest of us." He walked along side of the horse, making very sure that nothing unexpected happened to the Princess.

"I am actually riding a horse!" Shashi exclaimed, wild with excitement. "I haven't been on a horse since I was a little girl! This is so much better than riding in the wagon!" Shortly, General Wu Zhou saw her and came galloping back to her, his eyes were wide in total amazement.

"Shashi! This is incredible! You are riding!" he exclaimed.

"Yes, I don't have much control, so I might have to bite down like they are doing. This is so much fun, Wu. Once we get all settled in, you are going to have to take me riding often. Look at me! I am actually doing this." Princess Shashi was extremely proud of her achievement. After this, Shashi spent part of everyday riding along on Enrico's horse, which was conveniently much shorter than the usual Tashien bred horses, which stood as high as Louis' mare.

That night in their tent, Ilenakova commented as Enrico began massaging her arms and shoulders, "I sure am glad that you are back."

"Oh, you like my massages, do you?" he teased.

"Well, yes. It was terribly boring for me. I know that Shashi has said that we no longer need to appear as a kami while we around her, but we saw just how much her people believe that we are honoring her by being bound like this. Honestly, if I hadn't seen their admiration and respect with my own eyes, I wouldn't have believed it was so. I haven't the heart to disappoint so many of them. Still, it is a royal pain," Ilenakova commented.

"Kinky," Bianca added her appraisal to the mix. "Besides, I have an excuse to lie on Louis' shoulders all night long."

"You don't need any such excuse," Louis teased her and she grinned.

"Say, still no word about your mother and Bethany?" Enrico asked seriously.

"Nope, no one has been able to reach either of them," Bianca answered, growing serious herself. "I think Alessa knows something, but she is purposely not telling me. Louis and I have worked it out, Enrico. Once we get these folks to their new land, we are then going to ride along the coastline of the Desert of Desolation and go to Tan Lon Province and search for them ourselves. Want to come along?"

"Have you cleared this with home base?" he asked.

"Don't be silly. You know what they will say. We're going," Bianca said flatly.

"Enrico, we are making about twelve miles each day. How soon do you think that we will be there?" Louis asked. His knowledge of the local geography here was about nil.

"Twelve miles you say, well, let's see. I'd guess around October 20 we should be at the coast where the Dakar River meets the ocean, dividing the Arad from the Southlands. That whole area is still uninhabited, plus we found a grove of date and fig trees just on this side of the Dakar. Unfortunately, ladies, I ate all that I brought back with me. As far as I can see on just a quick tour, these people ought to be able to find everything they need to live well there. Well, except rice paddies; those will be a bit hard to create there. I suppose they could just import the rice that they need from Shansee," Enrico explained.

Bianca lay on Louis' shoulder, snuggling up as best she could. She thought, "Only fifteen more days of this, then I can head off to search for mom."

Five days later, the weather became noticeably warmer in the daytime. They had reached Juda Arad. Still, the nights were chilly, but the sun soon warmed everyone up as they ate breakfast. The warm weather certainly heightened Princess Shashi's morale considerably. She was now quite playful in the morning. She occasionally lifted a bit of food up to Wu's mouth, as if feeding him. He, of course, accepted it and hugged her. The change in their dispositions Enrico found remarkable indeed. Still, by evening, everyone was quite tired of riding, welcoming the relief of their tents.

On October 19, they reached the Dakar River where it met the coast. Here at its mouth, the river was shallow, wide, and easily forded. Enrico drew a quick sketch to show Princess Shashi and General Wu Zhou just where they were now located with respect to the desert and Tan Lon Provence. They were amazed. "We are really close enough that we could go there overland along the coast," General Wu Zhou observed. "Indeed, this place looks absolutely ideal for us."

The next morning, the tent city sprang up not far from the coast and close to the fresh water supply. General Wu Zhou now had to direct the construction projects, leaving Princess Shashi to deal with their supplies and organizational matters. Louis and Enrico took some time off to replenish their supplies, adding freshwater and all the fresh fruits and berries that they could find some miles from the ants who were building their new city. While they had plenty of rice, dried fish, and dried vegetables, they needed fruits, especially if they were going to head off towards Shansee.

That night as the four were getting ready for bed, Alessa contacted Bianca. *We've finally contacted them! They are alive and have escaped their captors. However, they have messed up again. Somehow, they got their lower arms cut off — something about being turned into a kami or some such thing. Bethany was not too clear on that. Also, they are pretty much lamed up, something about their feet's arches are now so high that they can barely walk. But that's not the worst of it. Their captors have gotten them all addicted to opium! We kind of thought something like that was going on, but we were not sure. They have been rescued along with San Min and four others who are all in the same condition. Right now, Bethany will be contacting us only when she is lucid, which is apparently only for a brief time in the mornings. The Forze Segrete members are arranging their escape. Dita managed to kill the man who did this to them, but he was the power lord there. Now chaos is spilling out into the streets of Shansee, but Jemma and Fina are all right and with the Forze Segrete folks and will continue their spying mission.*

Wow, mom screwed up again! Okay, we are just about done with our mission here. We are right at the mouth of the Dakar River. It is a short trip to pass by the Desert of Desolation and enter Tan Lon Province. We four are going to head there in a day or so to help rescue mom and the others, Bianca sent.

But we don't know where they are being taken just yet. Perhaps you should delay a few more days until we know better what their condition is and where they are heading, Alessa sent back.

Okay, but only for a few days. Mom needs rescuing again and we are really very close to Tashien. Yes, I know that the place is in turmoil and all that, but we have to get to them. Bianca was totally determined to come to her mom's aid.

Well, you are the closest of any of us to them, she got Alessa to admit and knew that they would soon get the okay to proceed.

Chapter 15 Crime and Extortion

Alessandra, a young dressmaker, added another pin. Kneeling, she was fitting the hem on the new dress she'd just made for Mrs. Atwater, who was standing patiently as she nearly finished. Just then, another person entered her shop, Alessandra's Fine Dresses. The blonde seamstress looked up from her kneeling position and her heart skipped a beat. Two young, ill-dressed men were standing just inside her doorway. "Thugs!" she thought to herself, but said, "I'll be with you in a minute." She hastily put the last pin in the dress's hem and rose to see what these two wanted.

They held daggers in their right hands, she noted as she approached them and her hands shook slightly. "Your shop needs some protection. We're that protection. Give us fifty gold now and nothing will happen to your store this week," the taller one said in an intimidating voice. The other snickered in a snide manner.

Alessandra gasped, "That's more than I make in a week!"

"You don't pay, bad things can happen — like this," the thug said. His dagger sliced through one of her dresses in her display window, cutting a six-inch tear in its bodice.

"Or this," the other lad added, cutting a foot long gash in the second dress on display.

"But I don't have that much gold here! Please, stop ruining my dresses," she pleaded, knowing that it would do no good.

"Get it. We'll be back tomorrow to collect. Don't have it by then, and your shop will have more damage than a couple cuts," the leader lad threatened. The two whirled on their feet and left, slamming the door and nearly breaking its glass.

Alessandra's knees nearly gave out; she grabbed hold of a table edge to support her. "Dear me!" Mrs. Atwater exclaimed. "Thugs! Just mean, vicious thugs! You ought to report this to the police, Alessandra."

"What can they do? How will I pay them? I don't make fifty a week," Alessandra was near tears.

"Say, I know just who might help. I do know many people in Velona. Are we done with the hem? Can I change now?" Mrs. Atwater asked. She was the wife of a wealthy merchant. Nearly fifty, Mrs. Atwater prided herself on knowing all the influential of Velona. True, she was more of a gossip, but someone had to speak out — that was her motto. Alessandra helped her change into her billowing cotton print dress, carefully sitting the new pink satin ball gown aside. She'd finish the hem sewing later.

"Now come with me, dear child. Yes, put your closed sign in your window. My carriage is just outside waiting. I *insist*, come on," Mrs. Atwater never took no for an answer. Her firm arm, clasped around the young dressmaker's arm, she pulled her towards the door. Distraught Alessandra barely had time to flip the sign in her window as the wealthy woman pulled her outside. "Ah, Leonardo, yes, lend us your hand please. We are going to 42 Hampton Way directly."

A half hour later, her carriage pulled up at the rot-iron gates. Several children were playing on the spacious lawn. An older woman, evidently watching them, came to the gate. "Hi, can I help you?" asked Sandra.

"Yes, Mrs. Atwater to see Mrs. Dianna Anka West Po, please. This is an emergency," she said, her voice full of important concern. Sandra smiled. This wasn't the first time this old gossip had dropped in for a visit. She opened the gate and sent Enyo to fetch Dianna. Well, Enyo was also Dianna, her youthful second body, so she was not surprised to find Dianna coming out of the front door long before Enyo had gotten to the door. Enyo, now nine, smiled at herself, that is, Dianna, and returned to the ball game.

The driver had pulled up by the front door and was assisting Mrs. Atwater to step down as Dianna walked up. "Hello Mrs. Atwater. What brings you to see me today?" Dianna had ink on her hands. She'd been busy making further detailed drawings for this new steam engine line with cars that was now under construction.

Leonardo next assisted the young dressmaker to step down. Mrs. Atwater said in a most urgent tone, "This is Alessandra, the dressmaker over on Ashway Lane. This is a most serious matter, and we simply must speak with you immediately and in private."

Dianna sighed; she was terribly busy with the drawings, but also knew that Mrs. Atwater was one of those people who simply would not go away until she'd said her piece. "Okay, follow me. Pardon me if I don't shake hands, they are full of ink. I'm in the middle of an engineering drawing for Bale."

They followed her inside and to the large study to the right, where Dianna had been working. The room was a complete mess of drawings and plans scattered about any available flat surface, including the floor. "Sorry about the mess, but Bale needs these plans finalized soon," Dianna explained, hoping the old gossip would get the message.

The older woman sat down in one of the plush chairs, motioning for Alessandra to do likewise. "Dianna, you simply must help us. It's Alessandra. This morning while she was fixing the hem on my new pink satin ball gown, two young thugs came into her shop demanding protection money, fifty gold a week. She doesn't make that much. Well, anyway, those two hooligans proceeded to slice up and ruin two of her dresses on display. They said that they would be back tomorrow for the money or else Alessandra's dress shop would suffer incredible damage. Now, Dianna, this simply *cannot* be allowed to continue. I happen to know that six other merchants on Ashway Lane are also being forced to pay this protection money. I know so because I *saw* the thugs collecting from the store owners while I was there. We simply won't stand for any more of this lawlessness, this intimidation of honest, hardworking citizens of Velona. So what are *you* going to do about it? I would have taken this directly to *Bale*, but I know our monarch is terribly busy." She finally wound down.

Dianna knew that Bale would not have the patience to deal with this busybody, and she knew that Mrs. Atwater also knew this. That's why she had come to Dianna, Bale's younger sister. She sighed, wondering how to get her handled quickly so she could finish these important drawings, which the construction engineers needed later today. "Cosima? Cosima, are you around?" she called out, keeping her fingers crossed.

"Coming," Cosima hollered back from her bedroom, where she was just finishing adjusting her fancy makeup. She and Alessa were now dabbing with using the latest of fashion statements, makeup. This they could now get away with, because nearly everyone was gone, excepting Dianna, of course, who really didn't care what the girls did, fashion wise.

Shortly, Cosima entered, wearing her Alexa high heels beneath a green satin ball gown, her long light brown hair draped over her right shoulder. Her cherry red, long nails were daintily visible, as she held her hands before her billowing dress. She wore matching lipstick and her hazel eyes were accentuated with the latest in eye makeup, a coal black liner. Right behind this fifteen year old young woman came her constant companion, Alessa, now thirteen, going on fourteen and nearly of age as she constantly reminded everyone. Alessa wore a blue satin ball gown with her Alexa high-heeled boots. Her makeup matched that of Cosima. They had been doing each other's makeup when Dianna called.

"Hello," said Cosima, as she noticed the two guests. "Mrs. Atwater, so pleased to see you once again. How is your cat doing?" She'd once had to sleuth for this woman. Her cat had gone missing, and she'd paid Cosima fifty gold to track down the cat for her.

"Why, she's just fine. I have you to thank for that! Yes, this is Alessandra, my dressmaker from Ashway Lane." They shook hands politely. Cosima noted that Mrs. Atwater had certainly been petting her cat this morning; she had several cat hairs on her dress. However, she also noted that Alessandra was quite distressed and surmised that the older woman had come about Alessandra.

Dianna quickly repeated what Mrs. Atwater told her, hoping that Cosima would take over so she could get back to her important drawings. "Yes, we must handle this immediately," Cosima said eager to get a new case. She also saw how annoyed Dianna was, and added, "If you will both step into my office, Alessa and I would like to hear the details, and how we may be of service to you, Alessandra." Dutifully, the two women followed the two teens to the study next to Dianna's. From the slow walking, Mrs. Atwater surmised that these two young ladies were also properly dressed, wearing Alexa boots, though she had no idea that they were wearing the "original" Alexa boots, made by the Grey Creatures and which had long ago been copied and mass produced by Alexa, who was now called Ania and who was currently off helping to sink opium shipments with Kali.

In contrast to the messy office of Dianna, Cosima and Alessa's office was immaculate. Even the desk smelled of polish. Cosima motioned for the two to have a seat on the plush, velvet couch, while she sat behind her desk and Alessa took her seat just to the side of the desk. Using her long nails, Cosima opened her notebook, picked up her pencil, and began writing. She looked up and began asking some basic questions, such as the precise address of her shop.

Then, Cosima had Mrs. Atwater describe the other similar protection payoffs that she had witnessed, which the older woman was dying to relate in full detail! Cosima took copious notes. When the woman finally wound down, Cosima at last spoke. "Okay, what time do you open in the morning, Alessandra? Nine it is. You may expect to see us there at that time. We will be arresting these thugs. If you ever have any others threaten you, send us word, and we will handle those too. Thank you very much, Mrs. Atwater for bringing this to our attention."

"But my dear, don't you need the police?" asked Mrs. Atwater.

"I am the police," Cosima replied. Her long nails and fingers deftly picked up her official badge and held it so the two women could view it. "See, I am *the* Detective Inspector of Velona. You have come to the right place."

"But dears, those thugs had daggers and who knows what else," Mrs. Atwater protested.

"Trust us," Alessa spoke up. "Those nasty thugs will be no match for either Cosima or me." Mrs. Atwater looked at the two elegantly dressed, high fashion young teens and didn't believe them at all, but she didn't want to offend them. Cosima and Alessa escorted them back to their carriage and reminded Alessandra that they would be there when she opened at nine tomorrow morning.

Once they had left, Cosima said eagerly, "The case is afoot, Alessa. Come on, we have more sleuthing to do yet today."

The two had been accumulating the various police reports of protection extortion for the last month, attempting to find a pattern in them, before taking action. "Usually, those being threatened do not come forward," Cosima pointed out to her assistant, Alessa.

"Because they are afraid?" asked Alessa.

"Precisely so. Thugs can be very persuasive against the common folk of Velona. As I said yesterday, the reported incidents are probably one tenth of the actual occurrences. Now let's see if those six that Mrs. Atwater witnessed are among the reported ones," Cosima said, diving into the stacks of reports she pulled from her desk drawer. Alessa took another pile and began searching as well, her long blonde hair continually falling over the pages.

"Well, none here. How about you?" asked Cosima.

"Nope, none here either. I see what you mean. Folks really are intimidated into silence by these men. We really must do something about this extortion racket," Alessa replied. "Go undercover, perhaps?" she suggested mischievously. She wanted to see some real action.

"I'm beginning to think so, Alessa. We should start making some plans," Cosima answered.

Arturo drove the two teens to Alessandra's Fine Dresses the next morning. The two teens wore their usual satin ball gowns and Alexa heels. They'd done up each other's makeup in the latest fashion and looked quite presentable, as Arturo held their hands when they stepped out onto the street. "If you will wait for us, we will have two prisoners shortly, I do believe," Cosima spoke quietly. Alessandra was just opening her shop as the two teens entered.

"Fine morning to nab two thugs," Cosima greeted the woman.

"Are you sure? I mean they had daggers and looked terribly strong," Alessandra replied very nervously. The last thing she wanted was to have the official Detective Inspector harmed in her shop.

"Oh they will hand over their weapons and not give us any trouble," Cosima replied absentmindedly. She was now gazing over the dresses that Alessandra had on display. "Say, you make some really nice looking gowns." She ran her hands over the blue velvet gown, feeling the fabric between her fingers and long red nails. "Say, how about making Alessa and me one of these velvet gowns. I just love the feel of the velvet. Alessa, what color would you prefer?"

Very pleased to get a pair of orders for her most expensive dresses, Alessandra began showing the two teens the various colors that she had in stock. The two girls began admiring the choices, "I think that your blonde hair would go well with this darker blue, Alessa," Cosima suggested. "Now which green do you think looks best on me?"

Just then, the two thugs entered the front door, daggers drawn. Cosima looked up and said softly, "Just stand there a minute. I have to choose my dress color first." Alessandra's fear rose as she saw them enter, but she was shocked to see the two ruffians suddenly freeze as if suddenly struck immobile. Cosima added, "They will remain motionless while I choose. What do you think, Alessa?"

"This green goes better with your eyes," she replied, and Cosima told Alessandra to make hers out of this one.

"Okay, let's get down to business," Cosima then said, putting her Detective Inspector badge around her neck so that she looked official. She and Alessa walked up to the stiff-standing men. "You will hand over your daggers now." To Alessandra's utter amazement, both thugs did as asked, hanging their weapons to Alessa. Cosima bent down and her long red nails picked a thread off one of the men's pant legs. "Ah, incriminating evidence. I do believe that this will match that dress there which you deliberately cut with your dagger yesterday." She pulled an evidence sack from her purse and deposited the strand.

She faced the two still frozen men and said formally, "You are both under arrest for extortion, criminal damage to property, and threatening the well-being of shop owners on Ashway Lane. You will turn around, walk out, and get into yonder carriage." Both men attempted to resist her, but she simply took control of their bodies and marched them outside Alessandra's shop, just as Mrs. Atwater came bustling up.

"Oh my! Yes, those *are* the two thugs that threatened her yesterday and cut up her dresses! How have you managed to capture them?" she asked completely astounded that the two men were voluntarily climbing into their coach, while Alessa was holding onto their two daggers.

"As I said, they will be no problem for your Detective Inspector, Mrs. Atwater. I've just arrested them and will take them in for questioning now. I must compliment you on having a fine dressmaker. Alessa and I have just ordered a dress for each of us. Her velvet dresses are simply wonderful. Thanks for pointing us to Alessandra's."

For once, Mrs. Atwater couldn't think of a single thing to say! She quickly entered the shop to chat with Alessandra and find out what all she had already missed. Cosima and Alessa climbed into the carriage, facing the two men. "Arturo, take us to Warehouse Number 52. I believe that it is currently empty. I wish to question these two men at some length."

Soon the carriage began rolling through the bustling streets of Velona, heading for the docks and the warehouse district. "Who are you? Where are you taking us?" the leader of the two spoke. Cosima relaxed her total control over the two thug's bodies slightly.

"As I said, I am the Detective Inspector of Velona and this is my assistant. You are both under arrest at this time. We are taking you to an abandoned warehouse where I can question you as I see fit. Alessa, please tie their hands behind their backs very securely." Alessa grinned and did so, though it was a bit awkward, dressed as they were and crowded into the carriage.

At the warehouse, Alessa pushed one of their daggers into the men's back to convince them to step out of the carriage. Arturo again held their hands so they could step out gracefully in their flowing dresses and heels. Alessa marched the men inside, following Cosima, who walked confidently into the currently empty warehouse. Later this fall it would be full of grain sacks ready for shipment to other countries.

Alessa walked them over to two chairs, which they had fixed up yesterday afternoon. Cosima took her position at the desk, where she had her notepad and pencils at the ready. Once Alessa securely tied them to the chairs, she walked gracefully over to her seat beside the desk. Cosima now began her formal questioning.

"Names," she asked first.

"We ain't saying nothing to you bitches," one spoke hostilely and spat at them. Cosima had allowed for this and his wet projectile fell far short of her.

"Okay, we can do this the easy way or the hard way. It makes no difference to us. Alessa, will you take one of their daggers. I believe that we will begin with the removal of mister foul-mouth's right ear."

Alessa flashed a coy grin with her cherry red lips, daintily picked up one of the daggers, and walked slowly over to him, her heels clicking on the stone floor. "Oh, I do hope your dagger here is sharp. I hate appendage removal with dull blades. Which ear did you say I should cut off first, Detective Inspector?" she asked once again flashing a coy smile.

"His right ear. He's not going to need it much longer," Cosima replied. "Do be careful, dear. Don't get his foul blood on your dress. Blood stains are *so* hard to wash out," she added.

"Wait! Ramos Seville. He's Ettore Bastio," the thug answered at last.

"Darn! Why did you have to open your big mouth?" Alessa complained. "You're spoiling my fun!"

"Now, then that is a good start. I happen to know that you boys are just too stupid to have thought up this protection racket scheme on your own. I want to know who thought it up and who is your boss?" Cosima asked, having finished writing down their names clearly on her pad. She looked up expectantly.

"None of your damn business, bitches. You will pay for this! You are both dead women! I swear, you are both walking dead!" Ramos screamed out.

"Not very polite is he? Well, when I am finished here with you this morning, you will be sent to Isla la Roca, our penal island, where you will spend the rest of your days. As I understand it, they are exceedingly short of women in that prison. I should expect that you both will soon become the bitches for those desperate, ruthless criminals in the Roca. Perhaps, Alessa, we should help prepare them for their new roles as prison bitches. Belay that removal of his ear. Instead, we should remove their man-ness so that they would be better suited for their new women roles in the Roca."

Alessa had tied their legs to the chairs so now she deftly used the dagger to cut through their belts. She cut into their pants to reveal their underwear partially. "You — you wouldn't dare," Ramos cried out.

"Oh darn, Detective Inspector. I forgot to get the fire going. The staunch iron is cold. When I cut them off, they'll bleed all over the place. I sure don't want to clean up that big of a mess. Can you delay a few minutes while I heat up the fires and get the iron hot so I can sear the wound shut once I cut them off?" Alessa asked.

"Yes, assistant. We can wait. We must see that these two pretty boys are properly ready to take on their new roles as Roca Bitches," Cosima replied. "Now then, where was I? Oh yes, I want to know who is your boss? Who thought up this extortion scheme, Ramos?"

"You — you — you can't do this! It's against the law," Ramos squealed.

"Perhaps you bitches haven't noticed, but I *am* the law here. And I most certainly can do this. Well, actually my assistant can, because she is very adept with a dagger. You won't feel too much pain, unless your dagger is dull. In that case, it's your own fault for not taking better care of your daggers. Now then, who is your boss and who thought up this scheme of yours?" Cosima repeated her question.

Alessa hollered from a distance behind them, "Please, Ramos, don't answer her! You'll spoil my fun! Keep quiet, please." She struggled to keep from laughing.

"Okay, okay. Keep that bitch away from us," Ramos pleaded. "Cardinal Reina Lano. It's his plan."

"I thought I told you to shut up!" Alessa said in mock anger from behind them.

"Excellent, Ramos. How and when and where do you meet with this Cardinal?"

"Saturday nights, after mass, he and his men come to a warehouse — around ten."

"What warehouse?" He quickly told her, and they heard Alessa's heels clicking on the stone floor returning towards them. She looked angry, as if they had spoiled her pleasure. Sweat dripped down Ramos' forehead.

"Very well. Alessa, free them from the chairs. We will take them to the city lockup and schedule them on the next boat to the Roca," Cosima replied, picking up her notebook and putting it and her pencil into her purse. Shortly, Alessa marched the men back out and into the carriage.

While they rode to the police station's lock up building, Ramos threatened her again. "When the Cardinal finds out about this, you are a dead woman!"

"When the Cardinal comes to the Roca to join you, perhaps you will be able to convince the others there to make him their bitch instead of you," Cosima retorted.

A while later, Alessa marched the men into the police lock up building. She handed the daggers over to the waiting man, while Cosima read their names and charges. "They are to be shipped off to Isla la Roca on the next boat. Hold them here until then," she ordered.

"Yes, Detective Inspector," the policeman replied, grabbing a large ring of keys. Just then, Ramos, though his hands were still tied, made a grab for his dagger and tried to hold it to Cosima's throat.

"Untie us and let us go," he screamed in desperation. Alessa's hand flashed out and landed on his shoulder's key location. Instantly, his arm became numb, the dagger falling harmlessly onto the stone floor.

"I have half a notion to make this permanent," Alessa said angrily.

"Bitch!" Ramos yelled. Alessa tightened her grip and then released it. His right arm was now permanently numb, though he didn't fully realize this yet. The two teens walked slowly out of the station and Arturo helped them into the carriage.

"Any trouble?" he asked.

"Not really. Home, please, we now have a whole lot of work to do and fast," Cosima explained. "No, cancel that. I need to see Bale first, then Chief Inspector Adolfo, and then home."

A half hour later, the two walked into the sprawling offices of Bale West Po, the monarch of Velona. Luck was on their side, Chief Inspector Adolfo was just coming out of a meeting with Bale. "Excuse me, Chief Inspector," Cosima caught his attention. "We've just captured a pair of thugs who have been extorting protection money from shopkeepers. We've gotten them to talk, and we know who is behind this crime spree. Would you join us with Bale for a minute? This is very sensitive information." He smiled and followed them into Bale's office.

"Back so soon, Chief Inspector," Bale grinned, looking up from his enormous desk. He saw and heard the teens following him and knew something was up. "Cosima, Alessa, my, you both look very fashionable this morning."

They flashed him a grin and the three took seats. Cosima then outlined what she had just learned. "Damn, this is bad news. The Cardinal is involved, damn," Bale cursed.

"Indeed, this is a problem," Chief Inspector Adolfo added. "We cannot officially arrest the head of the Church of Jehosanity here in Velona, because he is still a legal citizen of Megalos, not Velona. The best we could do is to expel him from Velona."

"That hardly seems fair for all the harm he's done to our people," Alessa exclaimed rather annoyed with this unexpected turn.

"Well, he's a dirty Holy Man," Cosima stated. "Perhaps, we should delay taking any action. From my deductions, there are two separate gangs that are involved doing the extortion."

"Right, that was my own conclusion," Chief Inspector Adolfo added. "You see, Bale, we believe that there is another gang down in the Little Tashien section of town extorting shop owners there. The one that Cosima ran into this morning runs their racket in the merchant district. I know of this Ramos fellow. He's had several run-ins with us before, fighting and petty thefts. He's always gotten off because his victims refused to come forward."

"Well, I found him guilty this time and sentenced him to the Roca," Cosima added. "He's off the streets now, but there are probably more in his gang. If I may be so bold, I believe that we need to gather more information on these gangs. Then, when the time is right, we capture all of them at the same time and ship them all off to the Roca. If you will leave the Cardinal to me, I also believe that I can see that he gets what he deserves. You both will know nothing about it."

Bale grinned; he liked the cunning of his adopted niece. "Excellent, what I don't know, I cannot be made to say. Yes, Chief Inspector, you and your Detective Inspector have complete authority from me to deal with this crime spree as you see fit. Do let me know when it is over so that I can make a public proclamation to that effect."

The meeting over, Cosima asked Arturo to drive them around the block where the clandestine meeting with the Cardinal was held. She wanted to see just what the layout there was. A plan was slowly forming in her mind.

Back home, she explained to Alessa, "On Saturday night, we are going to don some disguises and case the place. Our objective is to identify some of the thugs who are running the extortion scheme in Little Tashien. We don't fit in with all those yellow-skinned immigrants there so it is harder for us to do what we did today. I need to discover at least one of them and then we can visit Little Tashien and do a little spying for ourselves. Somehow, we need to find a way to apprehend all these criminals at the same time.

On Friday afternoon, Cosima and Alessa began to get ready for their double date. As usual, Gerardo West Po was taking Cosima to the formal dance at the Foundation. Tonight, he was bringing along a friend of his for Alessa. As the two slowly helped each other into their fanciest of Annelise ball gowns, Alessa said nervously, "I've never been on a blind date before. What do I do if he turns to be a pig or something?"

"I don't think that Gerardo would do that to you," Cosima replied. "If he turns out to be really bad, you could let others cut in on you or maybe pretend that you aren't feeling too well. I will play along and get Gerardo to bring us home. How's that? Gosh, this is awfully tight!" Alessa finally got her corset tightened up and tied off the laces.

"Well, it is only a twenty inch waist. I am glad we didn't try the smaller ones," Alessa said. "I don't think I could have tightened it fully."

A bit later, Alessa exclaimed, "You're right! This is so tight I can hardly breathe." Cosima finally got Alessa's fully tightened up. "Well, now for the rest."

Two hours later, both girls finally were dressed. Their hoops held their satin gowns out nearly fourteen feet across at the hemline. Their narrow waists fully accentuated their busts, which both fully appreciated. Both hoped that theirs would one day fill out like Dita's. Now they had no choice but to move slowly, wearing the extremely high heeled Annelise boots. "Remember small steps; that's what Dita always says. Small steps," Cosima reminded her sister. Now they brushed out each other's hair and set to work on donning the latest fashion makeup. They joined the others for supper, though they ate far less than normal.

At last, Gerardo knocked on their door. Gliding across their long hallway, Cosima insisted on being the one to greet him. Alessa followed nervously behind her. Sandra and Luisa both chuckled, "Were we ever like that?" Sandra asked. They and the many nine year olds were still eating, most demanding more pie for desert.

Gerardo wore his finest linen suit, white, with twin tails and black shiny shoes, and tall black stovepipe top hat, so popular among the fashionable men these days in Velona. He removed his hat and bowed to Cosima. "Wow. You look absolutely stunning tonight, Cosima."

She smiled and took his hand, glancing at the young lad he'd brought along for Alessa. "Oh, Alessa, this is my friend Arsenio Bartolo. Arsenio, this is Miss Alessa Brozena Malina." The lad was just over six feet tall, three inches more than Gerardo. He was thin and fifteen. His relatively short black hair looked freshly washed, slightly unmanageable now. He, too, wore a fancy suit; his was blue linen. His highly polished black shoes matched his tall hat as well.

He bowed and said shyly, "Good evening, Alessa. You look incredibly beautiful as well." Alessa took his hand, but realized that he was slightly shy. Well, she thought, at least he isn't a pig. He was rather cute, she decided. He whispered, "I've never been out with one dressed as fancy as you are. Forgive me if I don't quite know what to do. Why are we walking so slowly?"

She grinned and whispered, "We are wearing some very high heeled boots from Annelise. We can only take the smallest of steps. Here, I'll show you." She pulled back her giant hoop skirt so he could catch a glimpse of her very fancy black boots.

"Oh my!" he whispered.

"Yes, I do need to hold on to you most of the time," she whispered back.

"Oh, please do."

Gerardo had brought his own carriage and after the men helped their dates climb in, they joined them. "To the Foundation dance," he ordered his driver and they were off.

As they rode along, Gerardo chatted, "Well, dear, I've been busy this week, working out likely scenarios for what will happen when the opium supply is cut off."

"Oh do go on, let's hear them. Gerardo's always got keen insights into people's motivations and actions," Cosima explained to Alessa and Arsenio.

At the formal dance, the two couples joined many hundreds of others all pretty much dressed the same. That is, fancy ball gowns of the Annelise variety predominated, though some women wore the less dramatic Velona gowns. Uniformly, all the men wore similar fashionable suits. So much so, that it was hard to tell them apart.

Alone on the dance floor at last, Arsenio asked, "Alessa, are you also into all of those crime solving mysteries that Gerardo and Cosima are?"

"Oh no. I am more interested in fighting and breeding horses," she replied. "What do you do? Oh dear, this corset is so tight that I believe we will have to dance every other one. I need to catch my breath. Wearing this is just as mom told me. Sorry, Arsenio."

"Nothing to be sorry about, Alessa. You look gorgeous. I am an inventor. One day, I hope to be as famous as the incredible Enyo was. Bale West Po has already given me the commission to develop a prototype metal sailing ship based upon the steam engine design of Dianna. If my design works, as I believe it will, no longer will our fleets be at the mercy of the winds. No longer will they have to spend hours tacking into ports. They can just go zoom, right on in."

Alessa found this fascinating and encouraged him to tell her more. "I am also working on finding a way to harness and use the electricity found in lightning. Once I manage that, I have so many uses for it that I sometimes get way ahead of myself. We could all have lights at night and not have to mess around with lanterns or the dangerous gaslights. We might even be able to send messages long distances with it. I have already worked out a signal system, the Arsenio Code, I call it. Just as soon as I can get the electricity source ready, I can then present the long distance communication system, the LDCS, I call it."

Ten o'clock came in no time at all, as far as Alessa was concerned! "It's over already, but we just got here, Arsenio!"

"No," he pulled out his large pocket watch. "See, it is around ten."

"What's this thing?" she asked.

"Oh, another of my little inventions. It is called a clock because it keeps track of the time. Not terribly accurate, I am afraid. It loses five minutes each day. It is powered by a wind up spring. I have not yet marketed this invention because I must get it to work more accurately first." He slowly led Alessa to the large entrance, where Cosima and Gerardo were waiting for them. Alessa realized that she had been so engrossed with Arsenio that she'd not seen those two all evening long.

"Arsenio, you must come on in at the house. How about some tea? You can show your watch to Dianna. Perhaps she can give you an idea about how to keep it from losing the five minutes each day," Alessa insisted. Cosmia smiled, for she loved the idea of spending even more time with Gerardo, especially at their house.

A carriage ride later, the two escorted their beaus into their large estate home. The littler children were already in bed. Dianna was still up, plans spread on the kitchen table. She was sipping some tea, studying them. Cosima said, "You guys have a seat here in the dining room. We'll go make some tea and cookies. Back in a jiffy."

As soon as they were alone, Cosima whispered, "How is he? You seemed fascinated with him as far as I could tell. Not a pig, sis?" she grinned. She knew darn well that Alessa had not taken her eyes off him all evening.

"He's terrific! I really like Arsenio. I do hope he likes me. Do you think that he does, Cosima?"

"Does what?" asked Dianna, looking up from her plans. They had entered the kitchen at last. "Oh, how was your blind date, Alessa?"

"Perfect! He's an inventor. You have to meet him. Can I ask a favor of you, Dianna? He's invented a clock thing, which tells the time of day, but it loses five minutes. I sort of hinted that you might take a look at it and see if you can give him some idea how to make it work better."

Dianna grinned. "Okay, Alessa. The water's hot. Just made some tea." The girls quickly brewed a whole pot and put it and cups, napkins, and a tin of cookies onto a tray. Alessa carried the tray slowly back into the dining room, followed by Cosima and Dianna, who said, "Oh, you two must be wearing the Annelise boots." Cosima grinned. It was obvious; they walked far slower than normal.

"Arsenio, this is Dianna. Dianna, this is Arsenio Bartolo, the inventor," Alessa introduced them, while sitting the tray down. She and Cosima set the table and poured the tea.

"Oh, Arsenio, yes. We've met. You're the one modifying my steam engine for use on boats, right?" Dianna said, shaking his hand. The two began to chat about his all-metal boat until Alessa interrupted them by handing Arsenio his tea and a cookie.

"Dianna's agreed to examine your clock, Arsenio. Perhaps she can give you some ideas how to make it work better," Alessa re-took control of the conversation. The lad produced his clock and opened its back, revealing all manner of springs and gears. He explained how it worked, while Alessa sat there fascinated with his voice and enthusiasm. Dianna, on the other hand, was paying close attention to this invention of his.

Evidently, she understood what appeared to Alessa to be a complex device, because she did have some suggestions. Something about having one less tooth in this gear and one more on that one. She could have worked out the math herself, but she preferred to listen to him talk instead. Dianna then excused herself, claiming that she had an engineering obstacle to handle before morning. This track building was taking up more of her time than she'd originally planned.

Finally, Gerardo rose, "It is really late, and we must be going." He and Cosima embraced passionately. Not to be outdone, Alessa took hold of Arsenio and gave him a passionate kiss; his arms slipped around her waist and added to their brief passion.

"May I come calling on you, Alessa?" he whispered to her.

"Anytime that I am not busy, please do. Are you up for another dance next Friday night?" she asked keeping her fingers crossed behind her back.

"A fire couldn't keep me from it! Thanks Alessa. You are the first woman who isn't totally bored with me," he admitted shyly.

After they left, the two headed to their room. "Well, how did you like him?" Cosima asked eagerly.

"He's a dream! I think I'm in love," Alessa replied dizzily.

"Cool. We'd better get out of these tight corsets and heels," Cosima suggested.

The next day, the two spent hours working on disguises for their evening spy mission. Cosima's plan was to hide in an alleyway from which they could observe the entrance to this warehouse. They would try to memorize as many faces as possible, particularly those who were likely to be running the extortion plot in the Little Tashien section of Velona. Because of their long red nails, they decided to wear gloves to hide them. Donning their leather outfits was a good step, but Alessa needed a stocking type hat to hide her long, blonde hair. Soft boots would allow them to move silently through the alleys. Even though Cosima preferred not to carry a sword, Alessa insisted that she don one as part of their disguise.

Around eight, they had Arturo drive them to within two blocks of their destination and wait for them there. Quietly, like two shadows in the dark night, they stole to their observation point and took up their positions. Alessa would monitor their surroundings, providing protection for Cosima, who would concentrate solely on identifying the men who entered. Around nine, some began arriving. By the time that a carriage pulled up and the Cardinal and his Mano del Dio protection group of four stepped out, she had counted over two dozen men.

They were about equally split between those of Tashien descent and local thugs. Cosima whispered, "Watch out for my body. I am going inside to hear what's being said." Alessa acknowledged her and drew her sword, ready for action. Cosima slipped out of her body and headed through the front wall the warehouse.

She returned sometime later on, before the men began leaving. Quietly, the two slipped back down the alley and down the two blocks to where Arturo was waiting patiently for them. "Successful?" he asked as he opened the door for them.

"Absolutely. Interesting, somehow they have discovered that we two arrested Ramos, and they have placed a bounty on our heads," Cosima answered.

"Damn, that's not good at all," Arturo replied, becoming rather alarmed. Their safety was his responsibility. He was part of their Forze Segrete protection group.

"We are going to have to be far more careful in the future," Alessa stated factually, beginning to draw up ideas of how better to protect Cosima when they were active.

Back home, she shared the ill news with everyone. Sandra was quite concerned, "What if someone tries to break in at night while we are sleeping? This is not good at all. Luisa, Arturo, one of us is going to have to stand guard during the nighttime. That's all there is to it."

"Say," Dianna broke in, "I am having a really hard time running my Enyo body at the same time as I am trying to get work done, as you well know. I appreciate how hard you have all worked to keep my Enyo body relatively quiet. Why don't I have my Enyo body stay up nights with you and let it sleep in the daytime? That way, I won't get so distracted?"

Elena, Ania's daughter and Judger, spoke up. "Well, I ought to either start going with Cosima and Alessa or stay up nights with you guys too. I've been watching after the six kids, but this is more critical."

"Elena, you have been a huge help with the kids," Luisa answered. "With Sandra off at the Banca del Dio much of the day and Arturo dashing around with the others, I really do appreciate your help with the kids." Elena smiled; she knew just how helpful she had been, but this was a crisis. After some more discussion, they agreed that Enyo and Elena would stand guard over the estate at night. During the day, they would sleep. However, both were under strict orders that if they sensed anything amiss, anything at all, they were to wake Arturo and Luisa immediately before going off to investigate.

With so many gone, Alessa had moved into Cosima's bedroom for company. She missed Bianca. In their room undressing for the night, she said, "Cosima, we ought to eliminate these thugs as soon as possible."

"I know. This casts a different light on it. I will talk to Bale and Chief Inspector Adolfo tomorrow about it. In the meantime, we don't go out of the house without our blasters in our pockets," Cosima advised. She didn't know if these thugs had guns or not, but no sense in taking any chances.

On Monday, the two headed off to Alessandra's shop for a fitting of their new dresses. As always, Arturo drove them there and assisted them out of the carriage. Inside, their new velvet dresses were nearly finished. She had them change into them so she could adjust the hems. While she went about pinning up the hems, she commented, "You know I've seen a couple of thugs hanging around across the street. They seem to be keeping an eye on my shop. I'm becoming a bit nervous about them. What if they try to rob me like those other two did?"

"If they are there when we leave, we will check them out," Cosima attempted to relieve her fears. "If they try to extort money out of you, just let us know at once. Pickpockets are a fact of life, but this protection extortion racket is not tolerable."

About an hour later, Alessandra was finally satisfied with the final fittings and promised that they would be ready on Wednesday afternoon. Both girls thanked her and headed for the door. As they approached, Alessa spied the subtle hand signal from Arturo, who was leaning against their carriage, as if immensely bored with the long wait. In part, he was. However, his signal indicated trouble just outside.

As they exited, two thugs came rushing at them from their left, while another two came at them from their right, though one paid attention to Arturo and what he might do if the teens were attacked. All four had drawn short swords and one called out, "Kill'em."

The one nearest Cosima halted in his tracks, frozen into a statute. Cosima took over total control of his body. Arturo quick drew his blade and parried the second one to free up Cosima. Alessa whirled on her heels to face the two coming at her. She timed her move perfectly. As the nearest one began his exaggerated sword swing at her, she bent low and back stepped out of his way, while then launching into a circle kick with her left leg, aiming for the key nerve spot on the second man's side of his head.

Unfortunately for him, he saw her kick coming and tried to dodge. The tall spike of her Alexa boot missed the pressure point and landed straight in his eye. The force of her swing drove the narrow heel spike deep into his brain, while nearly knocking her off her feet as she fought to keep her balance and get her heel back out of the man's head.

The one who missed initially, turned to swing at her a second time, but in her efforts to free herself, she grabbed the short sword from the falling dead man and swung it upwards, cutting the man through his privates and into his groin. He dropped his weapon and fell clutching his lower parts. She didn't hesitate; she brought her follow through and sliced through half of his neck.

Meanwhile, Arturo parried his opponent and took advantage of the man's distraction. He plunged his blade deep into the man's chest, aiming for his heart. He pulled his blade out; the thug dropped to his knees, and then fell flat on the ground. Alessa finished it; she cut the frozen man's neck; he too dropped to the ground. "No sense taking any prisoners this time; they wanted to kill us," Alessa said angrily. She returned to each fallen man and stabbed each one, making doubly sure each was dead.

Alessandra watched all this from her shop and came out crying, "That's the ones! They were going to kill you! Are you all right?"

"Yes, we are unharmed, but I've got an awful lot of their blood on my shoes and dress. If it dries, it will be murder to get out. Have you got any water inside where I can wash out this mess before it stains my satin dress?" Alessa asked. Alessandra led her back inside.

"Gosh, Alessa can get angry," Cosima said, still startled that Alessa didn't hesitate to kill the one that she had immobilized.

"Best she had; he might have tried something again, perhaps back at the estate, endangering the kids," Arturo replied. "I'll move these bodies out onto the side of the street. The police can deal with them. We'll drop by and let them know that there are four less thugs to handle."

"Thanks for the head's up, Arturo," she replied, carefully stepping out of the way of the blood pools forming on the sidewalk. "Gosh, these spiked heels are terribly dangerous, aren't they?"

"I think she was heading for a pressure point, Cosima. The thug tried to dodge and got his eye in the way of her heel," Arturo explained. "I'm not a Protector, just a Loremaster, but it looked that way to me."

A half hour later, Alessa joined them; her dress was now clean but wet in numerous places. Arturo helped them climb into the carriage as usual. After a quick stop at police headquarters, they headed on home, where everyone wanted to hear about the battle.

"Honestly, it didn't even last a whole minute," Alessa tried to explain, though no one really believed her, not until Arturo backed her up.

Dianna teased her, "Alessa doesn't need to carry a sword anymore because she's got Alexa heels instead." Everyone laughed at her jest, except Cosima and Arturo who had witnessed that grim scene.

The next day, Chief Inspector Adolfo came by the house. "Cosima, this is becoming far too risky for you and Alessa. We are going to try to arrest the whole lot when they come for their Saturday night's meeting."

"Excellent. If I were you, I would have someone watching for the Cardinal's carriage. When it comes, have them warn him that a raid against some criminals is taking place and that this area is not safe for him. Don't let on that we know that he is behind this plot. This way, he will be in the dark. Right now, we don't want to take action against him. I have something else in mind for him later on. We'll be there to help if your men have trouble. Be careful. Some might be armed with guns," Cosima warned.

That night, both Gerardo and Arsenio dropped by to chat. "We heard about the attempt on your lives," Gerardo said the moment that Cosima came to the door. "Are you all right? Alessa too?" Both boys were very worried; she read their faces like a book.

"Come on in; yes we're fine, not a scratch on us, though the four who attacked us are quite dead now. Alessa took care of three of them."

"Hi Arsenio," Alessa called out from behind Cosima.

"Wow, you killed three of them?" Arsenio asked very surprised to hear this bit of news.

"I told you I am a fighter, a Protector to be exact. No way was I going to let some common thugs harm Cosima," Alessa answered him. "Come on in guys. Sandra says that we can't go to the dance Friday night. She thinks it would be too dangerous, and I happen to agree with her — professional opinion of course. There are some two dozen of these gang members who have been given orders to eliminate us, so the prudent thing to do is to stay here until we capture them on Saturday."

"Say, we could have our own private party," Cosima suggested.

"That's fine with me," Gerardo replied. "Maybe we can discuss my theories then as well."

"I'd love to," Arsenio added. "What should we wear? Should we bring anything?"

"Oh how about just everyday clothes this time?" Cosima suggested. "Do you like to play cards? We could do that and play some other games too." Rapidly, the foursome created their special party for Friday night. After they left, both teens were very excited about having their boyfriends over and set about cleaning up the entire house, which amazed Luisa. She'd never seen the two of them so into fixing everything nice and tidy before now.

Saturday night, Cosima, her Detective Inspector badge displayed on her chest, and Alessa stood at their usual hiding place at the end of the side alley. Dressed in their leathers, they waited for the action to begin. Chief Inspector Adolfo stood beside them. All were armed and ready for action. He had fifty policemen waiting in hiding nearly a half mile away. A string of policemen waited in a signal line. That is, per Cosima's advice, only these three were near the warehouse. When the Chief Inspector gave the signal to another policeman waiting at the other end of the alley, then that man would relay the signal to yet another one in disguise hiding about a block further away. This signal would then be similarly sent to a dozen more men until it reached the large batch with their wagons. The large force would then move in on the warehouse. The idea was not to alert those coming to the warehouse that a raid was about to happen. Cosima and the Chief Inspector were determined to nab them all.

At last, they spied a fancy carriage coming, the Cardinal's. Chief Inspector Adolfo gave the attack signal and then walked out into the street. Cosima and Alessa prepared to cover him. As the Cardinal's carriage pulled up, he called out, "Excuse me. Oh, Your Holiness. I must warn you that this area is not safe now. A raid is happening as we speak. I know that you must perform your Holy Obligations, but for your safety, I would not delay in this area."

"Why, thank you Chief Inspector for your most timely warning. We are on our way to deliver the Last Rites for a very sick man. We will not delay in this area. Thank you for the warning," the Cardinal replied. He gave orders for his driver to continue down the street. As soon as his carriage turned a corner and was out of sight, one by one, the dozen policemen came running up to their Chief Inspector. He gave them a sign to start surrounding the warehouse, blocking all exits. There were only two, but ten windows needed to also be watched, just in case. By the time that they were in position, the wagons and the remainder of his force arrived.

Once more, the Chief Inspector gave a signal and the raid was on. They smashed in the front door and some forty men charged inside. The sounds of confusion broke the nighttime stillness, then the clash of steel upon steel. A moment later, several gunshots added their muffled sounds to the ears of the two teens waiting and observing from the alleyway. Suddenly, they saw a window opposite their position shatter, and several thugs climbed out. The five overpowered the single policeman beside that window, but Cosima prevented one thug from killing the man. She forced him to drop his blade. The five made a dash towards the alley where the teens were hiding.

A pair of lightning bolts struck the two lead men who were running toward them, sending their bodies flying. The three behind them, startled by the unexpected lightning, veered to their right, heading straight for the Chief Inspector. Three other policemen, who had been watching more distant windows, took up the chase after them. Cosima saw one of them pull a gun, intent upon shooting the Chief Inspector!

"Damn him!" she called out angrily. She took control of the man's arm, forcing it to point the gun at himself, at which point it detonated. The thug fell to the ground before a startled Chief Inspector. Simultaneously, Alessa let fly an arrow from her short bow. It struck another of the thugs in the back of his neck, stopping him. The last man stopped running as he got to the Chief Inspector, who had his sword drawn. The thug dropped his sword and raised his hands, but it took the Chief Inspector several seconds to process the rapid, startling events. By then, the running policemen had come up to their boss and took over for him, carting the lone survivor to the wagon and tying him up.

Cosima and Alessa gave the Chief Inspector a wave of their hands, and he waved back, grateful for their timely assistance. At this point, some of the policemen began ushering captured thugs out of the front door of the warehouse and into the wagons. Chief Inspector Adolfo then ventured into the building to check on his men and their casualties. Inside, he found three of his men had been shot; one was dead. His men were tying up the last of the thugs.

"This one killed Jamison, Chief Inspector," one policeman notified him, leading the still struggling, but tied, thug toward the door.

"Hold a second. So you killed a police officer?" Chief Inspector Adolfo asked the burly man.

"What of it?" he spat at Adolfo. The Chief Inspector thrust his sword into the man's chest, aiming for his heart.

"No one gets away with shooting one of my men," the Chief Inspector snarled, spat on the rapidly dying thug, and then kicked him for good measure. The escorting policeman smiled; the justice of his boss was most swift and certain. He step was lighter as he went to assist others with their captured thugs.

After the last live criminals had been removed, Chief Inspector Adolfo ordered all the wagons but one to take them to the holding cells and to ship them all off to Isla la Roca in the morning. While his men now began to carry out the dead, he ordered the place thoroughly searched. They confiscated numerous money pouches. All told, the extortionists were about to deliver one thousand three hundred sixty-one gold to the Cardinal this evening!

As he was counting the coins, another thug was found hiding out, hoping to be overlooked. He was tied and forced to sit among his dead comrades. At last, Cosima and Alessa came out from their hiding place and entered the warehouse to get briefed on the outcome. Twenty-three of the extortionists had been captured or killed tonight. The three felt confident that most, if not all, of the two gangs of extortionists had been apprehended.

Later back at their estate, the two brought the others up to date, and Luisa and Sandra relaxed a little. The most serious threat to their charges had been eliminated. Cosima cautioned them all, "We should not relax our vigil. The Cardinal and his Mano del Dio men are still out there. They may try to assassinate us." That was a sobering thought and Elena and Enyo continued their nightly watch over the estate.

Chapter 16 Opium Troubles

"Yes, Alessa, Arsenio is nuts over you," Cosima revealed what she had weaseled out of Gerardo. Alessa giggled, she had so hoped so. He'd captured her heart, she was sure of that. Arsenio was constantly in her mind these days. So much so, that she found it hard to concentrate on much else.

It was Sunday and the two couples were going on a picnic to the train construction site just north of Velona. Dianna would be their chaperone, primarily because she needed to see firsthand the troubles that the engineers were having with the bridge over a river canal. Alessa wanted to wear her fancy dress, but Cosima insisted that they wear their cotton pants and tops. "We are riding horses and this is a picnic, not a dance." Alessa giggled.

Later, the two couples spread a blanket out on the hillside, while Dianna went to inspect the construction site below them. Arsenio chatted with Alessa, who lay on her back, resting her head on his lap. "You know, my clock is now working perfectly. I've invented a way that sailors can now know precisely where they are at in the ocean. If everyone adopts the longitude line through the center of the Holy Rose Church as the zero line, then with my clock, they can determine where they are at around the world." He chatted on and Alessa listened, fascinated by his inventions and their usefulness. Indeed, in five years' time, all ocean-going ships would use his clock as a key part of their navigation system, revolutionizing sea locations.

Gerardo explained his theories to Cosima. "When the opium supply starts to dry up, we can first expect the cost for the users to increase. When the shortage becomes more severe, the price will skyrocket. Now we will really begin to see a crime wave, as the desperate addicts rob and steal to get enough to pay for their next fix. Of course, when it totally dries up and there is no more coming in and all the dealer's supplies are gone, then we really have a problem with the addicts."

"Wildly out of control people?" Cosima asked.

"Yes, crazy people doing crazy things. I've heard that coming off an addiction like this can be really horrible. If there are only a few addicts, this might not be much of a problem. Do we have any idea how many people are addicts right now?" he asked. Cosima realized that she was lacking that critical detail.

"No, but we ought to make an attempt to find out," she replied. A bit later, the heady discussions gave way to passions, and Dianna returned to the picnic site and found both couples passionately kissing. She longed for Ania at times like this.

Mid-August, Cosima received word that the next month supply of opium was not going to make it to Velona. Bale took her advice and had a dozen of his men covertly watching the twelve known opium dens, which were legal to operate. Bale didn't dare make such illegal in Velona. Not only were they popular but also they would just go underground where he could not keep an eye on them. Besides, once Kali and Ania cut off the supply coming into Velona, the whole issue would become moot, or so he hoped.

By the end of August, the crime rate had nearly doubled, as many addicts turned to crime, desperate for their next fix. Bale had no choice but to double the police force. He allowed Chief Inspector Adolfo to deploy them as he thought fit. The wealthier citizens demanded more policemen on foot in their neighborhoods, protecting them, their wives, and children. Merchants, who were particularly being hit hard by the addicts seeking quick funds, demanded even more police protection. Chief Inspector Adolfo lost all patience with these people. His standing orders were quite plain. Any addict caught stealing or robbing was sent to Isla la Roca at once. They could rot in a dank prison cell and fight their addiction there. Heartless, yes, for he cared only for the victims of these desperate men and women.

Cosima received a new mystery crime to solve. Chief Inspector Adolfo had no men or time to spare on this one. With her badge prominently displayed on her chest and wearing her fine green satin ball gown with Alexa heels, she began walking up the driveway of the Boldovina Estate. Alessa in her blue satin gown was right behind her. Arturo again waited patiently with their carriage. The Boldovina's were well-respected and very wealthy. Augusto was an import-export merchant, while his wife was a patron of the arts, particularly the Laird Foundation, for whom she had been donating large sums over the years. They had six children, though they were adults now and married.

A servant, Adelina, met them at the door and led the two teens into the large sitting room, where a dozen fine paintings hung on the walls. All the furniture was top quality. Bibiana Boldovina was waiting for them here. She too wore a ball gown, her everyday gown as she called it. For many in Velona, this dress would be considered a very fancy gown to be worn at an extravaganza event. "Oh so good of you to come!" she rose and gave a hug to Cosima and Alessa.

Cosima sat down properly, took out her note pad, and began, "Okay, Mrs. Boldovina, tell me all that has happened here, please. Spare no detail, no matter how small and trivial it may seem to you."

"Just Bibiana, please, dear. Well I am so glad that someone at last is going to investigate this! Let me see. Why, I do believe it began about a month ago. First, some of our gold daily expense coins went missing. Lately, silverware and fine china are disappearing. Honestly, things just keep on turning up missing around here. It's like there is a mysterious gremlin in the house. Lord knows that we've searched high and low, but nothing has turned up." She rattled on and on in a confusing chatter.

"You see, we even thought that our servant, Adelina here, might be stealing our silverware. So Augusto has taken to locking Adelina in her room at nights. Still stuff keeps disappearing."

"I told you I wouldn't steal from you, Mrs. Boldovina!" the servant protested as she poured more tea for her employer.

"Well, I know, dear, but Augusto so insisted," Bibiana tried to mollify the harsh treatment of her servant woman.

"Okay, can you show me where these items were kept before they went missing," Cosima asked. She took out her magnifying glass and followed the woman from room to room. Some of the gold coins had been locked in a desk drawer. Here, she paused for a very close inspection.

"Ah, there are no signs of the lock having been forced open. A key was used to open this. Who has the key to this drawer?" she asked. As it turned out, they kept the key to the drawer in another drawer in a second desk nearby so that they could easily get at their daily expense funds when needed. The silverware came from the mahogany cabinet. Cosima spent an hour examining all the places from which things had turned up missing. All were here on the first floor of the estate.

Next, Cosima thoroughly examined all the outside door locks to see if any had been forced open. None showed any signs of tampering. Baffled, she then went around to all the outside windows checking them, especially the three large floor door-window combinations. Still, the detective found nothing unusual at all. As the two teens headed back inside, Alessa asked, "What does this all mean? An inside job?"

"Precisely. Now comes the hard part," Cosima replied, deep in thought. Back in the study, she asked, "Bibiana, is Adelina your only servant or do you have others, such as a gardener?" While there were two men who worked outside on the lawn and the many bushes and flowers, none had a key to the estate house. Cosima ruled them out; besides, they were around only once a week and clearly had no access to the house or its contents.

"So what do you think of our gremlin?" Bibiana asked.

"The culprit has a key to your house and is familiar with where everything is kept. There can be no other explanation," Cosima replied honestly. "Now then, I need a list of everyone who has a key to your home." She, her husband, and their six children, plus their wives and even Adelina all had keys.

"Should we change the locks?" the older woman asked.

"If you do that, do not give out any keys except to your husband, Adelina, and yourself. I suspect that will not be very practical. Please allow me to complete my investigation. I am confident that I can find who is responsible for the thefts. Now then, is there any other way into your home other than the windows and doors, which I have already seen? Like a secret door or such?"

"Well, no. Should we have one?" she asked.

"No, just checking all the possibilities. Could I possibly have a sample of the silverware and china to use as a comparison, please? I will return them when I am finished with the investigation." A few minutes later, the two teens walked slowly to the carriage, carrying some silverware and china samples.

As they began rolling, Cosima explained, "Well, this is an inside job. Someone in their family is desperate for funds. I suspect that it is one of their children. We need to have Sandra pull the bank accounts of all of them while we visit some of the pawnshops around Velona, looking for the missing items." Their first stop was the Banca del Dio where Sandra was hard at work correlating the bank records of all transactions larger than five thousand. Cosima gave her the names of the Boldovina family and had her do a search of their records.

Since that action would take time, the two headed off to canvas the many pawnshops in Velona. That took all the rest of the afternoon. At the very last one, they hit pay dirt. "Well, look at this, here is the mate to this fork!" Cosima exclaimed.

"Over here, this china set matches as well," Alessa pointed out, eager to be of assistance in the investigation. Cosima sent Arturo off to fetch Mrs. Boldovina, while she and Alessa proceeded to examine all the shop's merchandise. The owner was unable to give a good description of the person who had brought in these items, but did acknowledge that the same person brought in all the items the two had thus far selected out.

One cup held a special interest for Cosima. On its side was an oily smudge, finger print whorls were plainly visible and she began to have an idea. This cup, she kept aside to take with her, once it had been positively identified. When Mrs. Boldovina arrived, she was able to identify the whole pile plus a number of other items as having been stolen from her home. The pawn broker was dismayed that Cosima confiscated all the stolen merchandise, chiding him for buying them from a thief. He had little recourse for recompense; he was out the funds he had paid for these relatively expensive items. Cosima also told him that if the man returned with more items to pawn, he was to contact the police immediately.

After supper, Cosima experimented with the fingerprint and found a method to transfer it to a piece of white paper. She looked at the dark whorls for some time. Then, she began conducting two experiments. First, she wanted to know what composed this smudge. That identification was rapid. It was lamp oil. Next, she hassled everyone in the house, making them put some ink on their thumb and press it onto a white paper.

"What *are* you doing?" asked Elena, wiping the ink off her thumb.

"I am trying to see if people's thumb prints are different or the same," she replied. "See, so far, none are alike. I need to take a whole lot more, though. This may become very useful in crime investigations, you see." Elena didn't see, but went to eat her breakfast before standing night guard duty.

Sandra brought a copy of the significant finding of hers when she arrived at suppertime. Indeed, Cosima was right. Their older son, Bart, was in financial difficulties. He ran a lamp business. However, his company account had a single gold in it and his personal account was slightly overdrawn. Within the last month, he'd withdrawn every bit of money he and his company had. Cosima found this highly suspicious indeed. It had all been withdrawn as cash!

The next morning, she and Alessa called upon Chief Inspector Adolfo and asked him to come with them to Bart's Lamps. On the way, she explained her theory and what she was about to do. He found this most interesting indeed.

"Good morning. May I help you?" a young man asked as they entered the lamp shop. Various quality lamps adorned the many shelves as well as flasks of oil.

"We are looking for Bart Boldovina," Cosima said.

"That's me. How can I help you? I have many fine lamps here."

"Would you be so kind as to put your thumb in this ink and then roll it on this paper, please? Official police request," Cosima asked. He looked confused and had no idea at all why, but with Adolfo standing there, he did as asked. Cosima then got out her magnifying glass and held this print against the print she had lifted from the cup yesterday.

"See, Chief Inspector, they match identically," Cosima replied.

"By golly, they do match, incredible Cosima, amazing."

Cosima then said formally, "Bart, we have your banking records from your store and your personal records. You have withdrawn all of your funds in cash. You are totally broke. Worse, as you know, gold, valuable silverware, and even fine china have gone missing from your parent's home during the last few weeks. Yesterday, I found the pawnshop where they were sold for gold. I lifted this print here from one of the stolen cups. It matches identically to your thumb print you just gave me. This tells me that you were the one who stole and pawned all those items from your parents. Would you like to confess to Chief Inspector Adolfo here or should we take you to that pawnshop and let the owner there identify you?"

Bart began shaking and broke down. "I did it. I have to have money. I need it every day! It's the damn opium dealers; they keep jacking up their prices. I have to have some everyday now. Please, I didn't mean to hurt my folks. I just *have* to have it." He broke down and began crying, though his body began to thirst once more for his fix, which he still had not been able to get. Chief Inspector Adolfo arrested him and they headed to the Boldovina's residence.

Of course, the parents were terribly upset about Bart's thefts, but refused to press charges against their own son. "How do we help him? Buy him more opium?" asked a crying Bibiana.

"Right now, the price of opium is skyrocketing. Soon, all your money won't be able to buy any," Chief Inspector Adolfo answered her. "What we are doing with the addicts that we are arresting for thefts is to send them to the Roca and lock them in a cell. Let them work through their withdrawal. Some go crazy, I'm told. Some smash their own heads in on the stone walls. Some pull out of it. We simply do not have any medical cure for this addiction, ma'am. It might be best to lock him in a room somewhere and hope for the best." He wanted to give her more hope, but he refused to give her any false hopes in the process.

Crime solved, the three rode back to their estate, dropping the Chief Inspector off on their way. "This situation is growing worse by the day," he commented as they rode along towards his station. "I would encourage you to further investigate this fingerprint theory of yours. If you can show that no two people have identical prints, this could revolutionize law enforcement." She smiled and promised to work hard on proving it was so.

For the first two weeks in September, the two went to various well-populated areas of foot traffic in Velona. She offered everyone she met a gold coin if they would give her a sample of their fingerprints. By September 11, she had amassed a thousand set of prints and spent hours each evening comparing them. Alessa was pressed into the examination as well as Gerardo and even Arsenio, when they came by for a visit.

In the early morning hours of September 12, Elena woke everyone up. "Sandra, come look at little Bethany and Renzo. I think that they are sick or something. We're hearing an awful moaning from them." Sandra and Luisa rushed into the children's rooms.

Renzo and Bethany were thrashing around on their beds, moaning softly. Sandra, our Healer, set to work, trying to identify their illness. "No fever. Strange. They don't seem sick at their stomachs. The other children aren't sick, so that rules out some bad food, most likely." She tried three times to wake them up, unsuccessfully. At last, she had them moved into one room, where she could monitor them.

By morning, everyone was crowding around the kids' bedroom door, while Sandra continued to try to wake them up. She managed to get Bethany's eyes open, but she seemed "not there." "What's the matter with them?" Cosima asked, very curious about their illness. Indeed, everyone in the house was now worried about the two nine year olds.

"I just don't know. I cannot get them woken up so they can tell me anything. How strange," Sandra muttered, completely baffled by their mysterious illness. "Can you try contacting Bethany or Dita? Perhaps they can shed some light on this."

Alessa looked white as a sheet. "I can't get through to mom! This has never happened to me before. I can sense her presence, but I can't reach her. Something must be terribly wrong with them."

"Say, I cannot reach Dita either!" Luisa added, she had been acting as the coordinator of our various teams now in the field. "See if you can reach

Bianca and have her try to get a hold of her mom."

A bit later, Alessa cried, "She can't either. She tried to contact them both. What's going on? Mom's in danger somewhere, I just know it!"

"Calm down, Alessa. It is probably just a temporary thing. We can try again in a little while. Let's see if we can get either of these kids to wake up. Then, they could tell us what is going on in Tashien," Sandra suggested.

No luck, the two children continued to thrash about and moan, oblivious to the world around them. At last, she realized that for now all she could do was see that they were comfortable.

For the next two days, there was no change in their condition, and now Sandra was getting extremely worried. Alessa was in a near constant panic, trying every hour to reach her mom or Dita, all to no avail at all. "They are dehydrating fast," Sandra pronounced. "They've eaten nothing for two days. We must find a way to get some fluids in them."

Now they had something on which to focus their attention: finding a way to get liquids down their throats. At last, they worked out a method that worked. Luisa would hold one child in a sitting position. Someone would hold their mouth open, while Sandra carefully poured milk, water, broth, anything liquid, into their mouths. At least they didn't protest this and managed to swallow most of it.

Encouraged by this, the older three set to work, turning a regular meal into a liquid mush that Sandra could get into the two small bodies. This gave the three teens something on which to concentrate, though Alessa could barely do it.

At supper on the fourth day, Cosima suggested her theory. "Look, they are spiritual beings trying to run two bodies at the same time. I believe that what we are seeing here with the kids is similar to what Bethany and Dita are currently experiencing. That is, the kids are a mirror to their adult bodies in Tashien. Bethany and Dita must be somehow unconscious all this time. They must still be alive. If not, they would simply be here with us and their littler bodies. Since they are not, their adult bodies must still be alive, just somehow unconscious or totally out of it."

This seemed to be the best explanation available and was adopted for the moment. The two children needed constant care, constant watching. They were unable to do anything for themselves and their bed sheets had to be changed frequently as a result. It was imperative that Sandra get as much liquefied and nourishing food in them each day. Still, everyone's panic rose day by day as no change appeared in either child.

By now, Alessa had contacted everyone else who was out in the field. No one was close to them excepting Jemma and Fina, but they likewise knew only that they had failed to return from their visit to the Purple Palace. Alessa begged the two to charge into that palace and rescue her mother, but Fina convinced her of the true reality of the situation there. The palace was a fortified building and would take an army to get inside, during which they might just be killed outright.

Alessa desperately wanted to leave immediately to go rescue her mother, but Cosima pointed out that if she left now, it would take her many months to get there. By then, the situation may well have changed totally. "Besides, we have our own problems here, Alessa. The price of opium has now risen to stellar heights. Any day now, there will be none to be had at any price. We must be prepared for the chaos caused by so many addicts." Alessa realized she was right, but continued to try to reach her mother by telepathy a dozen times each day.

Days passed, with no real change in the two children. At last in the morning of the eighteenth day, Elena called out, "Everyone! Come quick! The kids are awake!" The whole household dashed into the kid's room. Bethany and Renzo were sitting up on their own, complaining that they were starving. Luisa rushed to get them something solid and nourishing, while Sandra began to talk to the two.

"Confused. Eighteen days we've been out? Where are we? Oh, in the Purple Palace, I see. Oh, we've been captured and had our arms cut off at our elbows. They've done something funny to our feet. We are starving, but we found San Min and four others, who are like us too. Food. She's feeding me," little Bethany talked somewhat out of it all. She was not aware of her surroundings or us.

Luisa rushed in with some solid food, and she and Sandra began stuffing both kids with as much as they could eat. At last full, Bethany began talking weirdly once more. "I feel this horrible craving coming over me. Yes, I need that pipe. Please. Oh yes, yes!" She and Renzo began rolling their eyes and moaning as if in an ecstasy of some kind and soon fell unconscious once more.

"I've seen that look," Cosima observed. "They looked just like the addicts do after they smoke their opium. I bet anything that Bethany and Dita are now heavily hooked on opium! Damn! Now what do we do?" Everyone looked at each other and then Sandra.

"I don't know, gang. I just don't know, but if they are, that explains much," their Healer replied with a sad sigh.

With tears coming down her cheeks, Alessa added, "But at least they are alive. I am going to contact Jemma and see if they can do anything to rescue them."

Beginning the next morning, a definite pattern began emerging. In the early morning both Bethany and Renzo were awake, rather alert, but very hungry. During this time, Sandra attempted to get as much nourishing food into their growing bodies as possible. The duration of this "clarity" period was short at first, perhaps an hour at most. Day by day, the period began to lengthen and the group learned more about what had happened to the two. However, since Bethany and Dita had much with which to deal, Sandra kept the relay of information to a minimum. She was just thankful for the opportunity to get sufficient food into the little bodies here.

No one was happier than Alessa to hear from Jemma on October 20 that both had been rescued and were doing as well as could be expected. Both were totally addicted to opium, which they had to have relatively frequently. Finally, Alessa could relax a bit; she was able to chat with her mom in the windows of opportunity when she was lucid, usually in the morning hours now.

This same day was the Inaugural Run of Engine Number One, as it was being promoted around the city. It was Dianna's big day. Her steam engine was finally ready for its maiden run. They had finished laying some ten miles of track. A turnaround loop was at the docks, and another such loop was at the northern edge of sprawling Velona. All of Velona's most important figures as well as countless others lined the side of the tracks to watch Dianna's invention. At the docks, three cars were loaded with gravel, wooden ties, and the metal tracks. Many, many wagons would be needed to move this volume of cargo from the docks to the current construction site just north of the city. Today, the three cars plus a fourth car carrying passengers would be pulled from the docks through the city to the north end. There, the three cargo cars would be unhitched and the passengers brought back to the docks.

Of course, the entire West Po clan would be riding in the car along with a dozen of the most influential men in Velona. Dianna was terribly nervous this morning and Cosima and Alessa went along with her to the docks. They would ride with them as per Chief Inspector Adolfo's request to have someone from the police department along for their protection.

When they arrived, Dianna's hand-chosen man to drive the engine, Domineco, already had gotten the fire in the boiler going and the head of steam was starting to build up. Bale and Lona, her sister and the High Priestess of Velona, were standing on a fancy platform. A dozen musicians sat behind them. Bale insisted that Dianna join him as he addressed the still assembling crowd.

At precisely ten o'clock, Bale, who now had one of Arsenio's new clocks in his pocket, began to speak. "Welcome everyone to the Inaugural Run of Engine Number One! Today marks a landmark change for Velona and the world. Dianna Anka West Po has unleashed her latest invention on us, the steam engine. Today, you will witness this first run. I call your attention to the last three cars, carrying crushed stone, timbers, and steel rails. Normally, many, many wagons would be needed to haul such a cargo. Yet, today, it will be done by one steam engine. Imagine the future as we add more miles of line and more cars and engines. With one train, massive amounts of Greenway grain can be moved from the far north to our docks. With one train, heavy cargo loads of coal, ores, and such can be brought easily across all the Sea Princes. The net result, ladies and gentlemen, is that Velona will continue to grow and become the number one importer and exporter in the entire world!" The crowd yelled and cheered and Domineco added a shrill blast from the engine's whistle to the noise.

"All this represents more jobs, more work, and more money for everyone in Velona!" Again, the crowd went wild with these ideas. The musicians began playing while the invited guests boarded the passenger car. It had bench seats and a canvas awning overhead, in case of rain. The engine itself had four main drive wheels, powered by the enormous steam pistons.

Dianna was a wreck with worry. Has Domineco check this and that? Has he done this? She had so many worries that Cosima gave up trying to attract her attention on to the crowd and the docks. "We should have made many more test runs," Dianna wailed. She wanted to climb up onto the engine where Domineco was at and take over for him, but Cosima and Alessa managed to restrain her impulse to do so.

"Look, your little engine works perfectly around the estate," Cosima consoled her. "So why won't this larger version work just fine?"

"Well, there are a thousand reasons," Dianna began to explain. Just then, with a mighty blast of steam, the car lurched and slowly began to move, shutting her up momentarily at least.

Gerardo inched his way to Cosima's side. "Hey, we are moving! Isn't this just the greatest thing? I mean it's one thing to ride around your estate on the little train, but this is something else. Wow!" She put her arm around him to steady herself, wishing that she had heeded Sandra's advice and not worn her Annelise tall-heeled boots. Alessa, who had likewise worn her pair, latched onto Arsenio as well. Keeping their balance on the moving car was challenging. No one was sitting on the benches.

The engine traveled a maximum of five miles an hour on this test run. At each street crossing, the loud whistle blew. Dianna hoped that people and horses would get out of the way. The engine could not stop at all quickly!

"Hey Dianna, how fast can it go?" someone asked her.

"It has a top safe speed of ten miles per hour," she replied. "No one would want to go faster than that, would they? Look, it doesn't have to stop at night. It can travel twenty-four hours a day, covering some two hundred forty miles each day. That's a huge jump from wagons that can make perhaps twenty or a carriage which can make about thirty." The asker was quite impressed with her figures. Once tracks were laid, one could go from Velona to Zargarb across all the Sea Princes in three to four days, twice as fast as an empty caravel could travel that path!

If all went well, the wealthy men who put up the funds for this would begin companies to produce more engines and cars. They would make even larger fortunes as a result. Now, Dianna simply worried, while Cosima, Alessa, Arsenio, and Gerardo enjoyed the fascinating ride, waving to the crowds lining the streets who were waving at them.

About an hour and a half later, they reached the northernmost end of the track with a side switch and turnaround loop. The train slowed to a stop and the back three cars were unhooked, before they headed back into the city and to the docks. Everything went according to plan and finally Dianna relaxed.

For the rest of the day, other people were given rides back and forth. In fact, for the next week, free rides were given, because many key people arrived to see the demonstration in person. One of these was Lionel d'Grange, the ruler of Fortress d'Grange. Naturally, when dignitaries came, Dianna was summoned to meet with them as well. Lionel was forty, fit, with a keen eye for detail. His judgment calls were seldom wrong. If this engine proved out, he saw that this would have a far reaching impact on the world at large. Hence, he was keenly interested, and Dianna gave him a personal ride, though she continued to allow Domineco actually to operate the engine.

"This is an incredible invention, young lady. Marvelous. I can foresee it having a giant impact on economies, if it does indeed perform as expected," he commented. "Of course, you are extending the track line up to your northernmost town, correct?"

"Yes, construction is ongoing, but it is going to take us some time to get that much of this track forged and then laid," she explained.

"What would you say to extending the track a little further to our border and allowing us to build it on through d'Grange? Perhaps we could even get permission to extend it into the Kingdom of Calgary as well. That would make it even more valuable a run, right?" he asked pointedly.

Bale, who was entertaining his monarch counterpart, stepped in, "Absolutely. We must run the line at least to Calgary, if not even further. Of course, you may also wish to have an engine and cars of your own, Lionel."

"Ah, now we are talking business! Yes, absolutely. Exactly how heavy a load can the engine pull?" he asked the key question.

Bale deferred to Dianna. "Well, sir, that all depends on whether the track is flat or if there is a grade to climb. Now, we honestly are not sure just how powerful this first prototype engine actually is. We carried three heavily laden cars plus a car full of passengers the other day, and it pulled them fine. Of course as you can see, the route here is nearly flat, no grades. We need to conduct further testing. Still, the run the other day carried the weight of some thirty wagon loads and could pull them around two hundred-forty miles in one long day, more than enough to get them from your place to ours in one day, sir."

"Incredible. Just remarkable. I would like d'Grange to be in on this initial deployment. If you can assist my engineers with the specifications of how the track is made and laid, we can work on getting our part done by the time yours reaches our border. Would it be possible for us to purchase an initial engine and say a dozen cars? It will take longer to load and unload the cars than it does to move them between our capitals. Simply amazing, Dianna."

Bale and Lionel began business discussions. Dianna sat back and enjoyed the early fall ride through the city and back again to the docks. A bit later, Lionel asked Dianna, "Say, I've been meaning to ask you if you have had any word from my son, Louis, who has gone off with your group to see about this war up in the Steppes. I do hope that he is not being a bother for your people."

"Oh quite the contrary, he is being of enormous assistance," Dianna countered. She spent a half hour filling Lionel in on the details that Bianca had relayed to Luisa and thus the rest.

"Now that is very enlightening! My wayward son has actually helped stop a war. I would never have thought that he had that in him. I am terribly sorry to hear that two of your friends are in such bad trouble down in Tashien. If you get a chance to relay any messages to them, please tell my son that I am proud of his accomplishments and that he has my permission to assist them in attempting a rescue of your personnel."

"I certainly will see that he gets your message, sir," Dianna replied. She had not told him that Louis and Bianca had fallen in love. Time enough for that when they returned; besides, by then, they might have fallen out of love. Bale did report to her the next day that Lionel had signed an order for twenty cars and one engine. He was also sending back with Lionel an engineer who would direct their track construction project. Initial estimates suggested that the two lines would meet at the border near the same date.

The next day, Bale again sent for Dianna. The monarch of Barcella was now in town for a demonstration as well. She was introduced to Andre and Felice Barcella. He was the grandson of the famous Jovanna Barcella, who had brought the country out of near destruction back into a great vitality, second only to that of Velona and possibly Zargarb. He was in his forties and saw the enormous impact this invention would have on transportation of cargo. By the end of the demonstration, he too wanted to purchase a large number of cars, an engine, and have tracks laid at least parallel to the Great Coastal Road across Barcella and on across eastern Velona and into the great docks of Velona proper. Dianna's grand design was beginning to bear fruit. Once rail lines linked these three countries, many others would desire to join in as well.

Dianna's problems were mounting. A better method of fastening the cars to each other had to be found, especially if the engine could pull more than the four cars thus far tried. The engine itself needed many modifications. It depended upon having wood or coal to burn and water. Refueling stations now needed to be created, but just how far apart remained unanswered. There were just not enough hours in the day for her to get all this handled. Then, she got a brilliant idea. "Duh! I have two bodies. Why not use my new one too?" After this realization and especially since Enyo was now staying up nights and sleeping through the daytime hours, she could put this one to sleep and use her Enyo body to work on more things! "I can get twice as much done this way!" Thus, of the six who were trying to run two bodies at the same time, Dianna-Enyo was the first to make a major use of the second body, her nine year old Enyo body.

Later that day, Cosima and Alessa were summoned to Bale's office, along with Chief Inspector Adolfo. Andre Barcella wanted to discuss the growing opium problem in his sector. First, Cosima outlined all that she knew about the secret drug dealing being done by the Church of Jehosanity. She pointed out the role that Cardinal Diego Estebano of Barcella was playing. Andre cursed when he heard of the Church's involvement. "This is criminal! They must be stopped!"

"We are working on it," Cosima replied, and she turned the meeting over to Bale. It was his position to tell Andre that he had sent one of his gun ships there, disguised as a pirate ship to sink the caravels bringing the opium here.

"So that's why there has been such a growing problem. Their supply is drying up! Well, now our increasing crime rate makes sense. What are we going to do about all this?" Andre wanted to know.

"Technically," Cosima answered him, "we are only legally allowed to document charges against the Cardinal and the Mano del Dio. Since they are still citizens of Megalos, they would then have to leave for home. We cannot actually legally arrest them."

"Damn! He should be made to pay and pay dearly for what he's doing! The damage to our people is huge," Andre fumed.

"We know, sir. We here all believe the same way. Still, there is the citizenship issue, if we wish to remain legal." She emphasized that last word. "Now if we don't, well. . ."

Bale said softly, "I think that all of us here are of the same mind. These men must pay for what they have done to our people. I've lost all patience and respect for this church of theirs and these men. When Cosima and Adolfo say the time is right, we are going to clandestinely capture our Cardinal and his assassins and ship them off to Isla la Roca, our penal colony on the tiny island off shore. No one will know anything about it, and I will make a big show of trying to find out what happened to these men. They will have just disappeared. The official rolls of the penal colony will list them under different names. In essence, then, they will merely vanish from Tarra, permanently. If you can arrange a similar scenario for your Cardinal, you are most welcome to send him to our penal island as well, Andre."

"Brilliant! I will take you up on your offer! How will we know when the time is right?" Andre asked.

"I will contact you, sir," Cosima answered. "Now, I am not entirely sure how this will all play out. Gerardo West Po and I have been working out likely predictions on what will likely happen next. So far, his studies and guesses have been precisely correct. I believe that the time will be fairly soon, perhaps within a month or so. As we know more here, I will let you know." Andre was quite satisfied with this arrangement and their part of the meeting was concluded.

On October 20, Luisa called for a family council. "Bianca has reported that her group has gotten the Tashien immigrants to their new land, just south of the Dakar River in the Southlands. They are now beginning to construct a sea coastal city there. She is asking for permission for her group to traverse the coast below the Desert of Desolation and head into Tashien and Tan Loc Province to rescue or aid Bethany and Dita. Do we give her our okay to proceed?"

"Jemma and Fina are still in Shansee?" asked Elena.

"Yes, they are still keeping tabs on opium shipments," Luisa replied.

"We might as well let them try it," Alessa said. "Bianca is likely to do it anyway. I know I would if I were there. My mom's in trouble too. Of course, I surely don't know how they are going to find them, since it's such a huge country."

The discussion was short lived. All agreed that the four should attempt to locate them. Sandra then asked, "Luisa, relay to Bianca that a Banca del Dio representative will be coming there shortly to build a Banca del Dio in this new city right away. That way, these people will be able to handle their banking needs very soon." Luisa agreed to do so.

Just then, Gerardo came looking for Cosima and the family meeting adjourned. "Hi Gerardo, what's up?" Cosima asked, after giving him a welcome hug and kiss.

"It's just happened! Just like I predicted, one of the drug dealers, one of those supplied directly from the Cardinal, has just been attacked and killed by distraught and angry addicts! As the eyewitness accounts go, they kept insisting that he must have a hidden supply somewhere and they wanted access to it. He didn't and they beat him to death. They've gone crazy and are doing anything imaginable looking for a fix. One down, eleven to go," he said very excited about the turn of events.

"This is really good news, Gerardo. It proves that your theory is still predicting correctly," Cosima encouraged him. Just then, Chief Inspector Adolfo arrived, rushing in great haste.

"Cosima, drug dealer Abramo has just been killed by a mob of angry addicts!" he exclaimed. "Oh hi Gerardo."

"Yes, Gerardo just told me. Did you capture the addicts?" she asked.

"Unfortunately no. They disbursed before our policemen got to the scene. I have sent out eleven of my men to spy on the remaining known dealers," he explained.

"Well, you may expect that as soon as the eleven hear about Abramo, they will either go into hiding, flee the country, or hide behind a whole army of security men," Gerardo explained. "At least that is what my theory is predicting. Will you let Cosima and me know if your spies observe these things happening or if they spot something else going on?"

"Absolutely. Perhaps the time is coming sooner than we expected, Cosima. I will be glad to be rid of these vermin," Chief Inspector Adolfo admitted.

"You know, I have an idea," Gerardo caught Adolfo before he left. "Velona ought to do a little service for these addicts. Why not post a number of official posters around the areas of the known dens? Have them list the known dealers. This way, the addicts who need their fix will know just who to contact."

"Oh, that *is* insidious!" Chief Inspector Adolfo acknowledged with a wry smile. "That will certainly put the eleven in the hot seat for their dirty dealings. I am sure that Bale will give us the okay. I'm off to see him now. Things may well become interesting later today. Keep you all posted." Smiling broadly and humming a ditty, the Chief Inspector left the estate.

"Gerardo, you are devious, but I love it," Cosima said and gave him a loving kiss. "Now when the dealers convince everyone that they no longer have the product, we can add one more name to the list, the Cardinal. When they storm his church, we are there to sweep him off to safety — the safety of Isla la Roca, that is."

"Yes, but we must be more devious than that. The other priests will know that we took him to safety. No, we need suspicion to fall on the mob of addicts, not the policemen. The Cardinal needs to see that his dealers are being mobbed and attacked so that he can grow worried that one of the dealers has talked to the mob telling them who sells the opium to him. Then, he will be primed for our action. We can hasten that along a little bit. I know someone who works for the newspaper that Ania started up some years ago. I think that I can convince him to add a little extra news in tomorrow's edition. Back in a while, love." Gerardo left to work his slight twist.

At nine the next morning, Chief Inspector Adolfo, a newspaper in his hand, knocked on the door of the rectory of the largest Church of Jehosanity in Velona. An adept cautiously opened the door. "Good morning. Chief Inspector Adolfo to see his Holiness, Cardinal Reina Lano. It is most urgent that I see him directly."

"Yes, this way. Nasty business — this opium business," the young priest in training commented as he led the policeman down the hallway to the Cardinal's main office, where he was just finishing his breakfast. "Your Holiness, Chief Inspector Adolfo to see you. Urgent business."

"Ah, please do come in, Chief Inspector," the scarlet clad middle aged man said as he rose. "Forgive the mess. I am forced to dine in my office. Security reasons, of course."

The adept closed the door, leaving the two men to talk in private. "I will be blunt. Have you seen the morning paper? I brought a copy in case you haven't."

"Yes, yes, this is a nasty business, isn't it," the Cardinal replied, a slight tremble in his voice.

"Well, yes, we are trying to deal with the mess, but we had no idea just how wide spread the opium use actually was here in Velona. We are grossly overworked now, what with these desperate addicts trying to acquire their next fix. That's what I've come to discuss with you. We both know that the newspaper has it completely wrong, claiming that one of the dealers claims that Your Eminence is the person who supplied the drug dealers here in Velona. Preposterous I say. Certainly not the Church's most Holy Man in Velona!"

The Cardinal visibly relaxed; the Chief Inspector didn't believe that bit of news. "Yes, preposterous indeed. Still. . ."

"Yes, that is why I have come. Bale West Po now fears greatly for your safety. These mobs are unpredictable and widespread. At first this morning, he was considering sending an army to surround your Church here to guarantee your safety. However, that was discarded because it would obviously interrupt your Church's Holy Work, and it would lend credence to that foul, slanderous accusation in the newspaper."

"Yes, I can see that," the Cardinal replied graciously.

"Bale then had a better idea. Perhaps all this is merely nothing to worry about."

"Oh, I am not so sure, Chief Inspector. Did not two of the drug dealers get beaten to death by mobs of angry, desperate addicts yesterday?" the Cardinal inquired, knowing full well that was in the papers and that Adolfo also knew about that.

"Yes, I agree with you and I convinced Bale not to do nothing. He's agreed that if a mob shows up here at your Church and rectory, he will slip you and your guards out of here to a place of safety until the police can get these mobs under control. He has a country house just up the coast a ways and has already sent word to a caravel down at the docks to be ready to receive you and set sail for his country home at a moment's notice. Of course, the accommodations there you will find are first class all the way, as befitting the monarch of Velona."

"Oh that is indeed most kind and considerate of him. I do believe that may be a wise course for us to follow, given this nasty business. I am most appreciative of his kindness," the Cardinal replied. He thought, "What a bunch of idiots! They have no idea that we are behind this uprising and the fools are now offering me safe haven. Idiots and fools. They are playing right into our hands as the Pope guessed they might."

"Excellent. Bale's prime concern is for your safety. I will leave one of my men wearing plain clothes here with you. Should anything happen, he will lead you to one of our carriages, which I will leave nearby, but out of sight from the street. The driver will be instructed to take you at once to the waiting caravel. In an hour, you will be totally safe and secure."

"Again, I must thank you and please thank Bale West Po for me, if I do not get the chance. We all are working for the betterment of Velona," the

Cardinal replied. Adolfo bowed and left. Shortly afterwards, a non-descript man took up a position just inside the rectory's main door, from which he could watch the grassy entrance area, where a mob would likely assemble, demanding an audience with the Cardinal. Adolfo then walked down the block behind the rectory to an alleyway to verify personally that the carriage was waiting.

Then, he checked on the fifty men waiting in wagons in the alleyway after that. If trouble came, he was prepared. At last, he walked back, climbed into his own carriage, and headed back to his office. There his staff gave him the official morning reports. "Ah, Gerardo was right," he muttered. Three dealers had already fled Velona for safety. Two had gone into hiding and his men lost complete track of them. Five were now holed up with dozens of fighters protecting their buildings and houses. He walked over to his large map of Velona. Red pins marked the deployment of his men this morning. Objective: keep an eye out for any mobs of addicts and report their movements to him. Was Gerardo right? Would the desperate addicts take the bait and head for the Cardinal's office?

Around eleven, the first notice that mobs were forming arrived at headquarters. At once, Chief Inspector Adolfo hopped into his carriage and headed for the scene to take charge. By the time that he had arrived where he'd positioned his wagon loads of policemen, an angry mob had already assembled outside of the Church of Jehosanity and was yelling for the Cardinal to come out or they would smash their way inside. As he ordered his men to deploy and arrest the mob, he saw the other carriage move out of the next alleyway. He grinned and then set to work, following his band of policemen.

As the large band of armed police began moving in towards the crowd, the addicts began to flee in all directions. By the time that Chief Inspector Adolfo reached the main doors of the Church, the mob had evaporated, dispersing down the other streets. With his men in firm control, he went inside to check on the situation. Father Janos seemed nervous. "Are they gone? Why would they attack the Holy Church?" he asked.

"It seems that your Cardinal was selling opium to the local dealers. Now the men that he has gotten addicted to his opium want more, and the Cardinal has not provided any more," Chief Inspector Adolfo explained, testing the priest.

"That can't be true, can it?" the priest asked, hastily crossing himself. "Scandalous. He left a while ago. No one seems to know where he's gone. He did leave two of our security men with us."

"As far as we know, it is true. Let us hope that that mob doesn't get to him. You know that they beat two drug dealers to death yesterday, don't you?" Adolfo planted more seeds.

"Yes, we heard about that. Tragic. Dealing in opium is a sin in our Church. If he has, we should notify our Pope and have him launch an investigation. If Cardinal Reina is guilty, then he will be defrocked and sent into exile. I will see that the Pope is notified of this today! I wonder where Cardinal Reina has gone?"

"Well, let's hope that he went somewhere safe. I will leave a number of policemen here on guard duty for the next few days. Hopefully, your church will not be damaged." Adolfo bowed and left.

When he returned to his office, the carriage driver had also returned. "It is done. Cardinal Reina is on his way to the Roca along with two of his Mano del Dio henchmen. He readily agreed to take off his scarlet robes so that he would not be recognized as he walked to the caravel at the docks. We do not believe that the three were recognized. His robes and those of his two henchmen are floating in the bay, and the tide will bring them ashore later. The drug dealers have been handled, boss."

"Excellent. I will go notify Bale and the others. Thanks." Feeling better than he had in days, Chief Inspector Adolfo left to visit Bale and then Cosima. Problem handled — at least that's how he saw it.

"Wow. That is good news. The Cardinal will be paying for his treachery," Cosima acknowledged, after the Chief Inspector told her and the others at the estate of the recent events. "I'll send this along to Andre in Barcella. Perhaps he can arrange something similar to the Cardinal there." He smiled and left.

"What did I tell you?" Gerardo smirked. "It worked out perfectly. When his robes wash up on shore, everyone will assume that the mob got to him at last. He is registered on the Roca under a false name. Only a few of us know the real story. Problem solved!"

"Oh no it isn't," Sandra broke in on their celebration. Everyone looked at her. "You've got a flock of opium addicts who are desperate for more and there is no more. There are a whole lot of very sick people out there that need help."

"I see what you mean," Cosima realized that she was right. "But how do we help them?"

"That's just it, I really don't know. We've never had to deal with something like this. Now we have Bethany and Dita on them too. We must find a way to help them and the other desperate addicts," she explained.

"Well," Alessa volunteered, "I am going to try our therapy on little Bethany whenever Bethany is lucid enough, probably in the early mornings. If I can get enough of her attention here with her little body, maybe I can help her without being down there in Tashien. At least it is worth a try."

"One of us should work with Renzo too, whenever Dita is awake enough," Cosima added. "Since Elena is asleep in the daytime now, I'll volunteer to work Renzo."

"We need some real patients here to study and experiment with to see if we can find better ways of helping them to come off of the opium," Sandra suggested. "Perhaps Bale can setup a free clinic where we Healers and doctors can see what we can do for them. As we figure things out, perhaps there will be a way we can also then help Bethany and Dita."

"Okay, I will go see Bale about it right now," Cosima replied. "Come on bodyguard." Alessa grinned and Gerardo followed them.

Chapter 17 Getting Unhooked

"Bart Boldovina! Sandra, we have someone for you to study," Cosima remembered the young married man who had stolen things from his parent's home to support his habit. "Arturo, let's go see him and ask him if he would like some medical assistance kicking his habit. Sandra can study him and use what she learns to help Bethany and Dita and the others too."

"Great, yes, that would be excellent. I'll make up the spare bedroom and get ready for him," Sandra replied, some hope returning that somehow she might be able to assist Dita and me.

Two hours later, the two returned with Bart. "Well, you are in luck, he still has a small quantity of the stuff left," Cosima handed her his precious bag. "His dad pulled every string in the book to get him even this much." Bart looked as if he were in dream land, but Sandra thought he was more like a walking zombie, as they led him into the spare bedroom.

Sandra began making observations and notes on his physical condition. Sandra noted that his pupils were constricted, his pulse was slow, and his breathing seemed uncommonly slow. Yet, he felt warm and relaxed and seemed extremely contented. That soon began to wear off, however.

Four hours later, he became very restless, his pulse rose significantly. From her point of view, he seemed to be delusional, worrying about police and someone who was following him. His anxiety level began rising, but soon gave way to a fit of crying, begging for another fix. When she didn't give him more, his muscles began shaking, almost as if having a spasm, she noted. This then led to a period of alternating chills and sweating. A bout of nausea and then vomiting followed. She noted that he definitely had not been eating well nor had a proper diet for an extended period. Later that night he couldn't sleep at all and began hallucinating wildly.

Sandra held onto his hand and then made a key observation. "I smell the stuff coming out of his pores! I wonder," an idea began forming and hand Luisa watch over him while she went to see Dianna.

"The opium is still inside his body; it's seeping out of his pores when he sweats, Dianna. I have an idea that may speed this whole withdrawal process. Can you make me a sauna in the basement by diverting a lot of our winter heating system into a small temporary room? I want to speed up his sweating greatly. If I am right, he will sweat out the residual buildup of the drug that is in his system far more rapidly."

"On it now; I believe I can have something rigged up in a few hours," she replied, eager to help. If Sandra was right, perhaps Bethany and Dita could do something similar to rid their bodies of this insidious drug more quickly.

Dianna got Elena, Cosima, and Alissa to help her while Arturo lent his strength to the heavier chores of the project. By morning, they had built a sweat room in the basement. A cold water barrel was right outside the door for cooling down when Bart would approach a heat stroke. Meanwhile, Sandra had Luisa begin fixing a proper well-balanced meal for Bart and had her take a supply of salt down to the sweat room. Sweating as much as she had in mind required periodic salt intake as well as cooling off baths.

Although everyone was exhausted when the morning came, Bart was still having such terrible withdrawal symptoms, that they ignored and focused on helping him. Sandra explained what she was going to try, but Bart mostly just groaned. Now his back was aching. With Arturo's help, they got him down the stairs and into the sweat room, which was as hot as a desert sun.

Since Bart was not really in command of his faculties, Sandra, Luisa, and Arturo carefully monitored him, while he sat sweating and shaking. Elena headed off to bed, along with Enyo. The teens yawned and watched after the other nine year olds, especially Bethany and Renzo, leaving the adults to deal with Bart and Sandra's experiment.

By the late afternoon, Bart was feeling lots better and gobbled down the food that Luisa had prepared. Then, he was tired and they allowed him to go to sleep. Elena watched over him during the night, allowing the weary adults finally to get some needed sleep.

By early morning, Bart was again suffering heavy symptoms, but they were not quite as bad as the previous day. Luisa managed to get him to eat a good, though smaller amount, of breakfast, before Sandra got him back into the sweating room.

When they ended for the day and supper, Bart was again clear-headed and ate well. Again, Elena watched over him during the night. When he woke the third day, his symptoms were still there, but Sandra and Bart noticed that they were markedly less in force. Now he began to see the sweating room as his salvation and needed no persuasion or force to enter it.

At the end of seven days, Sandra could no longer smell anything coming out of his pores and Bart no longer had any withdrawal symptoms. He felt clear headed for the first time in months. Besides thanking them, he made an interesting observation about himself. "You know, you have really saved my life. I now know that I am going to have to be very careful. Mentally, I still have urges to smoke it again, but that can be handled. I no longer have that awful physical craving over which I had no control." She thanked him for his observation and had Arturo drive him home.

Interestingly when Arturo returned, he handed Sandra a bag of a thousand gold. "His father insisted that I give you this along with his eternal thanks for saving his eldest son."

"Well, that's something. I think I will speak to Bale and use this to help setup an opium withdrawal clinic to help the many others fighting their addiction," Sandra decided. "We've proven this approach works, sweating it out and eating proper meals. Now let's see if it helps more broadly."

She and Bale setup a small clinic using the funds she had been given. During the next three weeks, she assisted three dozen addicts to overcome their cravings for opium.

Each day on the small riverboat was a challenge for us. Dita and I knew that we all absolutely had to be weaned from our intense cravings for the opium. Hence, we had poor Long Yan do his best to withhold our pipes from us for ever-lengthening periods each day. Yes, it tore his heart to see his beloved San Min begging, whining, and pleading with him to fetch the pipes for her. Heart wrenching yes, but highly necessary.

The fourth morning, while I was still lucid and not fighting my body's craving, Alessa joined Sandra with me via a Mind Link. *I have some good news, most promising,* Sandra explained. *I am treating a local man for heavy opium addiction. I have noticed that the drug has pervaded his whole body. I am having him sweat that residue out by using a sauna that Dianna has made. He must be given lots of salt and cold baths periodically, plus he must be given proper, nourishing meals too. It is working. Although it's only the third day of it, the results are very dramatic and quite visible. See if there is any way you can do something like that where you are at.*

We were in an enclosed cargo hold. They had a small heater that pumped warm air in here. Long and Bi were just getting ready to feed us our morning meal. "Bi, my friend back in Velona has come up with a way to help us all get off this damnable opium fairly easily." I explained what we needed. She got Kang down into the hold and we discussed how we might turn the cargo hold into a steaming sauna.

"I can use some of the gold of yours to lay in more charcoal, salt, and more food at the next village," Kang suggested. "Long Yan and Bi will have to carefully monitor you so that you don't get a heat stroke. You cannot maneuver well because of your feet, so they are going to have to help you constantly. I can bring a wash barrel down with cooler water and perhaps get some more at the next village. I believe that it is doable, though it will be hard on you."

"We have to get off this stuff," Dita growled. "I'm ready to do anything to make that happen!" The others agreed and they set about making the cargo hold into a sauna for us. "Long, forget modesty for now. We are going to be sweating like pigs. It will be far easier for everyone if we are mostly naked while sweating."

He grinned, "Yes, that will make it easier for me to get you into the cooler water when you are too hot. I am a modest man, but I must do all that I can to help you. I will endure anything to not have to light up those pipes for you anymore!"

With Bi and Long's assistance, we undressed to our panties. Kang and Long lowered the barrel into the hold and then slowly filled it with buckets from the river. All the while, the charcoal heater began to warm up the hold. Bi kept an eye on the heater, adding more charcoal as needed. Later, she fixed us our meals. By the time that we began feeling that craving coming upon us again, the water bath was ready and Long stripped down to join us. He had a large bag of salt and several water skins for us to drink as much water as we could.

Now the withdrawal symptoms began in earnest. We cried. We lost control of our muscles. Anxiety attacks became common. Yet, as the heat increased inside the cargo hold and our bodies began to sweat, that began to drown out our heavy symptoms. Sandra was right; this would work! Before long, poor Long began getting a real workout! As we got too hot, he had to pick us up and dunk us in the water barrel, put salt into our mouths, and help us guzzle water like mad. Occasionally, he had to cool himself off as well.

By suppertime, we were exhausted and very grateful to have the cargo hold covers removed and the cool evening air filling the hold. Now, Bi and Long had to dress us and then feed our ravenous bodies. Once done, all of us fell into a sound sleep, the first good sleep that we had had in a long time. For San, Chan, Dai, and Hon, it had been years since they slept this well.

The next morning, after we ate a good breakfast, the process began once more. By the end of the third day of this sweatbox therapy, Dita, Mei, and I knew it was going to work. None of us had had any opium for the three days and our heavy, overwhelming cravings were subsiding, along with our withdrawal symptoms. However, I now saw clearly that San, Chan, Dai, and Hon were going to need a whole lot more sweating time than we three did. Their bodies had been saturated with opium for at least three years or more.

After a week of sweating, Dita, Mei, and I were done. All the withdrawal symptoms were completely gone. We were free of the physical addiction part. However, we continued the process for the sake of the other four women who were not.

By day, Kang continued to walk the two oxen slowly along the riverside path. Frequently, he had to stop to allow other faster boats with larger teams to pass us. The better equipped riverboats were pulled by four to six oxen, and some even had teams to do the walking so that they didn't have to stop at night. Our progress up the Yonshu River was pitifully slow, but Kang and Bi didn't mind it at all. They had been doing this for nearly thirty years and loved the freedom that they had.

By the third week in November, we finally had the four women completely off of their addiction. None showed any more signs of withdrawal symptoms and their health and well-being were vastly improved. However, Kang pointed out that we were now at the large city of Giang, where we would need to leave the Yonshu and head west up the Yan River. "The city can sometimes be a bit wild. Stay on your guard," he cautioned.

Now free of her addiction, Dita moved out of her body and took up a guarding position on the bow, keeping watch over Kang. She feared trouble and we desperately needed Kang's help. In the afternoon, as Kang finally reached the junction and waited in line to make the turn with his oxen, two thugs came up to him.

"Hey, it's old Kang! Hey, old man, you gotta give us a gold if you are going to pass up the Yan," one demanded.

"Since when," Kang replied softly, becoming a bit worried. Both had nasty looking daggers in their waist belts.

"Since now, Kang. We will make sure you can make the turn, won't we," he said. His companion nodded.

Dita decided to act and not let this get out of hand. She picked up the bully and threw him out into the middle of the river. Seeing his pal somehow magically tossed into the river, the other one, who had been silent, turned and ran off into the crowded nearby streets close to these docks and oxen path. Kang looked around but saw nothing. Dita sent him telepathically, *My doing*. Kang smiled and continued his slow walk, pulling on his oxen once more.

As he continued to move along the path, Dita saw many other riverboats and teaming masses of people in the nearby streets. Crime was rampant here too, she noted, as she caught sight of several street fights, but didn't interfere. Because of us, Kang didn't want to spend the night here within the city, and he walked on until past midnight just to get clear of Giang before he tied up his oxen by a few trees near the river, some two miles outside the western edge of the city. After tying their grain bags to their heads, he came below to sleep.

This close to the city, Dita decided to stand guard over us all while we slept. She moved away from her body and positioned herself on the small bow deck where she had a good view all around us. Around three in the morning, she saw some movement along the shore among the low trees and bamboo reeds. Slinking figures, dressed in black, this caught her attention. Stealthily, they moved a few feet very silently and then froze, as if suddenly turned to stone. Then, they moved even closer. Dita became fully alert, somewhere in her mind was someone's warning about men dressed all in black. Unfortunately, she couldn't place it just yet.

Hand signals. Yes, definitely so. One made some tiny gestures and the other responded. Both were making their way towards this boat. Now the two were at the edge of the river, a mere foot from the boat, one at each end. A bit of silver glinted in the starlight. Weapons, these two had weapons strapped over their backs, perhaps fast drawing swords, she concluded. Both men froze once more, listening intently for sounds. We had one of the upper doors open to allow some fresh air into the cargo hold, where we were all sleeping. Up in the bow, Bi and Kang were sleeping in their small hammocks.

One pointed to the open cargo bay door and the other nodded that he saw it. While one gently placed a foot onto the boat, barely pressing down so as not to jostle the craft, the other mimicked him. Ever so slowly, the two men allowed their foot to take more and more of their weight until at last they were able to let go of the shore and slowly bring their other foot onto the deck as well. Dita admired their skill; the boat had only barely rocked a slight amount, no more so than it was from the occasional river wave.

The one over the cargo hold door peered down, and Dita watched his fingers counting the number of sleeping forms below him, while the other watched his fingers and made sure that Kang and Bi didn't stir. He correctly counted that there were eight of us below. The other man nodded, while the man who had done the counting silently drew his sword. Dita's mind finally made the connection. Someone had said to be extremely careful around men dressed all in black, for they were the Cao Bang, thieves and assassins. Now she acted. Just as the man was about to drop down into the cargo hold, she lifted him up into the air, moved him over the side of the boat, and put him down under the water, holding him there.

She put her full attention on the other man, who was staring in disbelief at what he'd just seen! He began to silently back off the boat. Just as he was about to step back onto the shore, Dita lifted him up and forced him underwater, holding both struggling men down. About a minute later, their bodies stopped struggling against Dita's force, and she let go of their bodies. Both lifeless bodies began drifting back down the Yan River towards Giang. Dita now rose up higher in the air looking for more of these assassins, but saw none.

In the morning, once we used the chamber pots, Bi brought us all breakfast. Dita then told us what had happened. Kang said a bit nervously, "Cao Bang assassins! Oh dear. Why would they be interested in my boat?"

"I don't think that they were interested in you, Kang," Dita answered him. "The one just stood watch to make sure you didn't wake up. They were very interested in us down here in the cargo hold. They were counting us and the count seemed to spark their interest."

San Min cried, "They must be after us now! I just know it. They know that we somehow killed Yuen Ming and they've sent the Cao after us! We're as good as dead now."

"No, San Min, you are very much alive," Dita countered. "I won't let them even get close to us. You have my word on that. However, Kang, I think that we ought to put some miles between us and here soon." He nodded and headed to the shore to get his oxen ready to pull the riverboat once more.

Soon, we felt the boat moving once more and I relaxed. Now it was time to begin handling their various traumas. During our extra time in the sweating heat, Alessa and Cosima had cleverly been working us through ours via our little nine year old bodies back home. It had worked well. We quickly re-experienced the pains of the operations, but it had taken our girls nearly two weeks of sessions before we finally erased the effects of the opium on our bodies and minds. I should comment that there were an awful lot of strange aches, weird sensations, to say nothing of unwanted emotions that we had accumulated via our long stretch of addiction. One by one, Alessa and Cosima ran us through these until all were gone.

Now it was our turn to do the same for these five. I took San Min first, while Dita took the easiest case, Mei Bi, who had just undergone the same trauma when we did. Chan, Dai, Hon, and Long watched our sessions with great interest. After the first sessions were done, the four wanted to learn how to do it as well. With a little coaching, Long began to do Dai, while Chan took Hon. Now each day, four sessions were off and running. Later on, Mei was handled and she took on Chan and Dita took over Hon from Chan.

By the time that we finally drew close to San Min's hometown of Nan Yan, all traces of the pain and trauma of the surgery was completely erased from us all, as well as most all the lingering effects of the long period of opium addiction with its accompanying strange sensations, aches, and emotions. During the evenings, Chan, Dai, and Hon in particular wanted to give us back a little something, which was fueled by Mei, actually. At the beginning, Mei felt bad that she had not been given the "extra" training in how to use her arms to further enhance her ability to give others intense pleasures. Thus, the three insisted each evening that they teach Mei as well as Dita and me how it was done. Of course, Dita and I had to be taught most everything that Mei already knew how to do as a kami. Now Mei at least felt that she was worthy of her new status as a zen-kami.

However, by the end of everyone's therapy sessions, they all had a completely different point of view about life. Each knew that they were a spiritual being and not a body, and that they had lived many previous lives. Further, they had all run into at least one incident where the Doll Creatures had enforced the aberration honor-system on them. Now this whole honor-based society seemed utterly false and pointless to them. They were all very alive, vibrant, and cheerful women, with one major obstacle, one major hurdle facing them and us as well: our arms ended at our elbows and our distorted, tiny feet, which made walking both very slow and required a delicate balancing act. We had most definite physical limitations now facing us, which we had yet to begin to address. This tied in strongly to their major question: what do we do now?

"Although others will look upon me as a zen-kami," Chan explained, "I no longer see this as something I want to do. I want to do something more important than giving bodies pleasure. Yet, what can we do like this?" She waved her short, conical arms. Indeed, while we no longer felt grief and resentment over our situation, we all faced that stark reality of physical limitations, particularly so for other the five women. Dita and I could deal with it, for we had done so before, well at least then we were able to walk, even if we had to wear heels. Now we were in a very different country with very different standards, one of which was that all seven of us would be automatically presumed to be zen-kami women. That is, we would be given the honor and respect that was quite high indeed, just less than that of Princesses and the Emperor and Empress, but along with that came the expectation that we would also deliver zen-kami experiences to others, which none of them now wanted to do anymore.

On the positive side, Sandra had verified that Jemma's transfer of sixty million in gold had gone through. The funds were now in my account. Following my wishes, she had set up an account for each of the five women and transferred five million into each of theirs. "We are incredibly independently wealthy!" was Chan's reaction, after they all finished letting out incredible squeals of joy and relief. Yuen had at last paid them for what he had done to them and with them.

"The money will allow us to live, but it does not give us any real purpose for our lives," Chan then pointed out. "At least, we can wear good quality clothing, eat well, and have a nice place to live. We can pay servants to assist us. All this is very important, Bethany. Without this, we would be doomed. Yet, I need more. I need a purpose, a goal."

"I could not agree with you more, Chan," I replied. "First, let's see if we can get some sanctuary for a while. Dita and I can help you all learn to do some things for yourselves so that you are not so hopelessly dependent on others. Then, let's see what we all can do about some really worthwhile purposes."

"Thanks. Long Yan and I want to get married before anything else bad happens to us," San Min teased me.

I admit, at this point in time I had absolutely no ideas of what purpose these women could have. I had no plans at all, except to try to be safe and sort out the incredible mess that we had entered. Well, I had found the nail and gotten the shoe onto the horse, using the Guardian's analogy. Now that I had the horse, I was at a total loss on where or who the rider should be, let alone where the battle that needed this rider was located. Instead, I had unknown assailants possibly hunting us down for unknown reasons. I had seven of us who could barely walk, let alone handle routine life things — excepting for Dita and me that is. I felt like yelling, "Will the rider of this horse please appear." I was more than a little frustrated just now.

Chapter 18 Aftermath in Shansee

Jemma paced the small room where Fang had put the two teens up. The thin bamboo walls at least stopped the torrential rains, which fell now almost constantly. "Monsoon season has come," Fang had explained. The rains were not what was bothering her, rather it was the chaos that followed in the wake of Yuen's death that had her stymied. Her job, detecting the next opium shipment from Shansee, was now on hold.

The various mid-level leaders of Yuen's organization were now fighting over the spoils of his empire. Indeed, his was a large one at that, with holdings in nearly every sector of life here in Shansee and even a large part of Tan Loc Province. The fighting between warring factions had spilled out onto the streets making travel there dangerous. So much so, that Fang now had to escort Chan Dai to and from her work at the Santi.

It was November 1. Rumors now suggested that Qiang Peng, Yuen's second in command had successfully taken over the two pleasure palaces, but could hold onto nothing more. She was more interested in Tao Shi, the aide who had muscled his way into controlling the opium trade of Yuen's. Would he attempt to reopen the trading deal with the Pope and his men? If so, when and where? Cooped up like this, she had no way of finding out.

Fina, on the other hand, was constantly practicing her fighting arts with her new boyfriend, Tian Wang. Zhen found her to be a very fast learner and the three of them spent most of their time in his academy practice rooms. Jemma hated fighting, well not so much fighting, as the fact that Fina had a boyfriend now and that Fina was a whole year younger than she was. The two of them had been letting their nails grow as well as their hair. On their own, more or less, both had decided to experiment a little and see how they would look. Now that Fina had a boyfriend, she spent far less time with her. Jemma finally stopped pacing. Yes, that was it. She was jealous of Fina spending time with Tian and not her. She chuckled and blew off that consideration.

Now Jemma focused her attention on just how she realistically could continue her mission: notifying Kali of opium shipments from Shansee. Cooped up because of the dangerous streets and the monsoon, she hadn't a clue whether or not more had been or was being sent. She felt as if she was letting Kali down. "How can I possibly continue the spy mission?" she asked herself and continued her pacing, confident that she was onto the real problem at hand. Of course, Fina had to learn all she could about fighting arts; her job was to protect Jemma.

A loud smashing, banging noise broke the sound of the torrential rains upon the bamboo and board roof above her head. It sounded like it came from the Academy's main entrance gates. She headed out to see what had caused it.

It was around five and Zhen Song was just wrapping up his daily lessons with his twenty students here at his Xian Academy. Tian and Fina were both sweating and leaning on their knees, catching their breaths from their workout. His other twenty students bowed to Zhen and prepared to gather up their things. Just then, the main gates were smashed open, and twenty-five figures dressed entirely in black burst into the main practice room. "Cao Bang!" yelled Zhen instantly recognizing these assassins. The figures all carried a curved sword in their hands, but formed into a line behind one figure that stepped forward and bowed to Zhen.

"Zhen Song. We know that you helped the seven zen-kami escape from the Purple Palace. We only want to know where you took them. Give us this information and we will leave. If you do not, we will take other means to make you tell us."

"Why do you wish to know this fact?" Zhen asked, stalling.

"Qiang Peng has put a hit out on these seven zen-kami. They are to be captured and brought before him to explain how it is that they were able to kill Yuen Ming. If they refuse to do so, they are to be killed. You have helped murders escape. Where did you take them, Zhen?"

Zhen laughed in an attempt to invalidate their assumption. "You are standing here before me telling me that zen-kami were able to kill the Master Yuen Ming? Not even I could do that. Surely, you are jesting me. What is it that you really want, Cao Bang?" He attempted to make this seem utterly impossible.

"Don't play games with me, Zhen Song. You and I both know that one or more of them has kijutsu powers. Qiang Peng knows this as well. This is your last chance to tell me before I take more forceful methods. If you do not tell me, my men may obtain what we want to know from Wen Dai, the publisher."

Now Zhen began to worry. These men knew of his close relationship with the Dias and Wen was not fighter trained and would likely be tortured or killed. Somehow he had to get to Wen before these men did, if he was not already too late! "Students, this is my fight. I order you to leave immediately by the back door," Zhen spoke with full intention. Many of them were youngsters, ill equipped or trained to fight such evil assassins. Most grabbed their bags and began running to the rear, leaving only two older teens and Tian, who stood beside Fina.

The speaker made a sharp downward motion with his sword, and his two dozen men rushed forward to attack Zhen, Fina, Tian, and the two other students. Coming out of that back room, Jemma heard this and prepared to fight as well, though she was far to the rear by over fifty feet. As the line advanced, Fina and Jemma saw both Tian and Zhen make a pushing motion with their hands. Suddenly, the charging line of men was pushed back and off their feet by some invisible force, as if a gigantic hand had suddenly pushed solidly into them. Jemma and Fina now realized that these two men also possessed kijutsu powers as well, part of their Xian skills, they assumed. Fina, Tian, and Zhen took this delay to get their swords out and ready.

One by one, the Cao Bang assassins got to their feet, recovered their weapons, and charged into the melee. However, the five formed a line of defense so that only two could attack anyone of them, except for Zhen and one of his teen students who were at either end of their line. Steel upon steel echoed over the sound of the heavy rain.

Jemma didn't hesitate. She chanted up a ball of fire and centered it on the back group of the Cao Bang. When it detonated, their clothes released giant clouds of steam. Screaming from the boiling pain, twelve of them dashed outside into the deluge to seek burn relief. Jemma could not unleash another because the remaining enemy was too close to her companions. Could she get a lightning bolt in through the door? She began to work out how.

Fina dropped one who was fighting her, but the other got a slice in on her left arm. She was forced to drop back a bit, and Tian again used a push kijutsu power to drive the others coming for her back across the floor. In the process, he too took a cut to his side from one in front of him. The two teens each killed one, before being overwhelmed by the strong, superior Cao Bang forces. Zhen killed two that had originally attacked him but was now fighting their leader, who was much more skilled. He too had to fall back a little.

Boom! Lightning flashed brilliantly in through the open doorway, the bolt striking the backs of three more Cao Bang, sending them flying into three others, knocking them down. Fina didn't hesitate; she stabbed the one who fell before her, while Tian did the same. Now the fight was more evenly balanced. Jemma next cast her illusion spell, centered on the apparent leader. In his mind, he saw three more bolts of lightning kijutsu power striking himself and his remaining men. He reacted, "Withdraw!" he barked loudly. Instantly, the remaining ten men bolted for the door as he did, leaving the Academy a bloody mess.

Zhen turned to see Fina grasping a bleeding arm and Tian holding onto his side, stemming the blood flow. His two teens were in bad shape; one was trying to stop the heavy bleeding from his fallen partner, though bleeding himself. Jemma rushed to Fina at once as Zhen dashed over to the heavily bleeding teen. Zhen again used some kijutsu power emitting a force from his hands. The heavy bleeding stopped. "Quick, bandage him tightly!" While the other teen began tearing up part of his torn shirt, Zhen began to bind his own wounds. He'd taken to slices to his arms. Though not bad cuts, they were bleeding heavily too.

"Here, hold this tightly, Fina," Jemma ordered and moved over to Tian. She saw that he needed her attention more so than Fina. Damn, she needed her emergency healing bag. While holding pressure on his wound, she moved out of her body and into her room. She latched onto her bag and brought it to here. The others saw her bag come floating out of her room over to Jemma's outreaching hand. Zhen smiled, "You have much kijutsu yourself, Miss Jemma."

"I have to sew up Tian and Fina quickly. Then, I'll get to the rest of you," she replied.

"I'll get boiling water, Jemma," Fina offered. "I can hold the bandage tight while I do it."

"Okay, Jemma, you are in charge, get these patched up if you can. I have to get to Wen before it is too late. I've got my arms tied up enough. If you can contact Fang and Chan, please do so. Tell them what has happened and to take extreme care. Get here as fast as possible." He bowed to her and dashed out into the torrential rains.

Jemma made the telepathic contact and relayed the messages. Shortly, Fina returned with the boiling water. Together they set to work, first on the badly wounded teen and then the others one by one. "You know something about healing," Tian commented as Fina and Jemma worked on sewing up his side wound. "Ouch."

"Sorry. Yes, we both do a little. Our Healer knows ten times more than we do," Jemma explained. "Now hold still, please." By the time that they finished up, Chan and Fang rushed in from the rain. Both women were soaked and very worried.

"Oh my god, this is worse than you said," Fang exclaimed as she stepped inside the ruined door and saw the dead men dressed in black scattered about the practice room. "Any word from Zhen and Wen?"

"Not yet. We've just finished getting us all sewn up. I've now got to go back and get some better bandages on them all," Jemma replied.

"Maybe we should go to my place," Chan suggested, extreme worry in her voice.

"Exactly what did Zhen say when he left?" Fang asked Jemma. She relayed his parting words. "Well, he didn't say that we should not head over to the Dai's shop. They are not back yet, so maybe he ran into more troubles."

"Let me contact him and see," Jemma replied and focused her attention onto locating Zhen. *Fang and Chan are back and want to know if they should head over to the Dai's to help you.*

Oh, no. Stay put and stand guard. They may well be back. I'm almost back with Wen. He will need your skills.

"He's nearly here with Wen. I think Wen is hurt too. Fina, more boiling water please," Jemma ordered. "He said for you to stand guard and that they might be back in force." The two took up positions beside the remains of their door. Chan was extremely worried about her husband, no doubt about that, Jemma thought.

In a few minutes, Zhen came through the pouring rain, carrying the body of Wen over his shoulders. Blood ran down his arms heavily diluted from the rainwater. "Put him over here on the mat," Jemma asked, adjusting the lanterns to give her maximum light, fearing the worst for Wen.

Fina came out of their small kitchen carrying another pot of boiling water just in time to see Zhen carefully deposit Wen Dai on the mat. Zhen's makeshift bandages were totally soaked and doing little good, so Fina set to work on him at once, while Fang hovered over her offering suggestions, meanwhile Jemma and Chan began to examine Wen. He had taken a terrible beating and his face was bruised and very swollen. He was unconscious, but Jemma didn't see any sword wounds on his body. "Zhen, was he just beaten up?" she asked. She needed far more data to treat him properly.

"I think his right arm is broken too. He was nearly unconscious when I got to him," Zhen grimaced in pain as Fina finally removed the last of his pressure-applying temporary rag bandages. Now she set to work on cleaning the two wounds and stitching them up.

"I believe that the Cao Bang forced him to tell them about Bethany and the others. He mumbled something about having told them before he lost consciousness," Zhen added.

While they were attending these two, Tian and the two teen students began dragging the enemy bodies outside, dumping them into the street gutter, where several burned bodies lay. Although Chan hovered over Jemma, Fang assisted the three and then stood guard, in case the Cao Bang retuned.

A half hour later, both Jemma and Fina had finished their work. Wen's arm was in splints, his mangled face had been cleaned, and a salve applied. "He's shivering. We ought to get all of you soaked folks into some dry clothes fast," Jemma ordered.

A half hour later, dried and with some hot tea inside them, Fang set to work on fixing something for everyone to eat. As they finally had dinner, Wen roused. Chan was at his side at once, helping him sit up and get to a chair. "I have failed you. They forced me to say that the zen-kami were on their way to Giang."

"You haven't failed us or them. You were beaten to an inch of your life, Wen," Zhen consoled his lifelong friend. "Against, the Cao Bang, you could not hope to withhold what they wanted to hear. At least you didn't tell them that they were actually headed to Nan Yan. It is not going to be safe around here. As soon as they discover that our seven are not in Giang, they will be back in force. Next time, we may not be so lucky to have so much kijutsu on our side."

"We're going to have to go after them, I mean Bethany and the others, aren't we," Jemma asked.

"Considering that they are virtually helpless and addicts to boot, yes, we are," Zhen replied. "Besides, we cannot stay here. In a week or so, they will be back in force. They have many days head start on us, yet we must go after them. I hope that we are not too late. Still, there is hope. The Cao Bang will only be little ahead of us."

"How will we go, dear?" asked Fang. "The monsoon season is here. The roads will be too muddy for a wagon or carriage. A riverboat will be too slow to catch them."

"We have no choice but to go by horse, though it will be tough to do in this rain," Zhen replied.

"Yes, but we have to keep these wounds dry," Jemma protested. "Are there inns where we can stay the nights?"

"We will have to stay at inns; there is no other recourse. The rains will ease off the further north that we get. Fang, you pack what we need. I'll take Chan back to their place and help her pack for Wen and herself."

"Zhen, you wear your oil cloak! Don't you dare get those bandages soaking," Fang replied. "Chan, you can wear my oil cloak. We are going to need some for the teens, Zhen. And where are we going to get horses on a night like tonight?"

"Have Tian and Jemma round them up. We're stealing the Cao Bang horses. The horses of the ones that died are still milling around just outside in the street," Zhen answered her, donning his heavy cloak which had an oil covering to repel the monsoon.

Jemma stuck her head outside and at once got drenched. However, she did see the horses and began to gather them up. Not knowing just where to put them, she led them inside out of the rain, tying them up just inside the Academy. Tian had ducked home to get his things, promising to be back in a few minutes. "Got to look after my Fina," he told Jemma, who grinned, but then growled as she had to fetch the horses herself. Once she had ten horses inside, she began going through the many saddlebags, discovering quite a few useful items, particularly more oil-coated cloaks. Should have had this a few minutes ago, she thought as she shook off the water from herself and then attempted to dry off a bit. At last, she headed off to change completely.

When Zhen and Chan returned carrying several large bags, both looked very worried. Dripping water onto the Academy mats, they took off their cloaks. "We are being watched," Zhen whispered. He motioned for everyone to head into the kitchen, located in the back of the complex where a stone wall would muffle their voices. Here, there was no chance that the Cao Bang milling outside could overhear them.

"They have left men to watch us. We are not safe here at all. I suspect that they may not have believed Wen fully," Zhen theorized.

"We are packed, but how are we going to leave without being seen?" Fang asked.

"I can handle the watchers," Jemma volunteered.

"Put them to sleep?" asked Fina. Jemma grinned.

"Okay, then let us pack up our things. We will need to bring along some provisions as well," Zhen decided to trust in this young teen. He was not in a position to go outside and challenge the Cao Bang lying in wait. There might be too many for him to handle, especially since his arms were now throbbing from the two wounds he had taken earlier.

Chan would have to lead Wen's horse, for it was all that he could do to hang on to the saddle. Zhen said, "I ride point and get us out of the city. Fang, you bring up the rear and make sure that we are not followed. Tian, Fina, Jemma, you ride between us and Chan and Wen. Look after them please. Jemma, can you lead a packhorse with all our bags on it?"

"Yes, will do," she replied. Now they set to work packing their gear and loading up the packhorse. An oilskin covering was securely lashed over the many bags to keep their bags as dry as possible. "I ought to go out alone for a bit to put the watchers to sleep," she announced. Zhen refused to allow her out alone, and he followed her. With the lanterns doused as if they were heading off to bed, Jemma quietly stepped through the shattered doors into the rain-filled night. She expanded her awareness and found three men were nearby watching the front of the Academy. A short chant later, she motioned for the others to begin to follow her. She led her horse out into the pouring rain, and Zhen pointed the direction. Again, she sensed another two men and put them asleep as well. Two blocks later, she sensed no more, and Zhen had them mount up. Fang handed Jemma the packhorse's reins. Now the group of seven began riding through the darkened streets of Shansee as the monsoon continued to pour buckets of fresh water down upon them.

Fina estimated that it was around ten when they left the Academy and more like midnight when the last houses of the northern section of the city fell behind them. The north road to Giang was stone. With this amount of rain, it would have been a muddy mess had it been dirt. Still, in the poor light and pouring rain, they dare not go faster than a walk. They could not afford to have a horse stumble. Three hundred miles lay before them just to get to Giang. Besides, somewhere ahead of them lay the Cao Bang, heading there to intercept Bethany and the others. Zhen could not risk running into them in the dark. On they rode, water flowing off them as if they were in a river.

By morning, Jemma, nearly half-asleep in her saddle, finally noticed that the rain had stopped. The sky, back lighted by the rising sun, looked ominous, but the heavy rains had ceased for a time.

As the rains let up, Phillipe Dumont at last checked out of the inn on Tiger Street. He mounted his horse and headed to the Xian Academy, full of hope that today Zhen Song would accepted him. Phillipe was sixteen and on his own. His grandparents had been part of the now long defunct Santi del Dio forces here in Shansee. After the demise of that organization, his father had remained here and married a local woman, Lin Sun. They had moved to a rural village west of Shansee, where Phillipe was born. They were now in their late fifties and at last had allowed their son to follow his dream of learning martial arts from some masters. Phillipe had long ago decided that he wanted to learn from the Xian Master, Zhen Song.

Now that the monsoon had temporarily let up for a brief time, he decided to venture from his inn, visit the Xian Academy, and see if Master Zhen would accept him as a student. However, when he neared the Academy, he knew that something was terribly wrong. Men dressed in black were secretly watching the place plus its main doors were smashed. He dismounted and began a closer inspection. "What has happened here?" He spotted several horses still inside the Academy and found traces of blood covering the mats. The place was deserted. He noticed that drawers were slightly ajar and clothes were missing. Conclusion: Zhen had fled after a large battle, probably with the Cao Bang. Quietly, he left and mounted up. He rode slowly on past the black cloaked men, and they made no effort to stop him for which he was thankful. Phillipe figured he could handle one of them, maybe, but why take the chance?

"He either fled the city or when into hiding," he said to himself, as he attempted to work out what had happened. He stopped for breakfast at Xia's. Over hot tea, he reflected on what he had observed. His grandfather had always said trust what you could observe with your senses. That advice had never failed him yet. "Ah, there were at least another half dozen horses inside the Academy last night." Images of the telltale dung piles came to mind. "Ah, so you have indeed packed and probably left with a party of a half dozen last night. Some are wounded. If you were going into hiding, why take horses? No, he must be fleeing the city. Now, where would he go?" It was monsoon season. The heavy rains would come again anytime. Cross country was out; they'd be into mud up to their ears. No, he concluded that Zhen either had probably stayed on the north road to Giang or had taken the coastal road. Swallowing the last of his breakfast egg roll and washing it down with the last of his tea, he decided on the north road to Giang.

He mounted up and headed north on Tiger Street, which eventually became the north road to Giang, which lay some three hundred miles to the north. He kicked his mare into a trot. "Make time while the rains hold off," he whispered to his mare. He began to estimate how far ahead his would-be master might be. If he left in the middle of the night, then it was raining heavily. Thus, he would be walking the horses. If they rode through the night, they would be tired and hungry by now and may likely be stopping at an inn somewhere ahead. How far ahead? It was now nine in the morning. Estimating ten hours of walking, that put them perhaps fifteen to twenty miles ahead of him. At his present pace, that put them around five hours ahead of him. A lot depended upon whether or not they would stop.

He decided that if they had wounded with them, they certainly would stop to eat and check on their wounds. How long? Well, he concluded that he might catch up to them by late afternoon, if the rains held off that long. He urged his mare into a slow canter for a time. Phillipe was determined to catch up with Zhen. Now his mind reflected upon what he would say when he finally met the Xian Master.

A couple of hours later, a small village drew closer. However, Phillipe noticed that a number of horses had left the stone road and headed off across the muddy countryside, evidentially bypassing the village. Curious, he kept his eyes open for signs after he passed through the village. "Yes, look, there come the horses back onto the road. Someone has definitely gone to a lot of trouble to go around this village. They did not want to be seen riding through it." He concluded this must be Zhen and his group. He pressed on. The same pattern held true for the next two small villages.

Late that afternoon, a somewhat larger town appeared, and once more, the tracks led off the trail. Now the rains came again, and Phillipe rode on more slowly, passing through the town. Anytime now, he half expected to see them up ahead of him, though his visibility was slowly reducing rapidly. However, this time, he saw no signs of the group getting back onto the road. After going several miles, he turned around and went back through the town and back to where they had left the road. Even though the rains were once more turning the ground into mush, he followed the clear trail, though with every passing minute, it deteriorated because of the rains.

Zhen pushed them on hard the next day, since the rains abated. Still, as the afternoon wore on, he knew that the large town of Sanloc lay ahead of them. This close to Shansee, he decided not to risk staying at an inn. Instead, there were small farms in the countryside around here. For a gold, a farmer would be very willing to allow them to spend the night in his barnyard buildings. Besides, all the wounds must be checked carefully while the light still held. So far, they had been luck that the rains had abated so long. He led them once more off the road onto the soft, spongy ground. Just north and west of the town, he spotted a large farmstead, whose out buildings looked large. He headed for them. As they rode up, he met the farmer and made his deal: one gold for one night in his barn. The farmer got a good deal indeed.

"We can stay here for the night. Everyone inside. Jemma, you start checking on all the wounds, while Chan and Fang work on fixing us something to eat. I will keep watch for a time, but I don't think that we are being followed."

"Okay, you heard the man; line up for wound inspection," Jemma said half in jest. She, like the others, was dead tired, having ridden all night through the monsoon rains and then nearly all day.

"I believe that my legs are done for, Miss Jemma," Wen said politely.

His face looked awful in the late afternoon light. Worse, he'd never ridden on a horse for so long, and his legs did indeed fail him. Fina caught him in time and helped him slip to the ground. Person by person, Jemma began examining the various wounds. She had to redo both bandages on Tian and Fina, because the rain had gotten in around their cloaks, soaking them.

She was just getting the old ones off when Zhen called out, "Prepare for trouble. Someone is coming; looks like he is tracking us! Damn!" He tried to draw his sword, but both arms were still aching from the two wounds.

"Got you covered," Fang came running up to him at the entrance of the outbuilding, stepping in front of him. Chan and Jemma joined her, wondering how bad this battle would become. They saw a lone rider, a young teen slowly following their trail, as it led to where they were standing. He looked up and saw them, swords in hand, staring out of the building at him.

"Hello. I am looking for Master Zhen Song," the lad called out, dismounting and walking up to them as the rain began falling down harder now. He was tall and thin; his hair was long and black, but he didn't quite look like he came from Tashien, and yet he rather did.

While the three women glanced around looking for others, Zhen stepped out from behind Fang. He bowed, "I am Master Zhen. What is it that you want of me?"

"May I come in out of the rain? I am Phillipe Dumont," he replied bowing as well. Fang, still watching him carefully, had seen no one else behind him or anywhere around the area, motioned him to come on inside. She kept her sword at the ready as he led his horse inside the outbuilding. He walked up to Zhen and bowed again. "I have come to ask if you would consider accepting me as a student."

"Phillipe, how did you find us?" Zhen asked quietly, though Fang and Jemma continued to keep an eye out for others and for treachery. He could not be Cao Bang, for they never appeared in public without their black clothes and mask. This lad was wearing traditional Tashien clothing, relatively expensive. That is, his shirt was cotton with numerous buttons; his pants, linen. His outer cloak was oiled linen.

"When I rose this morning, the rains had letup as they often do for a short period. I chose to ride over to the Xian Academy to ask you to accept me as a student. When I got there, I saw four Cao Bang watching the place and its door was smashed. Inside, I found some horses and a whole lot of blood on the mats. I noticed at least six horses were missing and concluded that some of you were wounded, likely in a battle with the Cao Bang, and that instead of going into hiding, your party chose to flee. I then guessed that it was the north road to Giang that you took and have followed your trail here, Master."

"How could you know that six horses were missing? Was our trail that obvious? We rode on the road," Zhen asked curiously. Jemma guessed that he might be testing the lad. Those were key questions.

"I found piles from six other horses but no horses. I spotted your trails when you left the road to go around the villages. I nearly missed this one and had to turn back when I could not find where you had returned to the road. I simply followed the trail here, but I believe you are safe. The rains now are washing away all signs of our passing. I was not followed by the Cao Bang, Master."

"You are most observant, young Phillipe. Come, share our quarters for the night. I would learn more of you. Chan, add a bit more to the food pot for Phillipe here," Zhen suggested. "Jemma is examining our wounds. Come and dry off." Fang decided to stand guard duty so that Jemma could deal with new bandages for Zhen as well.

Phillipe watched Jemma and volunteered, "Excuse me; I have some skill with such matters. May I lend you a hand, ma'am?"

Jemma looked at Zhen. Certainly, she didn't want anyone messing with her patients, but Zhen nodded his approval. She noticed that he was carefully observing the lad, so she consented to let him help. "See how Tian is doing. His got wet."

"Yes, I can see. We should be wiping it off with sterile water. The stitches look fine. Your handiwork?" he asked.

"Coming," Chan called out, bringing a tin pot of hot water to Jemma.

"Mine and Fina's," Jemma replied, thankful that he realized that they needed boiled water before they did much with the wounds. He followed Jemma's lead, wiping the wounds with a rag dipped in the water. Jemma handed him a clean cloth for the bandage and he tied the bandage on well. She noted that he did seem to know the right way to do this, adding to her curiosity about this strange lad. Together, they worked on Zhen last, while Fang finally closed the outbuilding's door. No sense allowing the lantern light to announce their presence now that the sun was near setting somewhere behind the massive cloud bank and torrential rains.

"Food is ready. I will help Wen," Chan announced. The group squatted on the ground and Fang handed out the wooden plates and sticks to everyone. The teapot was steaming, waiting for them to finish their rice, fish, and vegetables.

"Tell me about yourself, Phillipe. You seem wise for your young years," Zhen began over tea.

"I am sixteen, Master. My grandparents were from the Outer Lands, the Sea Princes, Fortress d'Grange. They were part of the old Santi del Dio organization. They taught me quite a few things before they passed away when I was twelve. My father stayed on and married Lin Sun. I am half Tashien and half d'Grange. Until five years ago, my father was an engineer who worked for the Imperial Palace. We traveled Tan Loc Province extensively when I was a child. I know the province well. When the chaos erupted, Lin and Emile settled down in a rural village some hundred miles from Shansee. There he said that we would be relatively safe. He still believes that one day this chaos will end, but until then, he is content to live a simple life with Lin Sun. Two weeks ago, he finally consented to allow me to come into Shansee to learn the art of Xian from your Academy, Master Zhen. I am here. I wish to learn, but I can see that perhaps I need to assist you first."

"How so?" asked a curious Zhen. Jemma also noticed this and paid close attention to his answer.

"It is obvious that you all are fleeing from the Cao Bang. That much is clear from the destruction at your Academy. I have also heard that the vicious Yuen Ming has been killed recently. His death has brought more chaos to Shansee, as they fight over the spoils. I think that perhaps your flight has something to do with Yuen's death. You are on the road to Giang. I cannot guess if that is your destination, only if it is, you are right to avoid the inns. I spotted Cao Bang watching for visitors in the villages that I passed through today. So how can I help? Well, as I said, I am very familiar with this province. If your goal is to get to Giang unnoticed by the Cao Bang, I know a number of routes by which this may be safely done."

"For such a young lad, you seem to know an awful lot about us. How is it that you suspect that the Cao Bang are after us and that we have had some involvement with Yuen's death?" Zhen continued to grill Phillipe.

"I am sorry, Master Zhen. I do not know much about your activities. I have listened to what others have said about various martial arts masters and believe that yours would be best suited for me. What I have said is speculation based upon some observations. The Cao Bang usually are interested only in significant events and things. They are not known for raiding a Master's Academy. Such is a most risky venture. They would only have chanced that if the stakes were exceedingly high. The only thing of news on the streets of Shansee is the mysterious death of Yuen Ming. I made the assumption based upon this. The north road leads to Giang. Well, it of course leads to many smaller towns and villages and then on into other provinces. I mention Giang only because it is the nearest large city."

"I know many of the back roads of the province. As I said, my dad used to be an engineer for the Imperial Throne. He built bridges around the province. We always traveled with him, so I do know my way around. If your destination is anywhere in Tan Loc, I can get you there without the Cao Bang knowing about your passage. The only times that my dad and I have ever seen them in some of the villages that I passed through following you were when they were on a mission and waiting for someone to appear there. At least that is what my dad always told me. You were avoiding those towns, ergo, they may be watching for you."

"I see, yes this makes logical sense, Phillipe. May I ask why you have chosen Xian and me?" Zhen asked. Tian also now looked sharply at Phillipe, this would be a crucial reply, Jemma guessed.

"My father taught me the use of the hana and hano blades. My grandparents taught me to observe. My mother taught me the balance of all things. Yet, I am not complete. Without a weapon, I am powerless, though I know I should not be. Since I was a child, I felt that I should be somehow able to move things away from me, rather like pushing them from me. I made many inquiries about the kijutsu powers of the different schools and have chosen Xian because the kijutsu that you master may be this push that I seek." Phillipe bowed to Zhen.

"Thank you Phillipe. Before I can accept you as a student, I need to test your current level of skills. However, this may not be practical for a time. My Academy has been invaded, and you are correct. It is not safe for us to be in Shansee right now. Both Tian and Fina are students of mine, but all three of us were wounded fending off the Cao Bang attack. It would not be fair to use either of us to test you just now. May I examine your hana and hano blades?" Zhen replied.

Phillipe carefully presented the larger blade and the smaller one. Both were the unique Tashien martial arts style of extremely sharp blades and of the highest quality. "Ah, Master Won-made blades. You possess a pair of the finest blades made in Tashien, young man." He handed them back to Phillipe. Tian, Jemma noticed, seemed very much impressed with the blades.

"Phillipe, wisdom suggests that I accept your offer of guidance. I will grant you conditional acceptance as a student, pending a thorough testing of your current skills. We need to get to Giang to check on some friends of ours, before the Cao Bang finds them. They are traveling upriver and are many days ahead of us. The Cao Bang may only be a day at most ahead of us. They beat some partial information out of poor Wen Dai here. He is a publisher, not a fighter. Admittedly, we had to leave shortly after they attacked my Academy and are ill prepared for the journey. Chan and Fang have only a limited supply of food with us. What would you advise us?" Zhen asked.

"Thank you Master Zhen," Phillipe bowed reverently. Lesser roads lead north towards Giang. The Cao Bang will not be watching them. They are used only by the wagons of smaller villages and towns for the most part. Dad built many of their bridges. There is a set of roads that we could use that parallel roughly the North Road. They lie five to ten miles west of the river. Traveling those will add perhaps another forty miles to the total trip, but we can stay in safety at inns. There ought to be no Cao Bang around. However, Master Zhen, there may be bandits around in these chaotic times. Also, as I have discovered, you may run into the soldiers of the various overlords out patrolling the areas that they now claim as theirs. The soldiers should pose no problems, but the bandits may take some convincing."

"I like your plan, young Phillipe. Tomorrow we will place ourselves in your hands. I must admit that I do not know the lands about us, as I should. While I have traveled the main North Road many times, seldom have I ventured off it, except to visit a larger town. Can you get us to Giang in say ten days by this alternative route?"

"Yes, easily," Phillipe replied. Zhen nodded.

"You should then meet the rest of us. This is my wife and fellow instructor, Fang." She bowed respectfully to the lad, who reciprocated. "My dear friends Wen and Chan Dai. This is my top student Tian Wang. We are charged with protecting these visitors from Velona, Fina da Cassa and Jemma Kato. Their adult guardians are on that riverboat under the care of a trusted river couple. More I will not say, for it is their judgment call what is divulged."

"Welcome Student Phillipe," Tian offered his hand. "Your blades are indeed the finest that I've seen. May you bring honor to them and their maker. Miss Fina is my partner now, and well, she has become my yellow orchid of spring," he grinned, and she blushed slightly. Phillipe picked up his not so subtle clue that Tian was highly interested in Fina.

Jemma decided that if Zhen trusted this young Phillipe, she ought to do so as well. He would certainly be asking about the Cao Bang attack on the Academy. "So your grandparents were Santi del Dio members?" Jemma nudged the conversation in a more interesting direction for her.

Sipping more tea, he replied, "Yes, they worked out of the inn that is now called the Santi. That used to be their home. When the organization gave the fortress back to Shansee, they moved out into an outlying village instead of heading back to d'Grange. I know that they loved it here. They could do some amazing things. I once saw them bringing down a bolt of lightning. That sure made an impression on me. I was five at the time. They had kijutsu powers for sure. I kind of figured that I may have inherited something from them, if kijutsu is inherited."

Phillipe then asked, "You know, I noticed a huge burn patch just inside your Academy, Master Zhen. Did the Cao Bang attempt to burn you out?"

Zhen looked at Jemma, unsure how much she wanted revealed. "Well, if you are going to be with us, you should know what you have gotten yourself into," Jemma answered. "Over two dozen Cao Bang broke into the Academy. It was just a few of us and some young students. I had to even the odds a bit. It was my ball of fire that you saw, Phillipe. I got rid of half of them right away and then had to cleverly bring a lightning bolt in through the door. That was a bit tricky to do."

"Had she not, we may will not be here," Zhen added, backing up her story. Phillipe's eyes opened wide and he looked hard at Jemma, wondering just who this young teen was.

Phillipe said, "My grandparents told me that the Santi del Dio was gone."

Jemma replied, "Yes, the organization has long passed into history. However, that does not mean that some of the powerful people within that organization are gone. Some of us are still around and quite active. I guess I had better start at the beginning or none of this is going to make any sense at all." She began by outlining just who we were and our dual mission to Tashien. Both Tian and Phillipe listened intently. Tian was hearing many details that even he had not known.

She described what had happened to Dita and me and that we had found San Min Wu. Both lads grimaced when they heard what Yuen Ming had done to us and the five other women. "Damn! He actually did that to them!" Phillipe cursed.

"Yes, they lost their arms at their elbows and have their feet somehow messed up," Jemma continued. She explained their opium addiction problem as well. "The boat is taking them to Giang and from there on up to San Min's home city of Nan Yan." She then told him how Dita had killed Yuen along with numerous other guards when they made their escape.

"Well no wonder the Cao Bang are on your trail, Master Zhen!" Phillipe exclaimed. So much now fell into place. "If we push it, I may be able to get us to Giang in eight or nine days, if you prefer," he added.

"Ten is fine. We all need the time to heal," Zhen replied.

"Okay. Jemma, are your mothers really on a gun ship that sinks the opium ships?" he asked.

"You bet. I was telling them when the shipments left, and they then intercepted them. Not one opium shipment got through until recently. Now that Yuen's dead, I don't know what's going on anymore. With all the street fighting, it wasn't safe to be out there spying any longer. Besides, Bethany and Dita now need our help far more. I guess mom and Ania can figure out some other way to find those ships, if any are actually being sent any longer," Jemma added.

"Well, I came looking for some excitement. I guess I have really found it. I give you my word, Jemma. I will stick with you until we get them to safety. That is, unless Master Zhen wants me to do something else for him," Phillipe swore.

"Your help is most appreciated," Zhen replied. "I hope that the Olin Masters in Nan Yan will provide them sanctuary there. If not, we could well be in big trouble, once the Cao Bang find out where they are. Honestly, they are really seven very helpless women now, though in times of clarity, Bethany and Dita can use their many kijutsu powers. Opium takes a terrible toll even on them. We should get some sleep now. We have many days of hard riding before us. I will take the first watch."

"No you are not, dear. You need your sleep too," Fang countered his order. "Chan, Jemma, and I will take turns. Now you crawl into the straw and rest." He did as she asked.

Later that night while Jemma stood guard over her sleeping

companions, she gazed long at Phillipe. What a strange fellow he was, intriguing actually. His thick black hair was as long as Dita's and nearly everyone else in this land. He had it nicely braided so that it was out of his way when fighting. Yet, his incredibly blue eyes marked him as different from the black and dark brown eyes of the usual folks in Tashien, to say nothing of his lighter skin color. That he was also cute only added to his mystique, she thought to herself.

The next morning after breakfast, they mounted up and headed out into the monsoon rains once more. Phillipe took the lead and they headed down a muddy farmer's road for several miles before it reached a larger north-south road. Here, Phillipe turned to his right and led them northward. The road was a graveled one, which he explained meant that it was a major secondary road. The lower level roads were merely dirt. Several miles later, they crossed over a stone bridge, a raging creek roared beneath them.

"My dad built this bridge, Jemma," Phillipe explained as they crossed.

"Hey, that's interesting. I wish these torrential rains would stop. I'm soaked again," she replied.

"In a few days we will be far enough north that we won't get such heavy rains," he explained.

He was right about the villages. During the day, they passed through three of them. Although they looked carefully, they saw no Cao Bang here. Hence, Zhen allowed them to begin spending their nights at smaller inns, which everyone appreciated. Warm food and cozy, dry beds were greatly appreciated.

On their fifth day, the rains ceased, though the clouds stayed densely packed and threatening to drop more rain. It didn't. Instead, they encountered a band of twenty-five mounted soldiers of the local overlord. They were only briefly stopped and questioned. On the sixth day, bandits struck.

As they approached a thicket of bamboo and dense undergrowth, a dozen poorly armed men rushed out demanding money. Fina, Zhen, and Tian all used their push powers to drive the lot back, giving them time to dismount and prepare to do battle. Up front, Phillipe dismounted and drew both weapons simultaneously. Fian and Tian were right behind him, along with Fang and Zhen. Jemma stayed mounted, holding their many reins, including Wen's, but was ready to fight as needed.

Zhen watched the style and moves of Phillipe as he rushed to engage the bandits. Both weapons flashed in rhythm and in the proper manner. His exceedingly sharp blades were no match for the poor quality swords of the bandits. The battle was short-lived. Half fled the scene as fast as they could run. Phillipe had downed four, while Tian and Fina each had one apiece. Zhen and Fang had yet to swing a weapon or make a move. She nodded to Zhen, who smiled. Both approved of Phillipe now; he had a good command of his two weapons, which was what Zhen needed to know.

"Well done, Phillipe. You have passed the test. Consider your conditional acceptance granted," Zhen said bowing to him. He grinned and bowed back. Jemma noticed that Phillipe was far more relaxed now that Master Zhen had fully accepted him.

At their inn on the ninth night, Jemma carefully removed everyone's stitches and inspected each wound. All were healing well. While she did this, Phillipe explained, "Tomorrow around three we ought to be entering the outskirts of Giang. Where are we to head?"

"To the forks. We will then travel up the Yan River. I will need to make some inquiries there. This will be the most dangerous part of our mission. Giang is a city of a half million, and the Cao Bang is sure to be watching for the boat and for us. We must take extreme care."

Fang suggested, "We could spit up, Zhen. I can take them to the northern edge to Zia's Inn, where we often stay. You could slip down to the river and make your inquires alone. It would raise less suspicion that way."

"I ought to go with him," Jemma suggested. "I can alter men's minds if they recognize him."

"Thanks, Jemma, but I had better do this alone. I can move as silently as the Cao when I have the need, and your skin color will give you away to everyone. Use your skills to help everyone get safely to the inn. If it is possible, it would be wise if none there at the inn remembered that we spent the night there," he deftly deflected her wish to come with him, giving her a new goal to pursue instead. Jemma recognized just what he had done, though, but accepted it.

As Phillipe promised, around three they paused on a low hill to get a good view of the large city down below them. The muddy Yonshu twisted and turned like a snake in the grass as it wound its way southward. The Yan River, twisting not as much and less than half the width, angled into the mighty Yan, near the center of the sprawling city. "If you like, I can take us around to the western edge, which may be closer to your inn, Fang," Phillipe suggested.

Both Fang and Zhen thought that was a good idea. Here they split up, Zhen headed on down into Giang, while Phillipe angled them along a side mud road to the west. Around five, they entered the city from the west and a half hour later, Fang stopped before Zia's Inn, where she and Zhen stayed when they were in Giang, which was rather infrequent. As usual, they took four rooms and stables for their horses. After eating dinner, Jemma carefully altered many memories of the other diners, before they headed to their rooms.

Zhen rode alone into the city, hiding himself as much as possible beneath his oilskin cloak. With its hood up, only the front of his face was visible. That evening was soon upon him helped him blend into the city. He made straight for the fork, where the two rivers met. Zhen knew quite a few old river men. As he rode slowly along the oxen path, he kept his eyes open for those whom he knew. As the hours passed, he gathered more and more information. Finally, around midnight, he arrived at Zia's Inn. Stabling his horse, he went up the stairs and searched for the right room. Fang had cleverly made a small mark on their door. He erased it as he entered.

Over breakfast, the next morning, Zhen outlined what he had learned from his river rat acquaintances. "The Cao Bang are definitely on the lookout for a riverboat heading up the Yonshu, but they are also now checking on the Yan as well. They do not know precisely what boat they are looking for or who is its owner. We have a big break on that one. Still, they are checking on every boat that is going upriver. Someone saw two Cao heading west out of town, presumably to check on other boats upstream. I believe that we will follow the ox trail and stick close to the river from now on. Kang's boat passed through here three days ago, so we are still behind them." They packed up and rode west out of town before cutting down to the Yan River bank and the heavily used oxen path along its edge.

They had only gone a few miles, when Phillipe spotted something in the reeds beside the bank. He halted and motioned for the others to come take a peak. A body dressed entirely in black had washed up among the reeds beside the bank. Unless one was watching the waters carefully, he or she would miss seeing the partially submerged body. "Well, done, Phillipe. Cao, no doubt of that. It looks like Dita got another one. Perhaps that was one of the two who headed west upriver," Zhen theorized.

Jemma took this break to contact me, and I relayed what Dita had done and our current situation. *Thanks for coming after us, Jemma,* I sent.

"Gang, Dita got two Cao Bang members three nights ago just a ways up ahead. They are now off opium. Somehow, all seven had been able to get completely off of it! Something about a steam bath. Anyway, they are running therapy sessions on everyone now, and Dita is always watching over them at night. We can relax a little bit," Jemma reported.

"When these two are missed, they will send out a larger force," Zhen explained. "We best be prepared to stop them. Let's see if we can close the distance a little." They rode on, passing many oxen teams hauling riverboats upstream. While the clouds looked threatening, the heavy rains didn't materialize. Phillipe explained that they were too far inland for the heavy monsoon rains of Shansee.

As they rode westward, the terrain gradually began to change. The low-lying lands that were so fertile and filled with farms and rice paddies nearer the coast gave way to rolling grasslands. Phillipe explained to Jemma and Fina that within a hundred miles, the foothills would begin. The entire western third of Tashien from the cold north to the swampy south was filled with steep ravines and rocky spines. Gradually, the elevation rose until at last it met the Helios Grande Mountains, an impassable barrier. In these foothills, travel was only possible up the valleys. Hence, many local overlords controlled the valleys. There were twenty of them in western Tan Loc alone and many more in the other provinces. Often, an overlord would build some kind of fortification at his main location, usually the largest town or village in that long valley line.

Indeed, any given valley line frequently ran for hundreds of miles, ever upwards towards the mountains. Nan Yan was the largest city in the west of Tan Loc, lying at the mouth of a wide, fertile valley complex that stretched westward for some three hundred miles. Nan Yan was also about two hundred miles south of the border with Wontun Province and two hundred miles north of the southern seacoast. About fifty miles before Nan Yan, the Yan River veered due north before turning again to the west at the city.

Now the party changed tactics, preferring to camp out along the oxen trail so that they could monitor the trail during the night. Zhen explained that their job now was to prevent the expected large force of Cao Bang from getting past them and thus preventing them from attacking the boat, which was still two days ahead of them. When they entered a town or village, often Fang and Chan would veer into the town to purchase more food and charcoal.

Days passed uneventfully. When they were about one hundred fifty miles out from Giang, that all changed. Fang called out, "Riders coming up hard from the rear!" At once, the group dismounted, hastily tying their horses to the shrubs near the bank of the river. They formed into a line, with Wen standing back with the horses. His broken arm prevented him from being useful for much else but keeping the horses together. Besides, he was not a fighter in the first place.

"If they are overlord soldiers, stand aside. If they are Cao Bang, we must stop them," Zhen ordered. Kijutsu first, we must make them dismount." Thirty seconds later, a band of twenty-five black clothed riders came galloping up the oxen trail. All wore black masks over their faces, Cao Bang for sure.

Zhen, Fang, and Tian focused and moved their hands outwards as if pushing something away. Suddenly, their push affected the front riders, knocking them from their horses. Others trampled over the fallen men and horses, effectively ending their gallop. Phillipe watched as many reacted instantly, dismounting and quick-drawing their hanos. Jemma and Fina each launched a ball of fire over the swarm; many men whose clothing erupted into flames dove into the river. The others knew how to deal with such kijutsu powers; they raced forward to attack the defensive line, knowing that no more kijutsu could be used against them when they were close to their opponents. Ten swarmed to face Zhen, Fang, Tian, Fina, Phillipe, and Chan. Jemma focused her attention onto those in the water and those still on the ground, recovering from the initial stopping forces.

These were highly skilled assassins and fighters, to say nothing of their martial arts skills. Chan was no match for one of these men and quickly had to do a fighting withdraw, taking a sword cut to her arm in the process. The heavy, dark clouds overhead were perfect for Jemma, who pulled down a bolt of lightning to eliminate the man who had harmed Chan. Wen, with his one arm, attempted to stem the blood flow from his wife's arm. Before long, both Tian and Fina also took some wounds as well, though they each had eliminated one of the Cao men before they had to retreat as well. Fang, Zhen, and Phillipe closed the big gap, fending off the assassins as best they could. Once more, Jemma used a lightning bolt to eliminate one who was attempting to exploit the hole in their line made by the retreating pair, who now began to put pressure on the worst of their wounds.

Both Fang and Zhen felled two of their opponents, but Phillipe's flashing double blades got four of these men. His last strike completely severed the man's head, cleanly! One assassin in the rear then threw a throwing star and struck Phillipe in his shoulder, forcing him to drop his hano. He could still use his shorter hana blade in his left hand, but he was forced back by flying circle kicks, against which he could not defend. Unfortunately, this left Fang and Zhen facing three each. As the swings and kicks increased, the two were slowly being forced back as well.

Jemma and Fina again pulled down a pair of lightning bolts, electrifying two, but still Zhen and Fang were forced back. He was tiring, and she was now making purely defensive moves. Just then, Dita, who had been notified of the attack by Jemma, appeared overhead. She'd left her body back on the boat and appeared above the battle. She picked up one of the men fighting against Fang and twisted his neck; then the other man's head twisted around in a circle as well, leaving Fang shocked. She could not believe what she had just seen. A moment later, the two on Zhen lay dead at his feet, their heads were twisted around facing their backs. Overhead, Dita smiled, but only Jemma and Fina could sense her presence.

Thanks Dita! You saved the day! Jemma sent.

Thanks for keeping these assassins from catching up to us, Dita replied and returned to the therapy session that she was running on the boat still way upstream from them.

"That was Dita. I asked her to come lend us a hand," Jemma explained.

"Where? I see no one?" Phillipe called out. "Their heads — like someone just twisted them around!"

"I don't believe what I just saw!" Fang exclaimed.

"Incredible kijutsu! Yuen had no chance at all!" Zhen replied.

"Can someone pull this thing out of my shoulder? I can't," Phillipe asked, in pain. Quickly, Zhen, Fang, and Jemma began assisting the wounded. After Zhen removed the star, Phillipe insisted that he help the others who were in more need. Holding his left hand over the small, bleeding wound, he picked up his hano and began making sure each of the

Cao bodies were dead by stabbing each in their hearts.

Chan, Tian, and Fina all needed quick treatment. First action, stem the blood loss quickly. Second action, get some water boiling fast so Jemma could go to work stitching them up. Wen lent his good arm fetching some firewood, and Jemma simply cast her fire spell onto it. The woodpile burst into flames, once more creating a stir among the others, who had not seen her do this before. Only four of the Cao who had dove into the river to extinguish their flaming clothes managed to escape on foot, running back down the oxen path.

It took Jemma two hours to get every wound properly attended and good bandages applied. "We should put a few miles between us and this bloody place," Zhen then advised. The somber, hurting group at last mounted up and rode on for another hour. As the shock of the battle finally settled on them, three were so weak that Zhen finally had to stop for the day. He and Fang did most of the work setting up their camp, while Jemma made her rounds, checking on each of the four wounded.

"You are pretty amazing, Jemma," Phillipe complimented her, as she looked at his shoulder wound. "Thanks for saving my butt back there. I got four, but as you could see, I cannot deal with their martial arts maneuvers."

"You are a hotshot with the swords, Phillipe. You got four yourself, impressive. I know I couldn't get even one of them," she replied.

"Supper," Fang called out at last. While they were eating, she said, "That was the most incredible use of kijutsu powers that I have ever seen or even heard about! Unbelievable! I would like to meet this Dita in person. She twisted their necks as if they were mere chickens! What kijutsu she must have!"

"Indeed, I am most humbled," Zhen added. "Never have I seen such kijutsu either. Jemma, please thank Dita for me. Without her aid, we may have perished back there. Yet, she is still on the boat. Such power in her kijutsu!"

"I will. She said for me to thank all of you for keeping the Cao Bang from reaching them. In their condition, they would be sitting ducks if the Cao got to them," Jemma remembered to relay Dita's thanks.

"Will they come back, Master Zhen?" asked Phillipe.

"The four that got away might possibly try a nighttime assassination attempt, but no, they will not execute a frontal attack. They might bring a hundred more of them against us, but I hope by then we are safely in Nan Yan. I'm sure that the Cao are not used to losing so many men in one small battle. This makes twice now that they have lost a couple dozen men attacking us. I sincerely hope that they take that into consideration," Zhen advised them.

From then on, two were always on guard duty at night. However, no assassination attempts occurred, and nothing at all out of the ordinary happened. A couple of days later, the river veered due north and the countryside began to change dramatically.

"Wow! Breathtakingly beautiful," Jemma announced, as she got her first view of the razor sharp peaks and the lush, green valleys there in the far west of Tan Loc. Now she could see why the only travel routes were up the valleys. While perhaps on foot one could climb the towering ridges, such would not be an easy task.

"Two more days and we'll be at Nan Yan," Phillipe announced. "When the river veers westward again, we are all but there!"

"None too soon for everyone," Fina commented.

On December 8, 752, they finally rounded the bend and saw the huge city of Nan Yan opening up before them. Just ahead of them, Zhen spied Kang's boat just now pulling up to the dock on the southern shore not too far from the Olin Monastery. They kicked their horses into a gallop, closing the short distance rapidly.

Chapter 19 How Do We Get There?

Loaded down with supplies, Bianca, Ilenakova, Enrico, and Louis finally headed across the Dakar River and out onto the shore of the ocean, just west of the looming Kathas Mountains. Steep, granite walls rose sharply on their left, leaving only a narrow shoreline upon which to ride. Their two packhorses were heavily laden with food and water, because they expected to find no fresh water until they had reached Tashien, some three hundred miles to the east. Once past the towering mountains, the Desert of Desolation lay to their left, a bitterly hot, arid land, without a single living creature or plant.

For fifteen long days, the group made their way along the seacoast, often having to dismount and lead their horses around and over massive boulder fields. At night, they camped mere feet from the ocean, though they soon got used to hearing the lulling sound of the waves crashing upon the shore. "It is very pretty," Louis admitted to Bianca. She agreed, if only they were not in such a hurry to get to her mother and help the seven.

On the November 8, they passed the last of the Helios Grande Mountains, where those impassable peaks touched the ocean and found itself no match for the ceaseless pounding of the ocean's waves. Now they were in Tashien proper, but were dismayed. Rugged foothills with tall, razor ridges totally blocked their inland travel!

After two discouraging days, they finally entered a small fishing village, where some hundred homes clung to the narrow coastline. Several more rose precariously on the steep, green hillside just beyond the sandy beach. There was no inn in this village, so long needed baths would have to wait, but they were able to resupply their nearly exhausted water supply.

More importantly, they asked about how to get from here to Nan Yan. To their dismay, they discovered that there was no path over these steep ridges. One old man drew them a map of western Ton Loc in the sands of the beach. "You go along the coast until you get to the beginning of the marsh lands, where the rice paddies begin. Further on down the coast, you will find a coastal road. At the marshes, you can then head north and traverse the foothills before they grow too tall to pass. You go straight north and you will find Nan Yan at the mouth of the Great Valley," the old fisherman explained. Unfortunately, that meant some four hundred fifty miles of coastline to travel before turning north another two hundred miles!

"Better get yourselves some oilskins," he added.

"What do you mean?" asked Enrico.

"Monsoon season is almost here. Rains all day and all night for weeks along the coast. Better get oilskin cloaks," he explained. A bit later, he had sold them six of his, having made triple their actual cost to him. He was a happy fisherman as the four rode out of his small village on down the coastline.

A few days later, they finally hit the western part of the Great Coastal Road and now could make far better time. Except for one thing, the monsoons arrived. Torrential downpours began and didn't let up for days. Visibility was poor and they made only slow progress, often they had to stop earlier than they would have because the next village and inn was too far to make before it got dark.

"Well, this is still better than sitting around being tied up," Ilenakova commented as the rain poured down on her, soaking her once again.

"I don't know. It was kind of kinky having Louis here feed me," Bianca teased.

"Hey, don't look at me," Enrico joined in the levity. "I was off galloping to the south. I wonder when this rain will let up? I've never seen this much rain before."

"Well, the good thing is that we don't melt," Louis teased them back. "Maybe we need to don three oilskins!"

"My leather reins and saddle are going to rot on me," Ilenakova grumbled. "I think mold is growing out of my leather pants." They all chuckled at this idea.

"Say in this rain, how are we even going to be able to tell where the marshes begin?" asked Louis. The ground beyond the road was a soggy mess. In many places, water was standing in small lakes.

"We keep asking in each village where we stop for the night," Enrico answered. "I am sure glad that we have inns. Could you imagine sleeping out of doors in this weather?"

"Besides being cold, we might get swept out to sea," Bianca made light of their situation. They all had a chuckle over this idea. None was actually talking about their actual stays in the different inns. That topic was worse than the weather. Uniformly, they found the people at the inn were in fear of unknown vagaries — though they had seen no Cao Bang and no overlords — or the people were in despair or grief. Some sat numb at the bar tables drinking the cheap rice beer, which only made things worse, Bianca thought. Some were so openly undeserving that they refused even the smallest of tips that the four offered them for the care of their horses. Perhaps the torrential rains had turned them all into an apathy, Ilenakova theorized. Rare was the man or woman who rose to open resentment over their lot in life or the state of Tashien or their village. Even rarer was the man who was openly angry or hostile. The bleakness of their emotions was matched by the bleakness of their coastal villages and life. The monsoon only added to their misery.

Finally late in November, an innkeeper told them to look for the north road out of this village. It would eventually take them to Nan Yan. The four were so happy to hear this news, that they gave the innkeeper two extra gold coins. He bowed profusely in thanks, wondering what he had done to earn this small fortune and instantly began to give the four provisions for their journey, which they didn't need. He just had to propitiate to them.

The change in direction bode well for the four. Now they no longer had the ocean on one side and steeply rising slopes on the other side. Here, the hills, while steep, were passable and green vegetation of countless plant varieties clamored for their attention. Off to their right lay the miles and miles of small rice paddy farms. On the highest bit of land rose the crudest of houses, often with bamboo outbuildings. Their fields were delineated by foot high walls of piled stones, removed by hand from the marshy fields they enclosed. Frequently, they spied snakes, some venomous, swimming around the water of the fields, their burrows temporarily flooded. All four were glad that they were not on foot.

The further inland they rode the more that the torrential rains lessened, until by the fourth day, the rain finally ceased. The four actually cheered when they left the inn only to find the rain had stopped that morning. Still the dark skies appeared ominous, but the rain held off. As they began riding north again, they noticed that the rice paddies had mysteriously given way to actual crop fields, which were not under water at this time. The farmsteads appeared a little more solidly built, though none was stone. Off to their left, they began to see wide valley entrances, which they now realized led one up hundreds of miles into those isolated valleys, ending close to the Helios Grande Mountains, now some three hundred miles to their west.

The road they followed was a dirt road, but it was not muddy as it had been when they first turned northward. While rain had recently fallen here, it was not the deluge that had fallen further south. Occasionally, they now passed some wagons hauling produce northward. Uniformly, the men and women riding in these were dressed in brown homespun clothing, often with a large number of buttons on their tops. Both the men and women wore their hair long — cutting it must be a sacrilege according to Ilenakova. Uniformly, their hair was black and thick and both sexes wore it in a single braid down their backs.

In Velona, passing a wagon would have netted the result of a cheery "hello" from those on the wagon, pleased to encounter other travelers. Here, somber faces observed them as they passed, even though they were obviously strangers to Tashien. Their faces reflected their feelings of uselessness, apathy, hopelessness, undeservingness, and even numbness. Occasionally, those on the wagons displayed real fear as the four passed them on the road. The degradation of these people was painfully obvious to the four.

Still the countryside was magnificent, and every so often, a stone bridge passed over a small creek or river as it flowed eastward to empty in the great Yonshu River. Three times during their northward ride, they encountered bands of soldiers, whom they learned were patrolling areas staked out by their various overlords. None gave them any trouble, once they stated they were heading to Nan Yan.

However, three days from Nan Yan as they finally approached the Yan River, a group of fifteen bandits jumped from the brush beside the road, demanding money. Ilenakova seemed in incredibly good spirits. As she drew her sword, she exclaimed loudly, "Oh great! A battle. I can't wait to slaughter these stupid men!" Bianca and Enrico also drew their swords, and the three easily dismounted, but Ilenakova had to do her flying dismount, placing herself at the forefront. Louis dismounted from his tall mare and drew out his large bastard sword. The bandits saw the huge blade of Louis and the charge of Ilenakova, and they decided to scatter instead. "Come back here and fight!" Ilenakova yelled after them. "You are spoiling my fun!" Bianca just laughed.

On December 9, the four finally rounded the bend to the west and saw the large city of Nan Yan before them. For several minutes, they paused and just took in the sight with their eyes. They were at the mouth of a wide valley. Ragged, jagged ridges rose skyward miles to the north and south. The quarter-mile wide Yan River flowed on past them, dividing the city in half. The valley and slopes were flush with green, even though it was December, though some brown was visible at the higher elevations on the slopes. The many houses looked like colored dots decorating the rolling, hilly landscape. It was a picture perfect, scenic sight.

Even from this distance, they could see that over half of the buildings were made from stone, probably quarried from the hillsides. Wooden buildings comprised the rest. As they began to enter the city from the east, they spied two great stone bridges over the Yan River, more like architectural monuments, though they were crowded with carts and people crossing. The Olin Monastery was on the south side of the river, where they were riding. Still watching the scene before them, they rode into the outskirts of the city, looking for the monastery and the rest of us.

Chapter 20 Sanctuary

The late morning was sunny, gone were the dark, ominous clouds. We were in the foothills where the monsoons didn't reach. Kang pulled his boat up to the river docks. He carefully looked around, but didn't see any Cao Bang watching for him or us. At last, he opened the cargo hold doors, allowing the sunlight and fresh air in on us seven huddled in the hold. Long Yan busily gathered up our meager possessions into that single bed sheet which we had used to cart them from the fifth floor prison. Bi now cautiously climbed out onto the front deck, her eyes darting about, fearful for everyone's safety. After tying a knot in the sheet, Long carried it onto the deck and handed it to Kang, who still stood looking around on the dock.

"Let's see, where was that Olin Monastery anyway?" he attempted to jog his memory. He'd actually only seen its entrance doors once. It lay further to the north, but just how far he wasn't sure. Long joined him, sitting the sheet bag on the ground.

"It is five streets over and ten up, near the southernmost edge of Nan Yan," Long replied to Kang's unspoken question. Finally, Long Yan was home. He and San Min Wu grew up here together, played as children, at least until her feet had been reformed into the proper Princess form as they were now. After that, he accompanied her everywhere, and the two had fallen hopelessly in love with each other. Far off to the north across the Yan River was the palace where she had lived before her abduction. Its stone walls and tall inner buildings were clearly visible, resting on the side of the sharply rising northern valley wall. It would be a two-mile ride through the city to get there from here. Actually, three-fourths of the city lay on the northern side of the Yan.

"Can they walk to the monastery?" Kang asked.

"Probably, but maybe we can find some riks to ferry them once we get out from the docks," Long replied. "Do you spot any Cao?" Long asked, worriedly. His greatest fear was that the Cao Bang would be here waiting for them to disembark. With seven women who could barely walk, they would be extraordinarily vulnerable once they left the protection of the riverboat.

"Not yet. Perhaps we are in luck after all," Kang replied. "Perhaps Bi and I should go with you to help them, do you think?" The two chatted for a few minutes, trying to work out a reasonable plan, though to these two non-fighters, nothing seemed at all reasonable, not with the assassins after them.

Just then, Long Yan saw a most welcome sight indeed. Zhen called out and waved at him! "Thank god! Zhen and the others are coming! We are saved," Long exclaimed, greatly relieved of the burden of trying to work out how to get the seven safely to the Olin Monastery and how to beg the Masters there to give them sanctuary, which they desperately needed. He called down to the seven that Zhen and the others were coming. I breathed a real sigh of relief. At last, we were not on our own.

"Okay, everyone, let's see if we can get over to the steps and then climb out onto the deck," I suggested.

Mei whispered, "Remember, very small steps." Indeed, already my short arms were swinging as I tried to keep my balance on the curved hull of the boat, made all the more difficult by its gentle rocking motion. Walking on my toes with virtually no heel support made movement precarious. I used my short arms for support and balance as I very carefully climbed up the six steps to the front deck. Bi saw me and grabbed onto my right arm to support me as I finally reached the deck. She helped me carefully cross the deck and Long lifted me over to the dock. At last, I was on solid ground in the fresh air and sunlight. Yes, it felt good. One by one, the others followed me, and Long sat them down on the dock beside me, as our riders reined in a short distance from us, starting in partial disbelief at we seven.

"Hi Jemma, Fina. We need rescuing once more," I jested. "Glad you all made it." I spied their many bandages and my levity evaporated, "Are you wounded? Are you okay?"

"We're on the mend. Had to keep the Cao from getting you," Fina answered, while Jemma gave me a hug and then Dita as well. Fina followed her lead and hugged us too. Then, Fina introduced Tian, whom we had not yet met, and Jemma introduced Phillipe. Then, it was our turn to introduce San Min Wu, Mei Bi, Chan Bao, Dai Son, and Hon Feng.

Zhen said urgently, "We should get you all to the monastery as soon as possible. No telling when the Cao might show up. Can you walk?"

"Sure," San Min piped up, "only we have to go slowly, and it helps if someone has their arms around us." Long Yan immediately put his around her waist and she smiled. They had done this for years before she had been abducted. Jemma took me; Fina took Dita; Fang took Mei; Zhen took Chan Bao; Chan Dai took Dai; and Phillipe took Hon. Wen and Tian took the reins of the horses. We said goodbye and thanks to Kang and Bi, who waved, as we slowly began our trek to the monastery.

Talk about moving slowly! The incredible high arch of our feet had us standing flat on our toes, and our walk was more of a four-inch shuffle than anything else. Long Yan and San Min were very used to this speed and led the way. Chan, Hon, and Dia were also somewhat used to walking, though only around that room on the fifth floor of the Purple Palace. Going a significant distance was new to them as well. Mei, Dita, and I had it the roughest, nearly wholly unused to walking this way. More than once, Jemma had to keep me from falling over. I nearly fell anytime that I tried to move a foot more than four inches from its previous location.

San Min seemed unbothered by it all. "Look, they've built a new store there, Long. How much we've missed these past five years! Oh, it helps if you look off at the things in a distance," she advised. I tried and found that did help, as long as I kept my steps incredibly tiny. "Long used to take me on long walks all the time," she chatted extremely happy to be back in her hometown.

"You should take a walk over the bridges; the view from their middle is very inspiring. Then there are the Central Gardens. Oh, Long, we must take them there to see it. We can spend a whole day exploring them," San Min explained happily.

"Dear, we have to wait until it is safe to go out. The Cao are still after us," Long reminded her.

My mind wandered. I estimated the total distance to be four thousand feet from the docks to the monastery. At four inches a step, I had to take some twelve thousand of my tiny steps. "Oh my god, this will be twelve thousand little steps! My legs and ankles will give out."

"Oh we must take a break periodically," San Min replied. "If you practice walking every day, eventually your muscles toughen up. Just don't be in a hurry and fall down. I made that mistake quite a lot when I was ten and eleven. That's when they did my feet, just as they did yours. Say, Bethany, remember when you were first here a century ago and they bound our feet? My servants had these training gowns that they gave you to wear, gowns that would not let you take too big a step. I bet those would really help you out. I wonder if we can get some of them made for you? Anyway, as I was saying, the secret is to take ever-lengthening walks every day. That's what Long and I did. Oh!"

She had just noticed that the people who were passing us and coming our way on the very crowded street were staring at us and whispering among themselves. I caught several repeating, "Zen-kami" and "Those must be zen-kami!" While Chan, Dai, Hon, and Mei smiled as they recognized their high status, San Min felt embarrassed. For her, it was a big loss of honor, from a Princess down to a zen-kami.

As soon as we had finally painstakingly traveled the five cross streets, Long spied riks! A few minutes later, we seven were being pulled along the last ten blocks. Our friends were extremely happy that our forward pace had so drastically picked up. As I rode along, I reflected on San Min's views. While these tiny feet were a very visible indicator of very high status in the Tashien society, I found them terribly annoying and most debilitating. Yet, I knew better than to say anything to the other five, especially San Min. Now I focused on the monastery ahead. Would we be granted sanctuary for a time or would we have to hastily make other arrangements? Dita knew that Bianca and her group were only a day from us as well. Soon, we would have four more to help us out, if we needed to find some other arrangements. If nothing else, we could head south and take them all out of Tashien, retracing the route that Ilenakova and Bianca had followed. Worried, yes, I was.

At last, the riks pulled up before the Olin Monastery of Nan Yan.

Jemma helped Dita and me out of the rik, and we all stared at the beautiful sight before us. The outer walls were white polished stone, though here and there green vines snaked their way upwards toward the ten-foot high tops. We stood before an enormous pair of black teakwood doors with a brass knocker in the shape of two dolphins swimming after each other, head to tail. Zhen stepped up and used the knockers to sound our presence. Tap. Tap. Tap.

Shortly, a bald headed man wearing an orange robe opened one of the doors and looked out upon our group. "Master Zhen Song of the Xian Academy of Shansee and party seek the sanctuary of Master Cheng Dau's Olin Monastery. The Cao Bang are after us," Zhen spoke for us.

"Wait. I shall deliver your message to Master Cheng," the man bowed respectfully to Zhen and the door shut.

I looked at Zhen and he replied, "This should only take a moment."

"I hope that we have a moment!" Fang called out. "I've just spotted a Cao Bang member watching us from two blocks back!" We all turned and saw the black clothed figure slip back into the shadows of an alleyway. Damn, I thought, so close.

A few anxious minutes and the door opened wide. The orange robed man spoke softly, "Temporary sanctuary is granted. Master Jian will be your caretaker and guide. You may stable your horses there," he pointed to an open-sided building where two horses were stalled along with a carriage. "Your journey has been long. Our guest quarters are yours. Please take the time to bathe. When you are in need of sustenance, notify Master Jian. Master Zhen, Master Cheng would like a brief word with you, before you join your companions. If you will follow me, Master Jian will assist your companions. I am called Hu, the Doorman. Welcome to the Olin Monastery."

As I stepped through the doorway, I felt a gentle touch in my mind, like the pedal of some flower just barely touching my skin. *Hello. I am Bethany Brozena Malina. Thank you. We need the help just now.* Yes, someone was touching my mind! I sensed a soothing calm coming from the other mind, as if blowing away all my worries and cares. I smiled and looked about me.

Two dozen men with a few women were sparring off to my left in this huge paved courtyard. Many were in their teens — their students, I assumed. Ahead rose a beautiful white stone building with a red tiled roof. It was a most unusual looking building. Consisting of seven stories, each layer was smaller than the one below it, with slanting red tiles extending out form its base to the edge of the lower floor. Each floor had many large windows and all had a flower box affixed to the walls just below the windows. I saw a man leaning out of one window on the third floor watering some plants, the last of the season, for winter was at hand.

Our Master Jian was in his twenties. His long black hair was done in the traditional braid down his back. His face was handsome and his form beneath his orange robes spoke of power. His voice was calm and gentle, but he was not the one who had just touched my mind. He said, "Rare indeed do we host such honorable guests as a zen-kami, but seven at one time is a first! You may lead your horses to the stables and then join us. I will lead our honored guests to their quarters."

"Master Jian, I guess now I appear as a zen-kami, but I used to be your Princess. I am San Min Wu," she corrected him. "I was abducted and turned into a zen-kami but now I have been rescued."

"Forgive me, Princess. I did not recognize you." He bowed low to her. "If you will follow me, baths are being prepared." We seven began our slow shuffle after Master Jian, who did not seem to mind our slow pace. "There are our students practicing. You probably can smell our fresh bread baking now." Indeed, the distinctive yeast smell from their bakery in the back of the complex now reached my nose. Master Jian chatted as we seven moved slowly across the open courtyard. At last, we reached the one floor guesthouse just to the right of the main five-storied building. However, the others now joined us, having unsaddled the horses and brought their gear back with them. Three men took care of the horses' needs for them.

"Ah, just in time," Long Yan whispered, as he slid his arm around San Min's waist for support. A lounging area was just inside the door, with couches, tables, and chairs. One door led to a dining room. Another door led to a large bathroom. The third door led to bedrooms, of which there were eight.

"Long, we are going to need some far better clothes than these traveling ones," San Min suggested once we were all gathered inside. "We should all look our best at long last. After all, we are now in a more civilized city. Master Jian, would it be possible for Long to bring a dressmaker here to assist us all with obtaining better clothing?"

"Of course, Princess," Master Jian replied.

"Dear, you get yourselves baths and I will return with proper clothing for everyone! At last, we are home and I am able to do something to really help everyone," Long said, his face breaking into a big smile. Wen Dai, his arm still in splints, decided to tag along. Now he had something he could do to help as well.

Jemma checked out the bathroom and announced, "Okay, there are eight tubs being filled with hot water. Let's get the seven into them first. Fang, you get a bath along with them. Guys, see about unpacking our stuff. See if you can find hairbrushes and combs." Jemma enjoyed being the one giving the orders for a change, even if they were domestic ones. I smiled and allowed her to be in charge of us. Chan, Fina, and Jemma ushered us eight into the bathroom.

"Really, I ought to help you with them," Fang protested.

"You can help us get them undressed and later with their hair,"

Jemma overrode her. "Bethany, what was all that about sweating to get rid of the opium?" They began to undress us and undid our long braids. It felt good to have my hair free once more. I realized that I did not like to wear my hair braided in the Tashien traditional way. Of course, Jemma had to examine my feet carefully, as did Fina with Dita's.

"Golly, it looks like they broke your arch somehow," Jemma suggested. While they gave us a good washing and did our long hair, we chatted about all that had happened to us. Mei Bi insisted on describing just how the sweating had worked miracles on us all. Two hours passed by rapidly. After much patting dry of hair, they set to work on combing it out.

However, Chan and Hon began to insist that they be allowed to work on our hair, using the brushes that they had taken from our captive room. "Look, we can do it. We are slow, but we've been doing it for nearly five years. Please, you take your baths now," Hon insisted. Jemma didn't actually believe her, but agreed. In fact, they all watched us closely, while sitting in the tubs. Hon showed Dita, Mei, and me how it was done. Holding the brush between their stumps, they used their body motion to do the work. Yes, they were pitifully slow and terribly awkward, but they were getting the job done. Satisfied, Jemma relaxed and took a good soaking bath herself. She knew as well as we that she needed to allow these women to do as much as they possibly could do for themselves.

By the time that we women were all finished, Long and Wen had returned, bringing San Min's old dressmaker with them, along with a large pile of clothing. So much so, that Long had to use one of the small push carts to bring the many packages back to the monastery. "Oh it's true, really true! You are back! I am so glad to see you again, San Min Wu!" her old dressmaker exclaimed as she entered the bathroom. "Oh! Dear me, what happened to you?" she now saw that the Princess was missing her lower arms and hands. Dainty cone shaped upper arms was all that remained for we seven.

"Everyone, this is one of the finest dressmakers in all Nan Yan, Hua Ju!" San Min explained. After introductions, Hua began unwrapping the many packages.

"I have brought elegant complete outfits for each of you, per Long's request. San Min, I do have some of those older training dresses that Long mentioned. I brought them as well as modern versions with the usual deep walking slits. Which should we use?" Hua asked.

"Oh my, look at this incredibly fine black silk hose!" Jemma exclaimed. "Now we get to look like they did, Fina!" While they examined the piles of clothing and accessories, San Min and I discussed the dresses. At last, I thought I would follow her advice and try the training dresses. Dita grumbled a little about having to wear a corset once more, but as soon as they slipped the silken hose on her legs, she shut up. Their feel was worth the slight discomfort. Indeed, Chan Dai, Fang, and our Velona teens had never worn such fine, silken hose before and chatted at length about how unusual it felt on their legs. Before long, we all were wearing colorful, silken dresses that highlighted our forms. The pencil skirts hugged our legs, highlighting them, but for six of us, there was no walking slit. I quickly discovered, as I had long ago, that I could physically not error and take too big a step anymore. I hoped that this would help.

When we all came out of the bathroom, the men gaped at us. Long's comment spoke what most were thinking, "Wow! San Min, you look incredibly beautiful!" Phillipe gave Jemma a big hug, while Tian did likewise with Fina. Zhen and Wen also gave their wives a passionate kiss as well. Jemma then ordered the men to hit the bath barrels.

While we were waiting on the men to bathe and dress in their new white silk suits, Fina explained, "Bethany, Tian and I are in love! I think that Jemma has fallen for Phillipe too." Jemma flushed. We chatted away as if we had not seen each other for years. San Min and Hua were in one corner and I could see that San Min was probably giving Hua an extensive list of new dresses to make for us. I smiled, it was good to see her so happy.

An hour later, the men made their appearance. They all looked handsome in their matching white suits with black ties and polished black boots. Jemma, however, again insisted on examining their healing wounds, making sure there were no infections. She also examined Wen's arm and concluded that he no longer needed to keep the splint on his arm. The bones had healed well. Now he only needed to begin exercising it to get the stiffness out.

Master Jian then brought us a large meal. Actually, five younger students carried the numerous trays into our dining room. "We can feed each other mostly if we use those special wooden spoons," Hon suggested.

"Please, Hon, will you allow us to do this small thing for you this time?" Jemma asked. Hon agreed. This was by far the best, most nourishing meal that we had all had in nearly six weeks! A most pleasant hour later, we finished our oolong after-dinner tea.

Master Zhen then said, "Master Cheng Dau wishes to meet with us all now that our bodies have been handled. He gave us temporary sanctuary here, but this meeting will determine if he grants it for a longer duration." We agreed to meet now and everyone rose to exit. Master Jian bowed to Master Zhen, when he opened the door and said that we were ready for the meeting.

As we filed out, Long Yan put his arm in its usual position around San Min's waist and gave her a quick kiss. "I'll ask him tonight," he whispered to her.

Mei Bi was taken by surprise, as Master Jian slipped his arm in a similar way around her waist, beneath her flowing black hair. "If you will permit me to escort you, Mei Bi? You are a rare flower, and I would be most honored to be your escort." She flushed and allowed him to support her.

Fina did the same for Dita, while Jemma supported me. Tian, Phillipe, and Wen supported Chan, Dia, and Hon, much to their surprise and pleasure. Not to be outdone, Zhen put his arm around Fang. However, I could tell that Tian and Phillipe rather wanted to have theirs around Fina and Jemma. As we began walking across the large courtyard, I quickly discovered that San Min was precisely correct in suggesting that we wear these old style training dresses, similar to the ones that we wore when we were here over a century ago. No longer could I easily over-step and thus lose my balance. Still, Dita and I appreciated the extra support from Fina and Jemma.

Quite a few men and women were outside, enjoying the late afternoon sun, and they all stopped to watch our slow walk to the main temple quarters. As we entered the main doors, I smelled incense and then that of a multitude of flowers. I saw pots lining the hallway and realized that come spring, the scents given off would be exotic indeed. This Master Cheng certainly had very good taste. Soon we entered a large meeting room. Soft mats were evenly spaced around the large room. A number of men were already here and rose as we slowly shuffled our way into the room. A massive round of mutual bowing ensued. These Tashien folks certainly loved their bowing, which took the place of our more customary handshaking. Well, handshaking was now definitely out for us, so we bowed with vigor instead. Slowly we were escorted to mats and allowed to sit down. Now, I discovered a new problem with these training dresses. With no walking slit, we were forced to more or less sit on our lower legs and then slide them off to one side. The others sat cross-legged.

Before us, Master Cheng Dau sat prominently. He was about fifty, I guessed, and he was the one that I had seen earlier water the flowers from the window. His hair was braided and long. He had a long, curved moustache and a goatee that reached down some eight inches. His face was oval and kindly looking, but I sensed a great power lay in this man, not only that of a highly skilled martial artist, but something more, something far more spiritual in nature. As his gaze met mine, I sensed his mind touching mine, filling me with a sense of peace.

"I am Master Cheng Dau. This is my Olin Monastery. You have met one of my seconds, Master Jian Li. This is Master Liang Dhow, Master Ning Chou, and Master Peng Dong. These four are my seconds. With us are two other guests. This is the prophet Yulin Wang and Elder Hui Bui of the High Council." I noticed that Hui Bui was quite old indeed. His hair was stark white and I guessed he must be at least seventy years old, perhaps more. I was pleasantly surprised to learn later that he was eighty-one years old.

"It is a great honor to have with us our Princess San Min Wu once again. At this time, I would like to hear a full and complete recounting of the events, which have happened. If you could be so kind to keep the tale in chronological order, that would help us understand. I sense an immense kijutsu power now in this room. Please, do not leave out any details," Master

Cheng asked.

San Min Wu began, relating her abduction and how she ended up in Yuen Ming's possession. Hon, Chan, and Dia were orphans who were working as kami for Yuen when San Min arrived there. All four underwent the knives of the surgeons at the same time. When they had recovered, the three then taught San Min the art of pleasure giving.

When our roles began, we could no longer go chronologically any more, since we were doing three different actions at the same time. Jemma described what she and Fina did, along with their mothers on the gun ship, Kali and Ania. Next, I related the adventures that Bianca, Ilenakova, and Enrico had had, based on what they had told me. I explained that they would be arriving here tomorrow and could tell their story in full, if desired. Then, I related what we had done to find San Min and how our mistake had not only led us to her, but had also gotten us under Yuen's surgeon's knives as well.

I noticed that Master Cheng was keenly interested in how Dita managed to kill Yuen and dealt with our escape. He was even more interested in how I had gotten us all off the opium addiction and the therapy sessions. Zhen then described his actions and added in what Dita had done to help them out in their last battle against the Cao Bang. We spent over two hours outlining our many adventures.

Now it was Master Cheng's turn to speak openly. "For quite some time now, we have been acutely aware that some massive kijutsu powers have been unleashed in Tan Loc Province. We are Olin Masters. We can touch minds, dispel emotions, and plant thoughts, though your telepathy far exceeds our humble means. We can lift bodies much as you can, Bethany. Allow me to explain more fully. There are some thirty different schools of martial arts here in Tashien. Many represent merely physical fighting skills. However, some also teach kijutsu powers. For example, Master Zhen Song is a Xian Master, known for their ability to push without hands. This power some of you have already seen. Ten of these thirty schools teach the use of kijutsu powers. Of these, only the Olin Masters teach of many such powers. Yes, we here are able to execute a dozen such powers."

"Yet, none of our powers can match those that your group possesses, Bethany. One of the Olin kijutsu powers is the ability to detect when kijutsu is being used. That is how we have known that something of major importance has been happening these past months, though we were unable to ascertain just what. At this time, I hereby grant you all and those who arrive tomorrow sanctuary here for as long as you need."

"We understand the unique needs of you seven. It is my wish to assist those in the most need. Bethany, you and Dita are surrounded by your own people. I will marry San Min Wu and Long Yan shortly. However, for the duration of your stay here, I am assigning my seconds to be the companions and assistants for the others of your people. Master Jian Li wishes to be with

Mei Bi. Master Liang Dhow will be with Dia Son. Master Ning Chou will assist Chan Bao. Master Peng Dong will help Hon Feng. Ladies, this is the highest honor that I can bestow upon you four, the assistance of my seconds. Always, a zen-kami should be shown such honor and respect. However, if you seven would remain with us a while longer, I have many questions that I would like to ask of you."

"But first, Princess San Min Wu, let me tell you a bit of what has happened here during the last five years. After your abduction, your brother, Ho Chi, took over the Royal Palace. However, as you know, he was arrogant and managed to make himself an enemy of the Cao Bang. He was assassinated three years ago. Now the Royal Palace lies empty, and the High Council has chosen not to elect any new Princess to live there. Indeed, the royal line has been nearly extinguished. Elder Hui Bui wishes to say a few words about this, Elder Hui?" he relinquished the forum to the aged man.

He spoke very slowly. "A great chaos has befallen our beloved Tashien. Old values are gone. New values that have appeared are dishonorable, wicked, or evil and cannot be supported by the High Council. The Tashien High Council has chosen not to attempt to elect another Emperor or Empress at this time because none who could be so chosen is worthy of that position or qualified or has sufficient physical means to bring the desperately needed order. While we could elect a few that are qualified, they would just be assassinated quickly. None has the armed forces necessary to keep themselves alive or to bring order to all this chaos. I too wish to hear more from you. With your permission, Princess, I will stay and listen." He bowed to her.

The others left us seven alone with the Olin Masters. Cheng asked, "Now, Princess San Min, please relate what your therapy sessions revealed and what your position now is."

"Oh that part is easy. I am an immortal spiritual being and have had other bodies before," San Min replied. She chatted about how she had been the Empress Sho Lin Wu. She talked about the strange Doll Creatures and their insistence on this whole honor aberration thing that so pervaded Tashien. "So now here I am. I am happier than anyone can imagine. I am strong and fit. All traces of the opium addiction are gone, as is all the pain from losing my lower arms. I am more alert and I think brighter too. However, what am I to do now? That is what all of us are trying to work out. You see, I was content to be your Princess, but now like this," she waved her arms, "I am demoted to only being a zen-kami. Indeed, as we walked here today, the people in the street looked upon me as just that, a zen-kami. However, I am not interested in being a zen-kami. None of us are anymore, for that matter. We want to do more in life, only we haven't yet figured out what that might be. Yes, we obviously now had a severe physical limitation, but we are all bright and alive. Surely, we can find some new goals. I want to help others somehow."

She gaily chatted on, "One thing we might do is to give others Bethany's therapy. It is the most valuable thing that we've ever received. Still, that seems like such a small thing. Me personally, I want to help our people. This insane chaos is destroying our whole country, bit by bit. I'd like to stop that if I could, but as you see I can't even hold a fork, so that's out. Bethany and Dita have promised to show us alternative ways of doing things for ourselves so that we do not have to be so utterly dependent upon others. We were planning to start on that when we got here, you see, to a place of safety." She finally ran down, though no one seemed to mind her explanations at all.

"Thank you, Princess San Min. How about you, Mei Bi?" Master Cheng asked.

"Well, San Min pretty much said it all. I was being a kami to earn a living. My parents died and that was the only thing that I could do to survive. I was treated well, clothed, and fed — only Yuen cheated us. He said that he was paying us, only we found out that he never did set up a bank account for us. Bethany and Jemma took care of that for us. I don't want to be a zen-kami, not really. I am not this body anymore, well I sort of am, I am using it, but I don't think of myself that way. I want to help, but none of us knows how we can yet," Mei replied honestly.

"Same with me," Chan added. "I used to enjoy being a zen-kami, but now it seems so trivial. There is so much more to life and I want to be part of it too."

"Only we don't know anything else but how to give pleasure," Hon added her thoughts. "I enjoyed being first a kami and then a zen-kami, but now I want to do something more worthwhile, only we don't know what that can be. We only know how to be a zen-kami. That's why we need to learn how to do things for ourselves, if that is even possible."

Master Cheng spoke again, "Thank you all for sharing your most personal thoughts with us. Now the evening has come. Perhaps, you would like to take a stroll around our courtyard. Masters Jian, Liang, Ning, and Peng, will you escort our esteemed guests please? I believe that cloaks will be needed. It is wintertime, and the evenings grow chilly here. Hiu Bui, Yulin Wang, and I have much to discuss among ourselves." He bowed to us all, and we began struggling to our feet. The four masters quickly assisted us, and we shuffled to the door.

Outside the meeting room, the four men fastened warm cloaks about us and then escorted us outside. Long Yan was there waiting for San Min and the two began to take their private stroll, chatting about just how soon Master Cheng would marry them. Dita and I wandered off by ourselves, our short arms completely buried beneath the cloaks. Meanwhile the four men and four zen-kami took their walks as well. I noticed that they went in four directions and Dita and I smiled. They would have some private time for once.

She and I leaned our heads on each other's shoulders and did our slow shuffle around the perimeter of the monastery. It was our first truly private time in months as well. "Sorry that my plan to have those kids help us find San Min backfired and got us in this pickle again, dear," Dita apologized.

"You've nothing to be sorry about, love. It actually worked. I don't know how else we could have gotten up there to where she was kept. You do look terribly sexy in your silk dress, you know," I replied.

She grinned, adding, "But you look absolutely ravishing! I was going to tease you and say just you wait until I get my hands on you, but I guess that might be too long a wait. Guess you'll have to settle for what we've got." She was teasing me, of course, so I stopped, and we passionately kissed.

We continued our walk only now she and I went extremely slowly. Our idea was just to amble. Neither of us felt any pressure to have to "hurry it up" so others would not be so put upon by our dismal speed. We suddenly realized this and chuckled to ourselves. "Say, now that we have the nail in the horse shoe on the horse, what's next, Madam Wid," Dita inquired.

"I don't know yet. Say, did you notice Master Cheng touching your mind today? He did touch mine," I asked. Dita had detected it as well. "These Olin Masters may have some powers that may somehow fit into the picture. Maybe they are part of the army."

"Maybe. Say, I will be glad to see Bianca tomorrow. I've rather missed her, you know. I hope I like this Louis fellow. What do I do if I don't? What if I don't think he's right for her?" Dita asked. I had no real answer for her on that one. Still not being in any kind of rush for once, we headed back to the guest house at our own speed, which we both guessed was about a quarter of our make haste shuffle that we had been doing until now. Around the time that we got near the door, the other four with their escorts arrived as well. From the color in their cheeks, I guessed they had enjoyed themselves. I also noticed that they too were ambling along nearly as slowly as we were.

Once inside, all four chatted about how wonderful their Masters were. More importantly, they had been shown that if they walked slowly, they could enjoy themselves and not worry about losing their balance and falling all the time. What I found fascinating was that all four men had asked the women to become their apprentice and learn the ways of the Olin Masters! If my suspicions were correct, if these women could learn these things, perhaps they would gain abilities to do things without their bodies as well.

A bit later, Jemma and Fina helped us get undressed and ready for bed. "Are you sure that you don't want one of us to sleep with you, Bethany?" Jemma asked for the fifth time.

"No, Dita and I can manage by ourselves. See you in the morning," I replied, a twinkle in my eye. This would be our first night alone together in months! Both of us now knew a whole lot more that we could do for each other and we did it. She and I both looked very contented the next morning when Jemma roused us.

After we were all dressed and ready for breakfast, to our surprise, the four Masters came with several others bringing us trays of food and tea. They each insisted on sitting beside their new apprentice and helping them eat breakfast. The topic of conversation was the coming wedding of San Min Wu and Long Yan, which would be held right after breakfast.

At that time, we all gathered in the courtyard. Now I could see that there were at least a hundred men and women here, a fair number of them were in their teens. The monastery was well guarded I concluded. Their ceremony was a simple one and soon Long was told to kiss the radiant bride. Finally, the two lovers were finally united before anything else could separate them. After the ceremony, we all gathered around them and chatted for a time. However, that was short lived. The four Masters then took their apprentices off for their first lessons. Dita and I decided to go for a slow walk around the complex, taking San Min's advice about walking practice.

Around noon, our other companions arrived at the gates of the monastery, and we were there to welcome them. Bianca's first action was to run over to Dita and give her a big hug and kiss, before standing back and staring at her new look. "Gosh, you look stunning, mom! Well, except for the arms and feet, that is," she gushed. After stabling their horses, Bianca introduced Louis d'Grange, the heir to his father's throne. Dita instantly liked him, and I breathed a sigh of relief. Dita, Bianca, and Louis began a lengthy chat, while I escorted Ilenakova and Enrico to the bathtubs. Jemma laid out some clean Tashien outfits for all four of them.

Bathed and now dressed like us, we lounged around on the couches chatting. Ilenakova commented, "I should have come with you guys up here. I haven't had but one chance to fight a battle. Here you guys are getting all the fun!" I knew that she was partially teasing us and partly dead serious. How boring she must have been being a kami all those weeks.

"So what's the plan? Do we go after these Cao Bang assassins now that we are all here in force?" Ilenakova asked, hopefully.

"Honestly, I just don't know yet. Somehow, we must find a way to get Tashien back on a better path," I replied.

"Well, it's pretty degraded around here," she admitted. "Honestly, we haven't seen a happy person until we got to all of you. It is as if the average person is in the pits! Honestly, Bethany, you should have seen the Tashien soldiers in Shashi Wu's army. They stood like statues while they were being gunned down by bullets! If they had not ordered flights of arrows, the riders would have hardly had any casualties at all. It was the sickest battle that I have ever heard tell of — really degraded beyond comprehension! I asked the general about it and his attitude and opinion and Shashi's too is that these soldiers are a dime a dozen, barely worth more than a rice paddy farmer. They've next to no value on human life, shocking beyond belief."

"I asked about the motivation of his soldiers. Guess what he said? They do it just to honor their ancestors. Stand up and take a bullet just to die. Insane, that's what I say," Ilenakova rattled on.

"I know, Ilenakova. We are facing a country of millions, and the vast majority is emotionally so far down, so close to death, that it is not funny," I agreed. "The question before us is how do we turn that around?"

"Hey Wid, that's your department. I am just a Protector, and it seems that you and Dita need lots of protecting," she teased.

"Don't rub it in," I growled and she laughed.

That afternoon, Master Cheng came to our guest room to make an announcement. "I have arranged for you seven to visit with some real zen-kami and to get some assistance from them. Trust me; this is very important for all of you. My four seconds and Long will accompany you. In addition, some of my warriors will accompany those of you who wish to visit the Banca del Dio to arrange for gold. Our carriage will await you in about a half of an hour." He bowed and left us in a bit of mystery. We attempted to get some more information from Master Jian, but he would only say that this was important for us.

The seven of us shuffled out to the waiting carriage, and the four Masters helped each of us inside, before they climbed on top. Bianca, Jemma, and some of the others headed off on horseback to visit the Banca to replenish our funds. As we rode out of the monastery, San Min and Long began pointing out the sights of this great city of theirs. I was impressed with the high arched bridge over the Yan River. The view from its crest was spectacular.

Soon, I realized that we were entering the pleasure district. We began to see kami walking among the crowded streets and the carriage pulled up at last outside one large stone building, the Green Emerald Palace. As the four Masters sat us gently down on the street, some of those passing by us bowed to us, including six kami, women who were bound with the usual silken ropes that were all too familiar to us.

Just as with the Purple Palace, the Green Emerald was elegance plus. The entrance doors were black teakwood with polished brass fixtures. The doorman wore an immaculate white silk suit and cordially opened the door for us. While we seven shuffled slowly inside, Master Jian went on ahead to notify the owner that we had arrived. A kami walked past us on her way outside; she paused to bow low to us, and we returned her bow. As we slowly moved along the entrance green, plush carpet, others also bowed respectfully. I did spot three bodyguards also in white suits watching observantly from discrete locations just inside this lobby area.

The owner came up to us with Master Jian. He bowed humbly and said, "Welcome to the Green Emerald. I am Shi Qiang Lu, the owner of this palace. My good friend Master Cheng Dau has asked me to have you meet with my two zen-kami. I must say that this is a very great honor for me to have so many zen-kami come to visit my establishment. If I can do anything to make your visit more pleasant, you only have to ask. My palace is your palace this afternoon. If you will follow me, I will take you to Lan Li and Sun Mi Lun." He bowed and we shuffled along after him. I noticed that he was used to walking along at our slow speed, which I found interesting. San Min and Long were in the front of our group and she purposely was not trying to move quickly. I say quickly, but you must realize that takes on a completely different meaning to us. Ours quickly translates to your very slowly and our slowly become excruciatingly slow for most people.

Finally, we arrived on the third floor, which was devoted to the exclusive use of the two zen-kami women. Shi Qiang Lu introduced us to the two women who we found lounging on a green velvet couch in the entrance room at the top of the stairs. Lan Li and Sun Mi Lun rose as we stepped into their room. Both women bowed to us and we, them. I estimated that they both were around forty years old or so. They wore identical green silk dresses, rather similar to ours, only they didn't wear corsets, but had garter belts to hold up their similar black silk stockings. Their shoes looked pretty much the same as ours and their upper arms were just as conical in shape as ours were. Both women were attractive and their long black hair was parted in the middle and draped across their shoulders and busts, just the way that we seven wore ours. In fact, other than the age difference, there were few differences between the way that they appeared and the way that we appeared. Strikingly so, I thought. Perhaps, there was an unwritten model that all surgeons followed in making zen-kami.

"Welcome honored zen-kami from Shansee. I am Lan and this is Sun Mi. Master Cheng has told us about your plight down in Shansee and has asked us to show you how we do things and to answer all of your questions. From what he has said, this Yuen must have mistreated you incredibly badly. Both Sun Mi and I wish to show you the true nature of we zen-kami."

Quietly, the four Masters and Shi Qiang went back down the stairs, leaving us seven to meet privately with these two zen-kami women. I was very much surprised and amazed. "Where do you live?" asked Chan, breaking the ice between us.

"Oh, we live across town with our husbands and family. We come to work here every morning around ten and return home by ten, but we work here only four days each week," Lan answered. "Master Cheng said that this evil Yuen kept you all locked in a room in his palace. That must have been just awful. Is this true?"

"Yes, we were total prisoners," Chan relied. "He promised us a thousand gold each week in pay, but he never paid us a copper really."

"Oh how awful! That is most despicable! He did you a grievous dishonor!" Sun Mi said very sincerely. "We are paid two hundred gold each week by Shi Qiang. He puts it in our Banca accounts, and we withdraw funds to help support our families, as we need it. My husband is an artist, a painter, so my funds help pay for our home and studio. I also do some watercolors when I have free time. I have two grown sons who have left the coop. With the money that we earn here, our lives have been such that we want for nothing."

"Yes, she is right. My husband and I have been able to afford a very nice stone house and a servant to help with things that I am unable to do. Honestly, I never did like to clean house, not even as a little girl," Lan admitted. "I have a boy who was a soldier, but he was killed. My daughter Min Li is now married and expecting a child soon. I will be a grandmother very soon now. My husband is a publisher of historical notes, but his job doesn't pay well, though he loves it. My income from being a zen-kami more than makes up for it. I am not an artist like Sun Mi is, but I enjoy calligraphy. I make very artistic signs in my spare time. I do it because I like writing the characters, not because I have to. We don't need any extra money. My bank account just keeps growing larger every day, though I do like to spend a good sum on fine clothes," she admitted her piece of vanity.

"She has made all of these signs you see on this floor," Sun Mi explained, pointing to one on the wall that read: Zen-kami: Lan Li and Sun Mi Lun. "We've worked together since we became zen-kami. How long ago was it, Lan?" she asked, rubbing her head with her arm.

"Golly, I believe it's been over twenty-two years now, Sun Mi! My, how time has flown," Lan answered. "Oh yes, there is one major rule that everyone must follow with zen-kami." This talk of years had reminded her of it. "Always zen-kami must be paired up. As you know, like this," she waved her arms, "we cannot feed ourselves, but with a partner, we can each feed the other. It is this way with many things. Where one zen-kami is unable to do something for herself, she is able to do that thing for another. So zen-kami must always be paired up. Sun Mi and I have been together since we became zen-kami so many years ago. We are together always, that is, when we are not at our own homes with our husbands and families. This rule must never be broken."

"Come, we must show you the tools that all of you should have received the day that you became zen-kami!" Sun Mi eagerly added. We rose and followed the two women. I noticed that they moved slowly, as had Dita and I the other night. Sun Mi noticed me noticing her and grasped at once my thoughts.

"Oh yes, you must learn to move at a comfortable speed, such as this. A zen-kami learns to move very slowly compared to others. We take the time to observe all that is around us, which the normal people fail to see in their hasty walking."

"Oh she is so right!" Lan added. "My husband and I just love to go for long walks around the city. We see so much that others utterly fail to see at all."

"She is right. Long walks are the best times for my husband and me. As we walk, we see so many things that others never see. He then paints them. I also make my humble attempts to render them in watercolors," Sun Mi added. "You learn to walk slow and put your full attention on the world beyond you. Then you too will see so very much of life. Some of it is not so good, but there is incredible beauty, if you only look. Going very slowly, you can see what others do not."

"Yes, a zen-kami never does anything quickly. Our world is like that of a snail that sees all and delights in all things," Lan added. "Here is one of Sun Mi's watercolors. Isn't it just beautiful?" We paused to gaze upon a pastel watercolor depiction of a garden with a waterfall and many springtime flowers. "That one took her six months to do. You must all learn to go slow and never think haste, for haste we cannot do and it makes for waste." She lectured us.

A bit later, we shuffled into their study room. "Here is our work room that we use when we are not with a customer. We usually see at most two women during the day and two men at night, though we never violate our husbands with these men, you see. No zen-kami or even a kami should ever be forced to do that. Only the lowly prostitutes do such acts; we provide pleasure, not intercourse. Ah, now here we have laid out the tool kit that all of you should have been given the day that you became a zen-kami," Sun Mi gestured to a large array of brass and copper tools that they had laid out on a table to show us.

Each one had a copper conical shaped band that slipped easily onto our conical shaped arms. "You slip them on like this," Lan demonstrated. "This one is a vital one as is this one. With the brush and comb attachments, we can brush out each other's hair." She demonstrated how it was done, by brushing Sun Mi's hair, adjusting it nicely across her front.

"This one is equally vital. With the attached spoon or fork, we can feed each other, though not ourselves. You can see why the vital rule must be that zen-kami are always in pairs. With these tools, we can care for each other's needs. Some attachments held a paintbrush, while others held a pen for writing the characters of their language. "With the hook ones, we can lift each other's dresses so that we can use the chamber pots," she continued her explanations. For a half hour, the two demonstrated their useful tools.

"How do we get these tools?" Chan finally asked.

"Master Cheng told Shi Qiang to get each of you a full set of tools. Shi Qiang told us that they were going to be delivered to the Olin Monastery later today. I do hope you get them. Honestly, Lan and I do not know how you have been able to get by without them!" Sun Mi exclaimed, her voice full of concern.

"We've had to depend on others for everything," Chan answered her. "Well, we did have some crude wooden spoons that Yuen gave us so we could feed each other and some hairbrushes. Those are terribly hard to manage, though we did. These will make so many things easier and even possible for us. Thank you very much for showing us!"

"You are most welcome. You seven have been most horribly dishonored," Lan put in.

"Say, is it safe for you to go out walking in the streets?" Hon asked. "We are so defenseless."

"Oh it is very safe. As we said, we both love to go on long walks. Don't you know that it is a high crime to bother, hurt, or injure a zen-kami? It is instant death to any who does so. A zen-kami is held in high respect in Tashien, though obviously this Yuen creature deserved to be killed," Sun Mi declared.

"Why did you decide to become a zen-kami?" Dita asked, curious about why anyone would desire to be like this.

Sun Mi answered, "My husband is a great artist. We were married when we were seventeen, and he needed funds so that he could create his art. I began earning extra money by working as a kami here. I soon saw that I could earn far more by becoming a zen-kami, and I saw the great reverence our people hold for them. So I wanted to become one myself, but my husband took a year to convince. He has been so wonderful to me all these years, but of course, I have also been so wonderful for him. Many of his paintings now fetch five hundred a canvas." She looked at Lan and added sheepishly, "Okay, I also love fine clothes and silk stockings very, very much. I have been able to afford the best. I know that this is vain and earthly of me, but I am being honest with you." She flushed a little.

She continued, "But Dita, there is more to being a zen-kami that you are thinking. I can tell that you think that we are foolish women for becoming as we are. You see us as helpless women who can barely walk. Yet, you also see us as very sexy women." Dita's face turned scarlet. She was indeed thinking that very thought. She was still holding the viewpoint of being a male.

"Our husbands see us likewise," Sun Mi went on with her accurate statements. "Yes, we know how to give others great sensual pleasures, but in return we have somehow grown. Dita, you will find zen-kami very keen observers. We miss very little, if anything. Go slow, and you too will soon discover this for yourselves. Bethany here does not see us as sexy women, yet you, Dita, see us much as our husbands do. Yes, some claim that we can read minds. We see it as seeing the real world as it really is. We can tell when someone is lying or is telling the truth. It is so plainly obvious to us. Sometimes the Olin Masters make use of our talents this way. Indeed, the Olin Masters highly respect us for our special skills of being able to see what is really present. Indeed, we often are used as soothsayers."

"San Min wants to really give pleasure to her new husband who has long been her supporting pillar, perhaps for years. She feels that she is owes him so very much, and that this is a small way that she can pay him back. Dia, Chan, and Hon, you three are an open book. All three of you so desperately want to find loving husbands who will respect you for what you are. You three give pleasure to others, but so terribly want to be able to give that gift to a husband." All three flushed beet red, embarrassed to have their innermost thoughts laid bare before the world. "Mei Bi, you most desperately want to learn how to actually be one of us, as well as to find a loving, kind husband."

"But you, Bethany, you are so very different. You seek only to find ways to help us survive better," Sun Mi read me.

"Yet, there is something far deeper," Lan interrupted. "Sun Mi. I sense that she wants to help all of us in Tashien, not just we zen-kami."

"Yes, I see that too, Lan, while she can see ways of helping the zen-kami, she cannot see how to help the greater," Sun Mi added. Now my face felt hot. These women certainly did have the skills that they claimed!

"How can we learn?" asked an embarrassed Chan.

"The Olin Masters have taken upon themselves to right the wrongs done to you. Follow their instructions, and you will gain what you are missing," Lan answered her. "The Olin Masters are the most powerful ones around. Have faith in them and their teachings, Chan."

We chatted a while longer and then the men returned for us. After thanking them all for so opening our eyes, we returned to the monastery. The four then went off with the four Masters to study, while San Min and Long sat down for a long talk about the future. Dita and I decided to take a walk around the complex, and Enrico, Ilenakova, Bianca, Jemma, and Louis joined us. Fina, Phillipe, and Tian were off practicing under the guidance of Master Zhen.

At first, our friends wanted to know what we had found out. Dita explained all that had happened. Then, I made as astute observation. "Yes, they have learned some incredible skills. Their powers of observation are as good as or possibly better than ours. Yet, have you noticed that the spiritual beings are actually stuck rather solidly inside their heads? Their methods of such concentration on fleshly bodies is not freeing them, but entrapping them more solidly. Contrast Lan and Sun Mi to Chan, Mei, Dia, and Hon, who are mostly now outside the backs of their heads. They are aware of themselves as spiritual beings and are torn between the world of the flesh and that of their native abilities."

"Yes, but where does this get us?" Dita asked. "Going as slow as we do and being as helpless as these bodies are, I can see how that rather allows them the time to actually observe what is around them. Isn't that an awfully steep price to pay for being able to observe the obvious?" she asked.

"Indeed, it is," Bianca agreed. "I wonder if the Olin Master's training will drive the four back into their heads once more? I hope not."

"Hope not what?" the quiet, yet commanding voice of Master Cheng broke in on our conversation. Bianca flushed and looked at me with a pleading look of help!

"We all thank you for arranging the trip to see the true situation with real zen-kami, Master Cheng. While we all now see what has been so terribly missing with us, we've seen the kijutsu of these true zen-kami women. Most impressive indeed. Yet, there are other ways to learn to observe the obvious around us without the need to cut off one's arms and cripple their feet. Still, they were exceedingly able with their skills, most impressive. However, we are all spiritual beings that inhabit for a time these fleshly bodies. We could not help but notice that Lan and Sun Mi were firmly stuck inside their heads. Chan, Dia, Hon, and Mei are mostly behind their heads and not stuck inside them. Bianca was hoping that the training your Masters are giving them will not force them back into their heads and into being a body once more, undoing our therapy."

He bowed to me and said, "You are most welcome. When I heard of your awful mistreatment at the hands of Yuen, I felt obliged to show you all the way that you should have been treated. I also feel obliged to see if some of that can be rectified, hence my Masters and their training. It is curious that you mention our spiritual nature. Prophet Yulin Wang has been telling us much about such things. What is unique about the Olin School is that in order to become master of so many kijutsu powers, one cannot ignore one's spiritual side. We believe that all such powers come from the being, not the body."

"Many of the other schools of the martial arts dwell solely on the physical aspects, tuning and using these bodies to their fullest. The fewer schools that teach one of the many kijutsu powers, such as Master Zhen's Xian School, must focus some attention to the spiritual side of man. Kijutsu powers come only from the being, not the body. I believe that you will find the four not returning to a position, as you say, inside their heads."

"I have come to tell you and Dita and the rest of your companions that you are all free to use your kijutsu powers here within the monastery walls any time you desire. I suspect that Dita would prefer to use them when she dines."

"We don't want to blow anyone's mind by having things just levitate," Dita hinted at our reasoning. "We got into serious trouble doing that once before and it cost us more than we've lost this time."

"Of that, you have no fear while within the monastery walls. Yes, beyond these sacred walls, the wise would follow the course that you have set. Within, you are free, for we accept and embrace kijutsu readily. Now may I ask you, Bethany, a personal question?" Master Cheng asked. I nodded.

"You have come to Tashien for more than just finding and rescuing our Princess San Min. I sense that strongly. Can you share that with me?" he asked.

"Sure, we also want to find some way to bring back stability to Tashien, to end these minor wars, to help your people find their true natures, and to better their lives. Admittedly, as yet I do not see how this may be accomplished."

"Thank you for being so honest with me. I will say this, Bethany: there are others who share your goals. You are not alone in this quest. Ah, it appears that the seven sets of zen-kami tools have arrived at last. Please accept this small gift from me to help ease your burdens," he bowed and excused himself to go meet the courier who was carrying a rather large box.

Somewhat later, we seven, aided by our friends, began experimenting with our new tools, designed especially for our unique needs. Some were quite similar in nature to those that my dad had invented for my mom in an earlier lifetime. Dita and I both appreciated the hook attachments, which allowed us to raise our dresses for each other. Chan, Dia, Hon, Mei, and San Min were extremely happy to discover that they could far more easily feed each other with the fork and spoon tools.

The next morning around ten a loud gong sounded, startling everyone. We heard men running out on the courtyard. Our group dashed outside to see what was going on, while we seven slowly made our way to the door. Ilenakova dashed back inside to tell us, "It's the Cao Bang. They are just outside the walls!" She grabbed several of her weapons and dashed outside and the others dashed inside to get theirs. We continued our slow shuffle and finally made it to the courtyard as the last of our folks, weapons in hand, ran past us to help defend the monastery.

I saw over a hundred men manning the walls, awaiting the start of the battle, which had not yet come. Master Cheng stood just outside the front doors of the main temple, while his seconds were organizing the warriors. Master Jian called out, "Master Cheng, one is holding a white flag. I believe he wants to parley. There are about a hundred men out there in black."

"Then, let us see what the Cao Bang desire," Master Cheng said. We seven continued on our slow walk into the courtyard. Hu, the doorman, opened the heavy gates and we all could see the large number of Cao Bang fighters in the street before the monastery. One of the men dressed in black was holding a white flag. Now he slowly walked up to the doors and handed his flag to one of his companions, along with his hano blade. He then walked through the doors and fell in beside Master Jian, while Hu closed and secured the heavy doors.

We were now over halfway across the courtyard as the two walked from the doors up to the main temple, where Master Cheng waited. I figured that this assassin would get a kick out of seeing we seven's unique shuffle as we tried to get to Master Cheng as well. I wanted to hear what this assassin had to say, no matter how silly I looked getting there. Of course, my companions swiftly moved in behind us, intent upon protecting us.

To my surprise, the Cao Bang man came up close to us and slowed down, giving us a bow as well. He followed along just at our sides and at our speed, though Master Jian kept close watch on him. The other three Masters also quietly moved into position behind us as well. At last, we stood close to Master Cheng. Both men bowed to each other, and the black masked man pulled off his hood. We got our first glimpse at his face, rather ordinary at that.

"Master Cheng Dau, thank you for receiving me. I am Gang Yo, leader of the Tan Loc Cao Bang. I wish to speak with you and these zen-kami from Shansee and those who have been protecting them, I believe that would be Master Zhen Song and his group," he requested politely.

"Granted. If you will all step inside and take tea with me," Master Cheng bowed and motioned for us to enter. Again, the men gave deference to we seven and we did our best to move as quickly as possible, but I thought it was pitifully slow at best. Still, we managed not to stumble and fall. We entered the main room where floor mats were already arranged and Master Cheng indicated where we should sit. Essentially, we seven and our companions were interspersed so that someone was at each of our sides to help us with the tea. Gang Yo sat facing us with Master Cheng just to his right. As soon as we were sitting, several servant women entered with trays of teacups and pots of oolong.

Gang spoke first, "Ah, so these are the mysterious zen-kami whom we have been following for quite some time. In case you are not aware of it, Qiang Peng has put a hit out on these seven zen-kami. According to him, these women managed to kill Yuen Ming and ten of his bodyguards during their escape from the fifth floor of the Purple Palace. At first, I thought that Qiang was joking, that he had some other reason behind his contract. We checked. Yes, Yuen had his neck twisted, nearly severed in fact. The fifth floor had doorknobs and locks. The main outside door also was locked, and yet after the escape, the locking mechanism was somehow jammed and had to be replaced. They left ten guards with their necks broken in a similar manner not only inside on the stairs of the palace, but also a trail of them going down the back alleyway."

"For days, I considered this to be utterly an impossible task for a zen-kami to have done, and I failed to believe Qiang Peng. However, during this long chase, I now believe him completely. I would like to ask the zen-kami if they did indeed do all this themselves."

Dita spoke up, "Yes, I did it. Yuen was about to rape me, and I twisted his neck around several times. I got us all out of there and had to kill the guards who wanted to stop us, though my wife had to lift our bodies down the stairs and such."

"Amazing display of kijutsu power," Gang replied politely and bowed again to Dita. "During these past months, the attempt to fulfill Qiang Peng's hit has cost us dearly. We've lost eighty-three of our men; some were very highly skilled fighters. The few survivors have reported seeing the most impressive display of kijutsu powers ever witnessed in Tan Loc. Balls of fire, bolts of lightning, mind control, push, and even the neck twisting, for want of a better name for this unknown skill, have been unleashed against us. Never in the entire history of the Cao Bang have we ever suffered losses such as this! Yes, we may lose one or two men, but never eighty-three!"

"Thus, I have concluded that at this time, we are witnessing the largest concentration ever of kijutsu power in Tan Loc. It would seem that much of this is coming from those from the Outer Lands. Hence, I came here personally. First, honored zen-kami, as of this moment, the contract on your lives is hereby voided by the Cao Bang. I have already returned Qiang's deposit. He will be upset, but he will be unable to do anything about it."

Dita replied, "Thank you. That is a relief. I had thought that we would be forced to kill every one of you to be rid of this contract." He smiled grimly and nodded.

"Second, it would seem that this huge influx of kijutsu power is coming from those from the Outside Lands. I would like to know your intentions here in Tashien and Tan Loc in particular. What are your objectives? Are you trying to take over our country?"

Dita looked at me with a look that said you answer this one. I replied, "We have accomplished our first mission, which was to help Long Yan find his lost fiancé, San Min Wu. We have found her, rescued her, and they are now married. Yuen was killed in part because he abducted us and turned us into zen-kami, and more importantly, he was holding San Min hostage against her will. Our second mission is to see if there is anything that we can do to help you stabilize your country and bring back order and personal freedom to Tashien."

"I see. May I ask why Outsiders are so interested in our internal matters?" he asked with a hint of hostility in his voice.

"You may ask. Your chaos has spilled over into the Outer Lands. Some of my friends here were just barely able to avert a huge war with some of your people who have fled your far northern lands into one of our allies' country. Also, your country's breakdown is impacting trade with the Outer Lands as well. It is in our best interests to help you bring order back to Tashien, and to achieve personal freedom for your people. Obviously, the ancient tradition of honoring ancestors is now beginning to break down broadly."

"You are not planning to use your kijutsu against us?" Gang asked, incredulously.

"Not unless we need to defend ourselves. We won't let others do similar things that Yuen did to Dita and me that's for sure," I answered, adding, "but if your Cao Bang start assassinating the good guys that we are trying to help, all bets are off."

Gang stared at me for a minute without saying a word. At last, he again bowed, "I believe that you are telling me the truth, that you have no intentions of trying to use your kijutsu to conquer our country. Master Cheng, you have given these people sanctuary. May I ask why?"

"Master Zhen is a friend of mine. These seven zen-kami have been horribly dishonored and mistreated. Four of the seven were made into zen-kami against their wishes. The Cao Bang have been hunting them down with the intent of further bodily harm. A zen-kami is nearly defenseless, just barely able to walk, with mere upper arms where we have hands. Such does not seem fair to me," Master Cheng answered.

Gang gave a smirk. "Put that way, it does sound unfair. So here we find ourselves. Just how are we to stabilize our country, as the zen-kami has put it, Master Cheng?" Again, his voice echoed a hint of antagonism.

"Alas, that has not yet been determined," he replied simply.

"The Cao Bang is not your enemy, Master Cheng. We, too, are experiencing great difficulties since the assassination of the Emperor and Empress. Chaos is as bad for our business as it is for yours. It is in our best interests to assist in finding a way to stabilize Tashien. In a little over three months, the dozens of overlords will be at it again, fighting petty wars with their neighbors over small bits of land to add to their control. We cannot turn back the clock and return to the old ways. There is no large army at anyone's control to enforce a leader's wishes on all Tashien as there used to be with Empress Pian Wu. Personally, I do not see how this can be done — the stabilization of Tashien," Gang admitted.

"Now, none of us do," I interjected. "Yet, we are open to any and all ideas. Gang, would you like to become involved in the decision making process?" I asked him directly without asking Master Cheng or Master Zhen first. Whether they liked my idea or not, any stabilization plan would have to be backed by the Cao Bang. That much was plainly obvious to me at this point.

Gang broke into a hearty laugh. "Master Cheng, your zen-kami here is most wise indeed!" Both Masters Cheng and Zhen smiled. "Of course I would like to be involved in the decision making process. This chaos adversely impacts us all."

"Indeed, Gang, it does. I accept your offer to become involved, Gang," Master Cheng replied, still grinning. "Indeed, this zen-kami is perhaps the wisest of all. Will you stay here in my monastery a while and join in our discussions, Gang?"

"Certainly, Master Cheng. First, I believe that we ought to defuse our forces. If you will permit me to retrieve my hano and disperse my men, I am prepared to stay here for some time," Gang answered him.

"Yes, we should all stand down. After the noon meal, I suggest that we begin our discussions. I will send for some others who may wish to join us. Bethany, will you please join us in our discussions this afternoon?" I nodded. The parley broke up. While the Masters and Gang headed off to deal with their forces, we seven shuffled slowly back to our quarters, while my companions tried awkwardly to go at our slow pace.

Chapter 21 Decisions and the Palace

After lunch, Master Jian and Master Zhen, who were to attend, walked with me back to the main temple. I quickly became annoyed with how slow my shuffling was, and I just picked up my body and moved it along quickly to the door, forcing the two men to break into a run to keep up with me. As I sat my body back down on the courtyard before the door, both men laughed as they joined me. "Ah, we have an impatient zen-kami, Master Jian," Zhen jested. I grinned.

This time, I was led to a second floor room with a south facing window. The sunlight filtered into the room, and mats were laid out in a circle on the floor. Teacups were properly positioned beside each. I was thankful for Zhen's assistance in helping me sit down easily. This training dress made such motions difficult. A walking slit would have been convenient just now.

In attendance at this first meeting were Masters Cheng, Zhen, and Jian. Gang and the prophet Yulin Wang joined us, along with the old elder Hui Bui. Zhen and Jian sat on either side of me, and Zhen assisted me with my tea. A large map of Tashien hung on the wall. I gazed at the unique geography. East-west ridges, impassible from the north and south, angled out from the Helios Grande Mountains about halfway across Tashien. I realized this limited north-south travel to the eastern half of the country, where the terrain was lower. It also meant that these overlords could hold up in their individual valleys defying any attempts to bring overall order. On the other hand, a large army could seal them inside their isolated valleys. Still, our solution ought to allow for these valley overlords.

As I sipped my tea while Zhen kindly held it for me, I reached a decision. These powerful leaders ought to know the truth behind their enslavement. "Where shall we begin?" asked Master Cheng, respectfully.

"At the very beginning," I suggested. The men looked at me and I continued. "Recently, we Outsiders have uncovered what has been happening here on Tarra. I won't discuss those issues that pertain solely to our portion of Tarra, but only what we've learned about Tashien. It is indeed a strange tale. Let me begin my stressing that we are all immortal spiritual beings that for a time inhabit these fleshly bodies that we see here. We are not our bodies. When these fleshly bodies die, we separate from them and go off to find a new baby body to begin the cycle over once more. If we are indeed powerful beings, one may look upon being forced to stay in these fleshly bodies, and even to consider that we are the body having lost all sense of our own selves, as being in a sort of prison."

I noticed that I had their complete attention and I continued. "Centuries ago, you spiritual beings who live in Tashien were being imprisoned in these bodies by alien creatures that looked rather like whitish doll bodies, standing some eight feet tall. Their bodies were not fleshly ones, but more like a child's rubber doll. They were not alive as we think of these bodies. They resided high in the Helios Grande Mountains. There they set up a number of electronic machines that sent out some kind of energy radiation that seemed to keep all the spiritual beings here in Tashien somehow pinned in these fleshly bodies, driving them to very low emotional tones, such as useless, apathy, hopeless, undeserving, and even numb. Worse, whenever a fleshly body died and the spiritual being became free of it finally, their energy beams forced them to return to the mountains where these Doll Creatures then further suppressed them downwards and attempted to convince them that their only goal in life was to honor their ancestors. With that as their only thought remaining, to honor their ancestors, they were sent back down to grab another baby body and continue their own imprisonment."

I noticed that Gang was looking rather ill. So were several others, but I continued anyway. "Now how long these Doll Creatures sat there in the mountains doing this I do not know. As you might expect, after centuries of this, they became bored. They shut off the energy beams, eliminated their doll bodies, and left Tarra, for good I hope. The moment that they shut off the energy beams is the precise time that the chaos began to erupt here in Tashien, some five years ago. With this continual energy beam suppression lifted, men and women began to move from their enforced emotional tones. Some have risen to resentment, hatred, and anger, lashing out against others. Many now doubt why they have been so long honoring their long dead ancestors, as that seems utterly ridiculous to be their whole goal in life. Others sense this, but have no other goals for themselves and so continue to attempt to honor their ancestors. That about sums it up, gentlemen."

Gang was definitely looking quite ill. Hui Bui also looked a bit green. Yulin was crying, while Master Zhen was nervously shaking. Only Masters Cheng and Jian had the least reactions; they were a bit fearful. "Okay, now that I have shaken you all up a bit, will you allow me and my friends to assist you in recovering from this?" Cheng nodded. I made a Mind Link quickly to Dita, Mei, Chan, Dia, San Min, and Hon. *I need your help. It is time that you practice your therapy session giving. Come at once to the second floor of the main temple.*

I wished that we all were not so movement-impaired, as I waited for what seemed an eternity for the six to shuffle into the room. Meantime, I told the men about what would be expected of them, to re-experience their traumas and tell their session giver what was happening as they went through it. Finally, from my point of view, Dita led the five into the room. Quickly, I got the sessions arranged. San Min sat beside Hui Bui and began running him. Mei took Master Jian, Chan took Master Cheng, Dia took Yulin, Hon took Master Zhen. I had Dita handle Gang, while I watched over the six ongoing sessions, lending a hand where needed.

Mostly, the incidents were quite similar. My story had most definitely re-stimulated their half-buried memories, which brought the physical pain and wild emotions back into the present. They all were re-experiencing one of the times that they had been forced to report to the Doll Creatures after their fleshly body had died. Zapped with electronic forces, ordered repeatedly to honor their ancestors until that was the sole idea in their minds, then forced back down from the mountains and into a new baby body — that was the sequence that each of the six were running.

Several complete passes over the entire incidents were needed as more and more of their unconsciousness and confusions surfaced and blew. Naturally, these first incidents did not fully erase, and in due time each of the six were asked if there was something earlier in time that was similar to this one. Of course there was. This had been happening to them for centuries.

Late in the afternoon, Master Cheng began laughing, having finally blown the whole chain of suppression events that had happened to him. Master Jian finished up not long after that. Both now watched the other sessions as they too began to end, when the realizations of their own decisions and postulates made back then blew as well. Master Zhen began laughing, then Yulin and Hui. The last one to finally blow off and erase the massive suppression was Gang, who declared, "Damn! I have been fighting the wrong people for centuries now! How stupid could I be?" He roared with laughter over his miss-identification.

"I do not have words enough to thank you for what you have done for us, Bethany. Truly, we have all been blessed with perhaps the most powerful kijutsu ever to be seen in Tashien," proclaimed a cheerful Master Cheng. Rapidly, the others joined in heaping praise and thanks upon we seven. Of course, they all wanted to know all about this therapy. Since it was dinnertime and hunger struck, Master Cheng sent word for dinner to be served, insisting the zen-kami stay and dine with them. I relaxed at last and allowed Master Zhen to feed me, while the others graciously fed the other five. Dita insisted on feeding herself, using her spiritual skills to lift the sticks. Of course, this display of "kijutsu powers" likewise impressed the men too. Dita later told me that she wanted to make very sure that Gang Yo knew that she had powerful kijutsu. She still didn't trust the Cao Bang assassin.

After dinner and another round of praise and thanks, Dita led the other zen-kami back to our quarters. At last, we could continue our discussions. Once more, I dominated the talks. "Okay, now that I have told you the history of what's been going on here in Tashien and now that you all have discovered that you are immortal spiritual beings and that what I have said about the Doll Creatures is true, we all are in possession of the accurate facts of the true situation here in your country. Now we can better decide what to do about it. I do not know what can be done to stabilize your country or how to bring about personal freedom here. Perhaps some of you can take over for me. I seem to have dominated the entire afternoon," I jested.

The six men smiled and Gang replied, "Such domination is most welcome. Your wife is most impressive." The six all chuckled.

Hui Bui spoke next. "If I may be permitted to speak?" Master Cheng nodded. "I am actually a member of the Tashien High Council. As you know, after the assassination of Emperor Banzhou and Empress Pian Wu, we chose not to proclaim a new Empress. We made this decision for two reasons. First, with the death of Pian, that direct line was ended. Princess Shashi remained in exile, but was now a zen-kami. While we could have chosen her, without her hands and long nails, she would not have been accepted at that time. Second, no one had a sufficiently large army to protect themselves should they be appointed the new rulers. We had no intention of appointing someone only to have them quickly assassinated as well."

"Hey, the Cao Bang was not behind the assassination of the Emperor and Empress Pian," Gang hastily pointed out. "It was done by one of the overlords of Wontun Province."

Hui continued, "Princess Shashi Wu lives, but she has moved her followers to the Outer Lands. Still, the High Council exists. With the revolutionary changes our country has undergone, at this time, the High Council could appoint a new Empress. I believe that there has been so much chaos that many would now accept a new ruler, if only to help bring back some order and stability. If we did so, it would additionally bring back some continuity with our past. So many are now questioning so many things that the appointment of a new Empress would be latched onto by many, much as a security blanket. Mind you, this could only be a stopgap action. Real change must somehow come."

"But who could be chosen as Empress?" asked Gang, curious about this possibility. "If we had a strong Empress and Emperor, perhaps stability might return."

"I have in mind San Min Wu. Because she has no hands, in many ways, the old ways of the Imperial Court would be broken. She may be seen as different, as a complete break with the old ways of the Empress. Admittedly, her husband is neither a politician nor a warrior, again, a complete break of tradition. Obviously, a new way of running our country must then be set in place. Still, if the people see that we now have a new Empress and Emperor, that alone may be enough to start bringing some stability to Tashien, allowing us to install the new way of running our country. In short, if we appoint a new Empress, it can only be a stopgap measure. We must be prepared to begin installing a new way at the same time as we appoint her."

Master Cheng asked, "But will the people accept what they see as a zen-kami as their Empress?"

"I have been giving that considerable thought, Master Cheng. I believe that we could try a little experiment to see how this would work out. Suppose that we here in Nan Yan put San Min Wu back on her throne as our Princess as she was before her abduction. We could carefully monitor how our people react to this. If she is broadly accepted as our Princess once more, then I believe that she would also be broadly accepted if appointed Empress," Hui answered.

Gang spoke up, "Yes, I like that idea, Hui. Put her back on her throne here in Nan Yan and see what happens. A few months should tell all, unless I am a terrible judge of people. However, Hui, she has no army. How can she protect herself in the Royal Palace? She must have protection. I do not want to see her assassinated, not after what I have seen her do with her kijutsu powers!"

"No indeed. These zen-kami are extremely valuable people, more so than any that I know in Tashien," Master Cheng replied sincerely. "They all must be highly protected. I am willing to summon all the Olin masters and charge them with protecting these zen-kami."

"Master Cheng, I will also offer all of my Xian Masters as well. We simply must protect them all. Perhaps if they were all residing in the Royal Palace here in Nan Yan they could be more easily protected."

"Thank you, Master Zhen. Yes, that was my thought; house them all in the Royal Palace. I could also send out a request to the other martial arts schools, asking that they also send some of their masters to assist us," Master Cheng added.

Gang spoke up, "I will likewise send a number of Cao Bang to protect them. When others know that the Cao Bang are supporting and protecting these women, few will dare take any action against them. We have a reputation."

Cheng and the others chuckled. He answered, "Yes, you do have a reputation that is well known. I am most grateful for your support, Gang Yo." The assassin leader smiled; he'd scored another small victory.

"Then are we all agreed that we should re-appoint San Min Wu as our Princess and ask the other zen-kami to join her in the Royal Palace?" asked Hui Bui.

All nodded, and I added, "With your permission, I and my companions would like to join them as well. We can offer a good measure of protection as well."

"More than accepted, Bethany," Master Cheng replied with a grin. "I would be disappointed if you and your companions did not. You are now intertwined in the history and events of Tashien, a web from which you will not be so easily freed." The men chuckled.

Hui nodded and said, "Then you may expect the announcement tomorrow. I will be responsible for gathering public opinion on this move.

By spring, we ought to know if she will be fully accepted as our Princess. If she is well received, then the High Council may act in the spring and appoint her our new Empress. We must be prepared to begin installing new methods of governing Tashien at that time."

Master Cheng concluded, "Excellent, Hui. Tomorrow, we will begin setting up protections at the Royal Palace. I will send out word to the Olin Masters. Master Zhen, you do the same with your Xian Masters. Gang, you do what you need to get the Cao Bang ready to assume their protection duties. Let us meet again after lunch tomorrow and begin to work out new methods by which Tashien may be governed."

Prophet Yulin, who had been mostly silent, now spoke softly, "My inner eye has been opened today. I must consult the Sacred Prophesies. Perhaps there we will find even more answers."

Zhen helped me up and asked if I needed an arm back to the guesthouse. "No, thanks Master Zhen. I know that you have urgent matters to handle. I can walk myself back." He bowed appreciatively and walked swiftly back to our rooms, while I contented myself to my three inch steps, shuffling along. When I finally got back, I found Bianca was doing Dita's hair. Jemma immediately insisted on doing mine. Naturally, the teens wanted to know all about the meeting. I asked her to assemble our group in my bedroom. While she brushed out my hair, I quickly told them what had happened, but urged them not to say a word about this to San Min or Long.

The next morning, Hui paid a visit to San Min and Long, talking in private to them both. After a half hour, he brought them out into our large common room. "I have an announcement to make." Hui Bui suddenly had everyone's full attention. "The High Council of Nan Yan has asked that San Min Wu resume her former position as our Princess. She has gratefully accepted the position once again, for which we are eternally grateful. She has stipulated that all of you move into the palace with her. Masters Jian, Liang, Ning, and Deng will also move in with their apprentices so that they can continue their studies of the Olin Masters. Master Cheng and Master Zhen will be providing palace security along with members of the Cao Bang, who are fully supporting the Princess." Everyone began clapping for San Min, who looked slightly embarrassed by all the attention.

After Hui bowed to her and left, she explained, "They still want me even though I cannot be a 'proper' Princess. The High Council knows that and says that is not a problem. I am just supposed to be me. I am so glad that you all will be coming with me. A wagon and carriage is supposed to pick us up after lunch. Oh, Bethany, the afternoon meeting of yours will be held at the palace. Someone is there right now fixing up a room for you seven. I am so excited! Now we can all get back to living life once more. You just must see the formal gardens of the palace. I do hope that they have been well cared for all these years that I've been gone." She merrily chatted away for several minutes.

After lunch, our things packed and ready, the wagon and carriage pulled into the courtyard. While we seven slowly shuffled out of the guesthouse and across the courtyard to the waiting carriage, the others quickly stowed bags and gear in the wagon, and saddled up their horses. I thought it a bit comical. Tthe others accomplished all these many tasks in the time that it took us to make our way to the carriage. Why these people saw our altered feet as a desirable thing was beyond me. I guess it is a cultural thing, but I had a notion it may have a deeper significance. I wondered if these people had a sadistic streak in them. It would fit, if the average emotional level was so terribly low. Could it be that men and perhaps women too got their jollies off on seeing women so nearly helpless? I realized that my mind was wandering now and came back to the present as we finally got to the carriage. I decided though to ask Master Cheng about this when I had the chance.

Hui had already sent out town criers to announce that Princess San Min Wu was returning to be their Princess once more. As our carriage began moving through the crowded streets, many people clapped, cheered and waved to us as we went by. Princess San Min waved her little arm out of the window, acknowledging their gestures of support.

The Royal Palace of Nan Yan occupied four square blocks. It was surrounded by a grey stone wall some ten feet tall, forming a natural barrier. However, we all knew that it could be climbed by assassins intent on getting inside. The northern quarter held the Formal Gardens, with the stables and servants quarters just below that, consisting of several stone buildings. The actual palace itself occupied the next quarter. The bottom quarter held several large rooms where large public gatherings where held and also the barracks for the palace guards. All the buildings were single-storied only and were made from the same grey stone, with red tiled roofs.

Empty now for over three years, the place had become somewhat neglected. The vast number of flowerbeds held as many weeds as flowers; vines had grown rapidly over some of the walls with some threatening to enter nearby windows. Now that winter had come, many dead leaves covered the grounds and flowerbeds as well.

Hui had already begun to assemble a basic staff for San Min. Two servants were hard at work cleaning out her old bedroom and two cooks were busy laying in stocks and scrubbing the kitchen areas. The palace building was a very long building, stretching three quarters of the entire length of the grounds. Out front was a huge courtyard, stretching from the formal gardens down to the south wall by the meeting rooms and guard quarters. Our carriage pulled up before the palace building itself.

Just inside the ornate doors was her old throne room. Dust lay thick here. Behind the throne, a door led into an extremely long hallway. Bedrooms and private rooms lined this long corridor. As we entered the hall, the first room on our left was the meeting room, where we would assemble shortly. The servants had already prepared it for us. To our right was San Min's bedroom. Next to that was the huge bathroom, while next to the meeting room was the huge formal dining room. Sixteen large bedrooms were just beyond the dining room. San Min insisted that I take the first bedroom after the bathroom, and that the other zen-kami take bedrooms as close to us as possible; this way, we would have a shorter distance to walk.

A half hour was spent while we picked out our rooms. Since each bedroom held two large beds, I asked Bianca and Jemma to sleep with Dita and me. I soon discovered that the four Olin Masters chose to sleep with their apprentices as well. However, Bianca commented, "Gosh, this place is filthy. I am going to have to clean before we can sleep in here!" I didn't relish the long afternoon that my friends were facing — tons of cleaning. Well, I justified, it would give them something to do.

San Min made one comment that I thought encouraging. "Well, there are going to be plenty of changes around here. I am no longer going to be carried around on that old divan as I used to be. Honestly, I can walk. That was a stupid tradition. Actually, now that I think about it, there are a lot of stupid traditions that I simply am not going to follow." I grinned and supported her.

Master Cheng arrived and our afternoon session was about to begin. As I shuffled to the meeting room opposite San Min's bedroom, I realized another barrier for us here in the palace: doors. While they gave Dita no problems, the rest of us would have difficulty with them. I resolved to practice on our bedroom door tonight.

As we seven sat down to resume our discussions, Gang spoke first. "We forgot about one key thing. Overlord Dang Ho now controls this valley, claiming dominion over it. Expect some trouble from him." Indeed, we had forgotten this aspect, that overlords now controlled all of these valleys. These were their strongholds, as they fought each other for control over the lower lands.

"By nightfall, we will have enough here to defend," Master Cheng admitted. "Yes, we will deal with him when the time comes. Now then, let's see what we can devise." All afternoon, they discussed ways of actually running their country. Before, the Emperor handled the fighting while the Empress handled all other matters. Their word was law and rigidly enforced, where they had sufficient force of arms to do so. Most provinces had their own local Princesses who dealt with provincial matters. Since they too had an army, their word was law there as well. Politicians and courtiers attempted to influence their rulers by any means possible.

Terra nova. That's what these men faced. None had any real ideas about how to govern such a huge country as Tashien without the use of the force of armies. They quizzed me about how the countries in the Outer Lands governed their people and which of those that I preferred. I quickly realized that I was out of my league with this and asked them if Jemma could join us, since she was a Judger and this was her specialty. At last, they agreed and Jemma soon joined us.

As she was barely of age, it took her a while to get these older men to take her seriously. After an hour, she earned their respect. She pointed out, "Yes, a benevolent monarchy is ideal. All decision making is in the hands of one person. The benefits are endless; however, the real problem is one of succession. We've seen enormous power struggles ensue when the benevolent monarch dies. What you need is a self-sustaining system here, one that will not have to be replaced when the Empress dies."

She continued, "Now of course, if you have a Council of Leaders, then you have a much wider array of new ideas and many now have a say in the running of their country. However, as you all know, in times of a crisis or battle, you don't want a group running it, but a strong, powerful leader."

Once she had finally gotten herself established with these men, I suggested, "You know, you have a golden opportunity that few countries ever have. You have the chance to create a really good, fair, and workable method of governing Tashien." They smiled; they'd already seen this aspect. Unfortunately, they didn't get much inventing done before they ended for the day and supper.

After dinner, Dita, Bianca, Jemma, and Ilenakova wanted to take me on a reconnoitering trip. "Got to know your surroundings, Bethany. Prime Protector rule," Ilenakova rattled off. She'd already ascertained the palace's strong points and weak points. "The weak link is that the perimeter walls are four thousand feet in circumference, impossible to patrol without a sufficiently large number of guards."

"Strong point," Bianca added, "is they keep out all but the most determined attackers. The walls are quite sturdy and not easily breached. We checked." I had no doubt that they had done so. "But she's right, with nearly a mile of walls, in the dark of night, you are going to need a guard about every fifty feet or so, if you want to take no chances of an assassin slipping over them. That means at least eighty guards on duty during the night shift."

"Yes, that's just the problem. The barracks can house only fifty men all told, including the day shift as well. This place is not going to be very secure at all," Ilenakova pronounced. "Now then, it is vitally important that we all know the layout of this place and where are the defensible positions."

"Yes indeed," Bianca inserted eagerly. "Mom and I and everyone else — we all checked this place out thoroughly today, well about as thoroughly as we could. There may be secret doors that we don't yet know about — things like that. Anyway, we need to show you around this place now. Mom will come with us, but we ought to put a cloak over you. It is starting to get cold around here. It is winter after all and Long Yan says we will get some snow soon."

"Yes, quite a lot compared to what we are used to having," Ilenakova attempted to take back the conversation. "Long says that you will find it most difficult to walk in the snow. He says that when any of you need to walk in the snow, you must have one of us supporting you. Apparently, San Min once took a bad spill when she tried to walk in the courtyard without him holding on to her. Now, let's get your cloak on and do this." She slipped a fur-lined cloak over my shoulders, while Bianca held my hair outside of it and then draped in nicely over my back.

Ilenakova steadied me, while Bianca supported her mother. "Notice that there are only two ways into this long hall, from the princess' meeting room at the front and the back door way down there at the other end," Ilenakova pointed out. "While we could defend here, it is more like a death trap with no escape. It is the same situation down in the barracks and in the servant's quarters as well. These three buildings are death traps, if we are caught inside." We began our slow shuffle through the throne room and out the front door of this main palace building.

The courtyard was approximately seven hundred fifty feet wide and two hundred fifty deep. Three long buildings occupied the remaining seven hundred fifty feet. The other two hundred fifty by one thousand feet at the north end was occupied by the formal gardens. "Let's head south," Ilenakova suggested as we shuffled slowly out onto the courtyard.

"Note that there is a twenty foot wide corridor down between the lengths of the three buildings and a similar path lies behind the buildings. Here the guards could patrol and defend the walls," she explained. I finally reached the first of these separating the palace building from the guest and guards building.

"This looks like a death trap alley to me," I noted. "If I headed down it, there's only the two ways out."

Bianca replied, "You're right. According to Long Yan, this was done intentionally to help trap invaders, but it obviously can trap us just as easily. The main thing, Bethany, is that if we are attacked, we are trapped here inside these grounds. There is only one way inside — through the main gates."

"At least they light lanterns periodically at night," Ilenakova granted them that much common sense. "We can see down these alleys at night. However, any good assassin will douse them as they slink along. Come on; let's show you the main gates, since those are the weak link, if the walls are ignored." We turned and headed some seven hundred feet to the gates.

Dita and I shuffled along at our snail's pace. Dita commented, "Dear, do you realize that we must take over two thousand tiny steps to get there from here?" We both groaned; this was over ten times what a normal person would need. "Oh, I nearly forgot to tell you, love, we are invited to a formal dance on Friday. Evidently, the wealthier folks of Nan Yan are throwing a welcome back party for their Princess."

Bianca bubbled, "Yes, and San Min is having several dressmakers come tomorrow, and she is giving us all a whole wardrobe of new, fancy clothes. Even the men will get them. She said it is just a little something that she can do for us all. I can't wait to try them on. I bet I'll drive Louis mad," she giggled.

"If he doesn't sweep you off your feet first," Dita teased her daughter. "Oh, Bethany, San Min also told me that at the dance, we will have lots of company shuffling. Apparently, many of the wealthier women also have had their feet made tiny like ours. I guess we'll just have to see that. Sure is a weird custom, but I guess I have to give them credit for ending that terribly painful foot binding that they used to do a century ago. I remember just how hard a time the Empress Wu had when she tried to walk. We used to have to totally support her, didn't we?"

"Gosh, what did they do to her feet?" asked Bianca.

"When she was a little girl, they essentially broke her feet and bound her toes up so they touched her ankles. They kept them bound that way so when we met her as an adult, she was essentially walking on her heels with almost no foot to keep her balance," I replied, remembering the nighttime walks that we had with her. "She couldn't really stand up on her own without holding on to someone. Grim. At least we can walk on our own."

As we approached the gates, I had to smile. There stood two well-armed men dressed all in black, complete with a black stocking mask over their faces. The Cao Bang. Another pair was just outside the gates. I noticed that the two men's eyes had been watching us as we approached them. Further as we finally drew close, I noticed they had bulges in their pants as well. Once more, I was glad that I did not have a male body.

"All is well, zen-kami," one of them spoke. "We will protect you with our lives."

"Thanks. It is good to have such brave men watching over us," I replied politely. I could see now that there was a very heavy set of bars securing the gates. Only a lengthy siege with a battering ram or a large gunpowder explosion could destroy them. That was some comfort.

As we turned to walk back, I commented, "Well, with the Cao Bang visibly present, I don't think that many would make any attempts on our lives. From what I have seen, the average person is terrified of the Cao Bang."

"Well, with good reason," Ilenakova added with a snarl.

Over the next few days, Princess San Min began hiring her staff. Many had previously worked for her and were very happy to have their old jobs back, none more so than the gardener, who lamented continuously about how disgraceful the formal gardens had become. He promised that by spring, they would be as the Princess had remembered them.

Four dressmakers also were hired along with what I thought was an excessive amount of new outfits for all of us. Of course, the teens just loved the look and feel of the thin black silk hose, just as we had done and still did.

By the end of the week, we women all now had a dozen different and fancy gowns, some in silk, some in satin, but none plain for every day. The men all had six new suits as well. At least one was white silk and one was white linen. The others were darker shades, but all were of the finest quality, complete with black polished, shiny shoes.

Since the Princess' jewelry had long ago disappeared after her abduction, she also bought more for herself and for all we women. Each one of us now had an emerald and gold necklace so that we would all match each other at the dance.

During these days, Jemma now sat in on the meetings, freeing me from that drudgery. Thus, I was able to meet some of the men and women who dropped by to meet the Princess. Most wanted to welcome her back and see what she now looked like, that is, as a zen-kami. To my surprise, more than half of these women, who I concluded were wealthy by way of the expensive jewelry that they wore, their very long nails, and their similarly small feet.

While we were sitting in San Min's throne room looking over fabrics for these new dresses, one of her new servants announced, "Lady Lian." I looked up to see a middle aged woman, very pretty with the usual very long black hair, walking into the room. She wore an expensive, light blue silk, slinky style dress with the usual thin black silk hose. However, her shuffling, tiny steps caught my attention at once and I found myself instinctively glancing at her arms. She sported bright red painted nails at least four inches long. Lian walked just as we seven did, slowly making her way over to us by the throne.

"Oh so good to see you again, Princess San Min! How long has it been, dear child?" Lian exclaimed. "At least five years now," she answered her own question. "Let me look at you. My, you do cut a striking figure as a zen-kami." She chatted away while she ever so slowly crossed the room.

"Bethany, this is Lady Lian. She used to take care of me when I was younger," San Min explained. She introduced Dita and me to Lady Lian.

"Thanks. I didn't choose to be a zen-kami; neither did my friends here. Yuen Ming in Shansee did it to us to keep me prisoner in his Purple Palace." Lian finally got to us and gave San Min a big hug, while San Min threw her arms around Lian as well.

"Well, San Min, you are alive and well. That is all that matters. We were so afraid that you had been murdered! At least the surgeons did you justice. You do look perfect. Your arms are just right," she said, sliding her hands down San Min's conical shaped arms to her small tips. "Just perfect. You look more radiant than I remember. And your friends, why, they are just perfect as well! That is something to be thankful for, now isn't it? I should say so indeed. By the way, Princes, you are going to the big welcoming dance on Friday, are you not?"

"Sure, I wouldn't miss it, Lian. Will you be there?"

"Of course, dear. I am helping to organize it. Say, what do you think of my new shoes? They are a variation of the fancy shoes that some foreign country makes, Annelise, I think it is called. There they have the most magnificent boots. Our cobblers have fashioned these especially for women like us, Princess. Oh, and you too, Bethany and Dita. Aren't these just gorgeous looking, and they are so shiny and match our hose so well, don't you think?"

We all looked at her shoes. They were shaped much like the ones we wore, but were made from leather and were black, polished, and quite shiny. The front part was more like a half-moon where our toes met the ground. However, instead of the tall wedge's sole meeting the ground about a quarter of an inch past the ends of our toes, a shiny high-heeled spike took its place.

"These are now the very latest in fashion for women like ourselves. For once, we can have just as shiny and polished shoes as our gentlemen, and they finally match our hose, which they should have in the first place," she explained.

"But are they harder to walk in?" Princess San Min asked.

"Oh no, dear. They are almost the same. Well, the heel is a little smaller than your wedge, but other than that no. You will see more than half of the women like us wearing them at the dance. You ought to get some too. I know. I will have the cobbler come around and fit you seven all with a pair. My treat, dear Sanie," she called her by her childhood name. San Min flushed; she obviously didn't like being called Sanie.

"Thank you, Lian. We would like to try them. They do look a hundred times better than our wedges. These really do not match anything that we wear," San Min replied.

"Perfect. I will send for him just as soon as I leave here. Now the men will really notice you, Princess. After all, they always do notice women like us in the first place. Only now with these shoes, you will get even more notices. But then, I am certain that as a zen-kami, you will be attracting all the men's attentions away from the rest of us." She was teasing, but I got curious.

"So men here in Tashien notice women who have small feet like we do?" I asked coyly.

"Oh, why yes. Hasn't the Princess explained that to you? I guess not. Well, in Tashien, Great Ladies all have very long nails, of course. Men do notice them, you see. Yet, if a woman also has small feet, why, they are found to be the most attractive of all! Well, that is except for the zen-kami, who gets everyone's total attention. In our country, small feet on a woman are considered the height of grace and beauty, a great honor, you see. Why, men just go nuts over women with small feet such as ours, you see, but a zen-kami, well, they are so rare that often they become the women of men's dreams. So very, very few could ever afford to spend one night with you, you see. Why, not even my late husband could afford to spend more than one night a year with one, though I know that he would have loved to spend far more. Well, I have to admit that I too spent one night a year with a zen-kami. He and I went together — such pleasures that she gives are almost unimaginable!"

"So men around here get off on seeing helpless women?" asked Dita, slightly annoyed with the whole conversation.

"Oh! No, no, no. Not helpless women, Dita, oh no. A zen-kami is *far* from helpless. Well, yes, I do see what you mean. In some ways, she is, but no one in Tashien knows how to pleasure one as well as a zen-kami! So she is not viewed as helpless by anyone, but rather a master at her craft, and also she is incredibly beautiful, such as yourself, Dita. Now yes, the regular kami do remarkably well, but trust me, a zen-kami really can read your mind and she knows just the right thing to do at the right instant to drive you just absolutely mad with pleasure! In our society, Dita, a zen-kami is held in the utmost awe and reverence. Only a Princess or Empress is held higher. So sit back and enjoy the reverence that others give you while they dress you, feed you, that sort of thing, and then give them back what they most desire, that which only a zen-kami can give." She felt very pleased about having given Dita some sage advice.

Dita, however, just had a revelation, which she told me about, after Lian left to send for her cobbler. "Say, I just figured it out, love. While yes, they are seeing women here as objects, as things, that is *not* the whole story. Look, they greatly desire to be receiving great physical pleasures and sensations. But what is that *actually* saying? I just realized when Lian was chatting that it means that they are considering that they, as a spiritual being, cannot create any such feelings and that only their bodies can generate it. The result: this stuff only locks them more solidly in the trap of their bodies! It is rather like attaching a lock onto the trap that they are in! They live for their pay — pleasurable sensations from the body. In Tashien, there are traps within traps within traps! These Doll Creatures sure knew how to entrap spiritual beings really well! I am impressed with their diabolicalness."

"Excellent observation, love. I also had one. She reminded me that here a zen-kami is held in the highest respect and honor. Perhaps that is to be our army. You know, we found the nail and repaired the horse's shoe and we now have the horses. Maybe the ultimate solution involves somehow the rare zen-kami," I theorized, though I had no ideas how.

That night as she and I got into bed, Dita whispered, "Okay, my love. I am now supposed to read your mind and know just the right thing to do to drive you mad with pleasure. Lian said so." We chuckled. "So prepare yourself, my love." She was dead serious, I quickly found out.

The next morning, the cobbler came, just as promised. He brought in a large box and carefully fitted each of us with a pair of the shiny, black high heels, made especially for the unique shape of our altered feet. I admit, I did like how well they blended with our hose and they looked great. We all tried them out and found walking only slightly more difficult, primarily because of the smaller heel diameter. Since we liked them, San Min ordered us each another five pairs, just in case we broke a heel. The cobbler explained that would not happen unless we took too large a step, putting an oblique force on the slender heel. As long as we walked in our normal shuffle, such would not happen. Nevertheless, San Min ordered the additional pairs, which the cobbler promised to deliver in three days.

After lunch, my companions headed off to assist the new staff while Dita, San Min, and I headed to her throne room. She had scheduled some interviews with several fighters who had answered Ling Yan's ad for the positions of palace captain of the guards. "We are early; they are supposed to come around one, but you know how slow we are," San Min justified. "Besides, I want you to help me judge these men." At least it gave us something to do.

We had just managed to get the doorknob turned by ourselves and were shuffling into the room when an angry man, well-armed, burst in the front door. "Ah so it is true, you are back, San Min," he growled, his face wrinkled in lines of tension, veins in his neck pulsed.

San Min nearly tripped, but by flailing her short arms, she managed to keep her footing. "This — this is Overlord Dang Ho," her voice squeaked slightly. San Min was taken by surprise. We continued our silly shuffle over to her throne chairs. She'd already gotten rid of the older divans that she'd used before she was abducted. No longer would she make someone carry her around as she had before.

"Well, you actually have become a zen-kami, San Min! I would have never guessed that you had left here to downgrade your position," he said, walking briskly across the room, standing before us as if mocking our speed. We'd just covered the five feet during the time that he had come all the way from the door! "Obviously, things have changed, San Min, though I didn't believe it when I heard them say that you had gone and become a zen-kami. I guess now that you will not have any objections to *my* continuing actually to *run* the affairs of Nan Yan and our valley. You *pleasure* people now, while I run things. Makes sense," he concluded very wrongly.

"You misunderstand, Dang, I was abducted and my abductors did this to me and my friends without my consent. I did not voluntarily become a zen-kami. During my absence, your constant misuse of power has only added to the overall chaos in our beloved Nan Yan and valley, to say nothing of the lands beyond here. Your time of power has officially ended. Our High Council has charged me with now running our city and valley. I give you a clear choice, Dang. Either you can be part of the solution or you can remain part of the problem. Personally, I would prefer you to be part of the solution," Princess San Min said very determinedly. I was quite surprised by her sharp, cutting response. While Dang was in anger, she was conservative in nature, hoping for the best.

Dang fumed, "You stupid fool! You cannot *do* a damn thing for yourself! Haven't you noticed that you are helpless in all things but pleasuring someone? I could kill you right where you stand and the two zen-kami by your side as well, and you could do absolutely nothing to prevent it. Do you honestly think that a couple of Cao Bang assassins and a few martial arts masters are going to keep you alive? Or prevent me from taking you out?" He fumed his anger and hostility towards her.

"Just so that you do not make a mistake, Dang Ho, if you tried to harm me, Dita here would have you dead before you even knew what hit you, that is, if Bethany didn't beat her to it. If you haven't heard, she killed Yuen Ming down in Shansee. There is an immense buildup of kijutsu powers around me, larger than at any time in the history of Tashien. Yes, I do know very well my own physical limitations that I am faced with every day. I don't want to be like this," she waved her short arms. "Yet, I still endeavor to do what is right and just for my people. So again, I am offering you a chance to be part of the solution, Dang. It is your choice."

"You foolish, foolish zen-kami! Well, I felt that I owed you a chance to be part of my solution, to live here in your little palace and pleasure people to your heart's content. I've given you that chance out of respect for your former position as Princess. The next time we meet, I will give you a chance to pleasure me. Good day, zen-kami." He turned on his heels and stomped out of the room, banging the front doors behind him.

Princess San Min commented, "Well, maybe he will calm down when he has a chance to think it over."

"I think that you are being overly optimistic," Dita growled. "He's locked in anger and open hostility. He will be back with his army, mark my words. Bethany, we should go alert the others." I decided that one of us ought to be around San Min at all times, so I left Dita to guard her and shuffled off to find the others.

Well, these new special high-heeled shoes definitely sounded my presence; telltale clicks announced my coming to Ilenakova, who was out in the courtyard making sure that Dang Ho left without doing any mischief. "Well, what did he have to say?" she asked as I slowly moved up to her position.

I quickly related the brief conversation. "You should have heard San Min; she remained conservative throughout and didn't react to his anger. I was very impressed with her. I am sure that Dang is probably going to return in force, try to take this palace, and eliminate this budding new governing body."

"That makes sense. I got that feeling from him as he left. Come on, let's see what the outside grounds look like," she suggested, putting her arm around my waist, beneath my long blonde hair. Slowly, we walked the long distance (for me, anyway) to the gates. The two Cao Bang guards bowed to us as we passed through them, and we stood just beyond the gates, surveying the frontal situation.

Sweeping my right arm over the open area here before the palace gates, I commented, "Well, an army could position a seriously large number of men here, couldn't they?"

"Yes, my guess, perhaps a thousand could besiege us from this position. Are you up for a walk? Let's walk around the outer walls," she suggested. "I don't mind going slow. I must size up the true defensive position here," she added.

Click, click, click. My new heels announced each of my three inch, shuffling steps. I resolved to not be in a hurry and actually found the walk much more pleasant to endure. She helped immensely by constantly pointing out the small details that could affect a lengthy siege of the palace, taking my attention off walking. "Of course, if Dang returns with a thousand men, we will have no choice but to use our Druwid powers against them. We are only a few," she pointed out.

"The thing to do with these huge armies of zombies is to eliminate their leaders, their generals and captains. Without leaders, they are not even a mob, if they are at all like Princess Shashi Wu's army there on the Steppes. Honestly, Bethany, you had to see it to believe it. The average soldier just stood there and did nothing until given a direct order to fire an arrow, for example. Thousands died and it had no slightest impact on their morale. Zombie army, I call them. Honestly, if San Min is going to form up an army, she would be wise to avoid using these kinds of soldiers."

By the time that we reentered the gates, I had walked nearly a mile, the longest distance for me yet and my toes ached from the thousands of small steps. Still, my legs and feet were toughening up, just as San Min suggested they would. I resolved to continue walking longer distances. However, Ilenakova and I discovered that only a few soldiers deep could stand before the three other walls. Many homes and businesses lay close to these other walls. Only the street was available on which army soldiers could stand to attack the walls. Still, a grappling hook could be used to climb over the walls and enter the grounds. From there, the enemy could enter the rear doors of the three buildings and begin wreaking havoc on us all.

"Well, Bethany, we've proved that this is a palace and not a fortress," she declared, "totally indefensible without a whole lot of soldiers." I agreed. We would need to plan carefully our defense should Dang Ho return with his forces.

"Now you and Dita could move out of your bodies' vicinity and do your things on them there beyond the walls, but the rest of us need to be able to see out there," Ilenakova thought aloud as we moved across the courtyard. "Perhaps we could get up on the roofs somehow. Then again, they might also simultaneously attempt to scale the walls in several locations. In that case, the rest of us would be busy repelling them. Bethany, this place is going to be hard to defend!" I chuckled, indeed it would be. We shared the news and our fears with all the others.

Thursday came dark and gloomy. The first big snowstorm of the season was coming, according to Long Yan and San Min. Around ten that morning a Cao Bang man appeared at the gates with an urgent message for Gang Yo. In my slow way, I led him to the meeting room and allowed him to open the door for me. He seemed agitated that I moved so slowly, and I stayed just inside the door as he rushed in. "Gang, the Overlord Dang Ho is moving an army of several thousand soldiers into Nan Yan from the north. They ought to be at the gates by early afternoon!"

"Damn, well it was to be expected," Gang cursed.

Master Cheng spoke softly, "We should get everyone into the throne room and discuss our defenses." At once, I began my shuffling out of the room, staying close to the hall wall, figuring the others would want to move rapidly. I was right; they flew out of that room! Jemma, however, paused and joined me.

"Well, looks like I'd better look after you, Bethany. Your relative immobility is definitely a factor," she commented.

"That and these," I waved my short, but aesthetic looking arms in jest. "Seriously, we have to keep San Min safe somehow."

A bit later, the four zen-kami, who were in a back room getting more of their personal training from the Olin Masters, finally shuffled into the large room. Their faces looked a bit pale, I thought. Suddenly, I sensed exactly what the four were feeling: helplessness. We were faced with a life threatening physical attack, and our peculiar situation now hit all four of them rather hard. San Min also emanated a similar feeling. They were unable to run, or move quickly, or defend themselves, short of batting with their upper arms, pathetic. Yes, that was the key word: pathetic! That's what they were feeling right at this instant. Master Cheng looked at me, and I sensed that he, too, sensed the very same thing.

"Chan, Hon, Mei, and Dia," Master Cheng spoke with an intention that I had never heard from him before. "Your job is to surround Princess San Min. If any enemy enters her throne room, you four combine your push kijutsu to keep them back. That is your job during the battle. If some of us get injured, we will bring them here into the throne room. Use your arms to put pressure on their wounds to slow the loss of blood. That will be all five of your secondary tasks, zen-kami. Long Yan, you and Wen and Chan will also remain here in the throne room. Your job will be to do what you can for the wounded. We will have all the servants in here as well; put them to work on the wounded as you can." I marveled at how his instant assignment of duties that they could possibly perform did wonders for the five women. Already, their strong emotions were subsiding.

I spoke up, "Dita and I will attack those before the gates. Someone needs to watch over our bodies in here. We will be out there before the gates. Dita will begin eliminating the leaders, while I handle the masses swarming the gates."

Master Cheng bowed to me, though Gang and several others looked at us in disbelief. He continued, "Our big problem will be fending off those who come over the walls. Expect them to attack the palace from all four sides. If we get overwhelmed, fall back to the throne room. We'll make this room our last defense, because there are only two ways into here. We ought to be able to hold them off for a long time."

"Mom," Bianca asked, "are we still to hold back on our powers or do we have free rein to let loose?"

Master Cheng gave Dita a funny look. She answered, "Master Cheng, we try not to be so overt in the use of our kijutsu powers. Yes, dear, you are all free to use any and all means on the attackers." Bianca grinned, nodding to Fina, a fellow Protector.

Next, he divided our forces among the four walls. He put one of his four seconds on each wall, along with five of his other Olin martial arts men. Twenty of them had already shown up in response to his summons. Tian and Fina took the back wall. Master Zhen and Fang took the garden's wall. Phillipe and Jemma took the front wall, while Louis and Bianca took the remaining wall. Enrico and Ilenakova were on the main gates. The sixteen newly hired palace guards of San Min were divided into teams of four and sent to join the others on each wall. Gang Yo divided his fifty Cao Bang into four groups and added them to support the wall defenses. Thousands against a handful hardly seemed fair, but then I remembered Ilenakova's assessment of their typical soldier and realized that we did have a chance.

The rest of the morning, the servants brought in supplies, boiling water, bandages, and finally our lunch, before they all came into the throne room and sat huddled together in one corner out of the way. Interestingly, by noon, ten more fighters showed up at the gates, requesting to be allowed to fight for their Princess. They'd heard of the army marching through Nan Yan and quickly rushed to the palace to help defend their Princess. San Min met each one personally, putting her arms on their shoulders and thanking them. Master Cheng then assigned them to the various walls.

After we all ate, Dita and I then moved out of our bodies and took up our positions. She and I perched like birds on the top of the main gates. Around one, we finally spied the army marching towards us. I quickly made a Mind Link to my companions and added Masters Cheng, Jian, Liang, Ning, Peng, Zhen, and Fang along with Gang Yo. *I am going to give you a bird's eye view of their forces until I need to take action.* The surprise I felt back from these others was expected, especially so from Gang. They were now seeing what I was seeing from a vantage point a thousand feet above the center of the palace. They could see the actual distribution and plans of the enemy army as it moved into their assault position. I figured this would give them a better idea of what we were facing and how to deal with it. I was right. Master Cheng thanked me; the other masters followed suit.

Overlord Dang Ho sent around two hundred men each to the three sides of the palace; their intention: scale the walls. Another thousand swarmed into the large open street and plaza before the palace gates. I noticed that a black flag hung on the outside of our gates. I later learned that this was the sign uniformly recognized as meaning this place was under the protection of the Cao Bang assassins. As the leading edge of the army approached marching in organized lines, they faltered upon seeing that black flag. Only the insistence of their leaders made these soldiers continue their march.

I also saw that they had lugged a huge battering ram along with them. As the soldiers began to spread out along the front wall of the palace, the ram on a wagon chassis became visible, being pulled by dozens of men. *I'll get the captains and look for their generals and Dang Ho. You mutilate the masses,* Dita send rather graphically. We waited.

Ranks upon ranks of soldiers stood at attention, awaiting the order to attack. At last, one general sitting astride a horse called out loudly, "Open the palace gates and surrender, and no one will be slain." Dita's answer came quickly. The man's head spun around in a circle, and then his body dropped lifelessly to the ground. Another gave the signal and several loud trumpet-like instruments sounded the commencement of the attack. The army surged forward towards the gate.

I sighed and went into action. I lifted the giant battering ram high into the air and then let it fall down to the ground, pulverizing a number of soldiers. Up I lifted it again and then down. This was getting too few men; a number had already thrown grappling hooks over the walls on either side of the gates. I picked up the hooks with men hanging onto them and gave them a toss. Now I just began picking up soldiers in a mass, forming them into a large ball about fifty feet above the ground. When I had a big enough ball, I gave it a pitch, sending them flying out of the city. I later learned that bodies were found up to five miles out of the city limits. Well, they would not be rejoining the fight anytime soon.

The more I pick and tossed, the more annoyed I became. Ants, I was dealing with an attack of ants, not men, literally. They were barely zombies in terms of their actions, useless and hopeless were these soldiers. I picked and tossed and picked some more.

As the hooks began appearing at the tops of the walls, my companions began letting lose their powers as well. Lightning blasts with thunderous claps of thunder smashed into soldiers who appeared at the top of the walls. Balls of fire dropped down on them on all three sides and a few even at the far ends of the front wall. They were careful to stay out of my way. As others reached the top of the walls, the Masters used their push kijutsu to knock them back down, crushing into others on the ground below them.

Little help, Bethany! It was the distant voice of Jemma. I looked down inside the palace. A large number of the soldiers had finally overwhelmed the defenders and had gotten inside. Now they were actually sword fighting as well as using martial arts to fend them off. Ilenakova was protecting the back entrance to the palace building proper. I grabbed and tossed the men opposing her and the others there like some giant machine tossing ears of corn, rapid fire. A bit later, there were no more here. I moved to the side wall and did the same, relieving our desperate fighters there and finally over to the garden wall, where Zhen and Fang were most hard pressed by dozens of soldiers. A minute later and they faced none. I went back out front and saw that they had regrouped and were trying it again. Once more, I began to pound them with the pretty well smashed up battering ram. I soon gave that up and began collecting and tossing once more.

Now I didn't see any standing soldiers, so I picked up and tossed the bodies lying all over the street and plaza before the gates. I even tossed a few horses; I was so out of control. I admit that I went slightly crazy once again. These soldiers I could not see as human beings, merely ants following their colony. When I could see no more bodies, I whipped around the inside of the palace and pitched those too, then grabbed even more, who were still around the three back walls. I tossed and tossed and tossed.

Bethany. Thanks for cleaning up the battlefield. Honestly, there aren't any more bodies or soldiers. You can stop now, dear. It was the distant voice of Dita.

But I don't want to stop, Dita. I am smashing ants!

We know, dear, but you have them all. You can stop now, please. She was begging me. I slowly sank back down and near my body once more. My eyes focused on the throne room and the bustle of activity going on. Wounded, people were treating the wounded. I had to help and focused on the here and now.

"Glad to see you are back," Dita whispered to me, giving my body a loving poke with her arm. "Come on, we are needed." We shuffled from our position near the throne out among the others. At least they were allowing us to do the actual treating of the many wounds.

Jemma called out, "Bethany, can you lend me your arms? Here, push this wound closed, while I sew it up." I squatted down and managed to do as she asked, and the blood from a Cao Bang man trickled onto my arms. I noticed that all five other were also doing similar things. Their arms were covered in blood as they held wounds tight for those who were doing the actual surgery.

I chose to tag along with Jemma, as she finished one patient and moved on to another. At last, we came to Master Cheng, who had suffered a small arm cut. He was one of the last to leave the battlefield after seeing all the others safely into the throne room. I held the wound closed with one arm, while applying pressure with the other. Jemma quickly began stitching.

"Most impressive, Goddess Bethany," Master Cheng said between needle pokes as Jemma went efficiently about the task.

"How many of our people died?" I asked, fearing the worst.

'We lost two Cao Bang men and five of the newly hired palace guards," he replied.

Jemma added, "We have several that are in critical condition. Bianca and Fina worked on them. They said not to hold out hope for those two guards. There, let me wipe off the blood and get a bandage on it."

"Thanks, Jemma," he replied. "Goddess Bethany, you and Goddess Dita actually won the battle for us. We should all be dead now. Your companions are incredibly powerful as well. I bow to far superior Masters." He did so. "Never has anyone seen such a display of kijutsu powers as we have been privileged to witness here this afternoon."

"Yes, but Dang Ho got away," Dita complained. "I never did see him, but I got all of his generals and captains. I wonder where the coward went?"

Gang Yo, nursing two sword wounds now nicely bandaged, joined us. "Don't worry, Goddesses. My men will return with his head before night. I've sent my men out after any others of Overlord Ho's men and lieutenants. I am sure glad that I was wise enough to join you and not be against you, Goddesses. That was beyond description. By the way, where did the fifteen hundred plus soldiers bodies go?"

"Er, I don't know. I just tossed them out of the city. I didn't want them to become projectiles landing on some nearby houses. Innocent people could have been hurt and their possessions damaged," I replied. "Wait, we are not goddesses, just people like yourself."

"Hardly," Gang Yo teased me. "Only a god or goddess could have done what you two did today, ignoring what your companions did. There must have been fifty lightning strikes and fifty balls of flames. You could conquer the world, if you desired."

"Sorry, we don't want to conquer the world. I hate fighting like that, but they gave us no choice but to unleash what we could to stay alive," I added, trying to justify my having slaughtered a thousand plus men. "There is no honor in killing a man, much less the thousand plus that I have done today. No, it is more as if I have failed in a very big way to have gotten myself into such a position where I could see no other way to handle the situation, Gang Yo. There are now a thousand plus men who have only added yet another trauma to their existence. I have forced them to have to start over once again with a new baby body. I take no pleasure in having done that. A true goddess would have found another way to resolve the conflict without adding yet more traumas to the lives of so many."

"Gang, she speaks with great wisdom," Master Cheng softly agreed with me. "There is no honor in killing a man. Yet, you should never fear to hurt another if the cause is just. This time, the cause is just. Bethany is quite right; we would have more honor had we been able to have resolved this peacefully."

"Dang Ho wanted to kill us all and retain sole control over Nan Yan and the valley. What other way than to defeat his army?" asked Gang. "I can see no other way than to kill him. His army is no more. His control is gone. Is that not what we desired?"

I tried a different approach. "Let me put it to you another way, Gang. You are not wrong at all, if you consider man to be these bodies that you see before you. Yet, as you now know, we are not these bodies; we are immortal and cannot die. Suppose that you kill Dang Ho. He will now have two new traumas added to those that he already has: seeing his mighty army destroyed by what he would call magical powers and the pain of having his body killed. Now, he goes off and gets a new body and it grows into manhood once more. While he may have forgotten analytically all this that has happened to him, the trauma still lays hidden from his conscious view. Now he meets you or me one day, and his unseen trauma causes him to lash out at you or me."

"Oh, I see. It is karma that we are dealing with here," Gang tried to pigeonhole this whole concept, rather than grasping the ideas themselves.

"Not karma, good Gang, unseen trauma that dictates our future conduct. Next lifetime, Dang Ho may become a fanatical killer of Cao Bang members, may become a killer of all holy men, misidentifying them as the source of the unseen carnage to his army, or may become an assassin of princesses or public leaders. Who can say what path Dang Ho will travel next? But you can be assured that because of the two new traumas he's suffered, he will be less able as a spiritual being from now on until the traumas have been erased."

Gang Yo looked introspective for a moment before he admitted, "Perhaps I have been on the wrong path myself." He didn't elaborate and I didn't press the point.

"Well, Bethany, now everyone knows that we are here," Dita teased me, lightening the mood a little. "No sense hiding our powers any longer." Jemma grinned, as did several others.

Bianca brought the five zen-kami over to us. Master Cheng was the last to be patched up. "Can you help me wash up our five helpers? No make that seven helpers," she added with a grin, looking at Dita and me. I saw the faces of Chan, Dia, Mei, Hon, and San Min and they beamed. Indeed, they had been useful, helping to save the lives of the wounded. Master Cheng noticed that I noticed this too, and he gave a slight nod of his head to acknowledge that I had noticed too.

Chan said, "Well, we may not be able to fight, but we can help with the aftermath. While it's not much, it is something that we can contribute. Now we are going to sit and watch over those who are in not so good shape,

Bethany. It is the very least that we can do for all these brave people who fought to save our lives."

"Excellent idea, Chan. That will give the others time to deal with other matters," I complimented her decision.

Mei added, "We actually did get to use our feeble push kijutsu once. One man actually made it inside here during the battle. We four kept him pinned to the wall and Bianca came in and took care of him."

Master Jian came up and put his arm around Mei. "Yes, my apprentice has done well today." She smiled and put her now clean, dry arm on his shoulder.

The kitchen staff headed off to make supper. The other domestic staff began to clean up the throne room, while the seriously wounded five men were carried to a vacant bedroom, just down the hall. The five zen-kami shuffled along after them, intent to sit beside the men in case some needed assistance or their wounds needed more attention.

The guards, who were able, headed outside and reported that it was now snowing. They gathered up the weapons dropped by the soldiers inside the palace and then the mountain of weapons outside as well. If nothing else, Princess San Min now had an armory full of swords.

Chapter 22 Prophesies, Dances, and the Offer

At dusk, Prophet Yulin Wang returned along with a messenger for Princess San Min. Because of the great battle, tomorrow's dance had been postponed a week. Once the messenger left, Yulin asked us get together to hear what he had found.

"In the Great Library of Nan Yan, I have been studying the ancient scrolls," Yulin began. I detected a note of excitement in him that I'd not seen before. "I went back to the most ancient of them and have spent days deciphering the old characters. I believe that I have found something of vital importance, especially in light of what happened here today."

"What?" asked San Min, becoming curious as well. Religion was not among her interests in life.

"The ancient Ulins, who lived in this very valley many centuries ago, were great priests; it is so written. One of their scrolls speaks of a Son of God who will come to us when darkness falls. I believe that the Darkness of which it speaks has come. We should look then for this Son of God!"

"And where shall we find him?" asked the Princess.

"Alas, that I do not know," Yulin admitted. "Yet, if he does come, we all may be saved."

"Saved from what?" asked San Min, becoming a little exasperated with the prophet. "Do all prophets speak in riddles?"

Yulin chuckled. "Aye, Princess we do. I am afraid that is because we can only see part of the whole picture. I say unto you that this Son of God will be coming to Tashien, and he will lead us to our salvations."

"Well, you have my permission to continue to search for him. Now, I will do all that I can to bring peace and prosperity to Nan Yan and our valley," she replied.

The next morning, she began the cleanup work. Hiring several hundred men, she sent them off to find the remains of the soldiers and see that they were buried. She paid the men well and they did a good job of the grizzly task. Word soon spread throughout Nan Yan that the dead bodies were found four miles from the palace out in the countryside nearly in a perfect circle centered on the palace. The people of Nan Yan began calling this miraculous event the Great Miracle of Deliverance. Further, they began to believe that their Princess was somehow a goddess herself.

Around ten that morning, Gang's men returned with the head of Dang Ho and several of his lieutenants who had somehow escaped Dita. Later, I heard that the Cao Bang had beheaded every single member of Dang Ho's extended family in retribution for the slaying of the two Cao Bang men. While I could not condone such actions, I realized this was one method they used to instill a terror of the Cao Bang among the general population.

Overnight an inch of snow fell, and by noon today, it had melted, washing away the blood from the battle. However, by late afternoon, the weather turned colder and the snow began falling heavily once more. Long Yan predicted that we would get several inches and he was right.

Most of the day, we spent making our rounds with the wounded, re-cleaning their wounds and applying clean bandages. We could not risk any infections. One of the critically wounded guards died despite our best efforts to save him. San Min had him buried with honors along with the others who had given their lives to protect us. All told, it was a somber day.

Late in the afternoon, Mei came running up to us. Okay, she couldn't run, rather she shuffled as fast as she dared, terribly animated and excited. Her face was flush as well. "Guess what! Master Jian Li has asked me to marry him!" She called out as she tried to close the distance to us, but couldn't wait to tell us.

"Congratulations, Mei Bi! He is a good man," San Min replied, opening her arms to give Mei a hug as soon as she reached her. "What did you say?" she asked the obvious, once Mei had finally made it over to where we were at in the throne room.

"Yes, of course, I am in love with him, though I told him that I was perhaps not worthy of him and that I would always be a liability for him. I move so slowly and need so much help with nearly everything." Mei answered. Just then a smiling, Master Jian entered the room and overheard her.

"I told her that a flower is never a liability. Mei is a beautiful and rare flower and I am totally in love with her," Jian exclaimed, forsaking his usual reserved nature. "I am so very pleased that she has consented to marry me, a humble Olin Master." Mei flushed and lowered her head slightly. "Bethany, I owe you so much that I will be forever in your debt. You have brought unto me the finest woman in Tashien!"

"What's that you are saying?" Master Liang Dhow called out. We turned to see Liang escorting Dia into the room. Master Ning with Chan was right behind them, followed by Master Peng and Hon. I noticed that all three women's faces were as flushed as Mei's. "Bethany, it is I and Dia who are eternally in your debt. I beg to differ; Dia is the finest woman in Tashien! She and I have an announcement. Dia has accepted my hand in marriage!"

"Ah, you are both wrong," Master Ning broke in before we had a chance to say anything. Chan is the finest woman in all Tashien and it is we who are eternally in your debt. She has agreed to marry me."

"No, you are all three wrong. Hon is the finest flower in all Tashien. She and I are eternally grateful to you, Bethany, for bringing us together. We are madly in love and this rare flower has agreed to marry me," Peng said proudly.

Everyone talked at once, hugging the four women and congratulating the four Masters as well. Master Jian explained, "The very first moment that

I saw Mei, I just knew that she was the woman for me. My heart nearly stopped when I met her. I am so thankful that Master Cheng has allowed me the high honor of working with Mei."

Master Cheng quietly stepped into the room, a smile on his face. "I see that I have not yet lost my touch." Everyone turned towards him. I gave him a questioning look and he bowed to me. "I have the ability to sense soul mates when I see them. I saw that Bethany and Dita were true soul mates the very first day I met you. I also saw these four couples were destined to discover that they too were soul mates. Yes, I so arranged it that they could discover this for themselves. Yet there are other soul mates here as well." His gaze took in Bianca, Fina, Jemma, Louis, Phillipe, and Tian. The girls giggled and I realized that he meant them as well.

Bianca took hold of Louis' hand. "Mom, we were going to tell you later on. We're going to get married as soon as we get back home." Dita looked very surprised, but I'd seen it coming. She hugged her daughter, who had to wipe off the tears trickling down Dita's cheeks.

"We are too," Jemma added, "but we wanted to wait and surprise our moms when we get back. That is, unless Ania and Kali come here first." For a few minutes, the room was filled with even more chatting, hugging, and well wishing.

"I will be marrying these four couples right after supper. While they could have a large, formal, traditional Tashien wedding," Master Cheng continued, "they have decided to have it simple. The four have no family to share their special day as your teens do."

"Yes, they do have family," I countered. "They have all of us." We all clapped, though Dita and I clapped with the ends of our arms. The four flushed once again.

"Well, if they are getting married after supper, we'd better get busy," San Min took charge. "We need to get them bathed and their hair done just right. Come on everyone." We women ushered the four beaming women off towards the bathroom. By the time that the call for supper came, we had them bathed and groomed. Wearing a new pair of the fancy black silk hose and dressed in their new white silk dresses with their new polished black heels, which matched their nicely brushed long, black hair, the four made their grand entrance, as we all entered the dining room at last. Their beaus stared lovingly at them and took them from us, seating their brides-to-be beside them at the table.

An hour later, all of us clapped loudly as Master Cheng finished his simple ceremony. A long round of hugs followed. Then, San Min shooed the four off to their bedrooms, while Long Yan began shoeing San Min to theirs, a big grin on his face. Not to be out done, Dita began pushing me towards our bedroom. A lot of welcomed pleasure happened that night.

During the week, Jemma made some definite progress with the leaders. Finally, the men decided that the optimum way to govern Tashien was two-fold. An elected High Parliament would make the laws for the country, while Low Parliaments would do so for the provinces. The High Parliament would consist of representatives from each of the four provinces, thirty from the various overlord controlled high valleys, ten from the largest cities, and one from the Cao Bang. These forty-five would draft and pass the laws of the land. To enforce these laws and to deal with foreign affairs and such things as wars, they would again elect an Emperor and Empress. However, they would serve only for ten years at a time and could not be re-elected to a second term, thus limiting their power. Members of the High Parliament would serve six-year terms and could be re-elected. The Low Parliaments would consist of all the provincial overlords and city representatives. In turn, they would elect the provincial Princess to carry out their laws.

On Thursday, this group gave a formal presentation to the rest of us. Essentially, we were their test subjects. If we could follow their plans easily, then they hoped that they would be able to explain and convince others. After Master Cheng and Gang Yo's presentation, everyone thought that they had a very workable proposal, which would give leadership powers to many, including the overlords.

"I have one question, no make that two," Princess San Min broke in. "Who is going to be the elected Emperor and Empress? And now that Dang Ho is gone, who will be the overlord representative from Nan Yan valley? No, make that three questions. How are we going to get everyone to agree to this good plan?"

I chuckled; she was an astute Princess. These were key questions indeed, ones that I wished answered as well. Master Cheng replied, "I can answer one of these, but not the others. How to get everyone to agree to the plan? Simple, the Empress will so order this plan to be implemented and followed. Now, her word is the law."

"Yes, but Master Cheng, we have no Empress at this time, not for five years or so," Princess San Min pointed out.

"Ah, just coming to that, Princess. We are going to have the High Council appoint one soon. She will then order the plan to be implemented and serve out her ten year term as Empress."

"Yes, I see. That ought to work, if the Empress has a strong enough army to enforce it," San Min added her agreement.

The elder Hui Bui spoke next, rather slowly. "The High Council has already chosen the new Empress." He paused and had the complete attention of everyone. "Princess San Min, the High Council has chosen you to be our next Empress. Will you accept this highest position in Tashien?"

"Me?" her voice cracked, and it sounded more like a squeal than a word. "But, but, but." Stunned, she had great difficulty formulating a reply.

"You are an excellent administrator, which is what we sorely need," Hui continued in his soft, slow manner. "You and Emperor Long will need to form up a real army with soldiers who can take the initiative. We need an army totally unlike those that we have always seen, such as those who attacked the palace last week. You see, the generals you choose and the army you form will hold those positions long after your term as Empress is finished. This will provide a solid continuity to the position and the High Parliament as well. Security too."

"The, the High Council wants me?" she finally found her voice and asked incredulously.

"Absolutely, Princess. There is no other who has sufficient credentials. You are a Wu and that alone will make your appointment widely accepted. Everything hinges on our choice for the Empress being accepted broadly," Hui explained.

San Min swallowed and said, "I can see what you mean. Okay, then I will accept it. Long, you are now going to be the Emperor. I will really need you now."

"Dear, I have always been at your side, except when you were abducted. I never gave up hope of finding you," Long replied, giving her a little hug.

"Thank you, Princess. We will make the formal announcement on the first day of the New Year. The High Council will see that the notice is given that day in all the big cities and to the overlords as well. In the meantime, you and Long should begin to establish your army. We will not move to the Imperial Throne in Zau until you have enough men to guard the Imperial Throne and certainly not until spring has come," Hui explained.

"Well, that is a good idea. We have three months to see about forming up a real army," she relaxed a bit. "Say, who then will become the Princess of Nan Yan? Who will be the overlord representative?" she asked.

"We are still discussing the overlord problem. However, the High Council will accept any suggestions you may wish to make for the new Princess position," Hui added. She smiled, she liked the idea of having a say in the choice to replace her.

Now with a solid goal in mind, Princess San Min asked Ilenakova, Louis, Enrico, and Bianca to help her assess the candidates, along with Fina and Tian, Master Zhen and Fang, and Phillipe. In this, Ilenakova, Zhen, and Bianca would play a pivotal role in her and Long's selections. Ilenakova's first suggestion was to pay the soldiers well, thus making the position a good career path. She set the base pay for the lowest foot soldier at fifty gold per month, more than five times what it had always been.

Fang and Tian reported that Nan Yan's army barracks was now empty. Overlord Dang Ho had taken it over several years ago. Now it lay empty and would be used to house the new recruits as they signed up. "Do those applying need to already be well trained?" San Min asked Ilenakova.

"No, they have to have the right attitude. A good recruit can be trained. Honestly, what has been passing for soldiers is a joke in any other country," she replied in her usual blunt manner. Tian chuckled, indeed they were.

Together, they worked up a help wanted poster and had a hundred signs made. In a week, they would be posted all over Nan Yan and in some of the villages further up the valley. Once they worked out the kinks, come spring, they would post similar notices all over Tashien. Meantime, Jemma and the others continued to work on their plans for the future, especially how to handle the missing overlord of Nan Yan valley.

Friday afternoon, we women began preparing for the large formal dance being held in Princess San Min's honor. She explained just how important this public outing actually would be. "All the important and wealthy people of Nan Yan will be there. We must all look our very best. I am afraid that many will be getting their first look at all of us and like it or not, first impressions are very important, especially if I will shortly afterwards be announced as the new Empress." We all wanted the dance to go well for her and hence, we took the whole afternoon off to get ourselves ready. Even the guys took time off to bathe as well.

Because San Min pointed out that winter was here, we were all to wear our heavier satin pencil style dresses. Dita groaned a little when Bianca tightened up her corset, but honestly, these under bust ones were neither as tight nor as restrictive as those from Annelise were. Our black silk hose and our shiny, polished, special black pumps were covered by a long, silk slip. Our satin gowns with leg slits were traditional, that is, they fit our bust and waist tightly and then fell straight as an arrow to near the floor, creating that pencil look. Mine was red satin, while Dita's was canary yellow, as you might expect. San Min's was sky blue. The teens had fun brushing out our hair, chatting all the while. They were looking forward to this dance more than the rest of us. For them, it promised to be an exciting evening out, while for San Min, it represented a far more vital affair.

After supper, looking our very best, the whole gang headed for the courtyard, where a dozen carriages awaited us. We wore heavy cloaks over our outfits and as I stepped outside, I realized why. A cold blast of winter air struck my face. Six inches of snow covered most of the courtyard. Since us women could not possibly walk in the snow and stay on our feet, the men graciously carried we seven to our carriages, and held the hands of the other women, who wore the traditional flat shoes.

A short ride later, the Royal Dance Theater loomed before us. Essentially, the hall was once enormous building with twenty chimneys poking their way skyward, smoke curls drifting slightly in the air as they rose. As each carriage drove up to the large six-door entrance, the men lifted us down and we moved towards the door, waiting until we were all assembled to enter. At last, with Long and San Min leading the way, we shuffled in our unique gait into the foyer. Here, our cloaks were hung in one huge storage closet, and the men were given a numbered receipt for easy retrieval at the end of the dance.

At last, we six women followed behind Long and San Min as they entered the spacious, well-lit dance hall. Decorations in rainbow colors hung from the rafters. Many streamers adorned the stone walls, creating a party atmosphere. Far off to the right were tables and chairs, while just beyond them a number of women manned a refreshment line. Far off to the left and upon a stage twenty musicians were warming up. Periodically around the room, twenty fireplaces crackled, adding warmth to the room.

As we entered, someone signaled the musicians, who played a fanfare as Princess San Min officially entered the ball. Wow. The place was packed with men and women. I saw no children at all. The vast majority of the women all wore similar pencil satin dresses with their long hair carefully parted down the middle and lying over their shoulders and bust. The men all wore fine linen suits, though whites, blues, greys, and blacks predominated. Uniformly, the men wore their long hair in a single braid down their backs. I estimated that there must be a thousand people packed in here.

However, what got my attention immediately was the sheer number of other women who were also shuffling as we, taking three-inch steps at most! Bianca estimated that of the five hundred or so women here, at least four hundred had small feet like we seven! I was stunned at the sheer magnitude of them. I had thought that this was just a thing that was expected of a Princess and the zen-kami, but now I began to see this in a different light. Women of importance and/or wealth all had similar small feet as we seven. For the first time ever, we did not feel out of place with our tiny, shuffling steps. We were the norm! Bianca and the others now felt a bit strange surrounded by women like us.

"Princess San Min, so good of you to come," exclaimed a middle aged woman as she shuffled up to us. "You are looking fit. I like your new look, zen-kami, isn't it?"

"Yes, Lady Lan, this is Bethany and Dita," San Min began the endless introductions. All night long, women shuffled up to us, often hugging San Min and insisting on being introduced to the rest of us, particularly we six. This was especially so with the men, who paid almost no attention to women or men in our group but we seven! We followed the lead of San Min, who always stuck out her short arm for others to shake and then hugged them, putting her arms over their shoulders, the closest she could come to a return hug.

Then, a young woman barely twenty shuffled up to San Min. She had the thickest, longest hair I had ever seen. Hers draped down below her knees! Dita kept a close eye on her, I noticed. "You don't recognize me do you?" her voice was angelic and soft. "I'm your cousin, Pian Li."

"Wow, Pian! You were barely this high when I last saw you," San Min replied, holding her arm down about four feet from the floor. "Your hair is magnificent!"

Pian's long red nails ran gently through her locks. "Yes, it just keeps growing. You look good yourself, cousin. When I heard that you were zen-kami, I feared that you would somehow look badly. Your arms, San Min, they are so elegantly shaped now. Your figure is just perfect. Can I talk with you later? I've missed you so and I'd give anything to catch up on old times."

"Absolutely, Pian. It's been too long for us all. Oh, this is Bethany and Dita; they are married and from Velona. They are the ones who rescued us from Yuen Ming down in Shansee."

"Wow, both of you look just fabulous. Do women in your country also have small feet like we do?" She took my arm in her hand, we shook, and then she hugged me.

"No, we don't. I'm afraid how we look is due solely to Yuen Ming," I replied.

"Well, you must at least give him thanks for doing such a fine job. Your arms are just perfect, both of you. My, Dita, you are perhaps the most beautiful woman here!" Dita held out her arm for the shake and then reciprocated her hug.

"Pian, I just love your hair! I've never seen any as long as yours. You'll have to tell me your secret for growing it so long," Dita complimented her. A proud grin outlined her angelic face.

"I'd love too. We'll talk more at intermission. I would love to dance with all of you. It's about to start soon now," Pian explained.

"Say, we don't have any idea how you dance in this country," I suddenly realized that we had no idea of their form of dance.

"Oh please, Dita, Bethany, you absolutely must allow me to show you. It is not hard, really," Pian suggested. I noticed that others were beginning to prepare as well, especially so, since we small-footed women moved so slowly. They formed into circles with around a dozen or so in each. We put our arms over the shoulders of those on either side of us. Pian was gentle and careful not to catch our hair. Hesitantly, I put my arm over her shoulder, but Dita was more than willing to do so. "This way, we each support the other. Now we all move two steps to the left, two to the right, two steps in and two back out. Once you get the hang of it, then try swiveling your body. It drives the men half mad," she giggled.

Dita sent, *I am half mad! God, she is exceptionally beautiful, don't you think? At times like this, love, I am so glad that I don't have a male body! My bulge would be so embarrassing!*

I had no time to answer her as the dance began, requiring my full attention. The strange sounding music was intoxicating, and we both soon began emulating the undulating moves that Pian had down effortlessly. I saw a number of our men covertly watching Pian as often as they could and I grinned. After three songs, we discovered that every other woman moved to join the circle on her left. Dita and I were soon parted with Pian, who whispered that she would join us at intermission, when everyone headed for the refreshments.

Shortly, even Dita and I found ourselves in different circles. The men and women quickly introduced themselves as we joined these adjacent groups. It was a marvel seeing so many of us shuffling in our unique way to move to the next group. I found these men and women were both kind and considerate, far above the normal that we had thus far seen here in Tashien. I chatted a bit with each of these strangers as we danced to the exotic music. Uniformly, I detected all harbored some resentment that was unexpressed. Beneath the surface of their kind faces lay something that greatly bothered them. I decided to see if I could find out what that might be.

When intermission came, I found myself far across the room from the refreshments area, but I caught sight of Dita and Pian, who were very close to the tables. I headed off to join the hundreds of us women who shuffled our way there. "Would you allow us to escort you, miss?" a middle aged man said, offering me his arm, while his shuffling wife offered me hers as well.

"Thank you, sure," I raised my arms and rested them on their shoulders, while theirs encircled me, steading both me and her. "I am Bethany Brozena Malina."

"I am Won Su and this is my charming wife, Li. I run a profitable import-export business."

"Pleased to meet you. What do you export?"

"Ah, only the finest in men's and women's clothing and accessories. What do you think of this remarkable paca fur neck liner on Li's neck? It comes from a place called Zargarb. Strange sounding name. Yet, it is the softest fur imaginable. Perhaps you know of this place?"

"Ah yes, I do as a matter of fact. It's not too far from my home city of Velona. And yes, the pacas are a docile, loving creature, kind of like a miniature donkey. I think it is a relative of the sheep, but then I am not that knowledgeable about animals."

"Splendid! Say, here is my card. I would love to open up a new line of exports to your Velona. Oh!" He suddenly realized that I had no hands with which to take his card and was very embarrassed.

"Just slide it down my front. I can have someone retrieve it when we get back to the palace. I would be very interested in opening up some trade with you. We all just love these silk hose and these dresses. I may even need more of these wonderful shoes as well." He did so hesitantly and then began to talk about how easily this trading could be arranged, explaining that it often took half a year for an order to arrive from Zargarb. "Always order ahead of your needs, you see. That's my motto, only I have a terrible time keeping enough paca in supply. Women love its feel and look." While he chatted away, I could not help but notice the hundreds of us all shuffling in a nearly identical manner towards the refreshments. I found it strangely comforting.

When I finally got close, Pian and Dita shuffled up to me. Pian was helping Dita and immediately volunteered to assist me as well. "I believe that we have enough pastries," Pian suggested.

Dita said, "Come on, love. Let's go get us some tea. We can bring it back here, and Pian can help us sip." We shuffled into the line and using the ends of our arms, held onto a fine china cup of a marvelous oolong. Carefully, we shuffled back to Pian, who was watching us carefully.

"You both did that so well! I am very impressed. I didn't see how you could manage to get your own cups. Splendid. Here. Let me help you drink. Dita has superb tastes, you know. She picked out the finest oolong in all Tashien." Pian chatted away, and we sipped the tea and gobbled the pastries.

"You know, love, this music has a three beat. We could waltz to it. Pian wanted to see what a waltz looks like, so I promised her that we would show her when the music starts again." I agreed and we chatted some more. A bit later, Dita added, "Pian is a remarkable young woman. She has studied history, politics, and even astronomy! Her boyfriend has an actual observatory, and she has invited us to come and view the stars one night soon."

"Oh yes, please, Bethany. You and Dita simply must come and view the stars. We just have to pick a night when there are no clouds or moon. I will send word to you when the time is right. If you can come then, that's perfect. If not, I'll let you know the next time that is right. I know that you are all very busy, but surely, you can get away for one evening. I know that you will not regret it. Only be sure to wear a warm cloak."

A bit later, the music began again, the signal for everyone to reform circles once more. This time, as Pian, Dita and I found ourselves being ushered into a new circle, Dita asked them to pause a moment. "We'll show you how we dance in Velona," she explained. She put her right arm on my waist; it obviously would no longer encircle it, while I put my right arm on her shoulder. We touched our left arms together at their tiny tips and began waltzing to the music. All the dozen in our new circle watched amazed at this new style of dance.

Shortly, Pian wanted to cut in, and she began to waltz with Dita, while a middle aged man joined with me. Only after everyone in this new circle had a chance to dance with Dita or me, did we all rejoin in their circle. This became the talk of those in the circle until it was time to shift to the left once more. An hour later the music finally ended, and the dance honoring Princess San Min was over. I was about as far from the exit as possible, and I was able to watch, as the hundreds shuffled along as I did, slowly to the door. Once more, I felt very comfortable around these people. I was certainly not out of place. In fact, one young man gave me his arm, insisting that he walk me to the exit and my companions. He gave me quite a few compliments, even though I told him that I was married.

Our group was actually one of the last to leave, primarily because I brought up the rear of those leaving. "Bethany! We just must do this more often!" exclaimed Bianca, when I finally drew close. Indeed, the teens were on cloud nine, having totally enjoyed the evening with their boyfriends. I knew that they had felt left out having to spend so many months cooped up in that Santi tower. San Min explained that winter dances were rather common and that we certainly could come to many more.

By the time that we got home, it was very late. However, Master Cheng was still up awaiting our return. "May I have a brief word with you and Dita?" he asked politely. Shortly, only we three remained in the throne room. "I wanted to let you both know that as an Olin Master, I have the ability to get your feet back to what they used to be. It is painful and requires six weeks to fully heal, during which time you have to remain off of your feet."

"Now that is interesting," I replied. "Thanks. After tonight, I can see that we ought to keep our small feet a while longer. I think when we are finished here and ready to head home, that would be a good time to do it. Too bad you can't regenerate our arms."

He smiled, "Yes, but that is beyond my powers. I waited until now to let you know that your feet can be restored. I wanted you to see how widespread the practice actually is and the caliber of the women who have had this done."

"Good idea. I was amazed, so many, and apparently, the most influential women have small feet. We will be better accepted if we continue to have small feet as well," I replied.

"Precisely my thinking as well. I bid you goodnight." He left us alone. After we entered our room, Dita and I both just had Bianca and Jemma remove our satin dress. We'd sleep in the rest. Dita coyly helped me onto our satin sheets and slipped in beside me. "I'm going to ravish you, my love!" she whispered, as we slipped around our slippery bedding. Later she admitted that she found Pian incredibly attractive. I had figured that out already.

After breakfast the next morning, Pian dropped by the palace. She brought several bottles of her special hair conditioner — her special secret for luxurious, long hair. According to her, it was responsible for her exceptionally long hair. She insisted on washing and applying it to our hair, making sure that Bianca and Jemma knew just how to do it right. We also set up a tentative date to visit her at the observatory. After she had our hair done, she then spent an hour chatting with her cousin, San Min.

With my hair now smelling slightly like jasmine flowers, I explained my findings to Jemma. "These influential and wealthy people last night are emotionally in resentment that they hesitate to express. I probed a little and discovered that they resent most of all the chaos that Tashien is now in and the many petty wars among the overlords. Such is terrible for business, according to the men. I believe that you can make use of them to help garner the support you will need for the reforms that you are helping to devise."

"Brilliant, Bethany! Thanks, that is critical information. We are meeting again in a few minutes. I'll relay that to the others. Good going, but then you are the Wid," she teased.

Bundled against the cold night and snow, Enrico lifted me into Pian's waiting carriage, and then he lifted Dita in as well. "All set to see the stars?" she asked. She too wore a warm cloak and Enrico adjusted the blankets over all our feet. He insisted on accompanying us. I had to accept, we couldn't easily manage this unless we used our kijutsu powers, which we continued to try not to use, though obviously we'd blown that during the battle two weeks ago.

"Wenhan Linhai is my fiancé. He's a brilliant scholar and an astronomer. He's been studying the stars since he was little. Of course, he thinks I was being foolish for having my feet done like yours when I was ten, but that has opened quite a lot of doors for me and also for him. It is hard for a woman to be taken seriously unless she is the epitome of beauty in the eyes of men. I've worked hard to achieve that, but I've worked even harder on what I am interested in, which is politics and the way societies operate. Well, then there is history too. I've read all the books that I can get my hands on. Anyway, now that I am taken seriously and everyone knows that Wenhan and I are to be married in the spring, they take him far more seriously than before as well."

"You know that he's discovered a new star? Yes, he first saw it as a child. He's been studying it all these years. He says that it was very bright at first, but now it is dimming down. Why, even Prophet Yulin Wang has visited him, asking about it. Yulin claims that it is a sign from God that his Holy Son now walks among us. Religion has never been my thing, so I don't know if that's true or not. Besides, if it is dimming, does that mean the son is dying?" Pian continued to chat as we drove through the snowy streets, heading to the northern edge. As we approached, I saw what must be the observatory.

At the top of a squarish stone building sat a hemisphere dome, silvery in color. Perhaps it was metal or else cleverly warped wood. Soon she pointed it out and her carriage pulled up at the door. I noticed the building had no windows. "No stray light can get in," Pian explained as Enrico helped each one of us down. Wenhan had already shoveled the snow from the entrance so we could walk up to the door, though Enrico insisted that we four put our arms around each other's shoulders just to make sure. Pian knocked and presently Wenhan opened the door.

He held a dim lantern. "So pleased to meet such Great Ladies," he bowed to us. "Dim light helps the eyes see better in the dark. Come inside." The first floor was his study and library. He had star charts spread out over several tables. Some were tacked to the walls as well.

"Tell us about this new star that you discovered," I asked by way of starting the conversation.

"Most honored to do so," he replied politely. He showed us a very long scroll on which he had documented the relative brightness of the star over a period of nearly twelve years. We could see that it had reached its brightest some ten years ago and was now gradually dimming out. Wenhan was very pleased to discuss it and showed us his star charts, which looked very different from the ones, which we were used to seeing. The constellations were completely different, but the stars were the same. He then became fascinated by our description of the groupings that we knew them by, and I promised to send him our star charts whenever I returned home. Actually, that Dita, Enrico, and I knew as much as we did about the stars greatly impressed him, and he talked at length about them. Pian listened and smiled, knowing just how much her fiancé was enjoying this meeting with others who shared his interest.

"Come, we will climb the stairs to my star-scope. It is made from glass lenses that I ground myself. With it you can see stars that are invisible to the eye, and it makes objects bigger," he explained.

We were faced with climbing a long set of stairs, something that we had not done since our escape from the Purple Palace, where I had just lifted us all down them. Pian came to our rescue. "Oh, it is easiest for us to go up sideways, like this." Facing the wall and holding onto the railing, she began sidestepping her way up the stairs. Dita and I put our stubby arms on the railing and followed her lead. Enrico constantly prepared himself to catch us if we fell.

"I told her that having her feet done was a foolish thing to do," Wenhan commented. "Still, she has done it, and I should not complain. Pian was right, as usual, because it has so greatly helped her and me as well." At the top was a black dome with a slit open to the sky. The stars were brilliant this cold, crisp evening. I guessed that our elevation was just under a mile high here in Nan Yan. In the center on a metal contraption was a long, brass tube. The skyward end, he explained, contained the five inch in diameter lense. A tiny eyepiece lense was near us.

For nearly two hours, Wenhan showed us the stars, as we had never before seen them. Some appeared as double stars in the star-scope, where they appeared only as a single star to our eyes. His was an incredible invention. "When I can get more money, I will build even bigger ones," he explained.

"How much did this one cost you to build?" I asked, very curious.

"Five hundred gold. If I can ever scrape together a thousand, then I will build one twice this big. Think of the wonders that I can see then!"

"I'll tell you what, Wenhan. Tomorrow, I will visit the Banca del Dio in Nan Yan and have twelve hundred gold transferred to your account. You build yourself a bigger one, and then when it is done, you carefully box this one up and ship it to me back in Velona. What do you say to that idea?" I wanted to get my hands on this invention! Okay, I had no hands now, but you get my meaning.

He was ecstatic as I suspected he would be. He bowed profusely, shook my arm, and thanked me many times. Even Pian was very pleased with my generosity. "Pian has done it once again. She has made the connections with the Great Ladies so that I can better study the stars. She is the finest woman in all Tashien!" Dita heartily agreed with him and I grinned at Dita.

It was after midnight before we finally crawled into our bed that night. Both of us were very excited about what we had seen. Dita commented, "You know that is a fantastic invention. It has many uses besides looking at the stars! Great thinking, love!" I gave her a loving kiss to shut her up and get her mind back onto me, which she did at once.

The next day around ten, Prophet Yulin Wang called on us. As usual, we were in the throne room with Princess San Min, who was getting ready to begin her interviews for prospective soldiers. Her ads were finally being answered. As expected, Ilenakova, Fina, Bianca, Master Zhen, and Fang were there as well, San Min was depending upon them to help her choose.

"Ah, Princess San Min, I have found the Holy Son of God! Allow me to introduce you to De An." A young man about twenty-one stood humbly behind Yulin. He looked like an ordinary man from Tashien, but perhaps from the lower portions of the society. He wore plain brown leather pants and brown cotton shirt with the millions of buttons. It was warm and practical dress. His black hair was done in the typical male ponytail, but his eyes were penetrating. Somehow, I had a vague notion that I knew this man, though I had never heard the name of De An before.

He took a step forward, bowed politely to the Princess, and said quietly, but with a solid conviction, "I have come to lead the way, Princess."

"Welcome De An. Lead the way to where?" San Min asked, a little annoyed with his vagueness.

"To the path of personal salvation and spiritual freedom. If you will be so kind as to give me your arms and close your eyes," he replied. From his intention, I knew that she would give them.

He took hold of her two short arms and closed his eyes, as if in prayer. When he let go of her arms, she opened them, and we all shrieked! There were her lower arms and hands, just as if they had never been amputated! She shrieked again in utter shock and surprise. She wiggled her fingers and looked at her beautiful six inch long nails. Then, she began feeling her arms and hands. "It's a miracle!" she exclaimed, as did the rest of us.

"Bethany, if you will be so kind as to give me your arms and close your eyes," De An said to me. I did as he asked. I felt energy surging at my arms. *The Guardian sends his thanks, Bethany. He also said to ask you when you are going to be able to do this for yourself? He was teasing, really. Do you recognize me now?* he sent.

Julie? Is that you? I sent back.

Yes, this is now my newest assignment. Thanks for getting everything set up for my appearance in Tashien. We will talk more later.

When I opened my eyes, there were my lower arms and hands, just as they were before Yuen had his doctors cut them off! While I reacted much as San Min had, De An moved before Dita and repeated his Holy Miracles. Shortly, Dita's hands were back, as if they had never been amputated as well. She also shrieked and gave De An a warm hug.

"Thank you, thank you," San Min tried to find words to express her awe, wonder, and appreciation. She had now a million questions flowing through her mind, but could only articulate her thanks.

"Most welcome, Princess San Min. Now I must visit the other four. Bethany, will you show me to them, please?" De An asked. I left the stunned Dita, San Min, and the others and led De An into the long hallway. Over the next five minutes, we all heard a similar shriek of surprise and shock coming from Mei, Chan, Dia, and Hon as well. Then, absolutely everyone stopped everything and followed De An back into the throne room, everyone was talking at once!

Tears flowed from the four Masters' eyes as well as Long Yan's. They had witnessed perhaps the greatest of miracles; their brides' quality of life had miraculously been restored, beyond all conceivable hope.

"I am the Son of God and I have come to show all the way to spiritual freedom," De An attempted to explain. "I believe that now there can be no question of the fact that I am who I say I am. The miracles that I have shown you are in the province of God."

Vic Broquard

Chapter 23 The Find

Shi Do's arms surrounded the supple body of Lin Lu, their lips met in a passionate embrace. "I love you, only two more days until we are united forever," the sixteen year old Shi whispered to his childhood fiancé. Shi was physically strong, as fitting the village blacksmith that he'd just become with the passing of his father. Always sharp-witted, his mind now soared to previously unthinkable heights. Something had happened a few years back, something that had lifted the veil of impossibility off his mind, freeing his thoughts, which now rose to unthinkable heights. He was going to marry his childhood love and create great works of iron art, the likes of which had never been seen in Tashien before now. Already, his artistic touch now adorned several of the wealthier villager's wrought iron fences. His eyes gazed lovingly on Lin Lu, her pure skin, long fingers, blue eyes, and most of all her thick, long black hair enchanted him, as they had since they were children playing in the dirt streets of Mong Yu.

Mong Yu was the last village of the Hong Valley, here in the far western section of Wontun Province where the mighty Jan River began as a trickle from the distant peaks of the Helios Grande Mountains. Home to nearly a five hundred, Mong Yu was a farming and mining village. Small terraces, outlined with low stone walls built from the boulders removed from the fields, dotting the steep sides of the valley on either side. Occasional talus slopes identified the location of the gold, silver, and iron ore mines. A single road left Mong Yu, following on down the Jan River heading eastward.

Lin Lu, also sixteen, ran her parent's farmer's market in the village during the summer and fall months. Always, her produce was carefully arranged in a most artistically manner, which she found appealed to her customers. Her stall always sold out first each day. Whatever had happened a few years ago had also affected her as well. During the long winters, she took up her needlepoint, creating extremely artistic decorations for the dresses that she made and sold. Now she dared to dream of becoming a great textile artist. Shi continually encouraged her to do so, as she encouraged his artistry in iron. Already she had her wedding dress ready, a traditional white silk, pencil gown adorned with a thousand multicolored lilies that she had sewn by hand, perhaps her greatest art work yet. Her parents had saved for a year to afford to buy her the silk for her dress. She remembered again the elation she felt that day when the monthly supply wagons brought the silk all the way from the Imperial City of Zau!

At last, Shi let go of Lin. He'd brought her lunch and now other women were beginning to arrive at the market square in the center of the village once more. Both had to get back to their chores. "We are almost out

310

of squash, Shi. Could you possibly make a trip up to dad's fields and tell him that if more are ready, I can sell them today," she asked. Only one squash remained of the dozen she had set out on display this morning. Ordinarily, she would not have asked him to run this time-consuming errand for her. Perhaps she felt a bit guilty because her parents had spent so much money for the white silk cloth. Perhaps she had a glimpse of the future and wanted to save Shi's life. Perhaps it was just intuition. Shi kissed her once more and rose.

"For you, my soul mate, anything. I'll tell them. Can I come by after supper?" She blushed, her mind filled with memories of their passionate evening hours together. She nodded demurely and Shi, feeling like he could conquer the world, headed off to the south. Soon, he left the edge of the village and began following the well-worn dirt trails of the many farmers. The Lu terraces were about two miles from Mong Yu and partway up the sides of the terraced valley.

Out of breath from the steep climb, Shi reached the Lu family. Lin's two younger brothers and younger sister were hard at work, helping their parents as Shi arrived. All looked up and Shi relayed his message. However, as they looked up at him, their eyes took in the scene of the village and sole road far below them. Unexpectedly, Shi saw fear in their eyes, and they began pointing. He whirled around and saw about fifty heavily armed fighters on horseback entering their village! Overlord Nangumo's long arm had finally come to Mong Yu!

For months and months, stories trickled up here to Mong Yu, evil, horrid tales of the evil Overlord's conquests. It had all started several years ago with the downfall the Emperor and Empress. Gone was the security of the Imperial Army, who maintained law and order. Power fell into the hands of the many valley overlords. Nangumo was more vicious than many, for he sought to control all of Wontun Province! Already, his forces had captured three neighboring valley overlords, subjugating them wholly. They'd heard that Nangumo would raid a village and steal whatever was valuable, but more importantly, he took away young men who were fit to become soldiers in his ever growing army! He also took young women that he fancied as well, though on their fates one could only speculate. Until now, Mong Yu had been spared, lying so isolated from the rest of Wontun Province, here within miles of the Helios Grande range.

"Lin Lu!" Shi screamed as he realized what was happening. "I've got to get to her!"

"Shi! Stay! They will only take you away with them to become a soldier in Nangumo's army!" her father cautioned his future son-in-law.

Shi didn't listen, but began running down the dirt paths toward the village. He could hear screams of terror and panic almost a mile from the village! From his altitude, he could see the soldiers dragging boys his own age or thereabouts out of their homes, tying them into a long line of captured prisoners. He prayed that Lin would find somewhere to hide! He had to get to her and protect her from these evil, vicious soldiers! Yet, he completely ignored the futility of his intention; he had no weapons. Indeed, he had no idea how to use a sword and never did get the hang of shooting arrows, though his best friend had spent hours trying to teach him how to hunt and shoot. If he could get to his blacksmith shop, he could grab a hammer. That would have to do.

He neared the edge of the village, when a horrifying sight sprang before his eyes. Waygon, his best friend, came running out of the village towards him. Two mounted soldiers were galloping after him, brandishing their swords at him! Waygon spied Shi and yelled, "Run! Run!" Shi froze as he watched the horsemen get close to Waygon. Shi knew he had to help his friend somehow, but how? He did the only thing he could think of: he picked up a rock from the low fence and threw it at one of the riders, who was now veering towards himself! It missed. He threw another and got lucky. The four-inch stone struck the rider in his face, knocking him out. The soldier fell off his horse, injuring himself far worse than the stone had done to him. Still, Shi was not in time to help his friend.

Shi tried to stop all motion, freezing the soldier's raised sword above the fleeing Waygon. While the image froze in his mind, it did not stop the real soldier. In horror, Shi saw the blade arc down and sever Waygon's left arm near the elbow! Shi threw four rocks in rapid succession and somehow managed to hit the attacker, knocking him from his horse as well. Waygon screamed wildly, as his arm poured out his life's blood onto the dirt beneath his feet. Shi had to act at once. He raced to his friend's side and tied his belt around Waygon's arm, hoping to stop the bleeding. Shock hit his friend, and Waygon slumped to the ground, unconscious, but Shi had gotten the bleeding slowed.

He heard more horses coming. What could he do? Shi did the only thing left for him. He dove behind the stone wall and hid, hoping the riders would not see him. Two riders came up, dismounted. One rounded up the two horses, while the other attended the two fallen soldiers. Shi held his breath, listening to the panic sounds of others in the village, helpless to help them, his friend, his love, or himself. Finally, the noise died down and Shi ventured a peek. The soldiers were gone; his friend lay where he had left him lying in the dirt path. Quickly, Shi went to Waygon's side. He was still breathing. Now, he knew what had to be done.

Memories of his father's actions came unbidden into his mind. Once when he was little, a man had had a mine accident and his arm was severed. He watched as they brought him to his father's blacksmith shop. His father had seared the stump with a red hot poker. That had stopped all blood loss. Quickly, Shi picked up his friend and struggled to carry him to his blacksmith shop at the western edge of the village. As he approached its front, he gagged and lost his lunch. On the ground were the bleeding bodies of his mother and younger sister, the last of his family. They had been killed during the raid.

Somehow, Shi got Waygon inside his shop and laid him on some straw. Hastily, he retrieved one of his red-hot pokers and took a deep breath. Only with great effort could he force himself to touch it to the stump of his dear friend's arm. He gagged from the stench of searing flesh, but he forced himself to hold it until the blood seepage stopped. Now, there was nothing more that he could do for his friend. He needed to find the village doctor and Lin! Lin! He'd forgotten all about her. He dashed outside past the bodies of his mother and sister, racing for the market in the village square.

All around him, older villagers and young children were standing around sobbing or crying openly. He did not count the number of dead lying in the streets. All thoughts now were upon his fiancé Lin Lu. He found her stall in the market. Produce lay scattered about, but there was no sign of Lin. He searched frantically for her, screaming out her name.

At last, one elderly woman came up to Shi. "They took her away with them, Shi. She was not harmed." Dumbstruck, Shi begged her to tell him what had happened, which the old woman did. Twice. Before she finished, the rest of the Lu family arrived, and she had to tell them as well.

Shi stared at the ground, unable to move or speak for a long time. At last, something within him clicked, and he swore, "I will get her back. I hereby devote the rest of my life to getting Lin Lu back to us!" Her parents, grief-stricken, nodded, but knew that this was just words. Lin Lu, the golden beauty of their life, was gone from them forever. Quietly, Shi walked back to his blacksmith shop.

When he arrived, he found two older women were attending to Waygon. They explained that the doctor had also been killed, and as his nurses, they were attending to the wounded of Mong Yu. "So many are dead," one said softly, as she wrapped a white cloth bandage around Waygon's arm. "So many are dead." The whole village was now in grief, no family was wholly untouched by loss this day.

A week later, the dead buried, Waygon was out of bed, though Shi waited on his needs. "You saved my life, Shi. I am honor bound to you now," Waygon said, as the two sat around the blacksmith shop. Shi had not done any further work since that day.

"You would have done the same for me," Shi replied absentmindedly. All his thoughts were focused on how to get Lin Lu back from the evil Overlord Nangumo. Waygon sensed this too, though such a rescue seemed hopeless to him, more so now that he had lost an arm. He couldn't shoot his bow anymore.

"I have to go after her and find her somehow, Waygon," Shi said at last, though he realized how hopeless the task was. Indeed, there was not a single sword in the whole village and few horses.

"How Shi? While we could get a horse and ride after them, how could we possibly take her back from so many well-trained, evil soldiers? I am now unable to help you. I can't ever shoot my bow anymore. No one even has a sword. Can you make us some swords?" Waygon asked, glumly.

"No, I have no idea how a good sword is made. I suppose I can hit them with a hammer, Waygon," Shi replied apathetically.

"We need the intervention of the gods!" Waygon said rather stupidly, as if there were somehow gods in the world.

However, the mention of that word struck a chord in Shi, a most desperate note at that. "Say, Waygon. What about those images you've always been telling me about? You know — the cavern in the mountains where godlike creatures lived." For years, in their idle hours, Waygon often told Shi about his vivid dreamlike images in his mind of a great cavern in the Helios Grande where strange, bulbous gods dwelled. In desperation, Shi began grasping at even such nebulous ideas as Waygon's ghostly gods.

"Well, if it is real, they might have some weapon that we can use against Nangumo and his men," Waygon replied, not at all convinced of this, however.

"What other choice do we have? I am sworn to get Lin Lu back. We ought to have been married by now. I can't see a hammer stopping all those swords. I know that I teased you a lot about your visions, but do you think that you could find this cavern place?" Shi asked.

"Shi, I am honor bound to try," Waygon replied. The two began making their plans. Shi sold off all the rest of his unfinished ironworks to purchase a horse to carry their supplies. Lu's family assisted them by providing a large supply of dried food. While Shi busied himself with scrounging the blacksmith shop for everything he thought might be useful to them on their exploration, Waygon spent his time recovering and thinking, trying to work out how they might find this cavern in the mountains. He was certain that somehow this very valley led to the cavern — well, at least in the general direction. Had it been in an adjacent valley, their trip would have been a very long one at that. They'd have to travel many, many miles to the east to get out of this valley and then back that same distance in an adjacent valley. Such a trip would take months and winter would be on them long before they hit the mountains.

The middle of August, the two friends finally set off on their quest. The Lu's thought the whole scheme would be the last that they ever saw of Shi Do. Still, they were honor bound to assist him and wish him well. The two teens, Shi leading the horse, walked westward out of the village. At first, they followed the few dirt roads that lead to the farmer's fields and to the more distant mines. Two days later, they left the last mine road behind them, heading on up the unexplored, rocky valley.

On either side of them, the craggy valley sides rose steeper and more inhospitable. Here, only mining could be done, if anyone really so desired.

As the days passed, the terrain grew increasingly impassable. Still, the two continued their upward climb. Neither was in a hurry, they were constantly searching for a cavern opening somewhere above them. Haste was not their worry, finding it was. Besides, Waygon's arm ached terribly and he was still recovering. Shi had to change his friend's bandages nearly every other day.

Some might say that these two were following a whim — a mere flight of fancy that had no factual basis in reality — gods who lived in the mountains. Such was certainly not real, though Shi clung to it tightly, his only real hope in rescuing Lin Lu. Waygon believed his mental images were real, just as real as the hard granite stone that surrounded him. These mental pictures swam about his mind as far back as he could remember. Parts of the images were blacked out, probably filled with something that he should not remember, he concluded. If these images were not real, then his whole life was not real, he believed.

By the middle of September, the pair was two miles high and into the Helios Grande proper. Often, they paused to look back the way that they had come. The view was spectacular! Jagged ridges at the beginnings of the many east-west valleys lay below them, like teeth of some enormous monster. Well a monster did lay down there, Overlord Nangumo. However, the nights grew very cold indeed; winter would come soon at this elevation. Firewood grew scarce as the trees, low and wind worn, fought against the elements for survival in this harsh land.

"There's the tree line!" Waygon pointed out. Both teens paused to see the well-defined demarcation line. "We'd better lay in a stock pile of firewood," he advised. Waygon had quietly accepted the position of advisor to Shi, who was completely out of his world of experience. Shi knew blacksmithing and village life. Waygon had often gone on hunts for fresh meat and was more of a backwoodsman than Shi. Thus, Shi began to rely upon Waygon's advice, now more than ever, which increased Waygon's self-esteem, which was pretty low, considering that he was now left-armless and couldn't even tie his own boots anymore.

The next day, their horse looking more like a walking woodpile, the two found that the gorge or valley had narrowed so much that if they extended their arms, they'd touch the steep sides of the granite walls! Yet, this was the day. "Look there!" Waygon pointed out.

"Yes! A black hole. Could that be the cavern?" Shi asked, suddenly becoming very excited. Could Waygon's dreams have really been real after all? Could this be the mountain home of the gods? Could he find a weapon he could use to defeat Nangumo? Many cross-thoughts flew through his mind in a rush.

"How do we get up there?" Waygon asked. "I don't think I can climb it without my arm."

"I don't think I can do it with two arms," Shi teased him. The two studied the rock wall before them for some minutes. "There is a seam that goes up. If I can drive an iron rod into that crack every so often, I can tie a rope to them for safety in case I slip. Once I get up, I can maybe pull you up with a rope," Shi decided at last. For an hour, the sounds of hammer upon metal spikes echoed in the otherwise stillness of this mountain cliff. Slowly, Shi ascended the near vertical cliff face that rose some fifty feet above where Waygon and their horse stood watching.

When Shi finally reached the top, he was surprised to find that there was a wide, level path that led around the cliff face. Duh, had they only continued up the narrow gorge, they would have come across it. "Is it the right cavern?" Waygon yelled up, his patience finally dissipated.

"Don't know, but I've found a way to get you and our horse up here. See if you can lead the horse up the gorge a bit more. I'll meet you there," Shi called down to his friend.

A bit later, Waygon called for help. "Shi, I can't climb and lead the horse at the same time. Little help."

A half hour later, Shi pulled Waygon up onto the path as well as the horse. However, the horse, seeing the incredible exposure, refused to budge along the narrow path. "Hey, put a rag over his eyes, then you can lead him," Waygon suggested. Ten minutes later, the two stood before the dark opening of the cavern. The opening was tall enough that one could have ridden the horse inside.

"Careful for bears," Waygon suggested, as the two peered into the darkness. Shi drew his hammer, though he thought that it would be of little use if they had stumbled into a bear's den. Bear versus hammer — hammer would lose. Shi led the horse just inside the opening. "Well, must not be any bears in here or the horse would have smelled it and reacted." Shi relaxed. "We should light our lanterns, Shi," he advised.

"What if the gods are still here?" Shi whispered.

"Well, it's been nice knowing you," Waygon teased, a bit of fear hidden in his jest.

"Is anyone here?" Shi called out loudly several times. His echo came back to him several times, adding to the spookiness of their venture. Hearing no reply, Shi finally unpacked their two lanterns and got them going. Leaving the horse here near the entrance, the two teens headed deeper into the cavern.

"Oh my god! This is exactly what it looks like in my dreams!" Waygon exclaimed. He didn't need to add, "We have found it." Around them lay numerous objects, all very strange to these two. Neither had ever seen anything like these things before. What they both found unnerving at first was that the instant they entered a new section of the cavern, some magical lights turned on of their own accord! Soon, they discovered that they didn't need their lanterns at all.

"We've walked into the home of some god!" Shi whispered, awestruck. "What is all this stuff?"

"I have no idea. It is alien. I hope no one is home or comes home soon," Waygon added nervously. The two wandered about for some time before returning to the entrance and their horse. Outside, the sky turned grey and snow began falling.

"No going back now?" Shi asked rhetorically. Obviously, they could not descend until the snows melted. Shi had a sinking feeling that would be months from now. "Well, let's go exploring. This cavern complex is huge. Look for anything that could be a weapon that I can use to defeat Nangumo and his army."

"Everything looks totally foreign!" Waygon exclaimed, as the two wandered about the maze of tunnels and chambers hollowed out of the solid granite mountainside. "Well, this must be the god's bed," he pointed out.

"If — if that's his bed, he must be a giant!" Shi gushed, staring at what looked like a bed, only it was twelve feet long and eight wide. An hour later, both teens slowly began to realize that they could not spend the winter here in the cavern. There was neither running water nor any food, let alone fodder or grain for their horse. While they were entranced with all the alien objects, both knew that they had to leave as soon as possible.

"Do your mind's images suggest anything that could be their weapons?" Shi finally probed. He was at a loss, having seen the whole complex now and finding no swords.

"Fix us something to eat and let me think," Waygon replied hesitantly. He closed his eyes and examined all of his confusing mental images of this place. Shi dutifully fixed them some bread, cheese, rice, and fish, using a good deal of their water supply in the process. As he worked, he wondered for the umpteenth time just how his friend could remember things about this place. He felt rather sick at his stomach; the place sent chills down his spine, even though the place seemed deserted. What if the god returned?

The two ate in silence. Waygon had not said anything yet, and Shi's nervousness only grew. As evening came, they unrolled their blankets. Both were unwilling to sleep in the god's giant bed, though neither mentioned their fears.

Shi slept fitfully, nightmares came to him. He thought he saw some rubbery doll-like god coming at him! It was saying something to him, but what? "Honor your ancestors!" Yes, that's what the god had said to him, and then he felt even sicker. He awoke in a cold sweat. Waygon lay beside him, also sleeping fitfully, Shi noted, and decided that perhaps this wasn't such a good idea after all.

Morning came none too soon for the two friends. Over breakfast, Waygon said, "Well, I think that the god used some kind of weapon in his hand. Looks like a small log or stick or something."

That image triggered Shi's nightmares, and he saw once more the images, which had so unnerved him during the night. Indeed, that god had held something in his hand, but he also wore some kind of girdle and a helm. After eating, the two began searching once more. Before long, they discovered a drawer that contained a pile of gold ingots. "We're rich!" Waygon exclaimed, and the two spent a half hour lugging the heavy bars to their campsite just inside the entrance. Then, they resumed their search.

Before long, they came across a niche in the bedroom's wall that they had not noticed before. Inside, were a cylindrical rod, a golden helm, and a metallic girdle. "Hey, Shi, maybe this is the god's weapon," Waygon suggested, picking up the rod and examining it. Not to be outdone, Shi picked up the girdle and helm.

He felt very curious and decided to don them, if only to impress Waygon, who was fiddling with the rod thing. The girdle was far too large for him, but he was shocked to discover that as soon as he had it fastened, the girdle suddenly shrank to fit his far smaller waist! Since nothing else happened, he donned the helm, which was twice the size of his head. To his surprise, the helm also shrank down to fit his head properly. "Hey, look at me, Waygon!"

The two had a good laugh. "You look like a fierce warrior, Shi. If nothing else, it looks impressive. I don't think this thing does anything." Waygon pushed a button. Suddenly, an energy beam came out and hit Shi in the chest. He flew across the room, landing on the giant bed, but was otherwise unhurt.

"Whoa! Now that was terrific!" Waygon replied, now quite excited! "We should take these things with us!" Elated that not all had been in vain, the two headed back to their campsite. Shi picked up the gold bars to begin to pack them into the saddlebags.

"Whoa! These feel light as a feather, Waygon. Here, how heavy does this one seem to you?" Shi asked.

"Really heavy, Shi, I can only lift a couple at once."

"Well, look at this!" Shi picked up all twenty bars with a couple of fingers only, impressing Waygon.

"Wow! Incredible. Those things must be helping you somehow, Shi. Come on, we ought to see if we can get out of here before the snow gets too deep," Waygon replied. Hastily, the two finished their packing and stepped outside into the open air and the incredible view below them. The afternoon sun had already melted yesterday's snow and the two led the horse back along the narrow path to the starting point of the extremely narrow gully.

Once clear of the slippery part, Shi began testing his newfound strength. To their surprise, he could lift giant boulders with one hand, though it took two to keep it properly balanced! Out of curiosity, Waygon pointed his rod at the three-foot in diameter boulder and pressed the button. To the shock of both teens, the boulder broke into hundreds of tiny pieces and flew off down the steep mountainside!

"I don't think we need a sword, Shi. With these we ought to be able to

318

fight Nangumo now!" Waygon suggested. Shi agreed. Now they only needed to get safely back to their village before heavy snows blocked them or their food supply ran out.

Chapter 24 He's Gonna Pay

Deep snow blanketed the high valley and village of Mong Yu. Shi Do and Waygon were the village heroes now. Each kept a gold bar for themselves and gave the rest to the villagers to help everyone rebuild after the vicious attack of Overlord Nangumo. Of the two, Waygon at least felt a bit like a hero. Now one armed, he figured he was pretty much useless in life and spent his time in the village pub, telling and retelling tales while basking in the praise doled out by the grateful villagers. Not so with Shi Do.

Shi avoided the limelight and spent long hours each day alone in his blacksmith shop. Gone was his will to create artistic ironworks. All his thoughts lay upon his Lin Lu fiancé. Images of her and her imagined mistreatment flooded his mind relentlessly. He had to find her and get her back somehow, but how? Nothing could now stand in his way, for the god's gifts would see to that. Yet, where had the wicked soldiers taken her? East. That was the only road out of Mong Yu. They had to have gone eastward, but where? No one really knew just where Overlord Nangumo made his home, at least not in this isolated village. His tone dropped to total hatred of Overlord Nangumo and his army of wicked men. Repeatedly in his mind, he envisioned tearing every one of those soldiers' bodies apart! "He's going to pay and pay dearly for taking Lin Lu!" Shi Do swore to his anvil. "If they have harmed her in any way, I will make my retribution as long lasting and painful as I possibly can! I so swear!"

In early January, it began, but not as Shi Do had expected. Six of the Overlord's soldiers rode into the village demanding a wagon of food be sent to Nangumo. Hearing the commotion going on outside, Shi donned his heavy cloak and set aside his fuming to see what was happening. He barely got outside when Waygon came slipping and sliding through the packed snow to find him. "Soldiers have come demanding food for Nangumo! Come on; let's get them!" he called out. He carried his god's rod, ready to put it to use at last.

The two headed back eastward toward the snow covered market square, where the soldiers were waiting for a wagon to be filled. Shi Do looked unusual with his golden helm half covered by his stocking hat. He carried no weapon. He didn't have to — he wore the god's girdle. Since he had first donned them months ago, he had not taken either one off. He couldn't. Somehow, he couldn't figure out how to take them off! He'd tried many times, but nothing he could do would remove them. It was if they had a mind of their own. Worse, they had begun to talk to him, telepathically, that is, feeding him ideas and fueling his hatred and desire for revenge! They had also given him some ideas about how to make the helm and girdle function. For that, he was grateful and had stopped even trying to remove them.

He thought, "Bellow loudly." Then, he spoke, not startled to hear his voice greatly magnified, "Overlord Nangumo's soldiers! You will pay dearly this time!" The six men, brandishing swords to hasten the scared villagers, whirled to face this new and unexpected threat. He thought, "Kill." He pointed a finger at one of the men and an energy pulse shot from his helm, blasting into the soldier. The man died instantly, his head was so badly crushed that he was no longer recognizable.

At nearly the same time, Waygon pushed his button while pointing his rod at another soldier. That soldier's entire body disintegrated into bloody bits, the largest of which was only a few inches around. The white snow around the wagon turned to crimson with his remains. The four remaining soldiers, unable to grasp what just happened, tried to charge into the two young villagers. Waygon disintegrated a second soldier, while Shi Do pointed his finger at two more. His helm activated and the two died instantly. Only one soldier remained; the elapsed time was about thirty seconds.

"You there, freeze!" Shi Do commanded; his helm activated and the man became motionless. "Where did the soldiers who raided Mong Yu last fall take all the prisoners, particularly the women?" Shi demanded to know. "Speak!"

The soldier's anger evaporated, as he fell rapidly down into hopelessness. His mind began to register the utter annihilation of his five companions. "Speak!" Shi Do commanded again. The soldier found himself talking rapidly, telling this teen where they had taken the captives. The men were forced into Nangumo's army and were in Zau being trained. Likewise, the women who were to become concubines were also taken to the Imperial City, where Nangumo now sat on the Emperor's throne. Waygon, recovering some coherency of mind, asked him where all the other soldiers were stationed. The answer did not surprise the two. In all the larger towns and cities on down the valley and into the Imperial City, Overlord Nangumo had stationed some of his forces to enforce his dominion. He now controlled three of the six valleys of Wontun Province and was planning on going after the other three in the spring, once the weather would cooperate. When the soldier finished, Shi Do thought, "Kill." He pointed his finger at the man; the helm activated, the soldier died instantly.

"Come on, Waygon. We are going after them now. I'm not going to wait for spring. We'll take their six horses with us," Shi Do decided at last. Having just killed four soldiers, his pent up rage had at last found an outlet. "They will pay dearly for this!"

While the villagers tried to hold another hero's celebration for the two, Shi Do ignored them and began packing what he thought they might need. Waygon, on the other hand, chose to accept their praise, thanks, and most of all, their endless supply of ale. When morning came, Waygon's head was throbbing harder than Shi Do's pounding on his door. "Come on, it's time to go," Shi Do called out.

Waygon staggered to the door and let Shi Do inside. The reality of what Shi Do planned now finally sank into Waygon's mind, like the blast of cold air, which struck his body. "Shi, with the god's things on you, no one can harm you. Me, I am a sitting duck. If we go attack the soldiers, I've got no way to keep them from killing me."

"You've got the rod," Shi protested. "Oh!" He suddenly realized the danger into which he was about to cast his friend. "You are right, Waygon. I must do this alone. I cannot take you with me. Surely, the evil soldiers will try to attack us, and while I'm impervious, you're not. I cannot have you killed. This is my battle, my fiancé."

Waygon breathed a sigh of relief. "Here, you take the god's rod. You might need it. I'll stay here and help the villagers get the spring crops planted. If you need something, send word, and I'll come. All right?"

"Sure, Waygon. Thank you for giving me a way to rescue my Lin Lu. I promise not to leave a single soldier behind my path. If some do miss me and attack Mong Yu again, send word to me, and I'll backtrack and get them too! I swear to you, dear Waygon, I won't return until every last soldier is dead, until Nangumo is dead, and until I have Lin Lu with me!" Waygon handed his friend the rod. For an instant, he had an image of the destruction that Shi would create. It startled him, but Waygon felt that it was entirely justified. After all, they had destroyed his life. What could he do with only his one arm now?

Shi packed two horses with as much food and supplies as possible, and headed east out of the village down the only road out of Mong Yu. Wagon tracks as well as horses marked an unmistakable trail.

A day later, a lone rider entered the next village. When he left, a dozen of Nangumo's soldiers lay dead. Shi learned that Lin Lu had passed this way and took heart in that. The villagers overheard much of this stranger's conversations with the soldiers before he'd killed them. Some began to spread the word on down the valley. By spring, word had spread everywhere of a lone Golden Warrior who was systematically slaying every one of Nangumo's soldiers, while asking about some woman named Lin Lu.

Chapter 25 Religion and Winter

Master Cheng touched our new arms, wiped an emotional tear from his eye. "Lord De An. Truly, my eyes have not deceived me. Your kijutsu is vast. I am most humbled to be in your presence." he bowed low to De An.

"No, it is I who must bow to you Masters," De An replied humbly. "For untold centuries, only a handful of spiritual beings out of all the millions in our land have attempted to forward beliefs and goals worthy of mankind. Those of you who teach others to use their spiritual abilities, the kijutsu, have kept alive a spark of our true natures all these years. Against overwhelming odds, you have continued to seek out those few who have not succumbed to the tortures of our jailers here on Tarra. Now that the constant suppression of our people has been lifted, the time is right for us to spread the word: the path towards our ultimate salvation is at hand. But this path must be walked by each individual. Neither you nor I can walk the route for others. Nay, we can only lead the way."

"What must we do, Lord De An?" asked Master Cheng. I noticed that he was very impressed with the miracles as well the proclamation of De An. His words resonated with the Olin Master.

"Master Cheng, you and the others here have already begun to walk that path. Bethany calls it simply her trauma therapy. Yet, it is so much more than that. To become free, one must walk that path, wherever it takes you. As you have seen, the walking requires the assistance of another. If we could have walked that path alone of our own efforts, we would have done so ages ago. No, the presence and direction of the giver provides the means for the walker to succeed," De An continued his explanation.

"I see," Mei grasped what he was saying. "I will volunteer to give as many therapies as needed. There is nothing more worthwhile in the world," she added. Quickly, Chan, Dia, and Hon also volunteered. I realized how could they not? All four women were looking for new goals in life, supplanting their giving others physical pleasure sensations.

Only San Min looked troubled. "I want to do that too, but I am supposed to become the new Empress," she explained.

De An replied, "Great women, I accept your offer of assistance." He looked at San Min and added, "San Min, yours is also a vital role. As I understand your new system of government, your posting as the Empress will only be for a few years. Once your term is finished, I will accept your offer to help with the freeing of others as well. You see, the problem of freeing our people is a two-fold action. We must provide a stable, calm, peaceful environment in which to work our miracles. As Tashien now stands, chaos rules, and I can only reach a very few. San Min, your work in establishing a safe, secure Tashien, will make it possible for us to work our miracles." San Min displayed a huge grin; she understood fully now.

De An continued, "There is also the matter of our personal security. As we go about our enormous task, many will attempt to interfere and possibly try to harm us. We all will need the protection of others."

"Ah, that's where we come in," Master Jian saw the need for himself and his fellow Olin Masters. "You may depend upon us, Lord De An."

"Yet," Master Cheng interrupted, "the Empress must also be protected. My seconds honor the school and me by assisting you and their new wives. I will do all that I can to ensure the safety of Princess San Min and help get the new High Parliament established and protected."

"Yes, you can count on the Xian Academy as well, Princess," Master Zhen pledged. His wife, Fang, nodded her complete agreement.

"Ours too, Princess," I added. "We will not leave Tashien until your country is back on the right track. Okay, so what's the plan?" I asked both San Min and De An.

Essentially, we divided into two groups to begin working out concrete plans for both the massive power shift and for the beginnings of the new religion. Seeing the seven miracles, Gang Yo was torn between his strong desire to become a part of the new ruling order of Tashien and his deep curiosity for De An and what he offered, spiritual rehabilitation. Yes, I knew that he looked upon this rehabilitation more as a way to gain even more power than true spiritual redemption. In time, I knew that his thirst for power would dissolve.

On January 1, 756, at a formal dance, the announcement of the new ruling orders were to become public as well as general population awareness of the seven "miracles" of De An. Elder Hui Bui would make the official proclamations known at the start of the dance. Of course, we seven would be visible with our arms restored. De An's religion would suddenly become very noticeable. Thus, during these last few days of December, we all worked on getting the plans ironed out, ready to begin their implementation. Both De An, San Min, and I knew full well that we had to be ready when the populace was notified.

Late one night, I finally got an opportunity to talk with De An or Julie as I used to know her in her former lifetime. In our bedroom, De, Dita, and I sipped tea and chatted. "How has the move to Dorota gone for the Guardian? Are you all making progress freeing them?" I asked.

"The move went well. Admittedly, our people did have some adjusting to do. All those armless women there — wow. Well, more than once the Guardian has spoken highly of the work that you all did there. He has started up a Freedom School in the seven major cities, where the Givers of the Holy Gift whom you trained are being given more advanced training. Soon, they will be delivering five thousand sessions a week to the people. While it will take years and years to free them fully, we are extremely hopeful for the future. Dorota may well be the first country of totally free and able spiritual beings on Tarra. We owe this huge step forward totally to your efforts there, Bethany, Dita."

He continued, "Now that we've seen to the elimination of these Doll Creatures and their suppression of Tashien, the future looks brighter than ever before. My task is to get those here who are the most able boosted up in their abilities first. I am hoping for a snowball effect. How else can we reach tens of millions of people, so many of whom are so emotionally close to death that it isn't funny?"

"Say, what did the Guardian mean when he said that I ought to be able to work the miracle and get my arms restored?" I asked, remembering his tease when De restored my lower arms.

"Dear Bethany, he was teasing you a bit there. Still, I will show you how it's done," he answered. Instantly, I paid total attention to De An. "Okay, close your eyes. I want you to create an illusion of a horse."

"Yes, got one," I replied, uncertain where this was going or what it had to do with my arms suddenly reappearing.

"Now, let's be sure it's your independent creation. Turn the horse purple and put yellow spots all over it," he requested.

"But horses aren't purple and they don't have yellow spots," I protested slightly.

"Of course, but make it purple with yellow spots anyway," he softly urged me.

"Well, okay. It's purple, but it looks weird," I replied.

"Good. We know that this is truly your creation, your illusion, right?" I nodded. "Okay, now let's get your horse good and heavy. Make it really solid."

After I said I had, De An continued. "The horse is in your universe, in your own space and time. The next step is to have another being see your horse. May I see your purple horse?"

"Sure, but I don't see what this has to do with getting new arms," I replied, feeling the light touch of De An now perceiving my purple horse.

"Thank you. Now two of us are looking at your creation. The next step is to make it solid enough so that everyone else who looks your way also sees the purple horse," De An explained. "When you do this — making it solid enough and deciding that all others can and will see it, then the horse will be real to them as well."

"Yes, but I still don't see. . ." I protested again.

"Okay Bethany. Do you agree that you have arms and hands?"

"Well, yes, now I do."

"Okay. Do you agree that everyone else who looks at your body will also agree that you have arms and hands?"

"Well, yes, I do now, after you remade them."

"That, Bethany, is all that there is to it. We all agree that something is real and so it is. What would you say if someone came into your room here and screamed about a large, mean black bear over there in the corner?"

"I'd say he's nuts," Dita spoke up. She, too, was following along with this whole discussion.

"He's crazy," I added.

"Right, because no one else is agreeing with him that there is a bear in this room. Reality is only that on which we all agree," De An explained.

"I get it," Dita exclaimed. "When I move out of my body to say twist another's neck, that action is very real in my universe. Since I have erased the reasons that I had been using to convince myself that others could not see this being done, others do see it, and that person's neck is twisted. Same thing with you, love. You pick up other people's bodies. You've erased the reasons why you withheld others seeing and agreeing that it was happening in the physical universe. Hence, others see the bodies being picked up. Simple."

"Precisely so, Dita. Precisely," De An went on with his explanation. "The key is the removal of the considerations and decisions that you've made in the distant past — decisions that your illusions of new arms cannot be physically real are what are preventing you both from doing so. I am sure that both of you can create an illusion of arms and hands that you prefer your fleshly bodies to have."

"Oh, I see. I must have some hidden, un-viewed decisions that this cannot be real in the physical universe," I replied, now catching on to the truth. "Wow. I certainly do. Honestly, what would life be like if everyone could go around totally altering their bodies at will? I mean, you get into a sword fight and are stabbed. The next instant, you re-create your body whole and unwounded. So much for sword fights."

"So much for guns and many other ways to control other people's bodies," Dita added. "Wow! I see. Where would we be if whatever we did to our enemy's body was immediately undone? Duh!"

"It would make wars and fighting totally senseless and useless," I added.

"Right, it would ruin the game that we are all playing here on Tarra. How else could you get justice from one who has wronged you or others?" De An summarized.

"Got it, you'd have to find a way to attack and harm the actual spiritual being," Dita answered. "Ah, like the Doll Creatures used to do with their electronic beams here in Tashien."

"Precisely so, Dita. Bethany, the Guardian knows that you have not yet had an opportunity to receive therapy along these lines — to remove the barriers you have to prevent you from suddenly creating new arms and hands. However, I will point out that your own power of creation is dependent upon your own power of illusion. If you are creating an illusion of your own, there is nothing unknown about or in that illusion. Cause is Knowing. Yet, when you look at someone else's illusion, he or she the cause of his or her own illusion, and thus from your viewpoint, there are some unknowns in that illusion. There has to be, since you are not Cause but Effect and he or she is Cause. Effect is Unknowing. Now suppose that you wish to agree with someone and you want to have things, like your fancy shoes. Someone else is Cause and you are Effect. If you are Effect, then you have sacrificed your own power of illusion, accepting his or hers in its place."

"Damn, that's heavy!" Dita proclaimed. I began to ponder his words. This was vital data that De An just gave us, only I was not sure how I could apply it now. De An smiled and left us to ponder his words.

The new year came faster than I expected. Honestly, we were all very busy helping San Min and her group get the plans for the new government ready to execute. Likewise, De An and his disciples and protectors were just as busy preparing their plans and getting one building in Nan Yan ready for church meetings and therapy sessions. After our usual round of baths and hours spent getting ourselves dressed and ready for the dance and the formal announcements, it was nearly time to depart! Our men all wore their finest dark linen suits, black, brown, and blue predominated. We women wore dark satin pencil gowns, with our usual thin, black hose and highly polished black heels.

As we shuffled towards the main throne room doors, bundled up against the cold winter outside, I realized that we seven were about to blow many minds. These wealthier and influential men and women who would be at this dance were going to see us with arms and hands, a miracle in their eyes. As I stepped outside, the cold winter blast chilled my cheeks. Snow was nearly a foot deep across the palace grounds. I realized that I had not been paying any attention at all to the weather. I had been engrossed in all the advance planning! Unable to take even one step in the deep snow without slipping and falling, we seven had to be carried to our carriages. With only our toes to support us, our feet constantly slipped out from under us. Here was another liability of this strange custom of Tashien women and their insistence on small feet.

At the Royal Dance Hall, once more, our entire group made its entrance at the same time; fanfare announced us to all those in attendance. I was surprised to see that the place was even more packed than it had been before! Tonight, well over fifteen hundred men and women crowded into the hall! At least seven hundred women also had small feet as we, and shuffling was once more the normal mode of walking.

Pian and Wenhan Li were waiting just inside the entrance. "Welcome, cousin!" Pian exclaimed as San Min shuffled inside, her arm around a proud Long Yan. "We've gotten married! Oh! San Min! You have arms and hands! My god! You all do!" Pian wore a dark red, satin pencil dress and highly polished black heels like ours. Her five-inch long nails matched her dress. Her thick, black hair was parted in the middle and draped over her shoulders and chest, falling before her to a few inches from the floor. Her facial expression changed from a proud look of a new bride to one of utter shock, as she and Wenhan stared at our arms and hands.

"Happy new year, cousin Pian! Congratulations on your marriage, Pian and Wenhan!" San Min replied. "Yes, we have had a Holy Miracle. The Son of God, De An here, gave us new arms and hands. It is such a relief to have them back. I am no longer helpless."

One by one, we all shook Wenhan's hand and gave Pian a warm hug. After she got over her initial shock, she whispered to Dita and me, "My, it looks like my potion is working. You hair is now down nearly to your knees."

"Wow. Yes, incredible, Pian. Thank you! We've been so busy," I replied honestly, "that we hadn't really paid that much attention to it."

Dita added, "Do you think ours will ever get to the length of yours, Pian? My, you look ravishing tonight." Wenhan grinned, still feeling that he had married the finest woman in all Tashien.

"Oh yes, give it time. Now you also should let your nails grow longer. I have a special lotion that I use on mine to help strengthen them and avoid chipping and brittleness. I'll send it by tomorrow." Both Dita and I noticed that ours had also grown to nearly four inches now, but we'd neglected to get them painted in the proper fashion. Now that I was in observation mode, I also saw that our girls had been letting theirs grow long as well. Fina's and Bianca's were about an inch and a half now, while Jemma's were over two inches. All three were dressed in their fancy satin gowns and wearing heels, holding onto their boyfriend's arms. My, our girls were really all grown up! How had time passed so rapidly, I wondered?

A fanfare stopped all talking. Elder Hui Bui climbed upon a raised platform, carrying a written speech. The entire fifteen hundred became very quiet, intent upon hearing his words. Evidently, they received a speech every new year's celebration, I guessed.

"Esteemed Ladies and Gentlemen of Nan Yan, I have quite the announcements tonight. First, the High Council has finally elected a new Empress. I give you Empress San Min Wu and Emperor Long Yan Wu." The crowd shouted and applauded for several minutes, before he could continue. "Nan Yan now has a new Princess. I give you Princess Pian Li!" Once more, the huge gathering applauded and cheered Pian, who blushed from all the attention.

Next, Hui Bui began to explain the new method of government rule. He explained the High Parliament and the Low Parliament system in detail, along with how they would work and the fact that the Empress position would no longer be for life but for a period of ten years. He announced Nan Yan's official representative to the newly formed High Parliament as well as the many members of the new Low Parliament of Nan Yan Valley.

Elder Hui Bui ended by also introducing the Son of God, De An. "De has given us seven miracles. Behold, Empress San Min now has arms and hands, as do the others. Please, talk with them about this blessed miracle from God and meet our Savior, De An. Now, let's let the dance begin."

As expected, we seven were bombarded with compliments, questions, stares, hugs, and praises all night long. Equally besieged, San Min and Pian handled their well-wishers with grace and dignity. I realized that both women would make powerful rulers. Hui Bui had chosen well. When the dance ended and we headed home, my feet were aching from the long hours spent standing on my toes. I had not been practicing walking as San Min had urged me to do. Dita and I promised each other that we would do so starting tomorrow, make that later today. It was now past midnight.

The next day, Pian and Wenhan moved into the Palace with us. San Min spent part of each day grooving in Pian on her new duties and responsibilities. She also taught her the many tricks that she'd employed all these years as their previous Princess, for which Pian was very grateful. I realized that here was a transition of power occurring. Instead of just being dumped into a new position, Pian received the benefit of a gradual change of power, guided by San Min. When we would leave in the spring, Pian would be fully trained and ready to help lead Nan Yan Valley. Jemma pointed all this out to me, by the way.

Pian also brought along her favorite hairdresser and nail specialist. We women now found our hair was routinely being pampered as well as our nails. Ah, the luxury of being in a power position, I thought.

In mid-January, De An and his group moved out of the Palace and into their own small building in Nan Yan. Their new Church of God building was an unpretentious converted warehouse. Their adopted religious symbol was a simple infinity sign over the main entrance doors. The four women now began delivering therapy sessions to those in need on a routine basis, watched over by De An himself. At first, I rather missed the company of Mei Bi, Han, Dia, Chan, and their four Olin Master husbands. That passed rather rapidly as news from the other provinces began coming into the Empress.

Indeed, the merchants and nobles of the other major cities welcomed this new transition of power. The numerous overlords did not, since they were in a continuous battle for controlling power themselves. Our biggest hurdle would be to overcome these overlords and their armies. Naturally, Empress San Min would have to have a large army herself.

During February, Empress San Min had each of overlords of the Tan Loc Province visit her here in Nan Yan. I was amazed at her efficiency. First, she outlined how the new system of government would work, carefully explaining the role of each overlord in its operation, both nationally and locally. "Of course, I suspect that you will want personally to sit on your local parliamentary seat," she coyly added. "Please meet with the other overlords and decide who will be taking your seats in the High Parliament in the Imperial City of Zau when it convenes for the first time on the first of June." How could they refuse?

Indeed, the constant warring among themselves for power and control of the rich farmlands of Tan Loc had extracted a heavy toll on all of these men. Given this chance for stability and an end to their warfare appealed to most all of these overlords. Those who grumbled about it also realized that if they chose to not participate, they would be left out utterly of the decision making process. None could afford that and all went along with their new Empress, if only for the time being.

Empress San Min later advised me, "Well, that went as well as I expected it would go here in Tan Loc. Now Dong Province, the ice land, will be even easier, after the mass evacuation of Princess Shashi Wu. Linyi Privince will probably also be easy to handle. Our real test will be Wontun Province, where twenty overlords have been viciously battling it out for control over our Imperial City of Zau. We may have to actually attack the Empress's Palace there to get it back from Overlord Nangumo."

The situation in Tashien now required a strong military force. Why? First, the preceding years of continual chaos and strife had to be ended before any overlords and others began spring offensives. Second, a strong hand was needed to ensure the smooth transfer of power to the Low and High Parliaments. Third, it seemed we would have to retake the Imperial Palace in Zau by force of arms from this Overlord Nangumo. Dita, Jemma, and I worked with both San Min and Pian as their advisors. Specifically, Dita and I helped them chose the right men and a few women for their ever growing army of "real" soldiers. That is, we picked only those who had a desire to fight, would be loyal, and who could think on their feet. We wanted none of the old style soldiers who were mere automatons on the battlefield. Jemma provided constant advice to both rulers on all matters not relating to their fighters.

Ilenakova, Enrico, Bianca, and Louis spend most of their time training the new soldier recruits. From these, they picked and then trained those whom they felt would be the best leaders. Having seen the old style army in action on the Northern Steppes, their goal was to guarantee a fighting army that could and would easily defeat the automaton armies that still existed under the leadership of the various overlords. Meanwhile, Fina, Tian, and Phillipe spent their time training under Master Zhen and his wife Fang. Their objective was to hone their fighting skills as much as possible. Yes, Bianca really wanted to also train with them, but chose to assist Ilenakova. Well, she also wanted to spend as much time with Louis as possible.

Chen and Wen Dai, alone, had little to do. It was not safe for them to return to Shansee and his publishing house and her job at the Santi inn. At my suggestion, Chen spent a good deal of her time helping the newly hired staff of both San Min and Pian get organized and functioning smoothly. Running the Palace in Nan Yan and eventually the larger Imperial Palace in Zau required a good deal of skill and wisdom. In fact, Chen began to love working with the domestic staff that were to accompany San Min to the Imperial Palace this spring. So much so, that San Min appointed Chen Dia as her Chief of the Imperial Staff, the top leader of the entire domestic staff. She also appointed Wen as her Royal Historian. He was so pleased with this turn of fortune, that he spent many hours each day traveling Nan Yan looking for books, scrolls, and supplies that would be needed to really firmly establish the Imperial Library in Zau. It had been pretty much ravaged during the last five years, since the assassination of the Empress and Emperor.

What of me? Well, with Wen needing to make many exploratory trips about the city, I decided to accompany him and do some shopping myself. Often, though Fang Song insisted on accompanying us. Actually, I was rather bored. Dita and Jemma were always very busy and thoroughly enjoying their new roles as key advisors. Hence, I decided to accompany Wen and do some shopping for us all. Don't let a woman go shopping when she has millions in her bank account! At least three times, I had to arrange for a huge crate to be shipped to Shansee and then on to Velona. By the way, one contained the star-scope of Wenhan with its five-inch lens. Already, he was nearly done with his new one which boasted a twelve-inch lens. Yes, I spent over a dozen nights at his observatory gazing at the stars with him. I learned a vast amount about the nighttime sky that I had not known before. While this was exciting for me, Dita and Pian accompanied us, but both usually chose to sit in the warm-up room chatting.

At least once a week, we women had our nails done as well as our hair. By the time that spring finally came, Dita and I noticed that Pian's hair care product had worked wonders. Our tresses now reached way below our knees, thick and strong. Likewise, our nails continued to grow even longer. I was surprised to discover that they were far stronger that I expected and rather chip-resistant. San Min continued to point out that we all needed to look our best when we finally setup court in Zau. We would all be at the focus of the attention of many vitally important and key men and women. Since we were "shaking up" the established rule in Tashien, it would be critical to maintain some ties to their old culture. Jemma pointed out the necessity of not changing their entire world. Such would destroy all traces of the universally agreed upon reality of Tashien rulers. Empress San Min would still look traditional with her long six-inch talons, long hair, and tiny feet. Our physical forms would appear as others would expect them to look. This would give them something to hang onto for support, while the methods of ruling totally changed.

Friday nights everyone attended the important dances at the Dance Hall. While this was actually our personal time, we soon discovered that many political deals and agreements were also made during these dances. San Min and Pian were constantly chatting with these important men and women. Some wanted to establish new trading deals with the Imperial

Palace, but most wanted to find ways to expand their various businesses, using San Min and Pian to further their goals. In return for their help and assistance, the two ensured the loyalty of these men and women. However, for the rest of us, the dances really were our personal time. It was no coincidence then that the dances followed immediately after we all had our weekly hair and nails done.

During these weeks, De An and his new followers continued to get their new Church of God established. The four women gave therapy sessions nearly every day. When we met them on Friday nights at the dances, Hon, Mei, Dia, and Chan always looked radiant and serene. Their self-respect was immense as was their confidence. De had chosen his disciples well. I did learn that when we left in the spring, De An would accompany us for a time, leaving Master Jian and Mei Bi Li in charge of his Nan Yan Church of God.

De spoke of his plans with me once. "If all goes as planned, I will establish Dia Son and Master Liang Dhow in Shansee, Hon Feng and Master Peng Dong in Lou Yang, and Chan Bao and Master Ning Chou in Zau. Still, I need to find more disciples. My goal is to establish a Church of God in all the larger cities of Tashien. Bethany, keep an eye open for likely candidates, please." I grinned and said that I would.

Around March 1, 756, the snows of winter melted and the first flowers of spring began a transformation of the Palace Formal Gardens here in Nan Yan. Purples, yellows, reds, and greens fought for our attention. Fresh fragrances swamped our senses when we went outside for walks. Yes, San Min was right to be proud of the Palace Gardens, though she found it increasingly difficult to consider that they were now Pian's Formal Gardens. In private moments, San Min wondered in what condition she would find the Imperial Gardens. Probably a total disaster, she speculated. An overlord would not be much interested in maintaining them, she theorized correctly.

On March 15, Empress San Min gave the order to begin the long journey to her Imperial Throne in Zau, Wontun Province. Our party was far too large to travel by boat. Her Imperial Army now consisted of two hundred fifty mounted soldiers. Thus, a caravan of carriages and wagons, accompanied by the hundreds of cavalry, would make the long journey overland. She estimated that we had to travel nearly a thousand miles to get there. As we finally shuffled out to board our carriages, Pian and Wenhan gave us all tearful hugs and well-wishes as did Master Jian and Mei Bi.

Holding back tears, Mei whispered to me, "Bethany, I cannot think of words to thank you enough for what you have done for me."

"I know, Mei. How about a hug instead?" She and I hugged each other tightly for a minute, before I was lifted into the waiting carriage. Dita gave Princess Pian a farewell hug as well.

Chapter 26 Signs of Degradation

From our carriage windows, we all had an excellent view of the countryside. While most chose to ride their horses, Dita and I rode with Empress San Min and Long Yan. De An and his disciples followed in another carriage. Once we turned east past the southern bend of the Yan River, the countryside turned hilly with the first shoots of green covering the land. She explained that this was horse country. Here horses were bred and exported to the rest of Tashien. Yes, the first few days of travel were enjoyable.

That soon changed as we dropped further in elevation into farming country. Low stone fences demarcated the hundreds of fields as we passed along the gravel road not too far from the riverbank. Now we could see the farmers working their fields. I looked in vain for plow pulling oxen, but saw only men and women tilling their fields by hand! Backbreaking work, they seldom looked up as we passed near them. Sometimes, children were also working the ground. Empress San Min pointed out that oxen and horses were expensive and a farmer, cheap. This was nothing compared to what lay just ahead of us!

The next day, we entered a small farming village that lay between the long Nan Yan valley and the one just to the south. As we approached Dolong, I sensed something was wrong up ahead, particularly when our carriage stopped. A grim faced Bianca rode up to our carriage. "Carnage ahead. Someone's butchered half of the villagers. We have to stop and lend a hand."

Long helped us step down, and I got my first view from some thousand feet from the village. I could see buzzards circling. Already those leading our group had dismounted and headed into the village, Bianca dismounted and tied her horse to our carriage. Then, she put her arms around both Dita and me so that we could somehow walk into the village on foot. Shuffling along on our toes over the rough gravel meant that we continually lost our balance and depended on Bianca to keep us upright. As we slowly reached the edge of the village, I spotted bloody bodies lying all over the streets and in doorways. Ilenakova, Louis, Enrico, Phillipe, Tian, Fina, and Jemma were already issuing orders, attempting to bring some order to massacre site.

"What happened here?" I asked Ilenakova as we finally got our feet on solid cobblestones within the village proper. She was issuing some orders to our soldiers.

"Massacre. Killed about four hundred men, women, and children. Got perhaps a hundred survivors and some wounded. Bodies are everywhere, Bethany. It's the grimmest crime scene I've ever seen," she replied. "Fina and Jemma are making a healing station out of the village pub. Soldiers are going house-to-house looking for wounded and survivors. I've ordered the survivors to be brought to the town square. Head on down this main street and you'll find the pub. Lend your healing skills please."

"Yes, ma'am," I teased her. Ilenakova was one of those people who instantly takes charge during a crisis. She grinned and turned to give a dozen soldiers additional orders. Bianca led us on down the street past dozens of rotting corpses. Flies buzzed around the fallen bodies, I estimated that the corpses had been lying here for at least a dozen hours, maybe more. The stench of death permeated the fragrances of spring, providing stark contrasts in olfactory senses.

"Ah, come lend a hand," Jemma called out as we three entered the pub. Already a dozen wounded men, women, and children had been brought here. Jemma had already prioritized them, and she and Fina were hard at work on the worst cases. All had various sword wounds, I noticed. Dita, Bianca, and I set to work at once.

Master Zhen and Fang soon brought in another dozen wounded. "Jemma, we think this is the last of the wounded," he said, trying to keep his voice calm and under control. I sensed his outrage and anger seething below the surface, however.

Fang added, "Bethany, Ilenakova wants a word with you as soon as you can safely take a short break." Her grim face hid her intense feelings as well.

After bandaging the woman's arm, I wiped off the blood from my hands and shuffled after her and Master Zhen. Outside, I saw around seventy-five survivors sitting in what used to be their farmer's market area. Our soldiers were passing around drinks while our cooks were busily making a lunch for everyone. Ilenakova saw me, and she and several others came rapidly over to me.

"Ah, thanks. We've learned what happened here. It seems that this is all Overlord Dongchan's handiwork. He and his small army hit the village about twelve hours ago, just before nightfall. This village used to be under to control of Overlord Ho Bu of Giang. Dongchan is making a power move to take over a good deal of Ho's territory. The spring offensives have already begun. More importantly, his forces are heading on down this road, deeper into Ho's territory. Permission to take the majority of our soldiers, gallop after them, and put a stop to Dognchan's butchery?" While this was crouched as a request, I knew that she was merely being polite in deference to my position as leader.

Before I could reply, she went on, "I will leave a burial detail behind. They will be strong enough to protect the Empress and the rest of you. You can follow along after us, once you have finished here."

"What does Empress San Min say about this?" I asked, not wanting to bypass her. This was her country, her army, and people.

Ilenakova grinned, knowing that she had me now. "I've already gotten her conditional approval, conditional upon your Okaying it as well," she smiled. I knew that I'd been had too. I grinned back.

"Okay, see to it. Well done, Ilenakova, only don't go getting our soldiers killed. We have so few of them," I gave her my Okay.

"We'll bring back the head of this Overlord, mom," Bianca promised her mother, Dita, as she prepared to join Ilenakova's attack band.

"Just kill him, dear. We are not stuffing it for our mantle," Dita teased her daughter. I chuckled at the grim Protector-style humor and went back to work on the wounded. Fina and Jemma also chose to stay, since there were too many in dire need of our healing services.

Mid-afternoon, we finally washed up, having tended to some thirty people. Outside at last, the warm spring sun shone down. The remaining soldiers had already dug a massive grave and had the hundreds of dead buried. Now they were taking a break eating lunch along with the grieving survivors. Empress San Min took me aside. "Thank you all for helping my people, Bethany. I've been gathering information. Those who survived are not even crying for their own slain relatives!" That got my attention.

"Please, you must take it. We must make amends with you, please, you must," one old man insisted. He'd been slowly carrying out the seed grain for this year's crop planting, trying to give it all to the Empress. If she accepted it, the remaining farmers here would have no crops to plant, further ensuring the village's demise.

"I don't know why you are even bothering with us, Empress," an elderly woman explained, as one of the Empress' cooks brought her a bowl of hot rice and fish. "We do not deserve such fine treatment."

"Why are you here? There is no hope left for us now, none at all. We're all dead," a young farmer whose fields lay next to the village explained. "It's just plain hopeless. There is nothing we can do now, nothing at all, except lie here."

A neighbor of his, who was sitting beside him, added her thoughts, "He's right you know. It's useless even to try. We are all just about the most useless excuses for people ever. I can't imagine why you are feeding us, Empress. You should just go on about your business and leave us here to our misery," she suggested.

So it went. The more that I chatted with the survivors, the more dismal their emotional tones struck me. All were barely alive, though their bodies were relatively healthy, as far as I could tell. "So you have noticed too," De An came up behind me and whispered softly, but poignantly.

"Aye, grim. They are below even grieving for their lost loved ones," I added.

"If you and your group will lend my disciples a hand, I will remedy this, Bethany," he suggested.

A few minutes later, Hon, Dia, and Chan joined Jemma, Dita, Fina, and me, ready to deliver loss therapy sessions. Amazingly, De An worked another of his miracles. Like a wisp of clean air blowing into a stifling hot room, he pushed off their heavy emotional cases. Heavy, black mental masses moved off some hundred minds, leaving them in grief at last, morning their lost loved ones. We seven set to work, but found the sessions easy going, thanks to the spiritual push provided by De An. By nightfall, reserved laughter replaced the hopelessness of the morning.

"Did ya miss us?" Ilenakova called out, leading our forces back into the village at sunset. I watched the hundred plus ride in, looking for casualties. "Reporting in sir!" Ilenakova teased both Empress San Min and me, giving us a fake salute.

"Report General Ilenakova Kato da Cassa," I teased her back, as Bianca and the others dismounted and headed for the waiting food pots.

Over a hundred of the Empress' new soldiers along with the rest of our group headed off after Overlord Dongchan and his mercenaries. Enrico smiled as Ilenakova automatically took charge. To Bianca and Louis galloping along beside him, he commented, "Well, it looks like San Min has a new general." Both chuckled. If fighting was involved, Ilenakova always took charge; it was her nature to do so. She just did not trust others to lead an attack without goofing it up.

Around noon, they passed by the enemy's campsite where they had spent the night. Louis and Ilenakova paused long enough to read the signs on the ground. "Only about an hour ahead of us," she called out and broke into a canter once more.

Phillipe yelled, "They are heading to the town of Xing, about two hours from here." Ilenakova nodded. His knowledge of Tan Loc Province was proving valuable once more. A little over an hour later, they spied their foes ahead. Around fifty mounted soldiers were nearing the larger town of Xing. As Ilenakova pressed into an all-out gallop, she observed the enemy forming into a line on the southern edge of the town of around a thousand people. Their assault plan was to form a cutting edge slicing through several city blocks. Well, that was about to change, she thought to herself as the wind flew by her face.

When she was within several hundred yards from the long line of mounted men, she slowed their charge to a canter. Already their enemy had heard their coming and had turned around to face this unexpected charge. She called out, "Let's soften them up a bit before we close. Balls of fire as you can!" As they continued to close, three flaming spheres dropped down onto the line of men, creating massive chaos. Burning men dove off their horses and rolled on the ground to put out the flames. Some did not rise again. Horses galloped off in all directions, fleeing the searing flames. Shortly after the busts, five Push spells also detonated, kijutsu from the various Masters. Most all the enemy was thrown from their horses, and Overlord Dongchan dismounted and screamed to his men to form up a defensive line.

Ilenakova, leading the final charge, galloped through the puny line, her sword arcing to the left and then to the right, felling all resistance to her charge. On either side, Louis, Bianca, Phillipe, Tian, and Enrico followed her, dismounting and charging into the confused soldiers. As expected, Ilenakova did her flying dismount before Overlord Dongchan and instantly engaged him personally. "Death is too good for you for what you did back at Dolong!" she screamed. Her sword flashed this way and that, faster than Dongchan could even parry. Twenty seconds later, her sword found the opening desired, and a red strip appeared along his neck and throat. He tried to speak, but no sounds came out, only a profuse flow of blood. Slowly, his body dropped to the ground, his life's blood gushing onto the dirt beside the gravel road. Only then did she look up at the rest of the battlefield.

She saw several others dispatching the last of these vile soldiers. "All right men! Excellent job! Well done, soldiers of Empress San Min!" She was quick to praise their efforts, though the new leaders of San Min's growing army were still awestruck with the whole attack, especially the valor of Ilenakova. They had experienced an entirely new way of fighting. Normally, each side would have formed a line and then charged into each other, hacking and slashing. None of the existing Tashien soldiers ever took any initiative. Now these new soldiers of San Min saw just what would happen if each soldier did take the initiative — a complete wipe out of the enemy forces. These new soldiers were learning valuable lessons.

"Okay, search them; confiscate what they stole from Dolong. Round up the horses, we'll take them back with us. Let's bury these bodies," she ordered. Now, she relaxed content to allow the new captains to issue the corresponding orders. Meantime, Bianca and Louis began checking on their own wounded soldiers.

Unable to find any, she called out, "Hey, anyone get hurt? Anyone need patching up?" To her and everyone else's amazement, not one of their men was seriously hurt. A couple reported to her to get some minor cuts bandaged.

Several hours later, bodies buried and horses rounded up, they headed back to Dolong. The red sun was nearly setting by the time that the group finally entered the village at last.

Ilenakova reported to San Min, "We caught up to them about two hours from here. Overlord Dongchan has gone to meet his ancestors. He had around seventy-five mounted soldiers with him. It took us longer to bury them than the battle lasted. Seriously, their soldiers are just like those that we saw back on the Steppes. Honestly, Empress, one of your new soldiers is worth at least a dozen of the existing soldiers. We've brought back the stolen valuables and supplies that they took from this village. That should help the survivors some," she added.

"How many of my new soldiers did we lose?" San Min asked worriedly.

"Not a one. We did take a few cuts, but nothing serious. Honestly, Empress, your soldiers did very well indeed," Ilenakova answered her.

"Ah, Jemma, you should have seen her," Phillipe eagerly said to his girlfriend. "Flying dismount and a lightning charge into the thick of things went Ilenakova, but not until Bianca and the others softened them up a bit with some balls of fire and a few Push kijutsu, which knocked many off their horses. Really, the only fight was with the overlord himself. Ilenakova took care of him singlehandedly. She is one heck of a fighter." The large group broke up into smaller ones, chatting about the events of the day and asking about what we had done.

The next morning before we resumed our journey, Empress San Min dictated a letter, which was copied a dozen times. She personally affixed her official wax seal to each document. A dozen couriers were sent off in many directions. Their job was to deliver her message to the other overlords ahead of our advance into the Imperial City of Zau. The essence of her order was that any overlord who attacked any other town or village would be sentenced to death as soon as she got to their seat of power. "I will not stand for any more of this butchery of our people," San Min declared as she watched her riders gallop off to deliver her first official proclamation.

This was the first time that I realized that San Min now had a very different point of view of her people. Gone was the widely held attitude that a person was of little worth because there were so many millions in Tashien. Okay, it was one person out of tens of millions who I knew had changed their attitude, but it was a start at least.

Several days later, I began noticing these rural farmers, which we could see from our carriage windows. Tending their fields, these men and women were preparing their spring planting. Centuries-old memories of us farmers of the Uru Valley came back to me. The sharp contrast in apparel now became very evident to me. Here, these farmers were exceedingly poor, and their clothing illustrated just how desperate their lives really were. Patchwork brown cotton pants and shirts predominated. One could scarcely tell the difference between the men and the women working in the fields. I began to wonder if even the clothes they wore had been handed down from generation to generation, a patch upon a patch to keep them wearable. The contrast between these farmers and those of the Uru Valley several hundred years ago was striking. Back then in the Greenway, we all wore well-made leather pants and cotton shirts. Women wore cotton dresses. The Uru farmers must have been considered incredibly wealthy compared to the farmers here in the Tan Loc Province. What self-opinion would one have if he or she knew that they could not afford a decent set of clothes? Grim indeed.

Periodically, we came to larger towns, whose population numbered in the thousands. Here we spent the nights at comfortable inns and made good use of their bathing facilities. After dinner, Dita and I often chose to take a stroll about the town. Bianca, Louis, Phillipe, Jemma, Ilenakova, and Enrico usually went along with us both out of boredom and out of curiosity. Because of our incredibly slow speed, the younger ones left us behind, while Ilenakova and Enrico kept their arms around us to steady our balance on the uneven ground. Now I began to see what Long Yan meant by seeing more when you walk slowly, and I did not like what I observed.

Put simply, bullies uniformly ran the towns! Intimidation ruled, not so much as force. That is, we frequently came across a bully who forced another to give way, hand over coins or produce, or even turn around and hastily go another way. "Those in hostility and anger are dominating the majority who are far lower," Dita observed correctly.

Ilenakova commented, "This is utterly incredible, Bethany. I swear that nine out of ten people around here are so degraded and have such a low opinion of their self-worth that they don't even stick up for their own best interests! Unreal!"

"The Doll Creatures were far more insidious jailors than the Grey Creatures," Dita observed. "They have turned tens of millions of spiritual beings into totally degraded beings, barely able to keep a fleshly body alive! Now, the Grey Creatures only forced us spiritual beings into these fleshly body's heads and then worked behind the scenes to foment wars and hatred. Still, antagonism and even anger is so far above these degraded people here that it's not funny."

"Hey, the other jailors — the Mantis Creatures — they were not this bad either," Ilenakova added. "I mean, even as diabolical as they were — you know, cutting off the arms of all women and such — still they were not this bad. Look, even though we were all forced into fleshly bodies and we had to go about living with no arms, at least we had our minds and our intelligence. Back then, Enyo and the others were far higher toned, even conservative perhaps if not cheerful about life and existence. Compared to these Doll Creatures, the mantis and the Grey Creatures were almost beneficent jailors!"

I laughed, "I never thought that I would think the mantis creatures were beneficent to us! Yet, Ilenakova, you are right. Compared to these Doll Creatures, the mantis were almost benign. I don't know how De An will ever be able to get so many millions boosted up into a recognition of their own spiritual selves. The ordinary person here has such a low self-respect, self-esteem, self-worth that it is almost beyond belief."

Dita put in, "You know, what scares me is that tens of millions of people here will have to eventually rise upwards through the hatred, anger, and hostility zones. I hate to think of the carnage that's going to be coming!"

"Well, I am certainly not helping," Ilenakova added. "I just helped knock the overlord and his soldiers back down by killing them. Now they get to acquire new bodies and start over only with more traumas added to their overall collection."

"True, but your cause was just, Ilenakova," I answered honestly. "They had to be stopped from committing further atrocities. There are no prisons here in Tashien to lock them up in, so we have to stop them from harming others anyway that we can."

"Well, no doubt about it," Dita put in, "Tashien has become a very lawless country!"

We continued our eastward journey towards Giang. I began to observe the farmsteads that dotted the landscape. Nearly all were mud buildings, adobe perhaps, and crude. These farmers were incredibly poor, although the entire civilization depended upon the crops that they grew. True, these rural people were exceedingly low emotionally, but I knew instinctively that in time and without further suppression, they would climb back up. Why? They were isolated and worked in their fields growing crops. This was both survival in nature and consisted of constructive, positive actions. Now that the Doll Creature's constant suppression had been lifted, in time, these rural inhabitants would recover greatly.

No, the overlords, the bullies, the thugs, the criminals, and the city dwellers were those that we had to worry about. These people would just continue their general suppression of others, not only in the cities but also the more rural areas, as we had just seen. As we approached Giang in early April, we were about to learn just how bad things had become.

Chapter 27 Future's Plans

Pope Christos held his annual Cardinal Conclave on March 1, 756 in Constanza City, Megalos. None of his cardinals had any word from the two missing cardinals. Cardinal Reina Lano of Velona and Cardinal Diego Estebano of Barcella had just vanished from the face of Tarra. Inexplicably vanished, that is. However, some suggested that Cardinal Reina had been the victim of foul play by the desperate opium addicts, who somehow found out that the Cardinal had been responsible for their opium supply.

Pope Christos had no choice but to appoint two new cardinals. Bosto Rems took over the Church of Jehosanity in Velona, while Eduardo Hels did the same in Barcella. However, he met with his two conspirators before talking with the replacement cardinals. In his private study where they could not be overheard, Cardinal Branco Beja of Vito and Cardinal Juan Malagon of Bonito asked him what was happening with the opium deliveries. None had come through since last year's October run, which had left Megalos in late August.

"Pirates! Some damnable pirates have gotten a hold of a caravel gun ship and have been sinking all our opium shipments! We are only out one million gold, while the dealers have lost many millions trying to get a shipment through to us. However, gentlemen, Shansee has undergone some kind of massive upheaval. Our supplier, Yuen Ming, has been killed. Apparently, he controlled nearly everything in Shansee. I have sent a contact to Shansee, and he reports that one Tao Shi has taken over Yuen's opium operation."

"The question before us, gentlemen, is should we continue this dealing in opium? I know that it has made us very rich, but the real goal was to bring down Velona and Barcella. That hasn't happened, not even when the opium supply dried up."

"I say that we should continue dealing. I know so far the opium addicts have given Monarch West Po a severe problem. Before Cardinal Reina disappeared, he reported a huge increase in their crime rate, and West Po was forced to more than double his police force. So I say that our plan was working, perhaps a little slower than expected," Cardinal Branco stated factually.

"I agree with him," added Cardinal Juan. "We need to give it more time. However, we cannot afford to have our supplies intercepted. Has this pirate gunship left our waters?"

"Who can say," Pope Christos answered. "Okay, I will go along with the plan for now. I will see if I can get this Tao Shi fellow to send our shipments overland. I'll send word when to expect the next shipment. However, if he won't agree to an overland shipment of his opium, then the deal is off. I will not risk having more of our expensive caravels sunk by these pirates."

"Your Holiness, what about our acquiring a gun ship of our own?" asked Cardinal Juan.

"Prohibitively expensive for now. I am looking to Demokritos ultimately to build a fleet of these gun ships. Let them bear the cost and the risks," Pope Christos replied. "Rather we need to focus on ways to expand our control over those who do not follow Lord Jehosa, particularly those within the Sea Princes. Gentlemen, I have given this considerable thought, and I believe that I have come up with a new approach."

Both men sat up and paid close attention to their Pope Christos, who continued his explanation of his new plan. "We have control of two of the eight Sea Prince Sectors only. The population of Vito and Bonilla are small compared to Velona and the others. Your armies are relatively small so we cannot go to war with the other sectors. No, instead, let's get others to do it for us."

"You mean to use Demokritos?" asked Cardinal Branco, trying to guess his Pope's plan.

"No, we have much more work to do down there before we can reasonably expect to bend them to our Holy Goals. Rather we can use the ten Greenway Kingdoms. Already we have our missionaries there preparing the way. We've accumulated a vast sum from our opium endeavors, now is the time to utilize some of that. Let's get some impressive churches built there and donate large sums to the various kings under the guise that we wish to help them defend their kingdoms. Let them use the funds to purchase more guns and cannonae. Endear ourselves to them; establish the Church of Jehosanity as their kindly benefactor. Once they take our sizeable funds, we will slowly begin to gain their trust. When they are sufficiently powerful, only a spark will be needed for them to declare war on the Sea Princes. Twenty years from now, gentlemen, our Holy Church will be in control of all the worth souls in this hemisphere, well, nearly so."

Both Cardinals praised his new plan. "Please, I am counting on you both to donate some of your profits to these new Cardinals that I am appointing for the Greenway Kingdoms."

"You can count on us, Your Holiness," Cardinal Branco declared enthusiastically. "Bonito and Vito will be seen as great benefactors to those in the Greenway as well. Brilliant. Between the opium and the ten kings, the Sea Princes are finally doomed to come under our jurisdiction. Then, we can begin to convert their souls." Pope Christos smiled and blessed his two cardinals. With those two donating their funds to the Greenway kingdoms, he was free to donate even more to Demokritos, which was his main plan all along.

After the two men left, Pope Christos began daydreaming once more. For some time now, he enjoyed relaxing late at night and imagining how his

Church could become the focal point for all religious endeavors worldwide. Tonight, as he often did, he reflected upon all that he had learned about Dorota, which had once been a "perfect society." He'd studied all of Pope Leo's private writings about his visit to that country, before they met their downfall. He imagined an entire country whose women had no arms and were so very dependent upon their menfolk. Obviously, the men had no time to squander on frivolous things, worldly things. No crime and deeply religious, that was an incredible combination indeed. Tonight, he began to look for the reasons that the Dorota religion had so readily disintegrated when it had tried to expand out to the rest of the world.

"It's all because they changed their religious dogma. If they had not recanted and continued to promote their holy actions of insisting all females be armless, why, they would have succeeded. I am amazed that the backlash against their doktors and elders was not any greater than it was. No, you cannot come into a country where women have arms and try to setup a subculture where all your women are armless. The two just do not mix at all, though I suspect that a gradual change would work."

He reflected on his Church's approach, their Holy Women of the Eighth Degree. By making such armless women feel that they had the highest honor that the Church of Jehosanity could bestow upon them, such was accepted by the women. Usually, he observed, only women of financial means, women of importance, were accepted for this special Holy Ceremony. He grinned. Without fail, the husbands of such women were universally now under the complete control of the Church. That was the main function of the Ceremony in the first place.

Ah, but could such a "perfect society" be created again, under the auspices of the Church of Jehosanity? If it could, perhaps the whole world could ultimately be transformed into a perfect society, one without crime, one that was deeply religious! Such a legacy would be monumental for any Pope to leave behind.

"It has to be patterned off of the old Dorota ways," he whispered a sudden realization. "Our Women of the Eighth Degree are very helpless and dependent upon servants for everything. Not so, those women from Dorota. No, I see it now. The path must be to emulate the old Dorota methods!" A new plan began to form in his mind, one guaranteed to succeed where Dorota failed.

Once the cardinals left for their homes, Pope Christos sent word for the three remaining Elders of Dorota still residing here in Megalos to come and partake an audience with himself. Elders Esais Cadmus, Damon Doros, and Ariston Horus arrived on time, very nervous. None of the three fully trusted the Pope and were afraid that some new calamity was about to befall them and their few remaining followers here on Megalos.

"Welcome most Holy Elders. Welcome. I am very pleased to see you. Have a seat," Pope Christos said in his most charming voice. The three hesitantly sat down across from the Pope, resplendent in his purple robes with gold trim. "I will get straight to the point. Our two religions are nearly identical, that has long been established. I want to see if together, you and I, can rectify the errors of our predecessors. I've studied at length the perfect society that you once had on Dorota, and I have found nothing at all lacking in it. Indeed, I see it as a model for all societies."

This was not what the three had expected from the Pope! "Well, yes, we had a perfect society, but the High Council totally wrecked it for all time," Elder Damon volunteered.

"Perhaps not, Elder Damon, perhaps not," the Pope said coyly with a hint of mystery in his voice. "Correct me if I am misunderstanding the situation. The downfall was two-fold. First, they renounced your ageless practices as a 'mistake.' Second, you tried to integrate your society within ours, in which women have arms."

"Aye, that is precisely what happened," broke in Elder Esais. "Our followers and women in particular were chastised and humiliated by others. Such nearly destroyed our women." His anger seethed.

"Precisely. Here we all are years later and little progress has been made. Elders, I have in mind a project of long duration, one that will establish just how correct your original perfect society was. We know that the best way for such a society to exist is in relative isolation from those in which women have arms. Here's my proposal. I would like to fund and support the establishment of a new perfect society, one that can be used as a model for the entire world to follow. I call it Hieras Anubis, the Holy Children, the Bambini del Dio, if you please."

"There is a town whose population has been very nearly wiped out by black savages. At this time, the savages are no longer interested in attacking those who remain. I want to pay those who still reside there to move elsewhere and to give that town to you, calling it Hieras Anubis. I want to move all of your devout followers and any others on Megalos who wish to join in the creation of this perfect society. Indeed, if it works out, I will even see if there are those down in Demokritos who also wish to join you."

"I will cover all expenses until your new town and its people are totally able to support themselves. Funding, Elders, is not a problem. You may have all the funds that you deem necessary to create our new society," he explained, noticing carefully the reactions of the three men. All were totally shocked and surprised by his grandiose offer.

"What, what is it that you want in return?" Elder Damon finally was able to overcome his shock and ask the key question from their point of view.

"I will send along a new Cardinal who will oversee and conduct religious ceremonies. He will be instructed to work with you to achieve a uniform blending of our two religions, which, as I said, seem to be very, very similar. All I ask of you is to do everything possible to create and achieve a 'perfect society' in this new land. When you are successful, I will ask you to expand your reach and create more such towns. Over the years, I envision our Hieras Anubis to grow gradually until it sweeps over all of Tarra! In the meantime, I would like for us to keep the news of this project just between us and those whom you decide you would like to take with you to the new town."

"Further, you will need a means of protecting your people. Therefore, you may expect an unlimited number of these new gun weapons and even some cannonae. However, I've just learned that an inventor down in Demokritos has just created a vast improvement on the gun. It is called a fucile, a rifle. It shoots its projectile a very long range indeed. I will see that you get a supply of these as well. You will also need a couple of caravels of your own for long distance trading as well as a host of coastal fishing vessels. Again, I will provide them. Honestly, Elders, if you agree to do this, I guarantee that you will lack nothing in the way of finance to achieve our most Holy Objective!"

"This is the most incredible offer that I have ever seen, Your Holiness!" Elder Ariston replied, totally astounded with his proposal. The three eagerly accepted.

"Excellent," Pope Christos replied, shaking their hands, sealing their bargain. "I will send Cardinal Krios Panos to meet with you later today. The town of Cape Hope will be evacuated within a month and ready for you to occupy. Undoubtedly, it will require much construction effort to get the buildings long vacant back to battery. If you feel that you need a team of workers to go there first and make repairs, let me know. I will send a caravel there on Monday to begin making the arrangements. If you like, you can send a representative along with them to see what must be done before you move into the town with your people. Also, let me know how I can best spread the word to others who may wish to join you in this Holy Project."

"What about your Women of the Eighth Degree?" asked Elder Damon. He knew that there were quite a few of these "helpless" women scattered over Megalos and Demokritos. Many were wives of wealthy merchants. Was the Pope planning to send those along too? Elder Damon didn't want any "helpless" women. Rather the opposite, the real women of Dorota were far, far from helpless.

"While some of their husbands might jump at this chance, seeing profits to be made, I don't believe that it would be wise for their women to join you, unless they agree to learn to care for themselves and renounce their attitude of being totally helpless women," Pope Christos replied honestly. "You cannot have some women in your society who will do nothing for themselves, requiring others to do everything for them."

Elder Damon relaxed and grinned, "No, indeed not. Our women are every bit as capable as your women. It's just that they have different ways of doing things. Yes, if a Woman of the Eighth Degree is willing to learn how to do things for herself, then we will welcome her and her husband."

Elder Esais added, "I'm relieved, Your Holiness. At first, I thought that you might just be trying to find a way to get rid of all the armless women on Megalos. You know, to get us all off your island permanently."

"Oh no, no indeed, Elders! I want to help create a perfect society! One in which there is no crime and everyone is most religious. It is my ultimate goal for the Church of Jehosanity to become the guiding beacon for all of Tarra. As I envision it, ours is just the first step. It cannot be done with Women of the Eighth Degree, because those women are very dependent upon others, unlike the true Dorota women. If we are successful, why, the Church of Jehosanity will help spread the perfect society to all of Tarra."

April 10, 756, the Pope's yacht returned to Constanza City. The remaining two hundred people in Cape Hope readily accepted the Pope's offer of three hundred gold to move to another town. The Elder's representative, who had gone with them, eagerly relayed how ideal the town actually was. While some repairs would be needed, he didn't think that the project needed to be so delayed. They could easily make the repairs themselves when they moved there.

During these weeks, the Elders and Cardinal Krios began preparing for the mass exodus. Three caravels were loaded with supplies, such as food, lumber, nails, and tools. Another caravel carried crop seed. Thus, on April 15, twelve hundred and sixty-three men, women, and children boarded a flotilla of caravels, ready for the ten day journey to their new town. In the weeks and months after this, another five hundred three would join them. Within six months, another seven hundred sailed there from Demokritos to partake in the creation of a new perfect society.

Incidentally, ten wealthy merchants and their wives also chose to accompany them. They saw the immense profits to be made if this society worked as expected. Pope Christos felt relieved in that at least ten merchants knew how to handle trading arrangements. He had no idea whether or not these men from Dorota knew how to deal with trading issues. By convincing these ten and their wives to go, Pope Christos felt vastly more confident in the outcome of the project.

Hieras Anubis boasted a population of two thousand four hundred sixty-six by October of 756. The old port town of Cape Hope was now transformed into Hieras Anubis, the great experiment of Pope Christos. The Pope carefully monitored the monthly progress reports that his Cardinal Krios sent and he was very hopeful of the outcome.

By May, he began work on Phase 2 of his Demokritos Project. Phase 1 had gone well. Emperor Kreon Demon and Empress Frona, a Holy Woman of the Eighth Degree, were now solidly backing the Church of Jehosanity. Yes, it had been ten million gold well spent, Pope Christos thought. Instead of the horrible mess that his predecessor Pope Leo had left him, he once more had leverage with the Emperor.

More importantly, via monthly reports, he had been following the actions and decrees of this new, self-appointed ruler. Emperor Kreon had done something never before seen in Demokritos: he'd appointed himself the sole ruler, bypassing the High Councils and the seven Kings and Queens. In fact, the Emperor was actually a fascist ruler, quite popular with the general populace of the country. This was their first Emperor who did not need the approval of the wealthy and powerful to remain in office. He and his Empress ruled as they alone saw fit, though both were careful always to put forth decrees that were popular with the common people of Demokritos, whether or not it was actually beneficial to the general population.

Now it was time to solidify his influence and begin to exert a slight push upon this ruler. To that end, Pope Christos prepared for his three-month's sea voyage to meet personally with Emperor Kreon and Empress Frona. Phase 2 of his plan was critical; if he succeeded, Demokritos would certainly be under the control of the Church of Jehosanity. This time, Pope Christos vowed, no mistakes would be made.

Chapter 28 Kali's Adventure

Meanwhile not far from Megalos, the Grande Pistola lay listless in the warm waters. Captain Dante lay on the deck of his gun ship, smoking his pipe, extremely bored. Ania and Kali joined him. "Well," he asked in a monotone, hardly expecting any change. No change, no action — that was precisely the case since they had sunk the Pope's caravel carrying an opium shipment way back in late October. Now it was early March and still no word of further shipments. Nearly six months of idle waiting had taken its toll on the crew and their leaders. True, they had to put into some Southlands' ports twice more for provisions, but that excitement lasted only a few days.

"No news is good news," Ania attempted to put a positive spin on their wait. "I just got verification from Sandra. There has been no Banca del Dio activity between the Pope and anyone in Shansee since last October. The opium situation has all but dried up now in both Velona and Barcella."

"Ah, then we can finally go home?" Captain Dante asked in a hopeful manner, eager to see some action, if only sailing home.

"Not just yet. Can you put one of us ashore in Shansee discretely? We want to see for ourselves if there really is not going to be any more shipments," Ania asked.

Dante sighed and rose; well, it was something to do at least. "Sure thing. Isn't that a bit dangerous?"

Kali replied, "Yes, but I am up to it. If you can slip me ashore in the middle of the night, I can do a little sleuthing and then get to that top room in the Santi the next day. Give me a week to see what I can learn. If I come up empty, then, yes, let's head for home. Bethany and the others are not ready to return, probably not for a long time yet. No sense for us to stay here doing nothing." Instantly, she wanted to retract her words! Doing nothing was precisely what they all had been doing for nearly half a year now!

However, the next day they spied a caravel flying the blue cross of the Church of Jehosanity heading eastwards. "Well, isn't this interesting," Captain Dante came alive at last. He passed the spyglass to Ania, who took a look herself, before handing it to Kali. "Could it be that the Pope is going to meet with the new opium dealers in Shansee?" he speculated.

"Well, looks like we are back in action," Kali suggested, glad the interminable boredom had ended.

"I'll shadow that ship from a good distance," Captain Dante explained. "We don't want to raise their suspicions." Indeed for the next two weeks, the Grande Pistola kept the other caravel just on the distant eastern horizon, barely visible, though not at all times.

On April 1, Captain Dante sailed close to Shansee, though maintaining an eastward course, as if they were headed perhaps for Dorota.

Spyglasses showed the Pope's caravel docked in the harbor of Shansee. Once out of sight of land, Captain Dante turned the ship due south and then westward, heaving too nearly due south of Shansee. Kali's plan would be executed under the cover of night.

Around two in the morning, the Grande Pistola slipped to within a mile of Shansee. Quietly, the dingy was lowered, and two crew manned its small sail. Kali, carrying one small bag, was their passenger. By three a.m., Kali, dressed in dark pants and cloak, slipped ashore, moving silently across the open docks area. She only had to put two men asleep as she passed them. However, she realized then that her clothes would instantly label her as a foreigner. No way could she easily spy on the docks area unless she bought some local clothing. If the streets were as unsafe as Jemma claimed, Kali ought not wander Shansee alone.

"Now what?" she thought. Quickly, she slipped into the shadows of the tall warehouse wooden buildings. Instinctively, she made her way to the warehouse in which the opium dealers stored their bales of powder ready to be delivered. Mentally, she thanked Jemma for telling her how to find this particular warehouse. As she approached it, three men stood guard near the main entrance even here in the wee hours of the morning. Quietly and discretely, Kali cased the perimeter of the building, looking for a way inside.

Memories of her previous lifetime as a member of the Demokritos' Kali gang of assassins came unbidden to her mind. Before, she had a whole network of men and women under her control to say nothing of knowing very intimately the layout of the large city. The differences between then and now were acute in her thoughts. While she had arms this lifetime and could speak crudely their language, Kali was completely alone and in a foreign city, unfamiliar with the culture as well as the layout. She doubled back after reaching the far side of the building. Other than a second story window vent, only the heavily guarded main doors allowed access to the warehouse.

Seeing no practical alternatives, she headed to the Santi Inn. Kali felt particularly vulnerable as she crossed the quarter mile of totally open and flat area before the Inn. Two men stood guard at the barred gates. Kali had a choice to make. These men watched her closely as she walked the barren road up to the inn. She could modify their minds or she could ask them if she could get a room this early in the morning. Of course, she would have to invent a reason to be traveling at four in the morning. She chose the latter.

"Good morning. Is this the Santi Inn?" she asked, pretending to be somewhat disoriented.

"Yes, ma'am. You are out early. It's dangerous to be out walking by yourself. Did a ship just arrive? Are there more visitors coming?" one guard asked.

"I'm the only one that I know of. I kind of got lost and turned around! Shansee is so huge! I am so glad that I have finally found the Santi Inn! Can I get a room this late or what do I do now?" she asked, playing a role of a confused woman.

"Sure, we'll escort you to the night manager," one guard replied. Escorted straight to the night manager's desk, the guard took no chances with her. "Lon, this visitor just arrived and needs a room."

Lon, a man in his thirties, looked up. He eyed Kali up and down, while the guard moved back to the main door, but did not leave. "We don't get many checking in at this hour. Did your ship just dock?"

"Well, no sir. I got lost in the huge city and have only now just found the inn. I would like a room please. I am staying a week in Shansee. Do you have quality room with a view of the city and docks? Perhaps that will help me learn my way around Shansee. It is so huge," she continued to use her ruse.

Lon explained their rates, but continued to query her about her arrival. Kali carefully sidestepped his direct questions and took a room on the top floor, the very one that Jemma had had. After paying gold for it, Lon explained that she would have to carry her own bags up to the room; no other night servants were available. He definitely took note of the fact that she had only one small duffle bag with her. As Kali climbed the flights of stairs, she realized that her arrival had been anything but clandestine. She'd roused the manager's suspicions as well as that of the guards. Not a good start, she thought. "I'd best be on my toes," she concluded.

The next morning, she went down for breakfast, following the information that Jemma had given her months ago. She found that the day manager had been informed of her arrival as well. He made polite inquiries about her as he explained the Inn arrangements to her. Again, Kali opted to pretend to have gotten lost on her way here. She knew that such was a lame excuse and probably did nothing to alleviate suspicions. So she asked, "What are the 'must see' sights for visitors to Shansee?"

"Well, you should visit the Purple Palace. That is our most elegant pleasure houses, though I am afraid that you will need to dress much better to even be allowed inside." He told her where she could find a dressmaker. The desk manager listed ten other sights for her to consider, and Kali dutifully wrote them down. He watched her do so and added, "You can get a rik to take you to these places. Just let me know when and I will see that one is here for you." Kali knew that she would at least have to visit some of these, though she was loathed to visit the Purple Palace alone. It was far too dangerous.

After spending an hour looking over the docks and the heavy day traffic, Kali decided to at least visit the dressmaker's shop and then take in some of the suggested sights. Failure to do so would raise even more suspicions. As promised, the manager had a rik waiting for her. Purposely, she had the driver take her on a tour of the docks before heading into the city proper and the dressmaker's in particular.

However, as they rode out of the Santi, she thought that she saw someone following them on foot! On her guard, Kali kept a diligent eye out as the rik moved into the dock area, swarming with men, carts, and other riks. The spy continued to shadow her, though he was good at his job. Only occasionally did she spot him ambling along about a block behind them. On the other hand, she did spy some men from Megalos walking with a group from Shansee. While the locals seemed to be fighter types, bodyguards, she guessed, at least one was very well dressed in a white linen suit. Perhaps that was the drug lord. Apparently, she'd guessed right, the Pope had sent an emissary to negotiate more opium shipments directly. At last, the rik pulled out into the main street of Shansee, heading for the dressmaker's shop. Kali spotted her shadow continuing to follow along. "Damn," she whispered beneath her breath.

The street climate had definitely changed with the death of Yuen Ming last year. Kali saw more thugs about than Jemma had told her about. She spotted robberies and extortion in nearly every block they passed through. She was not immune either, as suddenly a teenaged thug accosted her rik driver, who was forced to stop.

"Give me all your money," the bully advised, brandishing a short sword at her.

Kali gave a brief chant and said, "Never mind. Continue on your way." At once, the thug repeated her words, motioning for the rik driver to move on. As Kali looked back, she noted that the man who was following her had witnessed the attempted robbery and was now conversing with the thug. Damn, she thought again.

Twice more, she had to use her Druwid powers to avoid being robbed on her way to the dressmaker's shop. Jemma's prediction of the current situation was accurate, Kali thought, as she climbed out and entered the shop. An hour later, she stowed her bags in the rik and climbed in for the return trip to the Santi Inn. As they began moving into the flow of heavy foot traffic, she spotted her shadow following her once again. Hastily, she asked the rik driver to drive her by the Purple Palace. At least she figured this action would seem to back up the desk manager's story of her asking what sights she should see here in Shansee.

By the time that she arrived back at the inn, the hour was late. Still, her shadow was a discrete block behind the rik! Purposely, she made sure that the desk manager saw her packages. "Got the right kind of dress to visit the Purple Palace," she coyly whispered as she passed him and gave him a wink, as if to thank him for his sound advice. He smiled. All the while, she kept alert for the shadowy figure, but he did not enter the Santi. In her room at last, Kali relaxed before heading down to the dining room.

As she ate, Kali realized that even if she could somehow manage to acquire a peasant style dress, her bronze skin would alert everyone to the fact that she was from Megalos and not Shansee. She'd have to hide all of her skin to pull it off; perhaps a hooded cloak at night would serve. Daytime sleuthing was out.

The next morning, she again saw the Pope's representatives walking to the opium warehouse along with many local men and that man in white linen. Somehow, someway, she needed to overhear what they were discussing! The how remained elusive. She stared out the window for some time. Then, an idea formed. She saw a number of people fishing from the docks! "That's it! I'll go fishing. If I sit around there, I will be in a position to at least spy on that warehouse, if not overhear conversations outside the place. Brilliant."

She dressed in her light pants and shirt and headed down the stairs. "I'm going fishing this morning," she coyly said to the desk manager. "I haven't been fishing since I was a little girl. Where can I get a pole and bait?" The manager gave her a strange look, but provided her with detailed directions. After thanking him, she walked out of the inn, carefully checking to see if her unknown shadow was still around. By the time that she reached the main street and had passed that wide open stretch of land before the old Santi Fortress, she spied the man coming after her once more. Ah well, she could deal with him if he tried anything, she thought.

A half hour later, with a pole and can of worms in hand, Kali sat down on the edge of the dock about a block from the warehouse. From her position, she could simply turn her head slightly to the right and see the main entrance. While the heavy traffic continually moved past her blocking her vision of the warehouse, still she could observe. She dropped her line into the water and pretended to be relaxing and fishing on the fine spring morning. At least two dozen others were also fishing, so that she did not look too out of place.

After a time, she spied the Pope's men and the local man in white coming out of the warehouse. Carefully, she watched their movements and tried to catch anything that they were saying to each other. From a block away, she only caught a bit of their conversation, "horses will be here." What did horses have to do with the opium deal? Kali began pondering the significance of that snatch of data.

While she was doing just that, her line jerked. At the same instant, she spotted three men coming up stealthily behind her. One was the man who had been shadowing her. Kali made an instant decision. While she could have risen to her feet and prepared to defend herself, perhaps screaming to get others to come to her rescue, she decided instead to continue her guise of fishing. She began to pull in her line. "Oh, I've got one!" she exclaimed excitedly to no one in particular, though she sensed the three men were now very close behind her.

"Don't move woman! This is a knife in your back. Get up and come with us, we have some questions for you to answer," a rough voice said, speaking slowly, unsure how well she understood their language. Kali got up, holding her pole. "Just leave it," he added. Kali saw the speaker was the man who had been shadowing her. The other two looked like martial arts fighters. While she could likely evade the dagger pointed at her, she knew that she could not avoid their lightning fast moves. Now wasn't the time to strike, she decided.

"What do you want? Why the dagger? What about my fishing pole?" Kali continued to play dumb. One man kicked her pole off the dock and into the blue waters below. The dagger man pushed her towards the opium warehouse. She saw that the two men from Megalos were now watching them approach, along with the man in the white linen suit. Kali had a bad feeling about this confrontational meeting.

As she drew close, she saw that one of the men from Megalos was a Mano del Dio assassin, probably in charge of buying the opium. He stared hard at her. Whether the other one was an assassin or not, Kali couldn't tell. Perhaps, he was a priest in disguise. "Inside," the man in white ordered. Gruff hands pushed her inside the warehouse.

The building was one huge open space. Its center was filled ten feet high with stacked, one-foot square bundles of opium, presumably. Kali guessed that there must be some twenty-five thousand such bales, all neatly stacked and ready for delivery. The man in white saw her noticing the bales. "Yes, those are opium bales, lady. Twenty-five million gold worth, but they will bring ten times that on the street level. Take her to the rear and shut the doors."

Strong hands pushed her forward past the bales to the northeast corner of the warehouse. There, she was thrown into a wooden chair. "What is this? Why are you doing this to me?" she asked. The edge of fear in her voice was real. She saw a large grate on the floor just before the chair, the scent of sewage whiffed into her nose.

"I'll ask the questions, sit down. Tie her hands to the arms," the man in white ordered. Quickly, they fastened her wrists tightly to the wooden arms of the chair. The ends of the arms were wide and she found her palms were now flat on them, out before her. "I am Tao Shi. Who are you? Where do you come from?" he asked in a hostile manner.

"Kali. From Megalos originally, Galantas," she replied truthfully. Her bronze skin made that obvious.

"Good, Kali from Megalos," Tao replied with a snarl. "Now why are you spying on us? Are you with the pirates that have been sinking our opium shipments?"

"I'm not spying on you. I'm just visiting Shansee. What pirates? What shipments?" Kali lied.

"Bitch!" he screamed and slapped her across her face good and hard, stinging her left side. She wanted to reach up and feel her face, but her arms were completely restrained. She noticed another man fastening a rope around her waist, tying her to the back of the chair. Next, they tied her legs against the front legs of the chair.

"Kali of Megalos, I'll ask you once more politely, if you don't answer, then we will make you. Who are you working for?" Kali sat stone silent, defiantly refusing to say more. "Have it your way!"

Tao nodded. One of his men move over to her left hand, took a hold of her index finger. After a slight pause for dramatic effect, he jammed it up to her wrist, shattering the bones, leaving her finger lying against the back of her wrist. Pain! Kali screamed; whether or not she intended to do so, she shrieked in pain. Tao asked her again, "Who do you work for?" Kali continued to cry and scream in pain. Crack. Crack. More of her fingers now lay up against the back of her wrist. Excruciating pain throbbed in her left hand; she passed out.

Water. Someone threw a bucket of water on her face and she came too. She saw all her fingers and thumb were shattered, lying flat against the back of her wrist. "Who do you work for? Why are you spying on us?" Tao asked again. Kali just continued to cry and moan. Pain! Shattering pain struck her other hand, and she passed out once more.

Water. She awoke to cold water thrown on her face. Both of her hands were now totally crippled and useless, but the pain was almost unbearable. She fought hard to hold her hands immobile, as if that would somehow stop or lessen the pain. "Who do you work for?" Tao barked once more. Still, Kali did not answer him. Tao nodded and her torturer lifted up a heavy metal baton and he smashed it down hard on her fingers and wrist, shattering what remained of her fingers and hand and wrist. Kali screamed louder than she had ever known that she could. Searing pain shot through her left arm and overwhelmed her; she passed out again.

Water. The cold water brought her too once more. "You are running out of hands, Kali from Megalos. Who do you work for?" Tao barked, unrelentingly. Kali continued to cry and wail. Wham! The metal rod crushed what remained of her right hand and wrist, shattering the remnants of her fingers, the palm, and her wrist. Again, the pain was enormous, and she passed out once more.

She came too sometime later, though she heard voices talking. She opened her eyes a crack and noticed that her elbows were now tied tightly to the arms of the chair. She listened to the voices. "The horses have arrived as you can see. The overland shipment will begin as soon as they are loaded with your opium bales. It takes forty packhorses to carry your thousand bales, Prelate Axos. They must go single file along the rocky coast around the Desert of Desolation. Once they get into the Southlands, the cargo can be loaded into a few wagons for easier transport. Make sure that a caravel is waiting for them in New Barq to ferry them to your destinations. If it's not there, my men will unload it to the highest bidder," Tao Shi declared threateningly.

"Don't worry, our caravel will be there. Look for the blue cross flag," Axos replied. "If your men do not arrive, you will hear from us. It's imperative that we have a continuous flow of opium once we get it started again."

"I know, I know. Couldn't be helped. Damnable pirates! Did you ever find out who they were or why they were sinking the ships?" Tao asked.

"No idea. Like a ghost ship. We're still trying to find out, but no country is claiming responsibility or has publically announced the loss of a gun ship. Well, let's see the pirates stop an overland shipment," Axos snarled. "Now, let me have a go at your spy."

Cold water woke Kali up, although she only pretended to wake. Prelate Axos now stood before her, holding the metal rod. She saw her crushed hands; they looked swollen and terribly discolored, nearly black. The pain was throbbing with every pulse her heart sent out.

"Kali, who do you work for? Where are the pirates based?" Axos demanded to know. Kali sat rigidly motionless, as if somehow that would lessen the pain. "Damn, woman, your hands are a lost cause!" Kali continued crying. Axos slapped her hard on her cheek, breaking her lower jaw. Still she said nothing. Wham! He brought the rod down hard on her left foot, shattering her arch. She wailed in pain and passed out once more. After another water wake up, he again asked her. Wham! He shattered her right foot as well. As she passed out, Kali realized she was crippled up. She could not use her hands nor could she even walk anymore!

In a daze from the pain, she heard the voice of Axos once more. "Hell, we should take pity on you. Your hands are a complete mess. I'll do you a service, Kali. One day you can thank me for this." Unable to raise her head, she heard a swishing sound and felt an axe chop her left hand off at the wrist! A disconnected, blood-curling scream echoed inside the warehouse. Whack. Her right hand surged in pain, though she was now unconscious once more. She didn't see the men tightening two tourniquets on her lower arms.

Kali awoke. She was lying down; it was smelly and dark. The ends of her arms throbbed relentlessly as did her feet. Rats scampered back from their feasting on her arm stumps. She vomited. A bit later, she thought, "Where am I?" She tried to look around. A bit of light came from above her. She was in a long tunnel. Ah, the grate that she'd noticed before the torture chair was just over her head. She tried to sit up but couldn't in the confining space. She tried to push up the grate, but found she had no way to do it, no hands. Now she saw the crude tourniquets on both arms and gave up that idea altogether. It was still light. Was it even the same day?

"Before I die, I have to let Ania know what their plans are," she thought, focusing on her mission and not her plight, resigned to her death. It took all her concentration to make contact finally with Ania on the Grande Pistola.

Quickly, she relayed their current plans to smuggle the opium to the Sea Princes via an overland caravan along the southern coast of the Desert of Desolation. Then, she told Ania what had happened to her. *I'm in a sewer pipe inside the warehouse. I think I can crawl out, but I cannot get back inside the warehouse. I can't walk either. Just leave me to die, Ania,* Kali asked.

Don't be silly, Kali. We're on our way. Meantime, see if you can crawl down the pipe. Probably, they dispose of their victims by dumping their bodies down the pipe. I'll keep in touch when we make shore. We best come in under cover of darkness again. Kali learned that she had been unconscious for two days since her torture. She was thirsty and starving. Already the rats, which had been gnawing at her bloody stumps, began cautiously approaching her. She was about to try to make noise to drive them off when she heard voices coming from above her through the grate.

Tao said, "Well, tonight, dump several water barrels down the grate and flush her out to sea at high tide. That Prelate fellow sure was brutal, but honestly, I never had any intention that Kali would be allowed to live. Now that he's gone, we can dispose of her like all the others."

Kali fumed, "Damn him anyway! Suddenly inspiration struck! She remembered that there were quite a lot of lamp oil barrels around the warehouse, especially near the main doors. Besides, the opium bales were wrapped in cotton bags. The whole place was wood. Fire! Kali concentrated and then let loose with a barrage of balls of fire, the first few centered on the entrance doors and the barrels of lamp oil. She heard screaming and frantic action above her, but she continued launching her Druwid spells, though she could not see where exactly they all detonated. Only when she heard a raging inferno and no more voices coming from above her did she finally stop her casting. Much later, everyone learned that Tao Shi and six of him most trusted men died in the fire that consumed the warehouse and nearly twenty-five million gold in opium! Kali had her revenge.

Now a new worry got her attention! Heat and smoke began to reach her here in the sewer pipe. She knew that she had to get moving or she too would perish in the inferno. Using her elbows and knees, she began to move through the darkness, before she remembered to cast her blue light spell. "Ah, now I can at least see," she thought. On she crawled and slid down the pipe until at last she no longer felt the heat from overhead. Kali was beyond the warehouse proper. After resting her now bloody elbows, she continued making her way down the pipe.

An eternity later, Kali came to the end of the pipe. It was night. She heard yelling voices in the distance and soon realized that many men were now fighting the massive fire that she had ignited. She smelled the ocean and the rotting stench and knew that she was below the wooden docks. Here is where they dumped their fish entrails and other garbage. Using her blue light, she tried to see how far above ground the end of the pipe actually was — three feet. If Ania were coming, she'd never find her inside the pipe. Kali wiggled her way out and fell head first into the dump, frantically trying to break her fall with her non-existent hands. Her stumps hit the garbage pile, and the shooting pain once more knocked her out. Her body lay in the refuse mound about three feet from the rising waters.

Although it was only nine at night as the Grande Pistola came within a mile from the docks, the giant warehouse fire was highly visible. Flames shot up a hundred feet into the sky, threatening other nearby warehouses. Ania and three fighters manned the sailing dingy and headed in towards the docks. As they drew close, they saw hundreds of men frantically tossing buckets of water on the adjacent warehouses in a valiant attempt to keep them from also burning to the ground. No one paid the slightest attention to the lone sailing dingy, as it tacked up to the docks. None saw the four climb out and head under the docks or saw them return sometime later carrying the unconscious body with them. Quietly, the dingy sailed back out to sea.

As soon as the dingy was stowed, Captain Dante set full sails for home, though it would be many weeks before they could get there. Meanwhile, strong arms carried Kali below, and Ania and the ship's physician began examining her many wounds. "Looks like rat bites on her stumps," the doc suggested. "Gosh, she smells horrible. First, we best get her cleaned up! No telling what kind of infections she's exposed to!"

While they worked on stripping Kali and cleaning her body, Ania contacted Sandra. *Boy do we ever need a Healer!* She outlined the many injuries Kali had suffered and Sandra and Ania made a Mind Link so that Sandra could see for herself and give precise directions.

Sandra sent, *This is awful! You are going to have to remove more of her lower arms. Let's hope the infection can be stopped! Cosima is going to try to perform therapy on Kali via her other body here, Kallisto Ann. Her lower jaw is broken on her right side and both feet arches are crushed. How is her pulse?*

Weak, she's lost a lot of blood. Can we save her?

Sandra didn't answer. Once Kali's body was thoroughly washed with hot water, Ania began the additional surgery, removing another two inches of Kali's lower arms. She hoped and prayed that would be enough to stop the infection. Once that laborious surgery was done, she and Sandra discussed what to do about her broken jaw and feet. Sandra decided that the best thing for the feet would be somehow to fabricate a cast that would hold her arches in their proper position so that they would hopefully heal properly. While the ship's doc worked on concocting something for the two casts, Sandra, via Ania's eyes, examined the smashed left lower jawbone.

The bone was completely broken and the two halves easily moved as Ania put slight pressure on it. *We've got to immobilize her jaw somehow. Perhaps you can wire it shut with something. Make it so she can't move it. That's the best idea I have now,* Sandra sent.

Dawn came when Ania and the doc finally finished up their work. Kali had heavy casts on her feet, her jaw was wired shut, and heavy bandages covered her lower arms. She was still alive, but only barely.

Interestingly, back at 42 Hampton Way, as dawn came, Cosima took Kali's new body into a therapy session! All that day, Cosima ran Kallisto Ann through her torture, pain by pain. Three days later, Cosima finally finished running down each injury to a full erasure of the trauma. Kallisto Ann now felt terrific and relieved, but her Kali body was still weak and unconscious on the Grande Pistola. This had been the strangest of therapy sessions for Cosima, unique in many ways!

As the days passed, Ania fretted over the unconscious Kali, who was running a fever on top of everything else. She bathed her dear friend in cold water and sat beside her hammock constantly. How could she could get nourishing food into Kali once she regained consciousness? Kali had lost a lot of blood and still Ania could not get more fluids into her patient. On the second day, telltale red streaks began creeping up the left stump of Kali's arm. Ania's heart sank, blood poisoning! They had not gotten all of it. Once more, she and Sandra made a Mind Link and our top Healer carefully examined Kali.

She is too weak to withstand another operation. Yet, we must or she will most definitely die. Honestly, Ania, there is almost no hope at all for her, Sandra sent.

Mind if I join you? Kallisto Ann — that is, Kali from her new ten year old body back in Velona — joined them, along with the help of Cosima. *It's my old body there. Not much hope of it recovering is there?* she asked pointedly.

Kali, I wish I could say otherwise, Sandra answered her honestly, *but not really. It has lost a lot of blood, and we have not been able to get any fluids into it yet. There is an infection running rampant through the body, and the red line of death has appeared on the left arm. See here,* she pointed out.

I am so sorry, Kali. I ought to have gone with you, Ania cried.

Don't be silly, Ania. You and I both know that we would both be dead now and then there would be no one to stop that overland horse caravan. I am charging you with stopping them, Ania. I killed Tao Shi and wiped out their entire opium supply. Of course, someone else will step in, but there won't be any new opium for quite some time, Kallisto Ann consoled her friend.

I'll miss you, Ania cried, her grief overcoming her finally.

Silly, I am still here with our new bodies. We're ten and almost ready for action again, Ania. You be careful and get that caravan for me, Kallisto Ann replied, blowing a wisp of pure love to Ania.

I promise you that we will. What about your Kali body? Ania asked.

There, now you can toss it overboard. Kallisto Ann or Kali disconnected totally from it. As Ania and the ship's doc watched, Kali's body died. It was April 6, 756. Ania stared for a long time at her dear friend's body, just to make sure. Only when Captain Dante ushered her out of the cabin did Ania finally let go and cry. A few minutes later, Captain Dante and a very somber crew gave Kali Kato da Cassa a burial at sea with full honors. Of we six with two bodies, Kali was the first to get out of that bit of confusion. Now she could spend her full attention on her ten year old Kallisto Ann body back home.

"Okay, now what do we do?" asked Captain Dante. Ania wiped the tears from her face and headed below to get some tea; he followed her, respectful of her sorrow. A bit later, the two sat at the galley table. Ania finally spoke.

"We are not too far from Shansee. We should parallel the coastline and see if we can find them."

He replied, "Agreed. We need to know their numbers. Kali said that they were carrying a thousand bales. That means many horses. Won't they need to carry along food and water to traverse the southern edge of the Desert of Desolation?"

"Right. How can we stop them? We are too few," she asked, finally putting her mind on this final task for Kali.

Captain Dante chuckled, and then replied, "We can give them a broadside. That ought to soften them up considerably. Remember, we have fifty fighters on board. Come on; let's get to my navigational maps."

"Okay, Ania, my reckoning puts our location here, about two hundred miles west of Shansee. We ought to take them when they are crossing the coastline off the Desert of Desolation. That way they have only two directions they can go: east or west confined to the thin beach," Captain Dante suggested. Together, they made their plans. For several more days, they sailed northeast until at last they sighted the coastline of the Desert of Desolation. They were several hundred miles north of the giant island of Megalos. Now they waited patiently for the caravan of opium bales to reach their position.

Two weeks passed before their lookout gave the cry that the entire crew was awaiting, "Caravan ahoy!" Quickly, everyone rushed to the starboard side of the main deck, straining for a view of their enemy. Captain Dante, using his spyglass, carefully observed the snaking caravan, a long thin line of horses and men. He passed his glass to Ania.

"Looks like there are fifty men on horseback leading another fifty horses," he declared and began discussing artillery operations. Already, the gun crews had replaced the heavy lead balls that were used to sink ships by smashing a hole below the water line with anti-personnel shot. Essentially, they used modified cannone shells, consisting of bits of metal encased in a black powder metal ball. When the ball hit, the force of the hit would ignite the black power, which would then explode the ball, sending the deadly shrapnel flying in all directions.

Ania didn't like the idea of injuring so many of their horses, however.

When she mentioned her reservation to Captain Dante, he agreed with her. It seemed criminal of them to be injuring so many horses, just to also get at the men riding them. The two reached a compromise. Half of the guns would fire the modified shot while the other half would shoot the solid balls. "If they are smart, after the first volley, the men ought to let go of the horses that they are leading and flee for their lives. If so, we can land, destroy the opium, and be on our way."

Here in mid-April, the temperatures close to the Desert of Desolation were already in the high nineties, rising far higher the further inland that one went. The men rode single file along the thin strip of beach. While they were surprised to see a caravel anchored off the coast, they didn't see the gun ports that were hidden beneath the canvas covering. Boom! Boom! Boom! Fifty eyes turned to see the harmless caravel now a death threat.

Eight gun ports were clearly visible along with the black plumes of smoke from their guns. A bit later, the balls slammed into their long lines. Several exploded as they hit the ground, sending bits of metal slicing into bodies of men and horses. The solid shots occasionally struck a horse and rider, but mostly threw up sand and rock, which knocked a few from their horses, as well as frightening everyone. When the second volley came, the men finally reacted.

They dropped the reins of the horses that they were leading and galloped east or west as fast as they could ride. Here, the beach was sandy, and thus they vanished rapidly. Even in their panic, none was stupid enough to ride out onto the desert proper. Total duration: two minutes. With horses scattering in all directions, Captain Dante ordered his fighters to go ashore and mop up. Specifically, they were charged with counting the opium bales. He wanted none to get through to New Barq.

It took them a half hour finally to reach the beach. By now, the freed horses had stopped running and were milling around, looking for water and grass, none of which existed along this coastline with the Desert of Desolation. Because some shots had actually disintegrated the opium bales, the fighters found it difficult to obtain an accurate count. By nightfall, they had the beach scene under control and buried the dead men in shallow beach graves. When the tired men finally returned to the ship, they estimated that they had destroyed the bulk of the shipment. "Captain, we left the horses with their food, water, and grain supplies alone."

"Good. We don't want to be inhumane to the survivors by destroying their only water and food. Probably they will regroup, retrieve them, and head back home," Captain Dante surmised. He gave the order to set sail once more, moving the caravel away from the shore. However, he anchored such that he could still observe the shore via his spyglass. He wanted to make very sure of their success. By the next afternoon, he saw men returning and leading the horses back toward Shansee. Only now did he give the orders to set sail for home, for Velona, finally.

Chapter 29 Zau, the Imperial City

Ilenakova took the news of the death of her wife, Kali, very hard indeed. Likewise, Jemma, for Kali was her adopted mother. "We should have stayed back in Shansee," Jemma wailed.

"No dear, you were right in coming here. With the death of Yuen Ming, utter chaos broke out in Shansee," I tried to console her. "Kali knew well just how bad the situation in the city had become. Had you two stayed, we would have had to double back and rescue the both of you, assuming that you were not already killed. Kali knew what she was getting into when she headed ashore, and she wanted very much to put an end to the opium trade. She just gave the Church of Jehosanity a million gold loss and a twenty-five million loss to the opium dealers of Shansee. Besides, Cosima has already erased Kali's trauma, and Kallisto Ann is already back in action. Her other body is now ten, if you recall."

"Still, I'd like to slaughter them all," Ilenakova growled. While Jemma was coming to grips with the loss of her mother, Ilenakova was not. Her new ten year old boy body back home, Len, was still giving her a hard time concentrating on the present. More so now that he-she was beginning to want to practice sword battles. Kali and Ilenakova had asked for appropriate bodies so that they could have a proper marriage. Kallisto Ann and Len were those. Now that Kali had lost this body, I began to suspect that Ilenakova was now thinking along similar lines: ending this body's life so that she could concentrate solely on Len and her lover, Kallisto Ann.

Later when I had time, I took Jemma aside and ran a therapy session to help her deal with the loss of her mother. That helped her a whole lot, since it lay on top of the suicide of her birth mother.

Giang is the second largest city in Tan Loc Province, only Shansee is larger. As we rode into the city from the western edge, following the Yan River, the size of the city made an impression on me. Sprawling along the junction of the two large rivers, the Yan and the Yonshu, Giang was bustling with activity. The streets teamed with people, open air markets thrived, as did smaller shops. The sheer number of small stores dwarfed that of bustling Velona.

Overlord Ho Bu of Giang rolled out the red carpet for his new Empress San Min Wu. We all felt that the reception that we would receive in Giang would be a critical one. That is, would the warring overlords accept the new Empress and the new politics that had been unilaterally decreed? At this point, San Min had not the army to enforce her will against all the overlords throughout Tashien. If she was not accepted here in Giang, so close to her home town of Nan Yan, it was doubtful that she would be accepted elsewhere, compounding our problems of bringing order back to Tashien.

Once we reached the heart of Giang, where the Yan River joined the mighty Yonshu, Overlord Ho Bu had insisted the citizens throng the streets to welcome this visit by their new Empress. He was milking the passing of the Empress for all that it was worth, using her visit to enhance his political standing. Ho was a shrewd politician, we soon discovered. We passed cheering throngs of people. As we crossed one of the ornate bridges over the Yonshu, a volley of fireworks proclaimed the arrival of Empress San Min Wu to the entire city of several million. We were all impressed with the warm welcome, none more so than San Min.

Giang had no princess or palace proper, unlike Shansee. Overlord Ho Bu put us up at the finest inn in the city, the Golden Dragon, not to be confused with the Golden Palace, which was their equivalent of Shansee's Purple Palace of pleasures. We spent a week in the city; there was just too much business for San Min to handle to shorten it any.

Several things happened during this week. First, two hundred three martial arts specialists and Masters joined us. Word had been spread throughout Tan Loc Province by the Olin Masters. Their services had been politely requested, and they had assembled here to wait for our arrival. San Min was delighted, for she knew that one of these fighters was worth many, many of the traditional soldiers, which used to comprise the Imperial Army.

Second, thousands of young men and a few women lined up to seek an audience with San Min. They wanted to join her new army. Word had spread about the incredible pay that she was offering, and few could turn down a chance at such an income. Fortunately, San Min was able to allow Ilenakova and others to conduct those endless interviews. When we finally pulled out of Giang, Empress San Min's new Imperial Army numbered close to one thousand, though many were not yet trained in modern methods of combat.

Third, Cao Bang members reported to their leader, Gang Yo. Empress San Min learned firsthand just how lawless Shansee had become from these reports, if the death of Kali was not sufficient. Several of Gang Yo's men had come long distances to report on the situations in the northern large cities and provinces. Word had come to these northern overlords in time to prevent them from launching their planned spring offensives. Most all had adopted a let's wait and see what develops attitude.

"Empress," Gang Yo offered even more support, "the Cao Bang are at your disposal. I can round up two hundred men to send to Shansee to help bring back calm and order to that city." I saw this as yet another power play by Gang, further solidifying the legitimacy of his band. San Min also saw this, but she needed his help and accepted it. When we left Giang, his two hundred Cao Bang members along with a hundred of her Imperial Soldiers headed south to Shansee to bring back order one way or the other.

Additionally, De An also headed there, along with Dia Son and Master Liang Dhow. He promised to rejoin us as soon as he got those two and his church established in Shansee.

On April 12, we were again on the move, only our caravan now numbered well over a thousand strong. The Imperial City of Zau and the Empress' Palace was our next destination, as we headed due north. There were no large cities between Giang and Zau, but there were many large towns whose populations exceeded a half million. Twelve days and three hundred miles later, we crossed the border between Tan Loc Province and Wontun Province. The broad Lian River marked the border, as it too joined the Yonshu River.

Yes, slowly we added more soldiers to Empress San Min's ever-growing national army as well as a few more martial arts masters. While our fighters and Protectors spent the evenings teaching the new recruits proper methods of combat, frankly, I was bored. Dita tried to assist in the teaching, but because of her feet, such was impossible and she gave it up as well. Together, we moped around the inn. Even Jemma kept active, assisting Empress San Min with political details. Well, she is a Judger and that is what she is interested in doing. Boring for me.

On May 15, we finally arrived at the outskirts of Zau, the Imperial City from which the entire Tashien Empire had historically been ruled. Suddenly, things changed!

Overlord Nangumo controlled most all the entire central valley systems of this province as well as Zau itself. Over the years, his army had grown huge. Estimates put his forces at ten thousand or more. However, a large percentage of his soldiers were fanned out to the various cities and towns under his control. Yes, he had a strangle hold on this territory. By all accounts, he was mean and vicious, taking what he wanted when he wanted. Dita and I concluded that he was another Yuen Ming type.

Yet, the news that Empress San Min began to hear repeatedly was exceedingly strange. None of us knew what to make of it. Report after report came to her of a lone Golden Warrior who was systematically slaying Nangumo's soldiers. Some also reported that this Golden Warrior was constantly asking the soldiers about some woman named Lin Lu, before he killed them.

As we arrived at the outskirts of Zau, Empress San Min correctly called a halt to our advance. If this Overlord Nangumo was following traditions, he should come out to meet her and officially welcome her to the Imperial City. A huge celebration, similar to that in Giang, ought to have occurred as she subsequently entered the city. However, considering the size of his army, with hers being but a tenth of his, prudence dictated that she halt before the city and send in scouts to find out the true situation before entering.

Just as she was about to order scouts to enter Zau, a lone rider approached us. A well-dressed man, perhaps fifty, wearing a fine white linen suit and highly polished boots, rode up, and dismounted. "I am here to welcome Empress San Min Wu." Ilenakova and six of our new captains led him to her carriage.

When he walked up to her, Empress San Min offered him her hand. He bowed respectfully, took it, and gently kissed her hand, noticing her six-inch long, bright red talons. "Empress San Min Wu, I am most honored to receive you at this time on behalf of Overlord Nangumo. I am his Second, Gao Din. Please accept the blessings of the Imperial City. A welcome has been prepared for you. Overlord Nangumo has vacated the Imperial Palace, and it now awaits your arrival."

"Thank you, Gao. But where is Overlord Nangumo? How is it that he deigns not to greet me personally?" she asked politely, wondering just where he and his mighty army was located. Perhaps, he was waiting for her forces to enter the city and then ambush them all. She did not trust this overlord at all.

"You must forgive Overlord Nangumo. His life is in peril now. Perhaps you have heard of this Golden Warrior, who is systematically killing his soldiers and who is looking for him as well?"

"We've heard such rumors. What can you tell us about this Golden Warrior? Who is he? Where does he come from? Why is he after Overlord Nangumo and his men? How is it that one man can inflict such carnage and strike such fear in the Overlord?" she asked key questions. Empress San Min was quite blunt and sharp in her questions.

"No one knows for sure. From his trail of carnage, we believe that he began first in the far western valley of Mong Yu, the last village of the Hong Valley west of here. We have a few eye witness accounts, though none from our soldiers. This Golden Warrior enters a town and seeks out all our soldiers. He does not harm any of the townsfolk, only Nangumo's soldiers. So far, not one soldier in any of the towns that he has entered has lived! We are dependent upon the stories told to us by the locals," Gao explained, a strong measure of fear in his voice. His eyes darted about, never lighting on any of us for more than a split second.

"He wears some kind of strange golden helmet with large horns and a golden waist girdle. Some say that he carries a sword, but few report that he actually draws it when he kills our men. This is the strange part. He kills merely by looking at the soldier! A few bodies have been brought back to Overlord Nangumo to see. There is not a mark on them; yet they are very dead! We do not know how this is possible, yet it is so. Two thousand five hundred ten of his soldiers have perished thus far."

"Haven't his men tried to attack him back when he enters a town?" asked an incredulous San Min.

"Yes, of course. Overlord Nangumo has placed a ten thousand gold bounty on his head. Every soldier is now looking for this Golden Warrior.

Such is a most valuable prize indeed. Yet, not a single soldier has ever managed to inflict the slightest scratch on this Golden Warrior's body, though villagers have reported that they have certainly tried to do so. He is immune to their weapons! How can this be? How can a man be struck with a mighty sword and not be harmed in the slightest?" Now the real source of the fear in Gao became clear to us all.

This Golden Warrior was impervious to weapons and yet could kill without using a weapon. Such a combination was godlike and was certain to terrify the soldiers. Heck, even we were a bit unnerved by this description of the Golden Warrior!

"But what does this Golden Warrior want?" asked San Min, just as baffled as we were.

"Who knows? Yet, we have received many reports that this Golden Warrior always asks the soldier whom he is about to slay, 'Where is Lin Lu?' No matter what the soldier replies, he is then killed," Gao replied.

"So who is this Lin Lu?" San Min probed further.

Gao shrugged his shoulders. "No one knows! Honestly, Overlord Nangumo has asked everyone he can think of this question, but none of us knows who this woman may be. Yet, it is certain that this Golden Warrior is not going to stop until he finds this woman. At this time, Overlord Nangumo has gone into hiding. He never sleeps more than one night at any one place. He travels around frequently to avoid being found by the Golden Warrior. Still, he is not without a plan."

He continued in a hopeful manner, "The Golden Warrior is nearing Zau as we speak. Overlord Nangumo has arranged for him to be met with two thousand of his fighters just northwest of Zau. When the Golden Warrior comes, he will face an army of soldiers. We hope that they will be enough to kill him and put an end to this carnage."

"Interesting plan. Has this Golden Warrior attacked other overlords and their soldiers?" San Min inquired. I could sense that she was worried about our entering the city. Would he then attack us?

"We do not think so. Several times, he has been at the southern or northern edge of the valleys controlled by Overlord Nangumo and has encountered soldiers of these two neighboring overlords. To date, he has not harmed them, only ours. Isn't this the strangest thing?" asked Gao.

"Yes, it certainly is. However, Overlord Nangumo has brought this doom upon himself. His greed and viciousness towards our people has made him many bitter enemies. It would seem that he has made one too many enemies," the Empress replied.

"Nevertheless, we cannot stay here outside the city. We should enter and get settled at the Imperial Palace," San Min stated. "How soon can we do so?"

Gao bowed, "All is ready. I would be honored to ride before your entourage and announce your arrival."

A few minutes later, our caravan began to enter the enormous city. The last time I was here, over a century ago, we arrived by riverboat and could see little of the Imperial City. Now, I saw just how vast it actually was. Here was the single largest city on Tarra! At least ten million people called Zau home. From a hill before the city, we got a bird's eye view. Incredible. The city's tendrils stretched out for miles beyond the central hub some twenty miles in diameter, particularly along the Yonshu River, which ran north-south dividing the city in half. My group was speechless, as we got our first overview of this mighty city.

As we entered Zau traveling on the main paved road, throngs of people lined the sides of the road. Some were crowded onto rooftops as well. People waved green flags, the imperial colors. Many yelled and cheered, especially so once the fireworks began. Every couple of miles, a new volley of fireworks were set off, mostly making loud bangs, since it was daytime. It took us two hours to cover the ten miles to the Imperial Palace proper. Empress San Min received a royal welcome. We were now convinced that those who used to hold power in Tashien and the working class most definitely wanted a return to some kind of stability. They had had enough of the chaos of the last six years. It was time for a change. The new High Parliament methods were foreign to all, so they latched on to the Empress position that they had always had down through the centuries.

The Imperial Palace was a walled compound occupying four square miles near the heart of Zau. The outer walls, some fifteen feet tall, surrounded the complex, which was a square, two miles on a side. Yes, it was highly defensive in nature, not easily breached. Inside these outer walls, which boasted four enormous gate houses, were the stables and barracks for the Imperial Army. Thousands of soldiers could be garrisoned within the walls. Essentially, this was a mini-city within a city.

At the center of the square was yet another ten foot walled compound, a mile on its sides. Within these inner walls lay the actual Imperial Throne and living quarters for the rulers. We saw a large stable for all our carriages, a stone building that housed the domestic staff, another housed the Imperial Guards, a huge Imperial Formal Gardens, a giant Imperial Meeting Hall, and the actual Royal Palace itself, which rose some five stories tall. Each floor was smaller than the one below it; sloping red tiles formed the roofs up to the start of each new story. Quaint construction. It reminded me of the Olin Monastery building.

Of course, the palace already had a large number of staff running it. However, those people were hired by Overlord Nangumo and were likely loyal to him. San Min would have to hire her own replacements or accept some of those who already worked here hoping they were not spies for Nangumo.

"Wow!" Bianca exclaimed, as we climbed out of our carriages and had our first look at the impressive Royal Palace exterior. Similar remarks came from all of us as we entered. An elderly man, Xu Chang, greeted the Empress.

"I am Xu Chang, the Palace Steward. I am so pleased to meet you, Empress San Min Wu," he bowed low. After the many introductions and more bowing, he explained, "I am to give you a guided tour of the Palace, if you are ready."

We were. Emerald green hung everywhere, the royal colors, since the dawn of Tashien. Silken and satin curtains hung in nearly every room. The main entrance led to the huge throne room. Beyond that was a large meeting room, elegantly furnished. Next came the Royal Dining Hall so huge that it could service at least a hundred people at one time. The Royal Bath was out of this world. The main pool could bathe twenty at one time. Golden fixtures, mirrors, and the finest, soft cotton emerald green towels furnished the room, along with three dressing stations made of black teakwood and highly polished.

"Luxury beyond luxury!" Bianca exclaimed to her mom.

"No kidding," Dita replied.

"I don't believe it," Jemma added.

"Unreal," Fina commented, awestruck. "I wonder what the bedrooms are like?"

We chose to occupy the master bedrooms located on the fourth floor. The top floor consisted of observation rooms and sunrooms. "Wow love," Dita commented as we finally entered the bedroom assigned to us, "satin sheets, and mahogany furniture. Just wait until we retire!" I grinned and gave her a loving kiss to hold her until tonight.

Our first action was a long overdue bath as you might expect. Then, we all took off in small groups to explore fully our new home. Dita and I grinned as we watched the many young couples walking off, arm in arm, chatting excitedly to each other. Fina, Jemma, and Bianca would certainly have tales to tell the others back home. She and I began our slow shuffle as well, intent upon exploring this incredible work of art, this Royal Palace.

Over supper several hours later, Ilenakova brought us all back to the present situation. "Okay, it looks like our first major situation to handle is this Golden Warrior. Tomorrow, I ought to take some forces and head out to the west and check on the large army that lies in wait for him. I don't trust this Overlord Nangumo at all. Perhaps all this is sheer fabrication on his part."

"Make sure that everyone wears the emerald green sash, which identifies you as Imperial Troops," San Min urged. "Jemma, tomorrow we have our work cut out for us. Many important people will come for an audience, and I certainly could use your help."

Jemma smiled, she was enjoying this exercise very much. Her boyfriend looked bored and she hinted, "Phillipe, why don't you accompany Ilenakova and the others tomorrow? I will be tied up with meeting all these key people." The relief on his face caused Dita and I to chuckle!

Later that night, Dita and I were finally alone in our new elegant bedroom. As we brushed out our hair, Dita commented, "Wow, Pian sure has a good hair care product. Our hair is thick and it has grown so! Look, our hair is nearly down to our ankles now. Impressive, though it is starting be become a bit of a nuisance being this long, dear."

"I know, but I still love it. You look stunning indeed. Say, our nails are also growing better than normal. Pian sure does have some fine products. I wonder if she invented them or if someone pointed them out to her."

"You like my talons?" Dita said coyly, as I looked at her five-inch nails and she, mine. We hugged, kissed, and hit the bed.

The next day, Ilenakova and Enrico led a band of fighters to see for themselves what was going on to the west. Phillipe, Fina, Tian, Bianca, and Louis accompanied her, along with a hundred of San Min's new soldiers, including four captains. With little else to do, Dita and I decided to go for a long walk, strengthening our feet. San Min had always been encouraging us to walk further and further so that they would become strong. Now we had the time and the space. Arm in arm, supporting each other, we shuffled off on our slow walk around the inner complex. First stop, the Royal Formal Gardens.

"I wish our feet were normal. I hate walking like this," Dita complained.

"I know, me too, but in this country, I think we need to fit in with the upper class for a time yet. Besides, remember what Long Yan says. Go slow and see more," I teased her. Once we got to the gardens, we never left it all morning! Such beauty was beyond words. By evening, our toes were quite sore, as you can well imagine. We had been walking on our toes all day long.

Over dinner, Ilenakova told us that indeed Nangumo's army had formed a long barrier line, blocking the western approach to Zau. If this Golden Warrior came to Zau, he'd surely encounter them. She intended to go monitor them again in the morning. She, as were all our Protectors, keenly interested in seeing this Golden Warrior in action personally. Their professional curiosity was roused.

San Min explained that most all were accepting the new form of government, and she was already getting the members of the High Council appointed and briefed. "It will be days before I get them all briefed, though. Jemma is invaluable! I may not let her ever leave," she teased. Jemma giggled.

"Say, I learned some more about this Golden Warrior today," San Min continued. We were all ears in an instant. She grinned, and went on, "It seems that he has become a hero to those towns and villages that he has passed through on his way here to Zau. The locals there all hate Nangumo with a passion! He's done just about everything imaginable to these people, from robbing them to stealing their young men for his army to stealing their maidens. You can see why they view this Golden Warrior as their hero. In fact, once he had cleared out a town, they ply him with all the food and drink he desires before he rides off to the next town."

"Looks like Nangumo has made the wrong man mad," Ilenakova commented dryly. "I want to meet this hero." So did us all. I had far too many unanswered questions that needed answers.

She giggled and went on, "Yes, he certainly has. I have a theory that Nangumo or his men stole this Lin Lu woman from this Golden Warrior, and he is trying to get her back. It's just that I can't explain how no one can harm him and how he can kill the soldiers he has."

We all agreed that this made perfect sense and might well be the motivation behind the carnage. I realized that we definitely needed to talk with this Golden Warrior fellow. Probably Nangumo never even bothered to learn the names of the young women that he and his men kidnaped. I began also to wonder what happened to them later on, that is, were they later murdered? As I said, lots of questions and no answers yet.

"Oh, everyone, I forgot to tell you. I am holding our first social dance here at our Imperial Meeting Hall on Friday night, three nights from now. At least a thousand of the most influential and wealthy men and women of Zau will attend this first dance. Each week after that, I will invite others to come to meet us as well. So keep all Friday nights open for the foreseeable future, please." This met with everyone's approval! Never mention dances to women — we love them!

The next mid-morning, Ilenakova sent Dita and me a telepathic message. *Mind Link to me, Bethany! The Golden Warrior is riding up to this wall of soldiers right now! Hurry!* Quickly, I did so, and she and I began to see what Ilenakova was also seeing. Essentially, we two were watching through Ilenakova's eyes.

A paved road came running through the low hills before the western edge of Zau. Farmsteads dotted the landscape, very picturesque. The overlord's soldiers were on foot and had arrayed themselves across the road forming a huge U-shape, covering nearly a quarter of a mile up the sides of the hills surrounding the roadbed. I could not count them, but took her word that several thousand well-armed men stood fully ready for combat. Each one was desirous of earning that ten thousand gold for killing the Golden Warrior.

About a mile distant from the army and slowly riding down the road was a lone man. The sunlight reflected off his helm. Yes, it looked golden in color, and even from this extreme distance, the protruding horns were discernable. Something sparkled around his waist, but the distance was too great to tell what that might be. The rider paused, surveying the army before him.

It's suicide to ride into this army! Bianca sent to Dita and me. *He'll probably turn around. If so, Ilenakova and we will ride after him and see if we can chat with him.*

None of us expected what happened next! The rider continued to move on down the road toward the soldiers, albeit slowly, as if he had nothing better to do and all the time in the world. Ambling might be a better way to put his motion. When he was about a quarter mile from the men blocking the road, he dismounted and tied his reins to a block of stone marking the edge of a farmer's field. He then began walking towards the center of the U-shape, straight down the road!

A deadly volley of arrows flew; some two thousand came at the man from three directions. He ignored them, as if he didn't even see them. As we watched, the arrows bounced off his body as if he were wearing impenetrable armor. In fact, he wore only simple peasant leather pants and shirt! But now we could see that he also wore a golden girdle around his waist; it shimmered in the sunlight. The army only shot that single volley of arrows. Many were quite dismayed that not one of the arrows had the slightest effect on the Golden Warrior.

The Golden Warrior walked closer to the front line and then spoke to those directly before him. "Where is Lin Lu?" A few said that they didn't know anyone by that name, though most said nothing but drew their various weapons instead. Right before our very eyes, thirty men closest to the Golden Warrior suddenly collapsed, dead! Their bodies just slumped to the ground. Incredible! We'd seen him do absolutely nothing!

Then, the massive army swarmed into him, hacking and swinging. Dozens of men attempted to pummel him from all directions. Again, he completely ignored all the sword blows, which did absolutely nothing to him! "Where is Lin Lu?" he asked once more. No one answered and another twenty men dropped dead on the ground!

How is this possible? Bianca fairly yelled telepathically.

What's he doing? How is he not being killed? Fina seemed to scream to us.

This is not possible, Ilenakova added, awestruck with what she was seeing. Admittedly, I could not believe what I was seeing either. Good old Dita was the first to make some sense of this.

Gang, look not with your eyes. See if you can sense some kind of energy flows coming from him. Probably from the helmet or the waist thing, Dita sent calmly to all of us, including Enrico, Louis, Phillipe, and Tian.

More and more men piled into the attack, swarming down from the hills totally surrounding the Golden Warrior. He had to raise his voice to be heard above all the shouting and screaming that the overlord's men made as they raced to smash this warrior to bits. "Where is Lin Lu?"

Again, dozens of men closest to the warrior dropped dead before him. This time, several of us saw an energy beam shoot out from the man's helmet! Dita and I spotted it and helped the others begin to perceive the beam, as the warrior continued to ask his solitary question of those around him before he eliminated them.

Seeing that weapons were useless, the soldiers took a new tactic. Dozens of them jumped on top of the warrior, trying to crush him to the ground! I counted at least twenty men piled up on top of or hanging on to him. Surely, they would be able to subdue him this way, I thought. To my utter amazement, he let out a bellow and rose up, tossing all twenty men off of him, and then asked his question. Getting no answer, those twenty then died at once! This man had the strength of some super giant!

Now the soldiers were trampling over their fallen comrades, as new arrivals joined the attack on the Golden Warrior. However, I suddenly spied a man wearing an expensive white linen suit sitting astride a very expensive horse whose saddle glittered with gold trim. He was atop the southern hill, from which his men had charged down to surround the warrior. I realized, as did the others, that this was probably Overlord Nangumo himself, come to watch his army destroy his unknown enemy. It made sense. What human could possibly withstand such a force as he had arrayed here before the city?

For a number of minutes, we watched the carnage before us, a small mountain of bodies rose from the roadbed, until at last the battle shifted to the south of the road, trampling a farmer's field, littering it with dead bodies as well. After perhaps ten minutes, half of the initial force was dead. Any ordinary army that had just lost half of their men in ten minutes of combat without inflicting a single wound on their single enemy would have routed, racing from the battlefield, trying to save themselves. As Ilenakova had witnessed earlier, these soldiers were emotionally similar to those of the invaders in the Steppes. Instead of routing or fleeing, they simply continued to throw themselves into the fray and died as well! Dita and I just could not believe what we were seeing!

Told you so, Ilenakova sent us all. *It's just what the Czar's men saw when they attacked.*

Now I detected that the Golden Warrior also spotted Overlord Nangumo astride his magnificent stallion atop the hill just to his right. As we watched, Overlord Nangumo finally realized that his mighty army was not going to stop this madman! He kicked and pulled on his horse's reins, but the horse could only spin around in place!

As I looked more closely at this weird behavior, I spotted what could only be described as some kind of a tractor beam emanating from the warrior's helmet keeping the horse from carrying Overlord Nangumo away from the battle! Now I knew what I was seeing, though I did not tell my friends just yet. Okay, it was a good guess on my part, but it needed verification before I would tell the others. I continued to watch the carnage unfold.

Twenty minutes since the start, the last soldier fell to the ground, quite dead. Only the panicking horse and rider remained alive. The Golden Warrior began walking slowly up the hill, and Overlord Nangumo dismounted and drew his dual, super-sharp blades, preparing to do battle with his enemy.

"Nangumo! At last! What have you done to Lin Lu? Where is she? If you tell me, I may spare your life," the Golden Warrior spoke loudly. We could heard his conversation from Ilenakova's vantage point. Considering the distance, he must have been yelling, I concluded. I sensed an immense anger in his voice, though I could not see his facial expression. He was too far away and his back was turned to us.

"I don't know who you are talking about!" Overlord Nangumo screamed back at him. "Who is she anyway? Why are you killing off my soldiers? Who are you? Some god?" Fear. Fear emanated from Nangumo, who made a last ditch attempt to understand what was and had been happening to him. Gone was his self-confidence, his ruthless disregard for others, his hostilities. Terror had come finally to Nangumo, a terror he never imagined possible. In a flash of insight, he realized that he was now experiencing what many of his victims had felt during his six years of conquest. "Why? Why are you doing his?" he added.

"Your men raided Mong Yu and took my Lin Lu away with them. Where is she now? Speak, butcher, if you want to live," the Golden Warrior screamed back at the shaking man. I noticed that the Golden Warrior's emotions were sinking rapidly. Was he giving up?

"They took many women. I don't know them all. I don't know anyone called Lin Lu. You have the wrong man. I swear I would tell you if I knew about her. Please, you have to believe me. I didn't do this, please," Nangumo's emotions dropped further down. A sickly sympathy reeked from the man as he begged for his life.

Interestingly, the Golden Warrior's emotions also continued to drop. "Your men took her. You have to know what they did with her! You are lying! Tell me! Tell me now," he pleaded with Nangumo, as if somehow he could pull the information from the shaking man.

"I don't know her. I'm telling you the truth," Nangumo answered. However, he now realized that he could not answer the Golden Warrior's question. He couldn't tell him what he didn't know. Had his men done this? Probably, they had taken many women over these past six years. He had no idea how many. Perhaps she was one of those. If so, she could be anywhere, but more likely she was dead by now. He also realized that he was dead as well. He sunk into hopelessness and then into utter apathy. His sword arm slumped uselessly to his side, the super-sharp sword fells to the ground, their points sticking in the soft earth of the farmer's field. He waited his doom.

"Please, you must know," the Golden Warrior begged, grief in his voice. Though we could not see his face, tears streamed down both cheeks.

"Please."

"I don't know her," Nangumo said very slowly. His voice sounded distant and hollow. "Was that really my voice?" he wondered.

The invisible energy flashed. Nangumo's body slumped to the ground, dead before it landed. The Golden Warrior sank to his knees, holding his face in his hands. We heard sobbing, even from this distance.

Ilenakova, slowly approach him and offer our and the Empress' assistance to him. Get him to come to the Imperial Palace with you. Make sure that you have your Grey Creature blaster turned on before you go to him, I sent her. This was a risky move, I know. He could easily lash out at her, and her body would have no chance to survive his energy blast. Yet, we had to make contact. I thought of using telepathy on him, but figured the helmet might prevent the contact or he might react badly to it. I took a gamble on with her, risking her life.

"Bethany wants me to speak to him; watch out everyone," Ilenakova ordered, while Bianca made sure that her blaster was set properly. Ilenakova didn't hold much faith in these alien weapons, but took it with her as I ordered. Slowly, she wound her way on foot through, around, and over the massive pile of dead soldiers. At last. she began to move up the hill towards the Golden Warrior. He was now on his knees. Crying! Now she heard him sobbing to himself, his head buried in his hands.

"Sir, sir, may I have a word with you?" she said softly. Even though she was a hardened fighter, she still felt some compassion towards this man. Not because he was a skilled fighter; no, he'd done it all using these strange items that he wore. Instinctively, the man reacted, sending a blast of the deadly energy at her, as if lashing out at the world in his grief. The Grey Creature's blaster activated with the huge power surge, releasing an arcing glow in a sphere ten feet centered on her, nearly stunning her in the process!

"Whoa! Wow! Now that was something!" Ilenakova exclaimed, totally startled. She recovered, "Sir, I mean you no harm. I and others want to help you, sir. Please, the new Empress San Min Wu wants to help you. Please, sir?" he begged.

Her tone was just above his. He looked up with tearful eyes at this light brown haired, blue-eyed fighter. "I'm sorry. It's all been for nothing. Empress? It's hopeless. I've failed Lin Lu."

"Sir, perhaps you have not yet failed. You are still alive. With our help and that of the Empress, perhaps together, we can find Lin Lu. Please, sir, will you come back to the Imperial Palace with us and let us all help you?" Ilenakova tried to sound as diplomatic and helpful as possible. *Men!* She thought. *Honestly! They all abandon quests at the first setback!* I caught her thought and chuckled at her point of view.

"The Empress? She will help me?" he asked pitifully.

"I am sure that we and she will do everything possible to help you find Lin Lu. Please, will you come with us back to the Imperial Palace and meet with us and the Empress?"

"Well, there is no more hope really," his apathy now came through loud and clear. "Okay," he sighed. "I will come with you. There is nothing else that I can do now." He rose, and Ilenakova saw that she was about two inches taller than this Golden Warrior. While he had strong arm muscles, she saw that her legs were far more muscular than his. He was definitely not a fighter by training. Blacksmith? She conjectured. She pointed to his horse, and slowly he walked to his mare. Ilenakova hurried back to the others as quickly as possible. The pile of dead was quite an obstacle.

"Okay, he's coming with us to the palace. Soldiers, your job is to search the dead, confiscate anything that we can use. Bury them somehow and bring the goods back to the palace. I will send out some more men as soon as we get there," Ilenakova ordered. Bianca grinned; she liked seeing a woman giving orders to all the male soldiers, but she didn't comment. She held the reins for Ilenakova to mount.

Silently, the Golden Warrior followed our small group through the densely packed streets of Zau. Many stood and stared at this legend riding through their streets, though none said a word for fear of upsetting this emissary of death. An hour later, the small group rode into the Imperial Palace complex and on into the inner palace. Empress San Min Wu, Dita, and I, along with Jemma and several others stood just outside the doors waiting for them. We got our first good look at this Golden Warrior.

He was a young lad of seventeen at most. His upper body was physically strong, suggesting a blacksmith. His clothes were those of a poor rural villager. Still, his golden helmet and girdle dominated his appearance. As he walked up to her, his eyes finally focused on the Empress, and he appeared somewhat in awe of her.

"Welcome, Golden Warrior. I am Empress San Min Wu," she said, offering her hand, though she had no notion if the lad would know what he was to do. He didn't, but took it and gently shook her hand. He did bow, but with the helmet, he looked more like some court jester. "What is your name and where is your village?" she asked.

"I am Shi Do from Mong Yu, your highness." He said no more than what was asked; his apathy was still apparent.

"These are my dear friends from the Outer Lands," San Min continued the introductions. One by one, we were all made known to Shi. "Shi, it is lunch time. Would you care to dine with us and tell us your story? I am pledged to do all that I can to help you." He nodded and we three began our terribly slow, tiny step shuffle inside the palace. It seemed like forever for us to cross the spacious throne room and down the hall to the dining room. Inside, our small party was dwarfed in the enormous room. Once seated, servants brought in our lunch.

Shi ate as if he had not eaten for some days. Finally, San Min asked, "Okay, Shi. Please tell us all about your situation. Start at the very beginning so that we can better understand what must be done."

"It is hard for me to focus. It's this helmet and girdle. They are affecting me somehow. I cannot get them off me. Now that I have failed, I no longer need to wear them, but they are impossible to take off," Shi said fearfully.

"Okay, Bethany, I think this is yours to handle," San Min quickly pushed this problem off onto me. I grinned.

"Shi, how did you get them on your body?" I asked for starters.

"I just put the helmet on and fastened the girdle around my waist, but now they cannot come off. I have given up trying," he said apathetically.

I shuffled to his side and tried to gently lift the helmet off his head. It didn't budge, not even a fraction! Weird! I examined the girdle, but saw no means of unfastening it. It was as if the girdle had been formed around his waist in one piece. "Okay gang. This is weird. Little help," I asked. Bianca, Fina, Jemma, Dita, and Ilenakova came over to us and began examining the two items as well.

"Weird is right!" Bianca exclaimed as she tried to lift the helmet off his head. "It's like glued to his head or something."

We spent a frustrating ten minutes examining every inch of the two artifacts. We all knew these were alien devices. Oh what I would have given to have had Enyo, that is, Dianna, here now! Our resident engineer would find a way. Frustrated, I finally made contact with Dianna. *Help! We have the Golden Warrior here with us now. We need your help with these two alien devices. They can't seem to be taken off him. Can you lend us a hand?*

She giggled. *Okay. You will have to take me to him. I'm not any good moving around the world without my body in tow.* I latched on to her and together we moved above Shi's head.

Fascinating! Incredible find! Interesting! Yes, alien device. Bethany, you just **must** *bring this back for me to study! Promise me that you will do so!* Dianna was highly excited over this find, as I knew that she would be.

Okay. If it is possible, I will bring them to you when we return. Now can you find any way of removing them safely from Shi's head and waist?

Well, let me see. Dianna studied the helmet for several minutes. *Ah ha.* Yes, it is quite clear. Bethany, see these two pressure points here? While my body's eyes saw nothing, I, using spiritual being's perceptions did see them. They were quite plainly visible this way. *Just press both at once, and the helmet will likely be removable.* I allowed her the honor of pressing them and had Dita gently try lifting the helmet. It came off his head much like a simple hat would.

Around us, cheers broke out. "Thank you! Thank you!" relief flooded over Shi Do.

A bit later, Dianna pressed another pair of pressure points, and the girdle opened up and became very loose. Shi quickly took it off as if it were somehow poisonous! While Shi kept saying thank you over and over, I said,

"Dianna here did it. Hang on a second while I take her back home." While I was so occupied, Dita explained to the others, especially San Min and Shi, what I had done, namely brought our resident engineer and expert in alien devices here from Velona. They accepted it better when she mentioned kijutsu powers, however.

Since Dianna wanted to hear all about this man and the devices, I Mind Linked her to me, once I returned to the dining room. Quietly, I picked up the two devices and kept them by me under the table and out of sight.

"Thank you! I feel so much lighter now. My head's not so confused anymore. I think they were somehow taking over control of me somehow," Shi explained.

"I'm glad that you are doing better," San Min replied. "Please, can you tell us all about what has happened to you?"

"Last year, Lin Lu and I were about to be married. We've been in love with each other since we were children. She is a great artist too. I am our village's blacksmith. A week before our wedding day, Overlord Nangumo's men came to Mong Yu. We only have about five hundred people in our village. It is the last village before the Helios Grande Mountains, though there are a few mines further up the steep sided valley. Anyway, the soldiers came while I was out relaying a message to her parents in their fields. I raced back to the village, but I was not in time. My best friend, Waygon, was attacked and the butchers cut off his hand. I had to save him, and by the time that I had him stabilized, Lin Lu had been taken off by his soldiers. My Lin Lu," he mused.

"She has pure skin, long fingers, blue eyes, and most of all she has thick, long black hair. She is the love of my life. And now, she is gone from me," he cried again and we allowed him time to recover.

"Waygon and I decided to go after her and rescue her from Nangumo. However, no one has any weapons in Mong Yu. Waygon had visions in his mind of strange creatures with strange weapons. They lived high in the Helios Grande and he thought that he could find their home. Without any other options, he and I set out to see if his visions were true and if we could find some weapons that we could use to fight back and rescue Lin Lu."

He went on to describe how they had found this cavern complex full of alien things. They took the helmet, girdle, and hand thing from there. On their way back, the two discovered some of how they worked. Shi pulled out the hand held device, which shattered rocks into gravel. "With only the one hand, Waygon decided that he would only be a hindrance to me and so he gave me this device. I haven't used it because it turns a body into thousands of bloody bits, a real mess. The girdle gives me strength enough to lift huge boulders and toss them as if they were pebbles. The helm is another matter. Over time, it slowly seemed to speak to me, telling me how to use its powers. I can think a thought and it will somehow kill those that I intend to slay."

"All last fall, all winter, and now all spring, I have been systematically visiting all the towns and villages in our valley system, looking for any soldiers who might know where they took Lin Lu. After all this time and all those that I have questioned, the only thing that I know for sure is that some villagers saw Lin Lu on a wagon with other women passing through the village down from ours. After that, no one has seen her, not even Nangumo himself. I guess I have lost her forever," he sighed and looked pitiful.

Long Yan spoke for the first time. "I am Long Yan, you and I have much in common. San Min is my wife now." He launched into his own lengthy tale of his five-year search to find San Min. His tale definitely made an impression on Shi!

"Is it possible that you, Bethany, could find my Lin Lu? I will do anything for you if you can help me find her and get her back from those evil men," Shi pleaded. For the first time, I detected a trace of real hope in Shi's voice.

"Of course, Shi. My friends and I will do what we can to find her for you. After we have found her, in return, I would like you to allow us to keep these three alien devices and to have you show us this cavern in the mountains," I replied, striking the bargain that I had to have. Under no circumstances could I allow these devices and any others that might be found in that cavern to fall into any other hands. Honestly, the carnage Shi had inflicted during this past three-quarters of a year was unbelievable, putting it mildly.

"Keep them now. I have no need for them. No soldiers know what happened to my Lin Lu. I am a blacksmith, not a fighter. Yes, I can take you there. If I should die, go to Mong Yu and ask for Waygon. He can take you there too," Shi agreed.

"Deal. Now the first thing that we need is to know what Lin Lu looks like. With your permission, Shi, I will use my kijutsu powers to join with your mind and my friends. All you need to do is to remember how Lin Lu looked when you last saw her and we will all be seeing what you see. That way, we all will know what she looks like. Okay?"

Shi was awestruck. Someone was using real kijutsu powers on him! He readily agreed, and momentarily we all had a good look at his bride to be. I thought that she was rather pretty too. I also saw her artistic arrangement of her family's produce at their open air market, just before he kissed her goodbye. Lin Lu was also an artist, I suspected. I thanked him.

San Min then took him to a guest bedroom, where he could rest up. Along the way, she showed him the bathroom, insisting that he bathe first. She also saw that he received some new, clean clothes. Meanwhile, I took our group aside and began discussing how we could go about finding out what happened to Lin Lu.

We quickly realized that Shi had already eliminated all the personae that might have known or had some data about the abductions. "Hey, how about questioning his Second, Gao Din?" Dita asked. "Besides, someone ought to inform him that he is now the overlord." I agreed and we sent messengers out to find him and request his presence here at the palace.

"Look, we know nothing at all about the nefarious dealings of Nangumo," Bianca pointed out. "Anyone of a million things could have gone on, from taking her into his own home as a sex slave to outright murdering of her. We need more information, to say the least." Quickly, we all reached the same conclusion. We would have to wait for Gao, basing our hopes on what he might have to say.

Two hours later, a breathless and worried Gao Din came hastily into the palace. He was escorted to us in the dining room. "I came at once," he said worriedly. Lines of concern wrinkled his face. I knew that I had to put him at ease or we would get nothing useful from him.

"Gao, as you may have heard this morning, Overlord Nangumo was killed by the Golden Warrior," I began.

"Please, you must protect me from him!" Gao exclaimed. I saw at once that this was his primary concern.

"You may rest assured that the Golden Warrior will not be coming after you. You are safe; I give you my word and that of the Empress. Gao, but we need some information. By the way, you are now the Overlord taking Nangumo's place. San Min has so declared it. Congratulations."

"That is good news. Please thank the Empress for her generosity. I will fully support her in all ways," Gao quickly began to propitiate to us. I put a halt to that.

"Now then, we know that Nangumo had his soldiers raid villages and kidnap young men and some young women," I began.

"Yes, he forced the men to become his soldiers. He stationed the new recruits in towns and villages far from their homes so that they could not easily desert. Why?"

"Well, we are interested in the women that he abducted. What did he do with them? Were there many of them?" I asked.

Gao looked embarrassed, so I added, "I presume that he wanted to use them as sexual toys."

"Well, yes, yes he did. He took several to his home and forced them to become his servants as well. None of them is this Lin Lu that the Golden Warrior was asking about. I asked them all about that. None of them have ever heard of her. Why?"

"Thanks. That was wise of you to inquire. Now then, his men obviously kidnaped far more women than the few that Nangumo kept at his home. Where did those others go? What was the pattern that his soldiers followed when they kidnaped young women?"

"Oh I see what you want to know. Yes, well, their standing orders were to kidnap any women that they saw as particularly pretty."

"Makes sense. Then what were they to do with them?" I continued to press the issue. Gao squirmed, uncomfortable about talking openly to other women about such matters.

"Well, if they found them to be to their liking, they were to send them on up the lines," he answered.

"So those who kidnaped the women would try to rape them first," I stated flatly.

Gao squirmed even more. "Well, yes."

"And then what?"

"The ones found acceptable were delivered to the section captains," he answered. I nodded and he went on. "They tried them out next. If they passed inspection, the captains then sent the women on to Nangumo."

"Okay. What happened to those that the captains didn't find acceptable? What happened to the women who didn't please their original kidnapers?" I pressed him for what I thought may be the most critical information.

Gao squirmed even more. "Well, some were killed. I know that for a fact, but really, the individuals could do pretty much whatever they desired with those who were not going to be passed on up the lines."

"Does that mean most all were murdered?" Dita asked pointedly.

"Well, not really. There are other ways to get rid of an unwilling woman," Gao whispered. He was becoming more and more ill at ease with this discussion.

"Such as?" Dita asked directly.

"Well, there are those who would pay for them, if that's what you mean," Gao answered her.

"So the women who were not to be sent up the lines, were sold into slavery?" I pressed him.

"Often," he said quietly.

"Okay. We need a list of the men who would traffic in such women. Names and towns where we can find them," I ordered. "Make sure it is complete and then you can go. Thanks for being honest with us." I wanted him to feel relieved that this ordeal was over as soon as he wrote out the list for us. That way, he would be more likely to give us the complete list. A half hour later, he hastily left us.

"Well, now we are getting somewhere," Dita stated. "Undoubtedly, Lin Lu fought back against these lecherous men. Conclusion, they found her undesirable and got rid of her. The question is: did they murder her and bury her body somewhere or did they sell her to someone else?"

"This list has fifty names on it," Bianca mused.

"We need a map. Where are all these places?" asked Jemma.

A bit later, Ilenakova returned with a detailed map of Wontun Province. We highlighted the three valley systems that Nangumo controlled. Next, we put a red dot on Mong Yu. It was very close to the Helios Grande Mountains, far to the west of Zau, at least six hundred miles or more. Fina then placed pins in the towns in which these flesh traders dwelled. We had dots all over the three valleys.

"Gang, look. I think that we can initially rule out some of these. First, the adjacent valleys we can ignore. Gao said that the women first had to please their kidnapers. Lin Lu probably didn't. Even if she did, she certainly didn't please the captains, because they didn't send her on up to Nangumo. He had his army organized, so his captains could not be too far from the regiments under their command. Hence, let's rule out for now the adjacent valley systems. Further, we can rule out those places close to Zau. Mong Yu is a very long way from Zau. I think we can concentrate our efforts to say the first hundred miles from Mong Yu. It's unlikely that the captain in charge of the raiders of Mong Yu were stationed close to Zau."

The others liked my analysis thus far. We only had ten names on the list and eight towns or villages to search. Now we focused on the how of our quest.

"Well, we just cannot walk up to these slave trader fellows and ask them if they have bought Lin Lu!" Bianca pointed out the obvious.

"We can't just go nosing around their places of business looking for her either," Dita pointed out. "We did that with San Min and look where that got us."

"If we take enough force with us, we could force our way inside," Ilenakova declared. I knew that she would do just that!

Jemma giggled, "You need a Judger with you. Look gang, here's what you do. Have the Empress write out an official proclamation demanding a full and complete inspection of all such premises and personnel. That will give you total access to their site and women or they face Imperial repercussions."

"Duh!" I exclaimed and we all roared with laughter. Jemma volunteered to get it drafted and signed by San Min for us, leaving us to comment on her brilliant idea.

"Okay, now that we can get in, where do we start?" Dita asked.

"You know, optimally, we know that she was abducted around noon. We know she was transported via a wagon and can estimate travel speeds and distances. We also know that she was seen passing through the third village from Mong Yu and that there is only one road at that end of the valley. Ideally, we ought to start at that village and work our way towards Zau," I pointed out.

"Makes sense, dear," Dita added. "The soldiers need meals and a place to stay at night. I bet that they do not camp out of doors, not when inns and hot meals are not far away. I wager that they spent nights in the villages and towns along the way, probably robbing or extorting their stay from the various inns."

"Cool, mom. We should check with the various innkeepers as well. I bet that they can give us even better information on the kidnaped women

380

than the random soldiers that Shi questioned," Bianca added.

"We should start at the village of Luchuan, where she was last seen and head towards this next dot on the map, Zhenjing," Fina pointed out. "Are we going by horseback or by carriage?" She looked at Dita and me, wondering if we were still able to ride.

"Well, I'd like to ride," I answered her, "but Dita and I are supposed to be what they call 'great ladies' or 'important women.' So perhaps it would appear more acceptable if we two went by carriage while the rest of you rode horses. What do you all think? I'm sure that Dita and I could ride well enough. Our feet are just small that's all, but if we rode, we couldn't wear these 'important women' type of dresses or heels."

"Well, if you ask me, it may be wise to have two 'great, important ladies' along with us," Bianca replied. "That will add credence to the official proclamation. Besides, if we do find her, there is no telling what condition she will be in, and if we have a carriage, we can more easily transport her back here."

"Okay carriage for us it is. When should we leave?" I asked.

"How about on Saturday?" Bianca grinned. "Mom, Louis and I really want to go to this first fancy dance." From their faces, everyone wanted to attend this first dance on Friday night. We agreed on the date, and I set the others to begin making needed preparations.

Over supper, Empress San Min handed us the official proclamation. "I added a bit to it. Jemma and I were thinking that some of these places might be considered pleasure palaces. If so, we should also verify that the women are being paid an honest wage and that the owners are actually putting the women's funds into bank accounts. Remember how Yuen Ming cheated all of us zen-kami. This will give us a chance to verify that they are not cheating their women. If it works out, I will have others visit all the pleasure palaces in Tashien, verifying the same. If an owner is cheating his women employees, he'll be arrested and charged with crimes."

"Brilliant, San Min, brilliant," I exclaimed. Dita grinned; she was in full agreement with this idea too. She also insisted in sending along Captain Hei Michou and six of her new soldiers with us. Her idea was to make our expedition appear more formal, more Imperial in nature.

Friday night came. We dressed up in our finest, as expected of us, because tonight we were to be announced as her Imperial Advisors. Arm in arm, Dita and I entered the spacious Royal Dance Hall, as the meeting hall was renamed on these occasions. A band of two dozen musicians was already on their raised platform, warming up. Empress San Min and Emperor Lang had already organized their welcoming line. Jemma and Phillipe stood next to them; this was Jemma's grand idea: to welcome all the guests personally. San Min intended to do everything possible to endure a swift end to the chaos of the last six years. By making each of these influential and important people feel personally welcome, she hoped to gain their favor and backing.

"You stand after Jemma and Phillipe," San Min requested. The rest of our group soon entered and were asked to extend the welcoming line. Around six-thirty, the guests began arriving. For an hour, I watched elegantly dressed women of all ages, hanging on to the arm of their husbands or fiancés, shuffling into the hall; they had similar small feet as we. As we were introduced, the men never failed to bow deeply and kiss our offered hands. Likewise, the women took our hands in theirs. I've never seen so many long red nails before in my life. None of these women had nails shorter than three inches, unless one had broken. When the dance began at last, the room held twelve hundred women and as many men. Dita and I were astounded. Twelve hundred women had small feet and were forced to shuffle along as we did. Finally, I realized that this really was a custom in this land. Small feet and long nails denoted women of what one could call the upper class, the women of power and influence.

San Min and Jemma were elated when the dance began. They'd received thousands of compliments over their novel personal greeting of the guests. Evidently, this had never been done before and the men and women thought very highly of this gesture. She now was optimistic that the new methods of rule that she and the others were instigating would be accepted and would end the continual petty fighting among overlords and others.

For us, the actual dance was more than just fun. Dita and I lost count of the compliments that we received for our appearance. Both men and women loved our extremely long hair. We received several hundred spontaneous compliments for having our feet made small. "I am so impressed that you Velona women would have your feet made small to honor our ancient customs. Such consideration for our ways is so impressive." Variations on this theme came our way all night long, as we moved from dance partners to partners.

Dita was more impressed with the hundred offers that we received to come and visit their art galleries, their music recitals, pleasure palaces, and their wide variety of stores and salons. In a way, she and I regretted that we had to leave in the morning. However, we both promised to take them up on their offers once we returned from this next assignment. In fact, Dita began making a list of just what we needed to visit when we got back. By the end of the evening, she had well over one hundred places or events that we just had to attend. I was particularly interested in the rare bookshop that she had on her list, as well as the factory that made these silky, thin hose that felt wonderful to wear.

"Let's find this Lin Lu quickly so we can get back here and visit some of these places," Dita teased me.

Chapter 30 The Search for Lin Lu

Our carriage was loaded with spare clothes and gear of our party, leaving enough room for we two. Phillipe and Jemma gave us all farewell hugs as did San Min and Long. Ilenakova and Captain Hei Michou took the lead, with Bianca and Louis behind her. Enrico and Shi Do shared the duty of driving our carriage, with Fina and Tian riding behind us. The six other solders brought up the rear. We all wore official emerald green sashes, denoting that we were official Imperial Messengers. Dita and I were in charge of the maps and the coin box. San Min sent along enough funds for our expenses and then some.

We had a little over six hundred miles to travel to get to the last known sighting of Lin Lu in the town of Zhenjing, located near the start of the Jan River that flowed down into the mighty Yonshu River draining into the ocean in Shansee. Dita and my job was to plan our trip. We needed to end up at a town or village inn each evening. We had to calculate each day's travel to maximize the distance traveled and yet still have a place to stay that evening. Fortunately for us, Tashien is heavily populated, especially here in the bread bowl portion of the country. Towns and villages were between five and eight miles apart, especially paralleling the Jan River, which had its origin in the Helios Grande Mountains not far from Mong Yu, Shi's home village.

We were able to make about twenty-five miles each day, requiring twenty-four days to reach our destination, Zhenjing. Of course, we would then be backtracking the very towns we'd just passed through, looking for traces of Lin Lu. I estimated that we would get there by May 25.

Ah, spring weather! The days were pleasantly warm, often sunny. A multitude of delightful fragrances drifted through our carriage windows, pricking our senses and interest. We passed by fields which held hundreds of beehives, the honey district. The dairy district was obvious. Cows dotted the green pastures by the hundreds and several towns boasted the name of "Cheese Capitol." Of course, we had to sample the many varieties that the inn had on their menus. As the valley ridges far to the south and north grew more prominent, we spotted horse ranches, replacing the dairy region. Farther on, we entered groves of mulberry trees, where they raised the silk worms and harvested the silk from which their elegant apparel was made by hand. Dita and I promised to stop and visit one of these larger silk producers on our return trip. She wanted to see how they made such fine silk hose that we both loved to wear.

As the land grew rockier and the razor ridges more pronounced, we spotted numerous mines and smelters dotting the distant landscape. Indeed, the rising smoke marked the location of a smelter, even though we could not actually see it. I began to see why this central province was the heart of Tashien. While the wetlands of the far south by Shansee produced vast quantities of rice, one of their staple foods, this middle province yielded vast quantities of so many varied and necessary products. This Wontun Province was by far the wealthiest of all, rich in a vast array of products. True, the next province north of us, Linyi, produced far more gold and gems, but the climate was colder there. Here, the temperatures were nearly ideal, as was the rainfall. I no longer questioned why Zau was the Imperial City of Tashien.

Yes, it was an enjoyable three and a half weeks of travel. Dita claimed it was more of a holiday than a work trip. Several times, we both took a break and rode horses for part of the day, breaking the monotony. Overall, our group had a most pleasant trip to Zhenjing. Not so, after that. On May 25, 756, we arrived at the small town, and now began our search for Lin Lu.

We checked in at the inn where Shi Do had learned that Lin Lu had passed through this town. He'd never been able to pick up her abductor's trail from this town. Hence, here was our starting point. My first action was to chat with all the inn's staff. I needed to get a feel for how the kidnapers dealt with the transporting of their prisoners. While the innkeeper retold us what he could remember telling Shi Do nearly six months ago, I decided to chat with some of his maids.

It took a bit of skill, but I got them to remember and talk about what they had seen. Their male prisoners were kept chained in the stables along with their horses and wagons. One young woman had taken them down a bucket full of table scraps, which they ate greedily. One maid recalled overhearing the band's leader arguing with some of the women. Evidently, they had brought the women into the inn and to their bedrooms. They were chained and marched inside up to the rooms. One maid thought that the leader tried to make the women have intercourse with him. She'd overheard, "It'll go easier for you if you consent and be docile pleasure-givers." She had also heard the women screaming and a bit later saw the leader exiting the room, cursing and holding his groin. She guessed that one of the women had kicked him where it hurt. The group had left right after an early breakfast. She also noted that the women's clothing were ripped and torn that morning, lending credence to the leader's attempted assaults on them the night before.

After breakfast the next day, we headed back down the road to the next town. Since there were no other roads here, surely the raiders had gone this way. Dita and I began speculating as we rode along. "The real question, love, is what would they do to the women who did not go along with their sexual desires?" Dita pointed out. "As a man, I can say that first they would probably beat the women into submission."

"That would seem to be the case here. She did say their clothes were torn and ripped the next day," I concurred.

"Precisely. Now we couple this with why the women were abducted in the first place, and we can make more suppositions," Dita continued her line of thought. "Ultimately, the best of these women were being sent to the Overlord. Okay, we know that they only abducted pretty women, so we don't have to deal with unattractive women. That means, each of these women were reasonable possibilities, based on looks alone. Next, we throw in their willingness, temperament, and personality. Some may well succumb and do as they desire, hoping to somehow stay alive and perhaps later escape or whatever. From what Shi says of Lin Lu, she definitely would not have been the type to succumb, lie down, and take it. My guess is that she attempted to fight back anyway that she could."

"Ah," I began to see where Dita was headed, "so we need to see what they did to further convince them, and what they did to those whom they could not force to their will."

"Precisely, love. What do they do to them next? Well, I would suggest that they likely would try to beat them, rough them up a bit. However, they would not dare to hurt them physically, because then they would be valueless to the Overlord. Okay, supposing that Lin Lu was beaten and still didn't give in to their demands? That is the thread that I am considering, Bethany. She doesn't give in, so now what do they do with her? Likely many other women also didn't give in to their demands. They must have a routine method by which they handled that situation. Surely, it occurred frequently."

"You think that they outright killed those who refused to cooperate?" I asked, thinking we may be looking for a burial site.

Dita twisted her long hair between her long nails, deep in thought. At last, she said, "You know, that could be a possibility. However, I am putting myself in their position, the abductors. They've just kidnaped a bunch of women, ferried them miles from their villages, fed them, even tried to force them to their will, which ultimately failed. Kill them? Well, yes, but these are greedy men, men used to taking what they want, not losing things. I bet anything that if they had a woman that they could not coerce into going along with their needs, then they would try to somehow make a profit off her anyway."

"What do you mean by make a profit? Sell her?" I asked, trying to duplicate her thinking.

"We know that every town has some form of prostitution ring and many sport pleasure houses with the kami style women. I suspect that we need to look into these places to see if the raiders sometimes sold recalcitrant women to these men. While I don't see how they could make a kami out of an unwilling woman, Yuen Ming made unwilling women into his zen-kami. I'm sorry that I don't know much about how prostitution rings operate, love. Yet, it would seem to me that if the pimp left the woman walk the streets looking johns, there would be nothing to keep her from leaving town and heading back toward home. I know that if in such a situation, I certainly would just walk away. Even without money, I'm sure that I could find a way to get back home somehow."

"Point taken, Dita. We ought to look for grave sites and places where zen-kami may be found," I concluded.

"And any slave traders, if such exist," she added. We told the others of our conclusions and plans.

As we rode along the road, Ilenakova now had the six soldiers accompanying us fan out on either side of the road. Their job was to look for signs of gravesites, where the abductors may have buried those they killed. During the day, we passed through several small villages. None of these seemed hopeful places where women could have been sold into slavery. None had any kind of pleasure palaces and we saw no kami plying their trade either.

Ahead, we spied the town where we would spend this night. A mile from the town, we halted. Ilenakova called back, "He found a possible grave site." We climbed out and shuffled our way towards the others, who had dismounted and were making their way off between some low shrub brush. Enrico saw our plight, walking on your toes is intensely tricky on uneven, sloping ground.

"Allow me, Great Ladies," he teased and slid his arms around each of us, supporting and helping us keep our balance. He knew how much we wanted to see the discovery. We joined the others as they surveyed what appeared to be disturbed ground.

"Is she buried here?" wailed Shi, becoming distraught.

"Well, we have no choice but to find out," Ilenakova replied. "It looks rather shallow. Guys, please dig it up a bit." She relished giving this task to the soldiers, who snickered at her as a result. "Well, you guys have all the muscles," she teased them back. Everyone chuckled; her muscles were every bit as large as theirs were. A bit later, the two diggers revealed the corpse of a young boy and quickly covered him back up. We could tell it was a young boy primarily from his clothing. Shi was greatly relieved. A few minutes later, we entered the town of Dalong, whose population was over a thousand, so far the largest town from Shi's village of Mong Yu.

We stayed at the inn where we had stayed just a couple days before. Now we had specific questions to ask. The raider's trail led us here, for most likely they had stopped here on their way towards Zau. After checking with the innkeeper and staff, we gained no clues. None had any clear recollection of the raiders staying here some six months ago or more. True, the raiders had stayed here, but one time rather blended in with all the other times. No one had any real information. Dita then asked the innkeeper if there were any pleasure palaces in town. Surprisingly, there was the Golden Bee.

After dinner, we all headed off to visit the Golden Bee. In stark contrast to the Purple Palace, this place was a converted home, exceedingly small. We spotted only two kami on the street drumming up business. Neither was Lin Lu nor had they seen anyone like her. Inside, the proprietor, Peng Ho, cursed and grumbled as he read the Empress' proclamation that allowed us to ask him all the questions we desired, to search his place, and examine his pay records.

"What is this all about anyway?" Peng demanded to know. He was fifty and thin. His eyes flickered from person to person. "You going to disrupt my business tonight?"

"Not at all, Peng. Do you have any zen-kami working for you?" I asked outright.

"You crazy lady?" he asked in disbelief. "Look, Dalong is a small town. No one here could afford the services of such a Great One. I don't think any of us here has ever even seen a zen-kami. Okay, go ahead and search the place, only don't disrupt my few customers or intimidate them. Bad for business," he pleaded.

The main room held a group of local musicians. A dozen people were relaxing on soft divans, listening, absorbed in the enchanting sounds. The upstairs we found Peng's own bedroom and a large dining room, where six couples were dining in a romantic candlelight setting. His wife did the cooking and the serving as well. One of the kami, we learned, was his daughter. While we were checking out his establishment, Ilenakova chatted with the two kami and found that they were indeed paid nicely each week. Nothing was amiss here.

Once everything checked out, I paid him five gold so we could enjoy the pleasures of his palace — well, listen to the music really. This, everyone thoroughly enjoyed! As the evening wore on and Peng saw that he was making a tidy profit on us, he relaxed and became far friendlier. During an intermission while we were taking tea in the dining room, I explained what we were looking for, "You see, about six months ago, last fall, Overlord Nangumo's raiders struck Mong Yu and kidnaped a young woman, Lin Lu. We are trying to find her. She probably put up a whole lot of resistance to those men, who were attempting to force her to become a prostitute."

"Well, that's funny," Peng said cautiously. "Last fall, there was a man come by here — wanting to sell me two women real cheap. I told him that I don't buy women."

"What did he do after that?" I asked, becoming very alert, as did my companions.

"He asked me if I knew anyone around these parts who might be interested in buying some young, pretty women. So I says, 'You might try old Fung Su down in Gaikou.' Runs the Purple House there. If you're looking for a zen-kami, I hear old Fung has one. Also heard it costs five hundred a night for her services, mighty darn expensive, if you ask me. A kami is just fine for us rural folks."

"Thanks, that is a big help. Say, there isn't any place else between here and Gaikou where this raider could have sold those women?" I asked. Gaikou was a city really some seventy miles from here, several day's travel. Did we dare just head there? Might we miss some other clue along the way?

"Nah, only towns between here and there have an establishment like the Golden Bee. No, if he wanted to unload those young women, Gaikou would be the first place he might find someone interested," Peng replied. He seemed to be telling the truth and we accepted his data.

Back in our rooms later that evening, we discussed this new information. "We should be methodical," Ilenakova declared. "You know, search for more graves along the way. Check these other palaces. Perhaps one of them decided to buy the women and make their own zen-kami."

"Yes, but if they did so, no one could really afford the services of the zen-kami. Five hundred is the lowest price that I've heard for these women's services. I doubt that many locals could possibly afford such an expense," I countered.

"But we don't want to be backtracking all the time," she argued, and in the end, she won. We spent the next three days meandering back along the road from Zau, checking on the pleasure houses and looking for more graves. While we found one more grave, it too yielded a young man. Shi found this somewhat encouraging. At least she had not been killed thus far.

With a population of one hundred thousand, Gaikou was a sprawling city on the banks of the Jan River. A hub for local transportation of farmers produce, roads veered off to the north and south as well. We pulled in around noon and took rooms at the same inn that we had stayed in on our way to Zhenjing. After lunch and obtaining directions for this Purple House, our group headed off to search it. Although it was a mile from our inn, the day was warm and sunny, perfect for a walk. I know that the others became frustrated at the snail's pace that Dita and I forced upon them. Yet we shuffled along as rapidly as we dared. "Slow down and enjoy the day," Dita exclaimed contentiously. Bianca and Louis did just that, sneaking a few kisses behind our backs. Fina giggled and followed suit with Tian.

As we shuffled along, we received plenty of notice from other men and women, who paused to watch us walk. We also spied at least a dozen other small-footed women shuffling along the streets. Many carried shopping bags, some visiting the open-air markets. They too were closely observed by others as well. I realized that they saw us as Great Ladies, important women, influential if not wealthy women as well. Again, we were all reminded once more that in this society, women hobbled with small feet were looked upon as being of the highest social status.

Two blocks from the Purple House, we began to see kami walking the streets. Soon several came up to our group and began making discrete inquires of us. "Pleasure, Great Ladies?" one young woman asked.

"Not just now. Say, you work for Fung Su, correct?" I asked and she nodded. "Are you being well paid for your work? The Empress has sent us out to check on all the pleasure palaces to make sure the kami and zen-kami are being properly paid for their work. Down in Shansee, we discovered that the owner was not actually paying his women." She was barely twenty years old, if that, but very pretty.

"Oh yes, Fung Su pays very well. In fact, at home, I have now almost saved up enough to afford to get small feet myself! When I do, I will be looked upon as a Great Lady too, and I will be able to make even more money than I do now. Just ask Ai Bi." She chatted on, happy to share her good fortune with us.

Within the block of the palace, we found Ai Bi. To my surprise, she too had small feet like us and was shuffling very carefully along the street. With her arms tied in the typical kami fashion, she had to very carefully watch her steps, and I noticed that she took even smaller steps than we did. "Pleasure, Great Ladies? Ai Bi gives great pleasure to Great Ladies like herself," she asked us eagerly.

After a similar reply and questions, she related, "Oh yes, I am making almost twice what Cai makes, that's the woman you were talking to just now. She and I are good friends. Cai knows what I make each week. It is twice what she earns. I think that she will be able to afford getting small feet very soon now. Please, after you are finished with your work here, please allow me to pleasure such Great Ladies," she begged. I told her that we would consider it and we headed to the main doors.

As expected, two martial arts bouncers, well dressed however, stood beside the doors, keeping an eye on the many kami working the streets. As we approached, they bowed and opened the doors for us. Once inside, Dita and I found quite a lot of similarities between this place and the Purple Palace. This time, we showed the manager the Empress' proclamation and he quickly sent for the owner Fung Su. He was in his mid-forties, immaculately well dressed, sporting a long goatee and curled moustache.

"How may I help such Great Ladies?" he asked, noticing our feet, hair, and nails. I felt like some horse whose conformation was being examined. I showed him our orders from San Min and he seemed a little confused and bothered.

"But we have never been inspected. What is going on here? Why now?" he asked. Dita gave him our pat explanation.

"First, we need to see all of your kami and verify that they are actually being paid for their work," I explained.

"Well, that is obvious! Just ask them. Paydays are Monday mornings. In fact, three of my kami have earned enough to afford to get small feet themselves! Cai will be getting them too within a month, I expect. My kami are very well paid. Have you seen just how beautiful they are? Good wages attracts only the finest," he boasted. From what we'd seen, I had to agree with him.

"That is excellent and most admirable, most worthy of you," I played him up a bit and he relaxed somewhat and smiled for the first time. "Now then, do you have any zen-kami here?"

"But of course, Great Ladies. What would be a pleasure house without a pair of zen-kami?" he replied as if this was the most ignorant question yet.

We followed him up the steps to the third floor of this three-story building. We got a whiff of opium smoke when passing by the second floor, bringing back ill memories for us two. The decor of this floor was elegance personified. He introduced us to his zen-kami. "This is my wife Chani and Edan." His wife was forty and very, very pretty indeed, though she had the typical conical upper arms, ending at her elbows where they were barely an inch across. Her eyes were bright and her smile, infectious. Edan was thirty-three with enchanting eyes that never left mine!

We explained who we were and the Empress' proclamation. "So, do you both have sets of the proper zen-kami tools?" I asked.

"Of course, we could not live properly without them," Edan replied. Her voice was mellow, and I found myself wishing she would talk and talk! Hers was a voice one could listen to for hours! "Would you like to see them?" she asked.

"No, I believe you. Now, are you paid well for your services?" I continued our line of questioning, insisting on proof. Edan explained, "While I cannot handle actual coins, every Monday, Fung Su places them in my pouch before I go home to my family for the day. My husband handles my finances for me. Why do you ask such questions?"

Dita explained what had happened to the zen-kami in Shansee and both women were appalled. Now they understood and appreciated the Empress' proclamation, encouraging us to visit all the other palaces. Even Fung Su seemed upset over this unexpected news. He added, "That man ought to be slain for what he did! Zen-kami are as close to royalty as one can get without becoming a princess or the Empress herself!"

"Indeed, he was slain, I did it," Dita could not help but brag a little, though she didn't elaborate.

"You see, we are also charged with seeing if we can find a young woman who was abducted from Mong Yu last fall by Overlord Nangumo's raiders," I changed the subject. After giving him more details, I asked him if he had any information about them.

"Fung! You must tell them," his wife insisted. He bowed to her and bid us follow him. He led us to his first floor dining room and offered us all some tea. After seeing that we were all served, he then began to explain.

"Yes, it was late last fall, before the snows came. One of Nangumo's captains came to me. He wanted to know if I would like to purchase two young women. Prime zen-kami women, he claimed repeatedly. Okay, I had to see them. I admit it. He had them in a wagon just out front. Both women were very comely and would have been worth having as either a kami or a zen-kami. However, both women had been very badly mistreated. He claimed that they needed to be taught a lesson in manners. When I undid the blankets covering them, I saw why he had suggested that they be zen-kami candidates! He or his men, he never said who, had smashed both of their hands! Crushed them, probably stomped on them would be my guess, though I have never seen such wounds before. From their tears, I could see that they were in a good deal of pain, to say the least."

"I says to the captain, 'These women need medical attention right away.' He said, 'Well, for a hundred gold, both are yours. As I said, they are zen-kami material.' Now we all know that zen-kami are very special women. Normally, only the very best kami are ever offered such a position as zen-kami, and it is their free will choice. My wife became a zen-kami when she was twenty-five and the best kami in the city. So you see, both she and I were appalled at what this captain was suggesting."

"So what happened next?" I encouraged him.

"Well, I told him that these women needed immediate medical attention or their hands would very likely become gangrenous. I've seen that happen once to a farmer whose hand was crushed by a boulder, and he had to have it amputated. He asked where he could find such a doctor. Seeing how these women would likely need such drastic surgery, I recommended old Doc Yi. He's a strange fellow, some say he's crazy, but when it comes to such surgery, none can compare to his skill with the knife. Around here, he's famous for his surgery skills. He did both Chani and Edan's surgery. Just a perfect, prefect job, if you ask me. Very little scaring and magnificent shaping on both their arms."

I got directions on where to find this doctor and then asked, "Say, do you remember what those two women looked like?"

"Sure, why?" he asked.

"I have kijutsu powers. Would you allow me to look at your memories of those women to see if one of them is the one that we are seeking?" He gave me an awestruck look. For a second, I thought that he would refuse.

"Yes, Great Lady, if this will help you," he agreed. A minute later, I saw his images and joined the others in a Mind Link with me. Shi confirmed one of them was indeed Lin Lu, and he began sobbing uncontrollably. Surely, his Lin Lu was now dead or worse.

I had the soldiers and their captain take Shi back to our inn. Since Dita and I walked so slowly, I sent Ilenakova and Enrico off to check out this doctor and see if we could see him. Meanwhile, the rest of us finished our tea and began our slow walk home. We had not gotten but a block when the two returned, crestfallen.

"Sorry, it will have to wait until tomorrow evening, Bethany. Apparently, the doctor's services were needed in a nearby town. He's expected to return by suppertime. I made an appointment for us to see him then. He has a huge, relatively isolated mansion. I wager he is rather wealthy," Ilenakova reported.

An idea struck me, but I saw its source. Bianca and Fina were incredibly curious about just what went on in a pleasure palace. Cleverly, Bianca was trying to have me get the idea that we should spend some time being pleasured. I grinned and said, "You know, Fung was so helpful that I feel that we should perhaps spend some funds in his palace. He can then say that he entertained the Empress' party."

"Great! Wonderful," Bianca exclaimed, before I could back down. "Fina and I have always wondered just what these pleasure palaces are all about. Thanks Bethany."

I allowed her to think that she'd pulled this off, and we turned around and headed back inside. "Fung, we'd like to honor your Purple House. Bianca, Louis, Fina, Tian, Ilenakova, Enrico, Dita, and me — let's see. That's eight of us. We'd like the works, but no drugs, no opium. How much for us all?" I asked. The delight on Bianca's face was infectious!

"Oh my!" he exclaimed totally taken by surprise.

"We paid ten gold for the main floor of the Purple Palace," I added. "We heard that he charged a thousand for a night with his zen-kami."

Awed, Fung gave me a special rate of two thousand for all eight of us, but limited each of us to an hour with the zen-kami; dinner was included, along with a kami to see to our needs on the first two floors. Five hours later, the eight of us slowly walked back to our inn. Dita and I walked half as slowly as we normally did and no one said a word. All eight of us were completely satisfied. The music was both delicate and sensuous at the same time. So much so, that Dita and I spent most of our time lying on the divans enraptured.

When we were finally near our inn, Bianca at last was able to speak, "That was indescribable! Beauty and sensuous beyond all imagination. A zen-kami can be incredibly addictive! Unbelievable! Thank you, Bethany." The others shared her opinion; they all now had first-hand knowledge of the pleasure palaces, and why they played such a role in Tashien society. Further, they all realized why zen-kami were so highly respected. "I never knew that so much pleasure could come from our bodies," she added.

"Yes, but spiritual beings can generate far more. This is just another example of the diabolical trap setup by the Doll Creatures, gang. Make the body become the temple of pleasure and the being becomes naught. Careful what you wish for," I teased them.

Dita finally shared her deepest thoughts with her daughter, "Bianca, remember what you learned here and share similar things with your mate, your dearest love."

"I will, mom, thanks," she whispered back, giving her a warm hug and kiss.

The doctor's mansion was located near the southern edge of the city.

An iron fence surrounded his grounds, which covered at least a whole square block. The mansion was set back and surrounded by immense, tall evergreen trees. The building looked somehow ominous and very different from the usual architecture of the other homes in the city. Our captain explained that this mansion was probably one of the first homes ever built here, dating back well over a hundred years. Stone and wood construction intermingled; perhaps that's what gave it a spooky atmosphere. Or perhaps it was the diminished light from the dense trees. A long lane led to the doctor's main office portion of the mansion. Our captain led us and our carriage down the lane, halting before a set of overly wide doors. Here was the emergency entrance where patients were often brought.

Just inside, an office woman, perhaps in her late fifties waited for us. "Good evening. The doctor has arrived. I'm to take you to the visitor's room and he will join you there." She led us past his operating room, a well-lit room, very sterile. We could see many surgical tools arranged on a table, along with towels and linens. No doubt, here was where he performed his surgical miracles for which he was famous. In the adjoining room, we found comfortable couches lining one wall and a small table and four chairs. After showing us the room, she then left for home, biding us good evening.

Just when I began wondering how long we would have to wait to see this doctor, he walked in from another door that connected to the rest of his mansion. Doc Yi was sixty, his white hair still held streaks of brown from his youth. He was tall and thin, his clothes, immaculate, if not sterile. "Ah, good evening, Great Ladies, gentlemen. Elective surgery I see. For the Great Ladies? Yes?" he said. I detected a covertness in his voice and attitude. "Well, you have come to the right doctor. Yes, there is no finer skilled surgeon in all of Tashien. Why, I have spent my life researching amputational surgery. I have done extensive research on the most optimum removal of all appendages. Foremost expert in Tashien, I might add, published three dozen papers on the subject for the benefit of my colleagues as well as four books. Yes, you have picked the right surgeon. Come this way, allow me to show you my credentials," he continued to talk rapidly, ignoring us for the most part. He just assumed that Dita and I were here to have surgery, as zen-kami I guessed. We followed him into the next room.

The walls were lined with plaques, which bestowed all manner of honors on this doctor. Some were awards for saving the lives of prominent accident victims. Three tables displayed his many published articles, complete with extremely fine and accurate drawings and diagrams of the anatomy of arms and legs. Clearly, this man knew more about the appendages of a human body than anyone else on Tarra. His four books sat atop four mahogany book displays.

"You see here," he pointed out one of the sets of drawings that he had published, "the delicate and perfect shape of the zen-kami arms after my work has healed. This is before, this is during, and this is the result, perfect indeed. Would you not agree?" He didn't give us a moment to reply. "Now, the surgery will take one day, but the recovery period will be several months before your bodies are completely healed."

"Excuse me," I finally interrupted his steady stream of advice, "we are not here for surgery. Some of us are healers in our own country of Velona, fellow doctors one might say," I twisted the truth slightly. While we were not doctors per se, as Druwids we had some knowledge of the healing arts. Sandra, had she been here, would have been our comparable physician.

"Oh, excuse me, Great Ladies. Such a shame. Both of you would make the most exquisite zen-kami. Indeed, perhaps the very finest. You should consider it, you know. Why, with my skill, you two could become perhaps the finest zen-kami in all Tashien! Ah, healers you say from Velona? My, my fame has stretched to the Outer Lands already. Isn't that something? Well, I certainly know why. I know more about appendage surgery than anyone else in Tashien and probably the Outer Lands as well." My, this doctor sure had a big ego, but then from his work and fame, he probably was extremely good at what he did.

Dita jumped in, "Well, Doctor Yi, there have been times when we certainly could have used your expertise in our lands. Why the bloody carnage left after some of our wars was almost impossible to handle." She was remembering the First Holy Crusade for Religious Freedom, where we had to perform such surgery on thousands of wounded soldiers. Horrid affair.

'Yes, yes, I understand, though I hate working in such despicable situations. Why, men can so brutalize other men! I much prefer the accidents and elective surgeries. Do you realize that I have performed thousands of such surgeries? Do you have specialties yourselves or perhaps preferences? How skilled are the doctors in Velona? Perhaps you would like to acquire copies of my works with which to educate your own doctors. I suspect that my skill, my research, my knowledge surpasses that of your own Outer Lands' doctors. Am I right?" he rattled on and on.

"Yes, is it possible for us to acquire copies of your great works?" I asked. Whether or not this man was slightly off his rocker, the information contained in his works was most definitely extremely valuable! If nothing else, I had to bring this knowledge back to Velona!

"Oh yes, yes, indeed. Why, if you visit Hui's Books in the city, he has copies of all my works. I must say, publishing my works has made him a rich publisher. Yes, indeed. I am honored that you will share my work with the Outer Lands. Yes, indeed."

"Is it true that the smaller and tinier the stitches, the less scarring there will be?" asked Dita. She was curious. She'd often seen Sandra's incredibly tiny stitches, particularly in previous lifetimes. Dita, or rather Renzo in those days, was nowhere as skilled with his stitches.

"Ah, why yes, that is indeed so. Always make the tiniest, close-set stitches as you can, my Great Lady. Why just yesterday, I was called upon to perform emergency surgery on a farmer whose hand had been mangled in a farming accident. While he is not a zen-kami, still, I used my finest stitches on his stub. That way, when it is fully healed, he will have almost no visible scarring and can be proud of his arm. He will not need to hide it because it looks ugly. You see, there can be great beauty in what remains after surgery. I have spent my life teaching others always to make their amputations a work of art. Make the result so pleasing for the eye."

While all this was fascinating and potentially highly valuable, Doc Yi was not getting us any closer to our objective of finding Lin Lu. I decided to nudge the conversation more in that direction. "I wonder if we could see some of your results on real people, not just these drawings," I suggested.

"Ah, yes, yes, you just must. Visit the Purple House here in town. I did the arms of both of Fung Su's zen-kami — his wife, Chani, and Edan. Both are perfect in all ways. You must see them," he replied enthusiastically.

"Why, we have already seen both of those women," I answered truthfully. "They are absolutely magnificent. I saw no ugly scarring whatsoever. Your work is miraculous indeed, Doc Yi." I was getting frustrated; this line of questioning was also getting us nowhere.

Bianca, who had been idly flipping through pages of one of his book, came across a passage that intrigued her. "Say, it says here that you gained much knowledge and practice by working on research cases. What exactly is a research case," she asked innocently.

I noticed the doctor's eyes flickered wildly; his face reddened slightly. Evidently, she was onto a top topic. "Well, as fellow healers, you recognize the dire necessity to have bodies on which to practice, do you not?" he said somewhat defensively.

"You mean like recent accident victims?" she asked innocently, though I knew she was putting on an act. She too had observed his reaction.

"Well, not exactly. With accident victims, you are presented a wildly uncontrolled situation. In pure research, you need to keep all things constant except the variable that you are studying. Observe the results and form better theories, then test them out. I have spent my life perfecting these surgical methods. They have been proven to work best on test research subjects," he explained.

"Yes, of course," she agreed with him. "Where do you find your research subjects?" she asked the pointed question. I now saw where she was heading with her line of questioning.

"Why, Tashien is full of unwanted subjects — subjects who have no real lives of their own anymore. When I find them, I give them new, noble purposes for their lives — to further the advance of surgical procedures — procedures which not only save lives, but also bring a touch of great beauty and aesthetics to the final result — as witnessed by my results with Chani and Edan."

"Yes, the results on Chani and Edan are indeed most aesthetic indeed," I replied. "Last fall, Shi's fiancé was abducted by some of Overlord Nangumo's men. We believe that she was sold to someone here in Gaikou. We are charged by the Empress San Min Wu to find this missing woman. Might we see your research subjects? Perhaps she is one of them." I decided to be blunt about our motives at last. I was tired of beating around the bush with this doctor, who obviously had a low opinion of the value of a human life.

"Oh, I am sorry to hear about that. I do hope that you can find his fiancé. The hour is late, Great Ladies, and I have had a very long day of surgery with the farmer's hand. Perhaps you could come back another day?" he was politely excusing us. Our proclamation from San Min did not allow us to force this doctor to allow us to see his research subjects, if he actually had any. Another day would have to suffice. We thanked him and left.

As we congregated around our carriage, I was still suspicious. "Ilenakova, can I impose upon you to stay here around this place and keep an eye on things? Keep out of sight and don't let Doc Yi see you. Just be alert if he tries anything like disposing of his research subjects."

She grinned, "You bet! I don't like the sound of the way things went in there. He is so covert it isn't funny. Man, what an ego he has."

"Thanks, I'll send someone to relieve you in the morning," I promised and we left. Ilenakova slipped easily into the shadows of the dense pine trees, drawing closer to the mansion.

Back at our inn and sipping mead, Shi complained, "He must have my Lin Lu somewhere at his mansion!"

"We don't know that yet, Shi. Look, he is a famous surgeon. We just cannot go barging in there searching his whole place, not without probably cause. Be patient a little longer, please. Let us continue our search," I pleaded with him. He drunk himself into a stupor and had to be carried to his room.

The next day, I sent Bianca and Fina off to obtain copies of all Doc Yi's works. They returned with their arms full of articles and the four books. Fina then left to relieve Ilenakova, while we took over two tables at the inn and began looking through all the writings and drawings. Around noon, Bianca made a startling discovery.

"Look at this drawing, gang!" she held the latest article that Doc Yi had recently published, depicting the proper removal of legs at the knee in such a manner as to not impact the upper leg and to maintain the proper beauty of the remnants of the leg. We crowded around and looked at the detailed drawing.

"Damn! That sure looks like the images we've seen of Lin Lu!" Dita exclaimed. We all concurred; his drawing of the woman looked remarkably like the woman we were looking for!

"What?" the voice of Ilenakova broke in on us all. She'd just returned from her night of doc watching. We showed her the drawing, which looked remarkably like Lin Lu.

"Well, this doc is a strange one. It was after eight when we left him. He said that he was tired. But did he go to bed? No. The mansion has a basement. I saw him go down into the basement. He was down there for almost two hours! What could he be doing in a basement that long that late at night? Anyway, I did some sneaking around his place. His pantry is well stocked, from what I could see through the window at first light. He has a cook, and as I watched, she made breakfast for an army." We gave her a questioning look.

"Okay, large enough for a bunch of people. I saw Doc Yi eating, but then he disappeared for a while. Still, she made enough food for quite a few people, Bethany. Yet, I only saw the cook and the office assistant or nurse or whatever she actually is arrive this morning. That's three, but the breakfast would feed far more people, I'm sure of it. Then, Fina came and I headed back here. Something is going on inside there. I bet anything that he has Lin Lu in there. So what do we do now? Take him out?"

"We need to get a look inside; check out his basement," I concluded. "This is going to be tricky. He's a highly respected man, and yet if our theory is correct, a pure sadist as well, performing illegal amputations on unwilling victims, to say nothing of keeping them prisoners. As Jemma would say, tread softly."

"We don't know if he has victims in his basement, Bethany. He could well have a pack of dogs down there and is feeding them part of his breakfast," Dita pointed out.

"Well, you two can keep him occupied talking about his surgery techniques while the rest of us sneak in there and see what's in his basement," Ilenakova proposed. For once, she didn't suggest that we barge in there and force our way to the basement.

I reached a decision, based on the man's status in Tashien. "Okay, first, let's see if we can get him or persuade him to show us his research subjects. If that fails, then we go with Ilenakova's plan. Dita and I will keep him occupied, while the rest of you sneak a peek."

"Mom," Bianca asked, "what are we going to do if we find Lin Lu down there and some others as well?" Dita looked at me. I knew that she'd just ring his neck and be done with it. However, he was a highly respected surgeon. A conundrum faced us.

"I honestly don't know," I spoke what I felt. "If she is there, we certainly have the right and power to get her out of there."

"Another approach we could use," Louis suggested, "would be to keep an eye on him, and when he leaves, we break in and see for ourselves. If he's keeping prisoners there, we remove them and take them away with us. He'd be the none wiser."

"Hey, I like your plan!" Bianca praised her lover. "Say, we may need more wagons or carriages to transport them. I wonder how many there are?"

"Okay, okay gang. I can take a hint. You all watch over my body," I requested, feeling rather dumb that I had not thought of this before now. "I'll go take a look at what is in the basement now. Then, we will know what is there and can make better plans."

"Duh!" Dita exclaimed, feeling every bit as silly as me for not having thought of the simple answer as well.

I floated over the mansion of Doc Yi and spotted Fina hiding behind some trees where she could not be seen from the street and from where she could see anyone entering or leaving. I touched her mind. *I'm going inside to see what's in the basement. Keep an eye out, Fina.*

She grinned. *This is more like it,* she sent back to me. I floated on into the mansion and began looking for the way to the basement.

At last, I found it. Just off the kitchen area, a locked door led to the stairs. I floated on through the door and down into the dimly illuminated basement area. Part of the basement held all manner of junk. Doc Yi was one of these people who could not get rid of anything. After a bit of nosing around, I spied another locked door. On I went. Inside, I discovered the women!

I counted seven women, lying on mattresses on the floor. Then I saw why they were not on beds! I was shocked! I'd never seen anything like this before. I beat a hasty retreat back to my body. The others knew something was up; Dita said my face was white as a sheet! I'd found Lin Lu.

Chapter 31 Rescue and Salvation

"Did you see her, my Lin Lu?" Shi begged me just after I reanimated my body. The others looked at me expectantly. I weighted my answer. If they saw what I saw, they may well want to exterminate Doc Yi, especially Shi, who had already killed thousands of the overlord's soldiers. Still, they would soon see for themselves.

"Yes, our search is over. Lin Lu is in the basement along with six other women as well."

"Yes! We must rescue her at once! Come on; let's go!" Shi Do nearly knocked over his chair in his enthusiastic rise to leave.

"Patience, Shi. I have some very bad news to share. She is alive and well as far as I could tell. However, Shi, I need your promise not to harm Doc Yi. Lin Lu's life depends on our stealth. We must get her and the others back to the Imperial Palace as quickly as possible without anyone knowing their full story or seeing us, at least seeing us around this town. Do I have your solemn promise, Shi?"

"Yes, Great Lady Bethany, what must we do?" Shi calmed down and sat back down at our table. Still, he was restraining himself, I noted.

There was no easy way to break the news of what I saw; they'd see for themselves soon enough. I did my best. "We've all had our suspicions that Doc Yi was using these women as his research bodies. Well, we are right. All seven have been used in his research on amputation methods. We are going to have our hands full rescuing these women and caring for their unique needs while we travel."

"What did he do to my precious Lin Lu?" Shi wailed, clenching his fists. "Please, tell me. How badly is she. . ." He didn't know how to finish his question.

"About as bad as it can get, Shi. I'm sorry. Still, Shi, there is hope for them all if we can safely get them back to the Imperial Palace in Zau. Shi, I will do everything I can for them, including working miracles. Please have a little faith in me a little longer."

"I will, I promise. If not for you, I would never have found her. Please, what has he done to her?" Shi asked. I saw that the others now had a good idea of what I was about to say, though probably not as grim.

"She has no arms, and he's amputated her legs at her knees, Shi," I said as softly and gently as I could. Gasps came from all corners of the table, none expected this drastic a mutilation. Shi nearly fainted, tremendously crushed.

"There is another woman just like her. Only two women are capable of walking out of the basement. The others will have to be carried. I've never seen anything like it ever before," I added.

"The sadist! He ought to be given a taste of his own amputations!" Bianca exclaimed. Others echoed her sentiments, as I expected they would.

"We cannot touch him, not just yet and not without the Empress' permission. He is a very famous surgeon in Tashien. We cannot harm him without there being terrible repercussions," I explained. "I am certain that many other doctors and people will believe that he is quite justified in experimenting on them to gain the knowledge and skill to save other people. If we harm him, we may well become criminals in this land, doing great damage to the Empress and the other's plans to bring order back into the country. We cannot and dare not jeopardize that because of this insane doctor. Come, let's put our heads together, and figure out a way to get them out of his basement and back to the palace without anyone getting wise to us."

"We will need a second carriage," Ilenakova began planning. "I presume that you will want the five of us to start right in on giving them therapy sessions while we are traveling along. Enrico, Louis, you will become the carriage drivers. Tian, you will take my place riding point. Captain, you and your men will be responsible for our safety. Alert us if trouble comes. Now where will we get a carriage?"

"Can we even stay at inns along the way?" Bianca asked.

I rubbed my forehead. "I believe that we can sneak them into the inns, if we can cover them with cloaks. Also, they are going to need clothing. All seven are completely naked. I suspect that is to make it easier for them to deal with their unique situations. We will need chamber pots as well as blankets, just in case."

"Do you suppose that they are addicted to opium, like we were?" asked Dita.

"I've no idea. Sorry gang, I was so freaked by what I saw that I failed to totally observe their conditions. We will deal with that if needed. Don't worry, Shi, we have already figured out how to get someone off of an opium addiction."

He looked slightly relieved. "Now then, we should get the extra carriage and supplies immediately and be ready to rescue them the moment that the time is right," I ordered.

"When will that be?" asked Bianca.

"When he leaves the mansion for an extended period of time. That's when we strike. I presume that he will leave either his office woman or his cook to look after the women. I wish Jemma were here, she could simply put them to sleep. We'll have to make do. We cannot have them either seeing us there or knowing that it was us who took the seven women from the basement. We must leave Doc Yi in complete mystery about the disappearance of his research women."

While the others headed off to purchase what we needed, Dita and I returned to our room. While I watched over her body, she floated off to relieve Fina, telling her where to meet up with Ilenakova. Dita then kept watch over the mansion. Her objective: notify us when she saw him leaving for what may be an extended period.

"Early afternoon, Ilenakova had everything we needed acquired, and she was ready to execute our plan. Now we just had to be patient and wait for our opportunity. For us all, this was a long and difficult afternoon. Each wanted desperately to charge in there and rescue the women. Uppermost in our minds was the idea that he might be operating on one of the women while we sat here waiting! I didn't tell the others, that based on what I had seen, three to five other women were very likely candidates for additional surgery! I hoped and prayed that he didn't.

At suppertime, I relieved Dita so that she could have dinner as well. During the night, she relieved me. Shortly after breakfast, Dita returned to her body to eat as well. "Okay, the time is right. He has just left the mansion. I watched him pack some saddlebags so I think he will be gone a while." We let her eat while the rest of us got our things together. Ilenakova and the men got the carriages ready. Just as Dita finished, we were ready to head out.

"We need to park the carriages on the south side of his mansion. It's open country there. Hopefully, no one will see us," Dita explained. She and I climbed in and Ilenakova led our small party down the busy streets of Gaikou. The heavy crowds died out once we got nearer the residential area in the south of the city. We headed out on a southern road before veering to the west. She led us unerringly to the backside of the mansion, as I expected that she would.

As we got out of the carriage and the others dismounted, I explained further, "Remember, we must leave no trace of our coming and going. Wipe out all our tracks. Dita is going to disable whoever is inside, the cook or the office woman." Standing on the rough ground, I saw that we would have to climb over the fence and walk across the lawn to get to the mansion. Dita and I were going to have problems with our small feet. Thankfully, Ilenakova and Enrico already thought of this and lifted us both up and over before I could ask them.

"There you go, Great Lady," Ilenakova teased me. I grinned. Holding onto her, we headed slowly for the backside of the mansion. The thick pine trees hid us from view, if anyone inside the mansion was looking our way.

When we drew close, Dita left her body and floated inside. A few minutes later, she returned. "The cook is out. Thank goodness we all learned our pressure points. One small touch on the right spot, and she's out. Come on, to the rescue," Dita eagerly announced her small feat.

We entered through the back door and went directly to the kitchen. I led them to the basement door. "Ah, here is the key. Remember, we must relock it when we leave," I pointed out. I let Enrico unlock the door. My long nails would have made it difficult for me to do easily. Then, down the stairs we went. Again, Enrico opened the second locked door and stepped back.

Since the women were naked, our plan called for us women to enter first with some clothing. Once we had them ready, the men would begin carrying them up and out. I stepped into the room, followed by Dita, Bianca, Ilenakova, and Fina. The seven women looked up at us from their beds and gasped, startled. We were not the familiar cook.

"Hello. I am Bethany and this is Dita, Ilenakova, Bianca, and Fina. We have come to rescue you. Lin Lu, your fiancé Shi Do is just outside waiting for you. He's spent all this time trying to find you. You are all now safe."

Lin Lu stared at us and finally called out, "Please, just kill me. I'm helpless like this. Please, I want to die. I can't live like this, please."

"Me too, please kill me too," a woman about her age added. She too was missing her arms totally and had only her upper legs remaining. Soon, all the women were begging us to kill them!

"Please, don't let him cut off any more of me," the woman who was missing her hands and feet wailed. "I don't want to be like they are, please."

"First things first, we have to dress you, well sort of. We are in a hurry. We have to get you all safely out of here before the doc comes back," I explained. Hastily, they began to figure out ways to put some clothing to cover up their bodies, enough so that they would not be embarrassed when the men carried them to the waiting carriages.

We noticed that the women who had their lower legs removed now wore leather pads over what remained of their legs above their knees. Quickly, we saw that this was done to allow them to sort of walk on these pads. Lin Lu and her friend Zhi Jin had a terrible time of it, for they had no arms at all to help them keep their balance. Zhi Jin had been abducted along with Lin Lu from Mong Yu.

The other two women who had their legs removed at the knees in a similar fashion and who also wore the leg pads were Xue De and Ting Ding. Each was also missing one arm completely. Xue still had her whole right arm, while Ting still had her whole left arm. They explained that their job was to help the others, which is why they still had one arm and hand left.

Ying Huang had both her arms removed at the sockets, like Zhi and Lin. She at least could walk. I noticed that she had the most charming, green eyes, quite a beauty. Wen Dezhou was more like a zen-kami, with her lower arms removed. However, Doc Yi had gone a bit further with her, removing half of her upper arms before making them conical in shape. She too could walk.

Poor Yun Handan was the most recent arrival. Already she had had both hands and feet removed. She told us that Doc Yi was planning to remove the rest of her lower legs next, but had not yet decided whether to remove her arms at her elbow in zen-kami style or take even more off as he had done with Wen.

Once we had more or less gotten some clothes on them, I had the others enter and crowd in. Shi raced to Lin Lu, picked her up, and held her tightly, crying like a baby. "I'll never let you go again, Lin. I'll look after you now." She only cried and repeated that she wanted to die. Shi looked pleadingly at me.

I whispered, "It's the trauma speaking, Shi. Think about it. Who wouldn't want to die if they were cut up as these women are? Have faith in me, Shi. Let's get them all safely to the carriages."

The one armed Xue and Ting insisted that we bring along their many hairbrushes. These were their sole possessions, and they just could not be parted with them. I understood why and made sure that we brought them along with us. While the men began carrying the women up, out, and to the carriages, we women brought up the rear, re-locking the doors and making sure that we left no trace of our coming. At last, we shut the main doors and Ilenakova brought up the rear, wiping out traces of our passing across the lawn by using a branch.

A half hour from the start, we were aboard the two carriages and were moving at last. Dita, Bianca, and I were in one carriage along with the two worst cases, Lin Lu and Zhi Jin. Yun Handan was also with us, since she had no appendages left. Ilenakova and Fina rode in the second carriage with the others: Xue De, Ting Ding, Ying Huang, and Wen Dezhou.

Once we were safely on the main road heading east, I began a lengthy explanation of who we were and what was happening throughout Tashien. I told them about the new Empress and that she had sent us to find Lin Lu. Once I finished, Lin told us about what had happened to her and her friend, Zhi.

They had been abducted together that day. Later that night, the captain had tried to make them consent to having intercourse with him. Both had refused and had fought him, kicking him in his privates until he gave up. Twice more they had fought against his advances. At last, in frustration, the captain had stomped on both of their hands, shattering them. They had passed out from the pain. They had vague memories of being sold to Doc Yi sometime after that. At first, they were hopeful that he would fix their hands; at least that's what he said he would do. Both women were shocked to wake up from the surgery with their lower arms missing.

When they had recovered a bit, the doc had again put them under the knife, because they had resisted his advances and tried to escape, kicking and pounding on the basement doors. After that, he removed the rest of their arms. Still they tried to escape and their last surgery had left them without their lower legs.

Yun's story was much the same. Three months ago, she had been abducted, and she too had resisted all attempts to subdue her into a sexual slave. She ended up under Doc Yi's knives and woke up to find that she had lost her hands and feet. He promised to do further beautification surgery once she was fully healed. This beautification surgery, she subsequently learned would make her look like Lin Lu, but with short upper arms like those of Wen.

All three did explain that the doc had often said that they were helping advance the art of surgery so that other's lives could be saved. None of them actually believed this, though. Who would under the circumstances?

Next, I explained a bit about our special trauma therapy and soon we three began to run our three women back through their many traumatic operations, as well as their abductions. Meantime, Ilenakova and Fina were running Xue and Ting through theirs, while Ying and Wen listened in. They were in better shape; their legs were intact. We'd get to them as soon as we could. Yes, it took some confront on our part to sit there and listen to the horrors that these women had undergone, all in the name of surgical research!

Late that afternoon, we entered the town where we planned to spend the night. We put cloaks over the women, hiding all but their heads. Then, the strong arms of our men carried them inside and up to our waiting rooms. So far, this was working. A bit later, they brought up our dinner, and we took turns feeding the five who could not do this for themselves.

That handled, we women set about trying to get clothing adjusted to meet their needs. Yun could wear a normal warm dress, but we also put warm socks on her lower legs, just to make sure that she stayed warm. Similarly, Ying and Wen could wear normal dresses as long as we adjusted their sleeves.

The other four presented all manner of problems in fittings. We discovered that with their leg pads, the four were somewhat able to move around a bit. Whatever we did, I insisted that we not restrict their slim ability to move on their own, however slight it was. Bianca's idea of simply cutting the bottom half off their dresses proved most workable. Soon, all four were able to wear a warm dress.

At bedtime, Shi insisted that Lin Lu sleep with him. I thought this was an extremely good request on his part. Lin would need all the love and support that she could get. I took her friend Zhi to bed with me, while Dita cared for Yun. Bianca asked Ying to sleep with her, while Ilenakova wanted to watch over Wen. Xue and Ting could manage themselves, as long as someone helped them onto the bed; they at least still had a good arm. Overall, things were going remarkable well thus far.

When I sensed Zhi was asleep, I expanded my mind and found De An. *Hi. I've found more candidates for you.*

You have?

Yes. I gave him a very lengthy explanation and sent him some of my mental images of the seven women. *We should be back at the palace in about twenty-three more days. I don't have any right to ask this of you, De, but these seven women could definitely use some of your miracles. We will probably have their therapy sessions finished by then.*

Let me meet them and we shall see. I took this as a hopeful sign.

The next morning, as we dressed and got ready for breakfast, both Lin and Zhi again asked me, "Please, we cannot live like this. We appreciate all that you are doing for us. But look, what kind of a life can we have like this?" Lin asked.

Zhi added, "We are almost completely helpless. With our beds on the floor and the chamber pots there too, given a lot of time and effort, she and I are able to get up and go to the bathroom on our own."

"We sometimes fall," Lin added quickly. "Then, Xue or Ting has to come rescue us. Honestly, Bethany, we are completely pathetic like this. We both just want to die and have an end to this suffering. Please," she begged.

"That's incredible," I picked up on the only positive thing I'd heard. No sense trying to talk them out of this. "You are able to get out of bed, stand up, and walk? How do you do it?"

I ignited a tiny spark of self-respect, perhaps the only piece left to them. "Put us on the floor and we'll try to show you. We're pretty pathetic and we often fall," Lin replied. Dita and I sat them both onto the floor and stood back a ways. In doing so, both saw our small feet and just how slowly we had to move.

"We walk at least as fast as you do," Zhi noted, a strange look on her face. While we watched, both women wiggled and twisted, using their head and the side of the bed. With effort, both managed to stand on what remained of their legs. The heavy padded leather pads protected their stumps. With a twisting motion and careful leaning of their heads, both women managed to take a few steps out into the room on their own.

"You are incredible, Lin and Zhi. Amazing. If you will let us hold on to you to help you keep your balance, we will let you do some walking whenever possible," I suggested. Dita and I shuffled to them and put our arms on their shoulders, steading them. Together, we four walked around the room some. When we finished as the food arrived, we noticed that both women had a satisfied, pleased look on their faces. I took that as a good sign; I'd gotten their attention off their death wishes, if only for a moment. We had to feed them, of course, which didn't help.

While a few people stared at our men carrying the cloaked women down from our rooms and out into our carriages, they could not see the actual reason. So far so good, I thought. Shortly, we began rolling down the road once more.

Lin whispered to me, "Shi says that he still loves me and wants to marry me. I told him that I couldn't marry him as I am. I would be too much of a burden for him, but he won't take no for an answer. What should I do?"

"Lin, Shi's love for you runs deep. He's spent all this time searching for you relentlessly. The only real question is do you love him back." I pointed out. I hate it when I am put into the love-match making scenarios.

I'm just no good at this.

"Well, I do. We had planned to get married just before I was kidnaped. But is it fair of me to make him take care of me when I am like this?" she replied.

"People do many things out of love for each other. Take your current Empress and her husband," I began telling them about San Min Wu and Long Yan. When I finished, she had much to ponder, and we began therapy sessions once more.

Around lunchtime, we passed by an isolated meadow, brimming with golden flowers. Their flagrance was heady in the warm springtime air. Here we stopped for a picnic lunch. With the blankets spread out among the flowers, we all dined together. I saw the women looking longingly out across the beautiful meadow. "Shall we go for a short walk before we hit the trail again?" I suggested.

"We'd love to!" Xue and Ting chimed in together, forgetting their plight. The beauty around them was spectacular.

I took Xue's hand to support her, and together we moved slowly off the blanket and onto the soft ground. I moved even slower than she did. For the very first time, I heard a giggle from one of the seven. Dita followed suit, holding Ting's hand. Ting grinned and thanked her. Seeing how we did it, Shi helped Lin rise and got down on his knees so he was at her height. Supporting her, the two began to follow us. Bianca did the same with Zhi, who looked proudly for the first time. The other three followed behind us.

It was not a long walk in terms of distance traveled, but for these women, it was a life-giving walk. All seven began to feel alive after their long torture and imprisonment. Ilenakova had a tear in her eye when we finally returned. She whispered to me, "Brilliant!"

Slowly, the days passed by as we made our journey eastward towards the Imperial City of Zau. Just as slowly, the seven faced their pain, unconsciousness, and feelings contained within their many traumatic surgeries. After eighteen days on the road, we finished the last of their therapy sessions. All seven no longer had the trauma impacting their emotions or bodies. In fact, they had all run into their own personal encounters with the Doll Creatures, their jailers. Of course, they then asked many questions about them. Given this, Shi was able to explain how it was that he was able to go on his long quest for Lin Lu and killing Overlord Nangumo, who was ultimately responsible for Lin and Zhi's capture and torture. What we had not yet done, of course, was show them how they could live productive lives as they were now.

The last week of travel now became fun and enjoyable for us all. They were continually chatting, looking out of the windows, and asking a myriad of questions, especially about just how the therapy was done. As I suspected, all seven saw this as something that they could do by themselves to help others. I encouraged them, and we spent a good deal of time explaining how it was done.

While they were now rather cheerful and were no longer requesting their own deaths, their physical conditions constantly reminded them of how helpless and dependent they now were. We all resisted the temptation to tell them about our own brushes with similar physical situations. Why? I had no idea if De An could help them — they were missing so much — or even if he could. Certainly, these women's bodies were likely too old for Cosima's trick that she had used on our children's bodies, causing them to regrow our arms. No, false hope could crush them at this point. Instead, we suggested that once within the safety of the Imperial Palace, we would work with them to help them learn new ways of doing things. Already Ying and Wen were quite proud of the fact that they could use their feet to feed themselves mostly, gaining a little independence.

Finally, on June 20, we rolled into Zau at last. That they were about to meet the Empress of Tashien began to worry the seven. Embarrassed by their physical condition, their lack of appropriate dress, and the significance of so important a person, they worried and fretted. "She's going to look at us as if we are some kind of freaks," Lin Lu wailed. The others had similar feelings and words.

"Once we get you settled in at the palace, we can have proper, elegant clothing made for you all. The Empress does understand your situation. It is not my place to tell you just why that is, but when she explains her own trials, you will see that she truly does understand. While yes, people will be staring at you, for when has anyone seen women's bodies so mutilated as yours; no one will hold that against you. On the contrary, you fought back and did not succumb to their carnal desires for your bodies. You will be welcomed as heroes; that's my hunch, ladies. So be prepared to be honored as heroes," I tried to calm their anxieties as best I could without revealing too much at this time.

"Wow, Zau is so huge!" exclaimed Lin. All seven shared her awe; none had ever been in such a large city. The warm, late afternoon sun shone down upon the densely packed streets as we slowly made our way to the Imperial Palace.

"I can't believe that we are actually entering the Imperial Palace, let alone see the Empress herself!" Zhi said excitedly, as at last our carriages entered the outer wall's main western gates. "Wow! It's even bigger than I imagined. What will the Empress think of us? Why should she even want to see us? To give us her pity?"

"Zhi, if Empress San Min just gives you pity and sympathy only, I will personally eat your dress!" I teased her. She giggled.

After piling out of our carriages and getting into position to assist the seven, Enrico opened the door to the Imperial Palace for us. As we entered the Throne Room, musicians sounded a fanfare, much to my surprise. Empress San Min sat on her throne with Jemma on her left and Long Yan on her right. Phillipe stood behind Jemma, a sword at his waist. At once, I saw they had made some changes. A red carpet led from the doors up to the throne. Various tapestries now hung on the bare walls. San Min and Jemma had been busy. Slowly and carefully, we made our way across the long space to the throne. San Min wore her emerald satin dress and polished black heels; her long hair lay draped over her right front shoulder, falling below her lap. Her face was bursting from her infectious smile.

"Welcome, welcome all. I am so glad that you were able to find Lin Lu and rescue her and her friends. I am Empress San Min Wu, my husband, Long Yan, and my able Advisor from Velona, Jemma Kato, and her fiancé, Phillipe Dumont. Welcome indeed. Come, sit by my throne, and tell me all about what happened to you," she said enthusiastically.

She added to the four, "Ah, I see you four walk faster than I or Bethany or Dita." The four, not expecting such a compliment over their precarious steps, giggled slightly. Shi Do, walking on his knees to be at Lin Lu's height and better able to keep her upright, appreciated the newly installed carpet. "Lin Lu, you and I both are so fortunate to have captured the love and heart of such fine men. My Long Yan walked thousands of miles, all the way to Velona, just to find Bethany and ask her to help him find me. It took five years, but Long was tireless in his search to find and rescue me. Shi Do has moved mountains to find and rescue you, Lin Lu. You and I are very fortunate women." She grinned and Lin Lu did likewise.

We sat before the throne and chatted for over an hour. Then, San Min changed the topic. "Ladies, besides bringing back order from the chaos years, I am also setting up a new and hopefully better system of government. In addition, Tashien has been incredibly blessed with the arrival of the Son of God, De An, he is called. He is bringing spiritual freedom to our country. I and many others have been personally blessed with his miracles. De An and some of his disciples wishes to meet with you seven privately. If you seven will remain seated, we will let him come and speak with you privately. If you need anything, just call out, we will be in the next room. Bethany, Shi, the rest of you, please follow me. Phillipe, let De An know it is time."

She rose and we three began our slow shuffle out of the room, the others moved at their normal pace, making ours seem like a slow motion hop. As we three finally reached the door, De An was there. "Very well done Bethany, Dita. Thank you." We smiled, and he, Chan Bao, and Master Ning Chou entered and closed the door. As we three walked or rather shuffled along, San Min explained that already De An had established a modest church in Zau and installed Chan and Ning as the disciples in charge of the Zau Church of God.

De An sat on the floor before the seven women. Chan and Ning sat on either side of him. "I am De An, this is my disciple Chan and her husband and Olin Master Protector." Quickly, the seven introduced themselves. He continued, "Bethany has told me that you all have received our church's therapy sessions and have erased the recent traumas that have befallen you. Is this true?" Lin Lu answered that they had.

"That is good. Can you tell me what you have learned about yourselves as a result of the therapy sessions?" De An asked them.

"I no longer want to just die," Lin Lu ventured. "I mean like this, I am almost completely helpless, dependent for nearly everything. When they first found us, I begged them to kill me and put me out of my misery."

"Now that has changed?" De An probed gently.

"Yes, there is still one thing that I can do — that we all can do," she glanced at her equally helpless friend, Zhi. "We still have our minds and we have been learning how to do this therapy. We now want to help others by giving them this wonderful therapy. We all do."

"Ah, that is most admirable of you seven. What else have you learned about yourselves from the therapy sessions?" De An asked gently.

"Oh, we are not our bodies," Zhi caught on to what he was asking. "We are different and separate from the body you see here. We seem to have lived in other bodies years and years ago. We all fought and lost battles with some very strange things. They sort of looked like a child's doll, but they were enormous in size."

"Congratulations, you are among the very few here in Tashien who now realize that we are all sons and daughters of God, that we are all immortal spiritual beings. The goal of my church is to spread that awareness to all others in Tashien, to help them reach the same understanding that you seven have," De An explained.

"However, we spiritual beings are innately possessed of enormous powers, though most all have long ago forgotten how to use them. I wish to show this to you, to give you a priceless gift. Will you accept it?" De An asked.

"Yes, but we really are not worthy of a priceless gift," Lin Lu fumbled. "I mean, I cannot even hold it. Only Xue and Ting have a hand with which to hold your gift. I guess they could hold ours for us," she added, glancing at her companions for agreement. Zhi shook her head affirmatively.

De An smiled, "My gift is not something that you need to hold in your hands. Allow me to touch you." She nodded. De An placed his hands on her empty shoulders, closed his eyes. Yes, I wanted very much to be there and see just what he did. How did he do these miracles? I longed to know, but I respected his request for privacy. I heard a squeal through the stone walls and knew or imagined what was going on inside.

Lin Lu shrieked! She stared down at her arms. There they were, just as they had been before Doc Yi had begun his numerous surgeries on them. She wiggled them, touched them, and moved them about, feeling her body and face with her hands. Sheer joy illuminated her face. De An moved to Zhi and shortly she shrieked as well. From woman to woman, De An moved, until at last, all seven once more had the arms that they had had before Doc

Yi had performed his many amputations.

Next, De An restored their legs and feet. "Now at last, you are ready to hear the full stories of the Empress San Min and Bethany and the others," De An declared. For an hour, he outlined what had happened to the Empress and the others at the hands of Yuen Ming. Chan then related her side of that story and how she had been similarly blessed with the restoration of her arms and hands as well. As De An and I both expected, all seven wanted to become disciples of De An and help others with this incredible therapy.

When De An allowed us all to rejoin the women, Shi Do fainted. Lin Lu looked whole and perfect, as if nothing had ever happened. After getting him roused, he wailed and cried, thanking De An over and over and over, until Lin Lu kissed him to shut him up. He too swore to help Lin Lu and De An work more miracles throughout Tashien. Since it was now suppertime, we all headed to the large dining room. Such hope and joy shared over that meal was truly inspiring.

Now it was time for Shi Do to live up to his part of the bargain: to get us to the cavern of the Doll Creatures. We spent an hour that night chatting with him, getting specific details of its location. I know, it seems silly that we would have to travel that very same route once more! His village of Mong Yu lay some fifty or so mile further up the valley from where we had begun our search for Lin Lu. We were facing making the same journey once again, but it couldn't be helped.

Chapter 32 The Doll Creature's Cavern

The next morning, I made a decision. "Look. We really don't need to bring Shi Do along with us. He's just found Lin Lu and they want to be married soon. Both want to begin helping De An and I certainly don't want to separate them for another two or three months. His directions are very explicit and I don't think it will be possible for us to miss finding the cavern. Besides, he says that we can ask his friend in Mong Yu for help if we can't find the cavern. I say let's leave Shi Do behind this trip."

The others agreed. Dita asked, "Do we really need to take along San Min's soldiers this time? Perhaps, we could all travel there in just two carriages."

"Well, we will need to go by horseback the last ways," I added. "Still, we could bring along the horses with us and break the monotony by riding some of the time." Everyone agreed to this plan.

"Say, can we do some shopping before we go?" Bianca asked. We had all seen marvelous shops here in Zau and had money to burn. Okay, we all wanted to see the sights before spending another two to three boring months traveling across country once more. We decided to leave on July 1. Off shopping, we all went. I won't bore you with the thousands of gold that we spent during those marvelous days! Dita acquired a fine pair of traditional swords, a hana and hano. Me, I bought two dozen of these fine black silk hose along with several fancy dresses. I added some musical instruments and a number of historical books that outlined the history of Tashien. We shopped until we dropped during those days.

Finally, we had to leave on the long westward journey. We left the three Doll artifacts in Jemma and Phillipe's custody, which turned out to be a very wise decision. Before we could all leave Tashien for home, we just had to make sure that this cavern held no further surprises, no further alien artifacts that could be used to harm people. Off we went, Ilenakova, Enrico, Fina, Tian, Bianca, Louis, Dita, and I. We took our two carriages and brought along four more horses, tied to the rears of the carriages. When the carriages could no longer traverse the terrain, we would leave them and finish on horseback — a sound, workable plan.

Slowly the hot days of summer passed. Dita and I began to see a serious drawback in having nearly floor length hair. We tended to melt or so she claimed. Now we took to wearing our hair braided Tashien style. During these past months, our nails had continued to grow and before we left, we both visited a nail salon and had them done up properly, cherry red. Only now ours were approaching six inches in length, nearly that of San Min herself. We discovered this too was becoming a problem. Ordinary things were far more difficult to accomplish with such long talons. "I guess we've reached the extremes and should cut back," Dita suggested.

I chuckled. "Yes, too much of a good thing are we." To help pass the time, we began to play card games. Still, we all found it a tiresome trip; the heat was stifling inside the carriages. The last week before we got to Gaikou and old Doc Yi's city, we all began riding our horses just to get out of the carriages, though riding along with the hot sun bearing down on us was almost as unpleasant.

As we rode through Gaikou, I felt as though many eyes were spying upon us. Even Ilenakova felt uneasy as we passed through that city. Perhaps it was because this was the home of the sadistic Doc Yi. Once clear of Gaikou that feeling went away. Now the road began climbing with a much steeper grade. We were definitely gaining altitude. To the north and south, the green covered razor-backed ridges loomed higher, steeper, and larger, the valley floor grew correspondingly narrower. Still farmers managed to grow crops on terraced plots on the hillsides. At last, on August 1, we pulled into the last village on this westward road out of Zau, Mong Yu.

There was only one inn in the village with only four rooms, so we all doubled up. Bianca and Louis didn't mind this at all; neither did Fina and Tian. Ilenakova and Enrico grinned and shared a room. "Oh to be so young again," Enrico teased Ilenakova.

The next day, we spent purchasing food supplies for the rest of the journey, based on Shi's estimates of the number of days we would need to travel, about a month. Our carriages crammed with food and camping supplies, we rode out of Mong Yu, continuing on the west road, which was now only gravel. We could see the smoke from smelters and talus slopes from the various mines located precariously on the steep rocky ridges to the north and south of us. The air was cooler, and we were at least a mile high at this point, climbing higher with each mile we took. The grade, however, was still manageable, though our horses had more of a workout pulling the heavily laden carriages on up the dirt road.

A week later, we left all signs of civilization behind us. Gone were even the last vestiges of mining operations. The winter snows were too deep and the terrain just too inhospitable. A day later on, we were finally forced to leave the carriages behind. We stowed them and concealed them as best we could. "Duh, we forgot packhorses," Ilenakova teased us. We packed our stuff on the horses and discovered that four would have to walk! We all laughed and merrily began the last leg of this long journey. Dita and I rode, of course. It would be nearly impossible for us to walk over this rocky ground with our tiny feet.

After ten days of roughing it and trying to sleep on boulder-filled ground, our grumpy group finally spied the black opening above us and off to our left, a bit south. Although we saw the spikes the Shi had pounded in the cracks of the steep slope leading to the opening, we followed his advice and made our way on up the extremely narrow gorge. While the others went on foot, leading the horses, such was impossible for Dita and me. We had to ride. Just when the crack seemed to vanish, we spied the relatively flat ledge that arced around the sheer cliff face to the entrance of the Doll Creature's cavern. Again, Ilenakova followed Shi's advice and blindfolded the horses. Slowly and carefully, they led the horses along the ledge and into the dark tunnel opening. Dita and I clung to each other and shuffled our way along the ledge, being the last to enter.

As promised, I made a Mind Link to Dianna, our trusty engineer, so that she could see what I was seeing and offer many suggestions. After securing our horses and sticking a grain bag over their heads, keeping them content for the moment, we lighted our eight lanterns and began our search of the alien's cave complex. While the cavern's internal lights were turned on, we could use our lanterns to illuminate the dark recesses. Much was as Shi had described. We found the enormous bed and the cavity, which had held the golden helmet and girdle and found where they had discovered the gold ingots. The cavern seemed to be devoid of all else, except the strange instrument panel, which we suspected operated the suppression energy beams that had for centuries kept all the people in Tashien so low in emotional tones.

Bethany, there has to be more here. Look, if this is all there is, the person who lived here would be just bored out if their mind! Dianna sent me.

"Dianna thinks there may be more here. Check for concealed doors or secret chambers and the like," I suggested to the others. We all fanned out and began tapping on the walls of the various rooms. If nothing else, we had to be certain that there was nothing else here. We stopped for supper, compliments of Bianca and Fina, who tired of pounding on walls.

The next morning, we continued our search. Around noon, I decided to try something different. I imagined I was one of these creatures and pretended that I was walking in from the entrance. Now where would the most logical location for additional rooms be located, I asked myself. My answer was straight ahead of me. I tapped on the cavern wall there and it sounded hollow. A few more taps and I called out. "Hey, I think I have something here." The seven others rushed to my location, verifying the hollow sound themselves.

"Yep, something is behind this stone wall," Dita concurred. "How do we get through it?"

While the others began pushing, shoving, and kicking at the stone, Dianna had me stand back so she could see the whole wall, via my eyes. At last, the others gave up in disgust. Still, Dianna continued to look. *Say, there is the answer. See that indentation there?* She used my arm to point it out to me. *Try pushing or pressing there.* I asked Enrico to give it a try. He put his shoulders to the stone, pushing on that spot. A grating sound echoed throughout the cavern as the stone slid to the left, revealing another tall tunnel.

"Way to go, Dianna!" Ilenakova called out. Back home, Dianna flushed. Eight lanterns illuminated the long tunnel, but not for long. Dianna spied what she thought were light fixtures fastened to the wall along the tunnel. She had me push a button on the side wall near the stone door and these lights suddenly turned on, magic, I thought.

The tunnel led to three rooms. One was a study, complete with desk and chair, though they looked nothing like ours. The room was filled with interesting objects and Dianna and I ended up staying in here, collecting up what she thought was worth recovering and bringing back to Velona. The others fanned out to check on the other three rooms.

One chamber held all sorts of gadgets and devices, whose purposes or uses were entirely unknown to us. When Dianna saw these, she insisted that we bring all of them back with us. This room was a workshop, she concluded. The third room was a combination exercise room and storage room. However, Dita and I spied what just had to be a torque ball court on one end! We chatted over this find, ignoring the rest. For us, torque ball was our favorite game; we'd played it together for lifetimes now. "I wonder who invented the game," she commented. "Did the Dolls get it from us or did we somehow get it from the Dolls?" Neither of us had any idea, though.

In this room, Bianca discovered a large cache of gemstones, uncut, along with some additional gold bars. Now began the lengthy packing of all the items. Dianna wanted us to bring nearly everything back with us. In the end, Dita and I remained in the cavern while the others took eight horse loads down to the carriages before returning for more and us. We spent two weeks ferrying all the stuff down to the carriages. The last action we took we did at the request of De An. Using hammers, we eight smashed the machinery, which activated the suppression energy beams into small crushed bits. No way did De An want someone to reactivate those horrible beams.

September 1, we finally arrived at where we left the carriages and hitched the horses back up. Unfortunately, the carriages were brimming with all the stuff Dianna wanted us to bring back to Velona for her study. Enrico and Ilenakova lifted us up and we rode beside the drivers, Enrico and Ilenakova. The others rode the four remaining horses, down the canyon we went. For the horses' sake, I was glad that they were going downhill with this heavy a load.

On September 7, we spent the night at the only inn in Mong Yu, taking well needed baths as well and getting a sound night's sleep in beds for a welcome change. Then, we hit the road again. On September 14, we approached Gaikou once more.

"Hey, gang, I have a bad feeling about this. Stay alert for an ambush or something," Ilenakova called out from her driver's position on the lead carriage. Dita, who sat beside her, looked off in all directions, and I followed her lead. Indeed, she and I both felt like eyes were watching us. We picked up a definite hostile intention coming our way. Still, neither of us could spot its source. Then, we entered the city and the feeling passed. A half hour and we pulled up at the inn where we stayed. The feeling had gone and we put our attention on the tasks at hand.

Refreshed, the next day, we headed out again, facing the long three-week journey to Zau. Our thoughts naturally drifted to the distinct possibility that we could then head home to Velona. Our work here seemed to be winding down completely.

Chapter 33 Revenge

Doc Yi returned to his mansion, having changed the bandages on the farmer whose hand he'd removed a couple days ago. Panic swelled in his stomach the moment he saw his cook unconscious on the kitchen floor! He checked on her vital signs; she was alive. His eyes swept to the locked basement door. It was still locked, the key in its usual place. His tight stomach began to relax. Doc Yi took the key, unlocked the basement door, and descended, unlocking the inner door.

His eyes darted about the empty room! There were the seven beds, but no women! His test subjects, his experimental patients were gone! His stomach knotted tightly once more, threatening to expunge his late lunch. He swooned and sat down on one of the low beds.

"How could they have escaped?" he asked the walls. Slowly, he realized that on their own, they could not have left the basement period. Someone had raided his house and stolen his prized experiments from him! They had the audacity to relock both doors! Anger surged through his body, replacing the fear and terror and sense of loss. "How dare they! I am the world's foremost surgeon! They won't get away with this! I swear!" Doc Yi was mad, madder than he ever had been in his whole life.

Slowly, he went back upstairs, not bothering to lock the basement door. He bent down and woke his cook up, helping her to the couch. His interrogation of her yielded no additional facts. She was struck from behind and had no idea that someone had stolen his specimens, as she referred to the seven women he cared for in the basement. He retired to his study to think.

Who could have stolen his specimens? His mind drifted from surgeon to surgeon. At last, Doc Yi decided none of them would have done this to him. While some were at odds with some of his procedures, none even knew about his women. His office manager had never seen the women, only the cook and she was sworn to secrecy. She was loyal to a fault and would never have told anyone about them.

Then, he remembered the strange visitors who had been here days ago asking the strangest of questions. They just had to be the ones who kidnaped his specimens! Literally, there was no one else who might have known about them. It had to be those people. Doc Yi grabbed his cloak and left his mansion. He went straight to the pub that he frequented. There he spotted Meng Fen, a most unsavory sort, but a life-long friend. The two chatted and Doc Yi handed him a money pouch. Meng Fen rose and left hastily. Doc Yi finished his pint and headed home. It was full dark now.

He waited in his study for news. The hours passed. At last, Meng Fen knocked and Doc Yi quickly let him inside. "Well?" the surgeon asked.

"They left in a hurry. Some saw them leaving in two carriages, not the one in which they came. You are likely right, Doc. Now what?" Meng reported.

"Find out who they are and where they are from. Where they are going, if you can," Doc Yi replied, experiencing a bit of relief. He was now convinced that these foreigners had stolen his experimental patients, the perfect specimens of his surgical work. Why? That was obvious. They envied his marvelous work and wanted to copy it, to study his handiwork. Well, they'd not get that chance, he swore. Meng bowed and left. Outside, he grinned, old doc had given him a most worthy task indeed. Excitement rose in the thief-assassin.

Two weeks later, Meng finally reported to Doc Yi. As usual, they met at the pub, where their conversation was drowned by the crowd. "They are headed for the Imperial Palace in Zau, I am afraid. The two Great Ladies you mentioned are called Bethany and Dita, and some say that they are married. The others are merely part of their party, providing security and such. Rumor has it that these two have the Empress' goodwill and are working for her at this time."

"You have done well, Meng, as usual," Doc Yi replied, taking another long sip of his pint.

Meng drew closer, in a low voice, he added, "Some say that those two possess great kijutsu! Very great kijutu! Doc, you have most worthy opponents!"

"Kijutsu or not, I am not going to let them get away with stealing my valuable work!"

"All well and good, but they are going to the Imperial Palace, where they will be untouchable," Meng added.

"Anyone can be touched anywhere," Doc Yi pointed out. "It is just going to be more expensive to get them while they are at the Palace. How much?" Doc Yi grinned. Everyman had his price. He'd learned this lesson half a century ago. There is always a price.

"Expensive, doc. Probably at least ten thousand, maybe more. I'll have to see what I can do, who I can round up," Meng replied. He knew that Doc Yi would pay well for this retribution. Once this job was over, he could retire handsomely.

"Not a problem, Meng. Ten it is," Doc Yi answered just the way that Meng expected.

"What do you want done?"

"Well, if my specimens can be found, I want them returned to me unharmed. However, more importantly, I want those two brought to me, this Bethany and Dita of Velona. Since they are so interested in my surgical skills, I will make them living proof of my skill. I want those two brought to me here, alive. If they have to be wounded, so be it. Bring them to me alive so I can work my magic on them."

"This may cost you even more, you realize, taking them alive when they possess great kijutsu," Meng pointed out, seeing an opportunity to increase the fee.

"Cost is irrelevant, Meng. My work, my specimens are invaluable. Spare no expense, just bring them to me," Doc Yi argued.

Meng bowed. "It will take some time, but I am on it. I will get some helpers together tomorrow and leave for Zau. I'll stay in touch. I am glad that I can be of service to you once again, doc." Over the years, he had procured a number of specimens for the doctor and had later on disposed of them when they had died. Theirs was a symbiotic relationship — a big word that he'd learned from the doc.

By the time that Meng and his band of twenty accomplices were about halfway to Zau, he had learned a great deal about these foreign Great Ladies. Rumors had spread through the pubs and inns of amazing feats attributed to these two women. Some said that they had killed an entire army of soldiers, while protecting the Empress in Nan Yan. Meng couldn't quite believe that rumor. Those of the Golden Warrior — those he could believe.

As he and his men rode down the road toward Zau, to his utter amazement and complete surprise, he saw the very people that he was searching for coming his way! Two carriages lumbered down the road towards his band, which gave way and allowed them to pass. Meng carefully looked through the windows as they passed and saw the two women who had so wronged Doc Yi! Meng could scarcely believe his good luck. The doc had already given him twenty thousand, believing that they would have to infiltrate the Imperial Palace, a dangerous action in the best of times. Now, his prey were coming to him!

He turned his band around, and they began following the two carriages, but from an extreme distance. Meng was cagy and didn't want to arouse any suspicions. When they passed on through Gaikou, Meng knew that he had them. There was only one road out of Gaikou heading west to the end of the valley. Whatever their business there, they absolutely had to return this way and pass through Gaikou, no matter what direction they desired to travel. The valley walls precluded any other direction of travel. Meng hastily went to Doc Yi to report their phenomenal luck!

"Incredible! Incredible! Well done, Meng! Okay, we'll take them on their return trip through Gaikou. I will make my preparations. Bring them to my old farmhouse on the south rim. You know the place. It is isolated and no one will spy on us there. I will be there tomorrow and get my equipment setup and ready. Oh, such a glorious day is coming soon! I don't know how to thank you, Meng!"

Meng patted his purse, "You already have, doc. I'll send word to you when we spot them returning. It may be days before they return. We don't know where they are going or what or why. But we both know there is only fifty more miles of road and then the mountains take over. They will have to come back this way sometime."

Doc Yi shook hands with his old friend. Meng left to work out the details of just how he could capture two powerful kijutsu possessors. Meantime, Doc Yi packed up his equipment and climbed into his one horse carriage. He rode almost due south out of Gaikou, across dirt tracks that led to his parent's old home. It was deserted now, had been for ten years. He kept it as a place for his research and sometimes surgery appointments, ones that had to be done on the side without attracting attention. He spent the next few days cleaning and making his lengthy preparations. He, too, had means of protecting himself from kijutsu. Then, Doc Yi began to wait patiently for his revenge. Oh, it would be stimulating, he mused.

For days, Meng waited for the return of these Great Ladies. He took a gamble that they would again spend the night in Gaikou. This made sense because the next large town was more than twenty miles further east, much too far to cover in a day. He waited patiently in his hiding spot, carefully constructed close to the road. He lay beneath a brush pile, no one could see him from the road, yet he had a clear line of sight of all passing travelers. At last, his patience was rewarded. The two carriages came rolling along, four were now riding their horses just out in front of the two. Better still, the two Great Ladies sat high atop them along side of the drivers! He didn't bother to attempt to see inside of the carriages, merely noting where the eight were located. Most likely, they would use the same order tomorrow.

Once the last carriage could no longer be seen, Meng crawled out of his cover and returned to where his horse was tied, hidden behind nearby trees. He galloped into the city, entering from the south. He headed for the inn where he trusted they would be staying. "Totally predictable," he muttered to himself, as he watched them stopping at that inn. He headed off to gather his crew.

The next day, after breakfast, we again hit the road, heading out of Gaikou. I sat with Ilenakova, while Dita sat beside Enrico. The kids rode out in front of us, enjoying the cool early morning, fresh air. We'd gone a couple miles, when Ilenakova, Dita, Bianca, Fina, and I sensed danger. We called out to each other, warning each other of impending attack. Everyone was very alert; I kept looking in all directions, trying to spot from where the attack was coming.

Boom! Boom! Boom! An object landed close to Ilenakova and exploded. Simultaneously, an object was lobbed up beside Enrico and another between the four horses of our teens. All exploded nearly simultaneously. Just before the explosion, out of the corner of my eye, I saw men rushing us. The concussion of the black powder explosion knocked me out, but I felt Ilenakova falling off the carriage.

Boom! Boom! Boom! Dazed and confused, I heard another three rapid fire explosions and felt my body violently lurching backwards. A funny odor enveloped my head. What was that odor? In my confusion, I tried to focus on recognizing that smell. I couldn't hear much at all. The explosion had temporarily deafened me. Ether! Now I recognized that smell, but I blacked out at that very instant.

"Oh, do I hurt!" Bianca moaned, slowly getting to her feet. She'd been knocked off her horse after the first explosion. Knocked out, she only now began to come to, her whole body aching from the hard fall. Something was definitely wrong with her shoulder. As she came to, she looked and saw it was dislocated. She moaned and realized that she could not even move her left arm at all; the pain was just too great. She looked around and saw Fina, Louis, and Tian lying on the ground. Their horses were milling around some distance away. She glanced at the carriages and saw Enrico slumped over in the driver's seat. Ilenakova! God, Ilenakova! She moved as fast as she could to the back carriage. The front wagon wheel was squarely over Ilenakova's chest! Bianca knelt down and discovered that she was dead, crushed by the carriage wheel. She must have fallen off with the first blast and landed by the wheel. When the second blast came, the panicked horses must have pulled the wagon wheel onto her, crushing her to death. "Damn!" Bianca exclaimed to the world.

She moved back to check on Enrico, he seemed sound asleep. Strange. A peculiar odor still hung in the air by him, though she didn't recognize it yet. Now, she headed back to the other three, kneeling beside Louis first. "Thank god he is still alive," she said. Try as she might, she couldn't wake him. She checked on Fina and then Tian; both were breathing, a good sign. Water, her mind thought in slow motion. She headed for the carriage and returned to her three friends.

She struggled to open it with her one good arm and then let a bit of it fall on Louis' face. Almost at once, he stirred. "What happened? My leg, god it hurts! Bianca, thank god you are all right. My leg," he tried to say.

"Yes, it's broken. Lie there Louis while I wake the others," she suggested and gave him a quick kiss. She roused Fina and Tian similarly. Fina's right arm lay at a peculiar angle and Bianca knew at once that it was broken. As Fina woke, she too suddenly realized the same, crying out in pain, as she came to. Tian woke and snapped to his feet, ready for combat, before he could take in the whole scene before him. "Are you okay?" she asked.

Tian felt himself briefly and answered, "I think I have some broken ribs, nothing serious. Your shoulder — it's dislocated, right?"

"Yes, I can't move it. Fina's got a broken arm and Ilenakova's dead, crushed beneath the wagon wheel. Enrico is out cold, weird smell is around him," Bianca replied.

"Where's Bethany and Dita?" Tian asked, looking around at the mess.

"Mom! Bethany!" Bianca called out, suddenly recognizing that they were missing. She looked in all directions and called out again. No answer came. Repeatedly, Bianca yelled as loudly as she could, but they heard nothing. Neither one of us was anywhere around.

"Let's get your arm back in place," Tian suggested. Bianca cried out in a howl of pain, but felt immediate relief as her arm went back into its proper position. Now it was just sore. Together, she and Tian set to work setting Fina's arm and Louis' leg. Finally, the two went to see about Enrico who was still out cold.

At last, Bianca realized what made that odor. "Ether. They were knocked out with ether, used to put people to sleep during surgery. It's the latest thing to use. I've seen it once in Velona. They must have been gassed, and that's why he isn't recovering. I bet mom and Bethany were also gassed. I have to contact them and find out if they are okay or are hurt." She sat down and tried to relax and calm her racing mind. Eventually, she was able to reach out and attempt the telepathic connection. Nothing. She could reach neither Dita nor I. Reluctantly she got up.

"Find them?" Tian asked hopefully.

"Nothing. I think that they are still out cold from the ether. What do we do now, Tian?"

"See if we can get the carriage off of Ilenakova. We will have to bury her body somehow," he replied. Together, they managed to get the team to pull the wagon a couple more feet forward and off her. Both examined Ilenakova, just to make very sure.

What happened? It was Ilenakova. She had awoken and was hovering over them.

Bianca forgot and began talking to her body. "Ambush. Fina's got a broken arm; Louis has a broken leg. Tian has some busted ribs; my arm hurts. Enrico is still unconscious, but we think he is probably okay. Bethany and Dita are nowhere to be found. I think that they have been abducted again. What do we do?"

"Who are you talking to?" asked Tian.

Bianca flushed. "Ilenakova, she's here above us. Telepathy. I forgot and spoke aloud to her. There, she is joined with you too, Tian."

Damn, damn, danm! What a nasty time to get my body slain! Okay, kids. First, you have to get Enrico roused. Good, you have set the broken limbs. Get him awake, then Bianca, do a thorough search of the entire perimeter. Look for tracks and signs of what happened to them. They were probably carried off. I suspect that you will find wagon tracks not too far from here. I'll stick around and help as I can, but you know I don't do much without my body.

"Okay, will do, Ilenakova," Bianca replied.

"Hey, Bianca, you go do the searching right now. Tian and I will try to rouse Enrico. Louis, you keep a look out for more trouble," Fina suggested.

Bianca didn't hesitate. She began carefully examining the ground. Everything was confused this close to their group. However, some ten feet away, she found sets of footprints coming towards the carriages from both sides of the road. She estimated there were a dozen from each side. She also saw footprints leading back into the underbrush and trees. On one side, she found where they had tied up a number of horses, and there were two distinct tracks, one set coming and one set going back towards Gaikou.

On the other side, the south side, she also found where the horses were tied up, but she also saw wagon ruts. Again, they all led back towards Gaikou. Satisfied, she returned to find the two had finally awakened Enrico, who sat on the ground rubbing his head. "I'm okay. Damn, we were taken by ambush. Poor Ilenakova. I've let her down completely," he wailed.

No you haven't, Ilenakova sent him telepathically. *We were all taken by surprise in spite of our early warning senses. Just a freak accident, me falling off and the horses moving the wagon. Perhaps it's for the best this way. Anyway, we have work to do immediately.*

"You are right as always, Ilenakova," he said aloud, while still looking at her deceased form lying on the ground nearby. "First, we need to bury your body and round up the horses. Shall we go after Dita and Bethany?"

Bury it quickly; then we had better parley, Ilenakova sent to them all, rather startling Louis, unused to having her thoughts appear in his mind.

Enrico and Tian worked together to dig a shallow grave, and Bianca said a few words over her dear friend, before she began filling in the hole. Once that was done, grief suddenly began to flow over them. The stark reality of having just lost their dear friend and companion finally came home to all. They all cried for a time. Ilenakova allowed them a moment, but realized that time was becoming a problem. The longer they delayed, the further away Dita and I would be.

"Parley time," Bianca requested at Ilenakova's insistence. "We have to go after them, but we also have all this valuable alien stuff in the carriages."

"How much time has passed since the attack?" asked Fina, her arm was throbbing, but she tried to ignore it.

They all took some estimates based on the sun's position. They took an average of their guesses, which suggested that three hours had now passed since the attack. Just then, a farmer driving a wagonload of produce came up the road. He stopped and asked if they needed any help. They thanked him and said no. He drove on towards the city.

"Our most important task is to get these alien artifacts back to Zau and ultimately back to Velona," Bianca reasoned. "If these fall into the wrong hands, no telling what damage might be done. Yet, we have to go after mom and Bethany and try to rescue them."

"I'm pretty much useless," Louis commented. "I will have to ride in one of the carriages. My two coppers would be to send Bianca and Enrico off to see if they can find Dita and Bethany. Tian and Fina can drive the wagons on to Zau with me in tow. You two can always catch up with us, since the carriages go slower than you can on horseback."

His plan was quickly adopted. "Look, Fina, Tian, Louis, I am charging you three with getting these carriages with their cargo back to Zau no matter what. Guard them with your lives. Enrico and I will see about finding the others. Somehow, we will catch up to you, if we can. I'll keep in mental contact with you periodically. Enrico, let's ride!"

The two, now heavily armed, rode off to where the wagon tracks began. The two followed them until they joined the road about a quarter mile back towards town. Each took one side of the road and continued looking to make sure that the wagon did not veer off the road taking the two women to some secret place. At last, they entered Gaikou again. Each looked crestfallen at each other. In such a large city, wagons were nearly everywhere. Even here at the eastern edge, they saw five wagons, anyone of which could be carrying the two unconscious women! Bianca refused to say that it was hopeless.

"Let's think about this a bit, Bianca," Enrico suggested, taking charge. "This was done right by Gaikou. Who in Gaikou might want to ambush us and kidnap Bethany and Dita? Have we made enemies here? They didn't take a single thing from the carriages, though I admit we had the gemstones well hidden. Still, nothing was touched inside them. Robbery is not the motive."

"Enemies? Have we made any?" she asked confused.

"What about Doc Yi?" he suggested. "We did rescue the seven women he held prisoner in his basement, his experimental subjects."

"Good thinking. It must be him. Let's go to his mansion directly!" Bianca urged. Forty-five minutes later, they arrived at Doc Yi's mansion. There were no signs of anyone there. They knocked on the door, but no answer came. Still, Bianca had visions of us being held prisoner by this sadist, and the two broke in a side window and searched the entire mansion. They found nothing and no clues as well. Dejected, the two rode back to the inn where we had all stayed several times. They took one room and headed up to it to think.

"What do we do now?" Bianca asked, unable to withhold her tears any longer.

"We are stuck. Honestly, the trail is cold now. I think the best thing we can do now is stay here and keep trying to contact them with your telepathy. Once we can establish contact, perhaps they can give us a clue as to where they are located. Then, we can charge there to the rescue. Other than that, I admit I am at a loss. There are so many wagons moving around the city, we won't get anywhere asking about them. We don't even know who was driving it or how many or what it looked like; we're stuck."

"I know. You look after my body. I am going to shoot up high above the city and see if I can spot a wagon moving around outside the city. Maybe that will give us a clue," Bianca suggested.

A while later, she returned to the vicinity of her body. "No luck. There are many farmer's wagons nearby the city. No way to tell if any is the one we want. I guess you are right; I'll just keep on trying to make contact with them. Damn, damn, damn."

Shortly after noon, a lone wagon pulled up at the abandoned farmhouse. Meng climbed down and waved to Doc Yi, who heard him come and stood expectantly in the doorway. "Got'em both. No problems. Easiest snatch I can recall. Black powder bombs did the trick. They never knew what hit them, though I admit using the ether really worked well. Knocked them out immediately before they had the chance to use their kijutsu powers on us all."

"Well done, well done, Meng! Great job. Lend me a hand carrying them inside," Doc Yi ordered. He was elated, like a kid in a candy store with a gold to spend on anything he desired. Ten minutes later, both women lay on his metal operating table, side by side. He shook hands with Meng, who then left. What the doc did with these women was not his concern. No, the twenty thousand gold was. Well, make that fifteen thousand now; he'd paid off his hired help. Meng headed home to pack, planning to take a long vacation trip to Shansee and retire there, where it was warm in the winters; he could live with the monsoons.

Doc Yi looked at the two unconscious women lying on his operating table and grinned. "Oh, do I ever have great plans for the both of you. Yes, I do! You stole my test subjects, my works of art. Now, you two will become my crowing achievements. Subjects thirty-three and thirty-four were just perfect. Because you both apparently have mighty kijutsu, I must duplicate those subjects. I cannot have you wakening and using kijutsu on me. So it has to be done like those two, though I would prefer a different arrangement. I really enjoyed the look of subject thirty though. Those very short, conical arms were just delightful to look at, amazingly good looking, but completely useless for her. But then, this has never been about her, always about how good — how great she looked. Now you two will look even better than she, once I am done."

"I keep changing my mind, you know. Short conical arms really do look so wonderful on a woman. Still, you have kijutsu. Perhaps you can still muster some even with short arms. I cannot risk that. Okay, doc, time to go to work. Check their level of unconsciousness. Ah, bit more is needed I see. Okay, here we go. My lovely Dita, it is with great pride and honor that I do your first." He set to work.

It was full dark when he finished up with Dita. Standing back, he admired his handiwork. "Oh you are now so utterly perfect! Wait until you see your reflection in the mirror. Magnificent. Perhaps my very best work ever! I shall have to make extensive drawings and publish another paper on the surgery. Now to carry you to your new bedroom and home. You are so much lighter this way, you know." He carried her bandaged body down into the basement and laid her on the bed whose mattress lay on the floor. He double checked her depth of unconsciousness and gave her another whiff. "There, rest easy, my beauty."

Back upstairs, he checked on me. I was still out cold. "Ah, bit more for you so that you have a good night's sleep before I work my marvelous magic on you, Bethany. Tomorrow, you will have also become another magnificent work of art as well!" He gave me a kiss on my forehead, before retiring.

At dawn, Doc Yi checked on Dita, gave her a bit more to keep her sleeping, and then began his work on me. "Ah, I see you are still here and anxiously awaiting my artistry. Today, within hours, you will become yet another masterpiece of old Doc Yi. Why, your form will be absolutely exquisite my dear, just perfect in all ways! Yes, I give you my promise, when you wake up and see your new form, you too will agree that it is most artistic and most aesthetic. However, Dita has you beat in the attractiveness department. I do wish I could do something more to help you out with that, but I'm afraid I cannot alter your looks. Dita is simply stunning. Only now we have to add more qualifiers: try absolutely, exquisitely, artistically, aesthetically stunning, stunning beyond words. I am afraid that you will always be slightly less than she. I do give you my promise that you will be at least artistically and aesthetically stunning. I'll give you that much, Bethany. Now to work."

At noon, he finally finished. "There, all done, Bethany. Yes, I do agree with my own analysis. You are indeed now quite artistically and aesthetically stunning!" He picked me up and added, "And quite light and easy to move around too, I might add. You both will need to eat far less now. That's something. I hear women are always worried about eating too much. Well, that will not be a worry for you any longer." He placed me beside Dita on the low bed in the basement. He checked our depth of unconsciousness and put something over my nose yet again. Then all went quiet.

This data that I have just relayed to you came to light at a much later point in time, when finally I received a therapy session and recovered all that had been said to us while we were unconscious. During this time, I was stuck in an explosion. Repeatedly, my mind replayed the series of explosions. Each time, I seemed to be flying out of my head and off into space, unable to hold my position in space! Wild!

Daylight. Rice and chicken soup. I definitely smelled food. My stomach growled, my hunger intense. I opened my eyes. Oh, my shoulders ached and my thighs as well. My face itched, and I raised my arms to rub the sand out of my eyes. "God!" I screamed, as panic swept briefly through my stomach. I was sitting up on the low bed, a pillow holding me up. My arms were gone; tight bandages marked my arm sockets. My legs were gone below my knees; those thick leather pads encased my lower legs — the kind that Lin Lu wore so that she could somehow walk. My long hair lay draped over my left shoulder as I sat there completely naked and stretched out far below my form, down to where my feet had been.

Beside me, Dita moaned and came too as well. She let out a horrifying screech as she discovered what had happened to her body. We were identical in form, lying propped up, side by side on the bed. "That bastard!" she swore and then looked over at me. "I've failed you again, my love. Damn it anyway!"

"No, we were both knocked out, Dita. It's not your fault, but I'm really scared this time, Dita. I feel so helpless like this," I admitted, fear continuing to gnaw at my stomach as the harsh reality struck home more solidly.

"I feel so weak!" Dita said, mostly ignoring my admission. She was fighting down her own panic. "I can barely move. I'm really scared this time, Bethany."

"I'm too, so weak. I think that we must have lost too much blood at one time," I tried to force my mind to think instead of continuing to allow the panic to grow into terror, which it seemed to be about to do.

"God! I am really getting freaked out, Bethany. I can't move and my stomach is going in all directions. I gotta go to the bathroom soon. How can we? Damn! I'm shaking like a leaf! So weak, so hungry too."

Just then, we heard a noise above us and turned to see more light coming into the basement area. Footsteps, then the familiar voice of Doc Yi, "I'm coming, most beautiful ladies. I'm coming. I have some fine chicken and rice soup for you this afternoon." He came down the stairs, carrying a large bowl, steam rose above the ornate lip decorated with jasmine flowers. We both recoiled; more panic waves hit us both.

Weak as we were, our anger surged over the top of our fear. Dita exclaimed, "You bastard!" Doc Yi ignored her outburst completely, evidently used to such reactions to his surgery no doubt.

"Now then, I know that you both probably need to go to the bathroom and are also very physically weak," Doc Yi said softly, sitting the large bowl down. Without asking, he leaned over, picked up Dita, and carried her to the special chamber pot, one that we could reach with our now short legs. It was sturdily supported in a wooden frame. At least, he carefully kept Dita's now overly long hair from getting in the way. She growled, but used the pot. After placing her back on the bed, he did the same for me.

"Now then, chicken soup for the both of you," he sat down and offered a large spoonful to Dita first. She greedily accepted it. Then, he gave me a spoonful. Soup never tasted so good; yes, I was that hungry! While he fed us, Doc Yi continued to chat away, as if we were his fond patients.

"Yes, I have to apologize for your weakness. I've never done a quad amputation surgery before. You have lost far too much blood, for my liking. Normally, it is just one surgery at a time, you see, though occasionally, I've done both arms or both legs. Yet, in your case, I'm told that you both possess great kijutsu powers. I could not chance it and had to act as I have done. After all, you brought this on yourselves by stealing all my prized specimens, my glorious works of art. How can I show other surgeons the quality of my work — the aesthetic wonders that modern surgery can produce? No, you have forced me to create replacements. You must admit that your new forms are just incredibly perfect now, in all ways, breathtaking beauties to behold. Still, I must find some others to display the ultimate zen-kami look as well. I'm sorry that I could not use both of you for that. You see, I just couldn't risk your possible kijutsu powers and had to remove your arms completely."

"Now then, since all is done and all is now well, if you would like, I would be honored to show you something about how I and I alone can work these incredible surgical marvels. Would you be interested in seeing how it is done?"

Dita withheld her roaring anger and continued consuming all the soup that he fed her. My curiosity roused. "Yes, I would like to see how you do this butchery of women."

"Tisk, tisk, Bethany. By perfecting the art of surgery, all mankind benefits. In my long career, I cannot begin to tell you how many soldier's lives were saved. Sword combat can be horribly vicious indeed. However, I will say that the creation zen-kami has always been my favored surgery. You see, it all began when I was twenty." He continued spoon-feeding us.

"I had just opened my surgery practice when a man came to me with what he claimed was a very special surgical instrument. Indeed, it is very strange and has many unique powers, which over time I came to master. You see it there on that table." We both looked and saw a thick tube-like affair. It was blue in color, and even from this distance, I saw that there were strange symbols written on its side! Damn! Those were very similar to those that we had seen on the other objects we'd recovered from the Doll Creature's cavern! This was one of their instruments! An alien artifact.

"You see, it has an incredible feature that is invaluable in my work. When I make a cut into flesh, it sears the wound as I cut, preventing blood loss. Even when I cut through major arteries, the blade seals them almost as fast as I cut! Yes, in my various publications, I have had to outline in detail how others can duplicate my work using normal means available to us doctors. Still, the use of this blade has allowed me to perform many experiments and perfect the best, optimum means for surgical operations on limbs. Because of this unique blade, both of you will discover that your bodies will heal far more rapidly than normal. My own past experiments have shown that you will heal nearly three times as fast as you would have healed had I used my normal scalpels and saws."

"Oh yes, you are not completely immobile. Those special leg pads that I invented will enable you to walk, though you must be careful to maintain your balance. Isn't that just brilliant of me to have invented ways for those who have lost legs to be able to move about on their own? I should say so," he answered his own rhetorical question. "Now then, in fact, right now you both ought to be able to walk on them, though you might experience a bit of pain, as your legs have not fully healed yet. In a couple of weeks, why, you both will be moving around on your own just nicely."

He paused a moment and added, "Admittedly, Lin Lu and Zhi Jin did take months to learn to walk by themselves again, but they did learn. Of course, Xue and Ting learned very rapidly, but they still retained their arms at that time and could balance themselves well. Still, I am sure you both will be out of bed in no time at all. However, I will continue to feed you. Once we return to my mansion, my cook will take over until I can get some more specimens. I promise you that the next one will retain an arm so she can assist you both. I know Lin and Zhi appreciated that small kindness. You see, I am not all heartless."

"Don't worry. We won't be returning to the mansion for at least a month. I want you to heal fully and learn to walk by yourselves first. In the meantime, I will do my very best to find another and get her ready to assist both of you. You have my word on that. Until then, you will just have to put up with my cooking and caring for your needs. I took the liberty of not cutting your very beautiful and extremely long hair. I hope that it will not overly burden your freedom of motion. Your hair is so lovely that I just couldn't bring myself to cut it."

"Ah, I see that your appetites are strong indeed. Very good sign. The bowl is empty. Let's let your systems digest this amount for now. I have work to do upstairs, if we are to live here for another month. If this stays down, I will bring more solid food for dinner. In the meantime, you can rest, chat, or even begin to learn how to walk on your new leg pads. There should be very little pain if you do so. Remember, there will be no pain once your legs fully heal in a few weeks." He rose and stood back admiring us. "Golly, I do believe that I have done my very best work ever. The both of you are stunning beyond words! Be proud of your new looks, my ladies." He turned and left, climbing back up the stairs. We heard the door shut and a lock click into place. Why the lock, I wondered? We could not climb the stairs, let alone open a door!

Dita belched. "Well, I feel full. Have we got another alien artifact here?"

"Yes, good thing I had the egotistical sadist chat away. We have to get that thing away from him and off with the other artifacts — take it back to Dianna," I voiced my thoughts aloud. For a time, we both just lay there looking at each other and our helpless predicament. Time passed.

Mom? Mom? You awake? It was Bianca attempting to make telepathic contact with Dita, here in the late afternoon.

Yes. We are awake now, Dita replied. Hastily, she explained what Doc Yi had done to us. I felt Bianca's wild emotional reaction and sensed that she was now crying.

"Bianca's with us now. She wants to know where we are," Dita explained, though I had already surmised it was her daughter. She continued her report to me, "Louis has a broken leg, Fina, a broken arm. Ilenakova is dead; the carriage rolled over her. Damn! Damn! Damn!"

"Damn! Not Ilenakova. Doc Yi, your days are numbered!" I cursed. "Tell her we are in a basement of some farmhouse." I realized the second I spoke how useless this information would be to Bianca, who was probably desperately trying to find us.

Dita realized this and I sensed that she made a Mind Link with her daughter. I observed her moving up through the floor and out of the farmhouse. I followed her just to see for myself where we were. The green covered, steep sided, and rocky ridge lay just to the south of this farm. It was the last one before the ground rose too steeply to support reasonable farming. A mile up, we could see the farm country around us, irregular rocky foot high walls marking the farming plots, quite picturesque actually. Way off to the north, I spotted a town and hoped that it was Gaikou. Dita joined with me and suggested that we move over the town to see if we recognized it. I felt Bianca's sobbing in the background, though she was trying hard to mask it. I hoped and prayed that it was Gaikou. From Bianca's gasp, I knew that it was. All three of us relaxed finally; help was not far away!

I told Bianca about the surgical artifact — just how imperative it was that we confiscate it and take it back with all the other alien artifacts. Dita and Bianca both agreed wholeheartedly with that! Bianca then told us to hang loose, that she and Enrico would rent a carriage and come rescue us as soon as possible. We both found that very encouraging indeed and relaxed for the first time.

"What's that?" Dita asked sometime later. We both heard muffled talking coming from the floor above our heads along with a scraping sound. Just as we were about to move out of our heads and up to take a peak, Doc Yi came down the creaking wooden steps into our basement room.

"Ah, awake. Good. Hungry? I've brought you your dinner. I'm afraid that I will need to make this quick. I have surgery to perform yet tonight. Yes, as I promised, I have found you a caretaker. I will leave her with one arm so that she can take care of your needs. Open up, here's some chicken for you, lovely Dita," Doc Yi said with a proud, confident, twinkle in his eye. We both groaned; he was about to do this to yet another innocent woman!

At first, we instinctively ate slowly, hoping to prolong his stay here in the basement. Perhaps the young woman above us would wake up, free herself, and then escape before the sadist was ready to cut into her. Doc Yi, unable to hurry us up, began to chat with us again. "Yes, I will use my marvelous surgical tool over there once more. I believe that I will leave her left arm at her elbow, zen-kami style. What do you think? Won't she look pretty that way? Of course, her lower legs will have to match yours; otherwise, she'd just try to abandon you both instead of performing her duties with you both."

Dita snapped! She'd heard all that she could stomach from this sadist. "Damn you, Yi! Do you have any idea what it's like for women you've mutilated to live their lives?" She fairly screamed at him, taking him slightly aback for a brief moment.

"Oh yes, Miss Dita. You no longer have to work and slave to make a living. You are absolved of all responsibilities in life. You only need to look pretty — models of perfection; let others do absolutely everything for you. What could possibly be nicer? You have no more worries, no more cares, no more concerns. Why, you just have to sit there and enjoy life and all that the world has to offer you!" Doc Yi stated rather didactically, as if addressing wayward schoolgirls.

Then, he realized something. His face reddened, "Oh. Well, if you are worried about having sex, I will do what I can to remedy that." He went on with a rather graphic description of what he'd done for the other women whom we'd already rescued. "Yes, yes, I will see that you are pleasured just as much as you both desire. Have no worry on that account, Miss Dita."

"You are one sick man. Time for your lessons!" Dita cried out, angrier than I can ever recall having seen her. She moved out of her body, grabbed a tight hold on Doc Yi, pinning him against a pillar supporting the floor above us. She took hold of the alien surgical tool and moved various buttons until a cutting blade with a searing edge appeared. As I watched, she pulled his right arm out parallel to the floor and swung the alien tool down hard onto the top of his arm, about an inch from his shoulder socket. His arm dropped to the floor, as steam rose from the instant cauterization of the wound. He screamed in shock, pain, and utter surprise. Out went his left arm and down came the alien tool. Doc Yi fainted as his left arm fell to the floor.

Dita still held his body pinned to the pillar. Twice more, she swung the alien tool, removing his legs above the knees. At last, she plopped his body onto the foot of our bed, satisfied at last. "Never, ever mess with Dita!" she spat at him. She fiddled with the buttons, and the tool went dormant once more.

"Well, love, now he can experience what he's done to so many others," I said quietly, still a bit surprised at Dita's vengeance and anger.

"Oops," Dita said. "Guess I will have to feed you, my love." Doc Yi had only been feeding Dita before she attacked him. I was starving and readily agreed, as bits of chicken floated up off the plate and into my opened mouth. It tasted good, though I had to block the bloody images from my mind.

When we had finished the diner, she asked, "Now what? Wait until Bianca and Enrico get here?"

"I suppose so." What else could we do but sit there and wait?

Sometime later on, once it was full dark, Doc Yi moaned and awakened. His scream of recognition of his condition and situation was hideously loud and bone chilling! "What have you done to me? Help me!

Help me! Oh my god!" He began to bawl loudly and uncontrollably.

"Now you have a taste of what we and all the other women you've mutilated have felt. How do you like it, Doc Yi?" Dita sneered victoriously. He wailed and wailed like a baby, before changing into a pitiful moaning cry.

Up above us, we heard noises and a crashing sound. "Perhaps we can float up there and see if we can free the trapped woman," I suggested.

Dita agreed, and we two moved up through the floor and began floating from room to room, looking for the source of the noise and where the woman might be being held. Everything was pitch black! We followed the noise. At last, we entered what must be his operating room. Now we could see again. A young woman lay naked on the operating table, thrashing about and trying to free herself from the silk rope that bound her to the table, spread eagle. She had managed to knock an oil lamp off and the bowl had shattered. Flames roared against the wall where the oil had spilled. Worse, a keg of lamp oil was engulfed in flames! Any minute, we expected the keg to explode or erupt in a giant ball of flames, adding to the fire.

While I only move large objects and those rather crudely, Dita was the master of fine motions. She began working on the four ropes that bound the young woman to the table. She was half crazed, still partially under the effects of Doc Yi's drugs, though she was coming out of it now. One arm suddenly became free, and she reached over to try to free her other hand, while Dita moved down to untie her legs. Just as she got free, the keg exploded, sending oil flying over half of the room, almost reaching the young woman. She staggered out of the room, coughing madly from the acrid smoke. Dita and I pointed her in the right direction and made sure that she got outside the building, before we dove back to our own bodies.

"Damn! Damn! We are in a fine pickle this time," Dita swore. Smoke engulfed the entire basement now. Flames roared at the stairs leading down to us. I took a quick peak up the stairs, before rejoining my body.

"We're trapped! While we can lift and levitate our bodies out of here, Dita, we can't get them through the flames!" I explained, a slight panic in my voice, which I tried to quell.

Doc Yi coughed and wailed. "Help me! I can't move! Help, anyone help!"

"Nice feeling? You look so pretty, Doc Yi. Isn't it just grand that you must now depend upon others to do everything for you?" Dita snickered, driving her point home to this sadist who thought himself a doctor. His body shook in utter terror and complete panic.

"How are we going to get out?" I asked Dita.

She looked at the stairs and came to the same conclusion I had. "Can we punch a hole in the wall?" she asked. Not a chance. We were underground, no walls to break through. Already we could feel the intense heat coming from the burning boards over our heads.

Dita sighed. "Looks like there really is no way out of this bonfire for us, my love."

As much as I wanted a way out, I also didn't see any either. Both of us were now coughing like mad as well, drowning out the moaning and crying of Doc Yi, who thrashed about at the foot of our bed, feeling intensely his utter helplessness. Well, at least he got the chance to experience what his victims had, I thought.

"Dita, if there is no way out of this for us, could you please give our pathetic bodies a neck twist? That way, we will not have to suffer the agony of burning to death." I sighed; no way did I want to feel such pain.

Tears streaming down her cheeks and wholly unable to wipe them, Dita whispered, "Neither do I, but I won't do it until the last moment." Again, we coughed from the thickening smoke. Already, we felt the intense heat over our heads. The floor would soon drop the fire down on top of us.

Chapter 34 The Brotherhood of the Dragon

Dita moved out of her coughing body and prepared to give my neck a twist. No way was either of us going to go through an agonizing, hideously painful burning death! Just as I felt her touching my head, we both heard footsteps running down the steps to the basement. The smoke was so thick that at first we could only hear the person. I judged that the person was taking them two at a time. Dita stopped her actions and returned to her body, and we tried to see who was there. We knew it was not Bianca and Enrico. They were still miles away, bringing a carriage for us.

A man appeared before us, a wet rag over his face. His gasp told us that we were not quite what he had been expecting. His muffled voice called out to us, "Kijutsu?"

"Yes, both of us have kijutsu," Dita said between coughs.

Immediately, he went into action. He laid us both back on the bed, tore the sheets out and wrapped us up together into a tight bundle, our chests touching. Well, I could at least give Dita a kiss this way. His strong arms picked us up, and I felt him moving. Curious, both Dita and I moved out of our bodies to have a look at the fire. As he began ascending the steps, we saw a raging inferno at the top of the stairs! No way could we get through that! Our rescuer would be incinerated along with us!

"There is no heat. The flames cannot touch me. I cannot be harmed by these flames," the man chanted softly to himself, as he climbed the stairs towards the crackling flames. Crash! The floor above our bed fell, igniting the bedding. We heard the agonizing screams of Doc Yi, but could do nothing for him.

Freakish! That's the only way I can describe what happened as the man carrying us moved into the roaring flames at the top of the stairs! Involuntarily, I ridged what few muscles I had left and felt Dita doing likewise. Yet, our bodies felt only a small increase in heat from the flames, but our rescuer seemed wholly unaffected by them as he strode confidently through the licking, curling flames.

Only when he paused at the edge of the collapsed floor did he hesitate. I sensed a slight feeling of panic coming over him and acted. I lifted him up and moved us all over the gaping hole, setting us down on the far side of the room. Instinctively, the man began running through the smoke and finally dashed outside the burning farm house. Now I could see that the whole building was totally engulfed in flames, like some massive bonfire for a giant.

However, I also saw the alien surgical tool, if that was its true purpose, floating over to us out of the flames. Good old Dita refused to let this device be incinerated! The man kept on moving until he came to several horses. There we saw the woman whom we had helped rescue dressing herself in some spare clothes. Gently, the man placed us onto the ground and removed the sheet so we could breathe fresh air. Our naked bodies began to shiver in the chill of the evening air, but we both gasped and took in clean, refreshing, life-giving air at last!

"Oh!" the slender woman exclaimed as she first saw our mutilated bodies. "You found them, Xiong. Are they our goddesses? They must be, Xiong, they must be! Quickly, we must get some warm clothing on them before we ride." While he moved to his saddlebags, she fastened an oversized belt around her waist and spoke to us.

"I am Priestess Lian Ju Meiyan. Thank you for rescuing me from that evil man. My husband Xiong Meiyan has rescued you from the flames. You will come with us now." She was probably twenty-five, of average beauty, with braided long black hair and matching piercing eyes. From her tone, we knew that she was used to giving orders and getting her way.

Still coughing, I answered her, "I am Bethany Brozena Malina and this is my wife, Dita Malina. A few days ago, Doc Yi captured us and cut off our limbs. Thank you, Xiong, for saving us from a certain and painful death. Our friends, who are coming to rescue us, are nearly here and will take us back home to Velona, Sea Princess. They will be here in a little while, so you can just leave us here. We will be all right now that we are out of that inferno. Say, how come you and we were not burned horribly when we went through those intensely hot flames?" I was more than a little curious about that!

"Kijutsu," Lian Ju answered as she slipped a shirt onto Dita. "Xiong is a master of fire, as we all are to some degree. Often, he will walk unharmed over a bed of hot coals. Such is the test for anyone who wishes to become a Dragon. Dita, can you stand by leaning on me? I want to get these panties on you, if I can, so that you will be warmer." With a bit of assistance from Lian Ju, Dita rose on her two short legs, while Lian Ju got a pair of warm, cotton briefs on her. Meanwhile, Xiong slipped a warm cotton shirt over my torso and began buttoning it. I admit we both looked a bit weird with armless shirtsleeves dangling at our sides, but we were warm at last.

While Lian Ju began putting a pair of briefs on me, she added, "I'm afraid that we must take both of you with us. It is obvious that you two are our long awaited goddesses. You must come with us now. Besides, our enemies are near at hand, the Icemen. It was they who captured me and gave me to Doc Yi, who was going to cut off my legs and one arm. He said I was supposed to be your helper woman. Then, he knocked me out with some kind of drug that smelled awful. No, we cannot permit you to stay here. You must come with us. You must fulfill the ancient prophesy. We cannot allow you goddesses to fall into the hands of our enemies, the Icemen, who will claim you as theirs. You have saved my life back there on his operating table so I don't want to use my kijutsu to force you to come with us. However, if you resist, I will have to do so."

While she spoke softly, I sensed a veiled threat behind her words. *I can take them both out, if you want,* Dita sent me.

My curiosity was still roused. Who were these two? What was all this about? Who were these Dragons and Icemen? We'd heard nothing at all about either group. What did she mean goddesses? Did the Icemen also think that we would be goddesses too? What was going on here? I had too many unanswered questions, which overrode my feelings of helplessness just now.

Let's go along with them for the moment, Dita. We need to find out what this is all about. It could be important to the Empress, I sent.

Wids! Dita sent back jokingly. I looked her way, and she gave me a teasing smile.

Mom! We see a large fire on the horizon! Are you still okay? Bianca made contact with her mother, and Dita quickly joined the three of us together. Dita explained what had happened and our miraculous rescue.

The alien tool is lying on the ground near a tree where the two horses have been standing. Make sure that you find it and take it with you. Follow us somehow. I don't see a carriage, so I suppose they will somehow take us on horseback. Perhaps you should ditch the carriage and follow. Wids! Dita teased me once more. I sensed Bianca giggling.

"Look, Lian Ju, we've just had this major surgery a few days ago. Our shoulders and legs are aching and are only just beginning to heal. You'll need to change our bandages frequently, to say nothing of helping us with absolutely everything else. We are now so completely helpless," I tried to reason with her, indicating just what she was getting herself and Xiong into by taking us with them.

"We will deal with your bandages. Yet, you both possess great kijutsu, so use it to help yourselves when you need it," Lian Ju replied, too harshly for my way of thinking. After all, ignoring our spiritual powers, we were about as helpless as could be. Yet, I also sensed that she was being practical and not throwing huge amounts of sickly sympathy our way as I would have expected normal people to do with us. She was telling us subtly to do what we could for ourselves. Interesting, I thought, and wholly unexpected as well.

"We must hurry, Lian Ju. The Icemen may come here at any moment. The fire will certainly attract them," Xiong urged his wife, who finished dressing me. "I brought your horse, you take one, and I'll take the other."

He lifted Dita up and sat her in his saddle. Carefully, he draped her long hair out in front of her. While making sure that she didn't fall, he climbed up behind her. At the same time, Lian Ju lifted me up and sat me on her saddle. I held on tightly with my legs as I could, feeling very vulnerable. If I started to slip, I would have to use my spiritual skills to keep my body from falling off! She mounted behind me, sliding one arm securely around my waist. After draping my hair across my front side, she turned to Xiong and nodded. Both kicked their horses into action.

I guessed that it must be around nine or ten at night. Thank god they didn't trot! My body just could not take such bouncing now. Both horses moved easily into a loping gait, one that gave us a better ride, but where were we heading? How long would they ride? My lungs still burned from all the smoke I'd inhaled. I knew that I needed a bath and probably ought to have the bandages changed as well.

The cool breeze kept my face alert; we rode across the countryside, heading northeast. After a time, Lian Ju began talking again. "We were going to visit my mother, who was supposed to be dying — at least that is what the message had said. Now we know that it was just a forgery to lure us out of the Holy Temple. Mom was just fine, but when we left her house in town, we were jumped by twenty men. I was knocked out and woke up as they handed me off to Doc Yi. Yes, they were definitely the Icemen. Xiong followed their trail and found me just as I was coming out of the burning farmhouse."

"You see, I started that fire. After I learned what Doc Yi intended to do to me, I struggled to get free. Well, I did so once I woke up. He knocked me out with some kind of drug that smelled awful. As you know, I was bound spread eagle on his operating table. I started the fire in hopes that it would burn through the ropes tying me down to the table. Of course, being a Dragon Priestess, the flames would not harm my body. Unfortunately, the flames were taking far too long to reach my binding ropes. I do have to thank you both for helping to free me."

"You're welcome. But how come the flames do not burn you or your husband?" I asked, becoming even more curious.

"We are Dragons. Okay, we are all spiritual beings; we are not our bodies, we use them. Members of the Brotherhood of the Dragon spend their lives worshiping the Holy Fire. We train ourselves to become immune to heat and flames. You see, all physical life is based upon Fire. Without fire, human bodies would perish. Bodies use fire to cook, to keep their bodies from freezing, to warm their baths. Indeed, our bodies could not live without the Holy Fire. We train our whole lives to become masters of Holy Fire, forsaking these fleshly bodies, searching for a union with the Holy Flames, which gave birth to us all."

"Lian Ju, Dita and I also know that we are spiritual beings and not these fleshly bodies that we inhabit. I agree that fire is important to optimum survival of our bodies. You'll get no argument from us on that point," I decided to play along with her a little and see where this got us.

"Of course you must. Otherwise, you would have no kijutsu powers. I sensed that you two were very special the moment I detected your presence over me on that table. I admit that at that time I had no idea that you are *the* prophesy come unto us, Goddess Bethany." I wanted to query her more on this point, but Xiong intervened.

"Lian Ju, the road is clear. We will make for Yuanhey's place. He'll put us up for the rest of the night," he called out. We crossed the main road that led east towards Zau and rode on northeastward for a while longer. The terrain here was hilly but held many fields. However, in the darkness, I couldn't tell what crops were being grown, save corn. Around two in the morning, we pulled up before a farm complex, the home of an extended farming family, the Yuanhey's.

"Dita, Bethany, call upon your kijutsu to keep your bodies in the saddles while we dismount," Xiong commanded softly. A lone dog began barking, announcing our arrival. While Dita and I sat in the saddles scarcely daring to breath, holding our upper legs tightly to the sides of the saddles, the two walked up to the main farm house door and knocked. Shortly, a man holding a lantern opened it and the three talked in hushed tones.

Soon, Lian Ju and Xiong came back to us and carefully lifted us off and carried us into the house. The farmer gasped when he saw us, but said nothing. He led us into a back guestroom, where the two sat us down on one of the two beds. "Please, don't tell anyone about the condition of our two Holy Women. It is a matter of the greatest secrecy!" Lian Ju begged the old man. He nodded and asked what she needed.

Neither of the two wanted to wake the whole household. There would be far too many prying eyes and questions asked. Instead, Xiong and Lian Ju decided to handle our needs themselves. He carried in a large washtub while she began boiling water. The old man set about finding towels and a late night snack for us all.

"See if you can use your kijutsu to feed yourselves, while Xiong and I get the bath ready," Lian Ju asked. Well, it was more like a command really. Dutifully, Dita began moving the food up to our mouths. While we ate, the two brought many buckets of water, adding the boiling water when it was ready. By the time we finished, they stopped to eat a bite as well. Then, she carefully bathed each of us, washing the smoke stench from our hair as well. She was very gentle in removing our bandages, and we got our first look at how our wounds were healing. I detected no signs of any infections in either of us. At last, I relaxed a little.

Xiong then dried us off and patted out our long hair, before applying fresh bandages. "Tomorrow, we will tie up your hair into a bun so that it does not get in your way or ours," he explained. Finally, he tucked our naked bodies into bed and covered us up, rather as if we were his little children. As we drifted off into sleep, we heard them bathing themselves.

When morning came, the two helped us use the chamber pot, but then left us to feed ourselves. Lian Ju returned a while later with a sewing kit. "I am going to alter some clothes to fit your forms better." Later, we wore a shirt whose sleeves had been removed and the holes sewn shut. Underneath, we wore cotton briefs — a workable combination. The shirts were long enough to act as short dresses, which was all that we now needed.

This finished, I expected that the two would hit the trail once more, but I was wrong. "Lian Ju, we don't dare travel in the daytime with these two. Everyone will see their uniqueness. We must now travel under the cloak of darkness."

"I agree, Xiong. We cannot be seen carrying these Holy Women. Night it is," his wife agreed.

"Where are you taking us?" I ventured. "Is it a long journey?"

"Our Sacred Temple is in Quanhao, not too far from Luoyang in Linyi Province. It is about five hundred miles from here. Once we get you safely inside, you will be very safe. No one but a fellow Dragon can physically get to you there. You will see," Xiong answered me in a straightforward manner.

He continued, "You both did very well riding horseback last night. We will continue in that manner because we can travel much longer distances each day than we could if we had to bring you home in a carriage. I know that a carriage ride would be more comfortable for you, but we need speed. I believe that we can make at least forty miles each night. We should have you safe in about thirteen days. Now see if you can get some sleep. We have a long ride ahead of us tonight."

"Damn it, Enrico, I've failed mom yet again!" Bianca wailed to Enrico as they drove their carriage along the dirt track heading for the farmhouse of Doc Yi. "That bastard has cut off both their arms and cut off their legs at their knees. I've failed them again!"

"No Bianca, you haven't failed them. We were all taken by surprise in that ambush. We've done everything possible to locate them and get to them as fast as possible. What else could you or any of us possibly have done? I feel horrible that Ilenakova was killed on my watch. I was responsible for her safety too, you know. Yet, there wasn't anything that I could have done differently to have prevented it. We were just taken by surprise, that's the truth of the matter. Bianca, what is now important is for us to stay close to them to help them out when they ask."

"I suppose you are right," she sighed. He was, she knew that, still it didn't relieve the remorse that she felt. "Well, we did at least get the alien tool. It was right where she said it would be. I wonder how they managed to get out of that blaze?"

"Ask her next time you two chat, telepathically, I mean," he added. "Damn, this carriage is doing poorly cross country. We're going to have to swap the carriage for some horses soon."

The two were riding slowly along, trying hard to follow the faint trail left by the two horses carrying us some miles ahead of themselves. That it was dark greatly hindered them, for they often had to stop and use a lantern to verify that they were still following us properly.

Sometime after sunrise, they reached the east-west road. Here they paused and Dita made contact with her daughter. "Wow, now we know where they are headed and how. They are being taken to a town called Quanhao, which is not too far from Luoyang in Linyi Province. Mom said they would continue on horseback during the nights. Golly, I wonder how they can manage that as they are? Scary I suppose," she added, imagining us trying to sit atop a horse.

"We should take this opportunity to ditch this carriage, Bianca. Let's head west and find us the nearest town, sell the carriage, and get us properly supplied."

"Right. Makes sense. Say, I wonder how someone can be impervious to flames and heat? Mom said that all these Dragons could walk over hot burning coals. How is that possible anyway?" she asked. He shrugged his shoulders, impossible, he thought.

Around noon, the duo, now properly equipped for cross-country travel, paused beside the road where they had earlier left our trail. "Damn! It looks like some twenty others are also following them!" Bianca exclaimed.

"Maybe we have delayed too long," Enrico added worriedly. He too could see the unmistakable signs. "Let your mom know that others are following them. Let's make haste, and see if we can catch sight of whoever is following them." He didn't tell her of his sudden, dark thoughts about us. Twenty against two were bad odds, if it came to a fight. That these might be friends did not occur to Enrico.

Bianca contacted me, while my body lay trying to sleep during the long afternoon. *Bethany, we are again picking up your trail. We're on horseback and are prepared to camp out if need be. Are you aware that about twenty other people on horseback are also following your trail?*

No. But then Xiong did say that their enemies, the Icemen, might try to attack us. You two use extreme caution. See if you can spot who is tailing us. We are going to ride only at night; that should make it harder for them to follow us. I'll keep you updated on our direction of travel as best I can. We're at some farmer's place right now. Just be careful, Bianca.

Right, I sure don't want to lose my arms and legs like you two. Are you sure that you are doing okay? It must be awful for you and mom.

Awful, yes. Okay, well so far. At least we are alive. I thought that we were goners in that fiery blaze. I guess De An will have some more miracles to work whenever we do get back to Zau.

I sent her a good image of what this farmstead looked like, hoping that would help them find us more easily. The two rode on for several hours, passing by many working their fields. However, around five, they neared a small stretch of woods. "Look, the trail goes around that patch, but the twenty headed into the woods," Bianca pointed out.

"I bet they are making camp or have stopped for diner or maybe even the night," Enrico began making guesses. "I think we ought to go wide around these woods, unless you think that we should try to sneak a peek at whoever these are."

Bianca mulled it over. Two Protectors against an unknown twenty didn't sound appealing, especially since they had no back up, no one to help them if they were wounded. "We go around for now. It is more important that we stay close to mom than it is to find out who else is trailing them." They rode far to the west of the woods, rejoining our trail a mile further northeast of the woods. Both noticed that now only two horses were leaving a trail to follow. Conclusion: the twenty or so had to be back in those woods.

Just before dark, Bianca pulled up. "Hey, that looks like the farm down there." They were atop a small rise, gazing down on a large farm. Low rock fences marked the edges of over a dozen small fields surrounding the valley.

"Let's make a good guess which way they will head off after it gets dark. We position ourselves so we can get a glimpse of these two strangers who have them," Enrico suggested. Based on their direction of travel, the two skirted the farmstead and dismounted in a few trees on the opposite side of the wide valley, about a half mile distant from the farm buildings. The two fixed themselves a cold dinner, while watching the darkness fall.

"You know, they are going to have to spend each night at some farm along their route. I bet those won't be total strangers," Bianca theorized. After all, if someone showed up at our home with two women in the condition of mom and Bethany, everyone would be all eyes and wondering about them. If nothing else, they would raise intense curiosity."

"True. If they came to our home, I would be the first to want to do all that I could for the two. But Bianca, how could they know so many farmers and farmers at the key stopping points along their route each day? Are they retracing their original journey to visit her mother?"

"Well, if it was just us, we'd ride during the day and camp out in isolated groves at night," Bianca added her thoughts. "I don't think that they are retracing their steps, staying at somehow known farms. It would be easier and faster just to travel the main roads between here and there. I think that because they have mom and Bethany and because of their scary mutilations, they don't dare travel openly anymore. Maybe cutting across country would shorten the time to get to their temple place. I can see why they would want to travel by night, because no one is likely to get a good view of mom and Bethany. Still, I wonder how they will be choosing where to spend each night."

"Well, we know that all four of them needed a bath after being in that fire," Enrico added. "Perhaps they stopped here because they knew that they could get a bath in relative safety. Maybe after this, they will camp out, hiding among trees in the wild. I certainly would."

"Yes, but what about the people tailing them? Mom said that they expected these Icemen would be coming after them. Do they want to be overtaken in the wild?" Bianca asked, thinking hard.

"Perhaps you are on to something. If they were taken while they were in a building, they could be surrounded and trapped inside. It would be harder to trap someone if they were out in the open. I guess we'll find out near sunup," Enrico suggested. "Got your spyglass out?"

"Yes, I'll take the first watch. I want to get as good a look at mom and Bethany and their captors as well. Why don't you try to catch a little sleep? I suspect we'll have some action soon," Bianca replied, stowing the remainder of their gear into the saddlebags. Both their horses were grazing but ready to mount at a moment's notice. Enrico lay down, but only relaxed; he couldn't afford to sleep. At any moment, they would have to begin to trail the four. Besides, he missed the cocky, confident Ilenakova, now more than he ever had before. He was glad that Bianca didn't see his eyes water heavily.

Just after full dark, Bianca roused Enrico. "I see a man out saddling two horses. Here, have a look yourself." She passed the spyglasses to him. A bit later, he handed them back.

"My god! It is as bad as they said. Both are just like those two that we rescued!" Enrico whispered, a catch in his voice.

Bianca's eyes watered as she focused in on her armless mother sitting astride the horse, her legs were now less than two feet in length, barely able to sit in the saddle and with no way to hold onto the horse. She watched as Lian Ju sat me upon the other horse. Hastily, she focused her attention onto the two others. Both were skinny and neither looked at all like fighters, yet they were average height. She noted nothing unusual about them, though the darkness severely limited her observations. Perhaps when they stopped in the morning light she could get a better view. As she watched, both mounted and she relaxed. Bianca saw that both put one arm around the two relatively helpless women, making sure that they didn't fall off.

"They are coming this way; we best hide," she whispered. The two ducked behind some trees, and waiting and listening. Soon, the dull sounds of walking horses reached their ears. The pair passed about five hundred feet from their concealed position. Neither dared breathe until the horses crested the hill and disappeared from their direct sight. However, they did get a brief look at them.

"We shouldn't follow them too closely. It will be hard for us to tell when they stop. We certainly don't want to run into them," Enrico suggested as the two mounted their own horses. Bianca then relayed what they'd seen to both Bethany and Dita.

Twenty-two men are following you. All are wearing long grey robes, so it was hard to see much of them. They are about a half hour behind you now. We are giving them a lead on us because we don't want to run into them either. Is this a good plan? Are these the Icemen that you were warned about? Should we try to get ahead of this bunch in case they attempt to waylay you?

Good job, Bianca. You and Enrico are doing great. Let me see if I can get more info from Lian Ju. I smiled; indeed, she was becoming an excellent Protector. "Lian Ju, there are twenty-two men following us. They are wearing grey robes. Are these the Icemen that you were telling me about?"

"What? Following us? Xiong! Goddess Bethany is saying that twenty-two Icemen are following us. Bethany, any idea how far behind us they are?" Lian Ju asked worriedly, involuntarily tightening her grip around my waist. I knew that she was very worried about this news.

"A half hour to an hour at most," I relayed Bianca's estimate.

"Half hour, Xiong! What are we going to do? I will not let them catch me again. I don't want to become like our goddesses or even killed," her voice trembled slightly. I knew that she was actually in fear of these men. Her encounter with Doc Yi said it all.

"Let's try and put some distance between us and them," Xiong answered, though I knew that he really didn't have many options available. Carrying us was slowing them down. "I'll leave them a warning." I wondered what he meant by that, as both horses broke into a canter. Okay, I admit that Dita and I love to canter, though an all-out gallop is even better. Still, I was a bit spooked without having arms to hang on if needed or legs with which to grip the horse. The cool night air flew by my face; my senses were fully alert now.

A while later, we passed by a grove of trees. Here, Xiong slowed down and began a chant. A lone pine tree at the edge of the grove suddenly burst into flames. "There, that should serve as a warning to the Icemen," he called out.

I didn't like to see the tree burning. While yes, it did announce that the Dragons were ahead of them, it also provided a clue of our path as well as a time marker. I thought his act was rather foolish, but kept my mouth shut.

"Why are they after you, Lian Ju?" I tried to pump her for more information.

"I'm the Priestess for the Brotherhood of the Dragon. The Icemen are our worst enemies. I guess I should explain better. You see the world is a composite of four elemental forces: fire, earth, air, and water. From the dawn of time, many have worshiped these forces of life. Some of us believe that fire is the principle motivational spirit within all life. We are called the Brotherhood of the Dragon. Then, there are those who believe that the earth is the prime factor, the Brotherhood of Stone. Others believe that the air is more important, the Brotherhood of Air. The Brotherhood of Water believe that water is the prime source of all life. While we four are sometimes at odds with each other, we all know that the world is composed of each. Life cannot exist without portions of each."

"We devoted Dragons spend our lives working with and controlling fire. Indeed, the most elementary of our worshipers can walk barefoot over a bed of hot coals without harm. Likewise, the other Brotherhoods are masters of their elemental force. I've seen some men stay underwater for several minutes! I've seen some creating great gusts of wind that can knock you off your feet. Yes, we in the Brotherhoods have a kijutsu command over the four elemental forces."

"However, there are those who hate us and what we stand for — hate us with a passion. They call themselves the Icemen. Mostly, they live in the cold Dong Province, usually near Xin. Most of us in the Brotherhoods live in and around Luoyang in Linyi Province. The Icemen claim that bitter cold destroys fire, hardens water, and makes the air and ground unusable by man. Hence, they seek to destroy us. They sent me that message that my mother was dying. Their ruse worked. Xiong and I rode all the way back to Gaikou before we fell into their trap. They intended Doc Yi to mutilate my body and thus remove the Priestess of the Brotherhood of the Dragon. Thanks to your timely intervention that has been prevented."

"Now they have picked up our trail. Perhaps this time, they will just outright attempt to slay me, who can say," she finished up rather indecisive. That both of them were very worried was clear to me, but now I could offer no solution. I relayed all this to Bianca and Enrico.

Our horses were well lathered, and the two were forced to slow to a walk for a time. Xiong kept looking back over his shoulder, but the darkness was complete. The moon was new. Starlight yielded little hints to him, but not to Bianca and Enrico. They had slowly been closing the distance between the Icemen and themselves. Now they could see the backs of the men about a half mile ahead of the two.

Bianca's former lifetime's skills as a Sisterhood tracker returned to her. In the dim starlight, she was able to pick out our trail easily, quite unlike the Icemen ahead of them. What she and Enrico found most interesting was the Icemen's reaction to the burning pine tree. When they came upon it, both witnessed their reaction. The group paused a minute and a huge wall of ice surrounded the tree. Within minutes, the flaming tree was extinguished amid a volley of laughter and boasting. "Ice and cold wipes them all out once again," a distant voice bellowed out a counter-challenge, though we were far from this location by then.

"Well, it seems that these men can create ice, much like our ice sheets," Enrico whispered. "That makes them dangerous."

"Curious, the Dragons can create fires much like we can, while the Icemen create sheets of ice. I wonder what the other three groups can do? Bethany did say that Lian Ju said the air people could create blowing winds. Probably that is similar to our Push chants," Bianca concluded. "I wonder what the water and earth followers can create. Are these people also residing outside of their heads like us Druwids? If so, that would make them very formidable opponents."

"I don't like how this is developing," Enrico mused. "First we encounter martial arts masters, whose combat styles are killers. Yet, many also possess kijutsu powers, especially the Olin Masters. While these are now on the side of the Empress and ourselves, we know nothing about these new sects. How big are they? How much territory do they control? What is their goal in all this? Will they become an obstacle to the Empress and her re-establishing control over the chaos of Tashien?"

"We need a closer look at these Icemen, that's all," Bianca replied. "Whenever they make camp, let's sneak up on them, and observe them for a while. What say you?" He grinned. He liked this teen's style.

An hour later, the Icemen stopped. Bianca and Enrico dismounted and quietly snuck up for a closer look. The men seemed to be discussing the trail and were confused. "Are they still riding? It's nighttime," a voice complained.

"I don't get it. Are they going to ride all night?" another queried and coughed. Several more grumbled. Several more coughs broke the nighttime stillness. Overhead an owl flew past the group, who did not notice its flight.

"I get it. I think that they are on to us and are riding all night. Come on; let's see if we can catch them yet tonight," another voice said with a bit more authority than the others did. Still grumbling, the others mounted up. The two waited until the group had passed out of their sight before making their way back to their horses and mounting.

"Well, they are not stupid," Enrico commented as the two began following the group. "They've worked out the plan."

"You think that they will actually catch up to mom tonight?" Bianca asked worriedly. She then answered her own question. "Hey, they still are not cantering, just trotting along at best. No way are they going to catch up at this pace. Should we try to go around them or should we tail them all the way?"

"Let's tail them a while longer," he suggested.

Xiong pushed us as much as he dared without overtiring our horses. Around four in the morning, the first traces of twilight rimmed the eastern sky and I began wondering where we would stop this time. I think Lian Ju was wondering the same thing, she turned and asked, "Now what?"

"We covered more miles than I intended. Let's see if we can get permission to bed down in their barn. From there, we'd have a clear view of this ridge line so the Icemen won't be able to take us by surprise," he suggested. "Wrap Bethany in your cloak like I've done with Dita. That way, they won't see their actual bodies, just their heads. Let's try to keep the two concealed as much as possible. Far less questions that way."

Slowly, we rode down the hill and along the farmer's dirt track that crisscrossed his carefully tended fields. As usual, the farmer had removed the stones from his field, using them to form a low fence around each plot. Now the weeds had grown over them, giving a quaint appeal to his hedge line. Already we could see several people moving around the barnyard area.

One was milking a cow.

Xiong rode ahead of his wife and chatted. The milkmaid called out for her father and soon, he was holding a discussion with the elderly man. A gold coin made all the difference. He opened his barn doors and we rode inside. "Bring you food and drink after mom makes it," the farmer announced and closed the doors partway. When the coast was clear, the two dismounted and lifted us off the horses, sitting us down in the soft hay pile. They arranged cloaks over us to hide our unique shapes and then set to work on their horses.

Once we were fed, Dita and I fell asleep at once. It had been a nerve-wracking night ride for us. When we awoke the next late afternoon, our two captors were already up and saddling up the horses. After another meal, compliments of the farmer, we prepared for the long night's ride once more. By the light of the late afternoon sun, I got my first chance really to observe our captors. Both of them had skinny bodies. From the blackish expectorate of Xiong, I realized that his body was ill with the rotting lung disease! Lian Ju herself was not very healthy either. She had some lesions on her legs that ought to have been looked at and attended to months ago! Dita observed that both were solidly located within their body's heads, a fact that surprised her, since she had seen him conjure the fire that burned the pine tree. Neither of us knew what to make of it.

Meanwhile, the Icemen had continued riding all night long. As dawn came, they finally crested the ridge and looked down at the farmstead where we slept, though they did not know this detail. At last, so many of the Icemen were grumbling, they had to stop to rest as well. The group made camp in a grove of trees near the ridge line, ate some dinner, and began to sleep. Two guards were posted, each being relieved every two hours.

Bianca and Enrico camped on the far side of the grove. Although both wanted to go spy on these Icemen, Enrico insisted that he do it. When he returned two hours later, he outlined what he'd observed. "These are not typical strong, muscular fighters, Bianca. While they must have powers, their bodies are thin and gaunt. A couple have limps when they walk. I don't think they are very healthy, physically. I don't know what to make of that." Neither did Bianca. The ability to exercise spiritual abilities always required an alert, able being, one not stuck inside his or her head. Yet these Icemen were all plastered solidly in their body's heads! How unusual both thought.

As the sun set, I finally spoke up, "Xiong, the Icemen are camped among the trees along the distant ridge line. How are we going to escape them? Under the cover of night?" I wanted to alert him to their presence.

"Thank you Goddess Bethany," he bowed to me. "I am indebted for your timely warning. I will think of something." Lian Ju, on the other hand, looked panic-stricken. The Icemen were within attacking range. He thought for a minute and then began drawing in the dirt.

"There is a creek not far from here which flows to the east. We'll make for it and then head down it for a couple of miles. Then, we'll double back and continue our northeast route. That may throw them off our trail. I hope so anyway."

The horses were ready; carefully, the two placed us up onto the saddles. Gently, they mounted. Once again, I felt the secure arm of Lian Ju around my waist holding me steady in the saddle. Slowly, we rode out of the barn and headed off to the north. I sent Bianca our plans and asked her to bypass going east down the stream, but to make a trail to the northeast where we entered the water. Perhaps that would confuse them a little as well. She agreed.

"Qwan! Look! There they are! What? Who? They're carrying two women with them. Look at them! I've never seen anyone like that. Are they midgets?" one of the two Icemen guards called out to the other.

"What are they doing?" Qwan replied. "No, those aren't dwarfs. They don't have any arms at all. How can that be? Such short legs too."

"Looks like those women have lost their lower legs too. What evils have these two Dragons done now?"

"Rouse everyone! We must go after them and find out. Now we have proof that the Dragons are savages! We must take those helpless women from them. If we can get them, why, we can use it to raise enough anger to crush all four Brotherhoods at the same time!" Qwan growled, convinced that he now had his ultimate weapon of destruction — if only they could catch up with the two fleeing Dragons. Unfortunately, the sleeping men wasted a half hour getting ready to go after them. By then, it was very dark once more. That cost them dearly.

None saw Bianca and Enrico circling west of the farmstead and then rejoining our trail. When they came to the stream, the two did as I asked and crossed it, leaving a plain trail for the others to follow. The two waited a half hour some distance from the creek to see if the Icemen would take their ruse. The men did, following across the stream after them. Grinning, Bianca now set a course to the west to delay the men even longer. Only around midnight did the two finally veer to the northeast once more, galloping to make up lost time. We didn't realize it then, but their action created a five-hour delay before the Icemen finally found where we had actually left the creek. By then, we were many miles ahead of them, far too many for them to catch us that night.

Day by day, I noticed that the air grew chillier, and a few trees and bushes began changing into their fall foliage. Autumn was upon us. I had lost track of the date and finally asked Lian Ju. "We'll be in Quanhao on October 4, tomorrow, Bethany," she replied. Indeed, since we had lost the Icemen, her spirits rose. Or perhaps it was because she was so close to home and her temple. By now, our surgical wounds had fully healed, and we needed no bandages any longer. I was relieved that we had not gotten an infection during this unusual trip. That alone was a minor miracle in my mind.

Chapter 35 Of Temples and Kijutsu

She was right, on October 4, we finally entered the town of Quanhao, just north of the Binz River which separated Wontun Province from Linyi Province. Some fifty miles due east of here lay the provincial capital of Luoyang, which straddled the Binz and Upper Yonshu Rivers. As we rode into the city, I estimated that perhaps a half million called Quanhao their home. This was not a small city by Velona standards anyway. As expected, our bodies were hidden beneath cloaks with only our heads visible as we entered the city, teaming with people and activities.

Already the daytime temperatures were significantly colder than expected, until I realized that we were now at least a thousand miles north of Shansee. Winter would definitely come here. I also remembered the Empress' discussion of their ice province, Dong, which lay but a few hundred miles further north of here. I shivered a little beneath the cloak. Neither of our captors had brought along heavier clothing but I was promised a warm bath soon.

Still, the city seemed strange to my eyes. The people were all bundled up in heavier, layered clothing. Dark browns, aquamarines, bright reds, and off-whites predominated, though each person that we saw wore only one color of clothing. "Don't be deceived by their clothing colors," Lian Ju whispered. "Not everyone is a follower of the symbol's color. Dragons and those who support us wear red," she explained.

"Got it," I replied. "Aquamarines support the Brotherhood of Water. The browns, the Stones; and the off-whites, the Air. Right?"

"Yes, Quanhao is the center of the four Brotherhoods in Tashien. Each has its Mother Temple here, though smaller towns have lesser temples as well. Elemental worship is widespread here in Linyi Province. The Icemen live just north in Dong Province. However, I meant what I said. Do not be deceived by colors. Often, one will wear the guise of another, especially the Icemen. Please say nothing to anyone."

With increasing frequency, passers-by began nodding or bowing to Lian Ju as we passed them. I realized that they recognized their Priestess and her husband. Our captors were well known on sight; I filed that datum for future reference. About a half hour later, we drew near a huge, walled complex, with a rather ornate architecture. "The Royal Palace," Lian Ju said gruffly and spat towards the wall, but her shot fell far short of its mark.

"For centuries, a relative of the Empress has attempted to rule Linyi from here, the Royal Palace. Right now, our so called Princess is a distant cousin of the Empress San Min Wu. Diadan Wu is her name. As always, the Brotherhoods compete to attempt to convert the Princess to worship the Elemental Life Forces. Rarely do we succeed. Princesses are so utterly vain, so utterly caught up in their looks and appearances that they cannot worship anything but themselves." She spat once more. "Yet," she sighed, "we continue to make the attempt. However, now that we have you Goddesses, perhaps that will change." I began to wonder what exactly she meant by that remark. Had we suddenly entered a realm of political subterfuge once more?

Within twenty minutes, we entered a huge open square located in the very center of Quanhao. In its center rose four giant temples, each vastly different in appearance from the other. The red sandstone brick building had to be the Temple of Fire. Second tallest, it rose in eight jagged tiers or spires, each one becoming narrower with each floor. I guessed the topmost rooms were maybe six feet square, but offered a magnificent view of the city.

The brown granite building housed the Temple of Stone, the earth worshipers. The Temple of Water was aquamarine, as I expected. This building was only a single story tall, but five times the width of any other temple. Its blue roofs were undulating, giving the appearance of waves upon the ocean or a river. The off-white temple towered above the others, almost twice the height of that of the Dragon. While its main floor was large, probably to house the many worshipers who came for a service, and each floor above grew smaller, until the room at the top spire was again perhaps six feet around. Yes, the Temple of Air was circular in shape.

All four temples were in close proximity to each other, and the huge open square dwarfed the temples, which lay precisely in its center. What I found intriguing were the four color-coded paths across the square. Each led to the main entrance of the corresponding temple. While there was opposition between the four elemental fractions, they obviously also worked together as a whole. I found that to be an encouraging idea. They embraced the concept that the world needed all four working in a relative harmony for the survival of us all.

We rode up to the Dragon Temple's main entrance. At once, three red robed men stepped out and took the reins, while one helped their Priestess dismount. All stared at Dita and me, however. Quickly, Xiong and Lian Ju lifted us off and headed inside, where we would be out of sight of the public eyes. The entrance led at once into a huge Holy Chamber, as Lian Ju explained hurriedly as we walked rapidly across the huge room. As in any church, rows and rows of pews filled the space. The Altar of Fire demanded my full attention, however. It was spectacular; brilliant reds predominated, accented with tinges of orange and yellow, as if there were real flames rising from the altar.

Behind this Altar of Fire lay a set of descending steps. "Our followers and assistants live above in the upper rooms," Lian Ju said hastily. "However, those rooms are not secure. We must give you Goddesses our absolute best protection. We are going to the Inner Fire Sanctuary, where none but a true Dragon may enter. There you may relax and be assured that none but a true Dragon could possibly enter. You will be safe there, completely safe."

We descended some twenty feet; flaming torches illuminated the steps, also blood red in color. At the bottom, I felt a rush of heat and warmth. At first, I relished this! What was left of my body was overly chilled. Then I saw its source!

Before us at the bottom of the steps lay a bed of flaming coals! From wall to wall the coals burned, flickering deep red colors. Heat waves undulated before our eyes, distorting the view of the long hallway. "Dragon Flames are always here. The bed is fifty feet long. There is no other way past these but over the coals. Look," Lian Ju said, as she tossed a bit of cloth onto the coals. Instantly, it burst into flames.

"If one were to walk across wearing boots, they would be burned off the person's feet within a few feet. Only a true Dragon may pass this test. Yes, the other Temples have their Inner Sanctuaries similarly protected. Come, we will carry you across." First, both took off their boots and socks, holding onto them as well as us. Bare feet touched the coals, as both concentrated and chanted as they walked over this long bed of blazing hot fire. I was utterly amazed. If I had my feet and tried it, I would have had my feet burned off! No doubt about that! Dita was flabbergasted and said so. Fifty feet on down the tunnel, they stepped back onto solid rock once more. Both paused, as if catching their breaths.

"Over that bed of coals is the only way in here. Only a true Dragon can make that walk. Now you are very safe, Bethany, Dita. No one can harm you now," Lian Ju repeated. "Now, let's get you to my quarters, see about baths, and getting you your own private quarters. We have much to discuss, much to explain, but let's deal with our physical bodies first, shall we?" I didn't object.

We soon discovered that these Dragons loved warmth! This suited us, since we now had very limited abilities to clothe ourselves. In fact, the place was so warm that we only wore the lightest of silken clothing. Once we finished our baths and several women finished dealing with our long hair, we were dressed in the thinnest, finest red silk camisoles, which made our lack of arms extremely visible to a casual glance! Dita also claimed that they also revealed a bit too much, as they were very see-through in nature. We also wore red silk panties beneath our camisoles. Once our leather pads were again tightly laced, we were able to sort of stand up again, though neither of us had any real chances to learn how to really walk on our own.

"Do you want your hair in a braid or in a bun?" Lian asked as she stood back satisfied with the way our clothing looked on us.

"We are used to having it loose and flowing, although with our legs cut off, it is way too long," Dita replied honestly.

"Yes, I agree, Dita. Let's do it that way. If it causes too much trouble for you, I can always do it up in a bun for you." She gently draped Dita's thick black hair over her shoulders and down her chest, allowing it to bunch a bit on the floor before her. Then, she did my long blonde locks.

"Okay, both of you. From now on, you are to use your kijutsu as much as you need. I will not always be available to assist you. I know that you can levitate your bodies and move them, so I will not be carrying you anymore. Indeed, with your fabulous hair, I would recommend that you carry your bodies high enough so that your hair is above the floors. You will look positively stunning that way. However, I or one of my Dragon Maidens will assist you with your bathroom needs and help tuck you into bed at night. Other than that, please use your powers to help yourselves."

"Now then, if you will follow me, I will show you around a portion of the Inner Dragon Sanctuary, where you will be staying in perfect safety," Lian Ju ordered. We had no choice but to lift our bodies up and move them after her. Yes, she did turn around once to see how well we looked floating along behind her. I felt a little annoyed with our having to use our spiritual powers for such mundane uses, however, but I said nothing.

"Here is my private room. Next to mine will be yours. Ah, here are my Dragon Maidens, Ali, Chani, and Dan E." The three young women, barely out of their teens I surmised, bowed to us but also stared at us in complete awe and disbelief. After introductions, she had us enter our new quarters, which the three had been fixing up for us while we were being bathed and dressed. Our bed mattress was on the floor so that we have an easier time getting in and out. The decor was red satin and silk, varying shades, emulating flames. A pair of torches illuminated the room, which was small, about ten feet square. By the way, thus far, we saw no doors on any of the rooms, which suited us fine, if we were to be floating our way around the complex.

Next, she took us back out and down a hall to their dining room. A kitchen and pantry lay just to the left; probably they were just behind the stone wall our own room. Here we sat down and were served a good meal, the best that we had had in over two weeks. A number of other Dragons soon joined us and Dita and I became the focal point of everyone's sight, though none spoke to us aloud. That we levitated our food to our mouths attracted their full attention, but Lian Ju would not have it otherwise. If we wanted to eat, we had to feed ourselves by using our spiritual skills. Well, Dita fed us both, since she was the master of fine motions. I did most of the lifting and moving of our bodies around the complex.

After we ate, Lian Ju insisted that we all get some sleep. She promised to explain much to us in the morning after breakfast and her obligatory services to her fellow Dragon followers. After Chani and Ali tucked us in and extinguished the torches, Dita and I were finally alone for the first time since we were in Doc Yi's basement. However, Lian's room was next to ours and there was no door. We chose to whisper a bit. When our eyes adapted to the darkness, we found that the room was not dark at all!

Overhead, red glowing stars shone down upon us, as well as a fair number on the walls. Evidently, some kind of phosphorous absorbed the torch light and now was generating a night light for us. "This is really a cool bedroom," Dita whispered. "I like these satin sheets. We can more easily slip around in them as we are." We both wiggled a bit to get onto our sides and worked at getting our heads into a position so that we could embrace each other. Soon we both fell into a deep, relaxing sleep.

"How long do we have to endure this torture of having no arms and legs?" Dita whispered to me when we awoke. "I wish De An were here. I'm ready to be normal again."

"Me too, love. Me too. However, we best play along and see what is going on first. Here comes our helpers," I whispered back.

"Good morning Goddesses," Ali said softly in a humble and holy manner. She was treating us as if we were indeed deities. That came across solidly. We needed her aid in using the chamber pots and then per Lian Ju's wishes, I floated us out to breakfast. Okay, I admit that our appearance, two women floating into a room, makes quiet a statement. Again, all eyes, some thirty, followed our every move. I hate being the center of attention, but Dita did even more so. Both of us stifled our feelings and set about eating, fully anticipating the full explanation of the situation by Lian Ju once we were done.

"Ali, Chani, will you please brush out our Goddesses' hair? I will return once I give my sermon," Lian Ju stated. We had little choice but to follow the two back to our bedroom. For once, I relaxed and enjoyed allowing them to pamper our hair. Indeed, they did a very good job and our hair flowed out beautifully before us. Finally, Lian Ju returned and the explanations began.

"Follow me," Lian Ju ordered. "Few have ever entered our Most Holy Sanctuary, our Hall of Records." She made us move ourselves after her. It looked strange to see her in her fiery red silk robes walking down the equally red hallway with us floating along behind her a few feet above the floor in our red camisoles and our hair falling far below our dangling short leg stubs. Weird indeed, though we complied. We had little choice actually, if we wanted to discover what was going on here.

The hall ended at a round archway, the entrance to their Hall of Records. As we entered this holy room, we both felt a strong sense of deeply felt religious fervor emanating from the very room! Centered on the opposite wall from the entrance arch was her special flaming High Altar. "Holy Priestesses for centuries have kept our most Holiest of Flames burning. Never has it gone out. One of my tasks is to keep it burning," she explained as we floated into the room.

On the right wall, bookshelves rose from the floor to the ceiling, though many shelves were designed to hold scrolls, not books. A mahogany desk and several chairs sat before the library shelves. Ornately carved in a motif of flames, the woodwork was totally unique and impressive, to say the very least. However, our attention was called to the left wall, where an immense tapestry hung, depicting various historical scenes, we assumed.

"Oh my god!" Dita exclaimed, as her eyes fell upon the red tapestry. "That's us!" Indeed, in the first scene, two armless and nearly legless women with long hair appeared floating above and behind the four priestesses. Each of the priestesses wore different colored robes; one was precisely the same as the robes Lian Ju was wearing. I looked closely at the floating women. Stylized, that's how I later described these women. Their faces didn't look like ours, but then they didn't really look like a portrait of any woman, really. More stylized, done in a tapestry. Still, the resemblance was incredibly striking. Now I fully understood why Lian Ju was so taken with us. We appeared to be these two goddesses depicted in this ancient tapestry.

Yes, it was ancient. We both smelled a bit of mildew in the air. While the place was clean, it did have a slight odor of rot about it. Of course, now we both needed to know what Lian Ju expected of us, her ancient goddesses.

"In the Beginning, God created all of us, but we had no bodies, no forms. God then called forth the Holy Four Elementals. He mixed the Earth with the Water and formed fleshly bodies. God breathed the Holy Air upon the lifeless forms and gave life to Man. Yet, this was not enough. He called forth the Holy Fires, and Man was then alive and warm. Man lived and we took these Holy Bodies as our forms. God then appointed four women to be his High Priestesses to oversee and look after his Holy Creations on Tarra. As we all set foot on Tarra, God sent his two Holy Angels, San and Réal, down to assist and guide the four High Priestesses, that they may properly guide us all," Lian Ju explained. Her voice was soft and reverent, expressing deeply felt religious beliefs. "Those are his Goddesses, his Holy Angels you see there floating above the original four Priestesses."

"Here in the middle fresco is our present," she explained further. We saw four separate woven images. Each of the Priestesses had apparently gone their own separate ways, had their own followers. Yet, the images seemed rather chaotic. Some of the small figures seemed to be battling others. Some appeared to be thin and emaciated, perhaps starving. These middle fresco images did seem to reflect modern day Tashien, if you used your imagination a little. Lian Ju allowed us some time to observe closely these middle images, before she moved on to the last image on the tapestry.

Again, we saw the two Holy Angels, San and Réal, floating above the chaos. However, they appeared to be leading the faithful from the chaos of life into some kind of Holy Realm. "It is said that when San and Réal appear again on Tarra, they will lead the believers from the Chaos of Mundane Existence into God's Holy Realm, where we may once again become one with God, our Holy Father. Forgive me, Holy Angels. I am but God's humble Priestess of the Holy Flames. I do not know which of you is San and which is Réal. However, we are ready to receive our long promised Holy Salvation. San?" she asked me.

I could see no way out of this one. "Yes, you may call me San or Bethany, whichever you prefer."

Dita quickly followed my lead, "Réal or Dita, though I prefer Dita now." From her expression, I knew that Dita really didn't expect that she would continue to call her Dita.

"San and Réal it is then," Lian Ju declared decisively. "Now then. . ." She was interrupted by her maiden Chani, who had quietly walked into the room, her head bowed in great reverence.

"Priestess, Shan, Qian, and Wen are all demanding to see you and . . ." she faltered a moment, before finishing, "our Holy Angels. They are being most insistent."

Peeved, Lian Ju growled, "Well, okay. I wanted them to meet you later rather than sooner. Still, they must meet you, San, Réal. Chani, lower the barrier and allow them passage." She turned to us and added, "Come with me. The four Holy Inner Temples share a connecting passageway. However, each of us has an elemental blocking lock to prevent the others from entering our temple without our consent." We floated along after her to the hallway and took a left, entering a small ten-foot square room. Chani was already there, pulling down a level, which extinguished the flames, which blocked the secret passage into this room. She pulled another lever and part of the wall slid off to one side, revealing a well-lighted passage. Searing heat rushed out at us. Dita and I flinched from the unexpectedness of the blast, but the two Dragon women embraced it, as you might expect. I saw that the chamber ahead was really in the shape of a cross and presently a woman came walking determinedly out of each. They nodded to each other as they met in the center and moved directly towards us.

As they stepped into the flame-red small room, they stopped and gasped, staring hard at Dita and me. Well, if I saw us as we now were, I suppose that I would gasp too. Once they stepped into this small room, Chani shut the door and released the flame barrier once more.

"Then, it is true, San and Réal have returned!" the twenty-five year old woman dressed in brown, thin silk robes gushed. Her eyes never left us.

Pointing at me first and then Dita, Lian Ju declared formally, "San, Réal, I would like to present the other three Elemental Priestesses. This is Shan, the Stone Priestess. This is Qian, the Water Priestess. This is Wen, the Air Priestess." Their thin, silk robes told us at once which was which — brown, aquamarine, and off-white. All three women bowed deeply and in awe to us.

"We are your humble servants, mighty Holy Angels," Priestess Wen then said, her voice full of deep reverence towards us.

"If you will follow us into the Hall of Records, we can talk," Lian Ju ordered. Dita and I followed along after her, two floating half-women the length of whose hair greatly exceeded their body's height. The three priestesses continued to covert stares at us as we moved along using our kijutsu powers. Damn, I hated this more by the minute! I was loathed to display my spiritual skills so openly like this. I knew Dita felt much the same.

We floated into a pair of chairs, while the four arranged their seats across from us. Now we both had a chance to observe the four priestesses. Lian Ju Meiyan was thirty-three, with long black hair and eyes to match. She also had lesions on her legs, we noted. Her health was not so good. Shan, the Stone Priestess, wore the thinnest of brown silk robes, revealing her youthful twenty-five year old body. She wore her brown hair in a pair of braids down her back. We also noticed that her teeth looked to be in poor condition. Qian wore aquamarine robes of thin silk, which matched her eyes. Her light brown hair, parted in the middle, lay draped over her shoulders, stretching to her waist. Her hair attempted to hide several patches of rotting skin. She was forty years old. Wen was thirty-five. Her thick, long black hair was very similar to Dita's and contrasted sharply with her off-white silk robes. She walked with a limp, we noted.

Why are all four of them not in so good health? Dita sent me.

Dunno. Maybe we can find out. Damn, no hands to work our healing on them, I replied.

"Lian Ju, how did you find our Holy Angels? We heard that your mother was dying. Was that a deception on your part to keep us in the dark?" Qian asked, slightly hostile towards Lian Ju.

"The message we thought was real, but it was a ruse of the Icemen who captured me not far from my mother's home. Our Holy Angels freed me, but the farmhouse where we were being held captive was engulfed in flames. San and Réal intended to give up their fleshly bodies to save me. Once they had me free of the blaze, Xiong found me and I asked him to go into the inferno and rescued our Holy Angels. Together, he and I evaded the Icemen who were constantly on our heels and brought San and Réal here to the safety of the Dragon Temple."

Just then, the three Dragon Maidens returned with trays of tea, biscuits, and honey. Once again, Dita and I observed just how perfectly these women conducted their tea ceremony, placing each cup in a precise position, filling them in just the proper manner. Everyone seemed to be waiting for some event before eating. I bent my head in a curious manner towards Lian Ju. She smiled and said, "Your Holy Priestesses must not drink before the Holy Angels."

Dita picked up our cups and held them to our lips. We each took a small sip. Even though the three women continued to stare in awe at us, they lifted theirs and joined us. Still, they stared as the knife dipped into the honey jar and spread the golden liquid over a pair of biscuits, which then floated up to our mouths.

Qian then spoke again, "Lian Ju, how do we know that these two are the real Holy Angels, sent here by God? What proof do you have?" Ah, now that was a good question, I thought. Perhaps they had some test that we could fail and be done with this charade. I wanted nothing more than to find De An and have my arms and legs back! I was sick of being as I was.

"They are two. They have no arms at all, as you can clearly see. Their legs end where our knees begin. They have *immense* kijutsu. In fact, they need no assistance in living from us, but they have accepted our assistance with the chamber pots," Lian Ju answered her. "They rode on our horses all the way from my mother's hometown. What woman, who is as they, could possibly have done all that? Have you ever seen anyone like them? While we have heard that the women of Dorota have no arms like these two, those women do life's actions with their feet, or so I am told. Yet these two have no feet. Were you or I in their shape, we would be completely and utterly helpless in all things. I say that there cannot be any doubts at all that they are San and Réal."

"Yes, we accept what you are saying, Lian Ju," Qian replied, still not convinced. "Their skin is a different color from ours. How do we know that they have not just had their limbs removed in some elaborate hoax, possibly conceived by our enemies, the Icemen? Answer me that," she demanded to know.

Lian Ju answered her challenge. "Look, the Icemen left them locked up in the basement of the burning farmhouse, there to perish in flames. Only through Xiong's bravery were their lives spared. They know nothing about the Icemen, save what little I have told them. I cannot explain their skin color; I grant you that. As for their having their limbs removed as part of a hoax on us, well, look. We all know that limbs cannot be regrown. What women would ever consent to having their arms and legs removed? Once the hoax is finished, they would have to live the rest of their lives this way. No one would ever willingly do this to themselves, not for anything."

"Perhaps, they had no say in it. Perhaps, the Icemen captured two women and did this to them and then planted them in that farmhouse for you to find," Qian countered.

I spoke up, "We did not willingly give up our limbs. It was done while we were unconscious and had no say in the matter. No one would ever want to live life as we are now."

"Look," Lian Ju broke in, valiantly trying to convince the others of our authenticity, "Holy Angels must come down and take up a human body. Are not all our children born with two arms and legs? Of course they are. It has to be God's Will that has been at work to have their human bodies so altered to match the foreordained re-appearance of the Holy Angels."

Still, Qian was not wholly convinced. Seeing this, Shan spoke up, "What remains is their kijutsu. Holy Angels must have powerful kijutsu and of course be able to deal with the Holy Elemental Forces that we command. Can they create fire?"

"Where do you want it?" Dita broke in, rather annoyed with the direction the conversation was going. She didn't wait for an answer but used our Druwid powers to create a small ball of fire in the middle of the room, where nothing would be harmed. That caused them to think hard, all except Lian Ju, who saw this as proof positive. We were definitely in command of the Holy Fire.

Wen got into the act; she chanted and made a pushing forward motion with her hands towards us. Dita recognized that her actions were quite similar to her Druwid Push and she countered it by latching on to the far wall and then onto us. Our hair blew out straight behind our heads, but our bodies remained sitting in our chairs. Now Wen seemed completely satisfied.

Dita, fearing further spells or actions coming our way, piped up, "We can control the weather, but that effect takes time to materialize. We can cause the very earth to quake and shake, but that may well cause your Holy Temples to collapse. Please do not ask us to do that. We do not want to see these temples destroyed."

I was glad that my Protector spoke up. While I had no idea what kind of kijutsu the Stone Priestess might unleash on us, or what the Water Priestess might send our way, I didn't want to experience them. At least Wen and Lian Ju were totally satisfied about out kijutsu powers. However, eventually, someone would recognize who we were: those who had been helping the Empress San Min Wu. That alone might totally nullify these priestesses' views of us.

"May we have a say here?" I asked. The four nodded and I continued. "Yes, our human bodies were born here on Tarra. We came to Tashien from Velona, Sea Princes. At first, our goal was to find San Min Wu, who had been abducted and held prisoner. Yes, we have helped her rise to power and begin to create a new political organization for all Tashien, to end the reign of chaos that has befallen your country. Yes, we destroyed the overlord's army sent to slay Princess San Min before her ascendancy to the Imperial Throne. Yes, we are helping the Son of God, De An, spread the true word of God to all Tashien. Now it seems that we are here with you, and we are willing to also share the truths of God with you and your followers, if you so desire. If you do not wish us to do that, then please allow us to leave and return home to Zau."

Good job, love. Now they will surely see that we are not their Holy Angels and will send us packing. I can't wait to get back to Zau and have De An work his miracles on us again! Dita sent.

"You — you were the ones who killed thousands of the overlord's soldiers there in Nan Yan? You *must* be God's Holy Angels!" exclaimed Qian, deeply impressed with Bethany's revelation. Word of that battle had obviously spread up north. Instead of sending us packing as I had rather hoped — I too wanted my arms and legs back — all four were now convinced that we just *had* to be their long sought Holy Angels! My plan backfired; we were here to stay, trapped in these helpless bodies, forced to use our spiritual skills just to survive.

"We must make a formal presentation to our followers," Shan announced.

"Yes, we must, but I claim the right to do so first. After all, it was I who found them, rescued them, and brought them here," Lian Ju insisted. The four began arguing over just how the presentations were to be conducted and in what order. None wanted to be last in line to show us off to their congregation. Ugh.

Chapter 36 Intrigue, Religion, and Politics

Dita and I left the four priestesses arguing about how they were going to put us on display and we headed off to do a little exploring. First, we checked out her records hall. I wanted to see what clues I might find in the many scrolls and books that Lian Ju had. Unfortunately, we quickly saw that this would be beyond our spiritual manipulation skills. Without arms and hands, we gave up this idea in disgust. "I just want to get my arms and legs back," Dita whined.

We'd been through a lot, but this was just too much for her to bear alone. Tears welled up and began trickling down her cheeks. I wanted so badly to reach out and comfort her, to wipe them away, but had not the means. I, too, became overwhelmed with emotion and my tears joined hers. Together, we quietly slipped back into our bedroom and laid our half-bodies down on our bed.

"I'm getting sick of being cut up all the time," Dita sobbed. "I just can't take it anymore, Bethany."

"I know, love. Me too. But look at what all we have accomplished for so many others," I made a valiant attempt to cast our predicaments in a better light. "Besides, I'd rather have this happen to me than to my daughter or yours."

"Well, I have to agree with you on that one. I think that I'd go on a rampage if someone did this to Bianca or Alessa," Dita replied, pulling herself together once more. "I'd better check in with her."

Hi mom. How are you holding up? Bianca cheerily asked a bit later when Dita contacted her.

Dita didn't have the heart to tell her how she really felt, though I sensed that Bianca already knew or suspected. *Okay. We met the other three priestesses a bit ago. Honestly, we don't know what we are supposed to be doing for these people. What's up on your end?*

Bianca eagerly began her lengthy report. *We've scouted out the four temples. Enrico's a master at getting folks in the pubs to give us the scuttlebutt, the lowdown on what's been going on around here. It seems that your Elemental Masters are in big demand around here. They provide protection and security services for many of the overlords and even the Princess. The Dragons are in the most demand because of their powerful fire spells.*

Fina, Tian, and Louis are about halfway back to Zau now. They are doing okay; the cargo is safe. She says that their broken bones ought to be healed by the time they finally get to the Imperial Palace. Once they get the cargo boxed and sent off, they are going to head up here to us as well.

I chatted with De An, and he is heading to Luoyang shortly. He has asked us to try to figure out what's really going on in this province. He thinks that it is somehow different than the other two lower provinces. A couple of weeks ago, I had Empress San Min send word to the Princess here letting her know about us and you two. In another couple of weeks, the Princess Diadan Wu ought to know about us four and give us all the support we need.

Can you two hang on for a couple more weeks? Bianca finally asked what she most wanted to know. We suggested that we could.

Once the connection was broken, Dita sighed heavily, "Two weeks more of this isn't all. De An hasn't even left Zau yet. At best, he won't get here for another month, maybe more. Bethany, another month of this torture? I don't think I can take it. Your Protector is in big trouble."

"You have to, Dita. Look, I can't feed myself, and Lian Ju insists that we have to do that ourselves. I am depending on you, love," I tried to find a way to show her how much I was depending upon her skills. With an effort, she rolled onto her side, and we kissed.

At lunch, Lian Ju appeared in great spirits. "It's all settled. At the evening Service tonight, I will present you to our followers. Then, Qian will present you at her morning Service tomorrow. Wen will do so at her evening Service, and Shan will present you both at her morning Service the next day. They chose to go in age order, you see."

"What do we have to do or say at these services?" I asked, becoming a bit worried. We knew so little about these people, and what they believed in and expected of us.

"At these Formal Presentation of the Holy Angels, we will have two raised chairs behind me and the High Altar. When we give the signal, you will rise into the air, high up, so that everyone present can get a good look at the both of you. All our followers know well the prophesies of the returning of our Holy Angels. By seeing you as you are and seeing that you have a mighty kijutsu, their doubts will be vanquished. You will not need to speak at these four presentation services. After that, we four priestesses will meet with you and you can then tell us what we need to do to obtain Holy Salvation."

"Now, after the Service, some of our most devout and highly skilled followers will want to have an informal meeting with you. All of these are true masters of the Holy Flames. They will break bread and sip of the Holy Wine with you. Many of these are our most powerful Dragons, so do what you can to make a good impression on them. After the other three Services, the other elemental followers will also desire to meet with you and break bread. After those four meetings, you will have seen most all our best, most powerful and most devout followers. Admittedly, some others are not in Quanhao at this time. Their duties and assignments have taken them elsewhere. In the coming weeks, we will arrange for those who cannot meet you personally during the next few days to have an opportunity to do so. A personal meeting with the Holy Angels is of monumental importance to our devout followers."

"Okay, that sounds both appropriate and wise," I replied. "Will we need to give them any advice?"

"Not at this time, but you may bless them as you desire. Oh, one more thing. During the Service, we shoot flames towards the ceiling. As we do that, you are invited to also conjure your flames. Such will mean a lot to our followers, you can understand that, right?"

"Certainly. We will do our best," I answered. I hoped that the other three priestesses didn't want us to conjure water, air, or stone. I couldn't!

Later that afternoon, Ali and Chani brushed out our hair and made sure that we looked our best. After dinner, we followed Lian Ju back out over the fire trap, as Dita now called the protection barrier between the inner chambers and the actual public Temple of the Dragon. Two red chairs now sat above and behind the High Altar. To achieve this effect, several boxes were stacked on top of each other and a red velvet covering placed over them. The chairs sat atop these boxes. The only way to get to them was for us to levitate and move our bodies into the seats, further adding to the mystique.

A twenty-person choir, again wearing red robes, walked in and took their position on the far side. Their director nodded to Lian Ju, but then all of them just stared at us. Dita flushed and whispered to me, "I hate being stared at, now more than ever." I knew what she meant, but could think of nothing to say. We were both miserable, period.

When the first man entered, the choir began singing their hymns. Ah, this was more like it, I thought. Their music was enchanting, very different from what we were used to hearing back in Velona. Even more fascinating were the huge pipes on the opposite wall from the choir. Suddenly they began to sound as well, adding an incredibly low pitch sounds into the mix. Lian Ju explained that this was a relatively recent invention here in Tashien. It was called an organi-fundus. Two workers continuously manned the air pumps, which blew air over the bottoms of the pipes, causing the sounds. The player's keyboard activated stops, which opened covers of the pipes, allowing the air to sound that pipe. When a key was not pressed, the cover prevented that pipe from sounding. I just knew that we had to buy one of these and get it shipped back to Velona! I swear that the very walls shook when the lowest notes sounded!

The huge red Temple accommodated fifteen hundred worshipers at one time. Tonight, word had spread that the Holy Angels would be present. The Temple was packed beyond capacity. Many stood in the aisles, all eager to get a glimpse of their promised Angels of Salvation. At last, the music ended and Lian Ju began the most important service she'd ever conducted.

"Welcome to our most special Evening Service. As has long been foretold, God's Holy Angels have at last appeared, bringing God's Promised

Holy Salvation unto us, his faithful Dragons, his Holy Fire Worshipers. Behind me are San and Réal, the Holy Angels, just as God has so long ago promised."

"Eons ago, San and Réal came unto Tarra with God to help us, God's Children, adapt to his fleshly creations and create our lives upon this land. God, the Almighty, in his infinite wisdom, knew that over the many centuries, we, his chosen, would lose our way, become confused, make mistakes, and need his help and guidance to gain his Holy Salvation. Who among us is not guilty of at least one sin? Thus, in the Beginning, God told us that one day in the future, he would again send San and Réal unto us to help get us back onto the Lord's Holy Path, to regain our spiritual freedom."

"Finally, that wait is over. San and Réal have come among us once again, just as the Holy Tapestries depict. Like us, they forsake their fleshly bodies and strive for spiritual freedom and power. Indeed, their kijutsu is mighty indeed, for who among us would discard their arms and legs and still live normal lives?" We felt the intense stares of awe of well over two thousand men and women.

"Yet, San and Réal have discarded arms and legs to show all of us how unworthy these fleshly bodies are, just how unneeded our bodies actually are. Their spiritual power is mighty, beyond all measure, as bestowed by our God upon them. Let them be a beacon to all. Fleshly bodies are not wanted nor needed by God's Holy Children. Least some of you may doubt that they are San and Réal, imagine yourself without the slightest trace of arms and only the upper part of your legs. Would you be fully able to operate in life if you forsake them as they have done? Nay. I will be the first to admit that I would not."

"All our lives we have put our full and complete attention upon spiritual skills of the Holy Fires, forsaking our weak, fleshly shells. Many of you here tonight have achieved great powers and skills. From walking your feet over a bed of coals to the generation of Holy Flames — so many of us have achieved much. Now, San and Réal have come to assist us in the achievement of the Ultimate Salvation, our personal spiritual freedom finally."

"Let us pray and give our heartfelt and soul-felt thanks to Lord God, our Father, for his precious gift of San and Réal, his Holy Angels." I won't bore you with her lengthy prayer and even longer sermon. At the end of her sermon, she called out, "Now as the Holy Dragon Choir sings our most sacred hymn, let us raise our fires, our flames on high. Let us show Lord God that his children have maintained the Holy Flames all these years."

As the choir and organi-fundus began, hundreds of conjured flames shot up into the air. This was our signal to raise our bodies high into the air behind her, so that everyone could get a good look at us. We also let loose several of our own balls of fire. As we did so, hundreds of voices called out and cheered, giving us a warm welcome indeed.

When the hymn ended, Lian Ju spoke again. "Go forth and prepare to receive God's forthcoming Spiritual Salvation. As usual, those of you who have achieved Apprentice Dragon First Class or higher may stay and break bread and wine with San and Réal. Join us in the Community Room now. May God bless all of you, his precious Dragon Children."

With that, the hour long Service was over. Lian Ju moved towards a side door, beckoning us to float along after her, which we did. Many awe-struck eyes followed our every movement. In the Community Room, rows of tables and chairs awaited. Lian Ju had us sit on either side of her at the head table, perpendicular to all the many rows of tables. Once we were seated, many men and a lesser number of women began filing in, again staring at us, as expected.

Yes, we ate bread and sipped wine with the throng of around three hundred-fifty of them. More significantly, as far as we were concerned, each one was invited to come up to us and greet us personally. Dita and I got a close look at the most powerful of these Dragons. Of course, we couldn't shake hands or even give them a hug, but we at least said "God bless you" to each as they bowed humble before us.

Back in our room that night, Dita commented, "Bethany, there was not a healthy person in the lot of them! Every one of them had some disease, some malady, something not quite right with their bodies. Everyone was thin, like they haven't eaten properly or whatever. What's going on with them? Why are they all sick and not getting medical attention?"

I had no answer. These people were masters of powerful kijutsu themselves. After all, how many people do you know who can walk on hot coals without being burned? How many can conjure burning flames and so on? I also could not help but notice that every one of these people was stuck tightly inside their heads. We Druwids mastered conjuring of flames, but we were all located outside of our body's heads. Indeed, that had been a prerequisite for any Druwid training — the spiritual being had to be outside their body's head. In fact, I couldn't recall that we had ever successfully taught someone who was stuck inside their head to conjure balls of fire! This phenomenon was strange indeed. It only became worse.

Early the next morning, Qian came for us. It was time for the Water Elemental Service. She had us float along after her down the cross corridors and into her Inner Sanctuary, again far underground. Various shades of aquamarine dominated all the walls. Every room had a small water fall or bubbling spring flowing through it.

"I must change your clothing. You cannot be presented wearing our enemy's colors. She and two of her assistants quickly dressed us in aquamarine camisoles and panties, just as thin and fine as the red ones Lian Ju had given us. Once our hair was brushed out nicely, Qian took us to her chambers to await the start of her special Service.

"Just because Lian Ju has more followers than the rest of us is no reason for her to dominate God's Holy Angels," Qian began, somewhat agitated and still uncertain of our opinions.

"The four elemental forces ought to be in balance and harmony with each other," I hazarded an opinion, hoping to set her more at ease with us.

It certainly did! "Now that is what I like to hear. I told her so, but she didn't listen. Yes, harmony and together. You ought to spend alternate days in each of our Elemental Temples. I will see to it that you can spend the night with me. Tomorrow night with Wen, and the next night with Shan. Then, Lian Ju can have you for the fourth night. Yes, that will give us all equal opportunity to you, San and Réal."

"Oh dear, forgive me. I have never been around anyone who are as you — I mean without arms and legs. Are there things that I ought to assist you with?" Qian asked sympathetically, temporarily forgetting about her antagonism towards Lian Ju.

"If someone can assist us with the chamber pots, that would be nice. It is difficult for us to manage that. We do appreciate others brushing out our hair," Dita replied politely.

Then, for the next hour, Qian grilled us with volleys of questions that she insisted on having us answer. Were we born as we were? Did it hurt to have our arms cut off? Were we really from Velona? Why had we come to Tashien? Had God sent us? Why? On and on, she threw question after question at us, until at last she was satisfied. It took my having to lift her and her three maidens up into the air simultaneously to finally convince her that we had immense kijutsu powers.

Fifteen hundred plus gathered in her aquamarine Temple for her special Service. I just loved the huge waterfall that flowed continuously in the background. Water came down from the top of one wall and crashed into a pool at the bottom and flowed out through some underground passage way. I thought this was a marvelous invention and idea. Her Sermon was similar in nature and content to Lian Ju's. Likewise, we broke bread with around two hundred of their advanced members.

After a formal noon meal, Wen appeared and took us and our red clothing over to her Inner Sanctuary beneath the Temple of Air. She redressed us in off-white silken camisoles, which left Dita complaining that people could see her privates right through it. Well, she did have black hair. My blonde hair was not so noticeable. Wen ignored her protest, though.

Wen also bombarded us with many of the same questions that Qian had. She was pleased to hear that we would be spending the night with her, giving her even more time to chat with us. After their evening meal, we attended her special Service. Again, over fifteen hundred thronged into the Temple of Air to see us. We also met a little over two hundred of her most advanced men and women.

Late that evening, she had us follow her up to the Holy Room. This was her special room at the very top of the enormously tall tower. Here the room was barely ten feet across, windows open on all four sides. From here, the view was beyond description! The fresh, yet cold, night air flowed across our faces and bodies. Yes, we both were shivering in these thin silk camisoles, and were most happy to return to our underground room where it was warmer.

The following morning Shan came to get us. She dressed us in thin brown camisoles, stowing our other three sets in a silk bag for us. As her counterparts did, Shan asked us many questions, but dwelt more on how it felt to have bodies such as ours. Did we have emotions like other women? Did we have feelings and sensual perceptions? When she discovered that we were married, she gave us both a big hug. I had no idea why, however.

After spending the three nights in the other temples, we finally returned to the Dragon Temple. Now that we had a little time to ourselves, we compared notes. What struck us more than any other single thing was the fact that all of these more powerful people, the ones with whom we broke bread, all were not in the best of physical health! Some had lung infections that, untreated, would result in their deaths. Some had rotting skin lesions. Some had severe arthritis. The list of ills went on and on. Yet, they all commanded great spiritual powers, many were beyond our own skills, especially those of the earth, water, and air followers. Yet, unlike us Druwids, they were solidly located within their body's skulls. This, I just could not understand.

"Dear, you know that sooner or later, these priestesses are going to ask you about how to obtain their Holy Salvation," Dita pointed out. "What are we going to say?" I shook my head, for I had not a clue.

She was right. The next day, all four priestesses summoned us into the Hall of Records in the Dragon's Temple. "Well, we've presented to God's Elemental Believers God's Holy Angels, San and Réal. Now then, we four are listening. What are God's commands? What is it that we must do to obtain God's promised salvation?"

Have you ever been in a tight spot, nearly helpless and without a clue of how to handle the situation? Well, I certainly was this time. I did the only thing that I could think of: stall for time.

"Our Lord God has sent his Holy Son to Tashien. He now walks among us. He that will provide our Holy Salvation. I can say this much; he is now on his way here from Zau and will be here in a month, give or take. We have seen his many Holy Miracles." I saw all four frowning; they did not like what they were hearing at all. We were supposed to be giving them their promised salvation. I quickly added, "In the meantime, we are charged by God to discover all that we can about how his Holy Children are doing, now, at this precise moment in time. Per his instructions, we have seen how his Elemental Followers are faring. Yet, we are all God's Children, though many, many have lost the path entirely."

Their frowns changed to doubt. Emboldened, I continued. "Take your

Princess for example. Is she counted in the membership of one of your Temples? If so, why did we not meet her during the four Services?"

"Well, no she is not," Qian spoke truthfully. "When she was appointed to become our new Princess, we four attempted to bring her into one of our folds. Lian Ju has come the closest to netting her, though the Princess has not yet actually set foot in the Dragon Temple. Are you saying that all the people in Quanhao are to be considered God's Holy Children?"

"I see. Thanks. Yes, all of them are God's Holy Children, all people in Tashien, all people on Tarra for that matter. We are all God's Children, but so very, very many have totally lost their way, forsaking their own spiritual nature. So many believe utterly that they are nothing more than these fleshly bodies. So many have forgotten who and what they really are," I explained, keeping my non-existent fingers crossed that they would buy this explanation.

I saw the four looking at each other curiously. I continued in the same vein, "I know that you four have been working diligently, long and hard, to bring these lost souls back into God's Holy Light. There is so much more that we need to do, so many have completely lost their way."

"So what must we do?" Shan asked, rather overwhelmed by the thought that millions upon millions of people had to be convinced to join one of the four Elemental Temples.

"God wants us to discover for ourselves just what the true situation is here in Quanhao and all of Linyi Province. I am sure that you believe that Lord God is all knowing." All four nodded enthusiastically. "Yet, we are not God; we are only Holy Angels. If we are to prepare the way, we must know what the situation is. It begins with one person. We should like to meet your Princess. Perhaps we will be able to succeed where you have not."

"Yes, if the Princess is seen to join and support one of our Temples, perhaps that will encourage more to join," Qian offered, she saw at once the wisdom of my idea.

"Yes, but it is not safe for our Holy Angels to go to her Palace. Only within our Inner Sanctuaries can we assure their total safety," Lian Ju added, worried.

"Then, we should ask Princess Daidan Wu to come here. The Holy Angels would like to speak with her," Wen suggested. The four concurred, drafted a message, and sent a messenger to her Palace. Thankfully, the four allowed Dita and I time supposedly to meditate upon how to convert the Princess when she came.

De An! Thank god you're there. Help! We are in way over our heads here, I explained. Dita and I were lying on our bed, supposedly meditating. I joined with De An in a desperate attempt to get some guidance. I relayed what had happened and all that we had seen and heard.

He replied at last. *Bethany, you are right. Never argue religious beliefs with another. Every person has an innate desire and impulse to be right. To be wrong is to be dead. People must find a way to be right, even if they are blatantly wrong. Under no circumstances are you to argue with them about their beliefs or tell them that what they are doing is somehow wrong. That will never succeed and may get you killed.*

Duh! We already knew that with our many encounters with the Church of Jehosanity. He suggested, *First, go over with the four priestesses the Seven Aspects of Life.* He continued with what I thought was a brilliant plan. We promised to do our best.

The next day, word came that Princess Diadan Wu had agreed to meet with the Holy Angels. Bianca and Enrico relayed that word of the coming of the Elemental Holy Angels had spread all over town. We were the topic of conversation nearly everywhere. They overheard conversations about us in the market places as well as the pubs. Thus, I was not surprised that the Princess jumped at the chance to see precisely what was going on. After all, she was supposed to be the provincial leader and was still getting the High Parliament members chosen and sent off as well as establishing their Low Parliament here in Linyi Province.

Of course, the four priestesses now began arguing over which of them would host the Princess in their Community Room. "Excuse me," I interrupted their bickering. "May we have a say in the location of the meeting with the Princess?" That stopped them. All four bowed and allowed me to continue. "I would like to meet her in the Community Room of the Water Temple. Why? The sound of the running waterfall there is both soothing and relaxing. Such will aid us with the Princess, calming her and putting her more at ease. Don't you think so?" I probably shouldn't have said that last, and I regretted asking that. Thankfully, they agreed with me.

We donned our aquamarine camisoles and panties. Then, we six went over to Qian's Temple. They left us in the Community Room, while the four made their advance preparations. Little did we know that this would be the first time that any provincial princess had actually set foot in one of their four Temples.

The arrival of Princess Diadan Wu was obvious. We heard her telltale high heel clicks upon the stone long before she entered the room. From the closely spaced clicks, we knew that she too had small feet and was taking many tiny steps. One of Qian's maidens led her into the room. Because of her slow speed, both she and we got a good look at each other before she was seated across the table from us and the four priestesses.

Princess Diadan was forty, with long thick, black hair that fell to her waist. Her six-inch nails were painted bright red, as expected. She wore the familiar black silk hose with the highly polished, black high heels that we used to wear. Her silk dress was a deep emerald. Diadan was somewhat homely, but we soon saw that she was acute in her perceptions and a shrewd politician, and an excellent choice for her office as Princess of Linyi Province.

"I am Princess Diadan Wu," she said in a soft, but firm voice.

"Here in Linyi, we are called San and Réal. I am also known as Bethany Brozena Malina, and this is my wife, Dita Malina. As you can see, we can only bow to Your Highness." We both did so. I noticed that Shan grinned slightly when I mentioned that Dita and I were married and vowed to inquire further in private.

"Pleased to meet you. Your coming, I am told, has been long foretold. Something to do with their religious beliefs," she replied. "Life must be so very hard for women in your situation. I just cannot imagine how difficult the simplest things must be for you two."

"We manage by using our spiritual abilities, Princess," I replied. I sensed just how ill at ease she was facing the four priestesses and us. Shortly, tea was served. As usual, the tea was set before us in a "perfect" manner. The princess could not help but watch us as our cups rose on their own and we sipped from our floating cups. I hated to smash other's realities, but the priestesses left us no choice but to display our kijutsu.

After small talk over tea, I made a coldly calculated guess. "Priestesses, would you allow us to have a private chat with Princess Diadan, please?" Diadan's eyebrows raised, my guess was right. She would prefer to talk with us alone. Begrudgingly, the four priestesses rose and left us alone with the Princess. I heard them whispering among themselves as they left the room.

"There, now we can talk more frankly," I began. Diadan seemed relieved.

"You must excuse me," she ventured. "I've never been around such helpless women as you. If you need me to do something for you, please ask," she said nervously.

"Thanks, we will. Now then, we really do need to know what the true situation actually is here in Linyi Province. We've gotten one picture from the priestesses, but as you would expect, theirs is biased towards their Temple's needs," I said frankly.

Diadan smiled. "Wise women. Since you asked them to allow us a private chat, I will also compromise. What is it that you wish to know? The political situation here?"

We nodded. I asked, "You are not a follower of one of the Temples, right?"

"Yes, here in Linyi Province, the Four Elemental Temples do have a following, though by no means is theirs to be considered a majority religion. In fact, the majority of us really have little to do with organized religion per se. Yes, many worship sea gods, fertility gods and similar such imagined entities. Now I do hire a number of their Dragon men as part of my security forces. The various overlords do likewise. These Dragons command Holy Flames — impressive and deadly in a combat situation. I do employ a few from the other Elemental Temples as well, though their special powers are less effective in providing security."

She continued, "As Princess, I cannot be seen favoring and belonging to one religious group over others. Such is not politically ideal for a leader of the whole province, you see."

"Oh we fully understand and appreciate your position. It is one thing if you had been a believer and follower all of your life and quite another to suddenly join one of the Temples," I said coyly. She grinned and knew that I did grasp her position fully.

"Now as far as the High Parliament goes, of course the merchants are in favor of it and I've gotten most of the overlords to participate. The local parliament is still a chaotic mess. Everyone is vying for positions and demanding others not be allowed to participate. I would like someone from the Temples to step forward, support it, and become active participants in our local legislative body. So far, my requests have fallen on deaf ears," she explained.

"Understood. We will see if we can get them to join and participate," I offered. Diadan grinned, definitely appreciating our frankness and willingness to help her get Linyi organized. "What of the Icemen?"

"Oh, well, now that is a whole 'nother matter!" she exclaimed passionately.

"We know little of them. Where do they come from? Their agenda?" I inquired.

"They are stationed in Dong Province, the city of Xin, more specifically. You see, with the exodus of their Princess many years ago, three-quarters of the entire population of that icy, cold province are gone! That left a huge power vacuum. The Icemen are a small, isolate sect that worships the bitter cold. It is said that they control the cold and make fierce combatants."

"Worse, in the last two years, they have taken over nearly total control of Dong Province and are refusing to become part of the new order. They rejected the appointment of a Princess, as well as sending members to the High Parliament. This spring, they have begun raiding south of the border into our province. I have had to send some of my newly organized soldiers up to the border area at the request of the overlord there, who has been bearing the brunt of their attacks."

She continued, "Twice now, their raiding bands have even ventured all the way down to Luoyang! One of the items on the High Parliament's agenda is how are we going to deal with these bandits, for bandits they can only be, as they recognize no official laws of Tashien."

"What do they steal when they raid?" asked Dita.

"Gold, gems, food, clothing, nearly anything they get their hands on," Princess Diadan replied a bit hostilely."

"Do they consider themselves disenfranchised?" I inquired, basing my idea on what Ilenakova had told us about those who migrated through the Northern Steppes down to the Southlands.

"Possibly. Dong Province is considered a place of exile. Still, they ought to obey the laws and participate in the ruling of Tashien. If they don't, how can they ever expect to be other than disenfranchised?"

"Good point. Surely, the Icemen are not the only people still living in Dong Province. What do the others desire?" I asked.

"Who knows? My advisors suggest that the Icemen number a thousand at the very most. Yet, they are in total control of Dong, since the Princess left with all the regular army so many years ago. A blacksmith cannot hope to defeat an Iceman in combat, not with their cold-based kijutsu spells."

She explained further, "That's why I am employing so many Dragon followers in palace security. They are able to counter the Icemen's kijutsu more effectively than anyone else. I know that my own soldiers are just not good enough to deal with the Icemen. I've heard rumors that the Empress San Min has somehow formed up a new kind of army, a new kind of soldier, and that they are ten times more effective than our usual army soldier is. I wish I knew her secret."

"Would having some of her soldiers assigned here with you be helpful?" I saw an opening and took it.

"Oh yes, yes they would!"

"Okay. I need to send a dispatch to Empress San Min, then. Rats! I forgot, no hands. Princess, can you send the message for us? Tell the Empress to send about a thousand of her soldiers here for a while. Tell her that this is a request from Bethany and Dita. She will know what you mean and will send them as soon as possible. Also, ask her if she will send along someone to help you form and establish soldiers similar to hers. I am sure she will do so, as long as you tell her this request is coming from Bethany and Dita."

"Incredible! You have that kind of pull with our Empress?" she asked, her eyes wide open.

"Yes, we do."

"I will send it today. But what of your connection as Holy Angels to these Temples?" she asked, coyly. Ah, she was now fishing for some answers to her own questions.

"They are not a threat to your throne or to the governing of Linyi. They are on a quest for their own spiritual freedom. Within a month or so, the Son of God, De An, will be arriving here. This will be a major spiritual event for them, but such will have little or no impact on either your rule or the governing of Linyi Province," I put her at ease over the matter.

"Thank you for your frankness," she replied, accepting my explanation.

"Yes, there are many of us all working for the same goals: a healthy, prosperous, non-chaotic Tashien. You may count on us to do our part," I assured her. We then chatted a while longer, before I summoned the four priestesses.

Princess Diadan then said, "Thank you, priestesses, for allowing me the opportunity to discuss matters with your Holy Angels. I have found them extremely wise and very knowledgeable. Would it be possible for me to come by, say once a week, and chat with them further? They are extremely able women."

They looked at each other and Qian spoke first, "We would be honored, Princess Diadan. Yes, San and Réal are Holy Angels sent here by our Lord God." Diadan smiled and then bid us all good day.

Once she left, Qian asked, "Well?"

"As the political ruler, she is constrained from openly joining one of your Temples. Had she been a lifelong member, she could continue to attend. If she now suddenly joined, that would cause severe repercussions on her ability to govern Linyi Province. Do you follow me?" I explained and asked, not quite sure that they did. I was right.

"No, her personal salvation is more important than her fleshly body, which she is so utterly vain about," Qian declared in a most unflattering manner.

I decided that it was time to begin their education. "Priestesses, let me explain some things about God's creation, our world. God has given unto us the Seven Holy Aspects of Life. First, we should all be striving to survive as ourselves, to prosper in our lives, to do well, to achieve our own goals. Second, our families must thrive and prosper if we are to succeed. After all, our children are our future. Third, we all want the groups to which we belong to thrive and prosper. This is especially important for you and our four Temples. In this, I can say that you have done very well indeed."

All four smiled as I validated their personal efforts to make their Temples do well. I continued, "Fourth, we all need all mankind to thrive as well, for all of we humans are God's Children, though many have long forsaken him. Fifth, all plants and animals ought to thrive and multiply, for do not we depend upon them for our earthly needs? Sixth, the material world around us that God has created for us, our physical world ought to thrive and not decay. How can we do well if our world is in total decay? Seventh, we, as immortal spiritual beings, must thrive and prosper. Clearly, this aspect has long ago been forsaken by so very many of our people here in Tashien."

"A spiritual being must thrive and succeed on all seven of these aspects. They are all interdependent one on the other. If all plants died, then so would all animals, for do they not depend upon plants for their sustenance? If the animals disappear, so would all mankind, for our bodies depend upon both plants and animals. Can you see how these are all interdependent one upon the other?"

"Well, yes, I suppose that is so, but we are all striving for spiritual freedom. We want nothing to do with these pathetically frail fleshly bodies," Qian replied. Dita looked frustrated and slightly disgusted.

"Well, let's approach this from a different angle, Qian. Suppose for a moment that you were indeed a totally free, spiritual being. Would you have total certainty that you were yourself?"

"Of course I would."

"Okay. Would you also know that you were completely at cause, capable of the creation of nearly any effect that you desired?"

"Yes, ultimate power lies in a free spiritual being," she answered. The others nodded.

"Good. Would you have full knowingness, full understanding?" They nodded. "Would you not have complete trust in your abilities and would you not betray your own trust? Would you not in fact be truth, know truth instinctively? Would you be able to start, stop, and change all motion at will? Would you not so consider the future as endless and beautiful beyond all imagination? Would you be able to own your possessions, enjoy them, appreciate them, and be willing to share them with others? Would your actions in life naturally be the right actions?"

"Yes, yes, of course yes," Qian replied. "That is what true spiritual salvation means."

"Indeed that is so. Now let's take a hard look at just the opposite of this. Let's take a person who is very close to death. Do they not say apathetically that things are beyond mere right or wrong? Are they responsible for even their own bodies? Do they not feel like they have lost everything and thus own nothing anymore? Do they not feel like they are in fact nobody any longer? Do they even feel like they could possibly face the past? Can they start and stop objects any longer? Not at all. Are they prone to hallucinations, seeing things that we know are not real? Do they not feel that they have been betrayed and now distrust everyone and everything? Do they not consider that they themselves are the total effect of all life? Have they not felt that they are now lost and no longer of any importance whatsoever? Have they not decided that they can no longer know anything at all?"

Their solemn faces displayed their agreement with all of these. I hit them with my punch, "If you allow the Seven Aspects of Life to reach the bottom of near death, how then can you ever hope to achieve true spiritual freedom, which lies in the complete opposite direction?"

Four stunned faces stared back at me. I had just hammered home my point and at last, they began to understand, however slightly, the whole picture.

"We have come to announce to all of you that the Son of God has come to Tashien and is bringing with him the true path to Eternal Salvation for all of us," I ended with a bit of hope for them.

A sober Shan whispered, "I feel like I have somehow lost all of my illusions. Am I betraying my people? Perhaps lies are for the best," she added slightly angrily.

I could not leave her like this. I tried an experiment, "Isn't sometimes the true reality a real threat to you?"

She rose to antagonism, "Well, yes! Yes, it actually is a threat to me and to us sometimes! How did you know that?"

"Yes, but often it can be endured somehow, right Shan?" I asked becoming slightly bored. She responded well.

"Yes, now that you mention it, sometimes it can be born somehow," she yawned.

"As your Temple's Priestess, I bet you often have thought of good, imaginative ways to get others to do well in life. Am I right?"

She brightened up considerably. "Well, actually, I have done just that. You know, just last year, I had our members assist the stonemasons in the rebuilding of the palace's walls. The overlord wars had damaged them, you see. I encouraged our members to pitch in and help with the rebuilding. That worked out well and we even made a few new converts to our Temple as a result. Stonemasons often join our Temple, naturally. Wow, I suddenly feel so good. I don't know why, but I just do. Priestesses, maybe we can make this all work out for our people. Our dreams of Spiritual Salvation may just be possible!"

The other three gaped at the immense emotional change in Shan and realized that I had somehow done something very spiritual, almost magical, to her. The meeting quietly adjourned, and the four left chatting among themselves, Shan doing a lot of the talking.

Dita moved over and gave me a kiss. "Brilliant, Madam Wid, as always! Come on; let's raid the pantry. I'm hungry." Together, we floated off for the dining room.

During the ensuing days, the number of worshipers at the Temples continued to grow. More and more wanted to catch a glimpse of us, the Holy Angels. We had no choice but to sit above and behind the various priestesses as they gave their Services. Twice, Princess Diadan came to visit with us. On her last trip, she confided in us that she had received a private dispatch from Empress San Min telling her about us. Now, the Princess had a vast array of questions for us, including how we'd been mutilated and why.

Meantime, Dita and I continued to count the days before De An would arrive and give us our own miracles. Both of us wanted nothing more than to have our legs and arms back once more. We wanted an end of being the "show of shows!" We wanted an end to being so helpless.

Chapter 37 Betrayal

October 25 came, bringing with it the first heavy snowfall the season. Bianca reported that fact to us, as we were snug inside the warm Dragon Temple. De An was still a hundred or more miles south of Luoyang and would need to travel fifty more miles to get to us in Quanhao. Already, the priestesses were making plans to house De An when he arrived. Yes, we still were being openly displayed like some kind of trophies during their Services, bouncing from one Temple to another. To handle the larger crowd that demanded to see the Holy Angles for themselves, they staggered their times of Services. Now we had to be seen by large audiences four times each day!

At least, we did enjoy their music, and I did get Princess Diadan to order one of the finest organi-fundus for me. It was to be crated and shipped directly to 42 Hampton Way in Velona. One day in the future, I intended to learn how to play this marvelous instrument. In addition to the music, we both loved the sounds and smell of the waterfall in the Temple of Water. Other than that, we cringed before each of these public viewings. Bianca continued to encourage her mother and me, that it was only a few weeks more before we could be rescued. Dita and I retired for the night as usual, snug in our red room of the Dragon Temple.

In Dong, Meng Zhong listened to the latest reports from his Field Commander. "So the Elementals have their long prophesied Holy Angles now. The stupid idiots merely retrieved some pathetic women that Doc Yi cut up, calling them Holy Angels. Idiots." His anger glared. Then, his face brightened up.

"Say, this may be our golden opportunity to rid the world of these idiot Elementalists!" He called his aides together and drew up plans. "Secrecy, that's the name of this sortie. Call forth all our Icemen. Bands of twenty-five are to sneak across the border and head to Quanhao. They are to wear disguises, perhaps that of common peasants. Gather my Honor Guards, we leave tonight."

On October 25, Meng Zhong, the fifty year old ruler of the Icemen and all of Dong Province, stood looking at the four temples from the edge of the huge square. Snow was falling heavily, which only added to his chances of total success. Meng was patient, that is, when it suited him. Today, it suited him. Tonight, well, that would be another story. While he watched and waited, a man wearing a red cloak exited the Dragon Temple and waded through the half foot of snow already on the ground. Even from this distance, Meng saw that the man hated the snow and cold. He grinned, for he loved the snow and cold.

As the man drew closer, Meng raised his hand high. The robed man altered his course, now heading directly towards him. When the man finally joined him, Meng's men surrounded him and Meng motioned for him to accompany him down a side street. The Dragon obeyed. Few people were out this late afternoon. When they were at a relatively isolated location not far from the square, Meng halted. "Well, Xiong?"

"Tonight they are in the Dragon Temple's Inner Sanctuary. You promise that you will not harm them or us?" Xiong replied.

"Oh yes. You have my solemn word on that. I will not harm one hair on their heads. Here are your funds." He handed Xiong a large pouch filled with gems. Hands shaking both from the cold and from being so close to his enemies, Xiong checked on the glittering gemstones. Satisfied, he tightened the bag.

"You will keep your word, Meng?" Xiong asked, his voice faltering slightly.

"Yes, of course. We both know that they are complete fakes, merely unfortunate women who were cut up by old Doc Yi as part of his experiments. With your so called Holy Angels gone, you will be able to continue your religious beliefs as you always have. Any changes that they are suggesting will be lost. That's you wish, is it not?" Meng said with a snide smile.

"Yes, of course. They are bringing horrible change to all the Elemental Temples. They are destroying centuries of our beliefs and training. They are destroying us from within. Once they are gone, things will go back to the ways that they always have been," Xiong replied, hoping beyond hope that this would be the case. He'd seen and overheard much of what the Holy Angels had said. It was more than clear to him that these women thought that all the Dragon Masters were on the wrong path, completely! Xiong knew that this was not true. Long years he had studied and slaved, fought hard against his body to achieve the kijutsu powers of fire that he now commanded. Loathe was he to give that up! What would a Dragon Master be if he could not command the very elemental forces that he worshiped? This, he could not and must not allow. In time, perhaps Lian Ju would understand. If not, well so be it.

"You are right, Xiong," Meng replied. Xiong then turned to leave. He didn't see the dagger slide down Meng's sleeve, but he felt it piercing his back and into his heart. As he slid out of his dying body and looked down upon it from above, he finally realized what he had just done! In fear, panic, and guilt, he fled across Tashien as fast as he could go, with no thought of where he was heading. Meng bent over and retrieved his gems. "You'll not need these any longer." Meng chuckled evilly. His men dragged the body away and hid it. "Okay, give the orders to move to the staging areas." Three aides dashed off to deliver their master's orders. Meng waited patiently. Another hour and it would be dark. Give them a couple more to fall asleep, and this would be the easiest raid imaginable!

Around ten, Enrico made his way through the near foot of snow covering the streets. As usual, he was at the pub gathering information. Tonight, he had not liked what he had overheard. Many strange men were in town, strong men, some reported, likely fighters. Bianca had no desire to frequent the pubs if she didn't have to and had been letting Enrico go alone for the last two weeks. As he neared their inn, he began to notice hundreds of men moving down the streets heading toward the Temple Square. He caught glimpses of weapons and did not like what he saw at all. He hurried as much as he could.

"Bianca. Wake up. Something is about to happen!" he roused the sleeping Protector.

"What's up?" she replied, wiping sleep from her eyes.

"Hundreds of fighters are amassing at the Temple Square. I think they might be the Icemen about to raid the temples. Warn Bethany and Dita. Tell them to get the heck out of there. Grab your gear; we may be in for a huge battle!" Bianca snapped into action, strapping on her many weapons as fast as she could. Within five minutes, the two heavily cloaked Protectors headed out of the inn and waded through the snow towards the Temple Square.

"What are we going to do?" I asked Dita. Bianca had just awakened us both with a grim, dire warning. "We can't go outside dressed like this. We'll freeze to death in short order."

"We're in a death trap, if you had not already figured that out," Dita outlined our situation. "We're underground with few exits. Our only protection is that massive fire pit. If that is breached, then the soldiers can have free run of these halls, and we have no place to run or hide. Like I said, a death trap. Of course, the priestesses will see it differently."

"Can we get out of the temple ahead of the assault?" I asked, thinking that an escape might be our only way out.

"Not likely, unless you know how to disarm that massive fire trap. I sure don't know how. If we try to fly over it, our hair and clothes will ignite at once. We will be burned alive. Now we might be able to overcome some of the other temple's traps, but we don't know how to operate the mechanisms to open the doors. Like I said, we are a pair of trapped rats," Dita growled. "But I will protect you with my life, love."

"I know you will, Dita. Somehow, we have to get out of here. Let's move to the main firetrap. Maybe we can figure out some way to get across it." We lifted our pathetic bodies up and moved them silently passed the sleeping Lian Ju and out into the hallway. A few minutes later, we hovered before the massive flames of the firetrap, which was designed to keep us safe. Why didn't we feel so safe just now?

Meng, joined by his top twenty Icemen, the men with cold kijutsu that nearly matched his, paused before the entrance of the Dragon Temple.

"Remember the plan. Take out the Dragon's protecting the place. Make for the firetrap." They nodded. Nearby, his aides prepared others for the assault on the other three temples. Thanks to the information provided by Xiong, he knew precisely where he needed to go. Only this fire temple posed any real threat to Meng. Fire countered their kijutsu remarkably well. Water, stone, and air kijutsu could mostly be ignored or shunted aside. Meng raised his arm high and brought it down sharply. The signal given and relayed, they moved to the front entrance.

Here, two men planted their black powder devices, and they all stepped back. Boom! Boom! A series of explosions only seconds apart rocked the snow-stilled night, the snow dampening the sounds somewhat. The doors splintered and Meng and his men rushed inside. Thanks to Xiong, they knew precisely where the night guards were positioned and more importantly where the firetrap lay, the entrance to the Inner Sanctuary and their quarry: the Holy Angels.

Taken by complete surprise, the Dragon warriors had little chance, not against the powerful kijutsu of these twenty-one men. Even Meng launched one blast of cold against a guard. Soon twenty frozen statues of Dragon men stood in various positions around the main chamber where Services were held. With nothing more in his way, Meng and his men headed down the stairs for the firetrap.

"Well, there you are!" Meng said coldly. He saw us just arriving at the firetrap, but on the other side. "Don't go away. We are after you," he jested.

"Damn, retreat!" Dita ordered, and we flew back towards our room. We ran into Lian Ju, who was awakened by the explosions. She looked terrified.

"What's going on?" she shrieked.

"We are under attack. They are at the firetrap right now. They said that they are after us," Dita hastily explained. "Get us out of here now!"

"The firetrap will hold. I know it will," Lian Ju cried out. What else could she say or do? She now realized that there was nowhere to run — we were trapped here in the Inner Sanctuary. She raced down the hall to see for herself. Just as she saw the Holy Fires, she witnessed the combined effects of Meng and his top men. A giant blast of freezing cold came forth and landed on top of the flames. Ice sheets formed and solidified, extinguishing the flames.

With a smug look on his face, Meng walked over the top of the ice towards Priestess Lian Ju. "Give us the two Holy Angels, and we'll be gone," he called out. She refused and retreated, ordering us into our room. She took up a defensive position at her doorway, intent upon defending us with her life. We can't attack if we have to keep our bodies levitated. Thus, we sat the pathetic things on our bed and moved to support Lian Ju. Already she had conjured hot flames, forming a barrier against entry into her room.

As one man moved to force entry, Dita snapped his neck; he fell lifeless to the ground. Another came within striking distance, and I slammed his body against the stone wall, crushing his head. "Leave us alone or you will all die!" I screamed as loudly as I could.

Meng called out, "Lian Ju, surrender, and you will not be harmed. Xiong has already told us the positions of all your guards. They are frozen statues now. Don't worry. I killed that traitor for you. Surrender the Holy Angels, and I will leave you alone. You have ten seconds to make up your mind! One. Two. Three."

I never will forget the look of utter shock and horror on Lian Ju's face as his words struck home in her mind! Her concentration faltered; her barrier flames flickered and nearly went out. She was devastated beyond imagination. So were we, for that matter. The man who had rescued us from the inferno at Doc Yi's had betrayed us to the Icemen.

Get out of there, mom! Bianca fairly screamed telepathically to Dita.

We can't get by the Icemen; we're trapped in our room! We'll kill them all! Dita sent and moved around the corner to begin twisting necks. She snapped the man closest to her. "Ten," came the counting, confident voice of Meng. Boom! Psst! Two sounds reverberated in the rooms and hallways. I later learned that they'd tossed a stun grenade and an ether bomb. The former temporarily knocked us out and the latter put us to sleep.

Ever since the opium addiction had been handled, Dita and I were much harder to be knocked unconscious by things such as ether. However, we still had not had any chance to remove the ether and trauma inflicted on us by Doc Yi. There simply had not been any time when we were alone. Sandra couldn't do it with our children's bodies back home, since we needed our full concentration to deal with life here in the temple. Thus, we both went out like lights. The last thing Dita remembered was Bianca's scream. Thus, Bianca knew that we had been attacked.

"Damn, they've got mom!" Bianca swore aloud. The two were standing near the edge of the square watching perhaps a thousand men swarming the temples.

"Keep your eyes on the Dragon Temple, Bianca. That's where they ought to be bringing them out. How are we going to stop a thousand soldiers?" Enrico asked, feeling rather overwhelmed by the situation.

"If mom and Bethany are awake, they can help us. We stand a chance that way. If they are unconscious, we simply can't do it. Maybe they are trying to capture mom and Bethany. If so, we must follow them and find a way to rescue them."

The two watched. A few minutes later, men began coming out of the smashed doors. At last, the two saw men carrying what had to be our small bodies, wrapped in satin sheets. As they continued to watch, other men began moving out into the square leading countless horses. Then, a wagon entered the square and eventually pulled up by the men holding us. We were tossed into the back of the wagon and some blankets thrown over our unconscious bodies. Meng mounted and led the exodus. Within a half hour, all the Icemen mounted and rode out of the square, heading northward through town.

The two took that time to get their horses ready and to stow a few supplies and blankets on the backs of their saddles. Just as the last Iceman left the square, the lone duo mounted and followed from a distance. "We follow the wagon tracks only," Enrico ordered. Bianca merely cried; she'd failed to protect her helpless mother again, at least that's how she viewed it.

Slowly the wagon moved through the deep snow covered streets. This late at night and with the heavy snowfall, the streets were deserted. A strange stifled stillness lay over the city, black smoke clouds drifted into the night sky, mingling with the large, descending snowflakes, picturesque in other circumstances. Bianca and Enrico rode along following the unmistakable wagon trail, the easiest tracking either had ever done.

"How are we going to rescue them?" Bianca finally found her voice, though it still held a twinge of grief and fear. She fought hard to keep her emotions at bay.

"I'll be honest with you, Bianca. I just don't see how we can unless we have them helping us. We bide our time and stay as close as we can to them without getting caught ourselves," he said solemnly. They rode on into the snowy night. Visibility was only a few feet at best and they dare not use a lantern. Still, the wagon tracks were plainly visible.

Nine long hours later, as the dawn came at last and the snow ceased, the two crested a hill some eighteen miles north of Quanhao. Below them, they saw long lines of the Icemen, ambling along on their horses, half-asleep themselves. The wagon was in the center of the throng, moving along slowly through the deep snow. They'd hitched four horses to it to ensure that it did not become stuck in the deep snow. Fortunately, there had been no wind during the night and hence no huge snowdrifts, just over a foot of deep, wet snow.

Mom! Are you awake yet? For hours now, Bianca kept attempting to establish telepathic contact with Dita. At last, Dita replied!

I — I — I'm so-o-o-o c-o-l-d! She replied. We both stirred. I have never ever been so cold as I was at this moment! What was left of my body was shivering uncontrollably. Dita, likewise. As we both became oriented, we moved up and out of the blankets to see where we were at, leaving our violently shivering bodies beneath the flimsy blankets. Nearly a thousand Icemen, half asleep and plodding slowly across the country side, surrounded us. *If we don't do something immediately, our bodies are going to freeze to death, Bethany. Can we take all of them?* Dita sent me.

We have little choice. Damn them anyway! Okay, slaughter time, dear, I sent. I was still half out of it, very upset, and angry. Dita relayed our intentions to Bianca, who was to hold back until the path was clear to reach us.

Dita moved from man to man, giving their heads a nice twist, snapping them, killing them instantly. I, on the other hand, began moving down the ranks of riders, snatching onto a man and tossing his body as high into the sky as I could, then moving on to the next one. I guess Bianca and Enrico had quite a sight before them! From my view, it was simply a race against time. Our bodies were freezing to death. The faster we eliminated these men, the sooner Bianca and Enrico could attempt to get us warmed up. Time was not on our side nor was reason.

Meng suddenly alert and seeing his men magically flying high into the air, bodies crashing all around him smashed to death from the fall, whirled into action. He drew his sword and looked around, but saw only two lone riders on the distant hill, apparently watching. "Kijutsu!" he screamed, kicked his horse around, and headed for the wagon. His head swirled around several times, and his body fell to the ground, dead.

Bianca claimed that it took all of twenty minutes, but I had no way of telling. At last, there were no more men to toss into the air, and I calmed down. Dita likewise. We watched as Bianca and Enrico galloped up to the wagon, where our bodies lay beneath the blankets.

"Wake up, mom! Please wake up!" Bianca screamed at Dita. Our bodies were *so* cold! So lifeless! I had a very bad feeling about this, so did Dita, who moved over her body and felt it.

"No pulse. Bianca, we must have heat immediately. Start tearing off bits of the wagon and get a blaze going. I will begin rubbing them to try to warm them up," Enrico ordered Bianca, who was nearly hysterical by now, frantic with worry, and crying as well.

She tore off part of the sides and cast a ball of fire on them. Soon, she had a blaze going right there in the wagon's bed. Enrico, still rubbing our bodies through the blankets, moved us as close to the fire as he dared. They both worked as hard as they could to get us warmed up, but neither body showed any signs of life. Neither moved; no pulse came back. At last, Dita and I realized that we'd lost our bodies. They had been through more abuse than they could take.

Enrico checked long and hard for any signs of life. At last, he put his arms around Bianca, and whispered, "Their bodies didn't make it, Bianca." She bawled, pounding Enrico with her fists, but he held on to her. She collapsed in his arms crying heavily.

"We did all that we could to save them, but the Icemen let them freeze to death. Come on, Bianca; contact your mom. She's right here with us," Enrico said very softly.

Dita didn't wait; she joined with her daughter. *Honey, it's okay. You did your very best. We were just knocked out for far too long. It's over now. Now I need you to be very strong for us. I still need your help, Bianca.*

"What?" she said through her sobs, not recognizing that she was even speaking aloud.

First, we ought to be properly buried. Second, we need you to hurry back to Quanhao. Notify both the Temples and the Princess of this location. Have them send their men here to see what happened for themselves and to bury the many dead Icemen. Third, you must get that alien device back to Zau and join up with the others. They will now need your protection. Be strong. Remember, neither of us are really gone. We have our young bodies back home. Just don't go calling my Renzo body 'mom,' please. She tried for a spark of levity in an otherwise sad and somber situation.

Suddenly, Bianca sat bolt upright! "Oh! I lost my birth mother this lifetime too! That's why I am so grief stricken. Okay, mom." She wiped her wet face and relayed Dita's orders to Enrico, though I had already done so. Still full of emotion, Bianca set to about the tasks.

Together, the two dug a shallow grave and buried our stiff forms. Once done, they mounted their horses and headed back towards the city. This time, they rode as fast as they dared in the deep snow, arriving around noon.

First, they stopped at the Dragon Temple, where they found hundreds of Dragon followers gathered, making repairs to the doors and guarding the place from further attacks. Enrico said, "Excuse us. We must speak with your Priestess. It is about the Holy Angels."

At once, one of the red robed men rushed off to find her. A bit later, several armed men asked the two to come inside. Lian Ju, her eyes blood shot, looked forlornly at the two strangers. "What news have you?"

Bianca could not bear to talk about it, so Enrico explained what they had witnessed. The news that their Holy Angels had frozen to death hit her and those nearby very hard, as one might expect. That they had in turn slain all thousand of the Icemen brought new hope and wonder to Lian Ju. At once, she ordered a party to check out his report and thanked the two for bringing her the information.

While she was issuing more orders, the two quietly left and headed for the palace. There, they delivered the same message to one of the Princess' advisors. Satisfied they had obeyed Dita's second request, both headed back to their inn. After eating their first meal in almost twenty-four hours, they fell into a sound sleep.

In the morning, Bianca was still emotionally raw, but Enrico decided that they should begin their return trip anyway. Dita and I hovered over the two constantly. We were determined to make sure that nothing happened to them! While I also contacted everyone else and relayed the news of our bodies' deaths, Dita wisely Mind Linked to Enrico and via him began a therapy session on her daughter. Enrico also made sure that Bianca was not distracted as they rode along on the main road.

After a grief filled hour, Bianca finally erased the loss traumas and felt more cheerful about it. Still, she knew that she would miss her mother a whole lot. "Well, we all knew that this mission was fraught with danger and that our bodies could be killed. It's just that I really didn't think it could happen to mom or Bethany, not really anyway. They didn't stand much of a chance did they?"

"No, Bianca, they really didn't. Had those Icemen kept the two warm or had not kept them unconscious for nine hours freezing in the wagon, things might have turned out all right. Yes, fraught with danger indeed. Yet, we must make sure that alien devices get back home where Dianna can study them. Plus, we have the others to look after. I sure don't want to lose any more of our companions. We must be brave, but I do feel their loss and that of Ilenakova as well." His tears he could not suppress any longer. Until now, he had to be brave and keep the two on the right path. Now, his own raw feelings could no longer be suppressed.

Quietly, Bianca began a therapy session on Enrico, while Dita and I kept watch over them as they slowly rode along. By the time they arrived at an inn for the night, Enrico also felt more cheerful about the tragic losses he'd experienced. As they warmed up and ate a hot meal, Dita and I watched them carefully to make sure that the therapies had been successful. While they were still sober looking, the heavy emotional loss seemed to be gone from their minds. At last, Dita and I relaxed a bit.

Mind if I sit on your shoulder and watch the countryside go by? Dita sent her daughter the next morning as Enrico and Bianca began their southerly journey once more. Bianca soon felt her mother's presence on her left shoulder. For the first time since our tragic deaths, Bianca actually smiled. I did the same with Enrico, who definitely appreciated it as well.

Days passed by slowly as did the late fall countryside. The further south we went, the warmer it became. Entering Zau, we found no snow, only chilly fall weather. We arrived on November 20. A day later, the others arrived with the two heavily laden wagons full of the alien artifacts. Their broken bones had healed, and Fina had given both Tian and Louis therapy sessions, which greatly helped them heal more rapidly. In return, Louis managed to deliver his first-ever therapy session to Fina, and he was quite proud of his small achievement. While I would like to say that it was a joyous reunion for everyone, including Jemma and the others, our deaths prevented such.

Although we had kept in touch these past months, we all exchanged stories of our adventures. Even Empress San Min wanted to hear all about what had transpired with Dita and me. After a full day of catching up, our group met to make our next plans. Dita and I Mind Linked with everyone so we could give them guidance.

Jemma surprised even me. "Gang. I've decided that I want to stay here in Zau with Empress San Min indefinitely. Phillipe and I want to get married, and I want to help advise San Min. The situation here in Tashien, while it is improving, still needs guidance. It is a Judger's paradise. I hope you will all understand. I've lost Kali, my mother, too, and have no real urgent need to return to Velona. I have so much I can contribute here in Tashien."

You have my blessings, Jemma. I support you wholeheartedly. I am very proud of your decision. I sent to her and everyone else. She beamed.

Not to be outdone, Fina piped up, "Hey, I am staying too. I'm her Protector still. Besides Tian and I want to get married. So I'm staying with Jemma. Someday we will return to Velona, if only for a visit. I've lost my mom too, Ilenakova. So really, it is more important for me to stay and protect Jemma."

Congratulations, Fina. I think that is perfect. Say, can we all attend your weddings? Have you set a date yet? I sent. Both young women blushed. They hadn't.

Well, you had better marry soon. We are not leaving until we see you wed! I sent everyone.

During the next week, they boxed up all the artifacts and our many possessions. Six wooden crates nailed tightly shut were loaded onto a wagon, ready to accompany us on the long journey down to Shansee and then home to Velona. On December 1, the two happy couples were wed, and the next day, our party departed on the long return trip home.

We hired two drivers, one for the wagon and one to drive a carriage. Louis and Bianca rode in the carriage, chatting and spending time with each other. Enrico alternated riding with them and riding topside, visiting with the drivers.

Jemma continued to relay reports to us frequently. Indeed, the bodies of the Iceman Massacre were found and the attack became a legend in Linyi Province. The Holy Angels had wiped out the entire Icemen army. When the Empress' soldiers arrived in Xin, Dong Province, they were easily able to re-establish the new political machine being setup across all Tashien. The High Council elected a Princess for Dong and soon had representatives selected to join the High Parliament in Zau.

De An arrived in Quanhao, met with the Princess Diadan, and then spent a long time with the four priestesses and their followers. Evidently, he was successful in his mission, for we heard back little more.

By February, 757, our party finally reached Shansee. There we found a caravel waiting to make a return trip to Velona, compliments of Sandra. Mid-April, we finally sailed into the giant port of Velona, home at last.

Chapter 38 Home at Last

The instant Enrico walked off the gangplank, Luisa ran up to him, hugged him, and pelted him with kisses. "Don't you ever run off for such a long time again without taking me along," she teased him. Those two spent the next week in their bedroom, only coming out for meals and to use the bathroom.

Dita moved over her young Renzo body, which was now eleven years old, while I did the same with my Elizabeth Lilly body, also eleven. We hugged each other tightly. He whispered, "Now we can do this the right way." I blushed, only a couple more years and we would be of age once more and could marry again!

My fancy star-scope had already arrived from Tashien. Renzo and I unpacked it and set it up. We spent many hours looking at the stars with his marvelous invention. Yes, we all had much catching up to do.

As he and I looked through the scope, Renzo whispered, "Well, we did it, didn't we? We helped get a whole country out of chaos and back on track. Amazing."

"Yes, Renzo, we certainly did. Honestly, I don't want to go through all that again. I am totally through with having my arms cut off, legs too."

He laughed. "Me too. Only this time, I think that I am safe. You know that they only cut off women's arms, not guys." I chuckled this time.

"Say, wasn't Pian absolutely gorgeous?" he commented. I poked him in his ribs, and he laughed loudly and began chasing me around our yard.

The first of May, became the weddings' day. High Priestess Lona West Po performed the three ceremonies together in the Holy Rose Church. Lionel d'Grange gave away his son, Louis, to Bianca, while Tom West Po gave away his son, Gerardo, to Cosima. Dianna wept as she watched her little girl marry Gerardo. Alessa and Arsenio Bartolo also tied the knot. Ania and Dianna, the only two remaining of our original six, substituted for the missing mothers, and Elena played the role of bridesmaid for all three. We three eleven year olds were their flower girls. Yes, this was a very happy day for all and a new start on life for our three girls.

Bianca and Louis headed off to honeymoon at his horse ranch near Alta by the beautiful high country, the Paese di Dio. Cosima was promoted to Chief Detective Inspector, while Alessa became a Detective Inspector and bodyguard for Cosima. Bale appointed Gerardo to be his first Secretary of State so he could lend his immense strategic planning skills to the enormous task of governing Velona. Arsenio continued work on his many inventions, but now had the full financial backing of Velona. His prototype metal ship powered by a steam engine derived from Dianna's train engine was already under construction. His steam engine electricity generator contraption actually worked and numerous applications of electricity were under development.

Gerardo, Arsenio, and their brides were given a wedding present of a large estate in the center of Velona. Here, Arsenio had the space to develop his inventions. Plus, Alessa and Cosima were under one roof, where Alessa could better protect Cosima. Chief Inspector Adolfo insisted that Cosima be guarded at all times. Her incredible detective skills were vitally important to the city.

By May 7, life around 42 Hampton Way seemed very different. Yes, we six children still ran and played. Our parents, Sandra and Arturo Bartiana and Luisa and Enrico Angela, still watched over us, keeping us safe, our Forze Segrete protectors. However, only Elena, Ania's daughter, remained with us, she still did not have a boyfriend. Ania and Dianna still had the immense challenge of running two bodies at the same time. Ania quickly adopted Dianna's solution: have their eleven year old bodies sleep during the day while they worked and then have the children awake all night while they slept.

This way, Dianna claimed to be able to get twice as much invention work done each day. Indeed, with the arrival of all the new alien artifacts, Dianna could scarcely be pulled away from her study of them. Every day, I expected to hear of some new discovery she'd made about them. However, Dianna was unable to unlock their mysteries and eventually stored them away for later study.

Elena continued to play with us six children, relieving our parents, who were once more expecting babies. One day, as she sat on a swing with me, watching the others racing around the yard, I asked her, "Have you got a boyfriend yet?"

She sighed, "No, not yet, but I do know that I want to have lots of children. Honestly, Bethany, I have truly enjoyed helping raise all of you. I know that I ought to get busy and start finding a good use for my Judger skills, but I really like being a pseudo-mother."

"Well, there is no rush, Elena, you are only sixteen. You've got your whole life ahead of you. I'm sure that you will find the right fellow one day," I replied.

She sighed, "Yes, unlike my sisters, I am not in a big rush. Last lifetime, I had patience and it paid off handsomely for me. Somewhere out there in the big wide world is the man for me. One day, I will find him." Together, we continued to swing high on the swing set, watching the others dashing madly about the lawn. Just now, the world seemed at peace to us. I did have a gnawing thought, though: would it stay this way for long?
The End.

Other Books by Vic Broquard

Without Warning (fantasy)

The Trident Series: (fantasy)
>   Volume 1 The Trident and the Book
>   Volume 2 The Trident and the Scepter
>   Volume 3 The Trident and the Resurrection

The Adventures of Elizabeth Stanton Series: (science fiction)
>   Volume 1 The Evolution of the Path
>   Volume 2 The Great Messiah
>   Volume 3 Of Kings and Queens and Troubadours
>   Volume 4 Chaos in the Aftermath
>   Volume 5 Power Plays
>   Volume 6 Age of Exploration
>   Volume 7 Abducted
>   Volume 8 The Emperor and Empress
>   Volume 9 A Job Worth Doing
>   Volume 10 Degradation
>   Volume 11 The Second Crusade
>   Volume 12 When Worlds Collide
>   Volume 13 Dark Ages

The Lindsey Barron Series: (fantasy)
>   Volume 1 The Rod of the Apocalypse
>   Volume 2 The Board of Governors
>   Volume 3 The Crown of Moses
>   Volume 4 Dominus for President
>   Volume 5 The National Health Care Program
>   Volume 6 States Justice
>   Volume 7 Cross and Double-cross

Zoran Chronicles Series: (fantasy)
>   Volume 1 A Dragon in Our Town
>   Volume 2 Dragons, Power, Courts, and War

Planet of the Orange-red Sun Series: (science fiction)
>   Volume 1 When Kingdoms Fall
>   Volume 2 Dark Ages
>   Volume 3 Age of the Towers
>   Volume 4 Difficillis Exitus
>   Volume 5 Age of the Lords
>   Volume 6 The Renegade Tower

The Return of the Wizards: Twelve Companions – The Making of Wizards (fantasy)

www.ingramcontent.com/pod-product-compliance
Lightning Source LLC
Chambersburg PA
CBHW081226020726
47503CB00011B/2922